The viewscreen went dark. Sarah hyperventilated, trying to stave off the internal storm. She sank to her knees, forehead on the floor, and burst into tears, jerking mercilessly with the force of the counteracting medications.

I can't do this alone! I can't!

Sarah's trying *so hard* to keep her promise to Dmitri to behave, but ninety days of living by her wits is sometimes more than she can handle. She can't trust Uncle Tomas's kindness, Grandmamá scares the breath from her, and even her beloved Fearsome Four doesn't understand her needs. *If only Dimi were there!* It's going to take more than Tomas's good will and Dmitri's understanding to set Sarah straight. She'll need to rely on the one person she absolutely refuses to trust:

Herself.

BEST
OF
EVERYTHING

The Best things in life are worth waiting for

The **Best Intentions** series

Best Intentions
Best Efforts
Broken Trusts
Best of Everything

Also available in e-book format

BEST
OF
EVERYTHING

This is an original work of fiction. Names, characters, places and politics are the work of the author's imagination. Any similarity to persons living or dead is entirely coincidental.

With grateful thanks to my psychology professor,
Aurelio Torres, for sending me down the neural path
and
to my dad, Bob Staneslow, without whom
none of this would have been possible

"Saints help me, John, I'm in deep trouble. You never told me the child was blasted *insane!*"

A red flag waved in John Carver's mind. Tómas didn't fluster easily. "What do you mean, insane?"

"I thought this was just a matter of legal overreacting. They have two hundred pages of text discussing flashbacks and psychotic episodes and… and… reality testing, and… suicidal behaviors, and a whole host of other diagnoses," Tomas sputtered. "You told me you helped her through a depression. You never told me she was *crazy!* I can't bring someone like that into the house!"

"Calm down. How much time do we have?"

Tomas glanced at the chronometer near the screen. "They're holding a legal review in about forty-eight hours."

"Damn! I can't get there in time, even if I moley-beamed my way from stop to stop. What's the diagnosis?"

Tomas called up his notes. "'Traumatic stress, panic attack, paranoid ideology, attachment disorder, personality disorder, severe mood disorder, pathologic organic biochemical insufficiency, and self-destructive behaviors.' What the Hell does that mean?"

The psychiatrist sighed. "It means she hasn't made much progress since the last time I last saw her. Who's the doctor in charge?"

"Kyle L. Granger, Chief Medical Officer on the *Triumph*. They're here at the starbase."

"Have him send me his files. I'll skim them, then talk to him directly," Dr. Carver said, saving the name and commlink address. "Give me three hours, at least. Meanwhile, don't panic… "

"Don't panic? John, I promised I'd bring her back! I have a fortune riding on this! Don't forget, *I can't accompany her home!* And I can't send her home tied to a bed."

"*Don't panic!*" Carver repeated. "Talk with Dmitri, find out what's going on. You talked with her, Tomas. You judge character for a living. She can't be that bad if you and Vlad talked with her and didn't realize anything was wrong. She may have already recovered. Talk with her brother, talk with Sarah, then talk to me and we'll see where we stand."

"On very shaky legs," Tomas insisted.

7

Eight hours later, Dr. Carver's face looked a bit more positive. "I went over the file with the doctor there, and I think we'll make it. He says right now she's quite fragile, but the four weeks previous she was perfectly functional in her environment. He thinks the paranoia is related to fear of her situation, and the attachment label is because she refuses to cooperate unless Dmitri is present. It's not as bad as we feared."

"You're right. It's not as bad as I feared," Tomas said. "It's much worse! John, she's every stereotype of crazy I've ever seen in a horror cinema, only this was a live performance. I can't do this, John, I can't! I have no idea even how to talk to her. What am I going to do?"

"What's she doing? Describe it."

Tomas waved his hands. "As in begging people to shoot her. As in - talking rationally one second, and the next accusing me of dropping imaginary items. As in sniffing me like a wild animal. One second she'd act like I wasn't there, and the next she would ask relevant questions. I couldn't keep up."

"What did Dmitri say?"

"That she isn't normally like that, that she's very upset. She admitted the medications were making her irritable, and she wasn't sleeping well."

"She never does. What did Dmitri do?"

"He told her to stop the nonsense and pay attention. And she did."

"Don't give up, then," John urged. "We can do it. It's just got to be a coordinated effort. Get as much information out of Dmitri as you can. I'll walk you through the rest of it, step by step. I believe in her."

Tomas's face bore the waxen mask of someone about to be space sick. "God help me, John, because I'm going to need it."

En Route

Beep

The sudden noise in the stateroom made her jump. She hadn't been asleep, just lost in that nothingness of twilight, too afraid of not being alert to some lurking danger. Insomnia had plagued her on and off for years; it returned eight weeks previous and hadn't left, despite all the new medications.

beep beep beep beep beep beep beep beep beep beep beep

The hyperspace receiver wouldn't quit. The neurotransmitter sensors implanted in her arteries did their microscopic thing; the wave of medication took over in response to her adrenaline rush and her pounding heart began to calm, the panic to ease. Still, she couldn't. She just couldn't answer it. Not yet. She didn't have the strength yet. She pressed the pillow over her ears.

Leave me alone!

The noise stopped. She lifted a corner of the pillow. The *message waiting* signal blinked. Two full minutes passed, hypnotized by the flashing light, before she rose and hit the toggle.

A man's face appeared on the monitor. He was pleasant-looking, with hazel eyes that could be razor sharp or sympathetically kind. She knew him to be fifty-two, though he could have claimed ten years less. This time, his eyes were sharp enough to make her flinch.

"Sarah, this has gone on long enough," said the recording. "I am very concerned. If you don't wish to speak with me, please tell me, and I will stop calling. I know you have had at least five calls from home and you have not answered those, either. If you do not respond to this message within ten standard minutes, I will send a message directly to the captain of your ship and have him send someone to observe that you are not in need of assistance. Please, even if you have nothing else to say, let me know that you are all right. Ten minutes. Tómas Ivanóv, recording." The message ended; the screen went dark.

Ten minutes? That was four minutes ago! *Oh! Why is he doing this to me!* It was his own fault, sending her back to Earth alone like this. The last thing she needed was the humiliation of explaining herself to the captain of the starliner. Sarah bit her knuckle and flicked a different switch.

"Computer: last message, respond. Return call."

In seconds, the man reappeared on the screen. "Sarah! Where have you been? You had us very worried."

"I-I-I was washing my hands in the other room. I didn't hear the call."

9

"Sarah, this is the eleventh time I've tried to speak to you in two days. John has called you twice, Katya once, and Vladimir six times. Please don't tell me you have been in the washroom all that time."

"No sir. Uncle Tomas. Sir."

"Are you ill?"

"No sir."

"Then I'm afraid I don't understand why a sixteen-year-old girl cannot respond to an incoming message."

"I–I– " Sarah's face curled in a painful grimace and a tremor started in the muscles, spread down her neck, and ended somewhere off-camera in her arm. It happened sometimes, whenever she became very nervous or upset. It was a nasty side effect of the medication she was forced to take, forced by a court order. It wasn't a hard choice – admit she had some problems, accept treatment, or stand trial for attempted murder.

She had problems.

"Are you okay? Is that getting any better?" Tomas asked with concern.

"Yes, sir. Thank you, sir. The frequency is decreasing."

"I'm glad to hear that. Now, why can't you respond to calls?"

The tortured look returned to the girl's features. Her brother Dmitri understood her neuroses and allowed for them, but Uncle Tomas – Uncle Tomas didn't accept excuses like terror and fear and *I can't*. She breathed deep, calming herself so the medication didn't kick in.

"I've listened to every message everyone's sent. I just can't – I need more time to adjust. I can't bear to talk to anyone yet. Please tell them that I love them, and I miss them, and to keep leaving messages, but I can't talk to them directly yet."

"You want them to send messages, but you can't be bothered to answer them? That's poor manners, Sarah."

"I don't mean to be rude. I'm – afraid." She dropped her head and looked anywhere but the transmitting camera. "It's been a long time. I'm … ashamed."

"Ashamed? Of what? The last three weeks?" Uncle Tomas' eyes switched from sharp to caring. "Sarah, you don't have a single thing to be ashamed of. No one understands that better than your brothers and sisters. And you *need* to be talking with John. He's your doctor now. He can help you relax, if nothing else.

"All right," he relented. "If you don't want to talk to your family yet, that's fine, but you *must* answer *my* calls, okay? As your current guardian, it is *my duty* to make sure you are well. The easiest, most immediate way I can do this is to have direct contact with you. Do you understand that?"

The knot of Sarah's stomach pulled tighter. "Yes, sir,"

"Will you answer my calls, please?"

"Yes, sir."

"What about John's?"

Sarah hesitated. "If I have to. But only him! No one else."

Uncle Tomas smiled once more. "Fair enough. I will relay your messages, and I will call you at 0700 Universal Time. And you will be there to answer my call, correct?"

"Yessir," she whispered with all the enthusiasm of a prisoner on the way to execution.

"Okay. Until morning, then. Good night, Sarah."

"Good night, sir."

The viewscreen went dark. Sarah hyperventilated, trying to stave off the internal storm. She sank to her knees, forehead on the floor, and burst into tears, jerking mercilessly with the force of the counteracting medications.

I can't do this alone! I can't!

One

It was more beautiful than she could remember, swirling blue and white like some hand-blown glass holiday decoration dangling against the velvet blackness of space. So many years she'd searched the inky darkness, so many trillion kilometers, unable to see the planet but hoping for even a faint glimpse of the bright sun that burned like a beacon for her. It was a reminder of happier times, of brutal times, a time when family members and family bonds were taken for granted, when loneliness was unimaginable and emotional support only a handclasp away. She'd been pining for Earth most of her life, the place of warm but not suffocating summers, of snowy white winters, of leafy green trees and spacious houses with all that modern civilization could offer. Now it lay before her, so big it filled the viewport by her seat, growing larger with every passing second until the swirls became white clouds, the clouds gave way to pale sky, the sky deepened as the atmosphere thickened and the ground appeared. First brown and white, then the dots of cities appeared; buildings defined themselves. It should have been one of the greatest days of her life, but all she felt was dread.

Nerves burned at Sarah as the graceless orbital shuttle made its final decent toward the docking pad at Moscow Interstellar Spaceport. Even at the incredible speeds of the Davies Warp, the trip had taken forever. Two days on foot from their cabin to the Chessorak Research Base, fifteen days from Sigma Tau Ceti IV to Starbase 21, three days at the starbase, and a full week from the starbase to Earth. A week she spent holed up in her cabin, terrified at every voice passing her door, jumping out of her skin every time the hyperspace receiver announced an incoming message. She had no complaints about the accommodations whatsoever. Still, Uncle Tomas had wasted his money. She deserved *nothing*. She was returning to Earth branded insane; legally, mentally, criminally. She'd built a weapon in pure innocence; the court understood that. It was the holding seven people at bay and threatening to kill one of them, and not even remembering it, that everyone was rather touchy about.

She tried to bite a fingernail, but none were left. She'd never traveled alone anywhere except to school and back, but that was a lifetime ago, a host of neuroses ago. Certainly, as the tenth of thirteen children, she'd never been responsible for herself before.

Terror reigned.

She hid, safer behind the computerized locks and manual back-ups of her stateroom. When she wasn't weeping from fear and misery, she reread hundreds of pages' worth of printouts her brothers had written over the years, fingering the most recent pictures she had, wondering. So many years, so much pain, so much heartache. Especially heartache. Six years, eleven months, four days. She'd been separated from everyone for so long, it was hard to believe she was really going home.

At least, she called it home. She was born there, after all. It was Earth, it was Russia, her family was there, but she hadn't set foot on it in almost eleven years. *Earth* was a cozy memory, a childhood dream she remembered with the unabashed adulation of the preschooler she'd been. She was about to live in the home of a relative she'd only just met, in a strange city, under the most shameful of circumstances. If fear didn't get her first, the guilt of her crimes would. Panic attack not withstanding, it was hard to face your brothers and sisters after trying to kill your father.

The shuttle slowed to the merest crawl, then shuddered into place with a grinding *thunk*. A green light above the portal glowed to life, and the few passengers disembarking in Moscow headed for the exit. Sarah was the last to leave. Flipping her platinum hair out of the way, she shouldered her oversized desert-tan backpack by one strap, picked up her new metal travel case by the handle, and hesitated. The rest of her luggage and all of her brother Dmitri's had been shipped cargo; they would be delivered to the house. It wasn't right; Dimi's belongings deserved more respect than that.

"Gospozha?" The flight attendant's voice snapped her back. "Ma'am? Are you lost? Do you need help with those?"

"Nyet, spasiba." Sarah dragged her feet to the exit. No. The kind of help she needed would never be served by a flight attendant.

She'd been nine when forced to leave her family; her oldest sisters, twins, had been twenty-three, her youngest sister not yet a year. Everyone would be so much older. Her favorite sister, Katerina, was supposed to meet her in the spaceport. Katya was twenty-four herself now, married and with a baby of her own. Would they recognize each other? Would her husband be with her? What if they missed each other?

The boarding corridor opened into the vast main hall of the spaceport, teeming with thousands of travelers, both human and alien. Sarah shrank small inside her clothes, staring only at the colorful flooring. She'd been cooped up on ships and starbases breathing recycled air for three weeks;

13

her heart longed for the rain-fresh scents of the forests on Sigma Tau Ceti, for warm hay and axle grease and the vile stink of porshie shit. Her knees shook with each step until she wobbled.

She put the bags down to tuck her hair behind her ears. In all her nervousness she'd forgotten to comb it; it hung to her waist in a frizzy tangled mess. Ten, fifty, two hundred meters into the spaceport. No one said *where* Katerina was meeting her; it was a huge 'port.

"Sar'ina!"

Sarah's head snapped up, violet-blue eyes scanning the area. Ten meters away stood Katya, sweet, patient Katya, looking the same as she had seven years ago, but this time, instead of a desert robe to shelter her from Navara's searing heat, she wore a pink and white jacket to fend off the Moscow winter.

Sarah stared, afraid it was all a dream. "Katya?"

"Sarah!"

The fears of the last seven days melted, and for a brief instant it was as if nothing had ever changed. Sarah was still nine, Katya was still seventeen, and they were still best friends. The travel case fell from her fingers and she began to run, losing her precious knapsack a few meters later. They grabbed each other in a crushing embrace.

Kat kissed her several times on both cheeks. "Sarah! I can't believe it! Let me see you!" She tried to back up, but Sarah wouldn't let go.

Sarah fought down tears. "Katya? Is this for real? Am I just dreaming this?"

"It's real. Look at you! You're so tall! You're absolutely beautiful!"

Sarah blushed and stepped back. Tall, blonde, violet-eyed, athletic, nerves had pared any extra weight from her strong frame, leaving her lean and sculpted. She had – *filled out* – with more curves than she'd ever wanted, a trait that accompanied the girls of the taller side of the family. They were an embarrassment, a curse, an unwelcome symbol of feminine vulnerability that Sarah refused to acknowledge. She had few qualms against beating the daylights out of anyone who saw her as a target for unwelcome male attention. Luckily, she had her father's strong build to back her up, and none of her mother's petite delicacy. "I wouldn't go that far."

"There's your mama." A man walked up, a toddler on his arm. The little boy lunged for Katerina. She caught him in her arms with practiced ease.

"Mama," the child repeated.

"John?" Sarah stared, then was caught up in a hard shudder that shook her upper body for five long seconds.

"Ho! That was pretty bad. You all right? You're one of those one-in-ten tremblers, huh?"

"Yeah." Sarah felt the years melt away once more. *I am still nine! I am!* She wrapped her arms around the man, hugging him as fiercely as she'd hugged her sister. "John!"

"It's so good to see you, Sarah!" he breathed, returning the crush. "You've had us so worried."

"You left Starbase Four. Dimi tried to find you, but we couldn't."

"I hadn't heard from you in a long time. I came here to be with Kat. But we're here together now, aren't we." He took her hand firmly in his. Years ago, as a newly hired psychiatrist on the first solo case of his career, John had been Sarah's doctor, stupidly allowing himself to become over-involved with her very needy family. Now he would be Sarah's doctor again.

The court said so.

Sarah released his hand, allowing a shy smile. "John Carver! What on Earth have you done to my sister?"

"Unh-uh! It's Karverov now, at least professionally," he smiled back. "Doctors aren't supposed to get involved with their patients, so I had to settle for your sister." He slid his arm around his wife. "I took brazen advantage of her youth and beauty, but first she forced me to marry her so she could escape the drudgery of raising children."

"Stop that!" Katya kissed the baby.

"I was always trying to pawn you off on Valeria," Sarah remembered. "Katya was too young."

"Back then, maybe. Twelve years can be a stretch sometimes, but so far we're pretty happy with it."

Katya presented the baby proudly. "You haven't met Roman yet. He's just seventeen months."

He was a beautiful child, with round laughing cheeks, his father's brown eyes, and his mother's blond hair, but Sarah wasn't particularly fond of children. Roman curled his head into his mother's neck and peered at the stranger. Sarah smiled at him for Katya's sake and brushed her fingers across the soft cheek before turning to the father.

"We are talking about my *sister*, John! How could you *do* that?" She glanced at the baby and the implications of impregnation and childbirth, the horrible risk of death that Katya knew all too well. It had killed Mother, after all. Marriage, fine, but her trusted friend, her *doctor,* was – was – doing *That!* – to her favorite sister.

"You'll get over it," John said. "She was twenty-one when I married her. And you can't be any more protective of her than your brothers. For a

15

while there, I thought we were going to have to take David on the honeymoon."

"He was joking," Katya insisted. She jiggled the heavy baby on her arm. "Say 'Hi,' Roman. Say 'Hi' to your Aunt Sarah."

A shadow darkened Sarah's face. "Please don't put labels on my name. I can't begin to understand what an aunt is, let alone be one. Please don't make me into something I'm not. Just *Sarah*."

"Okay. Just Sarah."

Sarah shrank smaller. "I'm sorry. This is all very hard on me. It's going to take me time to adjust."

"Of course it is. I didn't mean to pressure you."

Sarah nodded and got control before a tremor struck. "I'm okay. It's just been a long six weeks. The worst six weeks of my entire life – can you believe that?" She laughed nervously, glancing at John through her bangs. "I'll bet you never thought *that* was possible, huh? You would have been proud of me, though. I came through it in one piece. See?" She held out her arms for examination.

No, she hadn't slashed her wrists this time. The burns from the energy field in her holding cell had healed without scars. He probably knew that. Doctors communicated about patients behind their backs.

John pulled her into another tight embrace. "I'm always proud of you, Sarah. It's over now. You're home and you're safe. That's what counts."

"How's Dimi?" Katya asked.

Sarah swallowed her guilt. Their brother Dmitri had been in charge of her during their exile. Sarah committed the crimes, but the court didn't think it was very smart of Dmitri to keep disassembled energy weapons in the same house with a sister who liked to tinker *and* had panic attacks. They were mad enough to lock him up to make him think about his error. There was some garbage in there about smuggling or no permit or something, too.

"Scared. I've only seen him more scared once, I think. He got three months on the weapons charges, and they dropped everything else. Just – one more way I've screwed up his life." She pressed her lips together for several seconds and held her breath, waiting for the warning tingle of the medication to pass.

She faked a smile before the anxiety won. "He'll be okay. Could – could we go now? I didn't sleep last night. I'm afraid I'll fall apart."

Katya took her hand. "You poor thing! And here we are, chattering away. I'll flag down a passenger car and we'll ride out to the flyer. John, grab her things."

Her brother-in-law scrambled to reclaim her bags. Sarah took the

16

backpack, but let him carry her clothes. She didn't care what happened to them, but the backpack held her most prized possessions, and she didn't trust anyone with it. She left the spaceport clinging to her sister, never looking back.

Two

"What's wrong?" Katya asked as the skimmer sped them through the skypaths two hours back to Minsk. "You look like you're about to be flightsick."

"I'm okay." Sarah sat immobile on the soft seat, eyes too bright in her emotionless face. The sky-blue flyer hit rough air and bounced unexpectedly for a second or two before the stabilizers kicked in. Sarah stifled a shriek, unable to catch a grip on the smooth seat. Next to her, Roman sucked his thumb sleepily, unperturbed.

John glanced back. "Nervous?"

"I guess. It's been a long time since I flew atmo."

"My wife and son are with you; I couldn't fly safer if I tried."

"I'm okay," Sarah repeated. "Can I ask you two a question?"

"Of course, darling! Anything!"

Only Katya could get away with such endearments as *darling*. You knew she meant them from the heart. Dmitri had called Sarah *Kid*, and when she was little she'd been Viktor's *Shining Star*, but that was it. She knew David's scornful *Bookhead* and *Thinktank* and *Monstermind* were meant with deniable affection, but it certainly wasn't *darling*.

Sarah knelt between the front seats. "What's it like? Uncle Tomas's house, I mean? Is it really that big house in the picture you sent, or is that an apartment building? Did Uncle Tomas return yet? Is it true he never yells at anyone? He doesn't like me, does he. Why wouldn't he come home with me, John? Why? I can't tell you how scared I was, all alone like that!"

John grinned. "Questions, questions, questions. I forgot about the constant questions. He was overdue when we left; he might be back by now. Of course he likes you! Why would he invite you to stay in his home if he didn't? And however nice Vlad told you he is, he's a thousand times nicer than that. I don't think I've ever met a nicer person."

"He's more than that, Sarah!" Katya breathed in awe. "He's *everything*! He's so knowledgeable, and genteel, and generous and caring – he knows just how to make dreams come true! And that's all one house, just his and Grandmamá's. It's absolutely magnificent, and you get to live there now, too."

"You sound like you've been brainwashed," Sarah said. "Nobody's that good, not even Viktor. What's she like – our Grandmother?"

John scrunched his face in comic exaggeration. "Not as nice as Uncle Tomas."

Katya slapped him on the knee. "Stop! You'll give Sarah a wrong impression. No, she's not as patient as Uncle Tomas, but she's still a very nice person. She just wants the best for everyone. She carries a lot of influence because of her position. She's very highly respected."

"And opinionated," John added.

"She's very high on deportment and etiquette. Just mind your manners and be polite, and you won't have a thing to worry about."

"As long as you agree with her ..."

Sarah felt her empty stomach cramp harder. "Oh goodness. I'm bound to screw that up at some point. I always do. What – What's everyone else like? I mean – How are they? You know – I mean – How do they feel about me coming home? Is – Val still mad at me? Will she let Dmitri in the house?"

Katya reached back to lift the downcast chin. "No one was *ever* mad at you, Sarah. Do you hear me? If the only way to bring both of you home was to live in a tent in Siberia, then that's where we'd be headed. Part of me doesn't blame Dmitri, but what he did, running off with you like that, that hurt her worse than you could ever imagine. Something in her died the day Dmitri said he wasn't coming back. Valeria wants you back more than anybody, so she can stop torturing herself. If it will make either of you more comfortable, she is willing to move out. All you have to do is say the word."

"No. That's not necessary. I don't want anyone put out because of me. As long as Dmitri's welcome, too. I couldn't stay there if he wasn't."

"He's been welcome since the day we arrived. It's *Dimi* who's kept this fight going," Katya reminded her.

"Coming up on downtown Minsk." John flipped several flashing toggles on the control panel. The craft descended and slowed. Tall gleaming buildings grew larger as they neared the city, and the ground-traffic crawled thick and steady between the towers. "Better get back in those restraints, just in case."

Sarah moved to obey, and Katya finished, "The point is, we love you both, with all our hearts, and we always have."

"I just – wasn't sure. After what I tried to do and all."

"Honestly, Sar – we don't care what happened, as long as you're back."

John chuckled, banking the flyer into a space in the city air-traffic. "There's an understatement! Vlad's made himself sick these last two weeks, waiting for you. If you look out the viewport there, you'll see the

19

clinic, that big white-and-glass one there. First floor is rehab and counseling, second is outpatient offices and administration, third is occupational and educational services, fourth is diagnostics, labs, and specialty supports, and fifth is reserved for inpatient. My office is 2-M. I'll take you on a tour tomorrow."

"I don't want to think about that right now."

"No rush. Same old rules still in place?"

"Which ones?"

"Hands off," John remembered. "No unplanned medications. Uh, beware of angry girl bent on revenge?"

Sarah caught a shaky breath, but the medication tremor seized her anyway.

"My goodness!" Katya said with alarm. "Are you okay? John!"

"I'm all right," Sarah said in a troubled voice. She would never, ever, revenge anybody again. She'd learned her lesson, a hundred times over. "John, that's not funny! I was a child then. A spoiled, undisciplined child! I'm as dark inside as a black hole. I do not need revenge anymore to poison people's lives, I just need to exist. Please do not remind me of that."

John Carver's eyes widened. "I'm sorry. I didn't mean to upset you. Take a look ahead." He slowed the craft to a crawl and dropped to a mere meter as they veered onto a side street. "Here we are."

Sarah peered out the side glass at the frozen countryside. *Snow.* How many years had it been since she'd touched precious snow? Four? Five? Trees, leafless and bare, rose up from the smooth whiteness. They still existed here, the ghostly pale trunks of her beloved white birches, interspersed with gray and black trunks of harder woods, so spindly when compared to the massive trees in Vandijoc. They passed a huge house, red bricks contrasting the snow.

"That's the Niametsky's," Katya directed. "And over there is the Zolotin's. They have a boy Sergei's age, but he goes to school in Vancouver. This is it."

And there it was, the house in the well-worn picture Sarah carried in her pack, looking like something out of a bedtime story. A snow-covered stone wall divided the property from the roadway. Above the gently sloping expanse of land, the *H*-shaped structure stood ostentatiously long, the masonry creamier than the pure white of the snow. Neo-Baroque decorations dripped from the corners of the windows, from the eaves, from the edges of the two-story veranda that stretched across the face like an open-air ballroom. For a single dwelling, it was monstrously huge. It was obscenely immense. To a girl raised by a brother in a little wood cabin, it was intimidating.

John eased the skimmer up the marked flyway toward that frosty winter palace, stopping under a flythrough so large four groundcraft could have parked under it at once.

"Here we are." He released the doors and retrieved Sarah's bags from the cargo space, while Katya hefted the sleeping baby.

"Something wrong?"

Sarah shivered against the vehicle, a long gray cloth wrapped around her shoulders. It was perhaps ten degrees warmer in Minsk than it had been in Moscow, but it was still *cold*. They had rarely needed coats in Vandijoc; the temperature almost never fell to freezing. She still wore the native clothing – a dark purple jumper over a cream-colored blouse, hand-knit stockings, and her best midnight-blue shoes, soft as velvet and as useful as a bedroom slipper outside. Not having to argue with Dmitri or her neighbor woman, Sarah had left off the uncomfortable undergarment that had corralled her blossoming chest. She was agitated enough without that pain. Besides, it wasn't like she had so much up top she needed it.

She didn't!

Sarah hugged her heavy pack and stared into space. The ache for Dmitri ballooned and crushed the breath from her. She hadn't realized how much she'd relied on his strength, his ability to slide in and out of social situations and let her remain comfortably out of the spotlight. She was about to be in the center of that spotlight, and he couldn't even coach her with a wink from the wings. John had to step close to hear her plead, "I can't. I can't do it. I need Dimi."

"Sure you can. Kat and I are right here. There's nothing in there to hurt you, only old friends. You want something for your nerves?"

"No!" Sarah shook her head hard, but her eyes held the look of a trapped animal. She summoned all her remaining strength and tore her foot from the frozen ground, moved it forward several centimeters and planted it before wrenching the other foot free, moving toward her doom.

She'd promised Dmitri she'd behave. She focused her attention on her "mission," memorizing the count of windows, estimating distances in her head, noting the architecture, scanning the open front yard to guess at the size, imagining what it must look like in the spring. If the yard matched the house, the gardens should be formidable. *Wouldn't Mrs. Al love them!*

"Welcome home, Sarah," Katya said, and led her inside.

The sight knocked her breath away. The cavernous foyer was larger than the entire cabin she'd spent the last four years living in – second floor included. Pink- and black-flecked stone gleamed under her feet. Suspended overhead, a fiberoptic chandelier three meters across shimmered with ten thousand cut-crystal shapes. Centered under the light, inlaid in the stone floor, shown a bright brass crest. On the far side of the entry, a massive wood staircase curved gracefully toward the second floor, as far removed from the narrow dusty stairs of the cabin as man was to an amoeba.

An old woman stood nearby, distinguished and regal in a silver-gray pantsuit. Ashen blonde hair framed a delicate face in sleek curves that ended under her chin. Her face was oddly familiar. The cheeks, the chin, the lips, the arch of the eyebrows... Take away thirty or forty years, add eighty centimeters to the hair and make it the color of sunshine, make the steely eyes bluer than the ocean, four or five centimeters shorter, five kilos or so thinner, add a radiant smile, and she would have been... *Mother*, Sarah realized. The woman had to be Mother's mother, Sarah's grandmother.

Off to the side stood a cluster of people. With a start, Sarah recognized one of the twins. Their eyes locked momentarily in acknowledgment, but Grandmother made the first move, stepping forward to greet the newcomer.

As Grandmother stretched out her hands to welcome her, Sarah dropped to her knees, forehead to the floor, the position of greatest respect and humility in the Sigma Tau Ceti culture she'd just left. Eyes closed, she hid behind the language barrier, mumbling a long stream of Tau Cetan Pelonishalak.

Mrs. Ivanov's impeccable manners were set back when her prey disappeared. She looked to the psychiatrist for an explanation. John shrugged, just as mystified.

"Please, my child. There is no need to lie on the floor. Stand up, let us see you." A manufactured smile embedded in Grandmother's face.

Sarah rose, bowing deeply several times and ending with a clumsy curtsey. "I bring you respectful greetings from the tranquility of Sigma Tau Ceti." She strung together as many large words as she could, hoping to sound as eloquent and pretentious as the hallway she stood in. "My brother, Dmitri Kirushenko, extends his heartfelt gratitude and regrets he cannot be here in person at this time. I am most humbly grateful for your offer allowing me to rejoin my family in your most magnificent home, and I thank you most sincerely. I shall gravely endeavor to ensure you do not regret your most gracious and hospitable invitation."

Grandmother's eyes blinked several times, until the practiced, cordial smile returned. "You're most welcome, my child! I've heard so very much about you. I'm delighted to meet you at last." She grasped Sarah's hands and kissed her cheeks, though Sarah stiffened at the contact and didn't

22

return the gesture. "I am Andrea Maximovna Ivanova, your maternal grandmother."

"Sarah-Irina Kirushenko, Ma'am," Sarah replied, starting to bow again. The bowing seemed out of place, so she tried the curtsey again, but that didn't seem right, either. Where was Dimi when she needed him!

"No patronymic?"

"No, Ma'am. Dmitri and I don't use one."

"I understand. Well, please, come in." Grandmother motioned to a woman in dark blue livery waiting by the wall. "Darella here will take your outerwear for you. Your family has been most anxious awaiting your arrival. I've had Marya set the sitting room for tea. Tomas is long overdue; I expect him momentarily."

Sarah barely had time to hand the servant her wrap before the tall twin at the side rushed to hug her.

"Remember me?"

"How could I forget you, Galina!"

"Are you *sure* I'm Galina?"

"Absolutely." Sarah hugged her sister back, not at all upset over the contact. "You were always fair to us."

Katya hugged Sarah again from behind. "Isn't she just beautiful, Gal!" She ran her fingers over Sarah's long, rough hair. "So tall!"

"She's got a ways to go before she'll qualify for tall in this family." Galina laughed, being one of the five siblings a meter eighty or more. "I'll bet you don't remember these two." She put an arm around each of the children next to her.

Sarah felt as if she should know the boy; he returned the look. He stood as high as her shoulder, with dark eyes and brown hair that wanted to curl at the ends despite the neat cut. *Ringlets*, she thought. *His hair should be longer and end in ringlets.*

"Nikky?" she gasped. "Nikolai? Oh my goodness! I would never have guessed, unless you were jumping on my bed."

Nikky gave her a polite hug. "We're not allowed to jump on the beds here. I think I kind of remember you. You didn't look like you, though."

"Because last time I saw you, I was probably younger than you!"

"Will you still be here for my birthday? I'll be eleven next month."

"I'm supposed to be." If she didn't screw up by then...

"My birthday's next month, too!" said the small girl on Galina's left. "I'm going to be eight!"

Sarah made a conscious effort to close her gaping mouth. "Marina?"

"This is Marina." Galina smiled down at the baby of the family. A

23

different mix than the other girls, Marina's hair had grown in a soft honey brown. She seemed a little tall for seven, but with a more moderate build.

"I don't remember you," she said, shaking Sarah's hand.

"You were just a little baby," Sarah remembered, then realized, "I watched you being *born!*"

"My mama died right after I was born, but she loved me just the same. I met my papa last fall, and he said that just makes me extra special," Marina recited proudly.

Galina steered the conversation away from their father. "Why don't we go sit?" She turned to lead the way, but behind the group, another tall figure clung to the shadows. She had Galina's height and Galina's face. She hung back, unsure.

Sarah stared back, mirroring the emotion. There was pride, and then there was cutting your own throat. She had to live in the house with everybody. How she greeted them would pave the way for everyone to accept Dmitri back. She had to make the effort, for his sake. She owed him that.

Head held unusually high, Sarah stepped forward. Here, after all these years, stood the very sister who had wanted to send Sarah away, the Traitor Twin who left Sarah and Dmitri behind in the blistering Navaran desert when the family returned to Earth. Here was the unmentionable Grand Enemy of the last seven years, in the flesh.

"Hello, Valeria."

"Hello, Sarah," Valeria replied huskily. "It's nice to see you looking so well."

Sarah hesitated, then leaned forward to give her eldest sister a token hug. "I'm sorry for causing the trouble that made you and Dimi fight."

Tears sprang onto Val's cheeks. "Oh, *Sarah!* You did *nothing* wrong! Not a thing! It was me, my fault. I am so, so sorry. Please forgive *me!*"

Sarah pulled away. "My brother took excellent care of me."

Valeria wiped her eyes with her fingers. "I can see that. I completely underestimated him."

"Yes, you did. I hold no animosity toward you, Valeria. I know you never meant for us to disappear like that, but it's not my forgiveness you need to seek. Dmitri is the one you wronged. He is the only one who can forgive you, and he doesn't do that easily. For the longest time you were his Number One enemy. I don't know if I have surpassed you on that list, but I know his pain is very slow to fade."

Valeria gave a wan smile. "He had every right. We'll have to hope for the best, won't we?"

"Good luck," Sarah wished. Val was still underestimating Dmitri.

"Come, everyone." Grandmother tried again, herding the growing crowd toward the spacious and airy reception room. "We can get reacquainted over tea."

The group hadn't managed a half-dozen steps in the right direction when another voice called out. "Sarah?"

The voice was deeper than it should have been, no longer a child's. Sarah clawed John and Valeria out of the way in her desperation to find the speaker.

And suddenly, after all the unending agony, the devastating loneliness, the gallons of tears, the hundreds of letters, the quintillions of kilometers, he was simply standing there, three steps from the bottom of the fairytale staircase.

Time stood still as reality took hold. It wasn't a dream, it wasn't a hyperspace video image or even a hologram. Vladimir, in the flesh.

Sarah's blood slid to her feet as her heart rushed to her throat. Her vision faded, her ears roared, her legs too weak to hold her up. Then the medication took over, canceling everything.

"Vlad? Vlad!"

It took Sarah two steps, but Vladimir cleared the three stairs in one leap to grab her in an embrace so tight their first several layers of molecules swapped electrons. Sarah screamed and burst into tears of joy, and Vlad joined her only a sob later.

"I can't believe this is real!" Vlad cried.

Sarah caressed his face. "Next time, we don't wait! Next time we run, just like we'd planned."

"Absolutely! Never, ever again."

"Never, ever! Look at you, Vlad!" She ran her hands through his soft hair, still damp from washing. His big brown doe-eyes with their beautiful dark lashes were still the same, but his face wasn't as round, there were angles in the cheeks, his jaw stronger, the skin under his chin irritated and red with a rash Dmitri, too, used to get from his beard inhibitor.

Beard?

Vlad?

There was a strength to him that had never been there before. "You're so big!" Sarah breathed in awe. "You did grow, after all!"

"It snuck up on me, every time I fell asleep," he apologized, returning her exploratory touches. "Look at you! You grew up, too! You look like a girl now."

Sarah laughed through her tears, hugging him. "And what was I before, a spider?"

"You know what I mean."

"Thank you!" she whispered. "Thank you for every word you ever sent me. Thank you for answering every one of my calls. You made it bearable for me. Because of you, I never lost hope. Even when I was at my very lowest, just knowing that you still cared kept me going. If it wasn't for you, I would not be alive right now. Please understand, I couldn't leave him. We were all each of us had left."

"I never lost hope, either. Never! Ask David! I thought about you every day, and I said goodnight to you every night. After Kat left, they were going to give that room to Marina, but I wouldn't let them. The other bed was supposed to be yours, and it was going to stay yours, and it still is yours, right now. My bed's right on the other side of the wall."

"Thank you." Never letting go, they folded to sit on the bottom steps. Sarah held his hand up, pressing hers against his, palm to palm, fingertip to fingertip. Their fingers were the same length now, though Sarah's hands were wider. Together they stared at the hands, then caught each other's eye and laughed.

Katya had been hugging her husband, leaking sentimental tears. She pulled away to kneel before the reunited pair, hugging them both together. A moment later Galina joined the cluster; Nikky followed a few seconds later to hug Galina; Marina hugged Katya. After hesitating, Valeria walked over. Marina let go of Katya to hug Val instead.

Andrea Ivanov stood alone, staring at the tearful pile of siblings, a Galactic-class hostess forgotten in her own home. The tea was cooling, the caviar losing its shine, and no one but herself seemed the least bit concerned.

John Carver moved next to her. "Take a good look," he said, watching the group with a warm, sappy feeling. "That's the kind of love that moves mountains. It's that kind of faith that works miracles. That's what family is all about."

Three

A Moonless nightmare, that's what it was. Social conversation wasn't the right word; conversation implied a voluntary two-way verbal exchange. In any future mention of those hours, Sarah would always refer to it as *the inquisition.*

She perched uncomfortably on a dusty-blue sofa in the huge formal sitting room, terrified of breaking the egg-shell-thin gilded porcelain cup that held her scalding tea. Vladimir sat close, holding her hand when it was free, or intercepting Grandmother's questions with stories of his own.

Vlad grabbed two cookies from a passing tray. "Try it! You'll love these." He held the confection to her lips.

Sarah smiled and allowed him to feed her a bite of the sweet. It was a crispy tube, filled with jellied fruit and vanilla crème, hand-dipped in a thick blanket of richest chocolate.

"It's like Heaven," she beamed, and pushed a loose crumb into her mouth.

"Is your tea hot enough, dear?" Grandmother asked.

"Yes, Ma'am!" Sarah turned too fast and spilled some of the burning liquid on her leg. Vlad blotted it for her with his napkin. "Thank you, Ma'am." She adjusted her damp skirt, knocked her hand against the cup, and sent her spoon somersaulting onto the blue carpeting. Mortified, Sarah abandoned the cup to the side table and grabbed for the spoon, but a servant's hand slid under hers and snatched it away first. "It's Darjeeling, isn't it?" she said painfully.

Andrea Ivanov seemed delighted. "Why, yes, I believe it is. I wasn't aware you were a connoisseur of teas."

"Everyone always drowned me with tea whenever I was sick," Sarah said, thrilled she'd said something right. "Mother was fond of Ceylon and English blends, while Father preferred the old Russian tea, but it was hard to get it outside of Russia, so he drank China black instead. Dmitri likes the Indian teas better, though his favorite was a special blend from the Armenian colony on Mellana IV. We couldn't get any of them on Sigma Tau, so we drank a local herbal tea. It tasted like a fresh-cut lawn with barley, but with enough sugars, you got used to it. It was much better than the medicinal teas. Mrs. Al – that was our neighbor lady who took care of us – pushed them on me once when I was getting coughy. It smelled like a field worker in the middle of harvest. I puked it up all over the place. She never tried it on me again, thank the Moons."

Nikky and Marina giggled. Vlad snickered. Grandmother merely pressed a hand to her chest. "Well, I shall be sure to make note of that," she said with a thin smile. "If Sigma Tau Ceti should be opened for exports, we shall specifically avoid medicinal teas. Darjeeling sits well with you, though?"

"Yes, Ma'am."

Grandmother steered the subject away from food. "Were you and Dmitri able to follow any of the recent Alliance elections, out there in the Epsilon quadrant?"

Sarah froze for an eyeblink. "We never paid a breath to politics. I can name the President of the Alliance, I think. Faramishulin Ojanikashi was the official in charge of Vandijoc, and Chinoor Tharnavasha was the Crown Lawman of Pelonishala, the Country-State we lived in, but that's as much as we ever followed things."

Andrea Ivanov coughed with discomfort. "Zharuminsky. Anatoly Germanovitch Zharuminsky is the current President of the Federation. Boris Ivanovich Irulin is the current Minister of Byelorus, and a good friend of mine. Veronika Petrovna Elodiak is the current administrator of Minsk."

"Yes, Ma'am." From the edge in Grandmother's tone, Sarah had the distinct feeling that she might be quizzed on those names later, and committed them to memory.

"Vlad said you worked for the Alliance, doing research," Galina said. "Were you in a research center, or just in a city?"

Sarah rolled her eyes. "Vandijoc's about as far from a city as you can get. Wilderness, more or less. We lived a kilometer and a half out of the settlement, half a kilometer from our nearest neighbor. We lent them our farmland and split the profits. We started out with three rooms to our cabin, but Dmitri built on three more. We must have cut down fifty trees for lumber. You should see me swing an axe!" she bragged to Vladimir. "I can split wood in a single blow. I'd pretend I was a Cossack soldier, brandishing my sword among the infidels. Of course, a sword would have been a bit more dashing than a boring old axe, but Dmitri would never have let me near one, even if we had one. I wasn't even allowed near his knives."

"Make a fist," Vlad asked, and he gave her bicep a hard squeeze. "Sun's Guns, Sar! I work out with weights and your arms are *still* bigger than mine! No matter what I do, you still do it better than me. It's not fair."

"I doubt that's true. I think we're a little big now to have a peeing contest," she reminded him, thinking back to the only time he'd ever beaten her at anything. Her stunning defeat infuriated her three-year old self for months. "To be honest, I think I will yield you that victory without a rematch. I hardly think I..."

Grandmother Ivanov cleared her throat sharply. Sarah stopped. Her eyes scanned the faces around the room. John's fingers rubbed his lip, but his eyes were laughing. Katya blushed at the carpeting. The old lady stared at her with strong disapproval, and even Vlad looked embarrassed.

Oops.

The silence was painful. Dimi would have been happy that she'd at least tried. Somehow, it was no surprise the old woman didn't approve of contests between the sexes – even preschool ones.

Change topics! Sarah bolted from the sofa to examine the huge painting above the fireplace. A black background burst with a frenzy of bold, chaotic chunks of colors, bombarding a pastel shape that could have been a stylized beanstalk, a limbless tree trunk, or even a vertical river.

"This painting is too modern for this room, I think," Sarah mused out loud. "It would look much more impressive by the stair in the main entry. Have you ever thought of putting it there? A portrait would work better in here, something brighter in tone and lighter in character."

Grandmother Ivanov joined her. "You are an expert on art, as well? Child, do you have any idea how much this painting is worth?"

Sarah gave it a critical eye. "If I were to guess, it's late twenty-first century. It's not – ?" She stood on tiptoe to squint at the signature. "Is this a Rayál? An *authentic* Rayál?"

"It most certainly is authentic!"

"Incredible! Gordon Rayál, first of the expressionist painters to arise from the ashes of World War III, 2024 to 2101," Sarah recited. "Known for his use of abstract color to represent emotion. There are only eight known surviving works, and at least two of those are partially destroyed. This painting is literally priceless!"

Grandmother actually smiled. "You do know something of art!"

"I've been to museums all over the galaxy, whenever Dimi would take me. Oh no!" Sarah dared to brush a finger over the bottom of the sleek frame. "This one's decaying, too! You're not hanging it properly. When was the last time you turned it?"

Andrea Ivanov's fingers tugged the jewelry at her throat as if it had tightened. "What do you mean, it's not hung properly? Of course it's hung properly."

"No it's not," Sarah contradicted with conviction. "Look here." She touched the edge of the painting. "Feel it. This little overhang? The paint has slid at least two millimeters. Any of Rayál's paintings must be rotated and hung upside down every six months to counteract the effects of gravity. There were no art materials manufactured in the immediate aftermath of World War III – they weren't a necessity to survival. Rayál used a medium he invented himself that included petroleum distillates, scavenged synthetic military lubricants, and powdered metal. It gave him the brilliant colors he was after, but his paint never fully dried. Even now, 200 years later, if you hang the picture too long in the same position, the painting will slowly slide off the canvas. It has to be rotated to keep the pigments in the same position. That's what ruined at least two of the surviving works, and it's starting to happen to this one as well. It can be chemically treated to fix the pigments, but that ruins the value. It loses the fragility that makes it so exceptionally rare."

Grandmother Ivanov's nostrils flared, but she kept her composure. "Well, I shall certainly mention that to Tomas when he returns. Is there anything you'd like to tell me about any of the other pieces in the house?"

The sugary tone hinted that Sarah had crossed some line again. "I haven't examined any other pieces that closely."

Andrea sighed with relief and beckoned her grandson. "That's easily remedied. Vladya, darling – you've been so eager for your sister to arrive, perhaps you would like to show her around the house." She said to Sarah, "It won't be as thorough as if I took you myself, of course, but perhaps Tomas can fill you in on the architectural and historical details later. Make sure he shows you where you'll be staying, dear. I'm sure you'd like an opportunity to freshen up, perhaps change out of your traveling clothes and into something more comfortable." The hostess smile returned to her aging features. "Go, children!"

"Thank you! Thank you for getting me out of there!" Sarah whispered in Vlad's ear as she threw her arms around his neck the moment they were out of sight of the sitting room. "Much longer and I would have died from fright."

Vlad's arms circled her waist. "Grandmamá's okay. She just takes some getting used to. Uncle Tomas is a lot more fun."

"I don't know him well, either, but so far I think you're right." Sarah grew overly aware of two short figures surrounding her, much too close for comfort. Her stomach quivered, the hair on her neck prickled, but she tried her best to relax before the medication noticed. They were only children. They should not have been threatening.

"Are you two in love?" Nikky asked.

Sarah pushed Vlad away. "No!"

"Then how come you keep hugging and kissing each other?"

"'Cause we miss each other, you asteroid." Vlad shoved Nikky in the head with the palm of his hand, a hateful gesture David had done to Vlad a thousand times a year almost since the day he was born. "You disappear for seven years and see what people do to you."

Fingers tugged at Sarah's skirt as Marina petted the fabric. "I like your dress. That color's pretty. Want to see my room?" She tried to slip her hand into Sarah's.

Sarah allowed the touch for a second before pulling her hand back. She caught herself before she could give her *Don't touch me!* shriek. The little girl had meant no harm, but still… Sarah knew from hard experience, a trusting child was a tragedy waiting to happen.

"You should not approach strangers like that," she warned Marina from the heart.

"You're not a stranger. Mama Val says you're my sister, just like her."

"That is true, but we've just met. Please give me a day or so to become acquainted with you. Only then might we become friendly enough to hold hands."

"Okay. Will you play with us?"

"I – I – maybe." The panicky feeling grew stronger, not weaker. A tremor twitched in one eye.

"Do you ski?" Nikky asked. "I'm really good at it. Dave and Serg have skis out in the hangar – you could borrow theirs, if you want."

Vlad saved her. "Get lost, both of you! *I'm* talkin' to Sarah! If you're gonna follow, then do it quiet. Come on." He grabbed Sarah's hand and dragged her down the hall. "You've gotta see the setup we've got in the Media room! It's like a private cinema!"

* * *

"Shhh!" Vlad giggled as he pulled Sarah along the secret access corridor. They huddled close, listening at the door panel. The tour had dissolved into an unofficial game of hide-and-seek with Nikky and Marina. With three official staircases and two official lifts, two sets of service stairs and a service lift connecting the basement with all three floors, they'd looped back on their tracks in hopes of losing their brother and sister.

"This is a change of pace," Sarah whispered. "Usually it was me leading you."

"Only til you learn your way. I figured I'd show you all the secret shortcuts, because I know when David gets home tomorrow he'll want to run the Fearsome Four through a round or two. This way you'll be able to beat him at his own game. You just have to be quiet. We're not supposed to play Commando in the house."

"I can't wait! I wish they were here now."

"I don't hear anything," Vlad said, listening. "This is a secret door in the north hallway, near the kitchen. Come on." He pulled the door aside and they burst into the hallway, quiet as mice. They would have made it unnoticed if it weren't for the fact that Sarah crashed full force into

Uncle Tomas.

Sarah shrieked. "Moons have mercy! I'm *sorry,* sir!"

Tomas regained his balance. "Sarah! Goodness! I hope you didn't hurt yourself."

She dropped to her knees before him, face in the carpeting. "I beg forgiveness, sir! I should have looked!"

"No harm done. I was just on my way to find you, Little Ghost. It's only fitting you appeared out of the wall. Please, stand up. That kind of groveling may have been standard on Sigma Tau Ceti, but this is Earth. You'll have the town talking."

"Yes, sir." Sarah took Vlad's hand to pull herself up.

Tomas smiled. "I see you two wasted no time finding each other. Are you happy now?"

Sarah turned to Vlad; he gazed proudly back. Tears of utter joy flooded to the surface. "Oh, yes, sir! It's like a dream!"

Vladimir lunged forward, grabbed his uncle around the neck with his free arm and kissed him heartily on both cheeks. "Thank you, sir! Thank you! It's absolutely, without a doubt, the happiest day of my life! This is how things should have been all along."

Following Vlad's lead, Sarah stood on tiptoe and gave Tomas the faintest of pecks. "Thank you, sir."

"As long as you're happy," Tomas said. "I apologize for being so late; there was a two-hour delay on the shuttle, and it took almost an hour to get clearance to moley-beam in from Moscow. Sarah, if you have a moment, I'd like to speak with you. We can use my office." He gestured down the hall.

Sarah's glow vanished as panic rose, sharp and cold. A warning tic twitched on her face. "Can Vlad come, too?"

"If he'd like," Tomas agreed, and Sarah allowed herself a thankful smile in return.

Tomas settled into his chair behind the desk. "So, you made your shuttle and met up with Katya without any problems. I told you you could do it."

"Yes, sir," Sarah agreed, simply because it was easier than explaining the terror she'd experienced.

"Did Vlad show you your room? My apartment is in the basement, but Mamá's suite is at the end of your hall. Anytime you need me, just give a buzz on the intercom. Is your room satisfactory?"

"Yes, sir. I don't think the Winter Palace could be as beautiful. You are far too kind, sir."

"It wasn't much. Katerina had the room done in pinks. Vlad said you preferred blues, so I simply ordered the color scheme changed. I haven't seen it yet, myself."

"Still, sir, I do appreciate it."

"I don't want to tie up your time, but I wanted to go over tomorrow with you. Breakfast is at seven sharp, so gauge your wake-up time accordingly. I'm sure David and Sergei will call later; they can't leave school until mid-morning tomorrow. I figured you'd want to be here, so I scheduled your appointment with John for nine. That should give us plenty of time."

Sarah's shoulders sagged. "Yes, sir. I'm starting that already?"

"John doesn't see patients on the weekends, and he's supposed to see you within forty-eight hours of your arrival. That leaves tomorrow. Is that a problem?"

Sarah shook her head. She could break her whole life into two parts – doctor times, and avoiding doctor times. "It never ends, does it?"

Vlad wrestled her shoulders annoyingly. "It's just a formality. John's just putting his name on the papers to make it look official. It's not like you're a real patient or anything. You just have to hang with him. Don't break a sweat."

Sarah summoned a tiny smile. "Maybe. It's the whole implication, that's all."

Vlad snorted. "Like we ever cared about that stuff! Nothing matters but the fact you're *home*. Now that you're here, everything will be fine."

Tomas consulted the computer for his notes. "We meet with your court systems manager in two weeks. Have they been in contact with you to go over any of the details?"

Sarah gulped and squeezed Vlad's hand. She didn't want to think about court. "No, sir."

"Well, I can tell you a few of them, if you like." Tomas tapped controls and called up a different screen. "As you know, I was given full custodial guardianship, though you remain a liability of the court due to your legal status. Your charges of attempted murder were dropped on the grounds of overwhelming mental instability at the time of the crime.

However, that makes you a high risk in the eyes of the law, requiring twenty-four-hour supervision by qualified persons. That means I can't leave you with Nikky and say that he's keeping an eye on you."

"I'm not letting you out of my sight," Vlad said. "I fell for that crap once, and I won't let it happen again."

Sarah opened her mouth to say she'd kill the first person who tried to separate them, but caught herself. Considering she was already under scrutiny for attempted murder, it might be more prudent to say something less violent, lest Uncle Tomas think she was serious. "Make sure you don't."

"You are required to undergo psychiatric counseling with a qualified physician – in your case, John – for no fewer than ten hours per week, until such time as you no longer demonstrate the unstable behaviors that make you a danger to others. Your progress will undergo monthly review by the court to insure your needs are being met by the process as it stands, and that you are in compliance with the prescribed plan of rehabilitation. Failure to obey any part of the decree, either by you, your physician, or me, can result in your removal to a setting that will ensure compliance. Any questions?"

Sarah gazed at her hands. This wasn't going to be much different than a full hospitalization, with no rights, no choices, no voice in what could happen to her, only this time she'd get to go home at night. She had no idea how much of a stickler for rules Uncle Tomas was. Would he forgive her if she slipped up, overlook an accidental mistake, or would he be on the comm to the court every time she forgot to cover her mouth when she sneezed? What people seemed to be, and what they really were, were too often opposites.

"I don't mean to sound rude, sir, but, Dmitri will regain custody of me when he returns, won't he?"

"I don't know, Sarah. That is a legal decision, not mine. Legally, his claim of guardianship never existed in the first place, and whatever title he pretended to have was officially revoked. Nonetheless, I promised Dmitri I would return you to him if that's what you both wished, and I meant that. If he wishes, I will start the paperwork the minute I know he's on his way."

The thought of her brother rotting in a prison somewhere on her account made the heartache of his absence unbearably strong, and she gave a painful sigh. "Please, sir, if you could give me a list of your household rules, I can study them to assure I do not inadvertently violate them."

Their uncle raised an eyebrow. "I've never made any hardfast rules

34

for the house. My mother doesn't allow running or shouting inside, but otherwise, as long you conduct yourself in a polite manner, you'll do fine. Keep in mind, we often entertain business or political associates, so be aware of that when you're walking about. Usually Arman, the house manager, has a schedule of who is to be here when and what room they'll be meeting in; I'll have him link you to the daily schedule as well."

"Thank you, sir. I'll remember that, sir." Sarah would have preferred real rules. *Be polite* had a million interpretations, and for every situation, 999,999 were the wrong ones. She fished a plastic card from the pocket of her skirt.

"Here, sir. You said I could return the unused amount when I got back."

"Yes, I did say that." Tomas slipped the bank card into a slot on his interface and called up the balance.

He frowned. "Sarah, this is everything you started with. You didn't spend *any* of it? I thought I made it clear this was yours to do with as you wished?"

She glanced up under the curtain of hair. "Yes, sir. As I tried to tell you, I already had enough to get me by. I thank you for your most courteous and considerate offer."

"I can't say I'm not confused, Sarah, but as long as you're happy with the outcome. There was absolutely nothing you needed, or wanted? There's a whole host of entertainments on an ambassador-class ship; nothing interested you at all?"

"No, sir. I had plenty of work to keep me busy, and nothing caught my eye." That wasn't *exactly* a lie. Nothing could possibly interest you if you never looked at the options. She had some money, but it wasn't even enough to buy her one restaurant meal on that damned luxury ship. The in-room replicator met her needs. Dmitri's money had been seized and frozen by the court until his sentence ended. She did have work with her she could have started, but she'd been far too upset to concentrate on anything like that.

"Well, I certainly hope you'll take better advantage of all the amenities in the house," Tomas said. "All work and no play makes Vanya a dull boy."

Vlad grinned. "Don't worry. I know what Sarah likes. I can take care of her. Don't worry about a thing."

"Ah! That reminds me." Tomas patted himself down until he pulled a small, flat box from a pocket. It was wrapped in blue and tied with a gold band. "This is for you, Vladimir, from Sarah. Unfortunately, she arrived home before me."

Both Vlad and Sarah seemed surprised. "When we were on the *Triumph*, you told me to make sure I gave it to him," Tomas reminded her.

Sarah gave a shy smile and nodded, thrilled Tomas hadn't misplaced or forgotten it. "I remember. It's a kiss."

Vladimir opened the gift to find a gold charm in the shape of two tiny lips.

"I hope you don't mind I took the liberty of having it gilded," Tomas said carefully. Tomas had been caught off guard by her unshakable belief that the gesture was three-dimensional and visible to everyone, so far as to accuse him of misplacing it. Whether Dmitri had gone along with Sarah just to pull his leg, or if Dmitri really believed it, too, Tomas didn't know, but at least with the purchased jewelry he could *find* the 'kiss' if he dropped it again. "I thought, that way, Vlad could keep it next to his heart."

It worked. The Mad Hatter was touched.

"Thank you, sir. That was most thoughtful. I remember it being bigger, though," Sarah said with disappointment. "I suppose it must have shrunk during the gilding process. Oh, well. It's the thought that counts."

Vlad hugged her tight. "It's perfect! David'll be so jealous!"

Four

D inner with Dmitri on Sigma Tau couldn't have been more casual. Barefoot, half-dressed, use a plate or just the table, use a spoon or use your bread to soak up your soup, it didn't matter much when they ate alone. It wasn't that they didn't know proper manners; it just wasn't a priority between them.

Sarah entered the formal dining room in Minsk, hand in hand with Vladimir and Nikky, weak with the expectations of perfection that would no doubt be thrust upon her. The long, lace-covered table suffered under a clutter of plates and glasses and pitchers and platters. Two candelabras burned in the center of the table, an homage to custom of the past rather than necessity in the brightly lit room. Everyone stood by their chairs, waiting for the stragglers. And this was only Thursday!

An empty seat waited at the corner between Uncle Tomas and Vlad; she slid into it. A servant placed a filled plate before her.

Sarah sniffed discretely at it. It was real food, not replicated, but she'd grown accustomed to Sigma Tau Ceti tastes and flavors. It would take time to reacclimate herself to the taste of Earth foods. Rare roast beef stared up at her, leaking contaminating juices on to the wafered potatoes cooked with onions and paprika and the honey-glazed parsnips. She had a water glass, and a glass half-filled with a deep red liquid.

Uncle Tomas stood, holding up his red glass in a toast before they ate. "To family reunions, both old and new. Sarah, it is with the utmost pleasure we welcome you to the fold at last, and hope you find as much happiness in being here as your presence has brought everyone. May your troubles be few, your successes be many, and if I hear one more whine out of Vladimir or anyone else, I shall leave Dear Mother Russia for good," he threatened with a laugh. "To family! May we always have a reason to gather."

"To Sarah!" Vladimir glowed, raising his glass as the table joined in. The golden kiss hung from a chain around his neck.

"To Dmitri," Sarah corrected when the cheering stopped. "May his accommodations be even half as nice as mine, and may he know how often he's in my thoughts." Although the red liquid looked far too much like blood, Sarah didn't wish to insult Tomas. She took a slight sip.

Tomas noticed her pucker. "You don't like the wine, Sarah?"

"Is that what it is? Dmitri didn't allow me to drink alcohol."

"Wine has a low alcohol content. A small amount of red is good for you. This particular one is French, a Chateau Rivard 2266," he said, turning the glass to watch the liquid sparkle. "A very good year for French wines. If you don't wish to drink it, that's perfectly acceptable. Not everyone here does."

"Thank you, sir." Sarah picked up her fork but her head remained bent, watching the table. She poked her food, testing small bits. Not having eaten breakfast or lunch, and having only picked at the afternoon tea, she was quite hungry, but nerves knotted her stomach. Not since the Mirabella Hotel had she dealt with so many pieces of tableware – plates that did nothing but hold the dinner plate, of all things! She wanted to dive into the spinach salad and devour the potatoes and fresh bread, but somehow, judging by the way Grandmother picked delicately at small portions, Sarah felt sure the bony old woman wouldn't approve of hearty appetites. When Vlad offered her another dinner roll; she took two and slipped one into her pocket for later.

Grandmother watched from the far end of the table. "Is there something wrong with your food, dear? If your meat has grown cold or is too rare, it is no problem for Marya to exchange it for something more to your liking."

Sarah stared with regret at the slices of striated bovine muscle tissue decaying on her plate. "No, Ma'am. Thank you, Ma'am. That's not necessary. I don't eat meat."

Uncle Tomas slapped a hand across his forehead. "I must have left my head on the starbase. I'm so sorry, Sarah! Dmitri told me you were vegetarian. I will inform the kitchen and they will plan for you accordingly. Please forgive me. Nadia!" he called to a staff waiting table. *"Pazhal'sta*, could you get Sarah another plate, without the meat?"

"There's no need for that! It's no problem, sir! It doesn't bother me! I'm used to it. Please! This is fine." She waved the servant away.

"Vegetarian? Nonsense!" Grandmother scoffed. "That's the finest Kazakhstani beef you'll ever see, raised on the most politically correct, humane breeding farms around, and personally inspected by Tomas himself. It passes every law, both civic and religious. There is absolutely nothing wrong with it."

"I have no doubt of that, Ma'am," Sarah insisted. "It's the thought. On Sigma Tau, porshies are used both as draft animals and a meat source. They take a baby porshie, perhaps only 125 kilos, and tie it to a post. You take a sharp knife, grab the head under your arm, and if you're any good, you're able to drive the knife up under the jaw and pull it across the baby's throat in one try, severing the arteries and the trachea all at once." She drew a finger around her throat for precision's sake.

"That is quite enough, thank you," Andrea Ivanov replied, but Sarah hadn't finished.

"...The blood sprays everywhere in a huge gush. It can't yell with its throat cut, so it bleeds silently, its mouth opening and closing, opening and closing, until it collapses in the dirt. If you're nice, you wait until it stops quivering before you untie it, roll it over, and make a slit ..."

"Tomas!" Grandmother commanded, napkin to her mouth.

"Sarah!" Vlad snapped. "You know my stomach! I don't need to hear that kind of stuff!"

"Sarah!" Tomas remained calm, but his manner said she'd crossed a line. "Your details are inappropriate conversation for a dinner table. While your objection is morally valid and I sympathize, next time, please stick to more general explanations. You could simply have said, 'I was disturbed by the butchering methods used on Sigma Tau.'"

"Yes, sir. I'm sorry, sir. I just wanted her to know my reasoning. I wasn't ignoring your meat to be rude. I simply can't bear to eat it." Sarah hung her head in honest contrition. "I'm sorry, Vlad."

Uncle Tomas sighed and dropped his napkin by his plate with more force than diplomacy would have allowed. He motioned to the kitchen staff. "Nadia, tell Marya I think we're ready for dessert now."

"Is that what happened to *our* beef?" Nikky stared in horror as the platters were cleared from the table.

John Carver reached for his wine. *"No!* That's Sigma Tau Ceti."

Sarah felt Vlad staring at her, unsure if he was mad or in sympathy. "What? I didn't even mention what Mrs. Al does to poultry... ."

* * *

Tomas took a seat for the ritual late evening tea in his mother's suite. Katya and John had left, Nikky and Marina were asleep, and Vladimir and Sarah were sprawled in his room, deep in conversation over a game of cards. All was as perfect as Tomas could ever want, and he felt damned pleased with himself.

He reached for a cup. "Well, Mamá? What do you think of our long-lost relative? Isn't she a charmer? The prettiest thing I've seen in ages, and smart enough for the Davies Institute. What did I tell you!"

Andrea was about to sip her tea, but she lowered the cup. "Good God, Tomas! Have you been in the vodka? I honestly don't know how to respond."

"Chush! How can you say she doesn't have the prettiest eyes you ever saw?"

"It becomes hard to notice the eyes when you're being assaulted by the rest of her," Andrea sniffed. "She's horribly rude …"

"She's very shy."

"… boorish … "

"Her manners are as impeccable as any of her siblings."

"I would prefer you feed her away from the table.

Tomas's eyebrows crept upward. "That was a little unexpected …"

"And those ghastly clothes!" Andrea pressed a hand to her chest. "How in Heaven's name can she hold her head up? I don't care how old she is or where she's coming from! She would hardly qualify as petite in structure. She needs some proper undergarments. She can't go around with her loose bosom jiggling like a roll of fat."

Tomas sighed with discomfort. "I'm aware of that, Mamá. That's what she wore where she was living. I'm guessing she doesn't have any other clothes."

"Then she shall have some tomorrow. Cover her with a coat and scarf, comb that awful hair, and I shall take her myself."

"I gave her a thousand-credit account, but she didn't touch it. I still don't understand why."

Andrea sipped her tea. "Only a thousand? It's not like you to be so stingy. That's barely enough for three good outfits, not counting accessories. She was probably insulted. If you expected her to get clothing, you should have offered at least five."

Tomas rubbed a pensive finger along his lip. "I don't think that was it. If anything, I think it might be pride. She and Dmitri are used to taking care of themselves. My guess is she doesn't want to admit she doesn't have anything else." He chose a small raisin scone from the plate between them and buttered it. "If she bought four outfits and wore them repeatedly, we'd know that was all she had."

"Oh, Tomas!" Mamá mourned. "You've really pulled one over on me this time. Maybe I should have let you have the dog you always begged for. At least we could have kept it in the hangar. *Borzhoi* are so big, but they do have a certain graceful elegance to them. A matching silver pair roaming the front lawns might look rather nice, don't you think? Perhaps you'd be willing to make a trade."

Tomas laughed and swallowed his bite of scone. "No, Mamá. The boys would love a pair of dogs, but I'm not about to trade Sarah for them. She's a little rough in places, but the basics of good breeding are all there, if you care to look. Give her some time"

"She's nothing but a… a… *kulak*! Did you see the condition of her hands? When you said farm, I assumed you meant in charge of personnel,

40

or maybe she oversaw harvester robots, or worked in a distribution office somewhere. When I saw those hands, I prayed she did soil research or product development or, Lord help us, mechanical repair. But no. Honestly, Tomas! What have I done to deserve this from you? She's nothing but a feudal *peasant*, scratching her food out of the ground with a stick! That fact cannot get around, Tomas! Do you hear me?" She pointed a finger of authority at him. "Come up with some title she can be trained to use instead – *Nutrition Production Specialist*, or, or, *Agricultural Production Engineer*. Something less … *primitive!*"

"Mamá! We are not going to *train* her like some animal! Of course it was primitive – it was a developing planet. Do not go out of your way to make her feel unwelcome. She *had* a title – Alliance Cultural Observer. She observed the local population and took notes, which the reports said she was quite good at. She also served as an accomplished translator. Dmitri said they did not farm themselves, but helped a neighbor for a cut of the profits, which is more your style. You're taking this a bit too seriously."

"I should hope it was a large share. The nails can be fixed until they grow in on their own, but it will take weeks of skincare sessions to scrub off those calluses," Andrea said.

"Back off a bit, Mamá, until she settles in. Sarah doesn't strike me as someone who is bothered by cosmetic imperfections. Give her a week, maybe even two, get her into some proper clothes, get her to –," he sighed, "comb through that mess of hair, and then we can polish her to your standards. It's a big change for her. Give her a month or two to get her bearings before you add her name to the social registry. Please."

"As you wish. Such a shame, though. Such potential for beauty. Her coloring's good, but she doesn't get that height or build from our side. I'm sure the coarse conversation and shameless conduct are also a product of the inferior blood."

"Mother!" It was impossible to tell from his tone if he was swearing or addressing her. He stood up angrily. "Sometimes you are so much like Papa, I feel like he's not really gone! After all these years, after all the pain over losing Maryana because of your self-righteous claim to centuries-dead nobility, how can you *still* see your grandchildren as being one half *in*ferior? Would you have said that about *my* son, simply because his mother was an American and not a pedigreed Russian like you? Can you really feel that Valeria or David or Sarah are less noble because their father's genes are more dominant? That Katya and Vladimir are inherently better genetically because they take after our side? You'll love Dmitri, then! He's more of your Alyatov blood than I am!"

Andrea's face pinched together in a deadly glare. "Don't get theatrical on me, Tomas. I could have accepted Maryana bearing one, even two children by that man, but we've taken care of *eight* of them! And don't forget the one that was murdered. And the one Galina's trying to locate. And when they sent us the body of the one that died, like a missing piece of a collection we were amassing. But wait! You've found two more to bring home! How can you stand there and defend a man that allowed his wife to breed to her very death? Your sister was not a strong girl. Her body was not meant for that kind of abuse."

"Because I've never met him! I don't know the rationale behind it," Tomas said coolly, "but if he loved my sister as much as their children claim, he can't have been all bad. Perhaps his breeding was not as perfect as ours, perhaps he *was* everything evil David claims, ... "

"He murdered his own *child*, Tomas!"

" ... but I *do* know that the combination produced the finest litter of children I would ever want to claim as my own!" Tomas held his head high. "If nothing else, I will grant him that much courtesy and respect! At some point in their lives, those children *were* raised properly, and I know these last two are no less wonderful than the other eight. I hope you can pry your heart open wide enough to see that. Now, I am going to check on our young guest and bid her good night. Do you wish to accompany me and make a good impression?"

Andrea's eyes were steely. Her mouth pressed into a tight line, showing the fine little creases accumulating once again around her lips. Another year or so, and she'd need another surgery to eliminate them. "Tomas, I believe you are treading a very fine line of insolence towards me."

"It's not insolence, Mamá. It's honesty. I realize this is my project, not yours, but if you left your private little suite and tried to involve yourself with everyone just a little bit more, you'd know I'm right."

Andrea rose to her tiny slippered feet. *"Tomas Severyan Fedorovitch!* Let us not forget by whose grace you and your entourage live here! This property does not become yours until my death, and even that fact can be changed. Someone must attend to business while you constantly take time off to pursue these philanthropic missions of yours! If the child had any grace and gratitude at all, *she* would be coming to bid *us* good night. As her guardian, you should have thought of that already." She stalked past him with a flounce of her diaphanous lounging robe. "Follow, Tomas. Let me remind you what constitutes gentility."

Tomas watched his mother's back progress down the hallway, then followed obediently. "Yes, Mamá."

Five

Andrea Ivanova would never admit that Tomas might be right, that she did subconsciously insulate herself from the tumult that had taken over in recent years. She simply decided that Tomas, breeding aside, was still a man, and a man was not the best role model for a wild young girl. This child would need her personal attention, her respected expertise in cultural etiquette, if she were to be turned around and saved from a feral life. She would invite the girl on a day-long shopping trip. They would visit the best boutiques in Minsk, travel all the way to the fashion centers of Kiev or Moscow, if necessary. They would have someone trim and condition the tangled mess of hair, cover the ragged nails with artificial ones, and start the tedious process of eliminating the thick calluses of the girl's fingers. Certainly, there was no pleasanter way to spend a day.

Andrea knocked on the bedroom door. She knocked again, louder. She tried the door, and it opened. "Sarah, dear?"

The bed was made, but yesterday's clothing and shoes lay scattered on the floor. The upstairs help didn't start on the bedrooms until seven. Andrea had only known the girl for a few hours, but she hadn't struck her as the type used to doing chamber work. The bed didn't look slept in. Perhaps Vladimir would know – the girl hadn't left his side for a moment the day before.

The room Vlad shared with Sergei was next down the hall. She knocked. "Vladimir?"

"Yeah?" came a muffled reply.

Mrs. Ivanov pushed the door open. "Vladimir, have you seen Sarah? I wanted to know if … " She stopped as her teenaged grandson sat up in bed, bleary with sleep. Between him and the wall lay an extra bedcover, a piecework design of alien fabric. Under the cover, her teenaged granddaughter stirred and sat up, looking to her brother with wide, nervous eyes.

Andrea felt her own eyes narrow. Perhaps her interpretation was wrong; she would need a second opinion. She strode into the room and addressed the house computer. "Intercom! Tomas, I need you in Vladimir's room, immediately!"

"Grandmamá? What's … ?" Vlad began. Next him, Sarah turned pale under the harsh stare, and pulled her blanket tighter around her.

Andrea held up a hand. "Don't move. Wait for Tomas."

Tomas appeared breathless in the doorway, having taken the stairs two at a time. "Mamá?"

"Take a look at what I found, Tomas. Her bed was not slept in last night. Please tell me I am imagining this. I didn't realize this is what you and Valeria intended to bring into my home."

Surprise registered on Tomas's face. "Vladimir? Can you explain this?"

Vlad stared back innocently. "Explain what?"

Sarah understood. In a flash she rolled over Vlad and off the bed. "I didn't do anything wrong!"

"We were asleep ... ."

"We didn't do anything wrong!" Sarah repeated.

Tomas kept his voice low. "I haven't said you did. Vladya, can you tell me –"

Vladimir clued in. He leapt from the bed, fully clad in green pajamas. "You think we were *sleeping* – ? Ohmigods." Vlad's face paled dangerously white, became deep red, then went back to white again. He clutched at his stomach. "We were *talking!* That's all! Sarah didn't want to be alone, so we talked until two or three in the morning! We fell asleep talking! That's all! I swear it on Mother's grave!"

Sarah twitched with small tremors. "I followed the rules! I didn't do anything wrong! Why won't you believe me? You can't do this!"

The loud voices brought Galina down the hall. "Is there something I can help with, Uncle Tomas?"

"Your grandmother found Sarah in bed with your ward."

"I brought my blanket! I followed the rules!" Sarah insisted. She dropped the bedcover and wrapped her hands in her hair to stop them from shaking. Her eye shivered with a tremor.

Galina laughed. "I suppose we should have warned you. Vlad and Sarah shared a bed from day one. Even after they were in separate rooms, we'd chase them back three or four times a night. We should have warned you."

Andrea's steel-gray eyes grew to metal disks. "You *approve* of this?"

"That's just the two of them, together at last."

"Galina, they're not little children anymore," Tomas reminded her. "I can't think of many cultures where seventeen-year-old boys sleep in the same bed with their sixteen-year-old sisters and there's not some experimenting going on."

"Yes, but in this case, I'm telling you from long experience, it's just them being them. They've been separated for so long, they don't want to miss a single moment." She rubbed Vlad's shoulder and gave him a

44

squeeze of comfort. A faint color came back to his face.

Andrea ruffled herself and fussed like an angry bird. "Utter nonsense! I did not see my sister for ten years; I did not go crawling in bed with her when we visited. Tomorrow you'll tell me the child was sleepwalking."

Tomas frowned with a sigh. "I'm afraid I'm going to have to make a ruling here …"

"Uncle Tomas, I *swear!* We were only … !"

"NO!" Sarah sank to her knees, head against the fancy carpet. "PLEASE! Not yet! I followed the rules!"

Tomas knelt down. "Sarah, please, sit up. Calm yourself. I haven't accused you of any wrongdoing. I realize you may be confused; I'm confused, too. Which rules are you referring to?"

Sarah rocked on her knees, seized with tremors. She crossed her arms over her chest and hugged herself as if cold. The tearful eyes darted several times between Tomas and the floor, sizing up his intent.

"Dimi's rules for sleeping in his bed," Sarah told the floor. "If I'm scared at night, I have to make sure he's awake, I have to ask him if it's okay, I must bring my own blanket and pillow, and I cannot get under his covers with him, no matter how scared I am.

"Vlad was still awake. I brought my blanket. He said it was okay. I'm sorry, I forgot to bring my pillow." She ducked as if fearing a strike. "He gave me one of his. He talked with me until I fell asleep. I never went under his blankets. Please don't send me away!"

"I won't let him, Sar," Vlad vowed. "If anyone should be punished, it's me. I'm older, I should have thought first."

"Shh. Easy, now. I don't want to touch you uninvited, Sarah, so please sit up for me," Tomas soothed. "Look up. I want you to hear what I have to say." The eyes began to glance his way, the sobbing breaths slowed. "Up-up-up."

"Sarah, I am not sending you *anywhere*," Tomas swore. "This is *your* home now, for as long as *you* wish to stay. The rules you mentioned are good rules, Sarah. Dmitri was very wise for making them. Galina believes you have done nothing wrong, and I have seen nothing to prove what you or Vlad have told me isn't true. I believe you.

"This is my house, though, and things work a little different here. I'm glad you told me your rules, but I'm going to have to give you some new ones to follow while you are here. If you are uncertain at night and feel you need company, you are free to crawl in bed with your sisters if they wish. But Sarah – from now on – I do not want you to be sleeping in or on your brothers' beds while they are in them, understand? Not even on top of the blankets, not even if you bring your own covers. If you wish to talk to

Vladimir at night when Sergei's not here, and Vlad agrees, you have my permission to sleep in Sergei's bed on occasion – alone, with the door open. If Sergei's home and you wish to join the boys and they both agree, you may bring your things in here and sleep on the floor, but no more in or on the beds with the boys. If they are asleep and you are upset and wish company, you are welcome to page me. I will be more than happy to speak with you, no matter what the hour. My schedule varies, and too often I am awake at night for business purposes. Vladimir can tell you, I don't bite heads off, even at two in the morning. But, for the sake of the younger children, I cannot allow sharing beds. Understood?"

Sarah gave a shuddering sob, but nodded. "Yes, sir. I'm sorry, sir. I didn't do anything wrong."

"I haven't said you did," Tomas reminded her. "Galina, why don't you help Sarah get ready for breakfast? Vladimir, I suggest you hurry, or you're going to be late." He stood up, present crisis averted. "Do you feel better now, Mamá?"

"No, I don't," Andrea Ivanova said firmly. "What kind of disturbed man invites young girls to sleep with them? This was not the kind of difficulty I envisioned when you spoke of her to me. We certainly cannot have … "

Tomas cut her off. "Mamá, this is not the time. We can speak further after breakfast, in private. I would prefer to wait until this afternoon, after I speak with Valeria and John, get their opinions, and talk things over with Vlad. Please, hold off right now." He steered her toward the door.

Galina held out a hand. "Come on, Sar. Let's see what you have to wear."

* * *

One by one, Sarah's insulation against panic disappeared: Valeria and Galina left for work, Nikky and Marina kissed everyone and ran to school, then Vlad left.

"I have weekly exams," he explained, holding her tight at the front door. And the front porch. And the front steps. "I can't miss them. I'll be home right after lunch. Promise not to go anywhere on me!"

Sarah forced a smile and shook her head. He walked backwards down the path to the street, waving. She waved back sadly, until Tomas called her in.

He didn't realize she had followed him to his study until he sat.

"Sarah! I didn't know you were there. Come in. Is there something I can do for you?"

No, the blonde head shook.

Tomas ran several computer screens, checking schedules. "We leave to see John an hour from now. We'll return at noon for lunch. Vladimir will return at 12:30, and Sergei and David are expected around one. You'll have the whole afternoon free to visit with them."

"Thank you, sir."

There was a long silence before Tomas looked up again. Sarah still stood at the door. "Sit down! Please! Are you sure there's nothing I can get for you? A cup of coffee, perhaps? Or tea! I'm sorry. Mamá said you're a tea drinker. A cup of tea?"

"No, thank you, sir." Sarah perched on the back sofa. It was the most comfortable piece of furniture in the room, but she sat as if balancing on nails.

The same blank stare, as if she were waiting for something ... Waiting for him to say the right thing, which was .... She could have been waiting for a public tram, for all Tomas knew. He felt guilty ignoring her, but he would be tied up all morning at the clinic; he'd hoped to catch a little work beforehand.

"Well, you're free to – drop a bone, as the boys say. If you have no questions, would you mind if I checked on a few things? It won't take long." Again, the silent, expected shake of the head.

Tomas tried to work, but found himself watching her. She never seemed to move, sitting patiently at attention.

"There's nothing else you feel like doing?"

"No sir. You haven't told me what I should do."

Aha! "Did Dmitri give you a schedule to follow?"

"No, sir. I knew what to do. You're in charge of me now. Dimi said I have to obey you. I don't know your routine. You haven't given me your list of expectations. Every time I think I know what I should be doing, one of your help beats me to it. I don't suppose you have firewood that needs to be split?"

"No, I know for a fact we don't." Tomas could imagine the furor if Mamá caught the girl wielding hand tools. "Until it's time to leave, you're free to do what you'd like – look around, explore the house. The gymnasium and pool are open, day or night. The library is well-stocked, and the media room is empty this time of day. I generally don't have a set schedule, but that's changed now. We'll see what plans John has for you, and we'll work our day around that, okay?"

A silent nod. Sarah eyed a large portrait on the wall, a photo of a younger Tomas with his arms around a laughing woman with golden hair and perfect teeth. "Is that your wife?"

"Yes. That's me and Lora, about a year before she died."

"Do you miss her?"

"Not a day goes by that I don't."

"Did you drink a lot after she died?" Sarah said in a distinctly accusatory tone.

Tomas thought back. "No, actually, I didn't. I was too much in shock. I talked to her just as she left work, and two hours later I got a call saying her shuttle had gone down. It took me a long, long time to get back on my feet."

"Is she buried here?"

"I scattered her ashes on a beach in California, in America. That's where she was from. We lived in New York, and we visited here, but her heart was in California, and I wanted her to be somewhere she loved.

He gave up on work. "You know, we have to fill out some forms and get your data processed at the clinic. Why don't you get ready and meet me in the foyer in fifteen minutes? We'll get a head start on the bureaucracy." To his relief the head nodded, and she left to ready herself.

The short ride to the clinic reminded Tomas of his first day with her at Starbase 21. Sarah sat mutely in the passenger seat of his Baltic Breeze, tensed as if to run, never looking his way once. She walked behind him as they entered the building, at best by his side. He gave her name at the entrance desk. She said nothing as he filled out questionnaires, filling in answers for him to questions he didn't know.

Tomas filled his name in under guardian, but watched as Sarah took the pad from him, erased his name from the space for emergency contact, and replaced it with *Dmitri M. Kirushenko, Gandron Rehabilitation Center*. She accepted him, but Dmitri was still first on her list. Tomas forced himself to shake off any jealousy. She'd been in his house less than twenty-four hours; what did he possibly expect?

He tried to be patient, but Sarah shuffled behind him on their way to the lifts, as if counting steps. She noticed the inconspicuous slots that stored the retracted security doors, examining them at such length Tomas had to prompt her. Even though the one-floor ride in the lift took no more than fifteen seconds, she melted into the wall of the car, as far away as she could get. She even *looked* physically smaller, as if she could escape by disappearing.

"There's nothing to be afraid of. You're already familiar with John. I'm sure he'll give us a tour." The beautiful eyes stared back, silent, expressionless. "This is it, 2-M."

John greeted her inside. "Sarah! Come in. How was your first night?

48

Tomas, you seem no worse for wear. You checked in with admissions, got your ID? Go ahead, take a look around. There isn't a whole lot in here. I'm not in my office much; I usually work out of the rec rooms down the hall." He stood back to give Sarah space.

Sarah nodded, poking, prodding, and prying into anything that would move. The closet behind her held nothing but John's coat; a wide cushioned bench set back in an alcove separated it from the lavatory door on the same wall. Under the cushions lay a solid platform; no deception there. The window on the next wall opened and shut on a slide switch; another control could darken it. It looked out onto the pedestrian walkways of the skychannel between the city blocks, boring and rigid and dull. A low table under the window held a basket of therapeutic manipulatives.

"Sarah, I don't think John wants you going through there," Tomas cautioned as she ransacked the desk in the middle of the room.

"She's fine," John allowed. "Sarah likes to know exactly what she's up against. She doesn't like surprises. I didn't forget."

Sarah noted the controls for the computer, but no matter where she searched, she couldn't find any hidden switches under the desk. The filing drawers near the desk held scores of computerized instructional disks, testing materials, and microcached medical reference journals. The bottom two were locked.

"Confidential files. Printscan access only. Sorry."

A nod accepted the information. The remaining wall held the door and several low shelves containing cases of testing materials and a gallery of displayed holos of his wife and son.

"Satisfied?" John asked. "If you'll remember, I'm a rather straight-forward type of person. Why don't you have a seat. I thought that since you and Tomas don't know each other well, we could spend some time getting everyone acquainted – see how things are going, maybe point you both in the right direction if you get stuck. How does that sound?"

John moved to his desk, but Sarah wandered back to the window, watching the traffic. The window wouldn't open more than thirty centimeters; far enough for fresh air, but not enough for escape.

Tomas took one of the chrome-and-brown chairs before the desk. Sarah glanced over her shoulder. Both men looked expectantly at her. She turned back to the window.

"Whatever."

John ignored the turned back. "So, Tomas. How do you feel your first day went? Any questions or concerns?"

"Very well, I think. She and Vlad stuck like glue the rest of the evening. I've never seen him happier. We did have a little bit of an incident this morning, though." Tomas' brow wrinkled, still pondering the scene. "Mamá called it to my attention. I didn't know what to make of it myself. I discussed it with Galina and Valeria; they found it amusing and expected, but I'm afraid Mamá's reaction may have been a little strong, and it seemed to upset Sarah."

"What happened?"

Tomas hesitated. "Mamá discovered that Sarah …had …spent the night with Vladimir …in bed with him."

"I was *ON* his bed, not *IN* his bed," Sarah corrected loudly. "Why am I the only one besides Vlad that can make that distinction? I told you, I followed the rules. I was *on* the bed, in my *own* blanket, and I followed the rules! It's not like she caught me with a boy! I did nothing wrong. *Nothing!* She had no reason to start trouble like that."

John chuckled. "Last time I saw him, Vlad wasn't exactly a girl, Sarah. Being human, that categorizes him as a boy."

"You know what I mean."

"Yes, I do. So, Grandmamá sees Vlad as a boy, but Sarah, Galina, and Valeria don't. What about Tomas?"

"It *seemed* innocent enough, and I've never known Vlad to lie, but I am a bit uncomfortable with it."

"How did you respond?"

Tomas recapped the highlights.

"If something's going to happen, it's going to happen with or without a bed, but that's not a bad compromise." John leaned back, thinking. "When I stayed at the Kirushenko's the one time, the last thing Valeria did before she went to bed was pull Sarah from Vladimir's bed. Putting one or the other back where they belonged was routine for them. I think Grandmamá simply stumbled upon a regression. They were traumatically separated; they're picking back up where they left off. It should taper off as they settle in again. If it continues or seems to be 'progressing,' then it might bear closer inspection. I wouldn't worry too much at this point."

"That sounds fair," Tomas said, but the window-shadow didn't move.

"How about you, Sarah? How do you feel your first day went? I know how happy you were to see everyone. What was your roughest spot of the day?"

Sarah turned, face somewhere between sad and angry. "Where do I stand?"

"In regard to what?"

"Everything."

"Everything's a pretty big category," John said. "Give me some parameters."

50

The eyes flicked toward Tomas. "Relationships."

"Specify. Person to person, person to place, person to situation ... ?"

An anxious line formed in the middle of the girl's forehead. "I already know I'm declared insane. I have no choice in what happens to me. I'm not even given a choice how I react, thanks to that mechanical spider inside me. I *want* to cooperate and get through this, but... past relationships aside, I'm coming in as an outsider. I want to know... where the loyalties lie. I mean – If I tell you something here in the office, how much of it will leak back to Tomas? If I confide something to Tomas, how fast is it going to get back to you?

"I mean, what instructions did you give everybody? Is everyone watching my every breath in case I do something that might be misconstrued? Are the staff counting the knives after every meal, ready to tackle me if one is missing? If I wax poetic, is Vlad under orders to report, 'Sarah was talking funny, I think she's going off the deep end.'? Where do I *stand?*"

"What is said to me in this building is absolutely confidential," Carver swore, "as far as is allowed by law. When you enter this building, any other relationship takes a back seat to my professional commitments. My friendship with Tomas disappears. My friendship with you becomes formal and professional. I might ask Tomas to clarify something – 'Sarah was upset, did something unusual happen last night?' 'Sarah seemed tired today, how do you feel she slept?' – but I will not ask him for a daily report. I can give him guidance, tell him what I find helpful, like knowing how it can take you several minutes before you're ready to ask something, or knowing how checking out a room helps you relax. I will not answer specific things like 'What did Sarah have to say about me ...' I won't do it," he promised. "I can call Tomas and say, 'Sarah was upset by her session today, give her a little extra space to sort herself out,' but gossip is out of the question. Not even with Katya. I think you know me better than that.

"As for everyone else," Carver said, catching her eye for an entire split second, "all we knew was that you were in legal trouble. We had no idea about the other until Tomas arrived at the starbase, saw the account of the incident, and saw the subsequent charge of insanity. We had twenty-four hours to come up with a plan that would hold up in court well enough to get you home. I spoke with Doctor Granger and assured him I was quite able to handle your case, gave him some pointers, explained certain relationships for him, and convinced him this was the very best arrangement possible. Tomas has read the reports from the *Triumph,* and I have copies here, but that's as far as it goes. I had no idea what shape you'd be in when you arrived. Based on the reports, I expected a lot worse. Your family believes the charges to be overblown and disregards the seriousness. I said you were very upset by everything and to give you some extra time and patience to settle in. If you want to tell anyone the details, that's your business. Is that fair?"

The worried wrinkle smoothed itself, but the sad look remained. "It's a start."

"I told you before, Sarah," Tomas said, "whatever I can do to make this time easier on you, I am fully committed to doing it."

"He's a pretty good listener, too." John winked, but the wary manner didn't change. "I've known him for a while now, and I've never known him to be unfair."

The head nodded without commitment.

John stood up. "Come on. Why I don't I give you the grand tour, and you can check everything out for yourself."

* * *

Sarah ran back to the neutrality of the window the minute she reentered the office, adjusting the opaqueness and peering at the city outside. It would become her routine, not to be interfered with. She glanced back to demand from Tomas, "Ninety minutes, right?"

"Without fail," Tomas promised as he left, and the head whipped back to the window.

"Pull up a seat," John invited. "What do you think?"

The figure at the window remained silent.

"Any questions for me? Anything I can go over with you? Schedules, information, protocols, medication?"

The back of her head swung side to side. She left the window and headed for the padded alcove bench, her back to the side wall, knees pulled up.

"I can't do this, Doctor Carver," Sarah announced with certainty.

"Clarify. Can't do what? Can't answer questions? Can't live with Tomas? Can't bend your arms without flexing your elbows? What?"

Sarah studied her fingers. "Everything. I can't do it. I can't start over again with this therapy nonsense. I have too many jars of worms, but they're labeled and sealed and inventoried. Most are past issues, and I'm not willing to take them down and open them. I'm sorry. The courts can do with me what they want, but they can't make me open them."

"What about the ones that aren't past issues? How recent are you talking? A date, if that's all?"

"Starting with the event that lead to my return. Those are recent issues, but I don't have the energy to sit through all this talk-game. My thoughts are my own, no one else's business. I have to be here, I want to cooperate, but I don't feel like talking."

"Three hours is a long time to sit here and stare at each other. I figured we'd spend our time in the rec rooms. I mean, if you don't feel up to that right away, that's fine. We can build up to it."

"I don't want *any* part of it," Sarah repeated irritably. "I can't do this."

"If you'd rather not work with me, I can find someone I trust for you. Generally, the rule is doctors don't treat family. I've never known you before as a family member, but I'll switch if you'd prefer."

"No! I mean, that would be a lot worse. I'd have to deny I had any worms in the first place. They'd tell me they thought otherwise, I'd be told I was in denial, labeled uncooperative, and they'd roll out the heavy drugs and formal behavior plans, and then I'd *really* have to put up a fight."

"So instead you're going to hide behind our friendship. I let you off the hook, which makes you appear cooperative, and on paper everything looks good."

"Thank you! That's the best offer I've had in weeks."

Carver laughed. "I think you know me better than that. When did I ever let you off a hook? I'd like to do my best to avoid those fights, if at all possible. Let's take it one day at a time, then. I'm sure there's plenty to talk about besides worms. If one just happens to fall out in the process, I promise to destroy it for you as fast as I can. Deal?"

Sarah slouched lower until she was nearly lying down. "Not really. Deals don't make a difference when you don't have a choice in the matter."

"I think I hear a worm right now. I don't have a choice, either. Court orders supersede me. Now, if I can show proof that the order is no longer necessary, that's something else, but I have to be able to show proof."

"Hmph!" Sarah sat up fast and stared directly at him. "John? Make me a promise! A binding promise! One you won't break, on your honor?"

"Let me hear it first."

"Promise me you'll make this office a safe place? Promise me you'll take my side when we're in here. No restraints, no drugs, no Security monsters? Not even City Security? Not Uncle Tomas or even Vlad if I don't wish it? Sacred ground?"

"This entire building is a safe zone, Sarah, but I understand. If I make that promise, what do I get in return?"

Her shoulders sucked inward until she seemed only half as wide as she'd been a moment before. "I promise I'll try to read you the labels on some of the jars."

"That seems fair enough. Providing that, if an intervention strategy is necessary, you will move out to the hallway on your own power. If I ask you to leave the office, you *must* leave, no matter how upset, on *your* honor."

Sarah searched for a trick, but couldn't find one. "Okay. Deal."

"I promise this is a safe zone, then." Terms laid out, Carver stood up. "Come on. Let's go down to the cafeteria. We'll get some tea or something."

"Why? I just establish this space as somewhere I can feel absolutely safe, and immediately you want me to leave it?"

"Sit here alone, then." By the time he reached the door, he'd gained a shadow.

The shadow stayed close, never more than a footstep away, down a floor and two long corridors to the cafeteria. Sarah didn't say a word, too busy looking in every direction at once.

"Put your ID card in here." John demonstrated, putting her card in the proper slot of the food replicator. "Once you're in the system, you can eat here for free, no matter where you're living. If you're on a special diet, the computer will respond accordingly. You're not, but your transfer files said you've lost close to ten kilos in the last few weeks. Combined with the vegetarian diet, I'd recommend something high in carbs and protein. Tea with milk and double sugar, and if I remember correctly," he said, showing her how to work the machine, "your old standby was chocolate pudding."

The ready light on the commercial replicator gave a colorful blink and the access panel slid away, revealing a tray with a cup of steaming tea and a dish filled with a creamy-looking brown substance.

Sarah pulled her card out of the slot. Her name and patient number stood out under a holographic ID portrait. "I'm sorry, John. I can't eat this. I don't know what this card says in it. Give me yours."

She took the doctor's ID. Copying his movements exactly, she called up an identical tray. She removed it, returned his card, and went to sit at an empty table at the edge of the room, back to a wall.

John followed a minute later with coffee and a bagel. "Is it the machine, the card, or me that you don't trust?"

Sarah stopped scanning the room with her eyes. "I didn't trust the food on the *Triumph*; I don't trust the food here. I don't know what information is being withheld from me. How do I know there isn't some code for additional medication to be manufactured in the food? Now I can't use yours again, either, because you could change it, have a special card you only take out for my sessions, in case I switch things again."

Carver stared harder than he meant. "Isn't that just a little bit paranoid?"

"I have to be," Sarah replied, as cold and calm as a Navaran. "I don't have Dmitri's social awareness. I must be extremely vigilant about hidden dangers, lest I be caught unprepared. I've never had to rely on myself before. I can't trust anybody if I'm to survive."

"You don't trust me?"

Sarah poked the pudding with a plastic spoon. "I trust you more than anyone but Dimi, John, but I can't allow myself to be lulled into a false sense of security based on past loyalty. I hope you can understand that."

"On a professional level, yes, but on a personal level, I guess I don't."

"Then it's a good thing you're a professional." She stabbed the pudding with her spoon and shoveled the heaping mound into her mouth. The texture was perfect, but the chocolate flavoring had a hint of flatness.

"So, all this time, you've been writing to Vladimir swearing undying friendship, but you don't trust him."

The eyes closed, the face fought to remain neutral. "Don't create worms, John! I cannot allow myself to be distracted. I've never been alone before. You have no concept of the level of fear that situation generates. If I can attract danger while carefully supervised, the danger to myself can only fester exponentially when left to incubate alone with my own incompetence!" The spoon bounced on the tray as her hands pressed themselves over her face. Sarah breathed deep and held it as the tremor passed over her upper half.

"That'sa girl," John coached. "Deep breath; let it out slow. Those should have gotten better by now. Sarah, maybe you don't realize it, but you're far from alone. You have the biggest support net of any client I've ever seen. Vladimir would lay down and die for you, if you asked. Katya would fight to the death for you, let alone David and Sergei. Tomas will do anything you ask. I hope you haven't forgotten the tightropes I've walked for you. I still have my rope-walking shoes in my office, should they be needed."

"Shut *up*, John!" Sarah stood and pushed the tray away. "Instead of helping me destroy worms, you're throwing them in front of me like confetti! No matter how many people you line up to tell me otherwise, the fact remains I *am* alone, I am *all* alone, and the only direction my diligence can be allowed to go is *up!*" She shot around the table and ran from the room.

Carver found her twitching on the edge of tears, just outside the cafeteria. She trusted him enough to wait. That was a start. "Let's go back to the office. It's a safe place."

55

Upstairs, Sarah made a dive for the alcove. Walls surrounded her on five sides there; unless they moved, she'd be secure.

Carver ignored her, instead placing a finger on the printlock of the file cabinet. A green light came on, and he opened the drawer. A quick scan of the numbers, and he pulled a computer card out of the file. He activated the interface on his desk. "Come sit."

"Why?"

"Because I asked. Take my chair. I promise, it's not a trap."

Sarah came to the desk, but didn't sit.

"Put the card in."

"Why me? You do it."

John rolled his eyes and sighed. He picked up the data card and stuffed it in the slot, tapped two controls, entered a number, and stepped aside. "Sit. Read it. It's your top secret file. Every possible thing I know about you is in there. Everything Dr. Granger transferred. All my old records from Rangler, just as I wrote them. You want to know if there are secret orders on your ID card, look under the last two weeks. You want to know all the court data, look under the last two weeks."

"Why are you showing me this? Is that legal? How do I know it's all here? How do I know you didn't hit something that shuttles data to a separate file so it can't be accessed?"

John studied her sadly. "Are you really that fearful? If so, we need to reevaluate your chem therapy. Paranoia isn't a side effect of a neuropump. Fifteen second self-check."

"What?"

"Fifteen second self-check. Look inside yourself for fifteen seconds, and tell me the first words that describe how you're feeling at this exact moment. Be absolutely honest. Every answer counts, and there are no wrong answers."

Sarah sat down at last, thinking.

"Scared?" she admitted. "Helpless. Terrified. Overwhelmed. Everything is so out of my control. I'm hoping it will ease over time, but until then, please understand I don't mean to be difficult. I'm just trying to figure out where everything sits."

"Okay. That's a good self-analysis. You'll get there. Hold on. You don't have to feel isolated, though. Remember, I'm here to help, even if all you want is someone to hold on to. Tomas feels just as helpless and uncertain as you do. He needs you to tell him what to do. Are your meds working? Do they help?"

Sarah paused. "Yeah. I don't like them, I hate the tremors like you wouldn't believe, but it helps. It dulls everything down so I can still walk and talk. If it didn't, I'd be a screaming mess in one of your inertia dampening rooms, twenty-four hours a day."

John squeezed her hand. "We won't let that happen. You're going to be fine."

Six

S arah was finishing lunch at 'home' when two hands clamped themselves over her eyes from behind.

"I can *smell* it's you!" she cried, and jumped up to crush her brother in an octopus hug. "Oh Vlad! You came back!"

"I do live here, you know," he said, and returned the embrace.

They sat in the huge lounge with Grandmother and Uncle Tomas, Sarah basking in the aura that was *Vlad*, when, down the hall, the side door gave a distant bang.

"Where the hell is she?" boomed a deep voice.

Sarah twisted on the sofa, trying to spot the speaker. Like a Minotaur loosed from its maze, David plowed into the room, shedding his coat onto the floor. He approached the sofa from behind and vaulted his long legs over it to land heavily between Vlad and Sarah.

"David Fyodor!" Grandmother gasped at the abuse of furniture. A house staff scurried to retrieve his coat.

"Ow!" Vlad howled as David's full weight came down on his hand and crushed against his leg. "Get off me, you Ursanoid!" He banged his free fist on his brother.

"So where is she?" David demanded. "Where are you hiding her?"

Sarah giggled. She tapped him on the shoulder. "I'm right here."

David feigned confusion. "You're not Sarah. Sarah's a snot-nosed little know-it-all, about this high," he held a hand up to how tall she used to be, "who can beat the living piss out of just about anyone I know."

"Better take that back or I'll have to beat the piss out of you!" Sarah tried to keep up the game, but she couldn't stem the tears of joy. "David!" She locked herself around his neck.

"Scout!"

"Get *off* me!" Vlad pounded.

"David, get off your brother," Tomas prompted, and David leaned just enough for Vlad to retrieve his aching hand.

A throat cleared behind Sarah, but she didn't pay attention. She rejoiced in David's big arms, arms that felt as large as tree trunks and twice as strong. The noise sounded again, more insistent. Sarah tried to see who waited, but David clamped her head against his neck.

At last a long finger reached out and tapped David. "Excuse me, it's my turn."

"Go to hell," David said.

Sarah pushed until David let go. The voice was too deep to be Sergei's, a grown-up's voice. She stood up, smiling shyly at her fifth-oldest brother. "Sergei!" *To hell with it!* One foot lightly touched the seat of the sofa as she leapt over it into his arms.

"Tomas, I will not see that again."

"Patience, Mamá."

After a small eternity, Sergei let Sarah slide to her feet. He looked so different! So tall! Tall enough that Sarah really had to look up to see him. His curly blond hair was the same, bushier than Mother had ever let him keep it, but on his chin! His chin sported a thin, dark blond goatee.

"That's so funny!" She grinned, allowing her fingers to explore the bristly hairs.

"Laugh while you can," Sergei said. "It goes away while I'm home, and I grow it back during the week. I have something for you." He opened his carryall and handed her a thick, worn volume with holographic photo spreads between the pages. It was the print book she'd lent him the day Valeria split them up.

"I've read it seven times, once every anniversary you told me to. It's every bit as good as you said it was. And I wanted you to be the very first to have this."

He handed her another volume, much thinner, bound in imitation leather, not generic plastic sheeting.

"*Weeping Winds*," Sarah read off the gilded cover, "A collection of poetry and drawings by – *by Sergei Kirushenko!* Sergei! You got something *published?*"

"You got them?" Vlad climbed over the couch to get a better view, too involved to hear Grandmamá's irate squawk. "Too tight for orbit!"

"My very own!" Sergei passed out copies to Grandmamá and Uncle Tomas. "It's been out on electronic preview for three weeks, and so far I've gotten three good reviews and one mediocre, so I can't complain. Here! Look here." He flipped several pages on Sarah's copy so she could read the dedication lines, standing alone on an empty page:

For Sarah,
who no doubt understands

Tears burned her eyes. "Sergei!"

"Wait." He flipped back to the inside cover. "I signed it for you, too."

For our Missing Man:
Don't ever leave home again.
Heartfully yours,
Sergei

"That's beautiful, Sergei! Thank you! Thank you so much, for everything! I'm so happy for you!" She hugged him until her eyes stopped burning.

"Yeah, yeah." David stood up and joined the group the proper way. "Leave it to both of you to cry over a lousy book when there's more important things at hand. Grab her, Serg!" He seized Vladimir by the shoulders, while Sergei guided Sarah to stand them back to back.

"Quick, Uncle Tomas!" David called. "Who's taller?"

Vlad waited for the humiliation to finish. "You are *such* a blood sucker."

Sergei measured with his hand. "Sarah's still got him beat!"

"It's very close; perhaps too close to call," Tomas said tactfully.

"Close as in five fat centimeters! She's *still* got you beat, Rodent!" David hooted. He let Vlad go.

"Yes, but I've stopped growing, and Vlad hasn't," Sarah made excuse. "And which of *you* is taller?"

David stretched himself up, towering over Sarah and Vlad. His shoulders were as thick and broad as their brother Viktor's had been, his arms even bulkier with solid muscle. His jaw had squared out, his hair uncharacteristically neat and short, giving him an air of social decency he'd never before projected. The powder blue eyes glanced over at Sergei, and David said sourly, "Mr. Long-legs, by three centimeters."

"A hundred ninety two and a half centimeters," Sergei gloated.

Sarah started to laugh, but was surprised to find herself bursting into tears with a tremor instead.

Vlad was the first to clutch her. "Sar? What's the matter? What's wrong?"

Tomas rose from the sofa. "Sarah?"

The tangly blonde head shook *no*. "Nothing's wrong," she said, trying to smile while being encased in the arms of three brothers determined to outcomfort each other. "It's just, I've never been happier in my entire life, and I don't have the slightest idea what to do!"

* * *

After school, Nikky begged Sarah to come outside in the snow, if not to play then just to watch him ski. David decided they would all go, but Sarah had no winter gear. She fit well enough in a larger ski jacket of Vlad's, and a pair of Nikky's mittens, but Vlad's pants were much too tight, and his extra boots too small. She settled for borrowing a pair of Valeria's boots, which fell off no less than five times during the mayhem outside.

Tomas found Val watching from the library window, the orange glow from the setting sun reflecting off the snow and turning the room a warm gold. He joined her at the window, laughing as Sarah ran from Marina, a handful of snow clutched in the younger girl's glove. Vlad caught a fistful of snow in the back of the head, thrown by David, and while Vlad charged after him, Sarah lay in wait and fired at David, who turned at just the wrong moment and caught it in the cheek. Sarah shrieked, trying to flee in the loose boots. Just as he closed in on Sarah, David was distracted by snow bouncing off the top of his head – the masterful work of Sergei.

"Happy?" Tomas asked.

"Yeah," Val sighed. "Even if I shouldn't be."

"Shouldn't be?"

"If I hadn't screwed up, this would be an every-day scene. It wouldn't be so special."

"If you can't put the past behind you, how can you expect her to?" Tomas posed. "The past is gone. The only thing you have to worry about is *this* minute, not the last one."

"I know. If I think of things that way, I *am* happy. I'm happy that *she's* happy. Look at her! It's like time stood still. You realize, of course, you're in deep trouble now?"

"How?"

Val gave an amused chuckle of foreboding. "Oh, you have no idea! You've reunited the Fearsome Four. The most fearless, daring, conniving bunch of hell-raisers this side of the Crab Nebula. They're bigger, wiser, and smarter than ever. If they get into full swing, you won't have a house left standing six months from now."

Tomas gave a casual shrug. David was chief troublemaker among the children, but all Tomas generally had to do was raise an eyebrow to bring him back in line. "I've heard about some of their exploits. I'm not worried. You yourself said Sarah's not a troublemaker, and even David, I think, knows not to fool with Mamá."

"Perhaps last week," Val said, "but that was with three. Now they have their Scout."

Tomas gave the group free rein over the evening. He socialized with the boys as often as his schedule permitted, joining in a game or sport match or taking in a program on the entertainment waves. It kept him in touch with them, what they did, what they liked, what they thought. Those times, he lost most of his authority and enjoyed his youth all over again. Sarah was a new cog in the sprocket.

They lay about the floor in Vlad and Sergei's bedroom, grazing on the tray of treats David swiped from the kitchen, showing off tattoos and playing a cutthroat game of cards. Sarah sat between Sergei and Vladimir, more shy with Tomas in the room but certainly not withdrawn. And she ate! Tomas had never seen her do more than pick at food, but she devoured more of the delicacies than Vlad and Sergei combined.

"Last one!" Vlad teased, dangling the pastry-wrapped cheese in her face before yanking it away. Sarah giggled and snapped at it. "Whoops! Can't have it!" he teased twice more before feeding her the morsel and licking his fingers.

David feigned revulsion. "Can you take it to a guest room or something? You're making me sick."

"You *are* sick!" Vlad laughed as Sarah tackled him with a spontaneous hug. They fell over on the floor. Sarah rolled over her brother until she straddled his hips, tickling him. Vlad bucked with squeals beneath her.

"*I'm* sick? I'm not the one tightening his bolt on his sister."

"David! That's quite uncalled for!" Tomas said sharply, and found himself faced with a whole new dimension of his niece he hadn't anticipated.

Sarah's head whipped around.

She rolled off Vlad and clawed hair out of her angry eyes. "You take that back, David Fyodor! How *dare* you! Is this how you've treated Vlad all these years?" She climbed to her feet, hands up and ready to strike. "Is that how you speak about *me?* You take that back or I'll knock you flatter than porshie shit in a downpour! I've done it before and I'm sure as hell not afraid to do it again!"

"Listen to her go!" Sergei crowed. "I'll bet twenty-five credits cold she can still kick your ass, Dave! You know better than to piss off a mama bear protecting her young."

"Stop! Stop, right there!" Tomas ordered. "No one move, no one say anything! Sarah, there will be no threats of violence in this house. David is out of line and owes his brother an apology, but that does not give you the right to threaten him with harm. Is that clear?"

"I will not stand by and allow Vladimir to be insulted like that. I never

62

have, and I never will. He should not have to endure a bully in his very own room." A hard tremor shook her from her cheek to her waist. Her hands flew to her face, and she fled in shame to the door.

David frowned. "What the hell was *that*? Sar? What happened?"

"Nothing to be concerned about," Tomas said. "Sarah's medication can make her a little jumpy, that's all."

"I was only having fun," David apologized. "You know that."

"Maybe to you, but she's not used to that anymore." Vlad glared as he rubbed Sarah's shoulder. He pulled her to sit on the end of his bed, but Tomas waved him away and sat next to her instead.

Sarah's eyes grew wide, and she leaned away as if to run. "I'm sorry! He's been through so much. There's no need for him to be insulted with disgusting lies on top of it."

"That may be true," Tomas said, "but it doesn't give you the right to make threats. I do not take threats lightly, not from anyone. Vladimir has been handling David more or less effectively for the past few years. While he may appreciate your defense, you will find another way to do it. Violence will not be tolerated, in any form. I also do not approve of vulgar speech. What you say to your brothers here in private is between you and them, but in public areas – outside personal rooms – you are to maintain a civil tongue. Is that understood?"

Sarah's chin glued to her chest. "Yes sir,"

"Just a friendly word of advice." Tomas patted her shoulder.

Sarah shot out from under the hand with a squeal to plaster herself against the wall.

Tomas folded his hands quickly. "I'm sorry, Sarah. My fault. I forgot. I'm sorry. Please, sit. I won't touch."

"I'm sorry," she mumbled. She peeled herself from the wall with great difficulty and sat next to him, stiff as stone. "I suppose I have to get used to it, don't I."

Tomas didn't abandon his sleep ruling, but in light of John's input, he tempered it a bit. He could guess what would happen. Sarah would slip into Vlad's room, and since Sergei was there on the weekends, David would object to being left out. He would point out he had an empty bed in his room that Sarah could use, but Sarah wouldn't go without Vladimir, and that would leave Sergei out. Tomas cut the argument off before it could begin: he suggested the four of them sleep on the floor in Vlad's room. Surely Mamá couldn't object too strongly with two very jealous chaperones and the door open.

Instinct told him he'd done the right thing when he made a final check in the early hours of the morning. Sarah and David lay on the floor head to head with Sergei and Vladimir, whispering sleepily in the dark, their four hands clenched in the center like a compass. Tomas felt more confident as he took the lift down to his apartment. First full day, two crises, and he'd handled them both successfully. She was skittery all right, but once she learned she had nothing to fear, he had no doubt Sarah'd settle in nicely. Even brash David had jumped and ducked when he first arrived. Spending time with the boy, doing things he liked to do, letting him show off his interests and abilities had done wonders for David's confidence. Perhaps it would work for the girl as well.

Tomas lay awake in bed, formulating a plan. Her IQ was exceptionally high. She liked science, but what else did the boys tell him? Museums. *Art or history? Botanical, textiles, old books, or transportation museums?* Here in the capital city, there were so many different kinds, he wasn't sure where to start. The Gagarin Institute had a program on early Solar System Exploration. The Greater Minsk Art Emporium had a display of ancient Japanese silks. The Federal Museum of Russia at Minsk had a vehicle on loan that once belonged to Tsar Nicholas. The East End Historical Society had a permanent display on the effects of radioactivity. Vilnius wasn't far; the city currently hosted an exhibit of Dutch Renaissance paintings.

He would do some research, print out schedules and simple itineraries, and present it to her on Sunday. It was a worthwhile idea.

Seven

Saturday was blissful, an entire day to be with those she loved most, but it left Sarah unprepared for the bombshell her brothers dropped on her late that night. From the minute David stretched, looked at his Chronolex and whined, "Uhh! And they won't even let us sleep late because of church tomorrow!", Sarah's stomach found a new way to knot itself.

"Right!" she laughed. "Like you ever set foot in a church! That's something I'd *pay* to see."

"Better find your bankcard," Sergei mumbled.

Vlad's eyes were the first clue something wasn't right. "He's not joking, Sar. Grandmamá makes us go. She says a gram of piety is worth a kilo of free advertising. 'It keeps you and your business on the minds of the community.'"

Sarah's forehead wrinkled in disbelief. *"Church?* The religious kind? Hallelujah, praise God, Saints-bless-the-unfortunate-among-us kind of thing?"

Sergei nodded. "One hour and ten minutes of up, down, left, right, kneel, sing, and stretch. And whatever you do, don't fall asleep, or Grandmamá will volunteer you to help with the services for the next month."

"Why? I haven't been to a church since we left Kiev eleven years ago! I don't remember what to do! She'll commit me to a convent or something!"

"Just do whatever we do," Vlad said. "It'll come back."

"Maybe I could fake a seizure. If I drank a liter of water just before we left, I'd wind up in the lavatory so many times I could pretend I was sick. Or I *could* get sick on the way there, and Uncle Tomas would have to bring me back. That's doable," Sarah reasoned.

"If I have to drag my ass there, so do you," David warned. "You'll get used to it. You learn to sleep with your eyes open."

Sarah couldn't see that happening. After the boys were asleep, she slipped over to the computer to read up on her alleged religion.

Two and a quarter hours of sleep after only four hours the night before, following on the heels of a three-hour night, which had followed a night of no sleep at all, left Sarah unbearably foggy. Sand filled her eyelids, her eyes felt hard as rocks, and she fought a crippling headache.

She stumbled to breakfast with her hair forgotten and her blouse misbuttoned, her velvety slipper-shoes but no socks. Her sense of dread – kept manageable by her medications – turned her taste buds to stone. She was discreetly trying to lick the jelly from a slice of toast when Nikky's fork made a sharp *clink* on his plate. The noise hit her weakened nerves like lightning and she gave a start, dropping the toast. It fell onto her chest jelly-side down and somersaulted into her lap, leaving a sticky trail.

Sarah closed her eyes and pressed the back of her fist to her mouth. A tremor shuddered its way down her body.

"Are you okay, Sarah?" Tomas asked. "You don't look well."

"I'm fine, thank you," she replied, and forced a cheerful look. "Just clumsy."

Vlad picked the toast out of her lap and dabbed at the jelly with his napkin.

Sarah took over the task. "I can get that. Thank you, Vlad."

"Maybe if you weren't up all night with the computer...," David let slip.

"I wasn't up all night!"

"I take it you will be changing your dress before we leave." Grandmother smiled thinly, but her eyes glared down the table at Tomas with crocodilian warmth.

Sarah shrank small in her chair. "Yes, Ma'am."

Tomas stopped her as the crowd left the dining room. "Sarah, may I speak with you a moment?"

"I'll meet you upstairs," Vlad said, and kept walking.

"I'm sorry about my dress, sir," Sarah said.

Tomas waved a hand. "Accidents happen. I've done that myself, too often to count. As you know, I'm in charge of your well-being. I know you didn't sleep much Thursday, and Friday you were up late with the boys. I would like to know what time you went to sleep last night."

Sarah summoned up the innocent charm that never failed to please. "The boys packed it in around one. I got to bed a little after that."

"How much later? What time?"

Withering wariness replaced the innocence. "I don't know. I wasn't watching the clock."

"What was the last time you did look?"

Sarah shrank even smaller. He should have accepted her answer by now and gone his way. "I – I don't know. Five-oh-five, maybe five-ten?"

"Sarah, have you had more than six hours sleep since you came here? In a single night?"

Sarah's eyes wandered everywhere but toward her uncle. "No, sir."

"More than four?"

"No, sir."

"Three?"

"I don't know, sir. Maybe."

Tomas's face didn't change, but he seemed disappointed. "Is anything wrong? Are you merely overextending yourself, or are you having difficulty sleeping? Is there anything I can do to help?"

"No, sir! Thank you, sir. I think I'm still on ship's time." She glanced up with a pleasant smile, selling the idea.

No sale.

Tomas's eyes seared into hers with remarkable perception. "That's not very healthy, Sarah. You need to sleep. I think we should mention that to John tomorrow. Perhaps he can prescribe something to help you sleep, just for a day or two, until you adjust."

"I will *not* be sedated!"

"I'm only suggesting … "

"NO!" Sarah snapped harder. "Under any circumstances, I will not do it! John knows that! He won't make me! You can't force that on me!" She winced as a strong tremor reminded her she was losing control. When it ended, she ran an agitated hand through her hair, then hugged herself, hard.

"*Shah.* Calm down. I am quite willing to leave that decision to you and John. However, unless things change tonight, I will mention it tomorrow."

"Yes, sir. Thank you, sir. I apologize for raising my voice, sir. May – may I go change now, sir?"

"Sure. Just remember, we dress a little more formally on Sundays!" he called as she vanished down the hall.

"She's coming, she's coming," Vlad said to the impatient crowd in the foyer. He pulled on his gloves as he clumped down the stairs. "She's getting her wrap on."

Tomas glanced at the expensive *Vsyochas* on his wrist. Twenty-nine minutes. To his relief, Sarah appeared a moment later.

Andrea took an aggressively deep breath and dug her nails into his sleeve. "You will *do* something with that child, and do it *now*! *Or I will!"*

The intense silence in the foyer said something was wrong, even if she didn't know what. Sarah clung to the railing on the last step, all eyes on her. She'd changed into her very best – an embroidered blue skirt and cream-colored blouse, every stitch painstakingly sewn by the loving hand of her neighbor on Sigma Tau Ceti. She'd wrapped herself in her long cool-weather wrap, pulling it around her shoulders, over her front, around the back, and tying the narrowing ends back around the front of her waist again. For Sunday's sake, she combed her hair and wove it into two long braids that hung down her back. Two rings decorated her hands; the ruby crystal was hers, though she'd never worn it before, and the silver band on her middle finger had been Viktor's. She gave Vlad a brave smile, though the look he returned was more of horror.

Tomas scratched the back of his head. "Sarah, I know ... "

Galina was faster. She stepped forward and ran her fingers over the embroidered hem. "Sarah! That's beautiful! Real handiwork? I can't imagine such skill! But feel it, Sar. It's so thin and delicate. It's quite cold out today," she said, though the temperature already read ten below, Celsius. "I'm afraid you'll freeze in that. Especially your feet. You don't have to dress *that* fancy for church. Come." She grabbed Sarah by the hand and started up the stairs. "We'll change you into something warmer. It will only take a minute."

"But ...!" Sarah found herself dragged.

The clock ticked, seven, eight, nine minutes. David hung on the banister at the bottom of the stairs, glancing at the time and the top of the stairs every fifteen seconds, while Grandmamá blistered Uncle Tomas's ears with choice words. At ten minutes, Galina returned, Sarah in tow, now clad in Galina's clothes. Sarah looked centuries better, but Galina was still fourteen years older, ten centimeters taller, fourteen kilos heavier, and more rounded in strategic places. Galina had brushed out the braids and held the hair back with a beaded headband. Sarah looked much more like the modern school-girl she should have been — waiting to grow into her clothes.

"I lent Sarah some warmer things," Galina explained, "but I can't find anything for her feet. My boots don't fit, Vlad's are too small, and David's are ridiculous. Her other shoes don't look right."

Tomas gave the feet a critical eye. "I'll be right back." He disappeared for a precious three minutes, returning with a pair of low white boots. "Try these," he said. "They're custom-fit, but they might work."

Sarah wriggled her foot into a boot. They were a little narrow, but they weren't falling off when she stepped. "They'll work."

"Good! Now run, everyone!" Tomas ordered. "We're going to be late."

The fears that seized Sarah the night before disappeared as they arrived in the city. Vlad's hand was forgotten as she entered the 200-year-old Cathedral of St. Nikolai, lost amid the spectacle of the lofty ceilings, ornate architecture, colored glass, and a blinding interior doused in gold leaf. There wasn't time to light a candle for mother or Viktor, but she followed the boys' lead, touching her fingers to her lips and then to the gilded icon on the wall of the vestibule. The rest became a blur. She drifted among the incoming crowd, exhaustion replaced by the glory of the soaring columns and bright paintings, mumbling notes to herself. Vlad and David steered her toward the family's seats.

Grandmamá sat on the aisle, the better to be seen, then Tomas. Vlad sat between Sarah and their uncle, leaving David and Sergei to elbow each other over the fact David had the preferred seat, Tomas's harsh glare not withstanding.

Sarah knelt backwards on the pew. "Too radical! Look, Vlad! See the scrollwork there? That's a hallmark of the Divine Revival period of 2084 to 2200. After that, things tipped the other way and began to streamline again."

Vlad nodded with blank acceptance. "How do you know all that?"

"I read it last night. Uncle Tomas? What year was this built, please?"

"Sit, Sarah. Around 2105."

"That's perfectly in line! Uncle Tomas? Those friezes back there – are they depicting the life of Saint Nikolai? Do you know who painted them? Were they original to the church or added later?" Sarah's hand shot out to point over the heads of the citizens behind them.

"Sarah! Please sit!" Tomas leaned over Vlad to tap her raised arm. "Do not point. Yes, it's Saint Nikolai. I don't know who painted them, but they've been here as long as I can remember. Shah!"

"What about the furnishings? Are these original as well?"

"We'll ask later, Sarah. The service is starting."

"But what about… "

Andrea Ivanov pretended not to see, closing her eyes and moving her lips in what looked like a prayerful manner, though the words were less than Holy.

"Vladimir, will you please switch places with your sister," Tomas said, exasperated.

"Not fair!" David growled. "I was sitting next to her! Move it, Rodent! I had her left side!"

"Go to Hell!" Vlad swore. "She sits with me!"

"Move, before I *send* you to hell!"

"Boys!" Tomas hissed through clenched teeth. "Enough! Vladimir, slide down. David, move over here next to me."

"At least let me sit between you and Sarah…"

"Sit, David!" Tomas pulled him over and handed him a prayer card. "You're disrupting the service."

David bit his lip and grumbled, stuck next to his grandmother – especially when Sergei leaned back and gave him a self-satisfied little wave.

If Sarah appeared more or less civilized through a church service, the morning's anxiety returned hard at the lunch table.

"My dear, where are the clothes you were wearing?" Grandmamá asked as Sarah took her seat.

"I returned them, before harm could come to them," Sarah said, now clothed in a pumpkin-gold Sigma Tau dress. "I don't need them now."

"The point was to keep you *warm*, Sarah," Galina said.

"I *am* warm," Sarah insisted, used to the inefficient radiant heat from the stove in her cabin in Vandijoc. "It's very warm in this house."

Tomas seized the chance to discuss the issue without causing grief. "Just the same, perhaps after lunch we should return to the city and get you some warmer clothing, at the very least some winter footwear and a coat. The boys can come with you, if you like."

The boys gave their vocal approval, arguing favorite vendors until Valeria hushed them.

Sarah stayed silent for well over a minute. "I – I don't think that's necessary, sir. What I have will serve me fine until spring. It's not that far away."

"It's January in Minsk, Sarah," Tomas said. "It's at least four months until good weather. Your wrap may feel warm, but you can't exactly play in the snow with it."

"Yes, but I can borrow Vlad's jacket for those times, like I did yesterday."

"It's *Vladimir's* jacket. There is no excuse for you not having one of your own. We will leave in forty-five minutes."

Sarah bent her head until her hair brushed her plate. "Yes, sir."

* * *

Sarah wound her way through downtown Minsk, lost inside an old jacket of David's, hand in hand with Sergei and Vlad. She followed Tomas's lead through six shops, shaking her head at everything he pointed out.

David shoved a pair of boots at her. "Here! They're perfect! You don't have to like them, just let me see you in them."

Reluctantly, Sarah accepted a single boot. The sueded gray fabric had an almost weightless gripper tread and a short heel. The shaft would come far up her calf, keeping out a considerable amount of snow. A sparkle shone in her eyes, and she sighed approval without realizing it.

Vlad nodded. "Those are really nice, Sar. You have to like those."

"That's an excellent choice," the sales clerk said. He took the other boot from David, pointing out the various features. "They're made in Murmansk from the latest developments in thermasuede fibers. The outer fabric is three-millimeter Texlan thermasuede, guaranteed against damage by snow, ice, water, or mud for five years. They're lined with nylasilk fleece for comfort, and will keep an internal temperature of eighteen degrees Celsius, at temperatures to minus fifteen."

Uncle Tomas took the first boot from Sarah, examining it. "Do you carry them in a forty-two?"

"We carry them on demand up to a forty-three. We can custom-order if desired, but it does take twenty-four hours for delivery. If you can buy a better boot for three hundred twenty-five credits, we'll give you this pair free," the clerk said with pride.

Tomas looked uncertain. "I wouldn't pay a credit more than two seventy-five. I have a pair every bit as good as these, with a higher cuff, that cost only two hundred."

The clerk rubbed his cheek with a finger. "I can give you the special shopper discount, ten percent."

Tomas handed the other boot back with a smile. "Thank you, anyway."

The clerk made sure no other patrons were close by. "I know for a fact we have these in stock. If you promise not to tell anyone, I'll let you take them for two eighty-five." He saw the hesitation in Tomas' face. "You'd throw away a deal like this for ten credits?"

"When you put it that way …." Tomas relented, happy enough with the bargain. "May we try a forty-two, then, please? Sarah … Sarah?" His ward was gone.

Tomas and the boys found her sitting on a display cube by the entrance, hugging herself.

"Sarah? Why are you over here? Try these on, make sure they're comfortable." He held out the boots.

Sarah looked away. "No, thank you, sir."

Tomas knew the unstated look of desire in a girl's eye. She'd shown more interest in the boots than anything else all afternoon. "These are quality footwear, and a very reasonable price. You seemed to like them a moment ago… "

"Not really."

"Sure she does," David said, bending to remove her shoe. "She's just playing polite. They're perfect, Sar. They'll look great …"

"NO!" Sarah smashed David's fingers with her other heel. He dropped her foot with a curse. "I said I *don't want* them! They're not what I'm looking for, and I don't like them!" She fled down a display aisle.

Tomas never feared an argument, unless it involved Mamá. He followed on her heels. "What *are* you looking for then, Sarah? We've seen a great number of styles and colors. What would you like better? Please, tell me, and I will make sure we find it."

Sarah gave a nervous twitch. "I don't know. I – I guess I'll know when I see it."

Vlad approached. His hand glided over her shoulder. "What's wrong?"

"Nothing's wrong! I don't like the boots! Can't I choose what I wear? Or is that part of my Declaration of Incompetence?" she growled at her beloved brother. "Subject is not to be unsupervised due to risk of injury! Subject is not to have access to sharp objects! Subject is not allowed to make decisions as to style and type of clothing she may wear …"

Tomas kept his voice low and calm. "Enough, Sarah. That's not true at all. If you tell us what you would prefer, we can help you find it. The store can find you virtually anything on the merchant network."

"I'd prefer to go home."

"We can go home as soon as you have chosen footwear and a coat."

"Then I shall hold you to that!" Sarah twisted away, walking as fast as she could without actually sprinting through the footwear display. Far below eye level, on the floor, she spied a pair of black boots, glanced at the electronic inventory card, and snatched them up.

"Here!" she said decisively as the group caught up. "If I must chose boots, these are the ones I desire. I will purchase these."

"You've got to be kidding!" David's face wrinkled in disgust. Even Vlad looked pained. "Sarah, those are polypoxyphene! You might as well wear plastic cups on your feet! At least plastic cups might have style to them or something."

"They are lined, waterproof, and rated to minus ten," Sarah read off the display card. "They are guaranteed not to leak for one full year. I will have outgrown them by then anyway. These or nothing."

"You have those in a forty-two?" Tomas asked the salesman following them. He returned the boot to the stand before he might be seen holding it.

"We have every size," the salesman replied with regret. "If I may say so, sir, those are our poorest seller, and they're currently on their final discount. Surely I can show you something of a more appropriate quality."

"You're not going to let her buy those, are you?" Sergei asked. "They're forty-credit trash!"

Tomas rolled his eyes and sighed. "The lady has spoken."

He walked to the end of the aisle where Sarah hung on Vladimir. They whispered together, nose to nose, as Vlad stroked her cheek with the back of a finger. He kissed her lightly on the tip of her nose; she put her head on his shoulder.

She pulled away as Tomas approached. "That is your final choice?" he dared.

"Yes, sir."

"Very well. What about outerwear?" Somehow, Tomas didn't think that would be any easier.

Sarah glanced at Vladimir.

"She can have my ski jacket," Vlad volunteered. "It fits her, and she likes it. I have two others I can wear."

Tomas grew impatient. "That's very generous, Vladimir, but there is no reason for Sarah not to have her own coat. Do you remember where you purchased it? Perhaps we can find another for her."

David brought over a beautiful sky-blue parka with white accents. "Try this. The color's perfect for you."

"*I don't want it!*" Sarah growled. She pressed her wrists to her temples and banged twice. "Take me home!" Her foot stomped once, and she turned her back.

"Sarah, you are in a public place," Tomas said softly. "Please keep your voice down. Why don't we take a walk, try another marketplace, and you can have some time to relax."

"I don't WANT to go anywhere! I don't WANT a coat!" Sarah tugged at her hair before being seized by a particularly hard medication tremor. It ran down as far as her leg, only the third time that had ever happened. She stumbled and would have fallen if Sergei hadn't caught her. The noise and tremor attracted attention in the quiet shop.

Enough was enough. He didn't understand, but Tomas knew defeat when he saw it. He'd been frightened by the girl's psychotic behaviors when he'd first met her not two weeks before; he was not prepared for an outburst in the middle of an upscale clothing shop.

"All right," he said with an artificial calm. "I think our time here is finished. Please come with me and I will walk you back to the flyer." He took her firmly by the shoulder and steered her toward the doors. "David, have the coat, boots, and some gloves put on my account. No, Vlad, stay here and wait for your brothers. Let me talk to Sarah alone." He took back David's extra coat from Sergei, who'd carried it through the shop.

"NO!" Sarah kept her voice below a shriek. "The boots! David! Nothing but the boots!" She tried to pull away from Tomas but he steered her outside. "Vlad! Help me!"

Tomas let go long enough to drape David's coat around her shoulders. Tears rose, but she didn't fight the walk back to the flyer. Sarah scrambled into the rear passenger area of the flyer as soon as the hatch opened, diving for the farthest seat. She gave a louder cry and cringed against the window as he climbed in after her and locked the doors.

Sarah raised her arms to protect her head. "Don't! Please don't touch me!" she begged. "I'm sorry! I'm sorry!"

"Shh, shh, shh," Tomas soothed. He crossed his legs, then folded his arms. "Relax, Sarah. I'm not going to hurt you. I'm not going to touch you. I'm not even angry with you. Put your hands down, please."

Sarah stayed crunched, but the arms came down to curl clenched hands to her chest. "I'm sorry!"

"I'm not asking for apologies. I would, however, like some sort of explanation. *Any* sort of explanation." He sighed. "I'm confused, Sarah. I want very much to make this transition easy for you, but *you* have to help *me* in that pursuit. I am not a telepath. I had hoped you would purchase some of what you needed on the starliner. Mamá wanted to take you to buy a wardrobe, but you were so involved with the boys, I didn't want to disturb you. There is no reason for you to borrow everything from your siblings when I am more than willing to provide you with whatever you'd like. You just have to *choose* something, Sarah! I promise not to fly into a rage if you say, 'I don't like the collar on that,' or 'I would prefer something in tangerine.'

"I don't understand what is going on here. Are you tired of shopping? Do you feel ill? Have we seen too many things today? Are there so many choices you can't pick? Are you upset by open places like the market squares? Is it *me* you dislike? Talk to me! Help me understand what has upset you. I promise, I will not be angry, no matter what your response."

Sarah rubbed her nose with a finger. "I chose a pair of boots."

"That's true. Thank you for that. But what don't you like about the other clothing?"

"I like my own clothing. I don't want anything else."

Tomas sighed heavily. He would not bang his head on a brick wall. "Fair enough. Let's compromise: I will support your decision to wear the clothing you have, perhaps borrow something fancier if necessary, but you will wear the coat David is bringing you when you leave the house.

You simply must have something warmer outside, Sarah."

Sarah sniffed and gave a nod. "Okay. But I keep my own clothes."

Tomas smiled in relief. "Thank you, Sarah. I'm glad we could reach an agreement."

The boys arrived at the flyer, pressing their noses against the girl's window and making faces. Sarah broke into a giggle. Tomas ordered the doors to unlock. "Let's get home."

At home, the difficulties evaporated without a trace, leaving Tomas dizzy with the change. Mamá's nagging questions and less-than-constructive 'observations' didn't help. There was no pattern, as far as he could see. Sarah was relaxed around the boys – except in display shops. She was consistently timid and shy around him – less so if the boys were around. *Was* it public places? She'd stuck close to him on the starbase. She did okay on Friday's trip to the clinic, but she'd been a mess on and off at home, too, so that theory didn't hold. *What, then?*

Vladimir was a sacred subject; he'd have to make sure David toned down his harassments for a while. Her assertion of vegetarianism was tactless, but hadn't caused any obvious discomfort until pressured. Certainly, there was no meat involved in a clothing choice. *Animals, though…* Tomas couldn't remember seeing any fur or leathers that possibly might have offended her. Color! He'd forgotten about color! She hated the color red. Perhaps she'd noticed something red that he'd overlooked? A red tag, a red lining? How in Heaven had Dmitri been able to keep up with it? He'd have to discuss things privately with John, see if this was 'normal,' or if he was even heading in the right direction.

Space, both John and Dmitri had instructed him. If she felt overwhelmed, give her space. Tomas gave her space upon their return, free time to seek comfort from her brothers, time without pressure to pull herself together. It sounded so good and professionally directed, but the space was more for him; he hated to admit, he was hiding in his study deliberately, on the pretext of checking on business. He did review the notes posted by his secretary, but he spent more time reviewing the museum directories he'd put together the day before. He would have to plan ahead on what to do if they rounded a corner and a red fur mobile set her to screaming.

No pressure seemed to be the key, for as Tomas walked the downstairs halls he could hear her laughter mix with the boys'. They sat in a cluster in the media room, Sarah in David's lap as they watched a comedy program. Tomas intended to join them, but they nearly trampled him in a sudden charge to the main lounge, Sergei having rediscovered a chess partner worthy of his efforts. He watched the game instead. With her brothers she seemed like any ordinary teen, chatting without care, giving as well as receiving insults in good humor, laughing and joking with ease. Anyone watching through a window would never have suspected a thing.

Sarah matched her brother's expertise play for play. An hour passed, but Tomas watched the players with interest. Sarah didn't seem distracted by his presence in the least. A little shyer perhaps, but she smiled and conversed without undue distress, tearing large holes in his latest theories. Several interruptions by Marina seemed to break her concentration, but no more than Sergei's, and, unlike David and Vladimir, she didn't angrily order the younger girl out.

Sergei perked up. He slid his bishop into an open square.

"Check."

Sarah frowned. She hadn't noticed that opening, either. She grabbed her king and moved him diagonally. Too late, she realized her error. Sergei's rook slid down the board.

"Check. I think that's mate, too," he said, studying the pieces.

She tipped her king in concession. "You win! I guess I'm out of practice."

"You'll beat him next time," Vlad said with assurance. "You always could."

"A good match, nonetheless," Tomas said. "Well done! I'm afraid you'd have me beat in the first ten moves. Sarah, if you could spare a few minutes, I'd like you to come down to my apartment after dinner. I have a surprise for you I thought we could discuss over dessert."

Sarah's eyes widened as if she'd overheard someone plotting her murder, and the smile vanished. She glanced at him, then back to the safety of the chess table.

"I – I was going to spend time with Vladimir later," she faltered.

"That's okay," Vlad said. "I promised to buzz one of my friends. I'll do that while you're downstairs. We'll get together afterwards."

"I don't want to keep you up too late …."

Tomas gave her an understanding wink. "I won't take long. Dinner should be ready soon, anyway."

"But… But… David said he would …"

David shook his head. "I'm sorry, Sar, I really can't. I blew off the whole weekend. I've got to get some work done before I leave in the morning, or I'll never catch up. Economediation's going to be the death of me yet. They give you six examples of failing economies and you have to write plans of corrections for each, taking into account a few million variables. I'll take a break around eleven to say goodnight," he promised.

76

The girl's face blanched. A medication tremor twitched across her face and into her shoulder.

"I'll play with you tonight!" Nikky offered with zeal. "Uncle Tomas taught me how to play chess."

"Sarah?" Tomas had seen enough of the tremors to know they were a warning sign. Somewhere, somehow, he'd missed the lightning strike.

"Yes," she replied distantly. "I just – I didn't realize it would be so soon."

"I couldn't see the point in waiting," Tomas shrugged. "John said you had no restrictions on activities. The boys go back to school tomorrow, and the house will be empty. You've had a few days to settle in. Your therapy runs only two or three hours a day, and John is willing to make that flexible." He spilled the surprise, hoping it would boost her spirits.

"I thought perhaps this week we could take some side trips, just you and I. Dmitri told me you like museums. We could hit Moscow, Kiev, maybe head all the way up to 'Petersburg and I'll take you to the Hermitage, if you'd like. In the coming weeks, we can try further excursions to Washington, or Paris, or Beijing. The Spaceflight Museum on the Moon is rather spectacular as well. What do you think?"

"Can I go, too?" Nikky begged. "I like museums!"

Sergei waved his hands with feeling. "You'll space out on the Hermitage! I spent a semester practically living there for two of my art classes. You could spend a year there and never get bored."

Sarah's eyes wandered, unfocused. She got up and paced the room. "Yes, sir? What difference does it make? Minsk, Moscow, Murmansk or the Moon, it's all the same."

"Sarah, you seem upset about something. If you'd rather do something else, please tell me, and we can make other plans."

"NO!" Sarah barked. She tugged her hair, hugged herself hard three times, then ran a hand through her hair, panting with stress.

"I'm sorry! I didn't mean to be rude. I am most grateful for your efforts. I can do it. I said I can, and I meant I can. I *will* do it! I never said I wouldn't!" Tremors jerked her face and shoulders, making her behavior seem that much stranger.

"Yo! Generate a stasis field, will you?" David exclaimed. "You're like a puppet in an earthquake! What's pulling your strings? If that's what your medication does to you, John can take you off it tonight. Come here." He grabbed her as she paced. His arms wrapped around her, but Sarah stiffened and fought him.

"No! No! Don't touch me! Let me go! I will! I will! I'll be ready! I can do it! I can!"

Vladimir pulled on David. "Let go of her! Can't you hear her? She doesn't want to be held right now."

Tomas was seconds behind. Sarah ducked and gave a cry of fear. "Let go!" he commanded, waving the boys back. "Let her breathe." Freed, Sarah ran several steps back, wrists pressed to her temples, trembling.

"I can do it! I can do it! I promise! I won't disappoint you! I know I can do it!" She gave a shriek as Tomas guided her by the elbows toward a chair. "So soon! So soon!"

"You need to relax, Sarah," Tomas ordered. "You're not making any sense. Sit down. Talk to me, and we'll work through what's bothering you."

Sarah wrenched away on the second step. "Don't touch me!"

"Sar?" Vlad tried. "What's wrong?"

Sarah exploded into tears. "I'm *sorry!* I'm *sorry!* I *can't* do it yet! I can't! I'm sorry!" In a blink, she turned and fled the room.

David frowned. "What the hell was that about?"

Vlad moved to run. "I'll get her."

Tomas stopped him. "No. Let her go for now. Maybe she just needs some privacy. Give her ten minutes, and I'll speak with her."

Marina entered the sitting room. "Are you done playing? Can I come in now?"

Tomas pushed his worry to the back of his head. "Sure, Princess. Come in. What have you been up to this afternoon?"

"Boring stuff. Jetta went to Mars for the weekend, Iliana's in Odessa, and you let Nikky in here but not me." Marina wandered to the chess table, where Sergei still sat. She picked up Sarah's pieces and put them in their starting positions. "How come Sarah gets to go outside without a coat? You yell at me."

Tomas turned sharply. "She went outside?"

"She ran out the door by the library. She's lucky Grandmamá didn't see her running." Marina reached to put Sergei's pieces back. "That's not fair. You told us she's just a kid, too."

The chess pieces bounced on the soft carpet as Sergei's knees hit the table. Vlad was first out of the room, the other boys and Tomas hard on his heels.

"The lights by the hangar just went on!" Vlad shouted from the library window. "She's heading for the trees!"

Nikky made a face. "Why would she go out without a coat? Doesn't she know it's almost dark? She's so weird!"

Vlad slammed his brother in the head. "Don't you talk about her like that! Get lost, will ya! You don't know anything!"

"Because no one ever *tells* me anything!" Nikky shot back.

"Easy, Vladimir," Tomas cautioned. "It's not his fault."

Sergei peered over Vlad's shoulder. "It's not more than minus five out. She's gonna freeze in that get-up she's wearing."

David headed for the door. "I'll get the snowcrawler and bring her back."

"No one's going anywhere. Let me handle this, please." Tomas addressed the library's interface. "Computer: security system. Activate perimeter security net. Rear property scan, infra-red."

The viewscreen lit up with a miniature map of the property in dark shadow. The four buildings, especially the main house, glowed with warmth against the frigid winter air. Only one other object did; a dot moving toward the top of the screen.

"I'll get her," Tomas said grimly, and pushed a confused Marina out of the way. "I don't know what I said to start this, but let me deal with it. Tell the kitchen to have some tea ready. Everyone else is to stay here and wait for me. Understand? *No one* is to leave the house." He stared extra firmly at David, who had a tendency to misinterpret directives he didn't agree with.

"Yes, sir," the boys promised.

Marina turned to Nikky, hands on her hips. "I told her she'd get in trouble!"

Eight

The cold air tore at the inside of Tomas's nose, burning his lungs as he jogged across the snowy tundra of the back lawns. Security lights from the house and outbuildings broke the winter twilight, but they couldn't penetrate the entire estate. Frozen slashes made by skis and the wider, motor-driven scars of David's snowcrawler gouged the snow into a shadowed jumble. From the lack of footprints, he guessed the girl had followed the hard crawler tracks; now and then a running step missed the path. Twenty hectares to run circles on, and she had to run for the trees.

A hundred thoughts came to him, too late to act upon. Tomas's modern thermal clothing and ankle-high shoes would keep his body warm, but he should have grabbed a hat to protect his ears. He should have grabbed gloves. The girl had no such protection – was she wearing shoes? Probably just those cloth ballet slippers from Sigma Tau. He should have grabbed a coat for her; at least a blanket. He'd taken off his *Vsyochas* wrist interface; there went any communication with the house. Sarah wasn't a small child; he doubted he could carry her all the way back.

The crawler's track made a sharp turn at the trees, but the footprints continued straight through the break that in summer was a gravel pathway. He sped up, his breath heaving clouds into the frigid air.

He could hear her wails over the crunching of his feet on the snow, and he slowed to a walk. The path opened to a clearing in the trees, ringed by simple stone benches. In the center stood the monument he'd had built, a family mausoleum. The ornately carved base stood four meters long, two and a half meters wide, and more than two meters at its cap. Rising another two meters from the top stood a bronze statue of a youthful man and woman, an arm around each other's waists. The man's other arm pointed skywards, and the couple's gaze followed the finger to look to the stars. Spotlights glared upward at the statue, illuminating the clearing. On the near side were engraved the names of the four deceased family members within, accompanied by eerie laser-etched portraits: Tomas' father, Fyodor; his sister Maryana; her young daughter Elizabyeta; her son Viktor. An expensive apology for shameful years of neglect.

Tomas's quarry knelt in the snow, plastered against the section of stone that bore her brother's likeness. Chilly red fingers clawed marble; they folded into fists and pounded at it while the girl shed explosive tears. She slid down the ice-cold stone until her head rested against the base.

It pained him, seeing her weeping by her brother instead of her mother, but Tomas knew Viktor had died brutally, and Sarah had been a witness. "I was told you were special to Viktor," he said aloud. "It must have hurt very badly to lose him."

Sarah screamed and twisted around, slouched against the tomb. Tears, snow, and spit glued her hair to her face. Snow wet her sleeves, and unmelted snow caked the folds of her skirt. The knitted stockings had slid to her ankles, and her legs and hands and face were red with cold. She pushed against the stone, gasping and coughing.

Tomas stepped closer. "Do you like my memorial? I commissioned the statue myself. It's very beautiful in the springtime, ringed with flowers." He squatted and offered his hand. "I didn't know Viktor. I'm sorry I never had a chance to meet him. Come sit on the bench over there, and you can tell me about him."

Tomas made the mistake of taking her hand. Sarah ripped it away and lashed out with a desperate kick, knocking him backward. She tried to crawl, but became tangled in the skirt. A tremor caught her, and she collapsed in the snow.

Tomas brushed himself off, undeterred. "My fault, Sarah. I'm sorry. I know not to touch." It was a ten-minute walk back to the main house. She would freeze by then.

"Sarah, I don't know what has upset you, but you need to stop," he said, kind but firm. "I don't understand why you are afraid of me, but if you don't get out of that snow, you will suffer frostbite, and that is both painful and dangerous. I am going to help you up, and we are going to sit on that bench. You don't have to speak to me, but you will sit there and calm down, and then we will walk back to the house and you will change to dry clothes of your choice. If you wish to hide from me, that is also your choice, but you will do it inside the house, where you are not at risk for exposure. Do you understand?"

No response. He stepped forward with determination, grasped the girl by her elbows, and hauled her to her feet. Sarah cried out weakly, unable to breathe from tears. She made only the briefest attempt at fighting; she was too cold, too tired, shivering too hard. Tomas half-dragged her to the bench and brushed the snow away. She folded over, face on her freezing knees.

He wiped the snow from her face, brushed it from her legs and clothes, straightened her skirt to cover as much of her cold legs as possible. "You're safe, Sarah. I don't know what's wrong, but I will guarantee nothing is as bad as you think. Good Lord, you're half frozen already." He arranged her in a sitting position and tucked a wet hand into her armpit. He breathed on her other hand, rubbing it, keeping the circulation moving. Between the crying and coughing and tremors and shivering, she couldn't hold herself up.

"Shhh. I promise, I won't hurt you." He put an arm around her to keep her upright; she stiffened and cried louder. "Try this – hold yourself up on your elbows, cup your hands like this," he formed her hands for her, "and breathe into them. That will slow your breathing and warm your hands and face at the same time. That's it. Good girl. Keep going. I'm going to let go now. Got it? Okay."

Tomas felt heartened by the slight cooperation. He slid an arm out of the sleeve of his pull-over sweater and took it off.

Sarah let out a strangled cry and tried to run. "No no no no," she sputtered. "Not … Vik!"

"Stop!" Tomas commanded, and dragged her back. He gathered the garment and pulled it over her head. "This is all-weather fabric, Sarah." He pushed one arm and then the other through the sleeves as if she were a baby. "It's rated to keep you comfortable to minus ten. It will keep you from freezing further on the walk back. My shirt's rated to zero; it will keep me for now. Tuck your hands inside the sleeves, keep them warm."

Sarah curled the ends of the sleeves around her stiff fingers. She struggled and caught a deep breath, nearly falling off the bench with the effort. A hard cough followed, and a long wet sniff.

Tomas watched in disgust as she wiped her face with the cuff, then ran most of the sleeve under her flowing nose. It was a beautiful sweater, an expensive blend of imitation wool and temperature-controlling synthetic fibers in a tan, cream, and heather tweed from a custom manufacturer in Edinburgh. He cleaned the sleeve with the wet hem of her skirt.

"It's dark, and getting colder. We need to head back."

Sarah slid forward and tried to stand, but fell to her knees on the first step.

"Come on. You can do it." He helped her up, supporting most of her weight. This time she didn't make a sound.

The tip of the gathering met them outside at the fly-through. Tomas recognized John's blue Starlight Skimmer parked underneath before he found him in the crowd.

"I trust this wasn't just a badly timed social call," he said, grateful for John rushing forward to hold up the other half of the stumbling girl.

"I wish," John said as they dragged Sarah into the house. "David called and said you were in trouble."

"I think that might have been a smart move. I don't know what's going on, but it's out of my control. Move, everyone!" Tomas ordered as he tripped on Vladimir.

Seeing the lights, feeling the warmth of the house, Sarah pulled away and dropped to her knees, shaking spastically. She burst into a new wave of tears, hugging herself. "Vik? Viktor? Dimi? Please help me, Dim! Dimi!" When no one replied, she screamed out, "DAVID!"

David surged forward. "Here! I'm right here, Sar! I'm right here." A house staff appeared with a warmed blanket, and he draped it over her.

"D-D-D-D-Dav-vid?" Sarah sprang and locked her arms around his neck. "I tried! I tried! I tried! I tried!"

John gave her a quick once-over with a hand-held medical scanner. "She's hypothermic. The medication pump overloaded and shut down. I can fix that. Get her upstairs." David hefted her in his arms; Sergei tucked the blanket around her.

"Val, get her into a warm bath. Not hot, just warm. Kat, give her a hand. Have the kitchen bring some tea up. I'll be there in a minute. Everyone else, stay down here." The hovering cluster burst into action.

"But, John!" Vlad protested, trying to follow David.

Carver turned him aside. "I know it's hard, but stay out of the way until I know what's going on. You'll be the first to see her, I promise."

"How about you?" he asked Tomas, waving his scanner. "You look pretty damned cold, too."

"Not as bad as she is." Tomas walked to the lounge. He headed straight for the liquor bottles at the back.

"Nothing tea and two shots of my best vodka won't cure. I'm telling you, John, it came up out of nowhere! It was like she saw a ghost, and it chased her right out of the house. All I can say is, thank God it happened now and not the middle of the night, or tomorrow there'd be another name on that tomb out there." He poured himself a shot of vodka, offered one to Carver.

John declined. Tomas swallowed his in a single gulp, feeling it chase the cold. He poured another but carried it across the room to stand before the huge fireplace. It burned clean artificial logs, but the heat they gave off was real.

"The boys told me she didn't sleep much last night, and she acted strange earlier today," John said. "That's one clue. Is there anything I should know about out there?"

Tomas toasted the backs of his legs. "Just a lot of hysteria and crying. It got worse every time I came close, but I think she reached the point where she was just too cold to fight any more. A word or two of gibberish, nothing more. I know she hasn't been sleeping well. Galina?" he called out the door. "While I think of it – get on the commlink, call that boutique on Universalni Prospekt. I want six sets of warm clothes delivered for her by seven tomorrow morning – whatever you think will fit. Shirts, pants, nightwear – anything she needs. Enough of this refusal to wear anything but those cold rags. And handkerchiefs!" he remembered as Galina hurried to place the request. "Order her a dozen – make it *five* dozen germicidal handkerchiefs! Blue, green, orange, white – I don't care if they have pink and yellow spinning Polish polka-dots, order them! She is not to leave her room without one." He heaved a stressed sigh and drained his second glass as a kitchen staff brought a tray with hot tea, followed closely by his mother.

John left, and Tomas collapsed on a sofa by the tray. The silence amplified the unspoken tension. He slid forward and poured himself tea, waiting for the inevitable comment.

"I told Olga to set dinner up as a buffet," Andrea said. "That way everyone can eat something when they have a moment."

"That was a good idea, Mamá."

Andrea stood behind the sofa and laid a thin hand on his shoulder. "Tomashka. I know you did this out of the goodness of your heart, but sometimes kindness isn't enough to set things right. There's a private hospital in Mozyr that's very discreet about their clientele. Perhaps after a few weeks' rest, you might try again."

Tomas slouched back to look up at her. He patted her hand. "I haven't given up yet, Mamá, but we'll keep it in mind if it comes to that. Let's see what John says. I'm afraid I may have been the cause, though I don't know how. She was perfectly happy, playing with Sergei." He waved a frustrated arm at the chess table in the corner. "I reminded her the boys were going back to school tomorrow, and she just – folded in on herself, like a house of cards. She hasn't left them for a second; maybe she can't bear to part with them. I told her it was perfectly okay if she wasn't up to sightseeing yet, but I don't think she heard me. This isn't what I expected."

Andrea looked down with a coolness borne of experience. "It never is."

* * *

Sarah didn't notice the tranquilizer John gave her, but it calmed her enough that the girls were able to get her to sit in the warm tub. She didn't notice him running scanners and tapping controls on a hand-held apparatus to reactivate and adjust the neurofeedback device implanted near her kidney. The tears stopped, but the hopeless sobbing continued, slow and soft.

Warmed and dried and clothed in her Sigma Tau nightdress, Sarah stopped at the back corner of the room and sank to the floor in a ball. When Katya tried to comfort her, Sarah pulled her down, too. She curled against her sister's shoulder and stayed there, motionless.

"I think Tomas got to her just in time," John said, checking the frosted toes. He pulled a thick sock over the foot and rubbed it familiarly. "The skin might peel in a couple spots, but I think she'll be fine. Now, about the rest of this... " He tried to get Sarah to look at him. "Val, give me a hand here."

Together they lifted the girl and helped her to the bed, but Sarah wanted no part of it. She curled up against the wall with her feet on her pillow, reaching for Katya's hand.

"Sarah, you have to keep warm," Valeria scolded gently. "Stay under the blanket." She stole the cover from the second bed and spread it over the girl.

John got down to business. "All right, Sarah. I know you well enough to know when something's really bothering you. You're not a baby, you're not in a hospital, and I'm not playing games. I need you to tell me what's wrong. I need to know if your attempt at freezing to death was accidental or deliberate." Getting no reaction, he motioned to Kat for his medical kit. He adjusted the airhypo and leaned forward.

Sarah squirmed just enough to make the task difficult. "No."

Katya held the arm long enough for John to reach his mark. "Shhh. It's only going to make you feel better."

"It's not a sedative," he explained. "I don't want you knocked out, either. It's just a heavy-duty anxiolytic. I want you relaxed. You should be feeling warm and heavy, maybe a little tingly right now. That's good. Go with it. Feel the warmth. Nice and warm. Everything in this room is peaceful, Sarah. It's a safe room. Everyone in this room knows everyone else quite well. There are no strangers here. Good girl," he soothed, seeing her take an extra-deep breath and sink into the bed. "Let your mind drift. Your mind is full of thoughts right now. Let them run. I'm going to have the girls leave, and we'll do some serious talking, just you and me."

Katya gave the limp hand a final squeeze and kissed her sister's cheek. "I'll be right downstairs."

Sarah stared into space, shaking her head as John pulled the reading chair to the bed.

* * *

Sergei, Vlad, and Nikky waited in the upstairs lounge, out of the way but still close at hand. Now and then someone would talk, usually Nik, but mostly they just sat and waited. David sat all of four minutes, crossing his legs one way, crossing them the other, tapping his fingers, jiggling his legs, until he finally had to move around. Granted, he wasn't about to bathe his sister, but in the midst of all her crying and craziness, she'd asked for *him*. She'd wanted *him* to hold her, not scrawny little Vlad. She may have written most of her letters to Vlad, but when she needed help, she'd called *him*. He should at least have been able to stay in the room. What if she called for him again?

Shit! He thumped his fists on the wall in frustration.

"I thought you were supposed to be studying?" Sergei said.

"So I fail Economediation. Big fuck." David punched upwards toward the ceiling lights. "It's not a requirement. I have enough points to graduate without it. If nothing else, I can take it again in the summer. Maybe I'll drop the whole semester. We haven't seen Sarah in seven years. I think I can spare four months of my life to make up for it. Uncle Tomas could use the help with her, anyway."

"You know damned well he'd never let you do that. Nobody quits last semester senior year."

"If you take a leave of absence, so am I!" Vladimir declared. "She wants me with her more than anybody."

"Me, too!" Nikky said. "I'm her friend, too! I can help."

David sneered. "Don't be stupid, Vlad. You're already a year behind. You miss any more time and Nik will be graduating with you."

"Sarah could teach me all that at home!" Vlad shot back. "She's smarter than any teacher!"

"Me, too!" came Nikky's echo. "She could teach me, too! If Vlad does it, so am I."

A door opening cut short the argument. The boys leapt for the hallway as Valeria and Katya appeared, a dozen questions flying at once.

"Shh! She's fine," Valeria said. "She's cold and she's tired, but John's talking with her. There's nothing more we can do until he's finished."

"*I* could have told you she was cold and tired!" David stabbed. "The way I remember, I don't think you should be the one judging Sarah's medical conditions."

"*David!*" Katya hissed.

Val's cheeks reddened, but she held her head high. "Very well then,

86

David. Next time, suffer in ignorance." She turned and went to spread the news downstairs.

"She'll be fine," Katya repeated, hugging Vlad extra hard. "She's in the best hands. It's probably going to be a while, though. Why don't we go downstairs and get some dinner? Misery loves company."

* * *

Two and a half unbearable hours passed before John paged Katya on the intercom, and another ten minutes before he appeared downstairs. He braced for the onslaught, arms raised for silence.

"Shh! Listen up! She's going to be fine. I know you want to see her but she's very sleepy and she needs to rest. Now, since I know you're not going to take no for an answer, I'll let you up in two groups, boys first, but not a second over five minutes. Kat's got strict orders to beat you out of there with a stick if she has to. She's full of medication, so don't expect her to talk. Don't pester her, don't question her, don't try and make her smile, just go in, say goodnight, and get back out so she can rest. I think she'll be a lot better in the morning."

Vlad didn't wait. His feet hit the stairs before David and Sergei cleared the room.

Tomas stood up, awaiting details. "She spoke to you?"

"We need to talk," John said without a trace of humor. "In private, and undisturbed. Why don't you grab a bottle of something good and we'll go down to your office."

Tomas nodded with a heavy heart. "I take it by something good, you mean something besides vodka." He walked back to the bar and regarded the selection. "That Australian rotgut you like? French Cognac?" He picked a fancy round bottle from the long rows. "This one's older than you are."

"As long as it's strong," John said. "We're going to need it."

Nine

Tomas sat on the sofa at the front of his office. "I take it things aren't looking good. I really thought she would be okay, until today."

"She will be, I think, if we can get this straightened out." John took the bottle of cognac from the table and poured two glasses. Tomas refused, but John insisted. "Take it. I've got to explain this in steps, and you'll want that as we go along, believe me.

"Actually, I'm rather impressed." He took a chair next to Tomas. "When she's that upset, she usually tears herself up – bangs her head, bites her fingers, cuts herself. They were still seeing that just a week ago on the space station. This time she didn't even tear her hair out. That means the medication's working."

"That's *working*? John, she nearly froze to death out there!"

"Accidental. She's coming from a forested area where the coldest temperatures never hit freezing. When she was frightened, she'd run outside and seek solace among the trees. She saw your trees and ran for them, forgetting what a Byelorussian winter is like. When she stopped running, she was lost in the dark."

"I guess that's good, but, do you know why? What did I say to make her react like that? I never meant to push her into anything. Dmitri said she likes museums. I thought time spent together, doing something she enjoyed, would make her less edgy. She's very polite, very obedient, but anyone can see she's not comfortable."

John swallowed a sip of cognac and put the glass down. "Here's where we're at. You can read her files all you want, the boys can talk about her all night, but you don't *know* Sarah. She's a brilliant girl, no question, but she is absolutely incapacitated by neuroses. They're nothing new. She grew up running from possible danger; it's automatic, without thought. Thoughts get in her head, sometimes good but sometimes bad, and she can't stop thinking about them – like convincing herself she caused her mother's death, then obsessing on it to the point of severe depression. These are old behaviors, Tomas. I want to make sure you understand that completely before I go any further," John emphasized. "*You* did not start this. We're going to discuss some pretty crazy stuff, and I want you to understand, under any circumstances, *you did not start this*."

"Okay. So it had nothing to do with what I said this afternoon?"

"Well, indirectly it did, but it really didn't." John waved the thought away. "Call it bad timing. Remember, I said she was brilliant. That's true, especially for academics. She's been teaching herself university-level courses the past six years, and she retains most of what she reads. Therefore she knows an incredible amount about literature, history, sciences and stuff."

Tomas leaned back and crossed his legs. "I've listened to her discuss several novels with Sergei. I have no doubt she can hold her own at the university level."

"She can, and more. Now, languages are her easiest subject, and sciences are what interest her the most, but her father was an archaeologist, and Sarah's very first lessons were in ancient studies. In their home, history was a way of life, a way of livelihood, and because of what her father did, history was *alive* for Sarah. It was real. It existed. The very proof lay right there in her living room." John cupped a hand as if holding an artifact.

"No doubt that fueled some of her interest, but what does history have to do with hysteria?"

John grinned. "Fueled it? It set that overeager preschool mind on *fire*! Bear with me, Tomas. I told you this would take some explaining. As a result, Sarah was a student of ancient history long before she ever knew there was a modern aspect. And that's the point I want you to remember right now, because it's very significant and we're going to come back to it."

"Ancient history," Tomas repeated.

"You better start on that cognac. Doctor's orders!"

Tomas picked up the glass, but only swished the liquid around.

"Here's part two, and this is where the trouble starts," John continued. "Sarah is a 170-centimeter walking guilt trip. She's being eaten alive by perceived guilt. She feels completely responsible for Dmitri getting into trouble with the Allied Fleet. As things looked bleaker and bleaker, she was desperate to save him. She would play the martyr, sacrifice herself, if she could just get Dmitri off the hook. She turned to the only friend she had left: Vladimir. All she wanted was the name of a good lawyer, one who could win their case and take payment on a long installment plan. Lo and behold, you intercepted her call. Then, to her utter horror, you showed up in person. Now, not only would Dmitri know she had gone against his wishes, but she had bothered you as well. Add another layer of guilt for making you come out there."

"She never asked me to go out there! That was my own choice! If they needed reinforcements, I would be in a much better position to bring them in if I was hearing things first hand. It had nothing to do with her whatsoever." Tomas sipped his cognac.

"That may be, but Sarah didn't see it that way." John's glass was empty, so he poured himself a second round; he deemed it his housecall fee.

"Now, she's relieved that these multiple lawyers, who have yet to discuss their fee with her, can cut a good deal for her brother, but she's still devastated by the fact she committed the crime but Dmitri's the one going to rehab."

"In the end, he *was* guilty," Tomas said, playing with his glass. "If he hadn't smuggled a forbidden weapon out of the research base, Sarah would never have used it. Dmitri knew that as well."

"I agree, but Sarah is fiercely loyal. Her vision stops at the point where she discovered the EPSAR and started to play with it." John shifted forward on his seat; Tomas mirrored the action.

"Here's where everything starts to snowball. What happened today is the accumulation of three weeks' guilt piling up. She's wallowing in guilt over Dimi, she's dying over the guilt of making you go out there, and now you've got custody of her, making her face her guilt every day. She said you tried to buy her dinner that first night?"

"Just a little café on the starbase. She declined a meal, so I ordered her a dessert instead. Dmitri said she liked sweets, and she hadn't eaten a thing all day."

"Guilt trip."

"That's ridiculous! I would have done that for a stranger off the street! I couldn't eat a meal in front of someone who hadn't eaten that day and not offer them *something!*" Tomas took a longer sip of the brandy.

"*You* wouldn't, but I told you, Tomas, this isn't about *you*. It's about *her*. She says she begged you not to send her home ambassador class, but you wouldn't listen. More guilt over what she saw as a needlessly extravagant expense. She didn't want your gift of expense money, but you refused to take it back. Guilty again."

"Oh, for Heaven's sake, John!" Tomas exclaimed with annoyance. "What was I supposed to do? She had nothing! *Nothing!* Alien costumes, travel bags that belonged in a refugee camp, and only pocket change for a week's journey. I'm her guardian; I have an image to uphold. Of course I gave her spending money! And she gave it all back. A thousand credits, hers to spend any way her heart desired, and she handed the card back with every credit intact. She couldn't have left her suite the entire time. I must admit, I felt insulted by that."

"She didn't leave her suite," John confirmed. "I'd doubt she left her bed. She told you she didn't want the money; you can only blame yourself there. She says you wanted her to stay in your suite at the starbase, but you allowed her to stay in the medical department of the ship when she asked."

"I'd hoped to spend the time talking, getting to know each other, but she was upset after the trial and afraid she might need medical intervention. She was having the implantation surgery for the pump in the morning anyway, so it made sense." Tomas rubbed his eyes. "I felt really bad about that. It was a missed opportunity to get things off to a good start."

"Don't, because you're going to feel a lot worse in a minute," John warned. "Somewhere, when you made that very innocent and polite invitation, two wrong circuits connected in that brilliantly paranoid mind. She jumped to a faulty conclusion, and became obsessed with it. Now, remember what I said about history?"

"She's a firm study in ancient civilizations."

"All this time, Sarah intended on paying the lawyer bill herself. When you arrived with three lawyers, she choked, but vowed to work three times as hard to pay it off. She tried to keep every additional expense out of the picture. She knew she was temporarily penniless, but no matter what she did, you kept upping expenses on her. She had the lawyers to pay for, she figured etiquette would demand she pay your travel expenses, and then you had the gall to send her home on a presidential starliner. You threw money at her, and then, to top it all off, today you forced her to buy expensive clothing. To her, she's already in debt for an astronomical sum, and you are doing everything you can to raise the bill."

Tomas exploded. "The debts are mine! You know me better than that, John! I was *overjoyed* to be able to help her after all this time. I would have carried her home on my shoulders if it would have helped!"

"*I* know that, *you* know that, but Sarah didn't – and still doesn't – know *you*. All this financial worry is eating away at her hour after hour, you say something perfectly honorable, and a fact of history enters her head, and she's seized by a new morbid obsession," John explained. "In ancient times, when a woman was destitute, had no property, no money, no place to live, nothing to eat, and no hope left, what was the one thing she had left to sell that might buy her a meal, or shelter for the night?"

Tomas shook his head, brain dulled by drink and the stressful day. "I don't know. Her firstborn?"

"Herself," John answered softly. "She sells her body for recreational pleasure. Believing herself in the same type of position, Sarah became convinced that was the only option left to her: to give herself to you, to pay for the debts she'd incurred."

It took several seconds for the ideas to connect. Tomas had started to pick up the cognac bottle. As the words sank in, the bottle slid between his fingers and fell noisily on the table. It clattered against his glass, knocking it over and breaking it.

"*What?!* She thought … She expected me to … Saint Nikolai, have mercy on me!" Tomas mumbled, crossing himself. "Mary, chosen Mother of God! John! I swear upon my estate, I never made such a request of her! I never made a suggestion or a – a hint! I could no more request such a thing from her than I could my own child! I would never *dream* of such a thing!"

John grabbed Tomas's trembling hand. "*I know that*, Tomas. No one is accusing you of wrongdoing. I told you, you are *not* the guilty party here. This is all about Sarah and her misplaced ideas. She admits you never made any direct suggestion of it. This is all about *her*.

"Trouble is," John continued, compulsively straightening the fallen bottle, "Sarah's not that kind of girl. She's very shy and modest, more so now than when she was young. Emotionally, she's very immature in that area. She couldn't bring herself to carry out the plan. On one hand, she's burning with guilt over being a poor relation who's deeper in debt every day and tearing her hair out believing she's allegedly bound by history to pay it off, and on the other, utterly unable to make herself do it. She's been struggling with the idea every hour since you put her on that expensive ship home."

Tomas walked over to the wall, trying to escape the news. He leaned against it with one hand, other hand across his mouth as if he were fighting his stomach. He stayed that way, motionless, letting his churning thoughts filter out. Carver gave him the courtesy of silence.

"So, every time I've tried to extend myself, to make her feel welcome…?"

John gazed at the coffee table with unfocused eyes. "Every time you've touched her, spoken to her alone, smiled or were friendly or just plain courteous, all she saw was an attempt at claiming your debt. Asking her to come to your apartment broke the camel's back. She couldn't take the strain any longer."

Tomas ran a hand uselessly over his hair. The pieces began to click. "She's never without one of the boys with her at all times. She sits in my flyer as far away as she can be. She jumps when I speak to her. *'I'm sorry, I can't do it, I tried,'* she said. I took my sweater off to put over her, and she screamed."

He shook his head, sickened. "The only words she said to me out there were, 'Not in front of Viktor.' *Not in front of Viktor.* I thought it was some craziness, but it makes sense now. My God! I promise the court to

92

take care of her, and four days later she's running for her life, terrified beyond reason I'm about to rape her in twenty centimeters of snow, in ten below zero temperatures. What was I thinking of, bringing her here?! I don't know anything about psychiatry! What the hell am I doing?"

"Not a damned thing wrong!" John answered with conviction. "From a logical point of view, you've handled everything perfectly, but logic doesn't work here. Welcome to Sarah's little world, where the daily special is an extra helping of fear, topped with an encyclopedic fact base and a side order of misinterpretation of social cues. We *never* should have let her come home alone, Tomas, never! I know we found out about her mental state too late to do anything, but it gave her a whole week with nothing to do but cement the ideas in her head. A whole week for her fears to grow out of control." He sank back defeatedly in his chair.

Tomas let his hands fall against his legs with a soft slap. "So what do I do *now*? How can I possibly hope to care for her if she's running in fear all the time? How can she possibly survive?"

"We're going to put a stop to it tonight," John said with authority. "Sarah's ashamed as all hell about it. It took me three different tranquilizers and a touch of narcotics to get her uninhibited enough for me to pick information from her, one damned word at a time. She's grateful to be here, but she's mourning Dmitri. He's been her entire life these past seven years – brother, father, family and best friend, all rolled into one, and rehab rules state no outside contact the first six weeks. While I've got her doped to the gills, I want to sit down together and hash this out. I think once she realizes your intentions are honest, she'll come around. Years ago it took her more than a month to really trust me. You've had four days."

Acid and alcohol backwashed into Tomas's chest, and he swallowed bitterly against it. If such false accusations got loose, his reputation would be destroyed, his businesses ruined. The girl may have been scared of him, but now he was every bit as scared of her, and he had much more to lose. For the first time in over a decade, he couldn't find it within himself to be the least bit cheerful in the face of difficulty. "You're the expert."

John peeked into the room. His wife stood up.

"She's still fighting, but fading fast," Katya whispered.

"Thanks." He kissed her as she slipped out the door. Tomas crept in after John.

John sat boldly on the bed. "Sarah? I'm back. I brought Tomas with me. I want this all out in the open, so there aren't any misunderstandings. I don't want you keeping that kind of worry inside."

Tomas managed a subdued smile, shielded behind the reading chair. "Good evening, Sarah. I'm glad you weren't seriously hurt."

The blank face turned away. The arms and head writhed, as if trying to escape a cocoon. *"Nooo,"* she breathed, more of a groan than a meaningful word.

John ignored it. "Tomas spoke to you. You need to answer him. He's in front of you. Look at him, please."

"Answer," Sarah echoed in a whisper. The head swung slowly back. "Thank you, sir."

Tomas beckoned John behind his armchair sanctuary. "Isn't she a little overmedicated? I've seen more animated service androids."

"No. The tranquilizers suppress the panic, but she's still feisty enough to fight. That particular narcotic leaves her extremely open to suggestion – hence the echo effect. She drifts if she's not focused, but she's quite aware of what's going on."

Tomas looked unsure, but nodded.

John returned to the bed. He motioned Tomas to sit in the chair. "Sit up, Sar. We need to have a little discussion."

The writhing increased. "No."

Carver wrestled her to sit up, knee to knee with Tomas, holding her in place with an arm. Sarah melted against him.

"Why don't you start, Tomas?" John prompted. "There's a lot to be said on both sides."

The environmental computer controlled the temperature of the room, never varying more than three degrees from its setting no matter how many persons were in the room, but sweat formed on Tomas's forehead. "Sarah... John and I were talking about your reaction downstairs earlier, and, he, uh, thought maybe we should, um, discuss that a bit. When you were playing with Sergei, and I mentioned ... "

Sarah covered her ears. "No."

John pulled the arms down. "Don't be a baby. You are in no danger here. Inside check. Are you nervous? Answer me."

"Answer. No."

"Are you afraid?"

Her eyes drooped as if she were drifting asleep. *"Afraid.* Should be."

"But you're *not* afraid," John said, relying on the drug-induced hypnosis to keep the suggestion implanted in her mind. "And you won't be. Now pay attention, and *listen* to what your uncle has to say. You were saying, Tomas?"

Tomas took a deep breath. "Sarah, what John told me this evening is... making me feel very bad inside. I loved my sister – your mother –

94

very much. We were very close when we were young – like you and your brothers. A part of her lives on in you – and your brothers and sisters, of course – and that makes *all* of you very special to me, you and Dmitri included. I care for you as much as I would my own child. The genes are the same. Coming to your aid on the *Triumph*, having you live here, buying you clothing or meals or entertainment, is nothing I wouldn't do for my *own* child," he insisted. "The idea that I would intentionally harm you or take advantage of my position – It makes me – absolutely *sick* inside!"

Sarah tried to stand, to flee, but John pushed her back with just two fingers. She turned away.

"I don't know what I said or did to make you think that, Sarah," Tomas told the back of her head, "but if I have conducted myself inappropriately, I apologize from the bottom of my heart. I assure you, it was quite unintentional. I meant only to make you feel welcome and at ease, nothing more. I only wanted you to be happy."

"Can you see that?" John coached. "Think back. Does that make sense? Look at him and answer."

The head turned more or less in Tomas's direction. "Yes."

"Sarah, I'm ... flattered, I guess, by what you had in mind, but not only is it unnecessary, I would never accept. What I did, I did of my own free will, simply because I wanted to *help*. It was voluntary; you are not in my debt for that, any part of it. I consider myself an honorable man, Sarah. Even if you crawled into my bed naked, I would not touch you. I would leave the room. You are a child to me, Sarah. That may appeal to some men, but not me. I know many women, on a dozen worlds, who are only too eager to entertain me. Do you understand that?"

The girl pulled inwards until she had folded up, chin to her chest, forehead on her knees, but she whispered, "I'm sorry."

"Don't be," Tomas said kindly. "I know this is very hard for you. It took quite a while for your brothers and sisters to adjust when they first arrived, too. My shoulders have been cried on by every one of your sisters – brothers, too, and they have yet to become too soggy to take on one more. All you have to do is tell me. If you feel uncomfortable approaching me directly, leave me a note with just your name on it, and I will come to you. We don't know each other yet, and I don't expect you to accept me or trust me or even like me immediately, but I'm hoping that, with time, we can come to be friends."

John watched for a glimmer of response. "What do you think, Sarah? Can you live with that? Would it be okay to have Tomas as a friend?"

"Friend? Yes."

"Then *tell* him," John urged. "He just told you a lot of heartfelt comments. How are you going to respond? What would you like him to know, while you're calm enough to say it? This is your best chance to set things straight. Talk to him."

Sarah squirmed, eyes closed, losing the battle against the powerful medications. Terror crushed by chemicals, the hypnotics urging her to comply, her uncensored thoughts rolled out.

"I'm sorry. I'm sorry," she repeated sleepily. "Never meant to offend. I want to like you. As a friend. Vlad loves you. He trusts you. Dimi said to trust you. I need your rules. I don't know what you expect without knowing the rules."

Tomas breathed easier. "I'm sorry, Sarah. I didn't realize it was that important to you. I will have them for you by the time you awake in the morning."

"Thank you." The eyes met his at last, sorrow lurking alive and ready inside them. "I'm happy here. I'm trying. Please don't send me away."

A wave of sympathy washed over Tomas, and he brushed a comforting hand over a cheek reddened by exposure. Drugged, Sarah gave no reaction, and he tucked her hair behind a scarlet ear.

"I didn't go through all the trouble to bring you here only to send you away. The boys would tear me to pieces. After Dmitri returns and completes his probation, if the two of you wish to leave, that's up to you. Until then, you're here for the duration."

Sarah nodded, too blunted to think of objections. After a pause, she fell forward to rest her head on her uncle's shoulder, hugging him with all the force of a dying butterfly.

Tomas rested his hands more than hugged her in return, just as uncertain about the touch. He glanced over her head to his psychiatrist friend, and raised his eyebrows in wonder. "We'll work things out," he promised. "You'll see."

Rules of Conduct

1) You will conduct yourself in a courteous and respectful manner at all times when in the public areas. Private areas of the house shall consist of personal living quarters or office areas when used for private conversation. Public areas shall consist of all other areas of the house and estate. Public profanity in any language is unacceptable.

2) You will notify me if something is upsetting you and you are unable to resolve the situation on your own. If I cannot be reached in person, a note on my mail, to my answering service, or a handwritten note placed where I will see it will suffice. I shall work hard with you to come to an acceptable solution, no matter how great or trivial the problem.

3) Running and rough-housing are not allowed in public areas, except when appropriate in the gymnasium or outdoors. There is to be no rough-housing, running, or careless play in or around the gym, pool, steam-room, or whirlpool. Voices will be kept to an acceptable indoor level.

4) Threats or violence towards others or toward the estate will not be tolerated. Violence or threats toward you by others will not be tolerated. Please report any instances of violence, actual or threatened, physical or verbal, real or implied, to me immediately.

5) Please report any incidents involving damage to property immediately, so the damage may be repaired.

6) You will treat the service staff with dignity and respect at all times, and you may expect the same from them in return.

7) You are expected to remain presentably groomed at all times when in public areas of the estate. Nudity is permissible only in your room or when appropriate in the gymnasium (private use of pool, steam-room, etc.).

8) You will follow the directions of persons in charge to the best of your ability. You will present any objections in a courteous and respectful manner. You will abide by the final decision.

9) Until the age of 18, you are forbidden from entertaining male guests in the private areas of the estate. You will not share beds with anyone in the household. Lewd, explicit, or licentious behavior in the public areas will result in expulsion of the guest and disciplinary action.

10) You are not allowed free access to household liquor stock. No one under the age of 16 will be served alcohol or other mind-altering substances. As you have 16 years of age, you are entitled to a small amount of alcohol at household social functions if you so choose. Excessive or rapid consumption, "contests," or public intoxication will result in immediate suspension of privileges. Consumption of alcohol or mind-altering substances, or being under the influence thereof, in the pool and gymnasium is strictly forbidden.

Tomas S. F. Ivanov

Ten

Sarah started at the gentle shaking of her arm. She blinked, trying to remember where she was. It had taken forever to fall asleep; was it morning already?

Uncle Tomas crouched next to her. "Whatever are you doing out here?"

Sarah sat up fast and pressed against Vladimir's door, blanket clutched tight in her fingers. She wanted to accept Uncle Tomas's profession of honor from the night before, but it was far too early to buy into it.

Better a cautious cat than a dead kitten.

"Vlad's door was shut and it was too late to wake him. I'm not in his bed."

"No, but you can't sleep in the hallway, either, Sarah. You have your own bed. Come, let's get you back there." He picked up her pillow and waved her in front of him. "Ladies before gentlemen."

"Age before beauty," she countered. He didn't look old, and she certainly didn't consider herself beautiful; that was just how the saying went.

Tomas merely smiled. "As you wish."

He walked four paces into her room. Sarah stopped at two, unwilling to let him stand between her and the door.

Tomas handed her the pillow. "Is there something that woke you? I can stay and talk, if you need."

"No! No. I just wanted to tell Vlad something. I guess it will wait until later." The chronometer on her computer screen glowed 3:36. *What was Uncle Tomas doing up at this hour?*

"Very well. Goodnight then, Sarah. I'll see you in a few hours."

"Goodnight, sir." Sarah asked the computer to lock the door after he left. She tossed the pillow on her bed and dropped wearily on it. She lay there, dozing, until Vlad knocked on her door at 6:30.

Three days into her first full week, and Sarah gained a routine. Vlad woke her the minute he did, and they had a full hour together. After he left, she fled to her room to read or study or send a message to Dmitri. He wasn't allowed outside contact for his first forty-five days, but she'd promised to send him letters, and this time she could use the video on the commlink. Let them pile up on the queue! She would keep her promise.

She also sent a message back to Sigma Tau Ceti, to her neighbor Mrs. Al and her son Charlie, who had been Dmitri's best friend. Sigma Tau was so far away the message would take more than a week to arrive, even by hyperspace transmission. From the receiving point at the research compound, it would take another two days for the message to reach the town of Vandijoc, and then the Aletneshfajas had to walk into town to discover it. Sarah had promised to write them, to ease their fears over her traumatic departure. That letter was, in some ways, more important to her than communicating with Dmitri. Dmitri would return in a few weeks; she'd never see the Al's again.

At 8:40 she met Uncle Tomas in the foyer, and he took her to her appointment at the clinic. John promised to take it easy for the first weeks, testing the waters, before setting up a final program. For the moment, he wanted her to be comfortable at the Ivanov's, and reacquaint herself with Earth culture.

"We've got some youth groups that meet here," he suggested. "Maybe you could sit in on a few of them, meet some other people your age from the area, find out what's popular with the teen crowd right now."

Sarah refused. "I have nothing in common with Earth children whatsoever, and I have never had need for social cliques. If I want to know what is considered 'solar' or what 'echoes' with current culture, I will ask my brothers. They are all experts on youth, teen, and young adult lifestyles."

"Yes, but it's still something to keep in mind," he insisted.

Uncle Tomas kept his promise, and they spent two afternoons wandering through local museums. Sarah gave her tentative approval of the idea, but preferred to start out slowly, staying in Minsk until she gained confidence in the arrangement. She tried very hard to take Tomas at his word that he would not harm her; and Tomas was just as afraid he'd do or say something that would be misinterpreted. Sarah entered her therapy session on Friday to announce proudly that she hadn't had a medication tremor in three whole days.

Tomas was but one step. More than thirty full-time house staff fed off the Ivanov payroll; some lived in rooms above the kitchen wing, some lived elsewhere, two lived in cottages beyond the vehicle hangar. So many strange people coming and going, knowing her business, being in her room, made Sarah feel inescapably surrounded, and she found herself longing for the interminable solitude of the great Pelonishala forest on Sigma Tau.

Sarah's true terror, however, stood 157 centimeters in heels, with stone-gray eyes that Sarah swore shot out invisible laser beams that cut people to ribbons. If she passed Grandmother in the hall, she froze in her tracks, bowing as the woman walked by. If Grandmother spoke to her, Sarah's voice froze in her throat, and she stammered dreadfully. One did not need to be a telepath to know Andrea Ivanov disapproved of her crazy granddaughter.

"I'm telling you, Vlad!" Sarah whispered in their hideout, the hidden service stairs behind the laundry. "She's like the old witch in the fairy stories! If this house sprouts chicken legs, I'm out of here!"

"You're taking it too hard," Vlad said. "She just has to get to know you. Relax. Maybe if you smiled more, she'd know you were happy."

The next time Sarah saw Grandmother, she broke into one of her most pleasant, practiced smiles.

"Why are you smiling like that?" Grandmother asked, lasers bursting from the cold robotic eyes to scan for trouble. "What have you done?"

The smile disappeared faster than light, and Sarah folded herself in until she was only half as wide. "Nothing, Ma'am," she whispered, and fled down the hall to hide under the desk in the library.

* * *

"I'm supposed to come to you when I have a problem, correct?" Sarah reminded Tomas on Thursday. "I have a problem."

"I'll do my best," he promised. "I've fixed everything from broken fingernails to transportation strikes. Does your problem fall somewhere between those extremes?"

"I believe so, sir. I will not attend church with everyone Sunday. I'm sorry, but I can't. I have reviewed the doctrines, and it would be hypocritical of me to pretend to believe most of it. I have been around the galaxy far too long to put my faith in such a specifically Earth-centric religious base. And I refuse to confess my transgressions. I already confess everything to John. I'm sure the celestial Spirits can hear me just as clearly there as they can in a church. If it is a matter of exposure to philosophical discipline, I will spend the equivalent time period studying philosophy and universal religious thought here at home."

Tomas's face lost its eagerness. "Well, that certainly poses a problem, doesn't it. Thank you for bringing it to my attention in a timely manner. It would not have been pretty if you'd mentioned it Sunday morning. Your reasons are indisputable. It puts me in a most difficult position, however.

"Mamá uses the church as a form of social launchpad. She keeps her name in the news just by sitting there for an hour a week, or by not being there if business takes precedence. She insists everyone else attend, since it increases her attention. If I allow you to defect, the boys will be right behind. And if you are not in attendance, it means someone must remain home with you. That is a problem as well."

"I'm sorry, sir, but I will not change my mind. If I can't feel it in my heart, I see no point in pretending. I cannot put up a false front like that."

"I don't expect you to," Tomas assured her. "I like the idea of philosophical discipline, however. There are dozens of religions here in Minsk. Perhaps I can assuage Mamá's objections by visiting a different place of worship each week. We would still be seen in the community, you would still be gaining an exposure to religious doctrines, and the boys wouldn't be off the hook, either. At the very least, it may hold back the flood a little while longer. Is that acceptable?"

"Could Vlad come with us?"

Even if Sarah meant only one, Tomas knew that any one brother would quickly turn into three or four. "Perhaps we could alternate, someone different every week. I don't think it would hurt Nikky or Marina to have their minds opened a little."

"That would be acceptable. Thank you, sir. It will give me something to think about all week, comparing things."

"I'm glad we could work it out," Tomas said pleasantly, but in her heart Sarah couldn't help feeling a little sorry for him, having to break the news to Grandmamá.

* * *

Sarah woke to the cold, clipped words shattering the silence. Grandmother stood in the closer doorway to the main sitting room, dressed for the day. Uncle Tomas stood next to her in a dressing robe, looking as if he'd just woken.

"Tomas, you will address this matter once and for all. This is a home where Statesmen come on holiday, not a kennel. Either train her to sleep in a bed, or I will insist you move her elsewhere. This is the second time this week."

Tomas blinked sleepily. Mamá had found her twice; it was actually the fourth time in as many days. He held up a hand to ward off further attack. "I will take care of it, Mamá."

When she left, he leaned on the concert grand that occupied the northeast corner of the lounge. "Is there something about your room you don't like, Sarah? First the hallway, then the dining room, the chair in the library, now the piano. Is your bed uncomfortable?"

101

"No sir." Sarah pulled her blanket around her shoulders. Sleep-spit shone wetly on the keyboard cover where her head had been resting. "I wasn't tired, so I came down to play the piano. I didn't think I would wake anyone. I'm sorry. I must have fallen asleep at the keys. Am I not allowed to play? Should I have asked first?"

"No, no. Play as much as you like. Mamá would just prefer you not sleep on it. Perhaps, if you are not sleepy tonight, you could find an activity to occupy yourself in your room, so if you fall asleep inadvertently, it won't be in a public place where Mamá will notice."

"Yessir. It won't happen tonight." She knew it wouldn't. The big boys would be home, and she could pile in with them.

"Come, I'll walk you upstairs. Vladimir will be up in twenty minutes, so you might as well get dressed."

True to her word, excited to have Sergei and David home again for the weekend, Sarah spent her second Friday night out of the hallways. Uncle Tomas seemed relieved, and even Grandmother seemed more pleasant at breakfast. The peace lasted until mid-Saturday, when Sarah ran upstairs to change into her new boots. The boys were in the vehicle hangar, and she was now forbidden from wearing her blue dress slippers outside. The household staff had done their best to resurrect the alien fabric, but the shoes had never quite recovered from their long run in the snow. She switched footwear and ran downstairs.

"Oh! There you are, Sarah." Grandmother stopped her in the hall. "I was looking for you. I would like you to meet Renata Yurievna Kapinski." She waved a hand to the woman next to her. The woman's blue-black hair was arranged as if it had been made of plastic and spun molded by machine. Open-toed shoes of clear plastic graced her feet, and the perfectly manicured nail of her big toe sported a shimmering emerald.

"Renata is my personal stylist," Grandmother continued pleasantly. "She comes to the house once a month to keep up on my skin and hair. I made arrangements for her to see you as well. She'll clear up those two blemishes, and we'll get your hair conditioned and cut to a manageable level. She can take care of those fingers for you, too. Having calluses like that may have been acceptable where you were living, but here in Minsk, people will notice."

The strange woman separated a section of Sarah's hair and pulled it forward with five-centimeter fingernails. "It's very dry. You'll need a deep conditioning. These ends are terrible. I'd take it off right at the neck. A good layering wouldn't hurt, either, for hair this fine. We might dye it a few shades darker, too. That color's fine for summer, but you're too pale to handle it in the winter. It bleaches the color from your face. I'll need three hours, but we can work on the skin and nails in between."

The nerve of the woman! As if Sarah were no more than a piece of art undergoing a critique before revision. She gripped her *zhopa*-length rope of tangled tresses. "I like my hair."

"Of course you do," Grandmother said, fluffing Sarah's bangs with her bony fingers. "And when it grows back, it will be thicker and healthier and as radiant as your mother's used to be."

Sarah gazed with increasing disgust at the Kapinski woman's fingernails, marbled green with fine gold lines running across them. Obviously she'd never pried *finashkani* tubers out of the ground with her fingers. Obviously she'd never kneaded sticky bread dough. Obviously she wasn't used to playing sports or wrestling with brothers. What could you possibly *do* with nails like that? Charlie would have laughed. The only thing those nails might have been good for was picking insects off plants. You could pinch them up tight on the ends of those blades and squish them without ever getting the mess on your fingers. The thought of gelatinous yellow bug innards on the ends of those dark green nails sent shivers up Sarah's spine. Those days were *over*.

She gave a half-hearted smile. "No, thank you. I'm happy as I am. Thank you for thinking of me."

Grandmother stopped her from leaving. "I've gone to great lengths to arrange this appointment. Renata is in great demand. You're a beautiful girl underneath that hair; with a little polishing, you'll be the envy of every girl in Minsk."

Oh! Uncle Tomas, where are *you! Help, Vlad!* "This is the way we wore our hair in Vandijoc. I don't want it cut. My hair was short once, and I looked like a boy. You should have asked me first." The fact that she looked like a boy never bothered Sarah; it was Dmitri's unexpected hack-job of a haircut.

"We don't have to go quite that short," Ms. Kapinski allowed. "Maybe just to your shoulders."

"I'm sorry, but I must decline. Good day, Ma'am; Grandmother." Sarah hurried off. She had to find someone to intervene before this blew up into a total mess.

"Sarah Kirushenko!" Grandmother commanded from behind. "Turn back this instant!"

Sarah stopped at the intersection of hallways. She didn't have the nerve to tell Grandmother to mind her own business and leave her alone. On the other hand, who the hell was Grandmother to tell her how short her hair should be? But then, it was Grandmother's house; Sarah was merely a guest. If she were rude to Grandmother, then surely Uncle Tomas would be upset, and then he'd tell John, and she'd go down on the books as argumentative, unstable, and unable to cooperate. Damn *everyone* for leaving her alone like this!

She whirled to face Grandmother, breath tight in her chest. "I will not change the color of my hair!"

Grandmother's words slipped through her clenched teeth like beads of refrigerator coolant. "Come back here. Your behavior is unacceptably rude. Your hair is disgraceful. You cannot be seen in public like that. I have the utmost faith in Renata to restore your hair to something you can take pride in."

Sarah backed away. "It's *my* hair! I don't want it changed! And I don't want ugly bug-killer fingernails, either!"

Uh oh! Grandmamá might kick her out of the house, but insulting a guest, no matter how weird, probably carried a death sentence.

Death by laser.

Shit!

Sarah bolted down the side hall to the flythrough.

Mercifully, the boys were just outside. David had brought his ground bike out from the hangar and was making a final adjustment under the seat. He closed it, put his headgear on, and sat down. The engine started on the fourth try.

Vlad was dressed to accompany him, sporting a heavy jacket and holding his helmet, waiting for David to give the okay. Sarah grabbed him on the run and spun him around.

"Please, Vlad! Please! Help me! Sergei! She's going to kill me! She wants to cut my hair off and dye it dark! I'd rather cut off my head! Please! Get Uncle Tomas! Get somebody! She's crazy!"

"Sarah!" Grandmother appeared under the flythrough, looking as deadly as her dainty self could manage. "You will come back this instant and apologize! Be assured Tomas will hear about this. Vladimir Vasily, don't you coddle her. Come here, my ill-bred child. Get out of my way, Sergei. Now!"

Sergei caught Vlad's eye, and from behind Grandmamá he pointed a finger at Sarah, then at David, waiting on his bike. It took two tries for Vlad to understand. He shoved his helmet over Sarah's head, stuffed her on the bike behind David, and clapped David on the shoulder. Sarah locked her arms around David as the front of the bike came off the ground for a second or two, then took off down the pathway at high speed.

Vlad cringed as Grandmamá found a new victim.

David's voice rang inside the helmet. "I take it that's you back there, Sar. It better be, 'cause if I find out you're Vlad hugging me like that, you're gonna be walking home so short you're gonna have to stand on your toes to see over the tops of your shoes."

The silver safety helmet digging into his back moved up and down.

"Hey, ease up, will ya? You're crushing my ribs. Sit back a little.

"I said ease up! Can you hear me? Is the interface working? I can't hear you at all. It works both ways, Sar. Just talk. The helmet picks you up automatically.

"What the fuck!" David pulled over at the side of the pathway, cutting the engine. Sarah leapt off the back. She caught her foot on the seat and stumbled away to sit on the frozen ground, skirts above her knees. Tomas had bought her several new outfits, but she would only wear them on Sundays or on formal excursions – and clinic didn't count. Nor was she allowed outside without a coat. *Two* broken rules. She tore the helmet from her head and lobbed it to the ground, then covered her face with her hands.

"What the – ?" David removed his helmet. He made sure the parking stabilizers were down and left the bike to squat before her. His manner softened.

He brushed away the tears. "Hey. What's the matter? You scared? You never been on a grounder before?"

The head shook sadly this time, and Sarah coughed on her tears.

"Well, shit, Sar! Why didn't you say something? I would'a slowed down. Don't cry about it. I've been riding one of these for years. It's perfectly safe. Just ease up a little. I have to breathe in order to pilot it. Come on, stand up. I'm not getting in trouble because I let you sit in the snow again.

"First off," he said, taking off the white jacket he wore, "put this on. It's made to take a beating. If you do fall, it will keep you from scraping. I don't have a second pair of gloves; just pull your hands inside the sleeves." He adjusted the jacket and fastened it for her. It was so loose she could have crossed the sleeves and tied them behind her.

Sarah sniffed and coughed again, clearing the tears from her throat. She felt better now that she wasn't speeding over open ground at 140 kilometers an hour. "Won't you get cold?"

"Nah. I got a good sweater on; it'll keep me. Besides, the shield screen blocks almost all the draft. Come'ere." He led her back to the bike.

He checked the readouts on the front display. "It's been giving me trouble starting. I'm going into the city to get a new buffer array. I think that's where the problem is. Here – sit on it for a minute. It's not going anywhere. Put your feet here. Here's your starter code input. Right hand controls the throttle, changes the amount of power output. Left hand controls the power supply ratios – you can click up or down depending on how much torque you want at a given time. Left foot," he put her leg in place, "controls braking speed, and right foot," he pointed, "is emergency reverse thrust. Touch that, and an inertia-dampening field is raised so the bike can drop 100 km per hour in three seconds flat without throwing you over the front. It's really pretty safe."

"I – I was unprepared. I'm sorry. I wasn't thinking. I just had to get away from Grandmother. She wanted to cut off my hair and give me talons for fingernails."

David picked up Vlad's helmet and handed it to her. "You could use some off. To about there." His finger marked a length just below her shoulderblades. "That's where you used to wear it, isn't it?"

Sarah nodded, flipping her hair back and pulling the helmet on. Yes, it needed to be trimmed, but it should be *her* decision, when *she* was ready to make it. And she wasn't yet ready to separate from Sigma Tau.

David showed her the passenger grips, and where to put her feet. He wiggled a connector under an access panel, tried, wiggled, and tried again before the bike finally started. He kept the speed down to what he considered a crawl.

"That better?" he asked through the helmet communicator.

"Yeah," Sarah managed to say this time. It still scared her to the point her chest hurt, but she was getting used to it.

"Hey – what do you say I take you to where I got my hair done? Cut just enough to keep the old lady happy. You'll catch on soon. I've found the best way to deal with Baba is to beat her to the punch."

Sarah giggled at the unrepentant use of the less-than-respectful word for their grandmother. She could imagine the furor if Baba heard him use it. "Okay."

David dropped the bike at a shop for a diagnostic, and they played tag for several blocks to where he promised she could have her hair cut as she wanted. Lightly conditioned and thirty centimeters shorter, her smooth hair danced just half-way down her back, making her head feel a kilo lighter.

"What's your favorite color, Sar?"

"Blue," she replied, until she realized David was whispering to the stylist and winking. After a considerable amount of begging on David's part, and a written promise from the stylist it would wash out on the first try, Sarah's reasonably long hair now sported bright blue dye on the last ten centimeters.

"Let's try something." He patted the seat of the bike. The repair had been minor, a corroded component in the starter relay. "Sit up front and I'll teach you to ride."

"Oh goodness, no! I can't navigate this! I'll break something."

"You can't break it," he insisted, pulling her on the bike in front of him. "Trust me. I even let Vlad pilot it now and then. I'm right here to help."

Trust me. Dmitri's favorite words, right before something went wrong. "I can't do this, David." Sarah's face twitched as the medication eased her fear, but the tightening of her chest made her cough. "I've never done anything like this before."

"Neither did I, until I did it." He leaned against her back, strong arms shadowing her on the controls. "Press the starter. Ease off the brake while you increase the power … " The craft lurched forward with a jolt. Sarah released the power control, stopping it.

"I did it! It moved!"

"Do it again."

Thirty minutes later, Sarah kept the bike in a straight line at the edge of the busy street path, unnerved by the hovercraft flying by.

"A little faster," David encouraged. "Keep the speed nice and steady."

She increased the speed slowly, sixty, seventy, eighty kilometers per hour. The blue ends of her hair banged against David's helmet. "I can't believe I'm doing this. Dimi will never believe me."

"So don't tell him," David replied acidly. "Keep boosting the speed. We want to get back before tomorrow."

Sarah flinched as a hovercraft hummed past, a meter from her elbow. "David, maybe you should take over. I could give it another try closer to home, where there isn't so much traffic. It's making me nervous."

"All right. Pull over at that intersection ahead. We'll switch … "

The helmet microphone picked up Sarah's scream with amazing clarity, deafening David inside the plastic shell. From behind a kiosk on the pedestrian walk, an untethered dog darted onto the edge of the roadway and stared at the oncoming speeder bike. Sarah panicked, twisting both the accelerator and the torque converter at the same time, sending the bike into high speed at the exact moment her foot slammed the brake. She cut the navigation bar sharply away from traffic before David could tell her what to do. The bike bumped over the curb, slammed into the kiosk, flipped on its side, spun, and smashed into a replicator-repair and sales shop. The dog took off at a run.

People rushed down the walk and out of the building. Hands reached out to Sarah. Forgetting about the emergency stop features, she'd been thrown clear on the first impact. She sat up and flung the helmet from her head, looking for her brother.

David was extricating himself, one leg caught under the horizontal bike. He wrenched it free with a curse, threw his helmet down, and got shakily to his feet, fighting off the helpers around him. He knelt beside her. "You okay?"

"I think so!" Sarah answered before bursting into tears.

"Hey, don't sweat it," he said as she cried on his chest. "As long as you're okay."

"I'm sorry! I'm so sorry, David! I killed your bike! I should never have touched it!"

David looked over at his Aeronavt Terrania 316-K Groundspeeder with a broken heart, a gift from Uncle Tomas for graduating Northern Academy in the top three of his class. He'd wanted that bike more than anything in his life. Seeing it lying on the walkway, wheel bent, bars twisted, was like the death of a close friend.

He clapped his fingers against her arm. "Bah. It's still in one piece."

A man spoke to them. "Hang in there. There's a medical team on their way. They should be here any second."

"Medical? We don't need that, we're fine."

"You're bleeding," the man insisted. "You should get that looked at. Germs'll kill you."

David glanced down. Road burn oozed heavy down his arm and leg, his clothes shredded and the skin scraped raw. Still, hardly worth a trip to a trauma clinic.

Sarah covered her mouth with her hand as if staving off another scream. "Moons above, David! I hurt you!"

David hadn't forgotten Sarah's terror of blood. "Don't you look at it! It's just a scratch, and I'll take care of it as soon as we get home. It's nothing! You hear me?"

He tried, he begged, but the medical team still loaded David into the transport and took him to the trauma center, Sarah clinging to his uninjured arm. She held onto him silently for the three-minute flight to the Trauma center. She held onto him silently for the ten minutes it took to see a doctor. She held onto him silently when he took his sweater and shirt off so the arm could be examined, but David caught her staring at the angry-looking patches on his side.

"You gotta get her out of here," David ordered the triage nurse. "She can't handle blood."

The nurse tried to escort her out, but Sarah froze, paralyzed by her fear of hospitals and doctors and medical equipment. Dimi would have understood, let her stay, talked her through it, but he wasn't there, and he wasn't going to be coming there, either. If David wouldn't support her, who would? She was all alone in a hospital. No one could save her.

She was already on brain medication. She was already certified as a breeder of bats for belfries. Maybe she wasn't supposed to be away from the estate. Maybe she wasn't supposed to be away from Uncle Tomas. Maybe she wasn't supposed to operate vehicles. What if she'd broken laws? They could arrest her for operating the grounder without a permit, and that would violate her terms for release, and that would violate Tomas's custody appeal, and they'd take her away and lock her up and she'd be screwed, screwed, screwed ....

Think! What would Dimi have me do?

Sit and wait for him, said her head.

"No," was the only word she spoke. She pulled away from the cheerful nurse and sat on the floor just outside the door, unwilling to move a centimeter, guarding the room until the moment David appeared again.

Would she like a chair? Was she hurt? Would she come with them to be looked at? She'd had quite a spill. Did she know where she was? Could she tell them her name, at least? Where she lived? Was there someone to contact? She was coughing rather hard; could they scan her ribs?

A few questions were answered with a nod, but mostly the blonde-and-blue head shook denial. Sarah waited, hypervigilant, for the falsely smiling psychiatrists, loaded hypos ready in their jacket pocket.

A familiar person raced down the trauma corridor just as David emerged from the treatment room. Sarah scrambled to her feet with relief. *Saved!* Or …

What if he was mad? What if she really had messed up something legal? What would …

Tomas hugged her breathlessly. "Sarah! Are you all right? What happened?!"

He brushed the hair from her face, shock replacing the worry when the bright blue tips waved like feathers under his fingers. "What happened to your *hair*? Sarah, your hair is blue! And half of it's missing!"

Uh oh. Sarah shrank small inside her clothes. She'd forgotten about that. Maybe she wasn't allowed to cut her hair. Maybe she …

"I kind of had them do that – It's not permanent," David explained for the moment. "I'm sorry, sir. They had no reason to call you. It was nothing! The bike flipped and I scraped my arm, and some idiot freaked out and called for a trauma transport. I could have treated it myself just as easily at home."

"It most certainly is something when I get a call looking for the guardian of a Sarah Kirushenko, because she was involved in a traffic accident and she's at a trauma center and they think she's in shock because she's unable to speak!" Tomas snapped. "I tell them they must have the wrong person, because my niece is at home. Imagine my shock when Mamá tells me she isn't! Do you have any idea what kind of trouble you may have caused? If that gets back to her court manager, I don't stand a chance!"

"I'm sorry, sir. I didn't think of that. Vlad put her on the bike just before I took off."

Sarah broke her silence. "It's my fault! An animal ran out in front of us and I swerved to avoid it and the bike fell over and I ruined it."

Tomas's surprise deepened. "What do you mean? David? You let her pilot your bike?"

"Well, not really," David hedged. "I let her sit in front, but I had my hands on the controls the whole time."

A physician approached, computer pad in hand.

"Are you the guardian? Perhaps you can get her to agree to be examined. She had a safety helmet on, but it's very possible she could be suffering a head injury."

Sarah met her uncle's inquiring stare. "I'm fine! I'm not hurt at all. Please, sir, I just want to go home."

Tomas weighed his responsibilities. "Well, she's quite shy to start with, and she gets even quieter when she's had a fright, so the fact she wouldn't speak to you doesn't surprise me. Take the jacket off; let's have a look."

Sure enough, the strong, slippery fibers of the bike jacket had done their work. The fabric was dirty and scuffed, but not a mark could be found save a minor scrape on her knee.

"She seems okay," Tomas said, "but I'll have my personal physician see her later this evening, just to be safe. Thank you for trying." With the signing of release forms, they were done.

"Thank you, Uncle Tomas!" Sarah whispered as they left. She wrapped her arms around him in an embrace from the heart, squeezing him from behind until she felt sure he got the message. He was on her side! He could have insisted on exams and tests and consults, called in psychiatry, but he didn't. He could have spoken to hospital security and filed a complaint that she'd left – run away – and broken her parole, ask that she be locked up. But he didn't. He understood her dying need to get out of

there, to avoid that exact kind of attention. He believed her! He agreed with her! He cared.

"Thank you for taking me home."

Tomas stopped walking. He tried to return the gesture, but she held him tight. "You took a year off my life, scaring me like that. You're lucky I have a soft spot for damsels in distress."

Tomas stopped the 'craft in the fly-through and got out. "I'd like to see you both in my office. Right now."

Sarah felt her heart clutch onto her ribs for support. She could hardly find the strength to move.

Her other brothers rushed up. Vlad hugged her. "What happened? Are you okay? You hurt?"

David stalked by, shredded sleeve flapping, the Nuskin bandage shining underneath. "Fine as fairydust. One big freakin' misunderstanding by some nosy do-gooder."

"I'm perfectly fine," Sarah apologized.

Sergei fingered her hair. "Son. Of. A. *Bitch!* What did he do to you?"

"We're not going to talk about that right now," Uncle Tomas ordered in his quiet manner, and pulled Sarah away by the elbow.

Vlad's eyes held sympathy. "She's gonna kill you."

Grandmamá met them as they passed the dining room. "Tomas, you're back. Thank goodness you found her before the media caught wind of it. Tomas, you and I need to clarify some issues with Sarah regarding … Tomas! *Tomas!* Her hair is *blue!*" Andrea sputtered.

"I am aware of that, Mamá. I shall speak with you in a short while."

A terrible, evil thought rose up in Sarah's mind, one of the awful, rude, amusing thoughts that always got her in trouble with Dmitri. She could never say anything like that to Grandmamá. Dimi would kill her. But socially conscious Dmitri wasn't here. She was with David, her bold and fearless commander of the Fearsome Four Survival Squad, and David didn't take *gavno* from anyone. He wouldn't expect her to, either.

As Tomas pulled her along, she reminded Grandmother, "My skin is too pale. David said it put color in my cheeks!"

Silence pressed on the room. Uncle Tomas leaned back in his desk chair, legs crossed, chin cradled between his thumb and forefinger. He didn't speak, he just watched. And waited.

David slouched in a chair before the desk. Sarah sat next to him, shoulders pulled in so tight they seemed to have disappeared.

It seemed forever before Tomas spoke. "David, I am supposed to accept the fact that you, as an adult, are responsible enough to know right from wrong, correct?"

David sat up and tried to look less guilty of irresponsibility. "Yes, sir."

"And am I correct in understanding that you are aware that I am in charge of Sarah's care and well-being, and if I cannot fulfill that responsibility to the satisfaction of the courts, I will lose that privilege and Sarah will be removed from this house and placed in a surrogate setting?"

"Yes, sir. Though I'd never let it happen."

"Irrelevant. I ... " Tomas bit his lip. It was a fine line to call, a delicate decision. "I'm not angry that you took Sarah into town, or even that you took her on the grounder. I believe you are responsible enough to pilot carefully with your sister's life at stake. However, I must insist that from here on, under any and all circumstances, planned or emergency, *I must be informed* when Sarah has left the grounds. Sarah, that rule is also applied to you: whether you are walking to the tramstop to meet Vlad, or you've packed your bags and are running away: *you must notify me*. If you so much as drop a candy over the stone wall, you *must notify me* before you attempt to retrieve it. Slip a note under my door. Leave a priority message on the comm. Ask the house manager to page me immediately. If such a situation arises again, I will be forced to take strong action, such as requesting electronic monitoring, which I'm sure neither of us wants. It is for your own safety, Sarah. I cannot stress that enough."

Sarah's hands wrung in her lap. "I'm sorry, sir. I didn't plan it. I wasn't running away."

"It is a simple courtesy. And David – if you insist on teaching Sarah to pilot your vehicles, it is to be done on the grounds of the estate, nowhere else. If you take her off grounds, it will be only in an enclosed passenger vehicle. Is that understood? Now, about this second matter ... " Tomas crossed his arms and sighed, a hint of amusement in his eye. "Who's idea was it to advertise a blue mood?"

"David's," Sarah said.

"Grandmamá's," David replied at the same instant.

David repeated Sarah's story. "Grandmother was chasing her through the house, trying to dye her hair. I simply took her elsewhere to have it done, in a color Sarah wouldn't mind."

"I see." Tomas accepted the answer, though perhaps *chasing* wasn't the right word. The world bowed to Mamá; Mamá did not chase after anybody. "You're dismissed, David. Please remember my rules. Sit, Sarah. I still want to speak with you."

David left, pausing to tug the peacock tips affectionately. Sarah closed

112

her eyes and cringed smaller as Tomas came around the desk to sit in the empty chair.

"Head up, Sarah. I don't relate well to shoulders."

"I'm sorry, sir," she said, and forced them downward. She reached into a pocket, retrieved a crumpled slip, and held it out to him. "I made them put it in writing the color will wash out on the first try."

Tomas chuckled. "That's fine. I'm more concerned about your difficulties with Mamá."

"Sir?"

"I don't need an investigation committee to know you are very different people. I don't want to put any more pressure on you right now than you can handle, and I know Mamá can create a lot of pressure."

"Sir! I – I – That's not true! I just …"

Tomas touched her arm. "Relax. It's no secret that Mamá can be demanding. I know. In fact, I've known it all my life." Sarah gave the faintest of nervous smiles as she pulled her arm away.

"I do not expect you to live up to Mamá's standards right away. For now, I expect you to be neat and presentable at all times. I expect you to be courteous and polite to everyone. You may change the color of your hair if you choose, but the color must be one that occurs naturally in humans – no sunset pinks, no glowing lavender. No blues. Your brothers know this, but now I'm informing you."

Sarah could live with that. "Yes, sir. It's not a problem, sir."

"I think the best thing for you to do is write your grandmother a letter of apology. It will not only look good on your part, but will show her that you have a sense of civility. You can leave it on her computer, if you choose."

"Yes, sir."

He brushed the blue hair off her shoulder. "That's all I wanted to say. I shall speak with Mamá and get her to back off. I must say, though, I do like this length on you. It is much more flattering."

"Thank you, sir," Sarah replied, and headed for the door. She stopped as he spoke again.

"Sarah, if I may say so without insulting you, I think the cold air has left the ends of your hair a bit dry. Perhaps you shouldn't wash it right away. It might not be good for it. It might need an extra day to recover." He gave a fast wink, as if afraid of being caught.

"Is – is that a direct order, sir?"

Tomas chuckled again. "Yes, I guess you could call it that, if you must."

Sarah returned his smile. "Yes, *sir!* Thank you, sir. I won't forget."

Eleven

Three days, and Sarah's hair once again regained its white-blonde lustre, the blue no more than an amusing story she relayed to Dmitri. The shorter length was easier to care for, and the ends didn't tangle in painful knots or catch in doors or chairs or under her *zhopa* when she sat. Sarah was pleased, Uncle Tomas was pleased, and even Grandmother gave an approval of sorts.

"It's an improvement," Andrea decreed. "Renata would have done better, but at least it's presentable. I hope they gave you instruction on how to comb it."

Vladimir had just arrived home from school when Uncle Tomas called Sarah downstairs. She left Vlad to change his clothes by himself and rushed down to find Katya visiting.

Sarah hugged her. "Where's Roman? Did you bring him?" She gave a hard, dry cough.

"No, I haven't picked him up yet. I stopped by on my way home. You're not getting sick, are you?"

Sarah rubbed hard at her nose. "I haven't adjusted to the planetary allergens yet. It's not bothering me that much. I already take more medications than I want. I'd rather just wait it out."

"I asked Katya to stop by," Tomas said from the sofa. "I know you get along well. I have some news for you, Sarah, and I wanted to see what you thought of it. I had some business come up today that I must deal with in person. I've tried every way I know to get around it, but I can't. I'm afraid I'm going to have to leave … "

"Leave?" A million reasons to panic jammed Sarah's head at once. "You're in charge of me! If you leave, that leaves … *Grandmother* in charge!"

"No, no. Your Grandmother couldn't do that," Tomas promised. "If you wouldn't mind, I thought perhaps you could stay …"

"What?!" Me? You're sending *me* away? Vlad's here! I don't want to leave!" Sarah's heart sank clear down to her feet. A tremor began, but she hardly noticed.

"No! That's not what he means," Katya squeezed in.

Hyperventilating brought on another cough. Sarah stood up. "That's not fair! You didn't give me any warning. *Please!* I *can't* leave! I'll do better! *Please*, Uncle Tomas!"

"I have no complaints with your behavior. I merely thought … "

114

"You can't do this to me!" Her foot stomped the carpeting, and before Katya could stop her, she fled the room.

* * *

"Dammit!" Tomas sprinted to the intercom control in the hallway. "Computer, security control, lock all exterior doors, authorization TSF Ivanov. We're not losing her in the snow again," he told Katya. "Come. We'll do it the hard way."

He activated the interface in the library. "She doesn't make things easy, does she."

"She just takes everything to heart," Katya said. "She's been so happy, she's afraid something will threaten that happiness."

"Computer, security. Building scan, display all inhabitants." A diagram of the house appeared, filled with blinking dots. Delete library," he said, beginning the tedious process of elimination. The intercom chimed next to him.

"What's going on?" Vladimir's voice demanded. Someone howled in the background. "Why are you sending Sarah away? I don't care, I won't let anyone take her! I'll call John! I'll call Val! I'll call Dmitri if I have to!"

Tomas felt a surge of indigestion begin. "It's a misunderstanding, Vlad. It can be cleared up if she'll just stand still long enough to let me finish a sentence. Stay where you are."

* * *

Sarah stood entrenched in the farthest corner of Vlad's room, his ice hockey stick held like a Tau Ceti axe, raised and ready to strike. They whispered back and forth as he dabbed the tears from her face.

"I'm not going!" Sarah yelled when Tomas and Katya entered the room.

Vlad shielded her. "What's going on? You're not taking her!"

Katerina walked fearlessly around Vladimir and pulled on the weapon. "For shame! How dare you threaten Uncle Tomas, when he's trying to be nice. I'm highly insulted as well! If you're that opposed to spending a night or two at my house, all you had to do was tell me, not jump into orbit screaming and crying."

Sarah released the hockey stick. "What?"

"You heard me, you thick-minded bookhead! I don't get to see as much of you as everyone else, so when I heard Tomas's problem, I asked if you could stay with me. We can make a party of it – a girl's night out. We'll eat nothing but chocolate and ice cream, and we'll stay up late talking, just like the old days. But if you're that dead set against it, you can stay here with Grandmother and practice listening without interrupting."

Sarah gave a deep hacking cough, still switching gears. Vlad wiped her face with the end of his sleeve. "At your house? With you? And then come back here?"

"I have to go to Mars for two days, Sarah, and I can't take you with me without a lot of red tape," Tomas said. "You'll have your regular appointments, but Katerina has volunteered to keep an eye on you in my absence. I only wanted to know if that arrangement was acceptable. I know you're not comfortable with Valeria."

"I don't like it," Vladimir objected. "She needs to be here at night. She doesn't sleep well unless she knows I'm here."

"Then why don't you join us for dinner?" Katya offered. "You can help her get settled, and then you can call her on the 'link before bed and say goodnight. Tomas will bring her to her appointment in the morning, John will keep her a little longer than usual at the clinic for me, and I will pick her up there in the afternoon."

Sarah blushed. "I'm sorry. I guess I overreacted. I just got scared."

"If you want to know the answers to your questions, you have to let a person finish answering," Tomas said. "I promised you you're here to stay, and I don't back out on promises. Now, do you feel you can be comfortable with Katya for two days, or should I try and make another arrangement?"

"Just two? Yeah. I can do that."

* * *

"Wake up. Come on. What are you two doing out here?"

Sarah's eyes flew open to a familiar if unwelcome sight. Uncle Tomas was in his night clothes, poking them. Vlad squirmed awake, entwined half next to her, half under her on the upstairs' lounge sofa.

Sarah unwrapped herself from Vlad's arms. "I'm not in his bed,"

"She had a bad dream," Vlad mumbled. "We came out here."

"That's well and good, but it's over now. Everyone back to their own bed." Tomas pulled Sarah up, then Vlad.

"I followed your rules," Sarah said. "I didn't do anything wrong."

"I understand that." Tomas escorted her to her room. "Thank you for obeying them, but good night now, Sarah." He shut the door and waited a full ten minutes, but it didn't open again.

116

Sarah could hardly sit still, unsure if she was more nervous about staying at Katya's or more excited. It would be hard to leave Vlad, even for a night or two, but she missed Katya almost as much. Valeria and Galina had left for university before Sarah turned four. Outside of the year they'd spent together after Mother died, she hadn't grown up with them at all. Marina wasn't yet a year old when they separated, and Sarah and Elizabyeta had been sworn enemies to the end.

Katya, on the other hand, was only eight years older. They'd almost always shared a bedroom, and much of the time shared a bed. Katya had been her mother in absentia. Katya bandaged wounds. Katya managed illnesses. Katya shared deepest secrets with her, late into the night. With the big girls gone, and her little sister studying practically the same classes, Katya had found a friend in Sarah, taming the diehard tomboy with a touch of femininity. Sarah was never a girly-girl, but she missed the sisterly closeness.

She wasn't sure about the Other Half, though. Sarah loved Kat, and she supposed in a way she loved John Carver – as a close friend – but Sarah wasn't sure if she loved them *together*. She was getting accustomed to seeing John in a social setting for dinner on Sunday afternoons, but most of the time she had to see him in a professional environment, a court-ordered Space Case for him to piece back together and keep from frightening innocent citizens. If she hadn't trusted him from before, Sarah didn't think it would have worked at all.

John and Katya lived in a small but comfortable home in inner Minsk, with just enough land to allow the parking of two small flyers, and a patch of yard behind it the size of Uncle Tomas's front porch. It was pretty and modern and unpretentious, devoid of breakables in the wake of Roman, and vastly different than the overpowering *status* of the estate. Sarah felt at ease almost immediately.

Sarah and Vlad hung around Katya's kitchen, sword-playing with carrots, keeping Roman out of the way, snitching almost as many bits of dinner as they assembled. John came home to find his brother-in-law balancing an olive on his nose, while his wife and sister-in-law tried to copy the maneuver.

"I can't even escape the crazy stuff when I come home," John complained. The siblings dissolved in laughter while Roman chased olives across the floor.

John listened to Sarah cough. "You sure you're okay?"

"More than fine! It's just allergies."

"Just the same, maybe I should run a scan on you."

"And I said *no*," Sarah replied in a tone that dared him to push the issue. "I didn't agree to stay here so I could be bullied around the clock."

"I'll turn up the humidity on the air system," Katya offered. "That should help."

Too soon, though, Katya chased Vladimir home and Sarah withdrew into herself. She shadowed Kat as she put the baby to bed, speaking only if spoken to.

Katerina dragged her to the guest room and shut the door. "Now it's girl time." She grabbed the control for the videoscreen on the wall and searched the menus for a suitable program. "What do you like to watch? Romance, comedy, adventure, or documentary stuff?"

Sarah shrugged. "I don't know. I only watch it when the boys pick something. Maybe a biography?"

"Here's one on Mozart. Good? Come over here and we can talk, just you and me," Katya said, dropping belly-down on the guest bed. She pulled Sarah down by the hand. "Just like old times. Are you ready to kill Grandmother yet?"

Sarah froze, eyes wide, but Kat laughed. "It's okay. I'm not going to tell her. I got off easy; I left for university after six months. I hated her at first, too. You feel like she doesn't see you, like you're just one of the multitudes that exist to serve her in her world."

Sarah nodded, relieved. "Like you're some great failure, and no matter what you do, it won't be right."

"It will get better. Eventually she'll figure out you've got enough of the Ivanov blood in you to make you worthy."

"I'm not so sure I want to be associated with it," Sarah said. "I mean, if it were just Uncle Tomas, maybe. He really *talks* to me – like when he took me to the art museum last week, and we had a real conversation. He knew enough about one artist, and I knew enough about that artist, and he actually debated several points with me, like a colleague or something. That was really nice. I mention art to Grandmamá, and all she mentions is the monetary value, not the style or anything. So far, I like Uncle Tomas a lot better."

"So do I," Kat said.

Four hours, three cups of tea, half a chocolate cake and a pot of ice cream later, with her nail stubs conditioned and painted, her skin exfoliated, and her hair combed and conditioned to a healthy sheen, Sarah readied for bed.

118

"If you'd feel better, I'll stay here with you," Katya offered. "I think that was my biggest adjustment, having a room and a bed to myself. I got really lonely at times. I think I missed you most at night."

"John won't get upset?" The single bed in Kat's pretty bedroom gave Sarah chills. What if John wanted Kat to …

No! John was a nice *person. He wouldn't make Kat go through that. He wouldn't!*

"Not at all. I already told him I would, if you wanted. He's happy to have the bed to himself." Kat slid into the bed and ordered the room to kill the lights.

Sarah snuggled close. Despite the filtered, humidified air in the house, the cough worsened when she lay down, but she disguised it as clearing her throat. She gave a contented sigh, and felt a magnitude of tension melt away. If she closed her eyes, they might still have been on Navara.

"I missed you," Sarah whispered in the darkness. "Dimi was good to me, but it wasn't the same. Boys don't understand the same things."

"I'm here now. What didn't he understand?"

"I don't know. Girl things. You know. Wishes and stuff."

"Boys?"

"No! I mean, I wouldn't have tried, anyway. The last thing I needed was him picking on me for nothing. But if I laughed at him when he was all stupid over a girl, you'd think I'd punched him."

Kat laughed. "That's a brother for you. Vlad said Dimi was married for a while?"

Sarah hesitated, but had to answer. "Yeah. She was really nice."

"What happened? Why didn't it work out?"

Despite the warmth of the room, Sarah shivered. Jaycelani Kirushenko would haunt her to the end of her days, a sad reminder of the evil that could lurk in the heart of a desperately lonely sister with nowhere left to turn. "I don't think I should be talking about it. That's Dimi's business."

"That's fair. What should we talk about, then?"

Sarah thought a minute. There were at least a dozen major topics she wanted to discuss with Kat, things she would never dream of discussing with any other soul. Katya wouldn't laugh, tell her she was weird, turn and share her secrets with everyone she met. It was easier to be embarrassed in the dark, where no one could see her face.

"Kat?"

"Mmm?"

"Can I ask you something really personal?"

"Of course!" Katya squeezed her hand.

"Keep the secret or die? Not even John?"

Katya chuckled. She leaned forward until their foreheads touched. "May I live to ripe old age."

Sarah tried several times, but the words wouldn't come out. She'd never, ever, talked about those kinds of things, not to anyone. Even the *thought* of the subject made her want to vomit. She couldn't talk to Dmitri about it; Dmitri was a boy and had no qualms whatsoever. He *liked* to talk about those things, but with other men, not a kid sister. Katya was the keeper of Sarah's deepest, darkest secret, the only soul she'd ever told. If she could share her fears with anyone, it would be with Katya. She took the chance.

"Kat, do you and John – *you* know. Do you … Do you do the … You know … that … *married* thing married people do? You know –after the kissing and stuff?"

"Married thing? You mean, make love?"

"Mm."

"Of course we do! You don't think Roman appeared out of thin air, do you? Why?"

"Nothing, I guess." Sarah chickened out. Even in the darkness, the subject was harder than she thought. Roman could have been conceived very harmlessly in a lab.

"Does it bother you? John and I being married, I mean? Is it hard, seeing him as a doctor at the clinic, and then seeing him here as my husband?"

"Maybe. Kat, were you … scared? To … do *It?* You know. I mean, after everything that happened at home. Do you really … *want* to do it?"

Kat giggled. "I *love* to do it! Sure I was scared, at first. I told John up front I wasn't about to rush into things with him. There's an age gap between us – twelve and a half years. And I wanted to make sure I was seeing him for the right reasons – not because of you or anything. We had a friendship over hyperspace for almost a year before I even allowed him to visit me. I told him all my worries – not because he was a psychiatrist, but because I wanted him to know those things about me, why I was uncomfortable with the idea. He didn't analyze me or give me advice or anything, he just accepted my reasons. We were engaged for ten months before I decided to take it further, because I didn't want to find out on my wedding night that I made a wrong decision. So, one night I surprised him. And oh! Was he surprised!" Kat laughed. "He was patient, and caring, and willing to let me take the lead. I found out my fears were for nothing, and it's been wonderful ever since. Do you worry about things like that? Because of what you went through?"

"Sometimes." Sarah backed off as her spine crawled. As always happened when the subject of her past came up, anxiety swelled, making it harder and harder to breathe. Next she would feel light-headed and start to shake, and depending on the situation, she might cry uncontrollably, get violent, or run away, maybe even all three. This time she couldn't. The burst of medication from the tiny pump flushed warm in her veins. The tremor washed over her as the panic eased.

Katya hugged her, unaware. "Trust yourself. If you're with the right person and you love them in your heart, you'll know it, and you won't be afraid. It will *feel* right. Love is very special when it's done right. Don't rush it. You have plenty of time, at your age. If he's not willing to wait until you're ready, then he's not worth your trouble in the first place. Remember that."

If Kat could overcome it, maybe there was hope for her, after all. "I'll try," Sarah said, and changed the subject.

* * *

Katerina stretched lazily as the dream slipped away, a silly nonsensical thing about Roman and catching a fish on a beach where there were blue glass mushrooms with white spots, and the presence of the mushrooms meant... The last of the dream evaporated with the last of her sleep. She opened her eyes and blinked at the morning light. She was in the guest room. Sarah... Sarah wasn't in the bed, or even in the room. Kat rolled the other way and looked at the time glowing on the wall. She blinked, unable to comprehend the four simple numbers.

Ten-twelve.

No!

One-zero-one-two. One three. She leapt out of the bed at a full run. *Where was Sarah?* Where was her *son!* A fast glance in the nursery showed Roman was not in his crib. Katerina flew down the stairs.

"Sarah?" She hadn't slept that late since ... since before Roman was born.

Katya stopped in the sitting room. Sarah lay on the floor, Roman bouncing on her belly, laughing. They were both dressed. And unharmed. And happy.

"Dobriy ootra, Katya!" Sarah greeted her cheerily. "I didn't know what you wanted for breakfast, or I would have made it for you. We were up kind of late, so I let you sleep."

"Thank you, Sarah," Kat said with relief. "You shouldn't have let me sleep so long, though." Roman toddled over; she picked him up and gave

121

him a kiss. "I didn't have you visit just so I could have a nanny."

Sarah got up from the floor with a series of painful coughs. "I didn't mind. I did it for years, too, remember? We had breakfast with John before he left, and then we played with the toys. I had to change him an hour ago," she wrinkled her nose, "but I found everything I needed. I got him dressed for you. Are those clothes okay?"

Katya smiled warmly and kissed her sister's cheek, kicking herself for ever being worried about either one of them. Everyone always blew Sarah's moods out of proportion. "Absolutely! Thank you."

Twelve

Tomas returned on schedule, easing Sarah's fears he wouldn't return at all. He was pleased to hear of her success, and praised Sarah for her responsible behavior. If, for some reason, he had to leave again, Sarah had a second haven. John was pleased to see her acting like a normal intelligent teen, without the anxiety and obsessions that plagued her, and told Sarah how good that would look in his report. Katya didn't see what the big deal was; Sarah had always been responsible like that. Vladimir hung on Sarah every waking minute; he hadn't slept, worrying about her. Sarah was happy that everyone else was happy.

She didn't want to admit she felt dreadfully tired, and the familiar burning pain in her chest whenever she breathed worried her. She knew damned well she didn't have allergies, but she'd caused so much trouble for Uncle Tomas in the last two weeks, and he'd been so happy that her visit had been trouble-free, that she hated to bother him with the fact she might be ill. It wasn't bad yet. Not that bad. Her immune system could still kick in and fight whatever virus had worked its way into her lungs. Sarah couldn't breathe at all if she lay down, and the headache tablets she asked Vlad to bring her did nothing for the fever burning her cheeks.

She slept a few hours leaning against Vladimir's door on Sunday, but Uncle Tomas chased her back to her room. On Monday night, she wanted to sleep in one of the lounging chairs in the library, but Tomas caught her sneaking down the back stairs by the kitchen. Coughing relentlessly, she managed to doze leaning against her bed. Tuesday morning, the virus won.

"Uncle Tomas! Uncle Tomas!" Nikky ran full speed into the breakfast room where the adults were eating. He yanked Tomas's sleeve. "Hurry! Sarah! She's choking! She's turning all funny colors and stuff!"

Tomas followed Nikky as fast as the boy could go, the twins and Mamá right behind.

Sarah slumped at the bottom of the stairs, Vladimir holding her up. Her back heaved with the effort of trying to draw breath. Her fingers clawed the floor, their tips a dusky grayish-purple.

"She can't breathe!" Vlad cried. "She started coughing and now she's blocked!"

Tomas wrapped his arms around the girl, feeling for the spot high on her belly where he could force the obstruction loose with his fist. "What's she choking on?"

"Nothing!"

"Sarah, stop. I'm trying to help you," Tomas urged as she stabbed him with her elbows.

Andrea watched in horror. "She's purple, Tomas!"

"No, she's frothing!" Valeria realized, seeing the foamy spit gathered around her sister's dark lips. Memories rushed back. "Her lungs! She needs to be drained!"

Val grabbed the weakening girl from Tomas and sat on the bottom step. She draped Sarah face down over her knees, pounding hard on the girl's back, from her waist to her neck.

"She's choking on fluid," Val explained. "Pneumonia! Feel her; she's hot as the sun. Vlad, why didn't you tell anyone she didn't feel well? Run! Get a towel or something."

Vlad shoved Nikky. "You heard her! Go!"

Nik didn't want to leave, either. He'd never seen anyone turn purple. "What kind of towel?"

"A hand towel, a disposable towel, a cleaning rag – it doesn't matter," Val said as a thick trail of infected spit wound from Sarah's mouth. "Hurry!"

Nikky ran.

Marina clung to Galina. "Is she going to die?"

"No, sweetheart, she's just sick," Galina explained. "There's infection in her lungs. Val's helping her make room for air."

Valeria banged softer as Sarah gave a drowning gurgle and vomited several mouthfuls of foaming spit into her cupped hands. Air wheezed in, and she coughed violently. Nikky ran back with a stack of cloth napkins; Vlad grabbed one and wiped Sarah's mouth for her. Tomas grabbed several others and cleaned her hands.

"I'll call Doctor Masarsky," Andrea offered, and pulled Marina with her.

Sarah coughed bubbles. "John!" she gasped. "Inhalers."

"John's a psychiatrist," Val said. "He's not licensed to treat pneumonia. You need a practitioner. Doctor Masarsky's very nice. He'll come right here to the house."

"Just need – inhalers." Sarah's color brightened, but she sounded as if she were breathing under water. She slid off Valeria into Vladimir's arms, exhausted, a napkin clenched to her mouth as she continued to cough in desperate bursts.

"Come, let's get you to bed." Tomas managed to lift her. Sarah hung a limp hand around his neck, too weak to argue. The heat of her fever burned through her clothes.

Valeria handed Vlad the pile of napkins. "Let me grab some things, and I'll be right up."

Sarah shivered with chills despite the blankets, raspy and uncomfortably weak. Vlad remembered the old standbys, stuffing two of his sister's precious thick textbooks under the foot of her bed, the incline helping the infected fluids drain from her lungs. With Sarah's permission, he instructed Uncle Tomas on her pneumonia routine.

"When you bang her back, keep your hands curved a little, and you can't bang too hard, because when her lungs are full, you could knock a lung loose from her ribs and collapse it." Vlad demonstrated the technique that shook excess fluid from deep in his sister's lungs.

"I'm not sure lungs are attached to ribs," Tomas frowned, "but I'll remember to go gently."

Valeria appeared, carrying a cup of sweet mint tea and a variety of common cold remedies. "Good news or bad news?"

"How bad?" Vlad demanded.

"The good news is, Dr. Masarsky will be here within an hour. The bad news is, David called, Grandmamá answered, and told him Sarah's sick. He insists he'll be here within a half hour. Be prepared."

"He's going to moley in? That's not like him. Sergei, too?" Tomas asked.

"I don't know." Val held out several chewable fever reducers. Sarah crunched them one at a time despite their small size. After every swallow she wheezed a hard, bubbly cough.

"You're going to be late for school," Valeria warned Vlad.

He shot her a harsh look. "Screw school! She needs someone used to her pneumonia. If she's better later, I'll connect to the classroom over the comm and sit in for a while."

"I don't think a day off would hurt too much," Tomas granted.

Scarcely twenty minutes elapsed before heavy footsteps sounded up the stairs and David exploded upon the room. He shed his coat and threw it toward the other bed.

"What the hell'd you do to her?" he barked in greeting. "Why the hell'd you let her get so sick?"

"She hid the fact from us," Tomas explained. "It got the better of her. Dr. Masarsky should be here any minute."

Vlad sat by Sarah's knees. "Move your ass," David said to him.

"Move your own!"

David promptly sat on his brother, who pounded him in protest.

125

"Get off him," Sarah wheezed. She pushed on David's leg.

Tomas barely had time to shoo David off Vlad when a house staff escorted Dr. Masarsky into the room.

He shook hands. "Hello, Tomas, good to see you again. So, this is the new one, no? It's nice to meet you, Miss … ?"

"Sarah," Vlad said.

Dr. Masarsky raised an eyebrow. "Well, Miss Sarah, I hear you have a severe illness."

"I want Dr. Carver."

"We've been over that, Sarah," Tomas said. "John will come by later."

Vladimir left her knee and sat by her head. "It's a bad case of pneumonia. She gets it a lot. She needs a Virasept mask with O-Vent, Alvekleer, and Axifen Mist inhalers."

"Thank you, Dr. Kirushenko," David sneered. "Maybe now you could let Dr. Masarsky give a second opinion."

"Thank you." Masarsky opened his field kit. Supplies and equipment filled the compartments, while monitor screens blinked to life as he opened the lid. He waved a scanner at the girl. Sarah started to protest, but got caught up in a hard cough that lasted a full minute. She went to wipe the resultant goo from her lips with a napkin, but the doctor beat her to it, scraping up a sample on a plastic collector and depositing it into the portalab slot.

"When did this start?" Masarsky asked, but Sarah stayed silent.

"She seemed fine on Sunday," David said, then realized the truth when he finished, "She spent most of the day reading."

"She had a cough last week," Vlad thought back, "but she said it was a dry throat from allergies."

"She had a severe chill the other week," Tomas reported, "enough to give her a touch of frostbite."

"Very likely that played a part." Masarsky checked his readouts. "Well, Miss, I'm afraid your young physician friend here is correct. You have a blue-ribbon case of bacterial pneumonia in there. Next time, don't wait so long. I'll give you a shot of Biostat, maybe a little Oxisist, too, and you should be on your feet in three days." He reached into his home-visit pack and retrieved a larger sprayhypo.

"No! I take inhalers!"

Masarsky frowned. "Mask inhalers are for small children. It would take a full week to achieve the same effect in only three days from the Biostat."

"It's just a quick injection, Sarah," Tomas said. "Surely you've had a number of those. It's quite painless."

"No it's not! I've had that before; I won't do it again! I want my inhalers! Vlad, I need my inhalers!" The protest ended in a choking cough.

"There is a certain discomfort associated with the Biostat," Masarsky agreed. "I inject it directly into the infected tissues. It's two injections, perhaps ten seconds each, but it's over in less than half a minute."

"How bad can it be, Sar?" David said. "You've been through worse. One minute, and then you're on your feet."

"If the mask'll work, why can't you just give her what she wants?" Vlad demanded.

Tomas gave permission to proceed. "If that's what's best."

"No! No! Vlad, get me out of here!" Sarah slapped hard at the airhypo. The instrument clattered on the floor.

"Lie down, Sarah," Tomas soothed. He reached around Vladimir to block her escape.

Masarsky retrieved the hypo. "Is she always this uncooperative?"

Tomas wrestled with Sarah. "She … has her days. She is very … opinionated."

"Perhaps if we cleared out the audience. Sometimes patients need to think for themselves."

"Come, boys," but Tomas got no further than waving his arm. Sarah gave a half-drowned scream and locked her hands around Vladimir's hips, kicking at the doctor. She buried her face against Vlad, coughing, coughing, coughing.

"I'm not leaving her!" Vlad insisted, holding Sarah just as tightly. He shifted her head a little higher on his belly.

"This isn't going to work," Tomas realized. "You're sure this Bio stuff is the best thing?"

"Absolutely. I've seen it work miracles, with minimal side effects."

Tomas sighed. "Sarah, I'm afraid I'm going to have to insist. It won't take but a minute, and then you'll breathe better. I'll talk you through it, if you'd like."

Sarah tried. She *tried*, but her body wouldn't cooperate. She struggled to sit up, to run, but the thick fluids bubbled up, causing her to wheeze. She doubled over with the force of her coughing and couldn't resist Tomas's gentle hands pushing her down. She kicked at the strange doctor, using up precious oxygen until her skin darkened.

Tomas suffered in sympathy. "Get her feet, David."

David pinned the weakening legs, protecting the doctor. He patted her knee. "Hold on, Scout. It'll be over in just a second."

The first shot was Oxisist, suffusing her tissues with oxygen transport

127

boosters, easing the suffocation and returning her color to normal. The second was the dreaded Biostat. Legs immobilized by David's thick arms, hands held firmly by her uncle, strength stolen by illness, Sarah arched her back and screamed as the doctor found the correct placement between her ribs and applied his torture.

"Shah, Sarah," Tomas hushed. "Count with me – *pyat, shest, syem, vosyem, ...*"

"Why are you doing this to her!" Vlad yelled. "That isn't her medicine! She needs inhalers! You're making her worse! She can't *breathe* like that!"

"Roll her forward, and I should be able to get the other side," Masarsky ordered. He wasted no time repeating the agony.

Released, Sarah rolled to the far side of the bed, back to the wall. She wrapped her fingers in her hair and began to pull.

"I don't envy you, Tomas." Masarsky threw the hypo in his kit with disgust. He dropped two small cylinders on the bed. "These are adult inhalers. The decongestant will loosen the fluid and shrink the swelling. She can use the oxygen booster as necessary. She shouldn't need them more than two days. I'll leave you some tablets to ease the coughing so she can sleep. Who's this other doctor she asked for?"

"John Karverov," Tomas admitted.

"That *Americanetz* at the psychiatric clinic? That explains a lot. I realize this was an emergency, but I suggest you let him handle this from here," Masarsky said dryly, picking up his kit. "I'm sure he knows physicians who are better qualified to handle her kind than I am."

"I'll be talking to him later. Thank you for your help."

"Get out!"

Four sets of eyes stared at Vladimir.

"I said get out!" Vlad spat, pointing to the door. His dark eyes burned with fire. "Every last one of you! First you ignore her, then you hurt her like that? I'm not going to let you insult her, too. You think because she's sick and can't stand up for herself, you can treat her like that? Traitors, every one of you! Get out!" He took his uncle by the shoulders and pushed him toward the door.

David laughed. "I'm not going anywhere. Who the hell are you, *mishka*?"

"You will if you know what's good for you! I said *get out!*"

"Vladimir!" Tomas said sharply.

"Please, Uncle Tomas! I don't want to get violent, but I will if I have to. I'm serious. Please get out and give her some peace."

David crossed his arms and puffed his shoulders out in silent intimidation. "You little bag of maggots! Who the hell do you think you are, ordering Uncle Tomas around? I've got just as much right to be here as you. Maybe you need a little reminder where you fall in the food chain around here … "

"David," Tomas beckoned. "Give them a minute while I show Doctor Masarsky to the door. Vladimir, I will speak to you alone when I return. Is that understood?"

"Clearly, sir."

Vladimir locked the door the minute Tomas dragged David from the room.

* * *

Tomas sighed into the videopickup. "You're the technical expert, John. How do I handle this? Vlad knows her a thousand times better than I do. He knows how to handle her illness, I don't. She's vastly more comfortable with him in the room. If I force the door and make him leave, she'll become upset, and I don't think that's a good thing, given her inability to breathe. They're so intensely close! The family loyalty here rivals the conflicts of the Middle Ages. I don't want to start a holy war stepping on toes. It took all my skills to convince David to go back to Moscow and get Sergei in person. I figure I've got two, maybe three hours before David breaks down the door and kills Vladimir."

"Step back a minute," Carver said. "You're a professional, Tomas. You know how to think like one. Loyalty has nothing to do with this. You are her legal guardian. You make the decisions regarding her care. If something should happen, do you think a court is going to give a damn that she wanted her brother to hold her hand? It's your house, your territory, you make the rules. You can take loyalty and comfort into consideration, but do it on your terms. If she chokes to death, it's not Vlad they're going to come after, it's you."

"You're right. I can stand up to premieres and presidents without a blink, but a pair of teens has got me hiding behind the tool shop."

"Don't look behind you," John said wryly," because chances are, I was hiding there first. I've got an hour or so before my next appointment. I'll be there in about ten minutes, and we'll work it out together. "

* * *

"I haven't changed my mind!" Vladimir shouted at the knock.

"It's John, Vlad. Sarah asked for me this morning. I'd like to talk to her."

"Are you alone?"

Some patients did better with as little extra information as possible, others liked to know everything. John's policy around Sarah was total honesty, no matter how difficult. "Tomas is with me."

"Forget it! Neither one of us wants to see him right now."

"It's all or nothing, I'm afraid."

A moment of silence followed, then a hacking cough before Vlad released the door. "You make damned sure he stays back. One touch, and she'll tear him apart."

"Easy, Vlad. It's his house; he has a right to be here. Sarah K.!" John said brightly. "I heard you pulled a fast one. You even slipped that past me. How are you feeling now?" He pulled the chair closer to the bed and sat down. Tomas stood behind him, features locked in an unreadable mask.

Sarah lay under her covers, head resting on her brother's lap while he stroked her hair. Next to them lay his hockey stick, the first potential weapon he'd come across on a fast dash to his room. Sarah kept a well-used napkin clutched to her lips, eyes bloodshot from tears. She leaned forward to put her arms around her trusted friend.

John gave her a brief hug. "Easy, now. Tell me what happened."

"I told them! I told them! Nobody would listen! I just wanted my inhalers. They took them away on the *Triumph*, so I had nothing to take when I got sick," Sarah snuffled, wheezing. "I hate Biostat! But he wouldn't listen to me. And David! David didn't back me up!"

"I yelled good and hard at Tomas for that." He took a scanner out of his pocket. "Can I have a look for myself?"

Sarah nodded. John passed his scanner around her ribs several times.

"I banged her a little while ago," Vlad said.

John did a double-take. "I beg your pardon?"

"I had to bang on her back to get the stuff out, about ten minutes ago."

John blushed. "It's called *percussion*, Vlad. Percussion. Congratulations," he told Sarah. "You've got the worst case of pneumonia I think I've ever seen. No wonder you scared Tomas half to death. You must have known yesterday what was wrong?"

Sarah nodded, caught by truth.

"Why didn't you tell me yesterday you didn't feel well?"

Shrug.

"There are two physical diagnosticians at the clinic, Sar. They're used to dealing with people who might be upset to be there. They'll work with you. And yes, sometimes you *can* refuse treatment. I would have stayed

130

with you, explained things. Yesterday you might have been able to avoid the Biostat. Masarsky's choice in using it was not unreasonable. For the severity of your infection, it was probably the best choice for outpatient treatment. So, what does this come down to?"

Carver waited, but received no answer. He tapped a finger on her knee. "It comes down to a communication problem, doesn't it. *You* did not communicate to anyone that you were feeling ill. Problem number one. I want you to practice saying, 'Uncle Tomas, I don't feel well,' once every hour for the next two days, and Vladimir is going to make sure you do it. Because of problem one, we arrive at problem two, you let yourself get seriously ill, which jeopardized your well-being, which led to being treated by a doctor you weren't familiar with, which led to a medication you didn't want, which led to a perceived need to use force. So who's fault is all this?"

Sarah averted her face.

"I think you know the answer to that. And you, Vladimir!" John said with anger. "What the hell do you think you're doing, locking her in here like this? I don't care what your opinion is, don't ever let me hear of you doing something so dumb again."

Sarah snapped back, protective feathers ruffled. "Don't yell at him."

"I can take care of her," Vlad insisted. "I know perfectly well how to handle her pneumonia."

"If you did, you'd have known just how sick she is," John countered. "If you were here alone, I would accept that answer, but when Tomas is here, he is, *without question*, the person who is to be in charge of any and all situations regarding Sarah's health and well-being. If you can't accept that, I'll have to make note of it in my records, and possibly take further action. It's not a game, Vlad; it's a court case. It's my ass on the line, it's Tomas's ass on the line, it's Sarah's ass on the line. If push comes to shove, it's your ass, too, for obstructing prescribed treatment. Sarah wants to be alone with you, that's fine, but you will not prevent a responsible party from having access to her, no matter what your gripe is. Is that clear?"

"Crystal, *sir*."

"Good." John smiled, more like his pleasant self. "Now, Miss, how about you lie down and let me show Tomas why you hate Biostat?"

Sarah settled under the covers. John tucked the blanket in close. "I'm going to ease this up," he warned, tugging slowly at her nightwear. "Just a few centimeters."

Sarah twisted away. "No!"

"Which no? No, don't touch my clothes, or no, don't show anyone?"

"I don't show my back to anyone," she reminded him, coughing. John knew, and her family knew, thick scars covered her back from a brutal whipping as a child. It was a private matter, not to be discussed. Uncle Tomas didn't need to know.

"Okay. Vlad, hand me a few of those cloths there. I'd like to check it out myself, if that's okay. How about if I drape off the exact area, not show a centimeter more than I have to? I think it's important that Tomas see."

Sarah considered it. The two worst scars had been surgically removed a few weeks before, but there were still dozens to go. "Promise?"

"Swear on my degrees." He had Vlad and Tomas step back, then examined the area. Using the nightdress, the blanket, and three of the cloth napkins, he draped off all but the spots he needed.

"This is what Sarah objected to." He motioned Tomas closer. Centered in the openings were fresh dark bruises.

Tomas took a sharp breath. "My God! That's from the injections?"

Carver nodded. "It's a large molecule and a thirty-cc dosage that's forced through the skin, the chest wall, and the lung tissue, to the infected fluid itself. Extra pressure is needed to pass through all that. The pressure pushes on tissue that's already inflamed. It certainly doesn't tickle. Those bruises extend right down to the lungs."

He patted Sarah's shoulder. "You can cover up now. Thank you." In a split second, she rolled over and covered the pain.

Vlad scowled at his uncle. "See! She wasn't trying to be difficult."

"Forgive me, Sarah," Tomas said. "I had no idea."

"Vlad's the only one who ever believes me."

"I don't?" John said.

"Yeah, usually."

"All right, then. Get lots of rest. If you feel any worse, call me, and I'll get one of our doctors out here. When you feel better I'll have you meet them, and you can pick someone there as a diagnostician. We'll skip our sessions this week, but I'll stop in to see you on my way home. Okay?"

"Don't go!" Sarah pleaded in a harsh wheeze. She grabbed his clothing. "Stay!"

"I can't, Sar. I have other patients. I'll come by again tonight. I know Kat will want to visit."

Tomas escorted him to the room's door. "Thank you, John."

"You'll catch on to it in time," Carver reassured him. To Vladimir, he pointed a stern finger. "I'm depending on you, Vlad. If you think she's having difficulty, don't wait. Get Tomas, get me, get somebody. Don't let her make you think she's going to be fine. It won't do her any good if

132

she's dead. And lose the hockey stick! There's no scientific proof it cures germs."

Any other day, Vlad would have appreciated the humor. He held his head high, but there was less challenge to his demeanor. "I can take care of her."

* * *

Exhausted by the relentless coughing and ravaging infection, aided by the regimen of medications, Sarah slipped into a deep, defenseless sleep. David and Sergei were home for the night, only a room away, and Vlad promised to stay while she slept. Halfway through the night, Sarah stirred, rolled over, and gave a forceful cough. The action woke her enough to realize light shone in the room. She opened her eyes to find Tomas sitting by the bed, a glowing compad in his lap. The lights in this half of the room were at quarter-power. He sat forward and put down the compad.

"You were resting rather quietly. Feel any better?"

Sarah pulled her covers tighter. "Where's Vlad?"

Tomas tipped his head toward the lump in the bed across the room. "He was just as tired as you were. I told him I would take the night watch. If something happened, I would wake him immediately so he could make sure I did things right."

"Let him sleep, then. He needs the rest. He tries, but he's not very strong."

"He's stronger than you think," Tomas wagered. "Are you hungry? I have tea here, and some light crackers and cheeses." He motioned to a tray on the central table.

"Tea, with double sugar. Please."

He poured her request. "Something to eat?"

"Crackers, please. No cheese."

"The protein will give you strength."

"Cheese is a mucus product," Sarah said, sitting up. "The last thing I need is more mucus in my throat."

Tomas arranged her pillows and handed her the tea. "I hadn't thought about that. Thank you for telling me."

Sarah sipped at the cup, grateful. She felt weak and chilled again, and the hot liquid was comforting. She knew Tomas was waiting, but she couldn't think of anything to say. She understood he had a right to be there, but she would have preferred one of the boys. Uncle Tomas made her feel … inadequate, as if she'd gotten sick just to be difficult. She hid the sickness to *avoid* being a problem, but only Vlad could understand that.

"Can I get you something else? Is there anything you'd like instead?"

"No, thank you, sir."

"Is the pain any better?"

"Yes, sir. A little." She glanced at her brother. "What time did he go to sleep?"

"A little after midnight. It was all he could do to keep his eyes open. Sergei packed it in at 11:30."

"He really does know what he's doing," Sarah told the cup of tea. "He wouldn't ever let me choke to death."

"I know that," Tomas said. "My concern this morning was that …"

He stopped as Sarah gave a sudden hard cough, followed by a gurgling wheeze. She sat up straight, but it didn't help. Tea sloshed onto the sheets as she coughed violently, only to choke on the thick fluid. She rolled onto her knees, trying to keep the cup upright as her face darkened.

Tomas rescued the cup and placed it on the table. He slid next to her and banged a hand between the heaving shoulders. "Is this right, Sarah? How can I help more?"

Sarah gagged, but the mass of tenacious fluid stuck in her throat, unwilling to move. Three thumps, a desperate gag, and the plug of goo came loose as she vomited tea and crackers onto the bed, along with a mouthful of infected fluid.

"I'm sorry!" she wheezed, groping for the oxygen-boosting inhalant. "I'm sorry! I didn't mean to do that! I'm sorry!"

"Shhh. Don't be sorry. Come sit." He tugged and dragged until she sat on the edge of the bed. "No wonder! You're hotter than engine exhaust. Your fever's back." He wrapped her in her Sigma Tau Ceti blanket and eased her into the chair.

"Here." He held out a glass of cloudy pink liquid from the table. "It's your fever reducers, just the way Vladimir said you liked them, powdered fine and mixed with fruit juice. Is lemonade good, or would you prefer something else?"

Sarah put the oxygenator in her lap and accepted the glass. Uncle Tomas seemed so pleased. How long ago had he crushed the tablets, waiting for her to awaken? She didn't have the heart to tell him the ones Val left were chewable and didn't need crushing.

"Lemonade is fine."

Tomas began to strip the soiled linens.

"I can do that!" Sarah struggled to stand, half-way through the doctored lemonade. "You don't need to bother!"

"It's not a bother. Believe it or not, I'm quite capable at household tasks. The staff free up my time from maintenance duties, but I have managed to live without them at various points in my life. I shall return in less than a minute."

Tomas returned to find Sarah clinging to the computer desk as she made her way back from the lavatory. "Let me help you." He dropped the clean bedding and slid an arm around her.

"I didn't realize I was that weak," she gasped, glassy-eyed. She allowed him to help her to the chair.

"You're quite ill, Sarah. Your fever is much higher than you think. You need all the rest you can get." He wrapped her well and moved the glass within her reach before making up the bed.

Tomas reached out to steady her arm as she transferred. "Easy does it."

Sarah pulled away, collapsing into the clean bed with a painful bout of coughing. Across the room, Vlad slumbered on. She clutched the blankets, feeling small and young and so very alone.

"It's not a crime to need help, Sarah," he said kindly. "I can't think of a single type of interaction that doesn't involve some sort of reciprocal give and take. Accepting help is not a sign of weakness, no more than giving it."

"Yes, sir. I'm sorry, sir. I know that, but … I *can't*," she grimaced from her cocoon. "I have to stay strong."

Tomas dared to sit on the bed. "Is that one of Dmitri's rules?"

"No. I just can't allow it. I'm trying so hard to do everything right. If I let just *one thing* slip, lose my concentration for even one distraction, I'll *fall*. I'll fall to pieces, and I might not *ever* recover." Tears welled onto her eyelashes, glistening in the feverish eyes but stubbornly refusing to spill over. They blinked away as she coughed.

Tomas reached for her hand. "Please don't be so afraid, Little Ghost. No matter how hard you fall, be assured, I will be there to catch you."

The woeful eyes lifted to meet his. "I know you would, sir." She lunged and buried her face in his neck, clinging to him. "I'm counting on it."

Thirteen

Tomas threw his hands up in frustration. "I don't know what else to do, John. I've done everything I can think of. Galina stayed with her last week until I was sure she felt better. Friday morning she was on her feet. She spent the weekend on Vlad's floor. I asked him to spy for me – something I swore I would never do – tell me if she actually did sleep during the night. According to him, she was firmly asleep within half an hour, and he woke her in the morning."

"So she *is* able to fall asleep and maintain a sleep pattern," John thought aloud. "That's a clue that it's not her medications. It's something internal. Kat said she slept fine at our house. She sleeps fine with the boys. If she was that desperate for companionship, she would have taken up the offer to room with Marina. There's something else going on."

"It's getting out of hand. I can't carry on business, open my home to friends or associates if I've got teens sleeping on my floor every morning. Let alone the pressure from 'above.'" Tomas sighed to the ceiling. It shamed him to admit he was driven to seek help more from the dread of Mamá's noise than the inconvenience of the problem itself.

"Sunday, the boys returned to school, and I woke her at 2:30 from the sofa in the media room. Monday, I put my foot down, saying I wanted her in her room and nowhere else. Mamá paged me at one a.m. because Sarah was sleeping on the floor, half in, half out of her doorway. Last night I reached my limit. I placed a chair in the doorway. I told her I wanted to see her spend a night in her bed, and that I would guard her door to make sure she was undisturbed."

"Did it work?"

"Like curing a hangover by banging your head with a rock," Tomas said grimly. "After asking her to lie down for fifty minutes, she finally did, only to sit up every time I blinked. I gave up at five, told her I was happy to know that she could indeed spend an entire night in her bed. I don't know if she slept after that. I don't know about her, but I'm damned well exhausted."

"I'm not sure that was the best idea, but it didn't seem to make things worse. I think she's just more relaxed around the boys. I don't think a sleep study is going to turn up anything helpful at this point. I think something to relax her a bit before bed is the best bet."

"She swears up and down she won't be tranquilized."

John shrugged it off. "She always says that. I just have to pick the right one and go over the chemistry with her. She fights things until she's tried them for herself, sees they're not as bad as she thinks. I think she'll see the logic in it."

* * *

Sarah stopped dead in the deserted back hallway. One of the doors stood open a few centimeters. Most of the doors at this end were always locked – the art gallery, the conference rooms, the access closets for wiring or environmentals. Vlad said this was the ballroom, but why would a ballroom be locked? Storage? It seemed stupid in light of the amount of space in the basement – Uncle Tomas's apartment, the gym, and the pool took up only one wing. Sarah took a step closer, sniffing the draft from the mysterious room. She checked the hallway for witnesses and slipped through the door.

The sight took her breath away. The cavernous room ran almost the length of the body of the house. Three crystal lamps, as tall as Sarah herself, swung from the middle of the frescoed ceiling. Three pairs of glass doors led to the wide covered porch, and between the doors the arched windows soared nearly to the ceiling, their carved caps and frames dazzling with gold and silver leaf. Across the length stood an immense fireplace, a decoration more than anything, framed by wide panels of stone mosaic depicting trees and doves; a huge portrait hung above it. Another concert piano stood in the farthest corner, this one white. Scores of chairs and folded tables lined the inside wall. Across the room, Anna and Darella chatted as they cleaned the carved woodwork, while a robotic cleaner ran its slow course across the scuffless flooring.

Sarah tiptoed in, mesmerized by the grandeur of the lofty arched ceiling. She spun around, trying to take in all the room at once, tripping on the floor cleaner as it swerved around her feet.

"Miss Sarah!" Darella called across the room. "*Vi ne prinadlezhitye zdyes.* This room is not for playing in."

"*Pazhal'sta!* I won't touch anything," Sarah promised. "It's like a palace in here! Why isn't this room used more? Why is it kept locked? Was this part of the original design, or added later? Why do you clean it if it's never used? Please, let me look around for a minute?"

"It's beautiful because no one comes in to mess it up," Anna said. "We clean it once a month so it is presentable at a moment's notice. *Iditye, seychas.*" She chased Sarah away. "You're putting fingerprints on the stone."

Sarah left the mosaic to examine the painting above. She stepped back for a better view, expecting to discover some other great work of art, but the subject matter caught her off guard.

There was no mistaking the painfully beautiful girl in the larger-than-life portrait. She stood on the curving main staircase of this very house, dressed in finery, slender young shoulders bare, jewels twinkling from her neck and ears and fingers. Her golden hair cascaded behind her, held back from her face by a narrow glittering band. Her ocean-blue eyes sparkled with life, and her smile radiated pure sunshine.

Sarah's family photos were tucked away in her backpack; most of them were from specific events in her life, and she took them out when she wanted to reminisce. Seeing her mother's face when she was so unprepared stabbed her like a knife. This was Uncle Tomas's house, or Grandmother's house; it was where *they* belonged, where *they* lived. *This was Mother's room* had little connection when Valeria and Galina were living there. *Mother's house* had been in Kiev, their big yellow one that she'd been so loathe to leave for Navara. While the taste and style of Uncle Tomas's house bore striking similarity to Maryana Kirushenko's preferences, there was nothing to confirm her mother had ever set foot there. Until now.

Darella saw the dumbfounded stare. "That's Miss Maryana, Mister Ivanov's late sister. She was such a beautiful girl."

"That's my *mother*," Sarah corrected, lost in the painting.

"I suppose so. I forget you're her children. You look like her yourself. You've got her hair, for certain."

"I could never even hope to be like her," Sarah mumbled, and sat down on the parquet to study the picture. Her mother had been thirty-two when Sarah was born; she'd been thirty-four in Sarah's haziest memories. She'd always been beautiful, and she'd always seemed happy, but in Sarah's lifetime she'd always been a grown-up and a mother and a wife and the mistress of a household. She'd never been as young as the girl in the painting. She'd never been that carefree.

"Please, Miss Sarah. You really don't belong in here. You're going to get in trouble if Mr. Ivanov finds you."

Sarah still sat quietly on the floor when Tomas poked his head in, looking for her.

"We've asked her leave, Mister Ivanov," Anna said, "but she won't move."

Tomas waved a hand. "It's not a problem." His footsteps echoed across the long room until he sat on the floor next to Sarah. "That was painted by an Austrian artist named Gerhardt Schulman, on the occasion of your mother's sixteenth birthday. I think he did a wonderful job, myself. He started around her birthday, and we got the final work just before the December holidays. A few weeks later she met your father. It used to hang on the staircase. Papa ordered it destroyed after your mother married, but Mamá and I hid it. After he died, I moved it here. I think this was your mother's favorite room in the house. She loved music and dance, and she loved a good party."

Sarah remembered her birthday, just four months previous. "On my sixteenth birthday, Mrs. Al made me a fruit cake with a baked-sugar topping. I wore the blue dress I wore yesterday, with no shoes. Dmitri gave me a textbook on comparative evolution, and Charlie gave me a bag of my favorite candy." She didn't mention the note in the bag that said, *'For sweetest girl I know.'*

"That sounds like a very pleasant birthday."

"It was warm, and muggy, and we had to keep the cake covered to keep the insects off," she added wistfully. "Whatever would possess someone to leave a place like this? To leave this for *Father*? I can't imagine what it was like to grow up here. We never lived in one place more than four years running; by the time Mother got things arranged the way she wanted, we moved again. I mean, Mother had fancy things and jewelry and stuff, and when she went somewhere important, she could dress more beautiful than anyone in the world. People would stop walking just to look at her. She could have had anything she ever wanted. Why would she throw it all away on *Father*?"

"Maybe she was doing what she wanted," Tomas proposed. "She was young, very outgoing, and wanting to be independent. I think the more your grandparents and I tried to steer her, the more determined she was to make her own decisions. Love does strange things to people. Sometimes you can be so in love with someone that you can't see beyond the love, to the side of people that isn't as desirable. Sometimes you see it but choose to ignore the weakness, because you think your love is strong enough to bear it. Have you ever been in love?"

It wasn't love! It wasn't! Familiarity and trust did not equal biologically driven lust. Homesickness was merely a manifestation of longing for the habituated situation over the physiological stress of the novel one. It had nothing to do with hormonally induced desires or distant worlds or people she'd never see again.

It didn't!

"No," she said with disinterest.

Tomas tipped his head. "Not even puppy love?"

"No!"

"That's too bad. I'm sure once you get out more in the community, find more people your age, you'll find someone quick enough. You're every bit as bright and pretty as your mother at your age."

Sarah shook her head. "I don't think so. I don't deserve it. I don't feel anything for anybody."

"Now, now! I don't buy that nonsense for a nanosecond. You demonstrate love to others all the time. Bring any one of your brothers or sisters around, and your entire face lights up with the love you feel for them. A blind man could hear it in your voice."

Sarah stared into space, thinking. The portrait stirred up too much inside her, knocked over one of the tins of worms she couldn't bear to look at, let alone fight closed again.

"She was dying, she was in pain, she begged me for help, but I wasn't fast enough," she announced. "My mother died and I didn't even cry. Not once. I was a horrible child."

Tomas heard the pain hidden in the words. "I've heard worse. You were very young, Sarah. I'm sure you were very frightened; I certainly would have been. No one blames you for that."

"It wasn't deliberate. It just never came out."

"Sometimes when people hurt very deep in their hearts, they're too upset to cry. Sometimes they don't cry until much later, when the pain rises back to the surface. It's never too late to cry about something that makes you feel sad. There are still days – the special days, like holidays and birthdays and anniversaries – when I miss Lora so strongly I still get tears, twelve years later."

Sarah nodded. There were so many days like that in her life. More than half had been erased simply by coming home, but the few that remained were deadly. She kept those days locked up, lest something crippling leak out.

"It's not good for me to cry about things like that," she said stiffly. "Sometimes I can't stop, and then everyone gets upset and I get in trouble. You know – the kind that results in doctors and stuff."

Tomas pulled a handkerchief out of a pocket and stuffed it between her fingers. He made sure he had one on him at all times. Sarah had her personal supply, but she never seemed to have one with her.

"I'll tell you what. I'll leave you alone for a while, let you think about it, and if you think you feel like crying, I want you to do it. Let yourself go. Then, maybe in half an hour or so, I'll come back. If you're crying and you don't think you can stop, I will help as best I can. Is that workable?"

Sarah's breath caught. She didn't dare. The tin of worms was bulging, straining. Explosive things were best left untouched. The cleaning help

140

packed up the floor machine and left. As he went to stand, she seized his arm with a cry. "Don't leave me! Don't leave me alone!"

"I'll sit with you all day if you wish." He stroked her hair. "You're not a bad person, Sarah. You're a young girl with an inordinate amount of pain, but pain is easier to bear when the load can be shared. If it wants to come out, don't stop it. Let it go."

Sarah stared up at the image of her mother, so unaware of the fate which awaited her. If she closed her eyes, she could still remember Mother's soft voice, remember Mother clapping for her when she learned something new, remember the glowing pride when Mother learned the Navarans would let Sarah stay in their school. She would never forget the look on Mother's pained, sweaty face as she lay in her own blood, close to delivery, or Mother's words of praise for calling for help so fast. The last words Mother ever said to her. So undeserved, in light of the results. Sarah'd tried, and failed. Mother knew that, she *had* to know that, but she'd forgiven her daughter anyway, because Mother was like that. How could Sarah ever be like her? Tears fought to burn their way up through her eyes.

This time, they made it.

* * *

The last thing Sarah wanted was yet another medication. She was opposed to tranquilizers, the shackles of the medical world, and had always managed to avoid them. As far as she could see, Tomas had no reason to be discussing her sleep habits at all. Sarah found herself growing angry over the intense scrutiny, and for the first time at the Ivanov's, her self-righteous and stubborn streak reared its little head.

Pig-headed tenacity had kept Sarah alive her entire life. Will to live allowed her to survive her premature birth; refusal to be defeated helped her survive years of abuse; obsessive determination helped her survive her exile. John had fought the demon and won, but it had taken unbearable anguish for Dmitri to reign as Lord and Master of the Devil itself, the only person, including Sarah, with that feat. A few weeks of kindness couldn't undo a pattern that had been deeply ingrained and highly successful for more than sixteen years.

"They're not working," Tomas said. "Two days. I chased her out of the upstairs lounge the first night, and last night she stayed in her room, reading."

Sarah glared from the other chair in John's office, irritable and furious. "That's not true! I read *until* I fell asleep. I did sleep!"

"What time, Sarah?" John said patiently. "When did you fall asleep, and what time did you wake up?"

"Vlad woke me at the usual time, 6:15. I don't know what time I fell asleep. If I was looking at the clock, I wouldn't be asleep now, would I?"

"Touché. Tomas, what time did you see her reading?"

"I checked on her at 2:45."

"So at most, you had three and a half hours sleep. That's not enough, Sarah. The body needs more than that to maintain itself." John waited for a response. When she gave none, he asked Tomas, "Are you sure she's taking the pills? She can be very sneaky about it. Sometimes you have to search."

"I took them!" Sarah snapped. She stood up to pace, keeping the chair between her and the others. "Now I can be accused of not cooperating with medications? I don't *want* them! I don't *need* them! I sleep *fine! I'm* not the one complaining! He says himself he has to wake me up to make me move! Why isn't *he* asleep at those times? No one's questioning *his* sleep patterns. I don't care what some dumb court says, I'm not a baby. I have a right to sleep when and if I want to. I think I'm capable of judging when I'm having a problem or not. Just leave me alone!"

She crossed her arms and scowled at John. "What are you laughing at?"

John squished his amusement down. "I'm sorry, Sarah. I'm not laughing at you. It's times like this you make my job difficult. On one hand, you are such a typical tantrumming sixteen-year old, I want to shout for joy. On the other hand, I know there's probably a deeper reason for your trouble that you will do anything to avoid discussing, and that *is* a problem. It's a symptom of something unhealthy, and I don't have any idea if it's harmless and self-limiting, or something malignant that's going to hurt you before we can catch it. Last time we uncovered something, you almost froze to death."

"It's harmless," Sarah insisted. "It'll *stay* harmless if you just stop obsessing on it. Worry about something else, something real."

"No stomping foot?" John said, remembering the old days. "I guess you could say that's a step in the right direction?"

It wasn't what Sarah wanted to hear, not on only three hour's sleep. On Sigma Tau, she'd had a dozen secret places she could hide to catch a nap; here she was forever under glass.

"No, I taught my foot a new trick." She swung her foot under the low table by the window, lifted it with a slight kick and flipped it over. The basket of materials on top spilled across the floor.

Tomas stood up with a shocked expression. "Sarah! You will fix that

142

immediately, and you will apologize to John. That behavior is not acceptable."

Sarah weighed her nerve, sure of John but not of Tomas. She walked over to the chair where she'd been sitting and turned it upside down at his feet. "I'm having a sixteen-year old tantrum," she said snidely. "Don't worry; it's normal." She dropped herself down on the padded alcove and put her feet on the wall. Her skirt slid up past her knees.

John sat unperturbed. "I think someone needs a few laps around the gymnasium. Do I need one escort, or two?"

Sarah stared at her raised feet. "One." An escort knocked at the door less than thirty seconds after John's page.

"Can't catch me!" Sarah took off for the gym before the man had a chance to touch her.

"I'm dreadfully sorry about that, John," Tomas said, righting the chair. "She's *never* been that rude before. Perhaps it's the lack of sleep."

John laughed. "Oh, yes she has. It's not the first time, and it won't be the last. Don't fix another thing. She has to make the reparations, and she knows it."

Tomas sat down, embarrassed. "I don't know what came over her. She's always extremely polite at home."

"I know *exactly* where she's at. Little Miss Sarah hasn't been swallowing her prescribed sleep aids and doesn't want that discovered. The attitude and tantrum are probably part legitimate – a real, understandable anger at not having a say in her own destiny, which is typical in an adolescent with a protracted illness of which they have little control. But the rest of it – the table flipping – is a ploy to change the subject and make us forget the topic of medication avoidance. I'll try again later. Meanwhile, you're going to have to rely on that politeness at home. You're going to have to search for pills, and I'm not sure how she'll react. I guarantee it won't be pretty."

Sarah obediently placed the pill in her mouth and drank the glass of water, watching Tomas over the rim. She finished the water, placed the glass on the tray, and turned to leave.

"Please wait, Sarah. I'm – required to examine your mouth to ensure you've swallowed your medication," Tomas explained, his own mouth too dry to spit. He didn't need a rampaging teen throwing his furniture and destroying his house. He produced a medical probe donated by John, and a fiberoptic light.

Sarah blanched whiter than the light. *"What?!"*

"I'm sorry. It's not my idea, but I'm required to do it."

"I swallowed it! I *swear*! I'm not lying!"

"I believe you, but I must now initial off that I've checked."

"That's all John's idea, isn't it? What's next? You'll be required to inspect my hygiene after I bathe? Am I allowed no dignity at all?"

"I would refuse such a request, and I would support your refusal to allow it," Tomas vowed. "I assure you, this is every bit as loathsome for me. I apologize for the indignity, but if you will cooperate, it will be over swiftly, and we can both forget about it."

"Until the next time!" Sarah opened her mouth and lifted her tongue to prove her point. "I told you, I swallowed it."

"I'm required to inspect around your gums."

Eyes flaming with hurt, she grabbed his hand and ran his finger around the edges of her mouth. *"Satisfied?"*

Tomas nodded squeamishly. "Yes, thank you, Sarah. You're free to go."

She didn't need a second invitation.

* * *

John opened the conversation. "So, how did yesterday go? How'd you sleep?"

"On my right side, with my eyes closed, in a state of unconsciousness," Sarah informed him. "Same as the night before, only with a lot of unnecessary humiliation on my part, and the part of my guardian. Unless you've decided to spare us the degradation, I have nothing to discuss on the matter. Next question?"

"Okay." It was easy enough to verify. "What did you do after our session?"

"I ate lunch with Uncle Tomas, since Grandmother was on business. Then I went upstairs."

"What did you do there?"

"Worked on my paper."

"Which paper is that?"

"The write-up of my plant study on Sigma Tau," Sarah said, feeling the subject to fall under the category of Success Stories, and therefore safe to discuss. "An officer on the *Triumph* said it was a worthwhile investigation, and I should write it up and submit it to a scientific journal. I've been going over my numbers one last time, making sure my statistics are correct. I just wish I knew someone like that here, who could check it over before I submit it."

"I could do that," John offered. "I'd be interested to read it, anyway."

Sarah made a skeptical face. "You've written scientific papers?"

John pretended to be hurt. "PhD in Recreational Therapy, remember? Designed, researched, implemented, and critiqued my own program, for one thing. I'm not as brilliant as you, of course, but I've had five papers accepted for publication since. One of them even involved you."

"*Me?!*" Sarah's deception radar jumped to high alert. "What did you write about me?"

"Relax. I never used your name. *Educational Programs as Recreational Therapy for the Academically Gifted, Three Case Histories,* in the Journal of Pediatric Psychiatry, 2265. You and two other smart young people I had the chance to work with."

Paranoia ended where jealousy started. "Were they as smart as me?"

"They were up there, but not quite as far as you," John assured her.

"And they were crazy, too?"

"No, just hopelessly neurotic. One had phobias over public places, insects, broken things, and the other was obsessive-compulsive about symmetry. But I want to see what your paper's about. Send me it over the comm, or bring it with you tomorrow and we'll go over it. Have you thought about where you'll go with your education now?"

The question surprised her. "No. I've always studied on my own."

"What classes have you read material for?"

"Oh goodness! I have to think. A lot." She rattled off a string of titles. "I'm still reading a text on comparative evolution."

John looked at the tally. "About thirty courses. That's pretty good. You've got a lot of different subjects there, too. Do you remember any of it?"

"Of course!" Sarah snorted. She remembered almost everything she read.

John tapped his fingers on his desk. "You need a minimum of forty courses for an undergraduate degree at the University of Byelorus here in Minsk. Twenty-eight would give you Junior standing. How many of those courses do you think you could pass an exemption exam on?"

"All of them! Of course, I wasn't able to do most of the laboratory portions of the science courses. We didn't get back to the Compound often enough for me to complete the work."

"If you're writing a formal paper on botany, I'm sure you'll pass the lab requirements. What do you say I arrange for you to speak with the admissions department of BGU and see what they'd require for you to get official credit for the work you've done?" He pronounced it *BeyGeyOo.*

"I could really do that?"

John chuckled. "Why not? See how far you get, and aim for a fall admission. We'll work on any missing requirements over the spring and summer. Maybe I can arrange with the teachers upstairs to supervise you on lab science an afternoon or two a week. That would get you out of the house a little more, too. Bring in your texts tomorrow."

Sarah sat, pondering. University was a big step, a *huge* step. It meant having to sit in lecture halls filled with strange men and women, listening to professors and asking questions, all by herself. She'd been begging for such an opportunity all her life.

She gave a tentative shrug of interest. "It doesn't hurt to inquire."

Within three days, Sarah sat in the admissions office of the University of Byelorus with Tomas. BGU was a huge university, with some 12,000 residential and 20,000 commuting students at the main campus there in Minsk. Sarah tried her very best to look calm and confident and not at all crazy, even if her insides squirmed like a box of overheated snakes. She knew the ruse of sanity wouldn't hold long – one look at her file, one realization she'd be taking the lab courses at a hospital school, and the administration would know what they were up against. That would be the end of that. She'd never have official letters after her name.

The director of admissions raised his eyebrows. "Four years in a Navaran school? That's quite impressive. Your entire educational record is rather remarkable. You realize, of course, we couldn't allow someone of your age to reside on campus?"

Sarah heard it as, 'We couldn't allow someone of your mental status to reside on campus.'

Uncle Tomas spoke for her. "Of course. It would be on a day-student basis only."

"Your claim of proficiency in eight languages is valid?"

Sarah forced her head up and shoulders down. "Every bit, sir."

"And you can provide references to validate your research work on the Pelonishalak language of Sigma Tau Ceti?"

"Yes, sir. You will find my name listed among the researchers on the Fleet database. Commander Guillaume and Lieutenant-Commander Dickerson will verify my work. I suppose I could ask Commander Ti'onam for a reference as well. He's a science officer on the explorer *Triumph*. He reviewed all my project notes, and he proctored my diploma exam."

The director made note of the names. "I shall certainly contact them. It's too late to begin any courses this semester, but I can look into getting you credit for your previous studies. I can arrange for you to take the final exams for the classes you claim to have studied. We will start with four; if you pass those to the satisfaction of the professors, we will continue with the remaining courses. If you do not pass at least three of them, we will consider your claims invalid, and you may enter in the fall with freshman status."

Sarah nodded, face devoid of any discernible emotion, good or bad. She could do it. Academic tests never bothered her; she looked forward to them. They were a mental exercise, a challenge, a chance to show off. She would floor them.

"That's most fair."

Fourteen

Elation over formal schooling made only a temporary diversion from the continuing struggle in the other areas of her life. Sarah could blame Tomas for the fuss that wound up adding sleep inducers to her regimen, but not the nightly searches; that was purely John's fault. What happened at home, though – *that* she blamed entirely on Tomas, and it would take a secret on his part, and an assumed miracle on hers, to make her forgive him.

Marya Fimofiev was a patient woman who, at 61, had let her hair gray naturally. She wore it conveniently short so as not to get in the way with her duties as kitchen director. For twenty-two years she'd kept the pantries stocked, juggled menus and staffing schedules, kept up on trends, hired temporary staff for small functions and directed the caterers for the large ones. She never bothered the Ivanovs with petty matters, so when she sought out Tomas Ivanov to discuss a problem, Tomas Ivanov listened.

"It's not that we wish to complain, Mr. Ivanov," Marya said. "We don't mean to cause trouble, but one of the issues, come the warmer months, could prove to be an issue of vermin prevention."

"Vermin?" Tomas mused. "I don't think I've ever seen so much as a fly in the house. Nonetheless, you know my stance regarding problems. It is better to get it out in the open than let it go unfixed, no matter how small."

"Yes, sir. Actually, there are two problems. The first is the state of the kitchen, sir."

"Is something wrong with the equipment?"

"Oh, no, sir. It's the condition we find it in the morning, sir. At least twice a week for the past month, the staff has arrived to find ingredients or dishes or spills littered about, when we know without fail it was spotless when we left."

"The boys making midnight raids again?" Tomas smiled at what had been a problem in the past, with three growing teenage boys.

Marya hesitated. "Perhaps one has occurred during the weekends, sir, but the rest have occurred during the week."

"I see."

"It's not the matter of someone raiding the stock, though we are going through an unusual amount of dessert ingredients. It's the matter of having to clean the kitchen before they can get to work that has the staff upset, sir."

"That's understandable. I shall look into the matter immediately. Please let me know the very second you find the kitchen in disarray again. I would like to see the matter for myself."

"Thank you, sir. The other problem was told to me by the housekeeping staff, but it involves food as well. Please don't think I'm trying to create trouble, sir, for I know the new Miss Kirushenko has had a bit of a time settling in. I don't know how she lived before, but she's keeping food about her room. Housekeeping is complaining because some of it has gone sour."

"Food? Like chicken legs and things? No, she wouldn't eat that," he corrected himself. "Dirty salad bowls? Lentils and rice?"

"Something like that, sir. Dinner breads, breakfast pastries, fruit, stashes of cooking chocolate and cheeses, and the nuts we use in recipes," Marya informed him. "Olga complained when they pulled a napkin of grapes from among the items in her closet, after they had turned to liquid. Come spring, that kind of compost will most certainly attract flies."

"That does pose a problem," Tomas agreed. "Thank you, Marya, for bringing this to my attention. I will speak to Olga, and I will speak to Sarah tonight."

"That's a lie!" Sarah fumed. She paced the study in neurotically fast laps. "Why would I do such a thing? There's more food here than I've ever seen in my life!"

"That may be true, but it doesn't answer the fact that housekeeping has removed a veritable grocer's market from your room." Sarah wasn't the cleverest of liars, Tomas had realized. If she was lying to avoid an inquiry, she oozed good manners and friendship. If she was lying to deny an accusation, she became vocal and defensive. This was one of those times, almost certainly conveying her guilt.

"Obviously someone must have planted it there. The upstairs staff doesn't like me. They look at me like I'm a deformed creature from a planet they've never heard of. One of these days, I have just the mind to shout *Boo!* and watch them run screaming."

Tomas leaned back in his chair with a patience gleaned from years of mediating boardroom shouting matches. "Not to make light of your concern, Olga Petrova has been in my employ for twelve years, seven of those twelve with your family present. I have never yet had a report of dishonesty on her part. I do not have any reason to believe my staff would suddenly start hiding half-eaten sandwiches among your underthings, chocolate pastries among your bath linens, or sacks of macadamias in your shoes. If you wish to have ready access to food between meals, I will have a variety of items of your preference brought to your room on a daily basis, but I must insist that you not leave perishable food about your room, lest insects discover it."

"I can't *stop* something I'm not *doing*!" Sarah shouted. "Just because you've never caught them in a lie doesn't mean I'm wrong! You believe them more than me, simply because I haven't been here as long? Is that it?"

Tomas sighed hopelessly. "Very well, Sarah. I have heard their side, and now I have heard yours …"

"And mine is the correct one!"

"In the meantime," Tomas said over her objection, "I would ask that *if* you choose to eat in your room, that you properly dispose of any remnants, lest I have to have your room treated for pests. Is that understood?"

Sarah snorted, arms crossed. "I understand exactly where I stand."

Dismissed, she ran to her room and locked the door. She stuffed her hand under the mattress, pulled out a small bundle of imported French caramel cooking cubes, and ate them, sulking, in her closet.

* * *

"Go ahead, you can take some," John told her, watching her eye the dish of chocolate truffles on the corner of his desk. Sarah had to suck on her lip to keep from drooling, but she was too stubborn to ask. "I put them there especially for you. I hear you've been rather hungry lately."

Sarah's head jerked up to give him a murderous glare. The hand in the dish released its cache of temptation with a raining patter.

"You heard wrong."

John shrugged. The strength of her conviction impressed him; he hadn't thought she'd be able to resist the treat. He pressed the concealed switch on the clip of his computer stylus. It would leave an electronic tracer at that point in the voice recording of the session, making it easy to cut back to important points for review.

"It's not something to be embarrassed about. Just make a list of what you like, and Tomas will make sure it's available."

"Hmph! You think Ivanov food is that great? Dimi and I used to eat in restaurants that make that stuff look like porshie swill."

"Is that true, or are you trying to impress me?"

"It's absolutely true!" Sarah sat up, wearing her best look of innocence. "Ask Dimi! He'll tell you! We went broke on some of those

150

meals. Places where the food was so fresh you could still smell the soil it grew in. Places where the desserts were twenty centimeters high and looked like they were made by an architect instead of a chef." She sighed dreamily, remembering. "Do you have any idea how much caviar costs on Arcturus?"

"So you're used to living the high life," John mused. "And you would bring the leftovers home with you, no doubt, and save them to eat later."

The attitude returned. "Of course not! You don't leave a restaurant like that with scraps."

"So what did you do if you were hungry before the next meal?"

"You're the one who keeps mentioning food. I think you need this more than I do." She pushed the dish of candy towards him. "I'm bored with the office today. Let's take a walk."

* * *

Nothing. Sarah would impart *nothing* as to reasons for her behavior. The best Tomas could do was have the staff make daily checks. He had a basket of fruit put on the table in her bedroom; she returned it to the kitchen, but the cleaning help found half a kilo of dried figs between the cushions of her reading chair. Surely it took all her will to place the tin of Danish butter-biscuits outside her door, unopened, yet the staff pulled a stash of Rainbow Rice Cakes from the depths of a potted plant in the upstairs hall.

Tomas had little choice but to lay a trap. After the help left for the night, he set the security system to chime his office when anyone entered the kitchen. At half-past one, the monitor beeped softly.

Tomas waited outside the kitchen. His ghost rummaged through drawers, cabinets banged, bare feet slapped softly on the floor. He let her become involved, then tiptoed in.

Sarah stood at a workspace in the vast room, clad in her nightwear, tasting from the bowl she was stirring. Powdery lines and sticky drops trailed the countertops and floor. She shook in a dash more salt, and caught sight of Tomas from the corner of her eye. She shrieked and ran clear to the back wall of the kitchen. A medication tremor shook its way down her body, calming the shock.

Tomas peered into the bowl. "May I?" He sampled the thick paste with the tip of his finger. "That's very good. It tastes like a future cake, or biscuit perhaps. With, let's see, cherries, white chocolate, and – What are these?" He picked out a lump and tried it. "Marshmallow? Mmm. Were you going to bake it, or eat it all like that?"

Sarah gave no reply, pinned against the wall.

"I forgot you had to make your own meals on Sigma Tau, so you're used to cooking."

"Am I in trouble?"

Tomas surveyed the messy workspace. "I'm afraid so. Not because you're using the kitchen, but because you lied to me about it, and lying is unacceptable, for any reason whatsoever."

There were seven doors out of the huge kitchen. The outdoor exit was closest. Sarah took a step toward it. "Are you going to whip me?"

"Is that what Dmitri would do?"

"No."

"Do you *want* me to whip you?" It had taken a full year to get her brothers to believe him when Tomas insisted he didn't hit people.

"No."

"Then it's unanimous. I do consider lying to be a serious crime, however, and I think the punishment should be rather stringent. Except for meals and appointments, you will stay in your room – alone," he emphasized, "and that includes at night."

"But it's Friday! David and Sergei come home today! Sergei's taking me to the theater! I get to sleep in Vlad's room! I can't miss their visit!"

"I'm afraid you will, at least part of it," Tomas insisted. "If you can behave yourself through Saturday, you may rejoin the family on Sunday. And clean up the mess you've made here." He pointed to the spills.

Sarah curled her lip. "That's not my job."

"I beg your pardon?"

"That's not my job," Sarah repeated, nose raised high. "My mother did not raise me to be a cleaning woman. That's what cleaning staff are hired for: cleaning."

Tomas fell speechless. Buried in the heart of the back-woods girl lay a scorching strain of aristocracy to make Mamá proud.

"No, the hired staff are here to keep order and perform functions that neither Mamá nor I have the time nor talent to accomplish. They work hard at their tasks, and they have every right to be upset when someone disrupts their work. Outside of a secretary or two, there are no personal servants in this house. To leave a mess like that is an insult; I will not allow such disrespect."

"I hardly see how that's a disrespect. If there were nothing to clean, there wouldn't be a service for them to perform. Mrs. Al and I fought long and hard over that point, but in the end she saw I was right."

"I don't care if it's wrong or right!" Tomas sputtered. "I asked you to clean up your mess, and I expect it to be done!"

Sarah's eyes narrowed. "I get it. If I don't, I get reported as uncooperative." She looked about for a wiper.

"That's not true." As far as Tomas cared, the mystery was solved, the matter addressed, the case closed. "It's not a matter of winning or losing. It's a matter of what's fair to everyone, and treating others with kindness and respect."

Sarah scrubbed the workspace clumsily. "Whatever you say,"

* * *

Murder, that's what it was. She stood accused of trying to kill people in a life-or-death situation and that was a crime, but Uncle Tomas could do this to her and the courts thought it was just orbital. The look on Vlad's face when he found out she was imprisoned for two days broke her heart. She didn't care if she was punished, it was the fact that Vlad, Sergei and David were being punished as well. It was heartlessly cruel.

Physical punishments could be merciless and painful, but eventually you recovered. Sarah knew that, and she knew emotional punishments were meant to be carried around like a branding mark year after year. But if Sarah despised anything, it was being caged like an animal. She'd been caught slipping away from school when she was little. She'd managed to bypass the security systems in the hospital at Starbase 4. She'd come close to escaping the hospital on Navara; she simply ran out of time. Dmitri had tried keeping her in, time after time, and all but one of his ways she could escape from quickly. They'd tried it on the *Triumph* and she'd escaped once, then nearly burned her skin off trying a second time. There were no guards on her door here, no energy barriers, no subdermal electronic tags to pinpoint her location. She was here entirely by choice, and that was the biggest thorn of all. She couldn't disobey Tomas. Even if he was wrong about the servants.

The balance of free will versus obedience to stupid, useless rules ate at her.

If she could just talk to Vlad for half an hour! How miserable he must be without her!

Sarah stared dully out the windows, too heartbroken even to study.

Windows?

On Sigma Tau, she could come and go out the second-story window of her bedroom as fast as if she'd used the stairs. No one would suspect that here.

Sarah opened the tall window and leaned out. The frigid air bit her face. It wasn't the same as the cabin: this window was three times higher, a long and disastrous fall if she slipped. A narrow ledge ran clear across the side of the house to the south wing, a private little highway under the bedroom windows. If she really wanted to, she could do it.

But did she dare?

Sarah shut the window and thought it out. Tomas never said she couldn't talk to Vlad through his window, so it wasn't really disobedience. David would be proud of her for running a Fearsome Four-style escape, and he'd know she hadn't lost her touch. *Yes,* Sarah nodded to herself. She could do it. She *would* do it. She pulled the chair over and climbed onto the window frame, looking down, down, down. It was a sobering height, but heights had never bothered her. She had only to go sideways this time.

Lord, it was cold! Bitterness radiated from the snow below, blew upwards under her dress in the chilling night breeze, freezing her legs and *zhopa* and toes. Sarah didn't dare wear shoes; the ledge was no more than twenty centimeters wide, and her heels stuck out beyond the edge. She had always climbed barefoot, gripping with her toes, and she needed that grip up here.

Belly to the building, she crept along a few centimeters at a time. The frozen cement hurt her feet; it wasn't like the clammy wood of the cabin at all. A decorative ridge of stucco separated the two rooms; she eased her foot around it and pulled her herself over with clumsy cold fingertips.

She leaned her weight forward onto her icy-stiff toes, out of handholds. She'd waited until after dinner, when Vlad was most likely to be in his room – and no one going to or from the hangar would notice her in the dark. Through the window she could see Vlad at the interface in his room, his back to her. She tapped cautiously at the glass.

Vlad picked his head up and said something to someone she couldn't see, then turned back to the computer. Sarah tried again, shivering so hard she could barely mold her hand into a fist. Cold had never bothered her like this, not until she froze last month. This time Vlad noticed. He gave a shout and Sergei appeared, disbelieving.

"How the Hell'd you do that!" Vlad exclaimed as he opened the next window panel. "You're going to be in so much trouble if you get caught!"

"Ah! That's the word precisely. *If.* In Vandijoc, I could do this faster than you could run down the stairs." Sarah shuffled the last few centimeters and reached for the window casing. Except her feet were numb, her fingers stiff, and she missed the edge of the window. She couldn't counterbalance with her freezing toes, and fell off the ledge with a knowing scream.

Sarah knew Dmitri had saved her from bad situations a dozen times at least, and she'd always told Vlad she would have died without his friendship all those years, but Sarah now knew, without a doubt, that Sergei had been born tall and long-armed for one reason and one reason only: to save the life of a sister who was too stupid to know better.

Sergei's hand had been outstretched to help her in the window. He saw her tip sideways and lurched the extra distance over Vlad to grab the neck of her dress. He nearly knocked Vlad out of the window in the process.

Sarah's screams could be heard clear across the frozen estate, but Vladimir's screams could be heard throughout the house. Sergei held her full weight in one hand and the window frame with the other. Two fasteners to the dress popped immediately, and the rest strained taut as she dangled three stories above the ground. Sarah grabbed his wrist, but her fingers were too cold to be of much help.

Sergei would have hit Vlad over the head to quiet him, but he couldn't spare even a foot for a kick. "Get help!" he yelled, and at last Vlad ran from the room to scream at the top of the stairs.

Two more fasteners gave, and Sergei let go of the frame to grab Sarah by the wrist. He released the dress to grab her other hand. "Stop kicking! I've got you! Walk your feet up the side!"

"I'm trying! I'm too cold!"

Sarah had an elbow on the ledge when David barreled into the room a scant second before Tomas, Vlad hard on his heels.

"Fuck!" David dove next to Sergei and helped haul his sister through the window. Sarah threw her arms around Sergei, weak with relief; Vlad hugged her from behind. The rest of the family appeared – Valeria and her boyfriend Adrik, Nikky and Marina, two house staff, and lastly Grandmamá, breathing hard.

"What in God's Holy Name was she doing out there!" Tomas demanded. "I want an answer, now!"

"Knocking," Vlad said innocently. "She slipped climbing in. Sergei caught her." Prayers and curses broke out among the crowd.

Sarah sat on the floor before her legs gave out. She gazed up at Vlad, begging forgiveness. "I wanted to talk to you. Just for a minute. I did it all the time on Sigma Tau. We did that at home when we were young. That was a Fearsome Four trademark."

David frowned on her like poisoned rain. "We aren't kids any more, Sar! We don't run from anything here! What the hell were you thinking? You could have *died*! I've seen you take a beating that would make me scream for mercy, but you're gonna risk your life for being sent to your room? Grow *up*!"

His rejection stung like Father's whip, and left her just as stunned. "I never meant to fall! It took longer than I estimated. I was too cold."

"She walked along the ledge – from her room to here?" Tomas said, astounded. "Barefoot? In February?"

Andrea clutched her chest. "Impossible."

Tomas peered out the boys' window. A window to the girl's room hung open, five or six meters away. He glanced downwards, where light from the rooms below shone out onto the snowcover. There wasn't nearly enough snow on the ground to break a fall from that height.

Nikky stared in unabashed awe. "That is *so* out of orbit!"

"Absolutely stellar," Marina agreed solemnly.

Tomas stood still, dumbfounded. He raised his hands as if trying to push back time itself. "I think we should all be grateful for Sergei's fast reflexes. Perhaps we should concentrate on that thought right now."

Sarah rubbed the feeling back into her fingers. "I'm sorry," she said with one of her best looks of repentance.

"Please. Please do not speak right now." Tomas folded his patience carefully and tucked it into a back corner of his mind lest it escape, too. "In fact, I want you to go downstairs with Valeria, where there are no ledges. Valeria, please take her to my office and sit with her there until I come to get her. I need a few minutes before I can deal with this rationally."

Valeria held out her hand. "Congratulations, Sarah. I think you've actually managed to push one of Tomas's buttons."

With a hug of thanks to Sergei and a lingering sad look at Vlad, Sarah left obediently, knowing she was *deep* in the compost this time.

* * *

"All right, everyone. Show's over." Tomas waved them toward the door. "Everyone out. Go."

"This is our room," Vlad reminded him.

"Very well. Please go to Sarah's room and shut her window for me."

He walked out to the second floor lounge on rubbery knees and sat, head in his hands. Mamá followed. He could feel a headache building fast, one of supernova proportions.

"That child is going to give me a heart attack yet. I don't know whether to be happy she wasn't hurt, or irate over her disobedience."

Andrea arched an eyebrow in disdain. "You seem rather determined to jeopardize your health. You're out of your element, Tomas. You're a well-meaning executive, not an animal tamer. You need to step back and reexamine your involvement. Should you fall ill with stress, who will step in to keep that creature in order? You can't expect John to do it; he has a business and family of his own. This is your project."

"Actually, it's more of a joint endeavor," he mumbled, rubbing the tension from his face. "Anyway, it's my concern, not yours. If you'll excuse me, I must go and consult with my fellow ringmaster."

"Thank you, Valeria, Adrik," Tomas said as he entered his office. "I'll take it from here."

"We'll stick around down here, just in case," Valeria said as they left.

Sarah sat on the back sofa, legs pulled up under her skirts so she could hug them. Her feet now boasted a pair of Val's warm socks.

"Over here," Tomas ordered, pointing to one of the chairs before the desk. After a pause, Sarah scurried over and threw herself in the chair.

He sat in his work chair, spinning around to face her with such hard-edged authority even Mamá would have sat down and shut up. "I can't tell you how absolutely incensed I am. I just don't have the words. If it wasn't for Sergei, you'd be dead, or close to it. Do you understand that?"

The head nodded.

"Words! I expect to be answered."

Sarah observed him through her bangs. "Yes, sir."

"I consider myself a fair man. You lied to me, I gave you a simple penalty of limited duration, and you've chosen to disregard that. I cannot look the other way, Sarah. I will have discipline. I expect my orders to be followed, without question. That's the way it is, the way it has been, and the way it will be tomorrow, as long as I draw breath. If you disagree with a decision, I expect objections to be brought up in a timely manner, either verbally or in writing, but my final decision *is* final, and it *will be obeyed*. Do you understand that? Repeat it to me."

"I am required to do whatever you say, unless I discuss objections with you beforehand, and I must accept the final answer."

"Correct. If you cannot, do you know what happens?"

"I have to leave."

"That is not my first choice, but it may be a reality we'll have to face whether I desire it or not, if I ever, *ever* see another stunt like that. Risks like that show that you are unable to accept limits, that you still act before you think, and that your actions are still placing you and others in mortal danger."

"I never meant to fall."

"What you mean and what you do are different things, Sarah!" Tomas erupted. "You *meant* to charge a handweapon for entertainment

157

purposes, but you created a potentially devastating explosive device. You *meant* to scare your father, but you risked the lives of seven people in the process. Intent is only a portion of action! If I swerve my flyer with the intent to avoid an air pocket and clip another flyer that crashes and kills six people, no one gives an atmospheric *damn* what my intentions were! Can you understand that?"

"Yes, but I just wanted to see Vlad for a minute … "

Tomas's shoulders sagged. "I don't care, Sarah. A punishment is not meant to be pleasant. It's supposed to make you remember that something *un*pleasant will happen when you do something undesirable. Because you cannot accept a simple punishment, I'm afraid I'm going to have to become much more severe."

The purple-blue eyes widened with fear. "Where will they take me?"

"I'm not that mad – yet. The problem does not seem to be the punishment – obviously, you were unhappy with my choice, which was the point. The problem is you are blatantly disregarding my authority, being disrespectful to me, and refusing to cooperate. I cannot, and will not, accept that. I have worked very hard to make this transition as easy as possible for you, but all I seem to create is dishonesty, and a subtle but distinct refusal to cooperate on the smallest of matters."

Tomas tossed his hands up in disgust. "I don't know what to do with you, Sarah! I have exhausted any logical means I know to get you to play by the rules. John is just as stumped. Neither of us wants to resort to putting you into lock-down residential treatment. It's come down to you. If you can't cooperate, I will be forced to take things to the next level, and there's not one person in this house who wants to see it go that far."

Sarah tugged the ends of the torn dress bodice closer over her blouse, and shook her head in silent agreement.

"John and I will give you one last chance. And to increase the likelihood of success, I will be consulting an expert in problematic adolescent behavior." The head lifted, just a little. Tomas caught the hint of sly grin, the faint chuckle to herself, saw the plan forming of how she would outwit the next challenge.

Figure out what she values most, then hit her hard where it hurts, John had advised him. There had to be something more valuable and less accessible than the boys, and Tomas thought he just might know what. He swung the chair around to face the computer screen.

"Computer: outgoing hyperspace message, video feed. Sender: Tomas Ivanov, imprint address. Destination: Kirushenko, Dmitri, Gandron Rehabilitation Center, Prima Vega, number …"

"What are you doing?" Sarah demanded.

"Consulting my expert. Perhaps you'd like to tell him yourself, so I don't accidentally omit the part about intent."

The look on her face was sheer panic. "You can't do that! His ban on calls isn't up! He's got six days left!"

"I will ask that it be overridden on the basis of family emergency. I can do that, and I do consider a second near-fatal experience to warrant emergency action." He returned to the computer. "Gandron Rehabilitation Center … "

"Wait! Stop! Computer, override!" Sarah called out. She ran around the desk and knelt before Tomas, the two remaining fasteners to the dress bodice straining. Tremors set in. "You can't do that!"

"I most certainly can."

"NO! You don't understand!" One hand slipped over the desktop to feel for the master power control of the computer; Tomas saw it, and shoved the hand away each time she tried.

"You can't tell him I did this! It would upset him! (*shove*) I promised him I'd behave! Please, please don't tell him I slipped up! Please, Uncle Tomas! (*shove*) I'll take whatever punishment you decide! I'll do anything! I'll follow your words to the letter! I'll – I'll write you a thousand-page apology! (*shove*) I'll – I'll clean all the laundry in the house! I'll scrub the kitchen with an eyelash brush! *Please, please, please*, don't tell Dimi I was bad!" Her hands left the computer and grabbed entreatingly at his.

"Control yourself!" he barked. She folded herself in, forehead to the floor, one arm trembling. "You brought every bit of this on yourself. You have no one to blame but you."

"I know that. *Please* give me one more chance! I won't mess up! *Please* don't tell Dimi!" She began to sob.

"Why? What will Dmitri recommend?"

"I - I don't know. He's already going to be so angry at me for sending him to rehab; if I make him any angrier, he won't come back and get me. *Please,* Mr. Ivanov! I won't ever go near a window again."

Abandonment. Tomas rubbed a finger over his lip. He'd stumbled on a weak spot, a very sore one, but how to exploit it to his advantage without damaging the girl?

"I'm not playing games, Sarah. If this is another lie … "

"I swear, sir! On Viktor's grave out there, I mean every word. I don't want to add a single bad thought to the burden Dmitri carries. You've been every bit as nice as you've said, I've been every bit as bad, and I will strive extra hard to do everything just as I'm told. Please don't tell him."

Tomas glared, long and harsh. "Computer, disregard message; end.

This is your last chance, Sarah. One refusal, just one, and I *will* contact Dmitri, and skinning yourself alive will not stop me. One more incident and I will request Dr. Carver find space for you on the residential floor of the clinic until such time as he can assure me you are able to accept limits and are not a danger to yourself. Is that understood?"

Sarah wiped her nose on her knee. "Clearly, sir. Thank you."

Fifteen

Sarah crawled back into herself, lest she feel inclined to be bold. She had no doubt her additional punishment was designed as a test of her commitment to keeping her word. She applied her stubbornation to it, determined to show she could not be defeated. In addition to an extension on her original punishment, she spent any unscheduled time from eight in the morning to eight at night sitting on a hard chair before the security cameras in the foyer with a sign around her neck. The first day it said *Disobedient*. The second day it said *Dishonest*. The third day she was *Disrespectful*. Punishment forbid her to speak when on the chair, so she used the time to go through facts in her head, thinking about her upcoming exemption exams. She got the point, Tomas' word was Law, but it affected her brother and sister even more. She knew she had Vlad's heartfelt sympathy, but the punishment scared the daylights out of Nikky and Marina, who watched with horrified empathy from the shadows of the stairs, and slipped her candies whenever they walked by. After three days Sarah was clear, but her bedroom windows were now locked.

One problem solved, but a world of them to go. John read her presentation paper and judged it sound. He helped her put the final copy together, along with a written recommendation Commander Ti'onam had given her, and helped her submit it.

"You realize it can take a year or more to see it published, even if they accept it?"

Sarah sighed. "I know. If Commander Ti'onam hadn't been so insistent, it would still be just a bunch of notes at the bottom of my bag. I can wait."

The university plan moved quicker. Sarah took her first mathematics exam – and passed. If all went right, she'd take exams over the next four months and her standing would be decided by the end of summer program. Academically, John knew Sarah was unstoppable. Emotionally was another story.

John's stylus dropped from his fingers to the desk with a frustrated *thunk*. "I don't know. By her rationale, she grew up happy, Valeria hated her, Saint Dmitri rescued her, they fell into a black hole for seven years, and you pulled her out by accident five weeks ago. I know she remembers. Every now and then she'll let something slip, but before I can get a word in, she's onto another subject or another activity, or she recants."

"She admits to studying during that time," Tomas said. "Perhaps that's a way around it."

John looked uncertain. "She'll discuss academics, but she's still holding something back. She looks forward to the exams, but I think she's after a validation of what she's done rather than a step toward more education. She won't commit to anything beyond the next seven weeks."

"Until Dmitri returns."

"Based on the reaction you described and their interplay at the starbase, I'd say she's biding her time. He told her to behave. She's waiting for the next instruction."

"Will that include 'go back to bed and go to sleep'?"

"I don't get that, either." John slumped over his desk. "She should be sleeping like a rock."

Tomas shrugged. "Not one night. I've found her in the hall, her doorway, the media room, under the desk in the library, and once under the dining room table. She sleeps in a bedroom only when the boys are home, and that probably isn't more than four or five hours, tops."

"With what she's already on, she can't possibly be fighting off the medication. And you're positive she's not countering it with something? Caffeine tablets? Anything from the boys? Have you checked her room?"

"No. I've always treated the children's bedrooms as their territory. I've never invaded their privacy like that."

"You might have to, in this case. Sarah's not simple; she's highly intelligent and strongly motivated. If she's dead set against a sleep-inducer, then you can bet your stock portfolio she'll find a way around it. Go over your routine again, step by step."

"I hand her the pill, she puts it in her mouth, drinks a glass of water, puts the glass back down ... "

"And the glass is completely empty?"

"Yes," Tomas insisted. "She allows me to search her mouth. I've never yet found any traces of the tablet. Then she drinks more water. She says they leave a bitter taste on her tongue."

"That's different. She usually prefers fruit juice with tablets so she can't taste them. How much water does she drink?"

Tomas raised an eyebrow. "Goodness. Close to a liter, I think. She claims juice makes the taste worse. They don't smell odd, but they must taste really awful."

"They're not bad at all." John tapped his fingers, thinking. "In fact, she specifically requested them orange flavored. A liter? What's she trying to do, dilute them? No, that wouldn't work. The kidneys would filter the water and everything would concentrate again in the bloodstream. What's

162

she doing with the water?" he wondered.

"What does she do after she's done? Bathe? Play? Exercise?"

Tomas hung his head. "The first few nights, she hid in the downstairs lavatory and cried so hard she nearly made herself sick. I felt so damned monstrous, making her go through that. Once, she gagged so hard I thought she'd vomit right there. I haven't paid attention the last few nights. I'm sure she's not far from a lavatory, though, after drinking water like that."

"That's it!" John shouted. He knocked against the desk so hard the computer screen sprang to life, blinking an options menu. "She's throwing them up! She's distending her stomach with water so she feels sick, then making herself vomit. All that water would come back easily. I told you she's a cagey pup! Now we just have to prove it."

* * *

Sarah swallowed her bedtime tablet in her uncle's office and chased it with an entire pitcher of water. She endured the required search, which had become briefer and briefer as nothing materialized. Stomach almost audibly sloshing with water, she made a beeline for her room, but Galina sat at the bottom of the stairs discussing wedding details with Grandmamá, blocking her way. Sarah sauntered around the corner to the large guest restrooms near the lounge and ballroom. She slipped into the farthest privacy stall, knelt before the sanitary, and stuffed three fingers deep into the back of her throat.

A knock on the door of the lavatory disrupted her.

"Sarah?" Tomas called. "Are you all right?"

"Perfectly fine! I'll be right out!" The fingers disappeared once more, and she gagged as quietly as she could.

"Give it up, Sarah," said a familiar voice, very close by. "I already figured it out." Carver peered over the divider from the next stall.

Sarah ignored him, successfully purging herself of the medication.

"All right, don't, then," he shrugged as Tomas entered the lavatory. "There's plenty more where that came from. I was right, Tomas. I guarantee she hasn't had a single dose yet."

Sarah wiped her mouth on the back of her sleeve. "And I won't. No tranquilizers."

"One way or another, you need to sleep, Sarah. Unless you're willing to get to the bottom of it, I'm afraid they're necessary. I hoped this would work. I don't think putting you on inpatient for a night or two is going to help."

Sarah slammed out of the stall; John exited his. "I really hate you, you know."

"Nah, I don't think you hate me," John replied easily. "I think you're just really, really angry at me right now."

Trapped in deceit, Sarah was in no mood for psychotherapy. "You think you're so smart because you hold power over me! It's my body and my life and my choice, and I will fight that point in court if I have to!" She glared at Tomas. "Or am I not allowed access to legal services?"

Tomas hesitated. "I would have to check the procedure with your court advisor. It would put me in a very bad position, but I won't prevent you, if you so choose."

John steered her toward the door. "Come on. Let's sit and talk this out."

"The answer's no!" Sarah spun and shoved her doctor-friend away.

"Sarah!" Tomas said sharply.

"Back off, Tomas." Carver pointed him to a corner. "No matter what happens, stay out of it. This is directed at me. Leave the room if you have to."

To Sarah, he beckoned, "You want to get into this? Let's do it. Either take the pills, or give me a reason to justify backing off."

"Because I said so, that's why! I'm perfectly fine without them. You used to believe me on those things."

John reached a hand to turn her toward the door, but Sarah swung a fist to block him. Working with the mentally and emotionally unstable, Carver, unlike Tomas, had long been trained to expect the possibility of violence. He grabbed the fist and spun her around until her back was against him. He crossed her arms so her hands were under the opposite elbows, hugging herself, while he gripped her wrists to hold them there. Sarah shrieked, she kicked violently at his shins, she swung her head backwards to smash him in the face, but John knew how to work the hold. Try as she might, Sarah was stuck.

"Give me a reason," John demanded, straining but in control. "Nightmares?"

"NO!" Sarah screeched, fighting to get a hand free. "Because I don't want it! Why isn't that good enough?"

"This is stupid, Sarah. It's getting us nowhere. If I let go, can we discuss this rationally?" The head nodded, and he released her.

Tomas braced as the girl shot towards him on her hands and knees, but he was more surprised to have her take refuge behind him, hugging his shins.

John brushed his hair back with his fingers, panting. "Now, what kind of compromise can we reach?"

* * *

Tomas sat up late, waiting for the call to go through. He and John had petitioned the court to waive the forty-five day ban on outside contact for new detainees, and it had been approved that morning. It was the last resort. The current compromise amounted to little more than Sarah agreeing to stay in her room at night. She'd been hiding, locked in her bathroom, and possibly sleeping on the carpet there. He doubted it was any more sleep than she'd been getting, but at least it was in her room.

Dmitri was allowed calls in just three days, but Tomas couldn't wait. The calls could not be for pleasure, though. For three days, they had to be in regard to Sarah.

The hyperspace call patched through three different departments. **ATTENTION: MONITORED TRANSMISSION** lit up in red print at the bottom of the screen. Dmitri's face appeared at last.

"Man! You look like Hell," Dmitri said. His skin was deep-space pale, his hair close-cut, and he wore a prison-issued T-shirt. "I'll give you credit; I expected the white flag long before this. She's really tearing you apart, huh?"

"No no no," Tomas said quickly. "She's doing quite well. I haven't had nearly as much trouble as I expected. John and I are hoping you can help us with just one question: *How in the Lord's name do you get her to sleep!*" He went over the problem.

"She goes through that sometimes, but she's never strayed farther than my room. What's her room like?"

Tomas described it for him.

"There's your problem, right there," Dmitri said. "It doesn't matter who's next door, it's who's not right *there*. She's trapped. She's either got to be protected by someone she trusts, have a secure lock, or have an avenue of escape. She's used to going out the window if she has to."

A light went on in Tomas's head. "She's already tried that. But if she's that worried, why doesn't she simply lock the door?"

"*You* have the master key. A lock won't stop *you*. If she sleeps, who's left to watch the door? Either find a way for her to lock the door, or accept the fact she isn't going to sleep much. Let her nap on Vlad's bed. She can live quite a while on minimal sleep. Don't make such a fuss about it. Accept it, and she'll settle down. I guarantee it."

"Thank you. That's worth a try. Tell me, Dmitri – did she horde food in strange places for you, too? It's driving the help crazy."

"It means she's worried about something. She may be afraid she's going to miss a meal, and keeps food hidden in case of emergency. You're not slipping medications in her food, are you? Don't ever do that. She'll stop eating completely."

"No, I never have. I don't understand why, though. There's always food available, though she never does more than pick at it. Thank you for the insight. I'm sure it will help."

Dmitri hid behind concern. "Hey – let me know how it works out? I mean, it's really good to hear a friendly voice, you know?"

"You can count on it," Tomas swore. "Thank you again."

"Thank *you*, for trying. Just – tell her to hang in there, okay?" The young man on the screen blinked extra hard and turned his face. "It won't be much longer. I'm glad she's trying, at least. Tell Vlad to take extra special care of her for me, okay?"

Tomas smiled. "He couldn't do better."

* * *

Sarah barged into the study without knocking. She marched directly to the desk, where Tomas was examining projected manufacturing expenses on Alpha Mensa. She stood before him, twitching and grimacing, something that hadn't been much of a problem for weeks.

"What can I do for you, Sarah?"

"Why is there a lock on my door? That new one up at the top? What is that for? Who put it there? What punishment has been created now? What's going to happen to me? *I want to know!*"

"I thought you might sleep more comfortably if you had greater control over the door to your room," Tomas explained. "Therefore, while we were out this morning, I had Assam install a lock that is not controlled by the computer. You must physically unlock it from the inside to allow passage. However," he pointed out, "it would be irresponsible of me to not have a system in place in case of an emergency. Should you fall, be injured, or be ill, there must be a way in besides an anti-grav platform to the window." He opened a drawer in his desk and withdrew a key tag on a holder. He held it out to her.

"There are two keys to that lock. I will give one to you, which you will then give to Dmitri when he returns. The other will be kept by Vladimir, which he must keep on himself at all times. Should you need help, he is the only person who will be able to override that lock. Not David, not Sergei, not the staff, not me.

"Of course," Tomas added, "your part of this bargain is that the lock

166

is to be used only during sleep hours. If you start locking yourself in there to avoid people or situations, the lock will be discontinued. And, of course, in non-emergency situations, you must unlock it upon request. Is that acceptable?"

Sarah stared at her uncle in utter amazement, the tremors and tics resolving. She had spoken to no one of the problem, not even Vladimir. Dimi would understand, but he wasn't here, and she couldn't explain it to him for two more agonizing days. Somehow, some blessed way, Uncle Tomas had figured it out. He wasn't laughing at her, he wasn't mad, he wasn't making fun. He accepted her fear, and simply wanted to help. Sarah didn't know whether to laugh or cry.

"Yeah," she whispered. "That's perfectly perfect." She ran around the desk to give Tomas a brief but crushing hug. *"Thank you!"*

Sixteen

"Sarah, please come to my office immediately," Tomas called on the household intercom. She appeared in less than a minute, apprehensive.

He waved a hand toward his viewscreen. "You have a call on a hyperspace channel. Someone wishes to speak with you."

Hyperspace? Who would speak to her via hyperspace? Every one she knew was here in Russia. Everyone except …

"Dimi!" she shouted, throwing herself into Tomas' chair. "Moons and Stars! Dimi!" Tears of joy flooded her eyes without permission.

Tomas laughed. "I thought you might want to take this one directly. Talk!" He left her to her privacy.

"Hey, Kid," Dmitri said with half a smile. He didn't seem mad, but he wasn't overflowing with happiness, either. "Behaving for me?"

What Dimi didn't know wouldn't hurt him. Sarah smiled so hard she feared her jaw might break. "I'm trying my very hardest," she swore. "What did they do to your *hair!*" Dmitri's beautiful black hair, for years so shaggy to keep up with the longer style on Sigma Tau Ceti, had been shaved within a centimeter of his head. He looked so *strange!*

He rubbed a regretful hand over the stubble. "They don't care much for style here. We're all supposed to look and dress like each other, because, after all, we're no better than anybody else."

"But you *are* better than everyone else there," Sarah declared. "You're the only one who's my brother."

"I know. Most of us are here for really stupid things, but I've got the best connections. I've got the shortest sentence of anyone here by three full months."

"You're still coming back in forty-four days?"

"Forty-four and counting." He squinted into the transmission camera. "Why the hell are still you wearing your old dresses? You're on *Earth*, for cryin' out loud! You hated those dresses."

Sarah's shoulders crept toward her ears, and she hung her head. "I wanted to ask you about that. I didn't have enough money to buy anything new, and none of my old things fit. Uncle Tomas offered to buy me clothes, but I didn't know if I was supposed to accept."

"He's your *guardian*, you asteroid! Right now it's *his* responsibility. Our money's frozen until I get out of here. Tell him to keep a separate account for you and I'll reimburse him when I get there. Just don't go overboard, okay?"

"Thank you, Dimi. Did you get the mail I sent? I sent fourteen so far."

"Yeah, I got 'em. Thanks. They helped, I guess. Guess you're living the high life, huh?"

Sarah caught the sarcasm. "No, not really," she said soberly. "Uncle Tomas has more than a page of rules I have to follow. I have to have a 'competent supervisory escort' if I want to set one centimeter beyond the yard. That amounts to Katya, John, the twins, or Uncle Tomas. Even David has to get special permission if he wants to take me for a walk. I don't think Uncle Tomas trusts him too much."

"I wouldn't. I know what kind of trouble he gets into. I'll probably get stuck with the same rules. How bad are they?"

"Not bad. Mostly just common sense and manners, and remembering to ask first. Talk to me, Dimi? Just – tell me everything about where you are?" Sadness crept over her like cloudshadow. "I'm so, so sorry."

* * *

Tomas found her, pressed against the plastiglass in the balcony doors like a moth yearning to be free. She stared resignedly out beyond the sloping lawn patchy with fading snow, out toward the city, toward the bleak gray sky that poured freezing rain. Only in her mind could she see through the grayness, across the blackness of space to the awful penitentiary that held her brother.

She sensed Tomas peripherally; it didn't hide the fact her face was wet. She held her breath to stop the tears; his hand started to reach out to rub her back, but he shoved it into his pocket. It was these quiet moments that worried him most. In the evenings she was chipper as the sun, helping with schoolwork, playing games with the younger children, or hanging around Vladimir, but during the long days when the others were away, she had too much time to think about the sadder things.

"What's wrong, Little Ghost? Please don't cry. Is it something I can help with?"

She gave the tiniest sniff. "I'm not crying. The weather is bothering my sinuses."

"I see. Well, I have a variety of sinus remedies downstairs, if you'd like. Or you could mention it to John. Perhaps he'll know something more appropriate."

"No, thank you. It will cure itself, I'm sure, in forty-four days."

"Ah. Well, we're at the halfway point. It's not much longer." He watched her struggle to stay strong in his presence, proud, dignified, and

169

oh-so-haunted looking.

"Sarah, it makes me very sad when I see you in discomfort. I know that when you used to feel... uncertain, you liked Dmitri to hold you. I realize the boys are at school, but – I want you to know that, if you ever needed ... *reassurance* like that, I am available to fill in for them. I know not to restrain you against your will."

The watery purple eyes closed for several seconds, then opened. They flickered sideways. "I thank you for the offer, sir, and I wish to express my sincere appreciation at the sentiment, but I cannot accept. It is not that I do not trust your touch. It's just that any pressure of ... *that* sort right now, would run a grievous risk of worsening my sinus condition. However, my sinuses ache only when I feel weak. I would be deeply grateful if I could draw upon some of your strength – through my hand." Her fingers twisted outward a centimeter.

"Of course." He slid his hand into her hers and gave it a friendly squeeze. "How's that?"

The crushing grip in return almost made him pull away in anger, until he realized it was wordless instruction. He matched the power of her grip, and sure enough, the crunch on his hand eased, the shoulders slackened in relief. She could relax her hold on life; he'd taken over the burden.

"Better?"

The head nodded against the glass. They stayed that way for several minutes, watching the cold rain turn the snow to slush, hands locked in an unspoken contract of trust.

"It rained in Vandijoc," Sarah said wistfully. "The rainy season lasted for months. It was cold then, too. Sometimes it would rain for days and days. Sometimes we'd get a break, and the sun would come out before the clouds returned. My room was upstairs. You could lie awake all night, listening to the rain on the roof. Sometimes it would pound so hard it would wake you out of a sound sleep. If it stormed, the lightning would highlight every crack in the walls. My room is upstairs here, but I can't hear the rain at all."

"You've got an extra floor above you," Tomas reminded her. "There's a powerplant over your head, and insulation and solar shingles and converters. My apartment is underground; I can't hear anything. If I'm not in the apartment, I'm in my office, and if I'm not there, I'm either en route in a transport somewhere or sitting in a conference room. I never pay attention to the weather."

After a moment, he unlocked the balcony doors. "Come on. Maybe it's time I remember."

On the balcony, the temperature hovered two degrees above freezing,

170

and a brisk wind gusted up the front lawn. It drove the icy rain backward under the roof, stinging like needles against them. They stood for several minutes, listening to the rain hammer the roof of the balcony in windy waves, until Tomas felt thoroughly chilled and damp, and brought her in.

"Perhaps you should go downstairs and get some tea to warm yourself," he cautioned as he locked the doors. "You don't need to fall ill again."

Sarah nodded. She still looked haunted, but the tears were gone. "Thank you. I have Dimi's permission to allow you to purchase some different clothes for me. If you would kindly keep track of the amount, he will reimburse you upon his return."

Was that what she had been waiting for, all this time? Dmitri's permission? Tomas felt incredibly stupid at the simplicity of the solution. "Of course. I could take you into the city right now, or if you'd prefer, we can wait until Vladimir is home and take him with us."

Sarah smoothed the limp skirt of the worn green work dress from Vandijoc, Pelonishala, Sigma Tau Ceti IV. There were soil stains on the hem that nothing had been able to eradicate, a repaired tear where she'd caught the pocket on a tree branch, grease stains on the front of the bodice, and the color had faded with the modern cleaning methods. Besides the fact it was cold and uncomfortable. A smile sweetened her face.

"Right now would be fine, thank you, sir. I hate dresses."

All this time ... All the tantrums over simple things like boots ... merely because she wanted permission first ... and she hated the damned dresses as much as Mamá. "We both need jackets before we go. Last one to the side door is a black hole," he said with a twinkle in his eye, and they ran in different directions.

* * *

"It was like a revelation!" Tomas said to John. "In that one instant, I had the key to the code. I understand now, how you call her an enigma. Nothing she says means what it does. Every word means something else; every idea is cloaked in symbolism. I think Dmitri is merely her translator, and I have a feeling everything will fall into place once he's returned. When I met them on the starbase, she did nothing unless he told her, and she did whatever he said. I don't think she can make a decision for herself, or at least won't until she can run it by him. I wish I'd realized it weeks ago."

John grinned. "I think you're right. Sarah's never simple. She'll drop clues, rattle off whole speeches, but a lot of times it's not what she's saying that's important, but what she's not saying. Sometimes that means more. You have to think in reverse.

"Congratulations, anyway," John leaned over the desk with an outstretched hand. Tomas shook it with a puzzled expression.

"If she held your hand for fifteen minutes, asked you to help her like that, then you're in," John explained. "You made it to her inner circle. You've officially gained her trust, tentative as it may be. Now the responsibility starts. There are levels to her inner circle as well – different levels of expectation. You have to maintain your position. Fail her now, and you'll never regain that trust."

"Talk about pressure," Tomas said half-heartedly. "What is she looking for?"

"I don't know. Everyone is different. We're all individual pieces to the puzzle, and the picture is her. David's in the inner circle, but she doesn't trust him with feelings. I'm close to the bull's eye, but she won't discuss some things with me, like romance or biology." He drew concentric circles on his compad to illustrate his point, filling in names as he spoke. "She'll discuss those with Katerina, but she won't discuss those missing years. Vladimir's able to touch that center seat, but she's very protective of him; she mothers him, and won't say anything she thinks would upset him.

"I don't know for sure where Dmitri stands, but I have a gut feeling he's got his foot on that center throne, and I wouldn't be the least surprised to find Sarah kneeling in front of it. There are numerous cases of people who are kidnapped who then fall in love with their kidnapper. I'm not saying she's 'in love' with him; more like hero worship. He was kind to her during a very difficult time, she transferred her trust to him, and in her eyes he can do no wrong. I've noticed some of that blindness in her denial of his guilt in the EPSAR incident.

"You know what you're doing," John encouraged. "Look at this morning – you realized the problem, but accepted it without comment. You didn't demand conversation or action or bore her with unsolicited advice. You let her take the lead simply by showing unconditional support. You lowered yourself into her well of despair and shared the grief without trying to change it. Show her there's a rope, but don't force her to climb it. That's the support she needs. She has a lot more self-awareness of her condition than she lets on. She usually knows why she's upset, and she knows what will ease it, and she knows if she can just manage to hold on, the pain will go away. Knowing that you're aware of what she's going through is a tremendous help. I think she's about to soar."

"Let's hope it's a trend," Tomas agreed.

Seventeen

S oar Sarah did. Knowing Dmitri would still speak to her, that he wasn't chained to a wall in some underground lair with moldy bread and sewer water, Sarah unfolded like a blooming rose. Tomas watched with delight as she shopped for clothing, running from item to item, excited by each new thing she encountered. In no time at all, in the first shop they tried, she found dozens of new items, from sweaters to gloves to hats to four pairs of shoes and two pairs of boots, and more clothes than she could carry. There were no tantrums, no denials, no tears or tremors, just smiles and laughter and joy. *And all it had taken was a word.* Tomas shook his head in amazement, hardly able to keep up.

She asked permission to wear one of the outfits home, clapping her hands when he said yes. He watched as she bid goodbye to her green dress, kissed it, and then asked the sales clerk to dispose of it. Once again Tomas felt the impact of the symbolism. Permission for new clothes – Earth clothes – meant Sarah wasn't going to be leaving anytime soon. She had Dmitri's permission to stay.

Sarah raced into the house, unable to contain herself. Grandmamá stopped her, a reprimand for running poised to leap from her tongue, but the girl never gave her the chance. She hugged the old woman, lifting her right off the ground, and gave her a kiss on her cheek.

"I can wear pants again!" Sarah cried, spinning around to show them off. Before Grandmother could recover, Sarah raced up the stairs to find Vladimir.

"Tomas!" Andrea pounced as he came down the hall. "Whatever you fed that child, it contained far too many stimulants."

A week went by, without incident. Tomas waited daily for the other shoe to fall, for a change in mood, for a word to be misinterpreted and set off some chain reaction, for the happiness to break, but nothing happened. Dmitri's weekly call came through on time. Sarah was waiting, full of happy chatter, eager to tell him about her new wardrobe, the latest thing Nikky had shown her, the difficulty of the test she took. Her spirits stayed high.

A second week slipped by, and Tomas uncrossed his fingers. He had started to believe in miracles when the boys put his faith in all of them to the test.

* * *

David pointed over Sergei's shoulder to the chart on the computer screen. "What about here? I don't have anything there."

Sergei twisted his bottom lip in his fingers. "I'm usually in the research library then, from 6:30 to 10:00 or so."

"Perfect. She likes that kind of stuff. Just have her back to my room by 11:00."

"Why do you get her every night? We can swap on Wednesday."

"Like hell we will! You've got a freak of a roommate; I don't."

"Like Tolya's going to bother her ... ."

"That's a risk I'm not willing to take, and if you took your head out of the dictionary, you'd agree with me."

Sergei bristled with thinning patience. "My friends are not freaks! Fine! She stays with you. At least I don't have to kiss my friends' asses to make them like me. Maybe you should warn Sarah about that, so she might possibly retain some respect for you. Then I get her for dinner on Tuesday *and* Wednesday."

"So she can get sick eating with those Spaceballs?"

"Look, you want to do this or not?" Sergei snapped. "You're not having Sarah every night and every meal as well. I want equal time, or it's not going to happen."

"What's not going to happen? How am I going to be with David every night?"

The brothers turned to see Sarah and Vlad enter the room, hand in hand.

"Why won't you be at school?" Sarah demanded.

The boys exchanged glances. "We were planning a surprise for you," David admitted. "We want to bring you up to school with us on Sunday. We're trying to work out all the details before we run it past Uncle Tomas."

"We figured you could come to class with us for a week, see what you think," Sergei said. "Get a feel for everything, so you'll know what to expect."

"Absolutely not!" Vladimir forbid. "She's not leaving here for an entire week. It's bad enough when she visits Kat, and that's here in town. She stays here with me, where she belongs. Besides, Uncle Tomas would never allow it. And she has to see John. She can't skip therapy."

"Take colder showers," David sneered. "I already asked if she can take a vacation from all that head-shrinking, and John said as long as he knows about it, it's fine."

"What do you think, Sar?" Sergei asked. "Would you come up to school with us? If Uncle Tomas says it's okay?"

"I'm glad somebody's asking my opinion." Sarah sat uneasily on Sergei's bed. "I don't know. It's kind of far. What if I have a problem? What if I get into trouble without meaning to, and it gets back to my court advisor?"

David put his arm around her. "Nothing's going to happen. We've got it all worked out. You'll be with me or Sergei every minute. Meals, classes, study breaks – you can meet my friends, Serg can take you to boring-ass poetry readings, and I'll take you sight-seeing in the old quarter. It'll be orbital."

"And when you get sick of David, you can stay with me," Sergei said. "I'll take the floor and you can have my bed. What do you say? If Uncle Tomas says yes, will you come with us?"

"I don't know." Sarah turned to Vladimir for advice, but he shook his head firmly. "I mean, I like the idea of going to classes with you, but …"

David slapped his leg. "Then it's settled. Let's go run it past The Boss."

* * *

Tomas approached the idea with all the caution of a risky business proposal. "Who's idea was this?"

"Me and Sergei's," David said, proud of himself.

"Is this something you'd *like* to do?" Tomas asked Sarah. He could tell by the way she held her eyes to the floor that it wasn't. He knew David; the boy's intensity could be overwhelming, and he knew Sarah rarely crossed her brothers, whether she agreed with them or not. Vladimir stood behind her chair, massaging her shoulders and shaking his head for her.

"It would be interesting to see what the classes are like," Sarah said, but she wasn't overly enthusiastic.

Tomas reviewed the boys' schedule. By the time he finished grilling them, the notes had moved from a simple class schedule to a ten-page minute-by-minute itinerary that looked more like a plan for a complex military exercise than a campus visit, but he knew how important details were to Sarah's peace of mind.

Tomas leaned back in his chair. "I will tell you straight out, I'm not comfortable with this. I would much prefer to bring her up there myself for a day before you try something like this. Moscow is out of state and out of jurisdiction. I am responsible for Sarah's welfare and her behavior. I would be sending an emotionally distressed young girl 650 kilometers with two boys straddling twenty, and trust them to take care of her in a variety of situations that she may or may not be comfortable in, for five days and nights.

"I don't mean that term in a derogatory manner, Sarah," he apologized, "I'm merely trying to convey the seriousness of this venture to your brothers. It's much more complicated than if they took Nikky or Marina with them."

"I understand, sir," Sarah said. "It's not exactly something I can deny."

"We do understand the seriousness of it," Sergei swore. "We just think she might like to try it. It fits with all her goals – peer socialization, educational opportunities, self-confidence … She's barely younger than some of the students."

"I'm aware of that. I didn't say it was a bad idea, just a complicated one. If Sarah wishes to go, I will give my preliminary permission, *but*: there will be a number of modifications. I will come up to the Moscow offices Monday morning and work from there while Sarah is with you. She will check in every twelve hours; at the very least, before bed and at breakfast. She is not to be out of your rooms past eleven p.m.. And I will have lunch with her on Wednesday myself. If she feels she has had enough excitement, or if I feel she is under too much stress, I will bring her home then. If all is well, she may stay until you return on Friday. Is that clear?"

"Wednesday is more than long enough," Vladimir said. "She needs time to work up to that."

Sarah reached over her shoulder and patted his hand. "I think it'll be okay, as long as I have the Wednesday option available. It's only two nights more. Is that okay?"

Vlad frowned. "I guess. I mean, I wish I could go with you, but I guess I can trust them. You'll call me every day, right?"

"Absolutely! Without fail. I'll tell you everything I learn."

"Then it's settled. Sarah may return to school with you after dinner tomorrow evening," Tomas decreed.

He called the boys into conference on Sunday afternoon. Sarah professed good spirits, but he knew better. Tomas hadn't seen her this upset in a while. She rearranged her meals on her plate, eating nothing. Whenever he saw her, she was wrapped around Vlad, desperate for reassurance. She might want to go, but she wasn't necessarily ready. John had been luke-warm over the idea, but he promised to support Sarah's decision either way.

David and Sergei found their uncle in his office, unusually humorless. He didn't sit down, nor did he offer them a seat. They stood in the middle of the room, not quite sure of anything.

"I want to make certain we understand each other correctly," Tomas said coldly. He stood centimeters before David, staring up from under his nose.

"Do not screw this up, David. I am trusting you with something far more important than a financial investment. If anything happens to that child that adversely affects her, I will hold you personally responsible, and I will make sure the court holds you responsible. Sergei is nineteen; while the same rules to apply to him, by court order he cannot be in charge. You are twenty-one; that responsibility is yours and yours alone. That child is to be treated as if she were as fragile as a soap bubble. You will pay strict attention to her at all times. If she seems upset, you will let her back off immediately."

Tomas circled the pair, watching, waiting to find some slip, some irreverence to make him believe there was a hidden reason for the visit, some possibility that the girl would be put at unnecessary risk, and he would cancel the trip.

"There will be no 'partying' while she is with you. No drinking. No double dating. She will not make plans to call or meet your friends at a later date, nor will she receive calls from them. No one; I repeat, *no one*; of *any* race or gender, except the two of you, is to be in the room with her at night, nor will you leave her alone, not for a second. You will keep her in sight at all times. There will be no cruiser racing, no airbike riding, no riding in private vehicles that you are not piloting, no target shooting at a weapons range. You and you alone are responsible for making sure she takes her oral medications, David," Tomas emphasized. "John will check her blood levels on Friday night; if she's off by so much as a vitamin, you will be held accountable. If she refuses, you will notify me immediately so I may document it. If she wishes to leave somewhere, or call home, or hide in your room, you will honor her wishes without hesitation, no matter how difficult a personal or academic situation it may put you in. Am I being received and recorded on a clear channel?"

"Yes, sir," David nodded, and Sergei replied, "Absolutely, sir."

"You can't hold us responsible for something out of our control, though," David protested, "like an accident that's not our fault, or ..."

"I will hold you responsible for each and every moment she experiences while she is out of my sight," Tomas ordered with finality. "Don't take her anywhere an accident is likely to happen. A soap bubble, David! Is that understood?"

"Yes, sir." David sighed as any possibility of fun flew out the window.

Tomas smiled at Sarah, hoping some of his optimism would transplant itself onto her. "Good luck. Listen to the boys, do as they say, and remember to call me, morning and night, and any other time you feel you need to talk to me."

"Yes, sir." The tension in Sarah's chin shoved her lower lip into the upper one. She lunged and wrapped her arms around him. "Wednesday, right?" her voice wavered. "You're going to meet me on Wednesday. If I want, I can come back here?"

Tomas felt her trembling, then the harsher, drug-induced shake took over. "I will meet you in David's room at eleven a.m. on Wednesday. We will lunch together, and if you wish, you may return here with me."

"And Vlad will be here?"

"Vlad will be here."

Sarah backed away, a tic in her eye. "You came and got me at the starbase and brought me here. If I want, you'll come and get me in Moscow and bring me back *here*. I know your access number by heart."

"It's not too late to stay if you're not sure about this," Tomas cautioned.

"I can do this. I'll be okay." She turned to Vladimir, hovering by her side. "He came and got me before. He'll be right there in Moscow. He's meeting me on Wednesday. That's less than three days. Sixty-four hours from now. I'll be okay. He said I can come back if I need to in sixty-four hours. I've been to Moscow before. That's still here on Earth. I could walk it if I had to. I could feasibly walk it in ... seventeen days."

"You don't have to walk it," Vlad scoffed. "*I'll* come get you, if you want." He put his arms around her, and she hugged him tight.

"Yo, save some for later," David said. "You're gonna get him all worked up. Come on, we have a two hour flight to make."

Sarah gave Vlad a final squeeze and followed David into his shiny red SkyDevil, where Sergei already waited.

Red!

David placed the ignition tag in the scanner and started the engines. The doors began to descend. As they reached the half-way point, Sarah dove under her door and scrambled to her feet amid the fiery sting of David's curses. Tomas and Vladimir met her on the run, halfway. She clung to Vlad, trembling and shaking.

"I love you," she whispered, kissing his cheek. "Sixty-three hours and fifty-six minutes. I'll be okay." She dashed back to the waiting flyer and

its impatient pilot, flinging herself face down on the rear seat and letting the doors seal her in.

* * *

David opened the door and threw his jacket on the second bed. "This is it. My not-so-loyal roommate moved in with some babe the end of September and I haven't seen him since, so I've got it all to myself.

"Bath's over here. Coldkeeper over there – mostly beer and Booster Juice, help yourself. You probably shouldn't have the beer, though. That bed's yours. We're not allowed food replicators in the rooms – too much energy drain or something. There's an autovend down the hall if you get hungry. What do you think?"

Sarah sat on the spare bed, hugging herself. "It's nice." It *was* a nice room, nicer than a number of places she and Dmitri had lived. David was no better at housekeeping than Dmitri had been; shoes mountained next to the closet, clothing consumed a chair, and the towering stack of research chips and papers and file boxes looked ready to collapse at the first breeze.

"It works." David dropped down in his desk chair and scanned his mail for anything important. "You feel like doing anything, or you just want to crash?"

"I don't care," Sarah replied lifelessly, and curled over her knees.

"You okay?" Sergei asked. "David's flying make you sick?"

"No. We go back on Friday, right?"

"Jesus Flying Christ!" David swore. "Enough already with the Friday shit! We went over that a thousand times on the flight here! If you didn't want to come, you should have said so!"

"What the hell are you yelling at her for?" Sergei growled. "What's the matter, Sar? You look cold. Are you getting sick again? Want me to turn the heat up for you?"

Sarah turned away, forcing the tears back into her eyes. "No."

David saw them. "Hey." He knelt in front of her. "What's the matter? You start crying on me and I'm gonna be in a heap of trouble. I'm sorry for swearing. I didn't mean to scare you or anything."

Sergei put an arm around her. "You don't want to stay here, you can come back with me. If I ask him nice enough, Anatoliy will leave for the night."

Sarah sniffed unconvincingly. "I'm okay. I can do this."

"I know! Why don't you call Vlad?" David suggested. "You should call Uncle Tomas anyway and tell him you got here okay. Talk to Vlad for a while. Tell him a bedtime story, so he'll think you're still there and

179

Galina won't have to walk the halls with him all night."

"I can call Vlad? You *want* me to?"

"Sure! I don't give a damn. Whatever makes you happy." David ordered the computer to set a call. "Just try to keep it under an hour, okay?"

Sarah raced over and sat down. "Show me! Which is the … Here? Okay." The face that answered the call wasn't the one she hoped for, but for the moment, it worked. "Hello, Uncle Tomas! We made it! I'm doing okay, but I like home, too. You're coming to see me on Wednesday, but David still says I'm coming home Friday. Is Vlad there?"

Tomas laughed on the viewscreen. "Slow down, Ghost! Well, you sound better than you did when you left. I'm glad you're okay. I'll await your call in the morning, then, and you can tell me how your night went. I should be in Moscow by nine. I'll get Vladimir for you. Goodnight to all of you, then." Tomas left, and a few seconds later Vlad appeared.

"How was it? What are you …"

Sarah's burst of chatter cut him off. "Oh Vlad! David said I could call you, all on his own! I didn't even have to ask! I miss you. I'm doing okay, though. This building's huge! Have you seen David's room? It's really nice. Uncle Tomas will be coming here in sixty-one hours and forty-three minutes. David still says we're coming home on Friday. Right, David?"

"*Yes!* For God's sakes, *yes!* Keep this up and *I'm* going to send you home on Wednesday." David threw himself down on his bed and pulled the pillow over his head. "Stop it, already."

Sarah went on for twenty minutes before ending the call with another check on Wednesday and Friday.

"Why do you keep asking about Friday?" Sergei asked

Sarah hung her head and sucked her shoulders inward. "Just checking."

"For what? You knew the answer the first twelve or fourteen times."

"To make sure you didn't change your mind."

David's scowl didn't help. "Why the hell would I change my mind? I've been going home every Friday afternoon, save a handful, for seven years. Why would I change that now?"

"You're afraid we'll change our minds and not go back?" Sergei guessed.

Sarah turned away, twitching, hands writhing until she pressed them to her face as the tremor hit.

Sergei's arms wrapped around her, and she leaned against him. "Don't do that. Uncle Tomas will be here on Wednesday. If you're really worried, I'll take you back in the morning. It's kind of late to head back now.

180

We wouldn't get there until after midnight."

"I like that house. I don't want to leave it. Everyone's nice there. I don't want to leave Vlad."

David rose from his bed, features clamped in a mask of smoldering anger. *"What did that bastard do to you?* What kind of fucking head games did he fill you with? I'll kill him!"

He grabbed her by the chin. "You listen to me, and you listen good! No one's keeping you anywhere! You're free to go anywhere you want. The minute you want to go back to Minsk, you tell me and you're on your way. You think we fucking kidnapped you here? Fuck's sake, Sar! What the hell would we do with you up here? I mean, I want you to visit and all, but I don't want you here all the damned time. I got a life to live."

Sarah ripped his hand away. "Don't you speak badly of Him, David Fyodor! You hear? I won't have it! I owe Dmitri my life and then some, and I will not hear Him wronged by another person who knows nothing about it! He did *nothing* bad to me! If this is a sample of what I shall be forced to endure, then take me back right now. I will not have you dishonor Him."

"No one's downgrading Dimi on you," Sergei insisted.

"Speak for yourself," David mumbled. "Fine. We won't talk about it. Now, are you going to stay, or what?"

"Just til Friday, right?" Sarah said with a gleam in her eye.

"Argh!" David pulled his fist back and pretended to aim a blow to her jaw. Sergei pulled her down backwards on top of him, as if she'd been hit, and the three of them dissolved into laughter.

Fear of permanent separation eased, Sarah settled down. Sergei left them at 23:30, and David sent her to bed.

"I've got to get some work done before tomorrow," he said as he sat at his computer.

"I could help you."

"Not on this."

Sarah sat on the side of her assigned bed, watching him. She always helped Dimi with his work, no matter what it was. There was never anything so pressing he couldn't take a moment or two to talk with her. But David seemed intent on his work, and she couldn't think of a single thing to start a conversation that didn't involve a day of the week. David was still David, her rough and ready master of mayhem and she loved him just as he was, but he wasn't … Dimi.

"David?"

"Mm?"

"I know I'm not supposed to share beds, because we're too big now and all, but, could we push the beds together, at least? That way I know you're only an arm's length away if I need you."

David was visibly annoyed, but he got up. "If you want."

Sarah lay in the bed, tired but watching him study. After an hour or so, he shook his head and stretched. He fished in a drawer and retrieved a small bottle. He tipped two tablets out and washed them down with water.

"Are those mine or yours?"

"Why the hell are you still awake?" he snapped, startled. He stuffed the bottle in the drawer. "They're mine! You're not the only one who takes vitamins, you know. I need all that A and E to keep my brain in gear."

"Oh. David? Are you going to bed?"

"Not for a while. Go to sleep."

The promise of classes kept Sarah together in the morning. David hadn't come to bed until three, and slept like the dead. If she were sleeping nearby, Dmitri would wake up if she so much as sighed. She held David's hand most of the night, stretching her arm across the beds, but he never once squeezed it back. She got up and dressed at seven, but David wouldn't rise. She made her call home and spoke to Vlad and Tomas. She poked David several more times and he promised to get up, but his head never left the pillow. At eight, he opened an eye, saw the time, and ran from the bed, cursing all way.

"We're gonna be fucking late for class," he growled, stuffing his compad into a carry bag. He grabbed more vitamins from his drawer and swallowed them dry.

"I need my meds before we go," Sarah reminded him.

"Shit! Where the hell did I put them? I know they came with us. Uncle Tomas made sure I had them." He flipped impatiently through a stack of data cards on his desk.

"David, I *need* my meds! I can't go without them."

"What for, anyway? I thought that's what that machine in you is for?" He kicked the pile of shoes, hoping.

"The neuropump manages the panic attacks," Sarah lectured, close at his heels. "The pills control the depression and the obsessive-compulsive behavior, and the vitamins replace things that are depleted by all the other drugs. It's really not a good idea for me to skip doses. Some of those things are carefully balanced and take a long time to get to therapeutic levels, and if I miss them the levels fall and it takes an awful lot of monitoring to get it all back where it's supposed to be, and if I do that the court will want to know why it happened and they won't like that. It will look like I'm not being responsible and stuff."

"I get it! Just shut the hell up." David grabbed his jacket off the bed, found nothing under it, and flung it toward the desk. It hit the edge and slid to the floor with a plop. A small vial rolled out of the pocket.

"That's them!" Sarah squealed with relief. She seized the jacket and stuffed her hand in the pocket, pulling out the containers.

David snatched the pills. "*I'm* in charge of these. And don't you dare give me a hassle about taking them, either."

They met Sergei for lunch at a hidden eatery tucked in the basement level of a student-supply shop. The food was third-rate at best, greasy and oversalted, but Sarah ate every crumb and more, snitching potatoes from her brothers when they weren't looking.

David tipped half his remaining potatoes onto her plate. "Marya's food's a million times better than this, but you never eat seconds on that."

"Because Grandmamá's not here to stare at me," Sarah confessed. "She watches every bite I take, like I'm responsible for her entire food bill. I'd starve to death on what she eats."

"Maybe she's happy to see you eat," Sergei suggested, stealing back a potato cube. "She lost half her stomach to a parasite she picked up on Centauri twenty years ago. She once said she misses being able to have room for dessert every night."

Sarah blushed, seeing the issue in a whole new light. "No one ever told me."

After lunch, Sarah followed Sergei to class. All through school he had recommended readings to her, and she'd hunted down as many as she could. She'd already studied basic philosophy, so Philosophy of Modern Culture was a breeze. There was a guest lecturer for Sergei's writing class: Darwin J. Ionan, author of *Movement in Literature: Fighting Stasis in the Novel: a Historical Approach.* The man spoke no Russian nor Standard English, so there was a perpetual pause every time he spoke as the mechanical translator processed his speech and converted it to Standard Russian. He spoke in a monotone, droning endlessly without pause. If the topic had been interesting, by the end of the lecture he'd managed to hammer it flat by voice alone.

Released from classes for the day, Sergei took her to the art studio. While his official degree would be in literary arts, his secondary concentration was art history, and that included courses in studio arts. While he'd always had crude sketches among his endless writings, it wasn't until he took classes at boarding school that he realized he enjoyed creating art as well as looking at it, and that he wasn't half bad.

From a storage slot, he pulled out the painting he was working on.

"Are you going to have Uncle Tomas hang it in the house when you're done?" Sarah asked.

Sergei choked. "I don't think anyone in the Ivanov household will want this on display." He removed the dust cover.

It was a large canvas, a meter wide. A woman sat, half-reclined, on a bed. Her nude back faced the viewer as she clutched a sheet to her chest with one hand. Long blonde hair poured from her head. Her other hand extended toward the outstretched fingers of another figure. The bearded man was large and rough-looking, dressed like a Cossack in black breeches and a red shirt open to his waist. From his other hand, dark among the shadows, hung a coiled whip. The figures were mostly painted, but the background was still in progress. Only a blind man wouldn't have recognized the figures as their parents.

"I call it *Shooting Stars*. I've given up on trying to make it photo-perfect; I'm not that good," Sergei explained. "I wanted to show a seduction, of lovers meeting secretly at any given time in history. I copied off some pictures Valeria had. If I'd used other faces, I probably would have done them nude. I've drawn nudes before, but there's something about trying to draw your parents naked that kind of screws you up inside. I like this better, anyway."

"I think nudity is supposed to do that." Sarah couldn't remember ever seeing her parents with less than swimwear on, and although she'd been privy to Dmitri's bare backside on several occasions, she couldn't remember seeing a totally naked human since Nikky was three. "It's a very intriguing concept," she said tactfully.

"You've started on the background," a voice behind them observed.

Sarah linked arms with Sergei and pressed close, but the newcomer's eyes studied the painting, not her. He was slender and smartly attired, with light brown hair and a black and white woven bracelet around his wrist.

"What was it your brother called it last week? The Rape of Decency? I'm surprised he hasn't put a fist through it, the way he carried on."

Sergei laughed. "Yeah. David absolutely hates it. Sarah, this is Anatoliy Gennadovitch, my roommate. Anatoliy, this is my younger sister, Sarah-Irina."

Sarah smiled politely for Sergei's sake, but she didn't offer a hand. "Pleased to meet you."

"The pleasure's all mine." Anatoliy stepped back for a better view. "Sergei, you told me your sister was visiting, not a Celestial Spirit incarnate. Your hair's a little short, but such a perfect shade of blonde. And those eyes! Break my heart: tell me that's their natural shade."

Sarah nodded, moving behind her brother since she couldn't get any closer physically. The three of them were alone in the storage area. Anatoliy was sizing her up with a very critical eye, and Sergei didn't seem the least bit concerned. *One finger*, Sarah thought ahead. *One finger on me and I'll floor him!*

"What do you think? Watercolor pink, green, and purple, a Differentia tunic to offset the hair, with magenta hose and sage green Forensi shoes? She's got that I'm-new-here innocence down perfectly."

Sergei laughed as Sarah pulled her sweater tighter and held it shut. "Anatoliy interned last year with a textile manufacturer," he explained. "Now he thinks he's a galaxy-class designer. I think you better switch that to black leggings, a plum tunic, and blue hikers. Underneath that face lies a mercenary who wrestled farm animals for a living."

"Not for a living," Sarah corrected. No one could seem to understand they *didn't* run a farm. "My official job was foreign observer and translator."

Anatoliy didn't hear. "Oh no, no, no. Black and purple is much too harsh – just a bruise looking for a victim." He sighed in distress. "Think about it, dear. You're a little short, but with that face and my designs and connections, I could make you a star on every runway in the Solar system. We'd make a fortune."

Sarah smiled nervously, unable to look higher than Anatoliy's wrap-around boots. She'd never been called short before. She'd always tried to make herself as physically inconspicuous as possible, and knowing the scarred condition of her back, any type of innovative clothing would be out of the question.

"Thank you, but I'm only here for a few days."

Sergei clapped an understanding hand on her shoulder. "Unless you're designing laboratory gear, I don't think Sarah's interested. You heading back to the room? We'll walk with you."

Sergei's building was a little newer, his room a little bigger, a good bit neater than David's. Art prints or photographs adorned most of the available wallspace, and more than a dozen copies of a promotional ad for Sergei's book of poetry. Cloth samples buried Anatoliy's desk, and a Martian tapestry covered his bed.

Sarah waited in the middle of the room. No one had told her where to sit, or even if she should. Sergei dug through his carry pack, unaware of her discomfort.

"Hey, Tolya? Throw me a *Kislo* while you're over there." He chose a card and popped it in the slot of his textreader. He flopped on his bed and caught the bottle his roommate threw him from their coldkeeper.

"Would you like one?" Anatoliy offered Sarah.

"Does it contain alcohol?"

"It's flavored mineral water with oxygen bubbles. There's strawberry and pomegranate left. I can mix it with vodka or something if you like."

"She's not allowed to drink," Sergei muttered absently, scanning his reader.

"The strawberry would be acceptable," Sarah said. "Thank you."

"Here we are, Sar. Come here." Sergei made room on the bed. "Read through this for me; let me know what you think. It's an essay I have to turn in on Thursday."

At last, Sarah had somewhere to sit and something to do. She took her fizzing water and sat, losing herself in her brother's work. Sergei moved to his desk and began classwork. She hadn't read more than two or three pages when the door pager buzzed.

"Open," Anatoliy and Sergei called together.

Two boys walked in without hesitation. "Hey, Serg." One of them parked half a backside on Sergei's desk. "We're heading to Vorag's for dinner. Coming with us?" Neither of them acknowledged Anatoliy, who observed wordlessly from his desk, nor seemed to notice Sarah, who froze, head bent toward the reader but watching the room from under her bangs.

Sergei glanced at the time. "Isn't it kind of early? I couldn't go until closer to six."

The boy at the desk noticed Sarah trying to invisible herself on the bed. He slammed his elbow into Sergei. "You didn't tell us you had company," he said with a wink.

"My sister, Sarah. David's taking her to dinner."

"You really his sister, or is he just trying to throw us off track?" the second boy asked.

Sarah nodded, clinging to the textreader as if it could save her life.

Sergei tapped a stylus at an old family photo fastened above his desk. "This one here."

"Nice to meet you." The first boy leaned forward to offer his hand. "Zivan Nikolaievitch Belodin."

Sarah shook his hand as briefly as she could, never looking him in the eye.

The second boy waved. "Nils Larsson. Remember you met me here first."

"You want to wait, I'll go after David gets here," Sergei offered.

"Can do," Zivan decided. He parked himself on the end of the bed, opened his carryall and dug out a reader of his own. "Did you read that sonnet by Tanoran yet? What the hell is he referring to where he says 'Intricacies fly free, where they enamored be'?"

Sarah lost her place in the essay, listening and watching. She moved up tight against the pillows, both feet on the floor, in case she needed to run. Neither boy seemed threatening, but she knew better than to rely on first impressions. Zivan discussed class with Sergei, while the boy with the Swedish lilt to his Russian dropped to the carpeting between the beds and unpacked work of his own. He must have known Sergei from an art class, for he took a large flatscreen from a case, advanced it through several images, and began to draw with a precision stylus.

A sharp whistle caught her attention.

"Hello? Approaching Earth, prepare for docking." Sergei and Zivan laughed at her.

"I asked if you were from Minsk," Zivan repeated.

Sarah blushed dark. "Yes. At the moment."

"How come you never came up here before?"

"I just got back. I was out on Sigma Tau Ceti IV, in the Epsilon quadrant."

"Never heard of it," Zivan decided. "What were you doing out there if your family was here?"

"I lived with another brother. He was a cultural observer out there," she said, wishing to the Moons he would stop talking to her.

"A diplomat job! Very cushy," Nils said. He shaded his drawing with a wider instrument.

The door buzzed again, and Sergei released it to admit yet another young man. "You've got to help me, Serg!" he pleaded. "Give me your notes for Myth? 'Vina's dragging me to a political rally all day Wednesday, and I've got to cram for Political Policy tomorrow."

"Yeah." Sergei dug through his workbag and retrieved a data card.

"Thank you *so* much! You just saved my ass."

"You couldn't pay me to touch your ass," Zivan said. "I'd have to fight Lavina, and that *suchara's* too damned vicious. Shit, Grisha! Your *yaitsi* must be bruised by the time she's done banging you."

"Note the order he put that in," Anatoliy said from across the room.

Nils laughed. "She bites at both ends."

"Hey! Hey!" Sergei objected. "Lady on board! Let her age a bit, first."

Zivan was the first to apologize. "Sorry. I forgot you were over there."

Sarah shrugged indifference. She was the only girl in a room with four men she'd never met before. If they treated that Lavina this way behind her back, how would they treat her? Could Sergei stop them if they got rougher?

"Lavina's a political activist," Anatoliy explained for her. "She can be a bit – aggressive, shall we say?"

Nils glanced up. "How can you complain about us if you're letting her loose with David? He uses more foul-assed words than a prison gang."

"Because he knows Uncle Tomas will kill him if he does," Sergei replied.

Zivan stood up and dug in the pocket of the vest he wore under his jacket. He reached up to a shelf over Sergei's desk and removed a small silver bowl carved through in an artful filigree. He removed the lid and placed a rough amber crystal in the bowl, then lit the crystal on fire. He replaced the lid and returned it to the shelf.

A light brown smoke seeped out. It smelled slightly sweet, slightly smoky, somewhat woody, as if an aromatic tree bark was burning. *Incense*, Sarah recognized. She'd seen all types of burning scents in her travels. This was pleasant, not choking but slow-burning and light. Sergei introduced her to Grisha, the unfortunate lover of Lavina.

"Could you look over here for a minute?" Nils asked Sarah. "I need a certain angle for a chin. Just a touch more to the right. Okay, hold it," he said, and sketched rapidly.

A half-hour later, Sarah sat on Sergei's lap at the desk, participating in an intellectual discussion on politics and feminism from a galactic viewpoint. Dmitri wouldn't have cared less. Anytime she wanted to discuss something like that with him, she had to teach him the topic first. Here was a whole roomful of people, all of whom already knew something and loved to debate! Her mouth opened, and words spilled out with ease. Not a trace of tightness pinched her middle; not a single tic disrupted her face. She was hanging on every word of Grisha's explanation of the cross-cultural interpretation of freedom when the door opened without a page and David walked in.

"Great freakin' Lord of the galaxy. The Spaceballs are plotting the overthrow of civilization again. What the hell are you doing, exposing her to this kind of ass lint? Fucking Hell, Serg! Don't you ever stop to think?" He waved a hand at the smoky air. He crossed the room in long steps, grabbed the incense burner, and emptied the contents out the window

"Hey! That was my rock!" Zivan protested.

"Congratulations. You finally mastered past tense." David tossed the bowl to Sergei.

Sergei caught it and placed it on the desk with growling sigh. "Why

188

are you starting shit?"

"Me? Where's your goddamned *brain*? Making Sarah breathe smoky shit, with her lungs? You trying to kill her or something?"

"I'm sorry, Sar. I didn't think … ."

"Bet your ass you didn't!"

"I'll kick up the enviro and filter everything," Anatoliy offered.

"It's just incense, David. It won't hurt me," Sarah said. "Even the Navarans use it."

"It's a *narc*, Sar! Yes it can! It could react with your meds."

Sarah jumped off Sergei with horror. She cupped her hands over her face, afraid to breathe. *"Contraband?!"*

"Not contraband," Sergei defended himself. "It's semi-controlled. You need a register card; you're allowed two stones a week. It's no worse than a glass of wine – it doesn't even make you sleepy. It won't hurt you at all."

"Of course, that's not to say four people can't combine a week's worth and get totally paralyzed," David stabbed.

"You would know!" Sergei shot back.

David pulled her away. "Get your stuff. You need to clear your nose. This room stinks of trash."

Sarah retrieved her jacket from the bed. "I have to go. I'll see you later, Serg. I really enjoyed our conversation," she told his friends.

David stalked to the door, impatient. His eye fell on Nils' drawing board, and he stepped closer. Today's work was beautiful, even if the details were only lightly sketched in.

For a crazy second, David's voice sounded exactly like Father's, low and deliberately threatening; Sarah froze in the middle of shrugging into her jacket. *"What the fuck are you doing?"*

"Hey!" Nils shouted. His board flew from his hands to hit the side of Sergei's bed and fall with a crash. "Fucker! My portfolio's in there! You damage that and I'll … !"

David grabbed Nils by his shirt. He lifted him clear off the floor and slammed him hard against the door. "You fucking *pervert!* I should snap your fingers bone by bone and twist them twice! Don't you *ever! Ever!* Put my sister in one of your sick drawings again, or I'll stab your pencil in one eye and out the other until there isn't enough bone left for them to attach implants!"

"Let him go!" Sergei ordered, using every bit of strength to push between David and his victim. Zivan stood ready as Grisha dared to wrestle David's arm, and Anatoliy's finger poised to page campus security if needed. Sergei rarely swore, never saw a need for dull basics when there were more unique and creative words to be used, but this time he felt justified.

"What the fuck are you doing!"

David let go of Nils and shook Grisha off with a vicious glare. He raised a finger to his brother. "I catch him in visual distance of her again, and not only will I inform Tomas of what you allowed to happen, but I'll file charges against him on her behalf."

"Could you at least tell me what's going on?" Sergei demanded, as confused as everyone else.

Sarah had fled to the back of the room when David threw the drawing board, but hearing herself mentioned she slipped over and retrieved it. She turned it over to see an unrealistically voluptuous woman wearing only a cloth tied around her hips. Her thick hair billowed back from her shoulders, leaving impossibly globular breasts proudly uncovered. She knelt, one leg outstretched, beckoning the observer with a finger. In her other hand she held a rope, and at the end of it, behind her, Nils had started sketching a tethered unicorn. It was a young man's erotic fantasy, except for what was unmistakably Sarah's face on the wanton figure, with a perfect chin angle to match the one she'd posed for.

"I don't look like this," she said, handing the board to Sergei. "Why would he draw me like that?"

"You don't need to know," David informed the room.

"Where's your respect, man," Sergei told Nils with disgust. "She's sixteen! You've got no right to add her to your collection. I think you'd better go. I don't know how long I can keep David from killing you, and right now I might not stop him. Maybe everybody'd better just go."

Zivan and Grisha moved to get their bags, while Nils crawled on the floor to retrieve his scattered materials. Sarah saw the other boys glance at the drawing, then at her, until Sergei erased it. The wonderful day dissolved into just another nightmare tainted by those... *boy* ideas. Not even here, among fellow intellects, was she safe. She fled to the farthest corner, hugging herself. David followed to comfort her.

"She's not a baby," Nils grumbled as he closed his carrycase. "You can't keep her locked in a box. I draw what inspires me. It's not like I asked her to pose like that for real."

David spun around. "You just don't know when to shut up, do you?" He moved Sarah in front of him and bent until he spoke beside her ear.

"What you need to remember is Sergei's friends are all brain-eating freaks of nature." He pointed to them one by one, starting with Nils. "See him? He's a spineless pervert and a freak. Don't go near him, don't look at him, don't let him look at you, and for God's sakes, don't ever touch his

190

hands without gloves, 'cause they're always in his pants. You have my personal permission to kick his ass if he so much as breathes in your direction."

"Yeah, and fuck yourself while you're at it!" Nils spat as he left the room.

"And don't go near that one, he's a revolutionary freak. Stay away from that one, he's sex-starved, and don't trust that one," David pointed to Grisha, Zivan, and Anatoliy. "No, I take that back," he said after pointing to Anatoliy. "You can talk to that one, I guess. I trust him if Serg's around. He's not about to hit on you."

"Oooh, I feel so honored," Anatoliy sneered. "Sergei! Let's celebrate! Your brother finally trusts me near a family member."

Sergei scowled. "Haven't you caused enough damage? Don't go dragging *that* into this!"

"Why would he hit me in the first place?" Sarah asked, wary.

"*Durak!* I mean, he doesn't like girls," David said.

That didn't make sense, either. "He's been most polite and pleasant to me. He made me a business offer, but when I declined, he let it drop and didn't pester me about it."

David rolled his eyes. He whispered in her ear.

Sarah's eyes grew to two purple-blue circles as she stared at Anatoliy.

Anatoliy nodded. "I have anything against you, it's just that our interests tend to run the same direction, if you know what I mean. It makes some men nervous. Kind of like your big bad brother there." He smiled at David with unmistakable loathing.

"Look, I was nice to you," David growled. "Don't you go fucking insulting me."

"The insults are free. The other – You couldn't pay me enough."

Sarah digested the information. She looked up again with the same incredulousness. "Sergei?"

"NO!" Sergei pointed a finger at her. "I know what you're thinking, and the answer's no. We knew each other from the studio, and we both needed a roommate before the rooming pool assigned us somewhere. This is strictly a friendship basis."

"He's such a tease," Anatoliy said. "Those long legs, that pouty lip, those thick blond curls…"

"Okay." Sarah felt dizzy, knowing it would be hours or even days before she could put everything straight in her head. Thank the Moons David was taking her out of there. She couldn't handle another shock. Oh, what things she'd have to tell John Carver! Vlad would never believe her!

"I guess I've just been out of society too long," she apologized. "I feel really stupid I didn't figure it out on my own."

Anatoliy shrugged. "It shouldn't make a difference either way."

Zivan gave a wave as he and Grisha left. "You know where we'll be."

"I'll see you later." Sarah waved to Sergei and Anatoliy as David dragged her out the door.

The last thing Sarah wanted to do was run off to a social engagement. She needed time to recover, quiet time to think things out and set herself straight. *Too much!* She pushed everything to the back of her mind before it got the better of her, but it wasn't easy. She ignored David's running editorial on Sergei's friends as they hurried to a restaurant in a posh section of midtown Moscow, just a minute's walk from the Galactic Embassy.

Five people awaited them. A girl no wider than a toothpick greeted David with a kiss. "You must be Sarah," she oozed, squeezing Sarah's hand. "Svetlana Ulmanova, of the Smolensk Ulmanovs. David's told us so much about you. How wonderful you could join us."

Sarah recognized the warm yet venomous smile; it belonged on Grandmother. She summoned a crocodile grin of her own. "Thank you."

They were shown to a table against the wall at the back of the restaurant. David held a chair for 'Lana, then took the wall seat. The other seats filled quickly. Sarah stood before the empty chair at the end.

"Sit down," David prompted. "What's the matter? Something on the chair?"

"No. I ... " *How to explain it without looking like a baby?* Dmitri would have saved the inside seat for her, letting her feel secure between him and the undemanding wall. The chair before her left her exposed to the entire restaurant, and not near David at all. "I'd prefer the inside seat, if I could."

David opened his mouth to say something acerbic, but snapped it shut again. "Whatever," and he had the girls slide down.

In no time at all, Sarah found herself bored, listening to a long discussion on opposing investment strategies as told in some professor's seminar. Lana spoke of her plans on going to Spain for the summer recess, which started another pointless discussion on the best places to spend a holiday, though none of the reasons seemed to go further than the quality of the food or accommodations.

Social, social, Sarah reminded herself. *Your contract says be social.* "I found the food at the Mirabella on Aquila to be superior to anything on Centauri," she volunteered, remembering perhaps the only good thing about that hotel.

Lana waved an indifferent hand. "It's not *bad*, but the Mirabella is so *showy*. I mean, if they put one more mirrored panel on it, the whole thing's going to reflect back into space and someone's going to catalogue it as a new star. I prefer the Sivona, three blocks over on the Garden Plaza. It's *so* much quieter. Who wants to deal with all that casino riff-raff, anyway."

"I can understand that." Sarah backed off on the subject. She tried again when the conversation turned to interstellar policy.

"But that's banned by the Constitution of the Alliance!" she argued one of the young men. "The Fair Trade Resolution of Article 56 states that planets with a population of less than 3 billion, or star systems with populations of less than 10 billion, quote, *must,* unquote, be given the same amount of representation as larger populations if their goods and resources are traded outside their system. Otherwise they'd be perpetually taken advantage of by exactly the type of proposals of which you speak."

The conversation came to a dead halt. David rolled his eyes.

"And you have a degree in interstellar trade?" the other boy sniffed.

"No, but I know the Constitution," Sarah replied.

This time David backed her up. "If she says it's so, I'd believe her. She would have finished school years ago if it wasn't for our brother holding her back. I'd pay to see her debate ol' Farhqart and put him in his place." The table broke out in shallow laughter.

Sarah forced a small smile. Even when she was eleven, the crew of the Chessorak compound listened to what she had to say and spoke to her as if she were a promising but inexperienced cadet. These people were not ready to see her on their level, no matter how much she knew. These people would have made Grandmamá proud. David hadn't struck her as their type at all; he wasn't like that, but he seemed to be able to bridge the gap.

"It's networking," David explained later. "I don't have to like them personally, but they're all headed for high governmental or corporate careers when they graduate. You make friends with them now, let them know where you're headed, and then in a few years you call them back up when you need favors and hope they remember you. I have other friends I hang out with who aren't afraid to cut loose."

It didn't seem to make much sense, but that was David's problem, not hers. As the night before, Sarah waited an eternity for David to go to bed. Once his exhausted breathing turned to snores, his hand limp to her grasp, Sarah let the floodgates of her mind nudge open, let the fears and anxieties and experiences of the day pour out, and she kept the tears to a minimum.

The second day went easier than the first. Sarah met Sergei at 0900, attended classes with him until noon, and traded back to David for lunch. David kept his promise and took Sarah sightseeing in the historic Red Square district. He tried to talk her out of meeting Sergei for dinner.

"He doesn't think," David grumbled. "You shouldn't be near the asteroids he hangs out with. They're all a worthless bunch of dreamers, with no marketable skills to back them up. Dreaming won't get you anywhere; it's preparation and foresight that pave the way to success."

Sarah laughed. "Listen to you, David Kirushenko! You sound like a propaganda poster. If your teachers in Kar Kuomi could hear you now, they might actually forgive you. I never stopped dreaming of home and I finally got here, didn't I?"

They met up with Sergei, only five minutes late.

"Where are we going?" Sarah asked Sergei when they boarded a packed tram for the far side of the city.

"I trust David about as much as I trust a Muphridian land shark. I don't need him making another scene, so we're going somewhere he won't find us. Don't worry."

Eight of his friends waited for them at the back of the Skyline restaurant, on the 87th floor of the Surikov Underwriters building. Across the river, the stalwart towers of Ivanov Industries, its guest suite holding no one less than Mr. Ivanov himself, glowed a comforting soft blue. Sarah greeted Zivan and Anatoliy, but didn't know the sharp-faced brunette with Grisha. To her relief, Nils was not among them. She took a floor cushion between Sergei and Anatoliy, more comfortable than she'd felt yet on her excursion. A little thrill shivered in her middle, excitement over the prospect of interesting conversation, and excitement over the fact David wouldn't approve.

Zivan tried hard to catch her eye. "What field do you plan to study?"

Sarah shrugged, used to looking anywhere but at someone. "I don't know. There's so many things I'd love to study. Probably science. Chemistry maybe, or biochem."

"Why would you want your name attached to a degree in science, when so much of our society has already been destroyed and perverted in the name of 'progressive' science?" Grisha's girlfriend, Lavina, scoffed.

"That's what interests me. I don't plan on developing anything that would destroy society."

"That's what every scientist says at the beginning. They said that before the early atomic wars, Lake Karachai, the Clone Uprising, the Tylumide gas cloud, *Synthecillus devistatum*, and Gods know how many other man-made holocausts. At some point, every scientific discovery will be exploited by someone bent on mass destruction, and it's the

194

galactic population who will pay the price."

"Who's to say I'm not the one to solve some of those problems?" Sarah said without offense. "Someone has to design the antidotes and vaccines and decontaminants. Not all science is bad. Not every experiment results in pain or torture or death. Sometimes problems exist naturally that need to be solved – such as the low birthrate on Sigma Tau Ceti IV – and science can help solve them."

"But see! That's *their* problem, not yours! It's another example of the UPA using its endless power to push their way into yet another developing planetary culture and cement its grip through promises of curing all their ills. What if they don't *want* their infertility cured? If their society has developed dependent on that fact, by curing one condition we could wipe the very reason for who and what they are. Where is the justice in that?" Lavina spat with conviction. "Independent Destiny means just that – *independence*."

In her head, Sarah saw the logic of the argument; it was the same reason she hadn't been allowed to carry out more intensive experimentation on her flowers, lest something unforeseen happen. In her heart, however, she knew the pain the Tau Cetans endured, endlessly hoping. Mrs. Al, who fussed over her only child like a shadow and never stopped wishing she could have had more. Moon-struck Jaycelani Sivalaxa Kirushenko, who would have gladly given one of her legs if she could have borne Dmitri a child, and for whom Sarah's horrible lie that Dmitri had abandoned his "other children" and didn't want hers was too much to bear. How could someone not want to ease pain like that?

"It's easy to pass judgment when all you know is a textbook concern," Sarah said at last, "but ideals become much grayer when you know the cultures and individuals and their daily lives. You raise an important point, but the problem will never be solved with blanket rules like that. No, we shouldn't interfere in other cultures, but if a friend of yours faced severe persecution, would you sentence them to torture or starvation on the principle of non-interference, or would you step in and pressure the government to uphold their right to peaceful existence? You can't have it both ways. There are many planets and cultures where slavery and tyranny are deeply entrenched, or the planets so physically and chemically destroyed the people are perishing. It's difficult to incite change in people who already have freedom and prosperity; perhaps you would achieve greater success by focusing your knowledge and energy into helping those people who need your guidance the most. It's one thing to read a subject and form an opinion; it is something else to experience the injustice first hand. Without that experience, we will never have the wisdom to have the right to make those kind of judgments."

Grisha stifled a laugh. "She's got you there, Vina. You wanted an internship for the summer. I think she just handed you a lead."

Lavina's mouth hung open, unable to form a retort.

"That's so profound," Anatoliy said with respect. "Where did you learn that?"

"It's something someone tried to teach me once," Sarah realized, remembering the politically knowledgeable but arrogant captain of the *Triumph*. *Was this the dawn of wisdom?* "I guess I never realized just how much I learned on Tau Ceti."

Punctual as ever, on Wednesday Uncle Tomas appeared at David's door as the chronometer on the computer changed from 10:59 to 11:00. For the boys' sake, Sarah controlled herself and didn't rush him.

"You came, just like you promised!"

Tomas raised an eyebrow. "You doubted me?"

Sarah smiled shyly. "No, sir."

The boys gave abbreviated versions of their activities during lunch, and Sarah filled the gaps with blameless statements. Tomas accepted the information without opinion, but the tension grew heavier as lunch ended and they made their way back to the dormitory.

"Well, Sarah. It's two hours back to Minsk. You seem happy and well enough. You may stay here two more days and return with the boys if you wish, or you can return home with me now. The choice is yours."

David was the bomb, Tomas had the fuse, and Sarah knew she was the detonator. *How to say it, without starting a conflagration?* She grasped a hand of each of her brothers and squeezed them as they all stood by the door.

"I've met some interesting people, visited some wonderful classes, and had some very educational experiences. Everyone has been most understanding and caring, but I think I've had enough excitement for now," she decided. "I'm not ready for this kind of life yet. I need to go home and pull it all together. At least now I know what to expect."

"Just two more days!" David pulled her away from Sergei. "There's a ton of stuff we haven't gotten to see yet. Don't back out now. You can do it."

She hugged him until he couldn't breathe. "I'd like to come back again before the semester's over, but I need to go home."

Eighteen

Sarah sat patiently on the stone wall, a sheet of plastic paper in her hand. She wasn't allowed past the wall without permission, but she was only *on* the wall, not past it. She'd been sitting faithfully all afternoon. Today was The Day, the day she'd be released from isolation and misery, and could truly celebrate returning to Russia, but she didn't know what *time*. Her patience didn't falter even as the sun picked up its march toward the horizon. She wouldn't let it. He *would* come. He promised. Dimi *always* kept his promises. He would come for her.

He would!

Sarah's heart seized as she heard the approaching buzz of a hovercraft gliding down the empty traffic lane before the property. *ОРЛОВСКИЙ КОСМОДРОМ* flashed in big letters on the side of a silver public transport car. The Orlovsky Spaceport Shuttle. It stopped at the gateway. Perhaps a minute passed before a hatch on the far side opened and a figure emerged, carrying a small travel bag. The growing pressure in Sarah's chest made it impossible to breathe. *Could someone actually suffocate from nerves?*

The shuttle pulled away. The slim man saw the brass plaque mounted on the stone post at the end of the flyway, the name Ivanov, and shook his head. He crossed the lane and stopped.

"Well? I didn't think I looked *that* different. All this fancy living make you forget me?"

Sarah jumped off the wall with a cry and wrapped herself around Dmitri's neck. He braced against the onslaught.

"All right. Enough already." He pushed her off after a hard hug. "Lemme see you. I guess they're feeding you pretty well." He slapped the back of his hand against her belly. "I haven't seen you that heavy since before Tau Ceti."

"That's a foul thing to say to a girl! I was underweight and nutritionally deficient when I arrived. I merely caught back up to where I was. Plus one kilo."

"Mmm."

Sarah held her paper up for him to see, a proud grin splitting her face. "Look! I finally got it!"

Dmitri eyed her Basic Education Diploma, unmoved. "*Da.* I got one, too. It was part of my rehab. I don't see what difference it makes. A stamp on a paper doesn't make me smarter than I was. I'm sure your scores were

197

higher than mine." He reached in the pocket of his jacket and retrieved a small tin. He opened it, removed a spotted tablet, and put it on his tongue.

A waterfall of guilt crashed down on Sarah. "Tranquilizer?"

"Breath mint." He held the tin out, and she took one. "Well, go ahead. Say it."

"Say what?"

"I couldn't forget seven years of nightmare in three months, no matter how hard they made me try. You've got that burning look like you're going to follow me like a shadow until I ask what's on your mind, so save us both the trouble and just get out with it, here and now. Go ahead," he said in a tone that forewarned of irritation if she didn't comply. "Because I may not answer it later."

Sarah hung her head. Dimi looked thinner than ever. His shorn head, something he'd never have done on his own, unnerved her. Chalk up losing his hair to her list of crimes. She didn't want to ask what had smoldered in the embers of her imagination for three long months. If he answered 'Great!' she'd know he was lying and he'd been miserable. If he said, 'Horrible, wha'ja expect?', she knew, medications or not, she'd explode into tears. She glanced up repentantly through her bangs.

"How was it?"

The harshness in his face eased. "Not so bad. I've been through worse. Mostly it was all psychological crap, trying to make me admit my fears and shortcomings and pinpoint exactly why I did what I did. Screw all of 'em. Given the same circumstances, I'd do it again. I'd just take the goddamned thing and bury it in the compost if I thought the 'Fleet would be poking around."

"That wouldn't be smart, Dimi," Sarah corrected. "Compost gets hot as it decays, and the heat might set off the charge … "

"Mud, then! You know what the Hell I mean."

"Yes, Dimi."

He stared up the rise to the house. "So, what's it like in there? Should I watch my back?" As he watched, the main door sprang open and a figure burst out, speeding down the path as fast as it could go. "Who the Hell's that?"

"Dimi!" the figure trumpeted. It stopped its headlong rush just before Dmitri decided he would have to step aside to avoid being run over. Instead, it grabbed him in a strong embrace, spinning him around as the boy attempted to stop fast. He banged Dmitri on the back before kissing him on both cheeks, then hugging him again.

Sarah danced with joy, trying to hug both at once. "I told you! I told you he'd get here!"

Dmitri stared in amazement. *"Vlad?* Vladimir? Cryin' out loud! You're almost as tall as me now! You actually *grew!"*

Vlad grinned until his dimples shown like divots. "Blame Sarah. She squeezed me so hard, I shot up fifteen centimeters."

Sarah shoved him on the arm, laughing. "I did not! But maybe I should."

"I don't doubt it. So, who's taller?" Dmitri had to know.

Vlad rolled his eyes. "Moons over Jupiter! Why is that all anybody can ever ask me?"

"I am," Sarah said.

"Sarah Kirushenko! Come up here this instant, or I shall inform Tomas!" A shrill voice carried down the rise from the front veranda. "You are beyond the wall."

"That's Grandmamá," Sarah said. "I'm sure she hates you already, because Moons know she hates me. Just kiss up to her real hard and you should be okay."

"Yeah, well, you're forgetting she's never met me, and there hasn't been a woman yet I couldn't charm the pants off," Dmitri said with confidence. He picked up his bag. "Not that I have any desire to see her with her pants off."

"Urk!" Vlad pretended to be sick at the thought. "Don't forget my stomach, Dim. You're going to shrivel my parts before their time." He gave a forced shudder, and his brother reached over with a grin to mess his hair as if he were still seven.

The old woman watched as they made their way up the long path and across the walk to the grand front porch.

Armed with her two favoritest brothers, Sarah pulled herself up tall, as pompous and proud as the woman before her. No longer could she be intimidated, not with Dimi by her side. *"Babushka*, may I present my brother, Dmitri-Mikhail Kirushenko. Dmitri, this is our grandmother, Andrea Maximovna Ivanova."

Dmitri bowed low, then took the cool, thin hand in his and kissed the back of her fingers. He looked the woman shamelessly in the eye and let his legendary lop-sided girl-killer smile creep across his face.

"It's an honor to meet you, Grandmother. Now I know why my mother was such a beautiful woman: she looked exactly like her own mother."

The iron face before him remained unmoved. Andrea took back her hand. "Perhaps, fifty years ago, but certainly not in your lifetime, young man. Your flattery is too forced to be honest, but at least your manners are creditable."

Dmitri raised an eyebrow. "Perhaps," he echoed, "but I stand by the sentiment. You make me think of my mother, and my mother was the most beautiful woman I've ever met. At the very least, please allow me to extend my humble appreciation at your willingness to care for my sister during my absence. I can't thank you enough."

Andrea's laser eyes burned at Sarah, but this time Sarah deflected the stare. "On that account, sir, you are correct. I'm afraid you'll have to thank Tomas, however. It was his doing. I do hope that you will wield a tighter discipline than Tomas could bring himself to use. Do come inside, before she catches another chill. I shall let Tomas know you've arrived. I'm sure he'll be most grateful to see you." She proceeded to the intercom in her office.

Dmitri took in the breathless grandeur of the entryway. "You must have pissed her off good," he said under his breath. "I thought I told you to behave?"

<I did!> Sarah whispered in Tau Cetan, lest Grandmother possibly hear. *<Honestly, Dim! That Old Bones scares my DNA from me. Every time I see her, I so scared I forget to breathe.>*

"Come on." She wasn't about to wait for Old Bones to return. She took his bag and pulled him to the stairs with Vlad. "I'll show you your room. I put your things where you always kept them, so you shouldn't have trouble finding anything. It's three doors down from mine, but I can run fast. It's got only one bed in it, but it's wide, like on Tau Ceti, so you'll like it. And bathrooms, Dim! Everyone has their *own* bathroom! And running hot water! And we never have to change the sheets; the upstairs help makes the bed every day. And they do all the laundry! You never have to worry about it."

"They'll even shine your shoes if you need it," Vlad added.

"This is it." Sarah placed the bag on his bed. "If you want, the staff will even unpack for you."

Dmitri checked the hall, then closed the door. "Shit, man! You weren't kidding about all that money stuff. Cryin' out loud! We really stepped in it this time, didn't we."

"It's like living at the Mirabella, but so far nothing bad has happened. Uncle Tomas insists he'll never hand us a tab at the end of the day."

"I've been here more than seven years, and he hasn't handed me one yet," Vlad said.

"That you know of," Dmitri added. He tested the mattress. "So, what's the deal? Where do I stand with everybody?"

"Galina lives at the end of the hall, but she spends a lot of time with her fiancé, Milos," Sarah informed him. "Should be no problems from her.

200

Val rooms with Galina. She has a steady boyfriend, too. I haven't talked to him much, but he seems okay. He's nice to Nikky and Marina, and they like him. I think she's afraid of you. You might be okay with her."

"She's not what she used to be," Vlad agreed. "She really wants you here."

"Yeah, right." Dmitri examined the drapes, then opened the window and surveyed the back lawns.

"Marina's got the front room next to theirs, and Nikky's got the front one across from you," Sarah went on. "I'm next to Val and Gal on this side of the hall, then Vlad and Sergei, and David's next door to you."

"Yeah? What's his story?"

Sarah bit her lip. "It's hard to separate the Attitude from what he really means, but, let's just say I don't think he'll be knocking on your door for a while."

"I'll take that as a good thing, then."

"He's only here on the weekends," Vlad said. "Around the corner is Grandmamá's suite. You should be okay with her, if you don't hold parties in here."

"What's with her?" Dmitri asked, checking out Sarah's arrangement of the drawers and closet.

"She just takes some getting used to. She's really old and into all that properness stuff."

"She hates me to death," Sarah insisted solemnly. "She can't accept the fact we were farmers and didn't exploit the economy as much as we could have."

Dmitri frowned. "We weren't farmers. We were cultural observers. You wrote the damned book on translation, for Moon's sakes."

"We lived in a farming community, and we got our hands dirty. That's unforgivable."

"What's with these?" Dmitri said, poking at the massive bouquet of roses on his desk. "Did you grow them yourself, or raid a greenhouse?"

"They're from me and Vlad. Ninety stems, one for each day we thought of you."

"I guess they can stay, then. Thank you."

A knock at the door interrupted them. Vlad let in Uncle Tomas.

"He's here!" Sarah grabbed Dimi around the neck, beaming so hard her jaw hurt. "He came back, just as he promised!"

"So I see. Dmitri." Tomas shook hands around Sarah and clapped him on the arm. "So good to see you again. Mamá said you had arrived. Welcome! You should have called. We would have met you at the 'port."

"I caught an earlier connector quite by accident. I didn't want to bother anybody."

"It would have been no bother at all. Is this room adequate? If you want something bigger, I can have your things moved to the suite in the front corner."

"This is more than fine. I've never had a room like this all to myself. It's perfect."

"If there's anything you need, anything you want made different, don't hesitate to ask," Tomas said. "Sarah took the liberty of arranging your belongings."

Dmitri nodded. "It's great. She remembered everything exactly."

"Good. Well then, I'll let you finish settling," Tomas said. "When you've had time to get your bearings, come downstairs and we'll talk. Sarah, can you show him to the study?"

"I'll show him *everything!*" She sprang and tackled Tomas as well. "He came back!"

Tomas patted her. "I didn't doubt it for a minute."

Sarah let go and hugged Vlad, unable to contain her joy. "Everything's going to be fine now. You'll see!"

* * *

In a way, Dmitri was dismayed not to find Sarah waiting for him in the hall after he met with Tomas. She'd brought him to the office by some roundabout secret way, and he didn't want to seem like an idiot asking for directions back to his room. He remembered the main stairs were in the foyer; so was that monster chandelier. He couldn't miss it, glowing like a fusion reactor down the corridor before him, and set off with confidence. Tomas had seemed pretty straight-forward when they'd met at Starbase 21 three months ago; his demeanor hadn't changed, but Dmitri wasn't ready to buy into all that nicey-niceness just yet. It would take more than chummy conversation and sharing secret shots of expensive illegal alien liqueur – fabulous, exotic liqueur! – before he could accept the man as he seemed. The fact Sarah had taken to him was a good sign, but Sarah's brilliance didn't usually extend to reading people.

As he reached the top of the grand staircase, a shadow caught his eye. Someone else was about to come down. One glance and his blood turned cold. A tall someone, with brown eyes and wavy gold hair. He'd been dreading this exact moment for years, dreaming of it, obsessing on it, perhaps. The moment that, when he wanted to admit it, might have been the whole reason he'd stayed away so long. They both froze, waiting for the other to make the first move.

No courtesy tainted his voice as he asked, "Which one are you?"

The woman flinched as if she'd been struck. She tried to smile. "Valeria. Welcome home, Dmitri. I'm glad you made it back. We've missed you."

Dmitri bit his tongue. This was Uncle Tomas's house, and he was a guest. This was a new start, a do-over, and he couldn't afford to blow it. "Thank you," he said coolly. "It's good to see Sarah looking well."

"Listen, ..." Val opened her mouth to say more, to air the apology she'd practiced for seven years, but Dmitri had already turned and gone to his room.

Sarah stood at the dinner table, waterglass held high. Her face radiated pure devotion. "To Dmitri! My fearless leader, my most patient teacher, my valiant protector, my deepest confidant, my truest friend. The best caretaker a sister could ever hope to have. To the person I owe everything: Welcome home, Dimi. May you rediscover the love that still exists here, as I have."

"To Dmitri," Vlad beamed beside her, "who let us stay in touch, and made the time bearable."

Cheers went up around the table. Dmitri did his best to let the adulations pass over him.

"Thank you. I'm glad to be here, I guess. I think the praise belongs elsewhere, though. I owe a world of thanks to Vlad for keeping Sarah busy all that time, and I owe everyone a huge thanks for taking care of her these last few months. She's a hell of a lot better than the last time I saw her. And of course, if it wasn't for Uncle Tomas's generosity, neither us would be here right now, so I guess the credit should really go to him. Thank you again, Tomas, from both of us."

Tomas shook it off as if he'd done no more than make a few calls, but he seemed pleased none the less. "As long as everyone's happy at last. Enough patting backs. Let's eat!"

"*Please*, Dimi!" Sarah begged her hardest, pillow in hand, blanket trailing behind her. She never needed more than one; the Ivanov house had heated floors and thermostatic sensors, not inefficient woodburners downstairs in the kitchen. "Just *one* night?"

"Don't be crazy! You can't sleep with me here!" Dmitri growled under his breath, unsure how thin the walls were. "I don't even have sleepwear yet! You know what everyone will think?"

"I explained your rules to Uncle Tomas; he understands. Besides, if you don't, I'll sleep in your doorway, and that makes Old Bones mad."

"I said, *No!*"

Sarah dropped her bedding on the floor and sat on it. "Then you'll have to throw me out yourself. I missed you, but obviously you didn't miss me. That's okay. I don't blame you. You have every right never to want to see me again… "

Dmitri pointed his finger at her. "Don't start that! You're not guilting me."

Sarah didn't say a word, just looked at him with her perfected look of innocence; part hurt, part sadness, part bewilderment, purple-blue eyes melting like a lost puppy's in a rainstorm.

He gave in with disgust. "Fine. But on the floor, and you shut your mouth."

"I always do."

Nineteen

Sarah peeked her head in John's office the following morning. "Look who I brought," she teased, then burst in with a squeal. "Dimi's back! He came back!"

John rose eagerly from his chair. "Dmitri!"

Dmitri shook the outstretched hand. "Hello, Dr. Carver. I can't believe it's really you."

"It's me. Grab a seat! Forget all that formal stuff. John is fine. I mean, hell, you're my brother-in-law now."

"Man! I got to get used to that one. I wish I knew before that Kat was marrying you. I would have sent you letters every week."

John laughed. "Only once a week?"

The exchange hurt, but Sarah smiled anyway. "You wouldn't believe how hard I've been working, Dim. I'm doing really well now, aren't I, John? Tell him! Tell him how hard I've been working."

"She's come a long way," he agreed. "I'm proud of her progress in such a short time."

Sarah couldn't have smiled harder. "See? I wasn't lying. I told him all about my plant experiments, and how we helped the Compound with their research, and how you bought me all those books to read and, Moons above! Remember the desserts we had at the Iqaqi Hotel on Aldebaran? He didn't believe me how wonderful that was!"

"Sarah's told me you two had some pretty wonderful times," John hinted, watching Sarah squirm and bounce and all but turn inside out in an effort to please her brother. She hugged him with exuberance.

"Easy." Dmitri pushed after a brief pat, and Sarah sat back for a few seconds. "Yeah, we saw our share. I mean, things stabilized a bit when we landed on Tau Ceti, but I think that was good. We were both ready for it at that point."

"And that was when?"

"Right after Viktor died. You watch your brother get gutted like a fish, you need somewhere quiet to get your head back together, you know? She didn't tell you that?"

Sarah watched her fingers twisting in her lap as if they were punishing each other. "I – I didn't tell him anything about that. I didn't want to talk about it."

"What have you been doing, then?" Dmitri demanded. "Playing

checkers? You at least told him about the ESPAR stuff, didn't you? *Didn't you?"*

"Some of it."

"Why the hell not? That's what you're here for, isn't it? With your precious Dr. Carver? I'm confined for three months, and you're playing games and talking about *desserts*?" Dmitri gave a snort. "Maybe I should come instead, tell John my side of things. How he should watch his back, and how to spot a lie."

Sarah's head snapped up. Her eyelid quivered with a tic. "I'd never do that! Ever! I haven't told John a single lie! I wouldn't! I've kept my promise!"

John watched the interplay with great interest. He'd learned more in five minutes than the last three months. "That might be a good idea. There are some things Sarah has great difficulty discussing. Maybe you can give me the highlights on some of them."

"No! He doesn't have to," Sarah interrupted. "I mean, don't take up his time with that. He just got back. Now that I know he's okay, I'm sure I can focus my full attention on things."

Dmitri nodded, unimpressed. "Whatever you need."

* * *

The *message waiting* light flashed on her mail queue after lunch. The letter wasn't translated, but she read it with ease.

To: Kirushenko, Sarah I., care of IVANOV\Minsk\Byelorus\Sol III\ 66015-98-93514-8ZX.

Forwarded by: Ennis, Hargan\ Survey Team 4\ Sigma Tau Ceti IV\UPA 63679001-99761/3.

Received/transferred Unified date 66013

Hey, Sarah! Everyone on staff here sends their regards. We miss you both! H.E.

THIS IS A CERTIFIED COPY
To my Moonshine girl
from Charshfenaki

Mother and I most happy to get letter from you. We most happy you safe and not in prisoning. Mother cry for weeks and weeks; she say prisoning terrible bad place for pretty girl, she worry very much. We happy Dimi-tri safe, too.

Old Porshie-girl Shinabat will have more baby next year. She very stubborn and mean, not want to work. I not like to work riding-porshie, but somedays I must. Work very hard and lonely without friends. No girls but Mother come to fields; I have no one to impress.

New families move into town, build tannery and shoe shop. That good for price of leathers. I not go to town much now. It not any fun without Dimi-tri. I see Jaycelani one time when I take urpintan to market; I tell her Dimi-tri gone back to his country. She pretend not to care. She find new man to marry. She say she have baby next year, too. I look, but I not see it yet. But you cannot hide such news. Mother will know.

Nobody move into your house. I walk to Chanchi, find Dikkerson. He say he sorry you have to leave so fast. He say you be okay. He say we can keep farming extra land if we want, no cost. We farm some. I not plant all of it this season. I cannot do all by self.

My heart cries for you, Moonshine. I cannot look at sky without thinking of you. Eyes like sky, hair like moon, face like sun. Please, make Charshfenaki happy, write more letters, like you do for brother. Please do not forget dear old friend Charshfenaki, who misses you very very very very much.

Friend for life,
Charshfenaki Aletneshfaja in Vandijoc

Sarah put her hand over her mouth, pushing back the emotion. She never expected him to write back. Charlie'd had some basic education, he wasn't stupid, but there was little time in his life for things like reading and writing for pleasure. Obviously, the letter had been important to him.

Obviously. She could hardly share the letter with Dmitri. The bit about Jaycelani, his ex-wife, might stir up bad feelings, but she didn't want to share the last paragraph at all. She'd tried everything she could to make Charlie forget about her, but he was as stubborn as a porshie when it came to that, and her own naiveté only made things worse.

It had only been a hug, a simple friendly hug on a Pelonishalak holiday last year, when she tried to be friendly and social, like Dimi wanted. She hugged Charlie, and in the Russian tradition gave him a faint kiss on his cheek. Charlie stared hard, grinning, and she witlessly smiled back.

"That was pretty damned forward of you," Dmitri kidded her later. "I thought you weren't interested in that kind of stuff? Don't tell me you're changing your mind about Charlie?"

She shrugged. "What stuff? It was nothing more than I'd give you or Commander Guillaume or anyone else to wish them Happy New Year. It didn't mean anything."

Dmitri looked at her funny. "In case you haven't noticed, which you obviously haven't because you never leave the damned cabin, these people kiss each other under the ear." He rubbed his fingers under her ear and along her jaw. "You might as well have shoved your tongue in his mouth! You never saw me do that to Jaycee?"

"No. I thought – that was just – whatever you were doing."

"It's a sign of serious interest. Man! You better go start explaining your way out of that one."

She lay awake all night, most of it in tears. Charlie was at the door right after breakfast.

<I go to town; you come for walk?> he asked with a new self-assurance.

"She'd love to," Dimi said and shoved her out the door, locking it behind her.

They were out of sight of the cabin when Charlie tried to hold her hand. She whirled around so nervous she almost vomited, but she tried her best.

<I sorry for what I do yesterday. I merely happy for holiday. I not mean for you to think I change mind about things. Dimi say I very wrong to do that. I terrible sorry.>

Charlie's face turned angry. His fists banged air like a petulant toddler, and he kicked the nearest tree.

*<Why you do this to me? I love you with every piece of heart, with eyes and head and chest and feet and hands! I **love** you, Sarrah! Why cannot you like* me*? You old enough girl now! I show you I can work hard, make good crops to buy you nice things. Three years I show you. You want me back off, I back off, I do anything you want, and you still not even look at me! I have face like porshie?>*

<No! No, Charlie! You have very pretty face. I tell you before, I cannot marry you. Someday I will *return to my home, and if I marry you, I cannot ever do that. You very nice boy; too nice to marry me.>*

<Tell me you not love me! Tell me!>

<Charlie... >

<Tell Charshfenaki you not like him at all, not even one little bit,> he demanded. He held his hands before her face, a centimeter apart.

<Charlie, you not... >

<Tell me!>

<Even if I say I like you, it not change anything!>

<You say it anyway,> he pouted.

Damn the whole planet and their weird ways! What idiot decided that Humanoids should kiss differently? They all seemed to mate the same!

<I like you, Charshfe,> Sarah mumbled, feeling as if she were slitting her own throat. *<You wonderful and always nicest person to me,* but **I not can marry you**! *Not you, not any other boy in Vandijoc! I not marry **anybody**! If I say I like you but not want to marry now, you will want to wait, but even if I return ten years from now, I still will not marry you.>*

<Even if you come back in thirty years, and I have other wife and many children, and you say, Charshfe, I marry you now, I will leave them and marry you.>

The tightness in Sarah's chest was all that kept her stomach from coming up. *<I marry no one. Never.>*

Charlie hung his head. A thought came to him, and he looked up with new hope. *<We not need contract. You know? We just practice, for real times later.>* *He slipped an arm around her.*

Argh! It was the practice *part she wanted to avoid most! Sarah knew enough about Tau Cetan customs to know that, with an abysmal fertility rate, teenagers fornicated like flies, with few social stigmas to direct them otherwise. A contract to fool around made things legally binding, but an accidental pregnancy was a blessing, and while such things almost always ended in marriage, a baby was positive proof that a woman was fertile. A single mother would have a long line of suitors to choose from, each proud to flaunt the baby as his own.*

She shoved him away with both hands. *<NO! If Dimi find out I do that without contract, he get very angry.>* *She lied, of course; Dimi would probably have been overjoyed.* *<You best of friend to him; I not make him angry with you. Second, if I say yes, then you will ask to marry again, and my answer will still be 'no'.>*

The playful, ever-hopeful look on his face melted into a

broken-hearted pout. Brawny Charlie looked so stupid and childish, standing there with tears in his eyes and his lip stuck out, she couldn't help feeling sad for him. He wouldn't have been more than eighteen or so on her planet. It wasn't his fault she couldn't tell him the real reasons, besides the fact fifteen was considered too young on her world. If she left him mad, he'd wind up telling Dmitri, and then Dmitri would get on her case for hurting Charlie's feelings.

She put her hand in his and squeezed it as a consolation prize. <I promise to you, Charshfenaki, if I ever decide to contract with somebody, for real or just pretend, you will be the first person I think of.>

Charlie's face glowed like noon sun coming out from behind a cloud. <I will wait!>

Sarah printed a copy of the letter as it was, then edited it down to three paragraphs and sent it over to Dmitri's mailbox. She folded her copy and stuffed it among the other letters in her old tan pack. Then she deleted the original from her mail.

The pain grew cancerously for over an hour before she gave in.

The house turned inside out over the deluge of tears – she hadn't done anything like that in weeks, and never quite like this – but Dmitri waved everyone away with a fatalistic calm. He sat on the floor, slid the crying girl onto his lap and rocked her. Sarah denied even Vlad permission to stay, but Tomas stayed on Dmitri's consent, watching and learning. Dimi needed just three questions to get a tiny nod. *The letter.*

"I would have thought a communiqué would make her happy," Tomas said.

"Why?" Dmitri replied over the top of Sarah's head. "Not to be rude, sir, but are you all so self-absorbed you think you're the beginning and ending of everything? We had a life, with real jobs and real responsibilities and real friends that we cared about. We were bound with ropes and dragged away as if we'd massacred a town, with no chance to explain and no chance to say good bye. Vandijoc was our home. Why shouldn't a letter from friends saying how much they miss us cause her to feel sad? She's *homesick,* for cryin' out loud!" He tried to look angry, but wound up as mournful as Sarah.

"Of course," he added, "I wouldn't expect you to understand that, having lived in the same house all your life."

"Not all my life," Tomas corrected. "It's just always been here to return to when needed. I am sorry. For seven years all I heard was, 'Get them back, get them back.' Not once, I'm afraid, did we ever stop to think if you *wanted* to come back."

Dmitri paused to wipe Sarah's face with Tomas's handkerchief. "We did. Just not like this."

Dmitri didn't see any need to bother John over a simple sadness, and sure enough, Sarah pulled herself together by morning.

"You may call me a ghost for haunting your thoughts, but I left ghosts behind on Tau Ceti just as well," she apologized at breakfast. "While you may travel the galaxy and visit your friends, I am currently forbidden from visiting mine. John can take his youth groups and shove them in his nose. I *had* real friends, and when I can stop mourning their loss, maybe then I'll be ready to make new ones, but not before."

Galina kissed her on her head. "Take your time. No one says you have to rush."

* * *

Day three, and Tomas began to see what could only become a growing issue.

He found her at last in the back hall. "Sarah, where have you been? I've been looking for you for twenty minutes. You haven't answered any of my pages."

"I went for a walk outside with Dimi. I showed him the hangar and some of the grounds."

"That's fine, Sarah, but the rule is you are required to notify me if you leave the house."

"It's okay. Dimi was with me."

"That doesn't excuse the fact," Tomas reminded her patiently. "I am your guardian, I am supposed to know your whereabouts at all times. We've been over this many, many times."

"But Dimi's back now. You're off the hook. He can worry about me again."

Tomas sighed. He knew what John Carver would say: *You know what's right, so bite off the bad spot and look the worm right in the eye.*

"Sarah, I know we're all in a difficult position until things get straightened out, but right now – legally – Dmitri is not your guardian. He has no more say in things than Nikky or Marina."

To his surprise – or maybe to his fear – Sarah didn't take offense. "Legally, he never *was*," she reminded him with a sweet smile of idealistic denial. "That's never made a whit of difference."

"It most certainly does. I *am* legally responsible, for you *and* for

211

Dmitri, until the courts decide otherwise, and they are now very aware he has no legitimate claim to you. I have no problem with you being with Dmitri and I am grateful he is able to help keep an eye on you, but my rules are still in place, and I still expect you to abide by them. And informing *me* of your whereabouts is highest priority."

Sarah's beatific Glow of Dmitri faded a notch. "But he's back now. He takes care of me."

Court or no court, Dmitri ruled. If Dmitri wanted to follow Tomas, that was fine, but Sarah followed Dmitri.

"I have no objection to that," he repeated. "Perhaps later today the three of us can sit down together and work out some new rules that will address everything. Just – keep telling me if you're leaving the house. If not for you, then so I know where Dmitri is, okay?"

"Okay."

The furniture in Tomas's apartment was more comfortable than that of his office, the setting far more relaxed and friendly, the mood he wanted most to convey. The last thing he wanted to initiate was a needless power struggle. "Sarah brought up a point today that bears some closer attention. You've been in charge of her for a long time, Dmitri, and she has a well-deserved devotion to you. However, I have been filling in as that authority figure in your absence. The question we need to address is what the three of us expect out of the current arrangement, and how to make it work to everyone's advantage."

Sarah was glued so tightly to Dmitri's side he had to push her away just to raise his tea to his mouth. "I don't understand."

"I know who Sarah feels is in charge of her," Tomas said. "Who do *you* feel should be in charge?"

"You're still her guardian, right?"

"Yes," Tomas said, relieved that Dmitri was conscious of the fact, "but I promised when you returned, I would return that duty to you if you wished. Do you want me to look into having Sarah's guardianship returned to you?"

"Of course he does!" Sarah smiled, then frowned, "Don't you?"

"Well, legally I never had it to begin with," Dimi said.

"What do you mean? You said that didn't make any difference! You put that in our contract!"

"I know, I know." He rubbed her arm before sighing. "I can't see giving her up at this point – it's only eighteen months more. I don't want to push you out, though; that's not right, either. Whether my claim was real or not, they legally yanked it on the *Triumph*. What do I do if they won't give it back?"

"They have to," Sarah decided. "I won't accept any other answer."

"That's a possibility," Tomas acknowledged. "What I can do is petition the court to grant a joint custody, have your name added on. I will start that process tomorrow. Until then, we need to lay some new ground rules. Dmitri, I have no problem with you having charge of her through daily routines. I'll give you a copy of the rules she follows; feel free to add any of your own that I don't know about. However, I will still take her to her various appointments. And you must inform me before you take her off grounds. It's simple accountability on my part."

"I'm not about to do that too quick," Dmitri said. "I've never held a pilot's license – real or assumed."

Tomas chuckled. "That's easy enough to fix."

* * *

It *was* good to be back. Vlad hung on Dmitri almost as much as Sarah, as well as Nikky and Marina. Sarah was right, Valeria was different, stepping aside to give him right of way and nearly bowing in remorse every time she saw him. Dmitri didn't feel the least bit sorry; in fact, he rather enjoyed it. He played up his manners and won Grandmother over. Maybe it was just Tomas's style of letting him settle in, but Dmitri felt comfortable with him. Tomas treated him as an adult who deserved respect despite a disastrous decision, and perhaps that was what made the weekend even more grating.

Friday came, and Sarah bubbled over about the boys. Sergei came to greet Dmitri as soon as he arrived, but no one else.

"Where's David?" Sarah asked. "He must have come in by now?"

"Who knows?" Sergei shrugged, but he shot her a look that said drop it.

David appeared briefly at dinner, dressed to kill.

Sarah left her seat to greet him. "Where have you been? Dimi's home! Come say hello!"

"Hi, how are you," David said from across the room, as if meeting a stranger he'd never see again. Dmitri started to rise, but David had already turned away.

"I might not be back by security time," he told Tomas. "I've got my bypass with me."

"Anywhere interesting?"

"Dinner and a ballet with Ivanka Paletin. That is, if my Number One girl doesn't mind." He hugged Sarah off her feet and gave her a loud kiss on the cheek, milking her affection.

Sarah hung from his neck, sucking up the flattery. She tossed her head in mock disdain. "I guess not. After all, you took me to the ballet two weeks ago. Don't do anything I wouldn't do!"

David opened his mouth to speak, but blushed instead. He held up a finger. "Don't hold me to that one," he said with a guilty smile, and left.

Sarah sat down before she realized it. "That's strange. He must not have recognized you," she said to Dmitri.

Dmitri allowed Sarah to blow it off, but he wasn't stupid. By the next day, the cool reception had become a cold breeze.

David's invisibility extended to Sarah, too. No matter where she searched the house that weekend, she couldn't find him, and his comm line went straight to message box. "He'll get over it. He missed you so much, he just doesn't want you to know."

"Yeah," Dmitri said sourly as they watched a program on the giant screen in the media room. "That's why he said all those nasty things in his letters. Well, you can just tell him to grow the hell up and get over it. I'm not out to start trouble, but I'm not afraid of it."

Sarah remained cheerful. "Don't be silly. He'll come around soon enough. I'll get Sergei to work on him. Give it a week. You'll see."

Twenty

I t wasn't unusual for Sarah to pick at breakfast; it was Sarah's admittance she had a stomach ache that set off a warning in the back of Dmitri's mind. Sarah couldn't be bothered with aches and pains. If she would admit to pain, then she thought she was dying. She disappeared after breakfast; an hour later, Dmitri went searching.

Her door was shut; he knocked as he went to open it. "Sar?" *Locked.* "Sar, open up."

Not a whisper sounded. "Sarah, open up or else!" He rushed to his room and returned with her key. He released the lock and peered inside.

The room looked typically Sarah even in this perfect house – the drapery pulled back as if someone had looked out a window, one shoe in the center of the room, the other half-under the bed, a butt-crease on the bedcover. He walked in. The bathroom door was shut. He knocked, then tried the door.

Locked.

"Sar? You in there? You know our rule on locked doors."

He banged hard on the door. "Are you sick? Answer!"

Valeria had a planned day off. She followed the raised voice, but hesitated at entering the room. "Can I help?"

"Can't hurt." Dmitri examined the door and frame. Modern electric pocket door, magnetic lock. It slid sideways; kicking it would do no good. "She's locked herself in and won't answer. We've got to get that door open, now. *Sarah!*" He banged again. "Answer me or I'm coming in there!"

Val hit the intercom. "Uncle Tomas, come upstairs, please! It's an emergency." She went over to the door. "Sarah, it's Val. Will you let a girl in? Please?"

Dmitri's stomach tightened with every passing second. He tried to force the door with his hands, but they slid across the smooth surface. Tomas appeared.

"There a release for this door? A key? Something? She won't answer. That's a real bad sign."

Tomas addressed the computer. "Computer: override all internal door locks, second floor; release. Voice authorization TSFI."

The lock released and Dmitri rushed in, followed by Valeria. He stopped short.

"*Shit!*"

Val gasped. "Oh my God!" In the bathroom's sink lay shards of glass.

Sarah sat in the sculptured soaking tub, knees pulled up to her bare breasts. In her clenched fist she held the broken stem of a goblet. Grisly puncture wounds lined the insides of her arms. Blood spotted the tub and wall, her hands, her knees, her chest, her face. Her left arm rested across her knees; dark blood welled up from the freshest wound. It fell with a faint *plink* to the discolored water below. Sarah stared fixedly at the drops, oblivious to the intruders.

"Get a towel!" Dmitri pulled Sarah to the carpeted floor, then peeled her fingers from the goblet stem and flung it out of reach. Valeria covered the naked girl, then wrapped two smaller cloths around the arms. She put pressure on one, while Dmitri held the other.

Dmitri peeked at the arm with a sigh. "Glass. She never used glass before."

"Crystal," Tomas corrected from the doorway. "Much sharper when it breaks."

"Why?" Valeria cried. "She was so happy, home with Vlad. Once you got here, her world was complete again. Why would she suddenly do this?"

Dmitri's eyes wandered the room, looking for clues. It had to be something bad for Sarah to be this desperate. She'd made it through everything else without crashing… *What could be bad enough to set her off?* Little was out of place in the bathroom, just the bloodied tub and her clothes on the floor.

The clothes.

The shirt lay dropped from where she'd stood, but the pants… The pants were rolled up and packed tightly into the farthest corner. That *wasn't* Sarah.

"Get her clothes."

Valeria shook the clothes out. Damp blood darkened the underwear and stained the seat of the pale blue pants. *"Ou yeyo dyela?"*

"Goddammit!" Dmitri shouted to the floor. "Goddammit all to Hell! *Her meds ran out!* She knew they were low. She wanted John to replace it when she got here. She must have lost her nerve. *Damn!* I should have called him myself, to make sure."

"What meds?"

"To stop *that*." He gestured to the pants with his chin. "She can't handle that … *women's stuff.* A doctor put her on a five-year medication to stop it. She knew her time was just about up."

Dmitri sighed. He lifted a corner of the blood-spotted towel. "I don't suppose these cuts are shallow?"

Val shook her head. "I don't think so. All this, just because of her monthlies? Should I call John?"

Dmitri nodded. Tomas took over the pressure on the oozing arm. Dmitri stroked Sarah's hair as she lay motionless, eyes open but not seeing.

He glanced up at Tomas. "They did warn you she really is crazy?"

"I knew of her past difficulties, but I've never seen anything like this." Tomas flushed, seeing the mat of scars across the girl's bare back and shoulders. "I would have tried harder to reach out. John told me not to push."

Dmitri petted the pale strands fanned on the carpet. "She not only talks *about* you, she talks *to* you, without making herself sick about it a week in advance. You reached her more than I ever expected, believe me. She even likes the name you call her. Huh, Kid? Ghost?" He twisted until he was in front of the unfocused eyes, brushing the cheek with the back of his fingers.

"We'll fix it," he crooned. "We'll make it stop again. Even if we have to get you off the planet to do it. Even if it means surgery this time. Hold on, Kid. I'm here. It's okay."

Val returned with fresh clothes. "John said to bring her to University Hospital. He'll meet us in trauma."

"I'll get the flyer and meet you downstairs." Tomas ran.

A private room waited for them on arrival. Dmitri sat on the exam table, Sarah curled silent against him. Valeria hovered close, reaching out every so often to run her hand over Sarah's back, or stroke her hair. Tomas stood by, wanting do something, anything, to make things better.

John Carver walked in. "Sarah! Imagine meeting you here. Is English okay, or do you really want to hear me murder some Russian?"

Sarah didn't blink, didn't look, but moved her head just slightly in a manner that could have been meant as a nod. He took it as a full sentence.

"I heard you had some trouble." He pulled a seat over and sat, motioning Dmitri to turn her forward. He unwrapped the bloody towels, expecting to see the same old scratchy slash wounds. The holes had stopped oozing but looked horrible, coated with clotted blood. Shock crossed his face before he could hide it.

"These look like stab wounds to me. That's not like you. Stabbing isn't a slow burn or a superficial slice. Stabbing is an act of violence, of anger, of serious intent. Can you tell me what happened to make you that upset?"

Sarah turned her face away slowly, expressionless and dead.

"She … " Dmitri started to answer but John stopped him. He wanted to hear it from Sarah.

"Well, you did a good job. Those are going to need some surgery." He produced a spray hypo, loaded it, and held it up for her to see.

"Anti-anxiety," John explained. "It will *not* put you to sleep. You will still be in control. It will just relax you, okay?"

The emotionless face shook *No*.

"Can I give it anyway?"

Sarah closed her eyes and allowed the inevitable.

The medication entered her arm with its evil pneumatic hiss. "Better?"

"No," she whispered dully.

Carver stood up. "Valeria, why don't you sit with Sarah and let me talk to your brother here."

"Sure. Will you let me sit with you, Sar?"

Carver motioned Dmitri out to the hall. Dimi kissed Sarah on the top of her head and tipped her over to Valeria. He waved at Tomas to follow.

"Me?" Tomas said with surprise. "This is your territory, I'm afraid. I don't have so much as a clue."

"You've been her guardian for three months and she lives in your house," Dmitri reasoned. "You've got as much right as anybody to know what's going on. You can't always prevent things, but I can teach you how to pick up the pieces."

"Thank you." Tomas followed them into the hall.

"Val told me on the comm you think she's menstruating and that's what triggered this," Carver said.

"Absolutely," Dimi replied, less embarrassed than usual. John knew what a mental case Sarah was; he didn't have to tapdance around it. "She can't handle it at all. She had medication to stop it, but it was running out. She was supposed to ask you to replace it when she got here, but I guess she never did."

"She did, through Kat, but I couldn't get many facts out of her, and I told her no."

"No?" Dmitri stared. "How could you *do* that to her? She came to you for help on something she can't bear to think about, let alone talk about, because she trusted you of all people to help her."

"She should never have been on that drug to start with!" John burst out savagely. "Whoever did that should be *censured!* There's a *reason* for age limits on certain medications, Dmitri! She's at high risk for endocrine problems, tumors, growths, mineral deficiencies – let alone potential sterility! Not just while on the drug, but *permanently*. Never, *ever* Norval Estrate in such a young child! And on a planet with limited medical

resources? You don't know how lucky she is!"

"She's not that young anymore!" Dmitri flashed. "It was that or watch her pull her eyes out of her head and knife herself! So you mean to say for the last couple of months she's been walking around knowing this would happen, and knowing every day brought her one day closer to her doom? How could you put her through that? That's cruel!

"Fix her arms, then!" he growled. "Fix her arms, and I'll take her elsewhere to fix the other! If it's one thing I learned in the last seven years, it's anything can be had for the right price, and there's always a way to get the money." He headed for the trauma room, but a hand on his shoulder stopped him.

"Just wait," John said firmly. "Finish hearing me out."

"I don't think I need to hear anything you have to say. She thought you were her *friend*!"

"Dmitri, let him finish, then make your decision," Tomas advised.

"Three minutes," he relented, watching the cheap spaceport Chronolex on his wrist count away the seconds. "Talk."

"Hear me out," Carver pleaded. "There are a hundred other, safer drugs that can do the same thing as Norval. Stopping the cycles won't solve the problem, it only postpones it. Either way, she should finish out the cycle before we stop it again. Let me admit her for five days, work her through it, find the underlying problem. You can't keep her on this stuff for forty years. Let's run some tests – brain scan, endocrine function, bone density... We'll knock her out with some heavy stuff, take the time to get a thorough physical exam, make sure she's really okay. If she is, we'll try her on something different, the same results with much less risk."

Dmitri shook his head. "I told her no more hospitals. So far I've kept that promise."

"I know your promise, and I'm trying to compromise. By law, I can hold her for ninety-six hours, with or without your permission. I don't see where she needs more than five to seven days. We'll get her in therapies eight, ten hours a day for the rest of the week, try a couple of different chems, and she's set to go. I can work with her at home if I have to. Visit as often as you want. Call it more of a precaution than a formal commitment. You can't watch her twenty-four hours a day. We can."

"I've done it for years, all by myself," Dmitri snapped, but he softened. "It's up to her. Convince her, and I'll stand by her decision."

"Fair enough." Carver could work around Sarah's objections easier than Dmitri's. They returned to the exam room.

"Well, Miss. Dmitri explained what he thinks the problem is. Is it possible his guess is correct?"

219

Sarah blushed painfully dark. She turned away, unable to answer.

"Here's my proposal." John waited for her to look at him. He tapped a finger to her nose, and she followed it back to his face. "You'll be here a few hours while we fix those arms and make sure you didn't damage anything. Because you're under court surveillance, I have to run a few chemical checks to make sure you're in compliance with your med orders. I know you are, but I have to show proof. We may have to make a few adjustments, because this shouldn't have happened. What do you say we make it a couple of days instead, until this thing passes, and we'll take it from there? Some basic tests, a different medication for the problem than you've been on, some talk about it, and you'll be home by Sunday, my word."

Sarah broke the eyecontact. "You're not talking a surgical floor, are you," she said thickly.

"No, I'm not."

Dmitri rubbed her shoulders, giving her strength. She eyed Carver with an infinite sadness, a weariness that ruled out a fight. "Lock-up again?"

"I'm afraid so. We're not talking about seeing gnomes living in your energy ports. You did yourself some serious damage. I have no choice but to start you out in High-Risk. I mean it, though – just until Sunday. And any visitors you want, whenever. I'll lift most of the rules."

"That's very nepotistic of you."

"As soon as we get your arms done, I'll take you upstairs. I'm going to get a surgeon in here right now. I'll warn you, though: you're going to be put out for this one. You'll be awake again a lot quicker than if we make you dopey and tie you down. I'll stay with you if you want, or Dmitri can, but that's the way it's going to be. Understand? Look at *me*."

Sarah glanced briefly and nodded. She reached behind and laced her fingers through her brother's; he squeezed the hand back.

"Val, why don't you have her lie down while I get some signatures on the consent forms," John said. "I can bring you home later, Dmitri, if you'd like." When they were out of the room, he added, "I'll get someone from Gynecology down here, and we'll do the other exam while she's out as well."

Dmitri gave in. "Okay. I'll stay with her, though. She'll want that."

"No problem."

"Do your best, John." Tomas skimmed over the computer form and signed his name at the bottom, then handed it diplomatically to Dmitri for his own 'consent.' "Whatever she needs, make sure she gets it."

"Absolutely."

Twenty-one

Vladimir tiptoed nervously onto the hospital floor, unsure what to expect. Sarah's vivid accounts of the patients from her previous hospitalization had left a lasting impression. Vlad had no idea how to deal with crazy people; Sarah wasn't crazy, she just worried too much. He hoped no one had beaten him here this early, especially when he wasn't supposed to be there. He didn't expect to meet his brother-in-law at the entrance desk.

"Vladimir! You're here kind of early," John said. "It's not even eight o'clock."

"No one would let me visit last night. Is she okay? Is she awake? Dimi said we could visit any time. Is that still all right?"

"That's fine. She was too groggy and upset last night, but I know she'll be very happy to see you. I was going to try a session with her in about five minutes. Maybe you'd like to do it for me."

Vlad's face wrinkled in disbelief. "Me? I don't know anything about that kind of stuff. I'm hardly the person to be giving advice to people. You'd be better off with David."

Carver laughed. "David gives a little *too* much advice for my needs. You're the perfect man for the job. She trusts you more than she trusts herself. How do you feel about going under cover?"

"Like spying on her?" Vlad was pretty sure John didn't mean something involving a bed.

"Not spying, exactly. More like a guide. There are monitors that will record whatever she says or does, so I can analyze it later. I couldn't get her to say two words last night. It doesn't matter what you talk about, but whatever she says, try and ask a question back if you can," John explained. "Keep her talking as much as possible, even if it's only about the number on your gym uniform. It might give me some insight for later."

Vlad wavered. Having an 'official' reason for visiting and not telling was kind of like a secret, and he and Sarah didn't keep secrets from each other. "Isn't that kind of sneaky? I don't think she'd like that. I wouldn't."

"Perhaps, but you want her home by Sunday, don't you?"

"Today would be better. If it'll help, I'll do it. She needs to be home." John clapped him on the shoulder. "That's the spirit."

* * *

Sarah sat at the table in the boring lounge, in hospital pajamas and robe, morosely staring at nothing. BGU Emergency Center wasn't a long-term hospital, so comforts were minimal – a videoscreen, bland reading materials, an interface with very limited access to anything, and private-listening music earsets. She wanted none of it. She was old enough now that she had no special treatment. The accursed nurses wouldn't let her hide in the lavatory, and chased her out all but ten minutes of every hour.

Tomas had visited last night, but she'd been so embarrassed all she did was cry. Dmitri stayed with her through the surgery, left, then came back later with Katya. Sarah was glad they came, but she didn't feel like talking. Not to anyone. Not yet. How could she ever go back when everyone would know what she did, and why? How could she ever face Uncle Tomas again? Or David? He sure as hell wouldn't understand. Dimi said he'd be back after lunch, too many hours away.

Sarah glanced sideways when she heard the door open. Force of habit, knowing where everyone in the room was at all times. She didn't expect to see her brother slip in, pale and frightened. She hugged the breath from him.

"Oh Vlad! You shouldn't have come. You don't need to see me like this. I'm so embarrassed, I could die."

He hugged her back just as hard. "We don't have secrets, remember? I never got to visit you last time, and I wasn't missing out now. Galina promised to bring me later, but I couldn't wait. *No one knows I'm here,"* he whispered. *"I skipped school!"*

Sarah's eyes opened wide. "*Vladimir Vasily Kirushenko!* How bold and devious and downright delinquent of you! I guess I should feel honored." She noticed the handful of other patients, some of whom were deliberately within earshot.

She grabbed Vlad by the hand, dragged him to the far corner, and sat on the floor. "Come on. It's quieter over here. You don't want to be around these people. They're *really* crazy."

"They don't allow you clothes here?" he asked as he sat.

Sarah twisted the edge of the robe in her fingers. "I don't want to get dressed. I want the world to go away. The nurses won't let me stay in bed. I wish I was home, so I could hide somewhere."

"You don't mean that. You don't want to see me?"

Misery leaked out in her voice, making her sound mournful. "I do. It's just – I can't bear to go back home, ever. The hired help will whisper worse, and Grandmother will definitely want me put somewhere else now. Someone might find out I'm a bad seed. And I stole and broke one of her glasses on purpose. With my luck, it was probably some rare historical

222

heirloom. Everyone in the house will know what happened, and that I'm too stupid to handle a basic bodily function."

Vlad feigned hurt pride. "I thought I was the King of Embarrassment?"

"That's different, Vlad. Wetting the bed and throwing up don't have to do with … *You* know … *Adult* functions."

"You can say the word now. You're old enough. David says it all the time to get Valeria mad. Say it." He poked her ribs with a bony finger.

"Ouch! I don't want to say it."

"Can't say it! Can't say it!" Vlad chanted, poking her.

"I can too!" Sarah almost smiled back, wrestling his hand away. "Stop! That hurts."

"Say the word."

"All right! Sex."

"So what?" Vlad said boldly, avoiding the word himself. "You're not the only girl in the world who does that thing."

"No, I'm just the only one out of twelve billion people on the planet that can't deal with it. Honestly, Vlad! Sometimes I think I'm so screwed up, I'll never recover."

"You know that's not true. Look how far you've come."

Sarah rolled her eyes. "Think about that statement, Vlad." She waved a bandaged arm in the air. "Where are we?"

"Well, yeah. But other than this, you *are* better – aren't you?"

"Sometimes. Then I think about it, and I know better." She fell silent for a minute.

"Vlad?"

"Mmm?"

"Can I ask you something … *personal*? You don't have to answer. I'd more than understand."

"No, I'll answer," he said with interest. "What?"

"Vlad?" Sarah tried to look at him, then looked away. *Of course he had. Vlad wasn't screwed up.* "Have you ever – kissed a girl? I mean, really *kissed* her? On the mouth?"

"You mean, like, making out?"

Sarah nodded.

"Sure. Lots of times. Naeima Chernega in the back row of the holocinema last Christmas," he said wistfully. "How about you? I mean, with a boy and all."

Sarah shook her head.

"Not even once? That's okay. I really am older than you, you know."

"Vlad? Did you ever … touch a girl? I mean, like, on the chest and

223

stuff? You know."

Vladimir eyed her strangely. "You're right. These are personal questions."

Sarah picked painfully at the robe. "I'm sorry. Please don't answer that. It's none of my business in the least."

He blushed. "No, it's okay. I… told Sergei about it, so I guess I could tell you, too. Just once, and they weren't very big."

Carver couldn't help but laugh from his secret spot in the observation room. Good for Vlad! He had more nerve than John thought. Teenage angst! From the console at which he sat, Carver could individually adjust any of the dozen small recording cameras hidden about the room's walls and ceilings. His subjects were partially hidden by the back of a chair, but he had a clear view from three angles. Sarah was opening up far more than he'd hoped. Vlad had his own natural way of handling her. Together, it was as if time had stopped, and they were both still only nine years old. It was hard to tell who was more innocent. Vlad had always been naïve and trusting. Despite Sarah's time-forged cynicism and distrust, she still believed blindly in those closest to her.

Sarah absorbed the information. "You liked that?"

"Sure, I guess."

"Did she object?"

Vlad stared at his feet. "No. Actually, she put my hand there. I don't think I would have had the guts otherwise. I mean, it was through her clothes and all," he explained nervously.

Another digestive pause. "No secrets?"

"Never."

"Did you ever … You know … Do *It*?" Sarah couldn't bring herself to look at him this time, rolling her hand in the air to carry the thought forward, like Dmitri did. "The big *It*?"

"Oh God." He turned away, watching the other patients across the room stare or squirm in various states of drugged control. "Promise not to tell? *Really* promise? Swear on Mother's ghost?"

"Yeah." Sarah turned the opposite way, studying the easy-clean finish on the lemon-yellow wall. "If you promise not to tell I asked."

"No. I haven't."

"Dimi has," Sarah confided to the wall. "Lots of times. I mean, he was married and all for a while, but girls just fall over for him. Don't tell him I told you that, though."

"No. I guarantee David has. He brags about it, but I never know if it's

224

true or he's just doing it to make fun of me. Sergei's always got a girl, and sometimes he doesn't come home until morning, but he doesn't brag like David."

"No," Sarah agreed. She gave a hard, depressing sigh. "But you expect to someday, right?"

Vlad flushed again. "Well, yeah, that *is* kind of on my list of goals. Preferably sooner than later, I hope. You?"

Sarah caught his eye for a short second, then hung her head. "That's just it, Vlad. I don't think I ever could. I'm so scared of anything like that I can't even bring myself to *talk* to a boy, let alone think of kissing one, or anything else."

"You got time. We're both still young and all, right? Did you ever want to? I mean – kiss a boy?"

"Doctor Karverov?" A nurse interrupted John, and he briefly lost track of the conversation. "The night shift had a question about Miss Kirushenko's insomnia … "

Sarah thought a minute. "I don't know. Maybe? I liked talking with this one man a couple of months ago, and he seemed to like talking to me. He was very educated, and I really looked forward to our conversations. Dimi laughed at me – not mean, just in fun, but I wouldn't go near him after that. Our neighbor had a thing for me. He was nice, but I was so scared because he liked me I just about got sick if we were alone together. I didn't want him thinking about me like that."

"It's not like you expect to kiss someone as soon as they talk to you. You don't just introduce yourself and then start kissing someone. It takes time to want to do that. It's nothing to be afraid of."

"I know that. That's what Dimi said. Told me I was stupid for being scared, and … Promise never to tell?" Sarah whispered in his ear, hiding her mouth with her hand so that Carver, in his remote eavesdropping, missed the crucial sentence and could only guess at the incident. *"He kissed me, right on the mouth!* So I'd know how stupid I was being, and that I had nothing to be afraid of. He meant well, but he wasn't exactly … *sober* at the time," she admitted. "He didn't warn me, and I spooked and kind of beat him up. If he'd told me what he was going to do …"

Vlad's face twisted in disgust. "Of course you freaked! You're not supposed to kiss your *sister* like that."

Sarah hugged her knees and rested her head on them. "It goes deeper than that.

"Can you keep a secret, Vlad? Really keep it to yourself, as a best

225

friend should? Never mention it to Sergei or David or anyone? Ever in your life, for any reason?" She reached for his hand.

"Of course I can."

Sarah flashed him a weary smile. "You never used to." She continued, much more seriously, "It's my very deepest secret, Vlad. My very worst one. Only Katya knows about it. Not you. Not Val. Even Dimi doesn't know it all. I couldn't tell him. Everything we'd been through together, and I still couldn't tell him. I still might not be able to tell *you*."

Vlad looked hurt. "You can trust me! We've been friends since birth. I'd never laugh at something that bothered you that much. You never laughed at me, and I did plenty I wish I could have died from, rather than know people knew about it."

Sarah let her head fall against his shoulder. "I know that. It's just the saying it part. I would absolutely die if someone found out." She took a deep breath and hugged her knees. "Remember, you promised.

"Remember when I was in the hospital the first time, and I told you how crazy the other people were? And how some of them were dangerous, and you couldn't always tell? Once, I met a patient in the hall, just for a few minutes. I didn't know it at the time, but he had a long history of ...."

She paused, unsure if she could continue, and whether or not she should. "*Harming* children ... in a very ... *adult* manner ..."

She glanced under her hair to see if Vlad caught her meaning. "Doing things meant only for *adults* to do. As in, *bedroom* activities...?"

Vladimir frowned. "*Adult* manner? Activities ... You mean he ... With *kids*?!"

Sarah met his gaze. Vlad's eyes could seem unreasonably huge when he was scared.

"You mean ... He ... With *you?!*"

"No!" Sarah shook her head hard. "No! He tried. They got him before he could. But he would have. He pinned me against the wall – *me*, the karate fiend that could lick even David. He crushed me until I couldn't breathe, and he kissed me so hard it hurt, and he choked me with his tongue when I tried to scream." She shuddered, remembering. She hadn't been nine for a month yet. She hadn't known *anything* back then.

"And ..." Sarah struggled, almost changed her mind. Vlad put his arms around her stiff shoulders; she buried her face against his neck and held on tight. "I tried! I fought *so hard* – you *know* how hard I could fight! But I couldn't stop him." She confessed the worst part in the softest of whispers. With her face away from the cameras, Carver missed her words.

Sarah held her breath as a medication tremor shook her. There. She'd said it. Moons help her if Vlad squealed.

Vlad held her so tight her ribs ached. "Oh my Gods. Why didn't you ever tell me! That's the most …! "

She clung to him, trembling, curled up small and vulnerable. "Would you have understood if I told you, back then? I didn't. Not really. I didn't connect everything until years later, when we were on Aquila."

"No, probably not. But of course you're afraid! I'd be afraid to kiss a lamppost, after that."

"Yeah." Sarah wiped her eyes on his shirt and sat up. "Now every time I think about kissing, I think back to that, and I become so terrified I can't even consider it. And all that brutal kissing leads to the … *sex* thing all the time, and *that* leads to babies, and babies make you bleed to death on floors from the same place I am right now. So you see why I can't handle this stupid thing? To me, it boils down to terror and death. I'd rather die my own way and get it over with."

Vlad shook his head numbly. "Man oh man. That's deep. I can't ... *Man!*"

"Yeah."

"I can't blame you, but I think Dmitri was right, in a way. Kissing shouldn't be brutal, it should feel really good. You have nothing good to compare it to, so of course you're going to be afraid. You need to kiss someone the right way – I mean, the right age and all, and nice the way it should be – and you'd probably get over it."

"I know that. Dmitri was always kissing girls, and touching them, and none of them ever looked unhappy or scared. But no matter how hard I try, I can't make myself get that far."

They sat quietly for several minutes, hands locked in support.

"Sar?" Vlad spoke at last, "You're not afraid of *me*, are you?"

"No. That would be like being afraid of myself."

"Sar?" he said uncomfortably, "What if *I* kissed you?"

Inside the observation room, Carver sat straight up. What the hell was the boy thinking? He'd just accomplished a miracle – pulling more voluntary information from his sister than Carver could dream. No. Absolutely not. John cursed the fact he sat a hallway away. He weighed his choices: run down there and blow the fact he was listening, which would destroy her faith in both Vlad and himself, and she'd never trust anyone again; page a staff to interrupt them and destroy the heavy rapport; or wait and see what happened. Tomas hadn't mentioned anything more about their relationship. The relief of Sarah's next statement wasn't enough to ease his concern.

Sarah gave a dry look of disgust. "You're my *brother*, Vlad. It probably breaks a dozen laws or something, besides being just plain *weird*. If anyone finds out, they'll probably lock you up, too."

"Doctor Karverov?" Another nurse interrupted the eavesdropping. "I'm sorry, but Dr. Belarkin at the clinic is on channel six. He says it's urgent, a patient named Eliadek."

John hesitated, torn between the call he needed to take – a chemically-addicted teen on suicide watch – and his current client, who despite a technical suicide attempt seemed more mature than he'd feared. Sometimes he wished reality had a pause button. "All right, I'll take it," he said, rushing out of the observation room. The faster out, the faster back.

"Think about it," Vlad said. "Just once. You'd know it didn't have a purpose behind it, you'd know I wouldn't hurt you, you'd know it in advance so you could stop if you wanted. You could relax and see it's not so bad. Just a plain kiss, nothing fancy. I don't want you to beat me up or anything."

"You'd do that for me?" Sarah felt honored by the amount of care in the gesture. There was logic to it. And she was pumped so full of tranq's anyway, she wasn't as likely to panic on him.

"If you want. And you promise never to tell. They'd beat the living *gavno* out of me at school. I'd never get to kiss a girl again. Not in this life, anyway."

"Of course not." Sarah consulted the wall. She trusted Vlad more than any person in the world, but... kissing a *brother* like that? That was like practicing kissing with a porshie. Dimi was bad enough. At least Vlad wouldn't taste like alcohol.

"Okay. Just once, though. And not 'til I say. Give me a minute to relax." She closed her eyes and took a deep, slow breath, then another.

Sarah braced herself. "Okay."

Vlad leaned in.

"Wait!" She pushed him away, eyes wide. "You're not going to use your tongue, are you?"

A look of horror crept over Vlad's face. "Gods no! That's disgusting! See, it's like this." He counted off on his fingers. "There's the nothing kiss, like when you meet someone and you really just touch cheeks more than kiss. There's the cheek kiss like you have to give Grandmamá whether you mean it or not. There's the really fast kiss on the mouth you sneak to a girl when you can't help but kiss her but you're not sure she wants you to. Next I guess would be the *real* kiss, then maybe kissing with your mouth open, *then* would come the tongue kiss. I've only done that twice. I don't know if anything comes after that. I'm talking a light number four, not a six."

"Just … checking." Sarah closed her eyes and swallowed hard. Vlad shifted position and started to lean.

Sarah's eyes snapped open. "What do *I* have to do?" she demanded.

"Nothing! Don't try to kiss me back. That's too much like real kissing. Just sit there."

"This time," she convinced herself, closing her eyes once more. "Okay. Go ahead."

Sarah couldn't stop her fists from clenching. She felt Vlad lean in, felt the warmth of his chest through her pajamas as he squished against her breast, felt the cooler, rougher touch of his clothing as it brushed her hand, breathed the comforting familiarness of scent that could only be described as *Vlad*. His lips pressed hers, soft and warm and firm; his breath fluttered hot and gentle on her face. Her heart pounded twice as fast as her lips stiffened, almost as if to push him away. He tasted of coconut lip balm and Shockwave star mints.

Vlad held it only a second or two, then sat up quickly, scrubbing his mouth on the back of his hand.

Sarah opened her eyes. "That's *it*?"

"What do you mean, *'That's it?'*! That was a good kiss! I can do that much!"

"That's what I mean, I guess. That wasn't threatening at all, really."

"It wasn't supposed to be, remember? Did you like it?"

"I don't know. I'll have to think about it." If she said no, she'd hurt his feelings. If she said yes, it meant she'd liked kissing her *brother*. It didn't get much more bizarre than that. "It – bears further investigation. I won't be so quick to rule out the possibility next time. But only if it's going to be nice and easy like that. Thanks."

"Don't ever mention it."

"Never. So, how everyone taking it? Please tell me they didn't call the boys home from school." She could just imagine David barging onto the floor shouting, "I want my sister! You bastards are holding her hostage and we want her released right now!" She could imagine him throwing her over his shoulder, pajamas and all, trying to carry her out.

"No. I don't think Val told them. I don't think she wants them coming home before Friday, but David usually calls home tomorrow, so be prepared. You know there'll be hell to pay when he finds out no one told him yesterday."

They talked for another half hour about nothing serious before Vlad figured he'd better get to school. Sarah hugged him without mercy.

* * *

John Carver waited for him by the exit.

Vlad's eyes grew over most of his face, and his heart dropped out of his body.

Shit! He'd forgotten about the monitors!

Shit! He said he skipped – He admitted he was still a – He *kissed* – *FUCK!*

The psychiatrist dragged him into an office by his hair.

"Don't you *ever* – *ever*! do anything like that again! I don't care *what* your intentions were!" Carver raged. "I know what you were trying to do, but *don't do it!* You have *no idea* what you're dealing with!"

"I-I-I didn't mean *anything* by it! Honest! I-I-I just wanted to help! For God's sakes, John! Please don't tell!" Vlad bent over in pain as his entire digestive system spasmed at once.

"I mean it, Vladimir! If she's that confused, *don't get involved! Don't* become her means for comfortable experimentation. She asks you to repeat anything like that you tell her *NO*, then *tell me!*"

Fear crushed Vlad's chest until he felt dizzy. "It's not something I'd ever do again! I-I-I just thought …"

Carver's pointing finger amplified his cold gaze. "I've seen it happen before, Vlad, to brothers and sisters not half as close as you. I *won't* let it happen here! I'm warning you: until I'm convinced it's not a pattern, *keep the physical contact to a minimum*. *No* hugging. *No* hand-holding. *No* backrubs. And above all, *no kissing*. *Nothing!* I see anything *remotely* like that again, I will remove Sarah from the house. Without wait or warning. I will not allow this to go a single breath further."

"Will you stop mentioning that!" Vlad shouted back. His stomach gave a warning gurgle, and he gripped it with both hands. "I get the point! There's nothing *TO* go further!"

Carver eased up. "Okay. Keep it that way. Don't forget. Keep the channels open. If she wants information, keep it general and nonpersonal. You think she's really stuck on something, tell me and I'll work on it with her, or find someone who can. Got that?"

Vlad nodded meekly. "You won't tell Galina, will you? That I was here and everything?"

"It's confidential material, occurring during a therapy session. None of Galina's business whatsoever."

230

"And you won't tell about the… personal stuff?" Vlad blushed hard. That was just about as deep a secret as he had. His most embarrassing moments were already public knowledge. "David'd never stop teasing me."

Carver smiled at last. "Get to school, Vlad. I'd be a lot more worried if you weren't."

* * *

She ran to greet Vlad the next day as he entered the floor after school. Sarah gave him a hard hug, happy to the core. "I'm so glad you came! Nobody came by this morning and I've had no one to talk to but specialists all day. It's terribly boring. Come, sit!" Her hand slipped into his and dragged him to a sofa. She curled her feet beneath her and bounced on the cushion, buzzed on booster medications. "How come you didn't come back last night? You promised you would! I called you for an hour, but you never answered. Tell me all you did today. How was class? What did you learn? Do you have work to finish? I could help you. Three more days and I'll be home. I can't wait!"

Vlad didn't return the embrace. He ripped his hand out of hers, petulant irritation on his face.

Sarah's glow faded. "What's the matter?"

"Nothing! You're – You're sixteen! Don't you think it's time you stopped holding hands with everybody like some two-year-old?"

"I'm sorry. If that's how you feel, I won't do it again."

Vlad grimaced. "I'm sorry. It's not your – Oh, forget it! I'm sorry."

Sarah touched a hand to his back but caught herself, and folded her hands instead. "What's wrong, Vlad?" she asked sweetly. "When you get that wrinkle in your forehead, it means you're upset. Yesterday I trusted you with my very worst, very deepest, most painful secret I ever had. What could be so much worse that you can't trust *me* with what's bothering *you*?"

"It's not that, Sar. There isn't anything more secret I could tell you. It's just – oh, *man!*"

"Tell me! I promise, I can handle it."

"John saw us yesterday," he confessed. "What I did? I got one hell of a rip-roaring lecture, and I'm not supposed to touch you again, and I'm not supposed to let you touch me, either. If I do, he threatened to tell Dimi and Uncle Tomas."

"What?! How? Did you tell him *why?* That it was okay? Vlad, I've been holding hands with you my entire life. I think I'm sane enough to

231

make *that* decision! Who the hell is he to tell us we can't?"

Vlad blushed and turned away. "John's afraid we might get – *romantically involved.*" He rested his elbows on his knees and let his head fall into his hands. "I'm sorry I ever suggested it."

"You're kidding! You mean like, lovey-dovey involved? Vlad, that's *sick!* You're my *brother*! We've been best friends all our lives! I mean, of course I love you, I'd die for you, but not like *that!* You told him that, didn't you? Is – Is that how you feel about me?"

Vlad's face was a pasty grey. "Gods no! I know you're a girl and all, and yeah, you're kind of pretty, I guess, but I don't think of you that way anymore than I'd think of a – a *grapefruit*! Please don't take that the wrong way."

"That's good. If you did, I'd have to beat the guts out of you, and I don't want to hurt you like that. *Sick!* They call *me* sick, but they get to make up stuff like that," she huffed. The Kirushenko temper welled up to turn her nerves to steel. She put her arms around him and kissed him on the cheek – more than a level two, but less than a level three. Someone had crossed the wrong person. Mess with her, fine, but don't ever upset Vladimir.

"Don't you worry, my little brother. I'll put a stop to *that* bullshit once and for all."

Twenty-two

"You're quiet."

Carver announced his awareness of the silent fish-eyed stare. Twenty minutes of sitting in the empty communal dining room of the psychiatric ward, and not a word. Sarah wasn't withdrawn; she was baiting him. He hadn't seen a hint of this kind of game since she'd returned.

"What have you been thinking about?"

Sarah smoldered in her chair. "Absolutely nothing," she said in a voice so icy it could have come from Grandmamá herself. "The court said I have to *attend* therapy. I am in attendance. There is nothing in the order that says I have to speak."

Denying she had to speak was still speaking. "Okay. I have a feeling it may have said something about cooperation, though."

"I am cooperating. I came in here without a problem, didn't I?"

"Yyyeeesss. So if you don't mind entering the room, then the problem must be with me."

"Now, why would I have a problem with you?" Sarah arched sideways across the chair. Throat to the ceiling, she drew up a knee, resting her heel on the edge of the seat. Her long hair fell seductively in a curtain behind her.

It was a very exposed, very vulnerable position, yet she held the pose as if waiting for comment. The more Carver thought about it, the more it seemed that's what she *was* clumsily attempting to project.

As no remark followed, she sat up, spinning the sheet of hair around with a sharp turn of her head, angry enough for the confrontation. "Vlad and I have spent the last seven years trying desperately to stay the very best of friends. Why would I have a problem with someone trying to break us up over a horrible, sick lie started by one of two people in this room?"

"Which lie would that be?"

"You've spread more than one?"

"I haven't spread any lies, Sarah. What have you heard that's bothering you?"

"I'm sick of all your psychotherapeutic *bullshit!* People incorrectly second-guessing me like some stupid child! I'm not stupid and I'm not a kid anymore! I shouldn't have to hear second-hand the sick, psychotic rumor that I'm trying to marry my brother."

Carver kicked himself mentally. *What was it on the recordings? No*

233

secrets? It underscored his feelings of uneasiness.

"I never said you wanted to marry Vladimir. I merely expressed concern over the appropriateness of yesterday's actions in light of how close you are."

"And how long have you been experiencing these fantasies?" Sarah said, well-rehearsed in therapeutic terminology. "I didn't realize voyeurism was a requirement for psychiatry. I don't remember seeing an observation window in the lounge."

"There isn't. I'm surprised you of all people forgot about camera ports. I seem to remember a certain child with an incredible knack for spotting hidden cameras, licking her fingers, and leaving so many prints on the lens covers the recordings were useless."

"Hmph! There are eight cameras in that room; we weren't near any of them. If I may be so bold, John, that's bullshit, and you know it."

"Do I? Teenage siblings don't generally kiss at all, in any form, especially on the mouth. Sibling rivalry exists for a reason."

"There is *nothing* between me and Vlad! Nothing we cannot do at a dinner table. *Your* table, if you want to be even pickier."

"Adolescence can be a confusing time. Hormones are switching on and off, there are great swings in brain chemistry as the body tries to move from childhood into adulthood. It's very easy to get lost along the way."

"I am *not* lost," she said arrogantly. "I am perfectly in control of that aspect of my life."

Carver held back a laugh. "Then you're the first sixteen-year-old in the history of humanity who is."

"*I'm* not just anybody." She flipped her hair in a daring show once more. A languid finger ran down her throat to hook the neckline of her shirt and pull it downwards, displaying a timid hint of cleavage. "But I believe we digress. We were discussing your obsession with incestuous relationships and your concurrent fantasies therewith."

"Right topic, wrong subject. Today's thesis discussion is on mid-adolescent hormone surges and socially acceptable methods of handling them."

Sarah blinked in mock confusion. "That's funny. That's not what was on the handouts at registration. I'm sure that's not the debate I signed up for. Oh, what the hell. I'm already here." She leaned forward over the table with calculated pose, the back of her hand supporting her chin.

Carver studied the change in demeanor. The naïve child had been replaced with a conceited, self-serving vixen whose very Attitude dared the opposer to battle her. If this was a portent of her impending maturity – He didn't want to be around when this butterfly emerged.

"You want to talk about *sssexxx*? *Fine!* Let's talk about it. We'll start with you! So tell me, John, how long have you and Katya been – what was the last idiom I heard? 'Powering up the Davies Drive' together? Hmm? I'll bet cash it was before you were legally bound, wasn't it?"

"My personal life is not open to discussion."

"How long did it take you to wear down her ability to refuse? How long did you *graciously* make yourself wait? How long did you nag her until she stopped saying 'no' just to make you leave her alone? She certainly didn't seem too eager to do It at seventeen ..."

Carver let his stylus drop with a clatter and pushed back from the table. "That's enough. If you want to discuss personal things with your sister, that's between you and her. My marital concerns are none of your business in the therapy setting and I will not dignify those questions with an answer. Like it or not, we are now family, and family doesn't treat family. I can give you advice, I can recommend people or treatments and explain them to you, but as of this very minute, I am no longer your therapist. I will no longer deal with you on a professional basis."

"Oh, *really*, John." The eyes rolled, and she gave a smug little smile. "Aren't you being a bit melodramatic? *You can't avoid me.* You see me here, and you see me at The Big House, and I've even slept at your house. *You're* the one who brought the subject up in the first place. It's not *my* fault you can't handle it."

Carver's irritation got the better of him. "Handle *what?* An insolent teen that refuses to discuss a problem that's tearing her apart? I navigated my adolescence more or less successfully a number of years ago. I *can* handle the fact that seven or eight of every ten teens *are* frightened of their emerging sexuality and the role it will play in their adult lives. I deal with them and their fears every day. Should they or shouldn't they, when and where and how and with whom? What's wrong? What's right? What's everyone else doing, and are they any different? Will they be laughed at? Are they doing it right? ..."

"John, John, John. You have a one-track mind."

" ... Is that what they're supposed to feel? What if they feel different? What if they don't like the opposite sex? What if their family objects to a Nalkarian partner? They're so caught up in the social aspects, they forget the bigger worries of pregnancy and diseases and abuse." John counted off on his fingers, spitting with determination to get his point across. "I realize you've been living in isolation, but eight or nine of those ten will explore their role through peer discussion, literature, or explicit videography long before they go through with anything. They explore various stages of sexual intimacy through group interaction, temporary one-on-one relationships, or through autoeroticism and mast - "

Sarah's shriek cut short his tirade. John had just enough time to shove his chair back and pull his knees up to avoid being hit by the table as Sarah took to her feet and flipped it toward him. The compad bounced on the floor. She grabbed her chair and swung it above her head, smashing it over and over on the table at Carver's feet. With an anguished cry, she let the chair fly across the room to land with a noisy crash. She turned and flipped two more tables in her run to the farthest end of the room. Throwing herself in the corner, she pounded her fists against the wall before sinking to the floor in tears. She banged her head two, three, four times, then collapsed into a ball, drained.

Carver unfolded, not quite sure what had transpired. She had every opportunity to injure him with the chair, but she hadn't. Despite her hostility, her anger was not directed at him. That was a clue.

"I think we may have touched a raw nerve here. How about you?" In poorly accented Russian, he said to the room, "*Interkom: pazhal'sta, send Doktor Petrova to this location, Kode tri, Doktor Karverov requesting,*" The backup was protocol, protecting him, protecting Sarah. Adina Petrova had been his first choice to work with the girl; what better time to slip her in than to watch him handle a major crisis? He crossed the room and sat on the floor near his patient.

Petrova poked her head in the door. John held a finger to his lips, then pointed to a chair. The new doctor sat, available to help if necessary, a third-party eyewitness to a sensitive situation.

"Maybe we should talk seriously, hmm?" Carver watched the curled back heave with sobs. After a minute or two, the figure pushed and rolled to a slouch. It pained him to see the frenetic jerking of her face and body as the neuro pump tried its computerized best to measure and counteract the rush of inappropriate neurochemicals.

"Deep breaths. Don't fight it."

"Make it stop!" Sarah sobbed. "I *hate* this, John! Take it out! I want … it out! I can't … be *me*! They have … no right to … tell me what I can feel! To force me not … to feel something!"

"I don't like it, either, Sar. I don't think it's the best thing for you and I don't think it's working right, but a court order is a court order. I can put through an emergency request, tell them you're having a bad reaction, but I have to replace it with something, and I need your cooperation for that. Think about that part, and I will have an answer for you by tomorrow. Okay?"

"Djyah!" she squeaked, somewhere between *da* and *yes*.

Carver clasped his hands around his knees. "I don't think that's what this is all about, though, is it? I said a lot of things. What part upset you? The idea of masturbation, or the subject of sexuality itself?"

The girl clawed the wall, but the wall would not allow escape. She hunched against it, coughing. The medications were winning. The hands moved as if trying to speak for her. Carver waited. The hands indicated the mind was working; he waited for the mouth to catch up.

"In ... order to do ... *any* ... of those ... things, I would have to a-a-admit ... to a ... *need* ... for such things."

No need ... John wracked his brain. "The general *idea* of sexuality, or a specific aspect of it?" The head nodded at the first part of the sentence. He thought out loud for her. "Okay. You would have to *admit* to a need for sexuality. You're not willing to *admit*. To not admit is to deny. I take it by the word *admit*, then, that at some point you experienced such a need and then denied it. Correct?"

"I don't know!"

"What makes you uncertain?"

Sarah trembled, cheek to the wall. "The Fleet officers staying with us – the youngest one was maybe Dimi's age. We talked a lot. I swear, John, that's all... it was! I just liked ... talking to him! But Dimi said I was ... acting dopey, I was showing off ... and I swear, John! I wasn't! I didn't know I was doing *any* of those things!" Her voice trailed off as she grappled with memories.

"I made sure I was the coolest, most reserved person I could. I didn't want him thinking about ... me like that. He tried ... but we never really talked again. So I don't know." She stole a sideways glance, sniffing hard and rubbing a tear.

Carver nodded. Teasing. Brothers and sisters did it every day, but the effects could be devastating. On the verge of making a giant step toward a healthy adulthood, she'd been set back to the beginning, or worse. The body screamed out adult, but the frightened mind still cried child, and the spirit was caught dying in between.

The sobs resurged; along with the medication twitches, she shook from head to toe. "And, a long time ago ... Our neighbor wanted to get – *friendlier*. Not in a nasty way," she corrected, wiping her nose on her sleeve, "but he – he *liked* me, and asked Dimi if he could walk me places."

"That's very nice. That's a compliment to you. That's a very natural thing, a first step in getting to know someone better."

Sarah grimaced. "But he *liked* me! The way *Dimi* liked girls! And I knew what Dimi did to girls he liked, because he did it all the time, with lots of different girls. And I couldn't! I couldn't let that happen to me."

The information raised a new concern. "Did Dmitri do these things in front of you?"

Sarah shook a vehement denial. *"No!* He knew it upset me. But sometimes – when he married – I would hide in my closet because it felt safe, but the other side of the wall was against Dimi's bed. If I was in there, I could hear everything. I never listened intentionally. I didn't! I had nowhere left to hide."

The siren-wail rose. "But I *liked* Charlie! I did!" she gasped. "He was kind, and polite, and didn't do anything I didn't like, and he looked so happy when we picked on Dimi together, and all he ever wanted to do was *be* with me! And I ran away! I ran away on him! I made myself bury it! I buried it until I didn't feel *anything*, and I *hated* that! He cried for me, and I wouldn't tell him … I felt that way, too!"

"So why did you do it, then? Why make yourself do something you hated and knew was wrong?"

Sarah gave no answer, but the hands clenched into painful fists of tension. The fists banged on the head, increasing their fury until John reached out and pulled one down. Sarah leaned against him and kicked the wall as hard as she could, growling and screeching.

"Get it out," Carver encouraged. "That'a girl. Fight it! Tear the *problem* to pieces, not yourself. Put the anger out with the compost; don't let it rot inside. You can beat it."

Out of breath, Sarah rolled to her knees and leaped at him. He flinched, but the arms only locked around his neck, seeking solace for the hysterical tears that burst forth. John glanced at Doctor Petrova as he put his arms around the girl, giving the comfort he knew she so desperately needed.

"You're strong, Sarah. Shshsh. Whatever it is, it can't hurt you in here. Show me which worm, and we'll squash it together."

Sarah wriggled away, retreating to the impartial wall. She kept her face down, curled up as small as she could manage. Heavy tears stole her breath.

"Be-cause I was *scared! hic* I … was … so … *scared*, John! Ev-ver *hic* since that … thing … at Rangler. I'm scared … of … *everything*! *hic* I'm … so scared … of boys … and men … and of … be*hic*ing … alone … because if no-one's … with me *hic* it … could happen again … or worse! That question *hic* … you al-al-always wanted … to know? *hic* The one… I would nev-ver … answer? Because the answer was … *yes*, John! It was *yes*! And it *hurt!* Fin*hic*gers! I know it was just *hic* … his fingers, but I was … so *scared* … *hic* and he didn't … *care!* I fought him … as hard as … I could … and he still *hurt* me! And if that … terr-i-fied me … that much, *hic...* how ... could I think ... of letting it happen to me ... v-v-vol-un-tar-i-ly, ... or doing... doing... what those girls *hic...* were do-ing... for D-D-Di-mi?" She gasped uncontrollably, unable to breathe, hands tugging at her hair.

Carver's face reflected his sympathy. He'd worried about that seven years ago, had seen the direction she was heading. He'd tried, but fingers stuffed the ears, and if he talked louder, she hummed or sang to herself, eyes closed, blocking him out. Now, after festering unchecked for seven years, the emotional wound was horribly infected, and would be much harder to heal.

"Tell me one thing, Sar, absolutely honest, no matter what. I *need* to know. It doesn't matter which answer you give, either one is *okay,* and the information will never leave this room. But I need to know, deep down, yes or no, absolutely confidential." He sighed, wishing he didn't have to ask it. "The way you felt about Dmitri's friend, the feelings you made yourself deny, do you have any of those same feelings for Vlad, even ones you might be trying to deny?"

Sobs devoured the squeal of fury. One hand rolled into a fist and swung at him. It was poorly aimed and powerless, and Carver deflected it with ease.

"NO! Once ... and for all ... NO! I *love* ... him! I'd give ... him my ... life if ... he needed it! But I DON'T... WANT... TO SLEEP... WITH HIM... LIKE THAT!" she choked. "STOP IT! STOP! Stop saying that! It's ... NOT ... TRUE! Leave ... him ... *alone!*" She gagged on the tears.

"Okay. Okay. I believe you. I won't ask again. Shhh. Come here," John soothed, and held out an arm. With a groan of misery, she tipped and let her head and shoulders fall into his lap. He smoothed her hair back from her face.

"Shh. It's all out in the open, and it can't hurt you again. You're going to be okay. If you hurt right now, it's from growing pains. You don't realize how big a step you just took toward fixing everything! You know you have a problem, you can already identify it, and I'd bet my money that deep inside, you already know how to fix it, too. You've already done the hardest part! We'll get you there, Kid. You're not the first person in the world to be so scared, and you won't be the last."

Sarah caught a deep breath. She grew heavier against his leg as her tension left, and she went limp with exhaustion.

"We're going to have to change some things, though," he warned. "I can't work you through this part. We're family now, and we're too close. It's not appropriate, I won't do it, and I don't *want* to do it. I want you to work with Adina for me. She's very good at working out those kinds of things. You're like one of my own; you're every bit as important to me as Roman, just bigger. I wouldn't trust you to just anyone, so keep that in mind. What you tell her will stay with her. She won't tell even me. I won't let her. Will you do that for me?"

"… Try!"

"And we'll drop our daily stuff," Carver continued. "You're more normal than you realize, Sar. You might not think so, but you are. I really want you in my group session, three afternoons a week. It's not the same as our one-on-one stuff. You may think you're ten, but like it or not, your brain and body are sixteen. You've never dealt with people your own age. It's time you did. Group's a good place to learn how they feel and how they handle situations that come up, like the ones you told me about. What do you think?"

The head gulped and nodded. A pager tone from the overhead speakers interrupted them.

"Doctor Karverov?"

"Da?"

"There are visitors here for Miss Kirushenko. Should I have them wait, or is there a time they should come back?"

"Kto oni?"

"Dmitri Kirushenko ee Tomas Ivanov."

"What do you say, Kid?" Carver asked. "Want to take a break? Are you up to visitors, or would you rather wait a while?"

"Now!"

"Send them down," he called to the intercom.

Sarah pulled herself together, wiping her eyes on John's leg and sitting up. It didn't help much, for as soon as Dmitri entered the room, she gave a loud cry and ran to him. Dmitri held her, surveying the destruction of the room.

"You all right?"

Carver stood and dusted off his pants. "I am *more* than all right! I am the best I've felt in months." He walked over and gave Sarah's hair one last affectionate fluff. "We just had a massive growth spurt, that's all. If she looks taller, it's because a huge weight just fell off those shoulders. But it was worth it, wasn't it?"

"You say so," said the muffled voice under Dmitri's ear.

"She's going to be okay. She's going to be *very* okay. If she works as hard as she did this afternoon, my guess is she'll be off all medication in six months, and the courts can go fly a sailplane when she turns eighteen."

Tomas looked doubtful. "That good?"

"Absolutely. Let me introduce you to Doctor Petrova." John waved a

240

hand to the dark-haired woman, who joined the group. "I called her in to observe some dynamics. Adina, these are Sarah's guardians: her brother Dmitri and her uncle, Tomas Ivanov."

Adina shook their hands. "Pleased to meet you."

"I'm going to have Dr. Petrova take over part of Sarah's therapy. She's more qualified in certain areas than I am, and I think Sarah'd be better off working with a female therapist for some subjects."

"That's probably not a bad idea," Dmitri said. Sarah was heavy around his neck; he backed up and sat on a bench by the door. She slid onto his lap, curling against him like a sleepy toddler. Tomas sat beside them.

"NO!" John barked. He took Sarah by the arms and dragged her off her brother, sitting her down between the two men. Her red-rimmed eyes stared at him in bewilderment.

"No more!" John ordered, pointing at Dmitri. "This is going to stop, and it's going to stop *now*! Sarah is not a baby. She is sixteen years old and should not be sitting on laps, especially her brothers'. And that goes for you too, Tomas."

"She doesn't do that with me," Tomas insisted.

"I don't care! Sarah is having some confusion as to what is considered appropriate behavior for people her age, and that kind of babying isn't helping matters at all. There are going to be some new rules instituted at home, and Tomas, it is up to you to make sure they are enforced. No more sitting on laps. No kissing brothers – none of them! No frontal hugging. No wrestling – ever. No sharing beds, or preferably even bedrooms. No handholding. And no discussing personal matters. General questions about handling feelings or situations or appropriate behavior, that's fine, but the gruesome details of our personal sexual exploits are more than she needs right now – and this means cutting off David and his stories about things real or imagined. Sarah needs some space to get her act together, a little less pressure put on her right now, until she gets on track. Understood? I'll work out the details, and we'll talk in a little while." He left the three to their visit, eager to speak with Petrova.

* * *

Dmitri paced the hospital conference room, poking at the various aesthetic but meaningless artifacts decorating it. He picked a colored glass egg out of a display bowl and rolled it between his hands.

"So ... what brought all this on? These new rules ... Are they hers or yours?"

John sat down. "My rules. She's sixteen. It's time she grew up. Did you sit on your sisters' laps when you were sixteen? Climb into bed with them when you were frightened? Hold their hands? Kiss them all the time?"

"I wouldn't know," Dmitri said acridly, replacing the egg. "I was abandoned at sixteen. I didn't have anyone to support me like that. I had to fend for myself."

"Point taken. When Katerina was sixteen, did she climb into bed with you or your brothers? Did they cuddle her on their laps? Or did she have other friends she went out with? Boyfriends, girlfriends, sweethearts, real or just pined for?"

"But she does that to all her brothers, not just Dmitri," Tomas reflected. "Even the girls, now and then."

"It doesn't matter," John insisted. "It's the maturity behind the behavior I'm concerned about, not necessarily the intent."

Dmitri adjusted the opacity on the room's window and gazed out over the hospital courtyard. Crocuses dotted the ground, cheering the end of winter. "Of course. Kat had more than Vik, but he had his share. And Sarah's so damned uptight, she hasn't had so much as one. She saw no point in trying to make friends with Tau Cetan girls, and Moons forbid she befriend a boy. She blamed it on that thing that happened to her – you know, back at your old hospital?"

"Which thing was that?"

Smart. Dmitri eyed Tomas. Secrets were secrets. He knew John knew, but… "What the hell. You know every other detail about her. You might as well know where all that insanity comes from. Just remember, it's a real deep secret to her. Never mention it."

"I know nothing unless she tells me," Tomas swore.

"The guy who grabbed her in the hall, and kissed her and stuff. She said it scared her so bad, she was afraid to kiss people. Poor Charlie loved her to death, but she was afraid if he liked her that much, he might do the same thing. I told her he wasn't like that – she knew he wasn't – but she wouldn't stop worrying about it. He cried over her for years. He wouldn't have forced anything on her if she was the last girl on the planet. But she wouldn't believe it."

Carver nodded. "Learning to trust again is a very difficult step, especially when the victim is in that age bracket. I tried to work with her on it back then, but she fought very hard to pretend the whole thing never happened. We filed the report as a third-degree assault, but it wasn't until today she confirmed my suspicion it was actually second-degree. I'd been afraid of that."

242

"Second degree what?" Dmitri clouded the window and glanced at his brother-in-law. "What was second degree?"

"The assault," John repeated. He poked a crumb of food from around the computer controls on the table. "She wasn't able to tell me back then, and I didn't want to push her and deepen her trauma. I refused to force her to submit to an exam. Today she admitted there was penetration …"

"*What?* What do you mean, pene – *What the hell are you talking about?*" The hair on the back of Dmitri's neck began to itch, and he felt the familiar frozen-steel fingers of disaster scratching at it. "It was just a kiss! Some crazy guy grabs her in a hallway, holds her against the wall, and tongues her hard without warning! That's all it was! *Wasn't it*, John? She said it was only a kiss!"

"Saints in Heaven!" Tomas breathed, afraid of the same conclusion.

Carver blanched as white as his shirt. He stood up quickly. "Oh my God. That's all she … ? I'm so sorry, Dmitri. I didn't realize that was all she told you. I am so sorry to spring it on you like that. Let me explain."

"All that nonsense when she first arrived – *that's* where that stemmed from, didn't it?" Tomas realized with horror. "From something despicable in her past? John, why didn't you warn me!"

"A lot of it, yeah, I think so," Carver agreed, but his attention was focused on Dmitri.

"It was *more* than just a kiss? Second degree … . John! You don't need a physical exam for a kiss! She was – *raped*?" Bile crept up Dmitri's throat, and he began to shake. He knew of Katya's secret, though she insisted it was her fault for being a drunken fourteen. But Sarah … "She was a kid! She was just a *little kid*!"

Memories flashed back – fears of the dark, of being alone, of strangers, the insane terror over Charlie's friendly affections, the almost desperate interruptions every time he tried to have privacy with Jaycee – the pieces of the puzzle slammed into place with crystal clarity. *And he'd yelled at her, ridiculed her, harassed her, threatened her, all because she couldn't tell him she'd been…*

"No!" John put a steadying hand on the boy's shoulder. "No! She wasn't raped, not as you're thinking."

Dmitri seized Carver by his shirt and shook him. *"How could you let that happen! She was a goddamned little kid! You were supposed to protect her!"*

Arms wrapped around him from behind, but they only held him in a tight embrace. "Let him go, Dmitri," Tomas said in a choked voice. "Being angry now won't change the past. Find out the facts, then you'll know where to lay blame. Then you can act as you feel you must. Come.

Come sit with me. We'll find out what happened together." He pulled Dmitri to a chair, and moved his closer.

John leaned against the table. He sighed and stuck his hands in his pockets. "I got there less than thirty seconds afterward. Two patients, two transport staff, they never moved out of visual range, and it still happened. It was not a case of rape in the first degree. She was held against her will while kissed and fondled under her clothing. The whole incident couldn't have lasted more than two minutes before someone saw. Simple touching would have counted as a third-class assault. Because, as I found out today, he did... violate her with his fingers, it's a second-class assault. Because of her age, it would have been a first class charge. That opened a whole new world of dangers she'd never known existed before.

"I'm sorry, Dmitri. I was every bit as upset and disgusted about it as you are. I wanted to kill him – and worse yet, I had the ability to do it. A slip with a hypo on a struggling patient, a wrong drug, a wrong dose, an accidental but fatal error... He was already facing sixteen proven counts of first-degree assault, and in my book and a few billion other people's he deserved to die more horribly than I'd do it, but I couldn't. I could do more to protect other children from the same fate by locking him away, not by getting locked up myself."

Tears formed in Dmitri's eyes, and he made no effort to hide them. *"Why?"* he whimpered. *"Why?"*

"She happened to be in the wrong place at the wrong time."

Dimi shook his head, whispering against his knuckles as he pressed his fist to his mouth. "No. All those times – I thought she was just being a brat! Why didn't she tell me? I thought she was just being mean and jealous. I yelled at her all the time. Told her she was being a baby, she had to grow up, it was part of nature. She was scared. She was only scared to death! And I was such a *bastard* about it!"

Tomas reached over and squeezed his shoulder.

"You didn't know," Carver said gently. "She'd buried the pain very, very deep, to make sure she never had to deal with it again. She couldn't admit it to herself, let alone anyone else. You realized she had a problem and you tried to steer her in the right direction. You did the best you could. You had no training for that, no expertise. It wasn't a problem you could have solved. The fact that she tried to make progress at all is a testament to your care and concern. She loved you, she respected you, and she trusted you enough to try. There's no chemical replacement for that. You already had the strongest medicine there is."

The last thing Dmitri expected to find as he drowned in guilt was praise and forgiveness. No one ever thought he could know what was best for Sarah; no one ever listened, no one ever believed in him. Not Val, not that star Captain, not the courts, not even John back then. Certainly the whole disaster that brought them home was living proof how far he could screw up good ideas. A whirlwind of emotions churning inside him, he fell forward on the doctor's shoulder, and let his guilt flow out with the tears.

* * *

Sarah lay motionless on the bed in her assigned roomlet, back to the door. She called it a roomlet because it was no bigger than the closet in her room at Uncle Tomas's house, just an assigned more-or-less private sleeping cubicle on the hospital floor. She heard the footsteps enter but didn't bother to turn around and look, still numb from the force of the afternoon's session. It was too late for guests, and she couldn't give a damn about the pesty nurses. She waited, but the footsteps neither left nor spoke. At last a folded paper fell in front of her face. She grabbed it and sat up quickly to stare at Dmitri.

Sarah opened the cream-colored Sigma Tau Ceti paper. The words were written in brown ink made from boiled tree bark, in her own near-perfect print:

> *I, Sarah-Irina Kirushenko, do voluntarily give ownership of my immortal soul to my brother, Dmitri-Mikhail Kirushenko, as partial payment for the terrible wrongs I have wrought him, until he declares the debt repaid and returns it to me.*

except that underneath it now bore new lines in black, in Dmitri's scratchy scrawl:

> *Paid in full*
> *7 April 2271*
> *Dmitri M. Kirushenko*

"What's this for? I didn't earn this back yet."

"Yes, you did," Dmitri said quietly. "I never should have accepted it in the first place."

"I'm ... happy, I guess, but I don't understand."

"John and I had a misunderstanding. I thought I knew what he was talking about, and then he started to discuss things I *didn't* know, and by

245

then it was too late. I found out the rest of your secret, Sar. I know what really happened in the hospital last time. I know what you told me about was only part of it."

Sarah's jaw clenched, and she stared angrily at the bedcover.

"Don't make that face. It wasn't John's fault. Why didn't you tell me?"

"It was none of your business! You weren't there. You couldn't do anything to change it."

"No, maybe not, but had you told me all the details way back when, I would never have treated you as I did."

"I didn't *want* anyone to know!" Sarah cried out, tears kept in check by a load of new chemicals. "I didn't want your stares or your whispers or your speculations or your worries, or any other type of differential treatment."

He sat on the bed. "With everything we've been through, have I *ever* done that to you?"

"No, I don't think so, but I'm not thinking too great right now. So help me, Dmitri Kirushenko, if you ever tell another soul any *part* of that story, I will kill myself, medications or no medications! Only two other people know, and they've kept the secret. I won't live with that information made public!"

"Well, make that four, because Tomas was in the room."

Sarah threw her hands in the air, just like Uncle Tomas. "I'm never going home! The whole world knows my worst secret! Uncle Tomas will tell Grandmamá, she'll tell all her friends, the servants will overhear and spread rumors, it will make its way completely around town, probably even onto the hyperspace headlines. *Leading Mystery Solved In Minsk; Crazy Child Tells All.*"

"He was in tears, Sar. He felt as bad as I do. In his line of work, if you can't keep a secret, you're out of business. I trust him with that."

"That's such a relief, Dim. How comforting to know *you* can trust people who know *my* secrets."

"I'm sorry," he said with a sigh. "I guess that's all I really meant to say. I'm sorry for ever treating you like I did. I know there were times when I tried to push you into things. I thought you were just fighting me to be a baby. I know there were times when I got really angry, and I said a lot of mean things. I thought a lot of worse ones. If you'd just told me half of it, I don't think – no, I *know* I wouldn't have done all that." He gave her a hard hug. "Please forgive me."

Sarah didn't fight the contact, but she didn't relax, either. "I've *never* talked about it. *Ever.* Until this week. And I *don't* want to talk about it.

246

Ever. But I have to." Hopelessness crept into her voice. "I have to talk about it because it's killing me inside, and I can't go on like this. I don't want to be like this forever, Dim! I want to be like you! I want to be able to enjoy life, not run from it; that every person I meet might be a deviant out to harm me, that every time I'm alone someone will hurt me, that every dark shadow hides a monster in wait. That every step in a friendship inexorably leads to fear and pain and pregnancy and death. I want to be normal!"

Dmitri held her tight. "You are, Kid. You can do anything you set your mind to. I've seen you do it. Listen to John, do exactly what he says, and he'll get you there. Any way I can help, let me know. I promise not to ask too many questions. I got a lot of making up to do."

Sarah hugged him back. "No. You're here, Vlad's here, and we're finally back in Russia. That's all I ever wanted to start with."

Twenty-three

It was one of the most difficult things Sarah had ever done, and like any major change, it happened so fast she didn't have time to build up objections. Dr. Petrova had John's infinite patience, listened without comment, never reprimanded, and let Sarah steer minimalist conversations as comfort allowed. It was just the subject matter that made Sarah want to vomit every time she forced herself into the office. John hadn't mentioned Petrova's specialty was sex therapy. In her heart Sarah knew it was for the best, and in a tiny corner of her head she wanted to succeed, but the mere thought of it made her want to hide under furniture and cry.

"Don't ever ask me what we talk about, or what she wants me to do," Sarah threatened Vladimir before he became curious. "Maybe in thirty or forty years, when I've had time to recover."

Within ten days, John presented Sarah with a medication specifically tailored to her present chemical deficiencies, and the neuropump and its embarrassing tremors disappeared for good. The new drug left her sluggish at the start, but the effect soon tapered. It supported her without controlling her reactions, and Sarah began to trust it.

"While we've got you belly-down on the table," John suggested, "how about I bring in a plastic surgeon and we get that back taken care of?"

Sarah perked up. "The scars? All of them?"

"Every one," he promised.

John's adolescent therapy group proved the hardest adjustment. Sarah could handle new medications, skin surgery, even the mortifying self-relaxation exercises Petrova wanted her to practice, but entering Group was like being kidnapped in a sound sleep and thrown into a wild stampede. Seven teens ranged in age from thirteen to seventeen; three conduct disorders, an adjustment disorder, a global impairment, an intractable psychotic, and an electively mute severe depressive. Sarah – whose files claimed she was depressed and self-mutilating, with an adjustment disorder, anxiety disorder, panic disorder, traumatic stress disorder, and court-supervised therapy under the auspices of temporary psychosis in lieu of an attempted murder charge – made eight.

Alta was the self-appointed ringleader, fully supported by half the room and ignored by the rest. A lanky, arrogant seventeen, he was everything David might have been – if David had never had a conscience. Oppositional, confrontational, disrespectful, charged four times for illegal narcotics, he was also sexually aggressive, a fact that terrified Sarah.

"Don't worry about it," John instructed her ahead of time. "There are two aides with me the entire time, giving a less than three-to-one staff ratio, which is very good for a group arrangement. Usually there's only one aide."

But Sarah had never met anyone so bold in her life. Her brothers teased her all the time, but they were never as openly pornographic as Alta. She lapsed into frightened silence.

Alta grinned when he saw her. "Son of a bitch! I've seen you in the halls, Chickie! What do you say we go at it slo-mo in one of the ID rooms? I'll teach you a whole new reason to scream."

Sarah pushed her chair over by the door.

"Cool it, Alta," John told him. "Back in your seat. Let's not scare Sarah off in her first five minutes. Who knows a better way Alta could have introduced himself?"

The reminders of social grace bounced off Alta's head. He spent the next five minutes licking his lips and winking. He started to squirm.

"Alta, is there a problem?" John finally acknowledged.

"Yeah, Doc," Alta said with a painful expression. "She's got my *huy* so greased I can't take it anymore! I gotta get some relief or I'm gonna die!" He made a show of unfastening his pants, and the room erupted in laughter.

"Alta, this your one warning," John ordered, making a mark on a wallscreen. "Fix your pants or leave."

Alta pretended to comply, then looked up helplessly. "I can't, Doc! They won't close anymore!"

John waved a thumb at the door and both aides grabbed Alta by the arms and escorted him from the room.

As he passed Sarah by the door, Alta managed to expose himself. "All yours!"

Two weeks, and Sarah found a routine. Arriving early, she sat hidden behind the door, waiting for the misery to begin. Mia, the young mute depressive, slipped in and sat in her usual place, also apart from the group. Mia cooperated for some activities, but remained pulled into herself. She glanced at Sarah from the corner of her eye.

Sarah noticed, performing the same maneuver on Mia. She broke her self-imposed silence. "You don't have to worry about me. I know exactly how you feel. Nothing's worse than people nagging you to talk when you just don't have the energy. I congratulate you on your resolve to ignore them. Don't give in. Don't let them force you into anything you're not ready for. It will get better in time. You just have to wait."

Mia didn't acknowledge her, but at the next session, she sat just one chair away. John noticed the move immediately, but Sarah held a finger to her lips. She understood in a way he couldn't.

She reached her breaking point at the eighth session. Sarah had to admit, superior intellect aside, she'd met her match in Alta. The more he harassed her, the more impassive she became; the more impassive she became, the harder he harassed her. She arrived at the room late; Alta was waiting. He jumped her as she walked in, grabbed her by the hips, and pretended to have sex with her from behind, moaning and laughing in front of everyone. Sarah screamed, then let her anger take over. She spun, all power in her fist, but Alta ducked. She didn't connect until he came at her again, laughing harder.

"You didn't tell me you liked it rough!" he goaded. "Beat me, baby! Make it hurt! Lower!"

Sarah stopped punching, confused. How could she possibly defeat him if he enjoyed punishment even more? Her pause allowed him to grab her again, and she resumed hitting him as hard and as fast as she could.

The room erupted. Three teens jumped in to cheer them on. Lara, the psychotic who believed herself to bear eighty-three eyes of the mystic Inaki, howled and tore off her clothes, the better to 'see.' Mia cowered under the activity table, crying. It took John and both aides to pull them apart as reinforcements were paged.

"Get him into a dampening room!" John ordered.

"You hurt my love-maker!" Alta shouted at Sarah. He unfastened his pants. "Kiss it!"

Sarah burst into tears. *"Screw you!"* she shouted at John. "Screw you and *all* your nut cases! I don't have to put up with this! I want to go home, right now, law or no law!" John had Dmitri called to retrieve her.

She returned for the next session flanked by two tall bodyguards, flexing their muscles threateningly. Alta was back, too, with an additional male staff whose sole job was to keep him in control.

"It's a nice gesture, guys, but you can't stay," John told David and Sergei. "This is a closed session."

"One minute," David assured him, unseasonably clad in a sleeveless athletic shirt that accentuated his bulky shoulders. He seized the chair next to Sarah, and with a straining grunt proceeded to bend and snap the tubular legs, one at a time. He held the last leg high, then jammed it through the plastic chair back with a deadly thrust. He dropped the wreck at Alta's feet.

250

"That's what happens to people who mess with our sister," David growled. He pointed at John. "Make sure it doesn't happen again." Sergei gave Sarah a pat on the back, and the boys left.

"Damn!" was all Alta said. "I'll bet he's hung like an animal!"

Sarah addressed the group for the first time. "I suggest you heed the warning. I'm here on seven counts of attempted murder, and I have no qualms making it eight."

John verified the fact. The level of direct harassment dropped. Sarah wasn't a part of the group socially, but she was bad enough to belong.

The next session, Mia sat next to Sarah.

It was a strange friendship, each accepting the other merely on the behavior exhibited during group. They never spoke during sessions, but partnered up for activities without a word, trusting in their silence. John wouldn't say a thing beyond the fact Mia had attempted suicide.

"I've got to be here early next time," Sarah whispered to her one day. "I'll have a half-hour to kill, bored in the gourd." As she'd hoped, Mia appeared not long after. It became the routine, a half-hour of silence between them, friends without the demand of conversation.

"Is it worse at night?" Sarah asked one day. Mia nodded slowly.

"It was for me, too. I'd hide in the smallest place I could find – under beds, in the closet, in a cupboard if I could fit. It made the emptiness seem more confined."

Mia nodded with understanding.

"Do you have any brothers or sisters?"

No.

"That's too bad. They make a big difference. My brothers are the only reason I'm still alive. Is it just a biochemical thing, or because of something really bad?"

The girl tensed up and turned away, but she gave a short nod.

"So was mine," Sarah admitted softly. "Something at home? So was mine. My father beat me so bad I'm still undergoing surgery, then my mother died, and my father killed my younger sister. I'm sorry. It took me eight years to get this far. Don't give up."

Mia's thin hand slipped off her lap to touch Sarah's fingers, the first contact she'd made with anyone in four months.

Sarah held the hand tightly. "You'll make it. It just takes time."

Twenty-four

S unday dinner had long been the few hours a week when the siblings
could gather as a group, once they'd started to spread apart. David
and Sergei were home, Katya, John, and Roman visited, Valeria's
boyfriend Adrik had been a semi-regular for two years, and Milos sat by
Galina. Now, with Dmitri and Sarah, they totaled fourteen, not counting
Uncle Tomas and Grandmother.

"While we're all here," Galina addressed the table, "I wanted to
discuss something that's really grinding me. I've spoken with Uncle
Tomas, and he supported my decision. I know not everyone will be happy,
but please, hear me out.

"Everyone's aware there are only nine weeks until the wedding." She
smiled as Milos took her hand. "And it is *my* wedding. I've thought this
through carefully, and I'm sorry if it causes trouble for anyone, but I have
to do what my heart tells me: I'm inviting Father to the wedding. He's
been staying with his sister out in the Caucasus, and I feel it's only right."

Katya broke the sudden silence. "I think that's wonderful. I'm sure
he'll be pleased. I didn't have that option, and I regret it."

Andrea Ivanov paled. "You're going to invite him here? To this
house? A murderer? The press will have a field day! It will sink our
business to the ground!"

David's nostrils flared as if he smelled a poisonous stench. "You're
kidding! You better make sure he's sitting at least two hectares away,
because I'd hate to see anything accidental spoil your day."

"I'm sorry if it makes things difficult for you, Dmitri," Galina said,
"and I do apologize. It's just …"

Dmitri waved her concern away. "It's your day, your guest list. I think
I can manage to behave for a day. As long as I know in advance. If you
didn't tell me and I came across him in the lavatory, then John might have
to find space for me at the clinic for a while."

Half the table broke out in laughter. "Thank you, Dimi. It really does
mean a lot to me. Sarah? Are you okay with that?"

Sarah had been staring into space, not even Vlad's inquiring touch
enough to cut through the mindlessness. The new medications worked
well; she didn't even feel like screaming.

"No. No, I'm not," she said to her waterglass. "Someone should have
warned me he was on the planet. I won't face him, not from any distance."
She placed her napkin on the table and stood up while she still had some

dignity. "Please have Marina take my place in your wedding party. I'm sorry; I must decline."

"Sarah, please! Wait." Galina rushed around the long table. Dmitri grabbed Sarah by the hem of her shirt, and she paused with her back to the room. "I wouldn't ask if it wasn't so important to me. I don't want to create more bad feelings out of what should be a happy occasion. I think the best thing to do is ease everyone into this, get the awkward stage over with before the wedding. Father's just as reluctant as you are. Therefore, with Uncle Tomas's permission, Valeria and I have invited him for dinner, two weeks from today, so we can work through any difficulties ahead of time."

"That's reasonable," John agreed.

Andrea was aghast. "You agreed to this before consulting me?"

"It's just a dinner invitation, Mamá," Tomas said. "I think the girls are very wise. And, after thirty-something years, I think it's time I met my notorious brother-in-law."

"I have a commitment that weekend," David lied. "I can't be here."

"You will find a way to work around it for a few hours," Tomas commanded in his ever-patient way. David's jaw clenched, but he held his tongue.

"Will that make it easier for you, Sarah?" Galina asked.

"I tried to *kill* him, Galina. *Dead.* Why would I want to eat with him, unless you plan to poison his food? It is your wedding, your dinner, your business. You have my sincerest promise I will not attempt to create a scene. Do what you want. It's your life, not mine." She wrestled free of Dmitri and walked stately out of the dining room, though the footsteps broke into a run as soon as she was out of sight.

Father.

How long had she run in fear from the very thought of him? How long had he terrorized her nightmares? Sarah thought she'd been able to exorcise the demon after so many years, but he turned up without warning in the safe haven of Vandijoc, fresh out of prison and looking to make amends. She'd panicked so badly she'd fired an energy weapon at him. Two hundred and five centimeters, a hundred thirty-six kilos thin, strong as an industrial crane with Rasputin's eyes and a drunken temper so foul as to make Genghis Khan mess his pants in fear. Sarah would not back down. She did not return to dinner, and would see no one except Dmitri or Vladimir, not even Tomas. She didn't want to suffer any apologies, lectures, or rationales about her decision. She did speak to John about it the following day at the clinic, with Tomas present.

"Let's get this out of the way, right at the beginning," Sarah said with a touch of Attitude. "I shouldn't even have to go over to this. I will not attend the dinner. The last time I saw Father I tried to kill him, and Dmitri and I have suffered ever since. Isn't that enough? I have nothing to say to him. I don't know what I said then, but I'm sure it wasn't pleasant, and I'm sure I meant every word. I won't apologize. I have tried very hard to move beyond that point in my life. Seeing Father across a yard is one thing; having to sit at a table and pretend to be social is an entirely different star system."

"You seem pretty firm on that," John said.

"Absolutely. Because I know in advance he will be there, I will have no reason to panic." Sarah raised a hand to pledge, "I promise I shall stay in my room the entire time, I will not harm or threaten to harm him, I will not see him, I will not speak to him, I will not make evil faces behind his back or attempt to humiliate him in any way. You may lock me in the attic if you wish; I don't want to know about him at all, except that he has left the grounds."

"You think you're ready to handle it, alone like that? Everyone else will be at the dinner, myself included."

"I have no choice."

"What about greeting him, and then … staying in the kitchen with the staff?" Tomas offered. "If you felt comfortable, you could join us for dessert, with no obligation to stay."

"I am trying my best to honor Galina's wishes for everyone else to reconciliate. I am offering progress: I will be in the same building with him. If I see him, even for an instant, I cannot guarantee that I wouldn't do something terribly embarrassing, and that would continue the bad feelings for everyone else. If, based on Dmitri and Vladimir's reports, I feel things went well, I might possibly move to the next step of visual contact, should Galina schedule further visits. For the sake of everyone involved, respect my wish?"

"Very well. I will leave it up to you," Tomas said. "If you wish to hide in your room, I will support that decision, provided you stick to your promise of not interfering. If you wish to be seen and not heard, or perhaps join us, you are more than welcome to do so. Your choice."

Sarah closed her eyes with relief. "Thank you, sir."

* * *

"They're here," David informed Tomas with a sneer.

Andrea's cosmetics stood out as she blanched and gave her son one last caustic look. "Did you tell Valeria to use the side door? I'd rather no one else know we are entertaining convicts."

Tomas tugged his perfect sleeves one final time. "They will use the front door. There is not a soul in this house who is unaware of his past mistakes. Like it or not, Mamá, he remains your son-in-law, and you shall treat him as such, if only out of respect for Maryana."

"I shall treat him with as much respect as they showed me." Andrea headed for the foyer where the crowd gathered, nose high in the air. Any further retort was cut off by the opening of the door.

Valeria entered first. She winked at Tomas. "We're here!"

Alexander Kirushenko entered behind her, Marina leading him by his giant hand, Galina and Milos right behind. His thick wavy hair was freshly cut and combed, Galina had chosen his clothing, and in his free hand he carried a single pink rose. Valeria had warned him Andrea didn't like beards, but the enduring shadow left when he removed it looked far worse than the beard, so he'd merely trimmed it close.

The dark eyes surveyed the crowd like the first day of classes, picking out the interested from those who couldn't have cared less. The scholar's mind drank in the foyer as if studying an ancient relic, noted styles, colors, curves, construction, tallied the worth in the back of his head. The total score weighed the big man's face, and he seemed to stoop under it.

Galina saved him from further awkwardness. "Uncle Tomas, may I present my father, Alexander Grigorevitch Kirushenko."

Tomas broke out in a wide grin, stepping forward to grasp the big man and plant a traditional kiss of greeting on his cheeks, which he couldn't have done if Sasha hadn't bent down to return the greeting.

"Alexander Grigorevitch, my brother!" He grasped the big hand as if they'd been lifelong friends. "Tomas Fedorovitch. I have wanted to meet you, sir, for such a very long time. A thousand apologies for not having invited you here sooner."

"I am known by Sasha," the professor clarified in his deep, rumbling voice. "I think this is the first opportunity where I would have been able to accept. I, too, have long wished to meet you."

"It pains me that it took us thirty years to set the date. May I present my mother, Andrea Maximovna Ivanova," Tomas said. He dragged her forward by an arm around her shoulders. "Mamá, this is Maryana's husband, Alexander Grigorevitch Kirushenko."

"Madame Ivanova," Sasha murmured, locking his dark, dark eyes onto her cold gray-blue ones. He bent forward to reach her hand. "I believe we have met before, though we were not properly introduced." He presented her with the flower. "I never met Tash without giving her a rose. This time, I give the rose to you."

Andrea was caught off guard as she accepted it, both by the gesture and by the emotions it stirred. The iron dislike with which she girded herself melted, and she gave him a gracious smile. "Thank you, sir. You are most thoughtful. I'm afraid our last meeting was under less than favorable circumstances." She blinked rapidly, tormented by the memory. Fyodor enraged beyond anything she'd ever seen, the violence of the security officers, Maryana's tearful pleas, her own fearful tears, and this man standing so strong and sure in the face of the nightmare.

"Papa!" Nikky bounded through the crowd to tackle his father. "*Pri'vyet*, Papa! Can you come upstairs? I want to show you my skiing ribbons."

Valeria pulled him away. "Perhaps later, Nik. After dinner."

Katya, ever polite, broke out of the pack and stood on tiptoe to give her father a brief kiss. "Hello, Father. It's nice to see you looking so well. Roman's asleep right now, but he'd love to see you later."

John held out a hand. "Mr. Kirushenko. It's good to see you again, sir."

"Thank you," Sasha replied shyly.

Sergei didn't hesitate, either, greeting his father with the double kiss, but Vlad still couldn't bring himself to do more than offer a timid hand.

"Welcome, Father," he mumbled, forever intimidated.

"Thank you, Vladimir."

Tomas' gaze bore down on David, prodding him.

"Sir," was the only acknowledgment he gave.

"David," Father replied, just as reserved.

Dmitri had hung back, but now came forward to shake the hand. "I guess I, uh, should apologize for the, uh, way our last meeting ended." He ran a hand through his hair and scratched the back of his neck. "I certainly didn't plan it that way. It was a little out of my control."

"It was not what I intended."

"She was already kind of edgy, with all those people out there and all. It just took her by surprise. She feels pretty bad about it. She knows you're coming today, even though she couldn't be here."

"That's good to know," Sasha agreed. "But, to be safe, perhaps I shouldn't sit with my back to a door."

Dmitri gave an amused half-smile. "You never know."

Tomas motioned his guest down the hallway. "Come. We have an hour or so before dinner, and Marya has prepared a stunning array of *zakuski*. Tell me, Sasha Grigorevitch – I have read your paper on 3-D in-situ reconstruction techniques, and I was wondering ... "

At Tomas's request, the table had been set with the Lomonosov china used on high formal affairs. Tomas insisted Sasha take the seat of honor, and took the corner seat himself. Dmitri sat to his right, as had become his standard place, but an empty seat gapped between Dmitri and Vladimir.

Andrea remained standing. "Where is Sarah?"

"We have already discussed that, Mamá," Tomas said softly. "Sarah felt it would be in everyone's best interest if she declined today's dinner invitation."

"I thought that issue had been resolved. Her father came to visit with his family. I cannot believe you would condone such disrespect, Tomas."

"She means no disrespect. I think we're all aware of Sarah's difficulties. She didn't feel up to this, and I agreed with her reasoning. Perhaps we should respect her wishes in that area."

"Nonsense!" Andrea huffed. She ordered a wait staff, "Leta, please find Miss Sarah and retrieve her at once."

"No!" Tomas countered. Leta waited to see who would win. "Mamá, I asked you to leave her."

"I do not wish to cause her further distress," Sasha rumbled.

"Maybe I should keep an eye on her," David volunteered, and pushed his chair back.

"Sit down," Tomas ordered. "Sit, Mamá. This isn't something society can fix."

Andrea took her seat. "I apologize, Mr. Kirushenko. I assure you, this degree of disrespect has never been tolerated before, and won't be again."

Sasha bowed his head. "It is nothing."

Dmitri leaned back in his seat as the dishes were cleared away, stuffed to the gills. So far, so good; he knew from hard experience if things were going too well, there would be a disaster building to counteract it, and the usual cause was currently unsupervised. The last time Sarah'd been left alone with Father around …. Dmitri didn't know if Tomas kept any weapons, but who knew if Sarah hadn't secretly assembled one lately?

"Please excuse me," he said to the table. "I just want to give a quick check upstairs."

"Mind if I come along?" John asked from the far end of the table. "I've got the same feeling."

"Make it three," David said, standing up as well.

"Sit down," Tomas said firmly. "They can manage quite nicely by themselves. You leave, and then Vlad will want to go, and then everyone else. Give her her space."

"Actually, I could use a little stretch right now," Valeria said. "It's such a nice day, perhaps we could have dessert on the back porch?"

Nikky seized his chance. "You could come see my room, Papa!"

Sasha glanced about, unsure.

Tomas caught the hesitation. "If he wishes to, Nikolai. If you'd like, Sasha, I can take you on a tour before dessert, and we can stop at his room."

"That would be fine. He said he had something to show me."

Tomas smiled warmly. "Wonderful! Nadia, we'll take tea and dessert on the back porch in half an hour. We'll meet everyone back there. Come, Sasha."

* * *

Sasha closed the door to the bedroom and leaned against it, blocking the exit. He said nothing, just stood, impassive as a mountain. It had not been his idea to tour the monstrous house, to rub the class difference in just a little harder. Nikky and Marina had left them; he had his host alone. It could very well be the only chance he'd ever have. Maryana had put great trust in her brother; Sasha hoped it had not been in vain.

"… worked from a photo Papa sent him…." Tomas stopped his monologue. He noticed the barricaded door. "Am I talking too much?"

"I have questions. I want answers," rumbled the deep voice.

"By all means. This is as private a place as any. Perhaps you would care to sit?" Tomas motioned to the bed.

The mighty figure wasn't impressed. "Why did you bring me here?"

"Here? As in the house? Galina wants very much for as many of her family as possible to be present at her wedding. She felt that a luncheon would be the best way to break the tension. If you mean this room, I thought you might like to see Maryana's room."

"I wasn't welcome in this *city* when Tash was alive. What makes you think I care to be here now?" Sasha demanded. "After being cursed and spat on for twenty-three years, after watching my wife's heart break, I'm supposed to embrace the people that hurt her the most? I am gravely indebted to you for assisting my children, sir, but it does not remove the agony Tash was forced to endure."

Tomas hung his head. "I am truly sorry. I did all that I could at the time. I was young, foolish, self-righteous, and very self-centered. Maryana's disappearance tore our house apart. My parents stopped speaking. They nearly divorced over it. I think mentally they did; they just never bothered to go through the paperwork. If you can believe it, my mother has been a much pleasanter person since my father died. If they hadn't found the remains of the aneurysm, I wouldn't have been surprised if my mother helped him cross over. She held him responsible for Maryana, to this very day. I think Mamá would have adjusted to the marriage in time. It was my father who couldn't."

"And you?"

"My sister and I were very close. It hurt very much to lose her; I couldn't understand it properly at the time. The little contact I maintained helped. I took comfort in knowing she was happy. When Valeria contacted me from Navara, I knew I had the perfect opportunity to reestablish contact, to start over. I couldn't bring my sister back, but I could try to make amends by helping her children. I am proud to be able to have them stay here. They are the finest group of children I have ever met, ever hope to meet," Tomas said with a hint of sadness. "I did not make them that way. Their parents did. Only a fool would acknowledge the influence of one parent and not the other. The feud died with my father, sir, and I haven't seen it since."

Sasha breathed deeply, absorbing the information. Thirty-one years was a long mistrust. "A long time ago – before Tash and I married – when they removed her from school – I was assaulted by a number of men as I left work. I still carry a scar from that beating." He rubbed the thin line that ran across his nose and under his left eye. "I was warned to stay not only away from Tash, but this side of the city, or next time would be worse. Were you one of those men, or did you just order the assault?"

Tomas shrank backwards with a shocked expression. *"What?* I swear on my sister's honor, sir, I never ordered any such thing! This is the first I have ever heard of it. Violence is not my style; it never has been. If I had been so inclined, I would have fought you legally – taken Maryana off world, gotten an order of restraint, something to that effect. Even Papa couldn't find an address for you until it was too late. I was not involved in any attack on you, sir, at any time, in any form. I will sign a statement to that effect, and offer a substantial reward to anyone who can prove I was."

Sasha dropped his cold stare. "Tash swore you hadn't. She claimed it was a friend of yours, one who had his own eye on her."

Tomas thought back. "Petya, perhaps? More likely Ilya Turyalin. He envisioned himself a mercenary. I haven't thought of him in years. I'm very sorry if you suffered on his account. If I had known, I would have stopped him."

"I never touched her. Not until we had a marriage contract in our hands. Should she have wished to back out of our relationship, I didn't want her to have regrets."

"That was most noble of you," Tomas said distantly. "However, I don't think it would have changed Papa's mind. He'd worked very hard to make his fortune. He wasn't about to lose it by the news of Maryana's decision hitting the gossip columns. You can laugh at that concept all you want, but this lifestyle isn't as easy as you might think.

"I have the power to collapse the economies of six different worlds, all in a single hyperspace call. It would cost me some reliable income, but I can. To protect themselves, the companies I have business with, and all my competitors, watch my every breath. I cannot step outside this building without a smile on my face or someone will write that I look troubled. Economies will fluctuate as people try to guess why, and I can lose a fortune depending on that decision. If I have to cancel a social function because of sheer exhaustion, there will be wild speculations in the headlines. If I sell off a venture because I feel it is draining capital, the trade lines will scream I am in financial trouble. If I meet with a government official simply because he's an old friend, someone somewhere will scream bribery. Privacy is the most expensive luxury I pay for," Tomas insisted. "Don't be surprised if someone prints something about your visit today. Eventually someone will discover who you are, and I'll read all about someone else's interpretation of my alleged motives. If I have any motive today, Sasha Grigorevitch, be assured, it is merely to attempt to make amends for years of neglect. You are every bit as welcome here as your children, any day of the year. Make no mistake about that. If anyone tells you different, they are in error."

Tomas stood, pensive, hands in the side pockets of his sweater. "We're a lot alike, you and me, Sasha."

"In what way?" Outside of both being human men, Sasha couldn't think of a single thing they might have in common, let alone several. They moved in different worlds. Hell, it could have been different galaxies as often as those worlds crossed. Wealthy people weren't even sent to the same prisons as regular people, if they were sent at all.

"Many ways. We're both educated men, for one thing, very close in age. We both know what it is like to lose the woman we love more than anything in the world. Lora was pregnant when she died; we never got to hold our son, even once. We both loved my sister, and we both suffer the pain of her loss. And we both take joy in her children. I don't think the differences are very much after you take those things into account. I think that's more than enough common ground for friendship."

The big man nodded at last, the hard tension in his face easing as the long-imagined threat diminished.

"Come, then!" Tomas moved toward the door, and Sasha stepped aside. "I'm sure we're holding up dessert. Actually, you took the smart way out, I think." He shook a finger at Sasha with a gleam in his eye. "That's twenty-three years you didn't have to deal with Mamá!"

Twenty-five

"She's not up there," Dmitri said as he clomped down the stairs. "Not in her closet, not in the bathroom, not under the beds or behind the drapes. And before you ask, I checked the passage in the south wing, my room, and Vlad's as well." He rested his hands on his hips and sighed. He had enough trouble keeping track of Sarah in a six-room cabin; Dmitri'd lost count of the rooms here after thirty. "She won't go far; she's too nosy. If I thought she dared, I'd say she's directly over that dining room, boring a hole through the floor to spy on him."

"She's not in the sauna or gym. Let's sweep down here again before we ask Tomas to run a security check," John suggested. "She can't enter his apartment. Maybe she went outside."

The rooms off the back hall were locked except for the empty media room. The library turned up no leads. Back in the main hall, deciding their next move, both men heard a faint clink of glass hitting glass, followed by a female voice speaking something John didn't understand.

"That's her." Dmitri dashed around the corner to the lounge, John right behind. In the very back, in the alcove by the hospitality bar, Sarah knelt on the floor, hidden from view. She scrubbed at the carpeting with a handful of cocktail napkins.

Dmitri sneaked up behind her. "Spill something?"

Sarah spun on her knee, ready to run. Fear turned to anger when she saw the speaker. "What are you doing in here? How did you find me?" She rose and leaned nonchalantly against the bar.

"I should probably ask the same of you. Only two people on this entire planet can curse in Tau Cetan, and it wasn't me. And you should be ashamed of yourself, by the way. I have half a mind to tell Tomas what you said."

"Do you really think I give a damn? Leave me alone!"

"What are you hiding, Sarah?" John inquired. He watched her twist and pose in great contortions, trying to block their view of the bar but look perfectly natural at the same time.

"Nothing! I came in here to be alone, and I don't need people harassing me. Get away!"

Dmitri pushed her aside to reveal an open bottle of vodka and a partially filled glass – not a little vodka glass, but a large one meant for cocktails. He eyed her sadly. "You know better than to touch that stuff."

"Leave me alone!" She broke his gaze long enough to snatch the glass and drain it before he could stop her. "You drank it at my age."

"I didn't drink it like *that* at your age." Dmitri pried the glass from her fingers. Up close, he realized it hadn't been her first, either.

"That's not a smart idea, Sarah, considering the medications you're on," John said. "You shouldn't mix them. How much have you had?"

"Enough to start and not enough to stop," she declared. "As you're so fond of saying, Dmitri, 'Drinking's not a bad thing; it merely gives you the strength to do things you wouldn't normally be able to do.'" She grabbed the open bottle and tried to get it to her lips, fighting Dmitri's counterpull for all she was worth.

"Like say hello?"

At the familiar deep ring of voice, Sarah let go of the bottle; the recoil just missed Dmitri's head. The three of them watched as Father and Uncle Tomas crossed the lounge.

"Sarah?" Tomas said, "I don't recall giving you permission to touch my liquor stock. That's not something you're allowed access to."

Father continued his slow approach. "It's a lie, Sar'ina. I know. Even if you drank every bottle here, it won't change a thing. The strength you get is fleeting. It leaves you weaker, so the next time it can steal even more of you away. While it pulses through your veins, you're invincible. You can face anything, do anything. Never feel pain, regret, sorrow. But when it wears off, you find nothing has changed. You're as weak as ever, and now you're ashamed of it."

"Get away!" Sarah backed up, but the alcove was a dead end. She tried to slide behind John for protection, but John moved sideways, leaving her exposed.

"Get away from me! If it weren't for you, I wouldn't need to. I won't go back. I won't! I won't live that way again! I won't let you hurt Vlad again."

"Go back to *where*?" Sasha snorted. "I'm going to stuff everyone in my two rooms in Stavropol? In my hotel room in Minsk? I am forbidden custody of my children. It's strange how you feel I am going to hurt Vladimir, but Vladimir is man enough to speak to me, take a meal with me. If I recall, the last time we met, *you* tried to harm *me*."

"And I will do it again if you come a step closer!" Fright filled her eyes, but Sarah took on a fighting stance, hands poised.

Dmitri tried herding her to the side. "Let me take her upstairs. Nobody needs this today."

Inspiration struck John. "No! It might be *just* the thing we need today! Tomas, Sasha, I don't want to usurp your visit, but if you're willing, we could try resolving this once and for all. I don't know how long we'll need, but there's a technique called flooding therapy. Now that we actually have Sarah and her father in the same room, we simply lock the doors and let them fight it out. There's a lot of pain and anger in this room. If we can cut through even half of that to arrive at some sort of awareness, I think everyone will rest easier tonight."

Tomas shrugged. "I have no set time schedule. I would say it's up to Sasha. It's his business. However," he tipped his head, "at some point we *are* going to have to come to some sort of peace. Galina wants her father at her wedding; she wants her sister as an attendant. If that's to happen, they must both be in the same room. Sasha, it's your decision. Would you want to address this now, or would you be willing perhaps to come back another day to work things out?"

"There is nothing to work out!" Sarah spat. "Get him away from me! He's lying. He's biding his time until we least expect it, and then he will strike! If he didn't want me dead for what I said in court, he'll get me for trying to kill him."

Sasha's ruddy face darkened above the beard. "The best laid plans can crumble to dust before you are able to carry them out. If you feel the conditions are right, then I am willing to work things out now."

"Great." John swung into action. "Tomas, close the doors and lock them, please. No one in or out until we're done. Sasha, take a seat wherever you like. Sarah, come with me."

Tomas got to the doors as some of the crowd headed down the hall to the sitting room.

"What's going on?" Vlad said as Tomas closed the doors in front of him. "Why are you shutting the doors? Why's Sarah in there?"

"Your father and Sarah are speaking with John," Tomas explained. "David, I'm counting on you to keep everyone away until they're done. No interruptions, whatsoever."

"With *him?*" David fumed. "You can't do that to her. I won't allow it!"

"Tomas, this is hardly the time for …" Andrea objected.

"Not now, Mamá. Have your tea on the portico," he suggested, and shut the doors.

Sarah pulled away from Dmitri. "What are you doing? Let me out of here! Right now! You can't keep me prisoner. I have rights! Dimi, I want to leave! Uncle Tomas, *please!*"

"Stop it, Sar," Dmitri whispered. He helped John drag her from the doors. "Do you know how bad you look? I won't leave you."

"I won't do this! Get him out of here! You can't make me talk to him! It's not in my contract!"

John and Dmitri dropped her on a sofa. She struggled to stand, but John pushed her down. "If she gets up, sit on her."

Sasha limped heavily to the other end of the same sofa and eased himself down.

Tomas noticed the increasing difficulty. "Would you be more comfortable in a different chair?"

"No, thank you," Sasha insisted. "Height and weight have destroyed my hip. I'm scheduled for a replacement in two weeks. The knee has been rebuilt already."

"I'm sorry to hear that. Best of luck," Tomas wished him.

Carver sat on the marble-topped sofa table to face his subjects. Grandmamá would have screeched, but Tomas said nothing. "Okay. Sarah, you've had outstanding issues with your father as long as I've known you, and your feelings seem to have intensified. No one is denying you have good reasons for your anxieties, but no one is leaving this room until you face up to some of this, and make at least a preliminary truce."

"Make a truce with *what!*" Sarah stabbed a finger at the other end of the sofa. *"That?* I'm supposed to make a truce with a person who whipped his children like recalcitrant porshies? A drunken … bastard who can't *remember* his worser crimes? Don't push Grandmother's religious dogma on me! I've seen Hell and I managed to escape, barely alive! And do you know who was in charge? He was!"

She pulled her feet up until her knees were under her chin. "I have nothing to say to him, ever."

Sasha's face remained expressionless, but he pointed in return.

"Do you see that face?" he told John. "That's the same face she had as a little girl, when she was mad. She would have every chance to run but she'd choose to fight, even when she knew she would lose. That's what she's doing right now."

Dmitri gave a chuckle. "The stamping foot comes next."

"Traitor," Sarah sneered.

"I cannot defend myself," Sasha acknowledged. "What you say is truth. I accept that. I could sit here for a year telling you everything I regret, but it won't fix those regrets. I could plead with you to accept my apologies, but you will not accept them. It troubles me, however, that you cannot move past that. It took several years of therapy to make that move, but I did do it. To suffer once is a regrettable tragedy. To force oneself to suffer over and over is stupidity. Until you walk away from the pain, you will never have peace."

"Who are you to offer words of wisdom? What do you know of pain?"

"Far more than *you*."

The comment was more forceful than warranted, the deep voice reverberating like an earthquake, but Sasha's features remained impassive. "I know what it's like to hold my wife as she draws her very last breath, hear her whisper undeserved forgiveness to me. I know what it's like to wake up in a detention cell without knowing how I got there, to learn I'm being held on charges of murder, that I murdered one of my own children. I have to wait a day and a half to learn which one. I know how it feels to find out in the middle of a murder trial that I tried to harm a daughter I had only the highest respect for, but have absolutely no memory of it. I will not trivialize what you and your brothers and sisters went through, but there are worse things in the world than close calls. Than even death."

Sasha wrestled with something inside. The dark beard twitched, as if his words couldn't decide to stay silent or be spoken.

"I should have known better, but I did not connect anything until Rehab. In the name of therapy, I was forced to relive some very harsh facts, ones I would have given anything to avoid digging up, but this time I was made to examine them from the outside."

"Hindsight always has perfect clarity," Sarah charged acidly. "Too bad we weren't born on Venatici, with eyes in the backs of our heads."

Her father sighed heavily. "Let me tell you something I've never told anyone, outside of counselors. Not even your mother. I could not tell her. She was no older than you when I met her, and she'd known only happiness, like a flower in a hothouse." Sasha's eyes roamed the grandeur of the huge room, but his face didn't pass judgment. "She'd grown up here, surrounded by love, and beauty, and happiness. To her, cruelty was being too ill to attend a social function. Violence was an argument over who made the best *zakuski*. Insensitivity was forgetting to greet a guest. Your mother was always a Lady, fit for the company of Tsars and Emperors. How could I tell her that her mother-in-law was nothing but the cheapest form of whore?"

Dmitri hadn't been paying too much attention. He had no desire to socialize with Father, and underneath everything his heart was siding with Sarah, but he was trying to keep the peace for Tomas's sake. He knew what Father said about Mother to be fact, but the last sentence spun his head around. It wasn't drunken instigation; it was sad, it was bitter, it was purposely intended and intensely disgusted. It was the very first time Dmitri'd ever heard his other grandmother mentioned, and the accusation took his breath away. He left his spot near Sarah and sat next to Tomas.

Tomas, too, heard the change in tone, for he walked to the bar, returning to place an iced glass of liquid on the table next to his brother-in-law. "Just lemon water," he reassured him.

"*Spasiba.*" Sasha gave a grateful nod. Sarah oozed contempt, pretending to ignore him, but she'd stopped sniping, so he continued.

"My father was a factory technician on a month's holiday down at the resorts in Sochi. He stopped at a club his first night there, and fell in love with one of the dancers. My mother was in her thirties, tall, with blue eyes and curly hair. It was brown, but she kept it heavily streaked with blonde. She was recently divorced, with two daughters to support. When my father offered to buy her a drink, she accepted."

Sasha paused to sip his water.

"Three weeks later she was pregnant with my sister Ana. She didn't want another child, didn't want to be married again, but my father talked her into both things. Six years later, I was born. If Ana wasn't wanted, my arrival was worse.

"My mother fed off the wild side of life. She hated being chained to a family," Sasha recalled. "She'd throw things, hit us, scream to the world what a bastard my father was for keeping her down like that. Several times he caught her visiting other men, and they would scream insults for days. By the time I turned seven, he'd had enough. I woke one morning and he was gone. His clothes, his shoes, his work bag, his photographs. Erased, as if he'd never been there. And that's when I found out what Hell is."

"Hmph!" grunted the far end of the sofa.

"Your mother and I had a good marriage. We never had a disagreement in front of our children, and we never let it progress to a fight. We respected each other. She understood me like no one ever has. Even in the worst times, she helped hold me up."

Dmitri shook his head in wonder. "That always amazed us. No matter how mad you were, no matter how bad you were hitting someone, she could walk right up to you and you would walk away with her like you'd forgotten we were there. If anyone else had done it they would have been knocked flat. I think that's why things got so much worse after she died. The few times we tried, somebody got hurt."

Father nodded, understanding it to be true. "Now imagine if she had died when you were very young. My mother regretted being married, but it gave her financial stability. Without my father, she lost even more freedom. She had to work harder. My half-sisters were grown, but she still had two children around her neck. She tried to go back to dancing, but no one wants to see a forty-eight-year-old mother of four on stage in nothing but body paint. She was reduced to serving tables, which she considered an insult. She'd meet people at work, sometimes bring them home. Other times she wouldn't come home for days, out with the people she'd meet. She liked to drink, and she got involved with chemicals. I drank too much, but I stayed away from chems." He glanced at Dmitri as if to defend himself; Dimi confirmed it with a nod.

"She couldn't keep a job after that. When she didn't have enough credits for the chems, she'd take it out on us. Vodka bottles leave nice wide bruises, and they don't break, even on the tenth swing."

"Ow!" Dmitri cringed in sympathy. Tomas grimaced, but John Carver had heard such things before.

"Some of the drugs she liked were fumigants – you had to heat them and breathe the fumes. One of her favorite punishments was her heating rod." Sasha brushed his hand over his arm. "If you look, you can still find some scars."

"My God!" Tomas exclaimed in horror. "I can't begin to imagine… !"

"That's nothing," Sarah sneered. "Did you know you can be hit with a whip twenty or thirty times and it still doesn't break? Don't talk to me about scars!"

"Whips don't break bones," her father pointed out. "The very worst happened when I was ten. After that … I don't know. Part of us died that night, and we woke up as new people." Sasha looked ill. He paused, as if gathering his nerve. "Nothing was the same.

"Mother had frequent male guests. Some stayed an hour, some stayed several weeks. Some were nice – buying us little luxuries to win our favor, or giving us money to get lost. Some we had bad feelings about, and we would stay out all night in winter rather than be in the apartment with them. When I was ten, my mother hit a bad stretch, out of work and depressed for several months. She started to offer her *experience* in exchange for cash, or whatever chemicals she needed at the time. One day a man came by, one of mother's suppliers. She'd run up a considerable debt, and he wanted his credits or he threatened to break a bone a day until he got it. Mother offered him her services; he refused. He knocked her around while we hid. I don't know if she was more scared of him or of losing her chems. She called my sister Ana out."

Sasha picked up the glass of water and drank from it. He played with it in his thick hands, staring at the slice of lemon sitting crookedly on the melting ice. His head stayed bent, but his eyes glanced at the men in front of him.

John Carver met the wounded gaze. Abuse went in circles; it didn't start with Sasha, but it would hopefully stop with his children.

Sasha steeled himself. "Ana was fifteen or so. She only went out there because she thought Mother needed help. Ana tried. She tried, but there was only one exit from the apartment, and to jump from the window meant a fall onto hard pavement. I was big for ten, but I didn't know what to do. I tried, but I was beaten back to my room." He paused again, lost in the memory.

> *Ana burst into their room, making little hysterical cries. She dragged the one clothing chest in front of the door and threw herself in the corner, running her hands over herself as if brushing off bugs.*
>
> *"Ana? What happened?" he'd said, afraid enough for both of them. He pushed the hair out of his frightened eyes and knelt next to her on the floor. "You want some water or somethin'? I got half a bag of crackers; you can have them if you want. Ana! You're bleeding …!" Only then did he realize she wore nothing but her shirt and her underwear.*
>
> *A fist pounded on the door, scaring them both.*
>
> *"Anastasia! Come out here, sweetheart," crooned Mother. "I just want to talk to you, kitten. It's nothing to be upset about. You get used to it. You'll want it soon enough. Open up, kitten!" The artificial patience disappeared. "Goddammit, Ana! Don't be such a baby! Open the goddamned door!"*
>
> *Ana shook. "I want to die, Sash. Please! Please help me die!"*

Sasha's face grew dark with anger, his hand squeezing his waterglass until it looked about to break. "The unforgivable whore that birthed me sold her *daughter's* flesh."

Not a sound crossed the room, not a cough, not a wheeze, not a whisper. Even Sarah sat immobile, eyes wide, remembering a time not so long ago when someone had offered to purchase her for an evening.

Sasha breathed a seemingly endless sigh, drained. "That was forty-five years ago, and I still hear her screams in my head." He downed the rest of his water in a single gulp, but it remained only water.

John Carver glanced behind. Tomas's eyes were clenched in anguish. Dmitri stared at the floor. John caught his eye, and he tipped his head toward Sasha.

Me? Dmitri pointed to his chest, twice as frightened. John nodded.

Dmitri dragged his feet over and took the cushion next to his father. What the hell could he say after that?

He licked his lips nervously. "I'm – I'm sorry, Father. That's – definitely worse than anything we ever went through. I mean – sometimes it *felt* that way when it was happening, but – I can look back now and see that it wasn't. We never thought how things might have been worse. Like you said, you never got into chemicals. We always had a nice place to live, and enough clothes and food, and there was always someone around who could get Mother if we thought it was getting bad. We never thought about things from your point. All we saw was our side."

"Understandable. As I said, I never told your mother."

"Thank you," Tomas choked. His fist pressed his mouth as if stifling a belch. "Thank you for not telling her. She was such a naïve soul. Such things would have destroyed her."

"Precisely."

"I – I know Elizabyeta was an accident," Dmitri admitted. "I was there. You were too drunk to get out of the chair. You didn't know she was hurt that bad; none of us did. And Kat – well, that might have been a lot worse if it hadn't been for Viktor, but there *were* a lot of us around, and that made all the difference."

Sasha accepted the forgiveness. "I wish I could have thanked him for that."

"It would have meant a lot to him. Instead, you beat us for it. I mean, I'm sure there were times when we really *did* deserve some of what we got, it's just… Sometimes you went overboard. I mean, Sarah's a perfect example… ."

His father winced. He rubbed his eyes with his oversized fingers, then shook his head, as if chasing away fatigue. "Of all the atrocities I have committed, that one I remember. I felt sick about that. I still do, every time I look at her. I –." He stumbled, searching for the right words.

"I should have turned myself in for counseling then. I was so scared. I couldn't bear to look at her. I'd had trouble with my supervisor from the first day," Sasha explained. "He was a third-rate archaeologist who'd earned his position by seniority, and there I was, fresh from my success at Gamma Europa, awards still coming in, but he was the head of the department. He made it quite clear who was in charge and who would remain in charge. He'd been excessively rude that day, telling me I'd better watch myself, because a woman like your mother wouldn't put up with an unemployed Neanderthal like me. I hated him for that. My wife was none of his damned business. I stopped to drink on the way home, hoping to erase the anger before I got there. It helped, but underneath I was still upset. When Vladimir spilled his water, it was like one more insult."

He eyed Sarah, her chin high in arrogant denial. "Then you ran up, yelling and hitting and calling me names. With all my credentials, with all my success, I still could not seem to command respect from so much as a schoolchild. All that rage took over. I know now it was directed at my supervisor. Unfortunately, you took it for him.

"When I realized what I had done, I hated myself," Sasha faltered. "More than I can explain. I was afraid you would die. I was afraid to take you for help – I couldn't lie around it. I was afraid someone would report me. I was afraid of myself." The great lip wavered; the chin under the beard gave a shiver.

"I wanted to apologize. I did! But every time I saw you, I wanted to cry. I stopped drinking, let myself cool down. I'd always felt guilt towards you. After that, I was afraid of you."

Sarah laughed bitterly. "Oh, yes! You just ran in fear from me, cowering in closets and trembling under beds at the sound of my footsteps, holding back the tears in school when sand got under your clothes and scraped against all that raw tissue. Oh, the terror in your eyes when I walked into a room! Remember, Dimi? Remember the power I had? Once. Only once did I *ever* have that power. And Dimi was the one that paid for it."

"That's a very interesting point, Sasha," John said, intrigued. "Why did Sarah make you feel guilty? If she was six when you became afraid of her, what did she do to make you feel guilty before that?"

"It was my fault," Sasha insisted. "Starting with her conception. Sergei was supposed to be our last child. They underestimated his size, and Tash had great difficulty with his birth. They warned her she shouldn't have any more children. They weren't sure she *could* have more, so we got careless, and we got Vladimir. Tash planned on being sterilized at that point, but Vlad was very sick as an infant. We were so distracted, we never took care of our problem. Eventually he had surgery on his stomach and he started to gain weight. He aged us five years in five months."

"I kind of remember that," Dmitri reflected. "I certainly remember him throwing up everywhere."

"He still does, on occasion," Tomas said.

"We had eight children, a sick baby, and Tash realized she was pregnant again. It most certainly was not planned, and I blamed myself."

He handed his empty glass to his son, gesturing for a refill. Dmitri moved to comply out of old habit, filling the glass with ice and adding water and lemon from the bar in the back of the room. How strange not to add vodka to the water!

"Now, because of our size difference – my weight and strength

271

compared to hers – whenever Tash was expecting, there were several weeks when the doctors felt it would be best if we refrained from … physical contact."

Sarah clamped her hands over her ears. "I don't need to hear this pornography!" She flexed them just a little, allowing her to hear without looking like she was.

"We almost made it through that point with Sarah, but there came a time when we … lost our control," Sasha said delicately. "It sent their mother into labor, several months early. They had to deliver Sarah then, or she would die. Her lungs weren't ready, and it was weeks before she could breathe air. As soon as she did, she got sick. Tash tried to take the blame, but I should have known better. There was no excuse. Every time Sarah got sick, I blamed myself."

Sarah glared sideways at him. "So you abandoned me to the mercy of hospitals, without visiting me even once? Guilty people faun over the people they've wronged. They don't ignore the injured party."

"What good would it have done to stand in a hospital and stare at a baby on a respirator? All it did was make me drink. It was better on everyone if I just stayed away."

"If it was 'Byeta you would have!" Sarah accused. "She was your favorite for everything."

Sasha's thick features clouded over. "Elizabyeta? Elizabyeta was *nobody's* favorite! She looked like an angel, yes, but she had the blackest temper of any child I have ever met. When Nikolai was a baby, 'Byeta would pinch him until he cried. When your mother would go to pick him up, she would be standing there pretending to comfort him like a saint, until your mother caught her. When he learned to walk, 'Byeta would push him down. Eventually, Tash had you and Vladimir watch over him. That took some of the pressure off your mother, and she had more time to tame Elizabyeta."

" 'Byeta was *that* bad?" Dmitri said, surprised. "I mean, she and Sarah fought and all, but I didn't know about her and Nikky. We thought Mother did that because she couldn't be bothered with Nikky."

"No! No!" Sasha shook his head insistently. "It was for his protection. She knew Vladimir wouldn't hurt a fly, and she knew how protective Sarah was about Vladimir. When she was pregnant on Navara and so sick from the heat, she was grateful she could rely on them.

"It's hard to pick favorites among your children. The very first time I ever held a baby, Galina was a minute old, and your mother already held Valeria. I was terrified. I could handle priceless, fragile relics with ease, but I was so scared of breaking this little baby. We learned as we

272

went, twice as fast.

"Vladimir was so frail Tash hardly ever put him down, until Sarah came along," Sasha explained. A wistful smile formed behind the beard. "They were so tiny we put them in the same crib, and they found each other like two blind puppies. That was the very first time Vladimir ever slept through the night," he told John proudly. "He was fourteen months old. I can't tell you how much that meant to us."

"That must have been a tremendous relief," John said with parental sympathy.

Sasha turned back to the sofa. "Believe it or not, Sarah, of all our special children, *you* were my favorite. You had the bluest eyes of anyone I'd ever seen, and you were so *frighteningly* smart, we felt like new parents all over again. No matter how we tested you, you managed to do it. Your mother taught you languages, and you took to them like a bird to the air. Sometimes, if I was doing field work, or there was something interesting going on in the labs, I'd take the older children to see. You'd look up at me with such hope in your eyes and say, 'Me, too?', and I'd take you along. You'd ask hundreds of questions, trying to get out all those big terms in your little baby voice. It was very endearing."

Sarah gave a dramatic roll of her head. "Oh, it was *very* endearing. He loved to favor me when it came time to beat on someone."

"Sarah's told me how those trips were a major influence on her interest in the sciences," John told his father-in-law. "They were very important to her."

"That was confidential material! You have no right to say those things to anyone!"

"That's hardly a secret," Dmitri said. "I mean, when you think about it, yeah, there were good times. More when we were young, but we had fun. I can remember soccer games at the Kiev State Fields. We saw every circus that came near. We were always going to watch you give lectures, and there were trips to important sites and discoveries, and we traveled everywhere," he remembered. "I mean, the celebrations after Gamma Europa were unbelievable in themselves. Like stuff that only happens to celebrities. The day you bought the holovision, I thought you were the most incredible father anyone could ever have. I guess we just lost sight of all that after we got to Navara. We just missed home."

"I'm sure that was more than half of it," Sasha agreed. "We nearly returned that first week. If we had, I have no doubt whatsoever your mother would be alive today."

"What about you, Sarah?" John asked. "Can you remember a time you enjoyed? Something that made you happy?"

"Enjoyed *what*? Having my face slapped so hard it strained my jaw?"

"You can't think of a single instance, in nine years, where you weren't happy for even five minutes?" John raised his eyebrows, knowing. "Not one time, not one thing that seemed special, or made you happy, or made you feel good?"

"No."

"Her birthday every year," Dmitri offered. "She counted the days from hers to Vlad's, because for a few weeks they were the same age, and they'd pretend they were twins, too."

"You are such a *traitor!*" Sarah squealed with fury. She twisted sideways on the sofa and pummeled her brother with her feet. "You are no friend of mine."

"Never said I was." Dimi moved back to Uncle Tomas's couch. "Look through her bag upstairs. She's carried around pictures and bits of junk ever since we left Navara. Nobody carries around reminders of bad times."

"One thing, Sarah, and I'll let you off the hook," John promised. "Just one thing from your childhood that was special to you."

"Nothing." Sarah rubbed her face. The vodka swam through her head, flushing her cheeks and watering her eyes. The room dissolved into a pregnant silence that grew heavier with each passing second.

"My ring," she mumbled. "I liked my ring."

Sasha looked puzzled, but Dmitri filled in. "Right after the excitement started with Gamma Europa. You bought everybody solid crystal rings in some shop there. Mine was blue. I still have it upstairs. I have Viktor's, too. His was purple."

"What color is your ring, Sarah?" John asked.

Sarah laughed, but she looked ready to cry. "Red! Can you believe that? A bright crystalline blood red. I guess it must have been a warning."

John smiled. "Maybe it was. But I think we're starting to touch on some common ground."

"I have *nothing* in common with him!"

"You keep drinking like that, you will," Dmitri said, more serious than he cared to admit. "I've only seen you touch alcohol three times, and each time you wound up drunk. In fact, if I remember right, the last time, you were so tanked I had to put you to bed because you were out cold! If that didn't bring back bad memories… "

"You're just a spigot of lies today!"

"There were five other witnesses. "

"I'm not like that!" Sarah jumped to her feet, fists raised and ready to defend her honor, but John pushed her down with ease. "One incident does

not make me a permanent drunk like that one over there! If I were you, I wouldn't go around bragging about an unencumbered liver!"

"I didn't claim that."

John intervened. "The point is, Sarah, if you keep doing that, you *will* wind up on the same path. You have more in common with your father than you want to admit, and it's a simple test to find out if the susceptibility to alcohol is part of it. You've both had difficult childhoods at the hands of an abusive, alcoholic parent. You both have a bit of a hot temper. You both are prone to episodes of depression. You both have pasts filled with things you regret – "

Sarah couldn't hold back. "Regret?! He doesn't regret a damned thing! A whole bunch of sob stories, that's what he's told you! If he had any regrets at all, he wouldn't have beaten me like he did! He's full of *shit!*" Her breath caught as soon as the word left her mouth. She'd cursed in front of John before, and Dmitri'd heard plenty, but she'd never used that kind of language near Father.

John pushed past it. "And you've never done anything you've ever been sorry about? You've never done or said a single thing you were ever sorry for? Never made a mistake? Never wished you could have done something a different way, made a different choice? You've never had a regret in your entire life?"

Dmitri crossed his arms with a soft snort. "I could give you a possible list, but they'd be just a bunch of sob stories. Right, Sar? I can't think of single thing she might regret, but then, I'm not perfect. The person to ask would have been my wife, Jaycee. She was a much better judge of things like that."

Sarah withered at the bitterness in Dimi's voice. "You're not fair," she whispered.

"I just spent three months in rehab, remember? I know all about that denial crap, too. *I* know the truth. You're the one who's got to live with it."

"It's not easy to be forgiven, is it?" John said gently. "No matter what you do, no matter how much you throw yourself at the other person's feet – even promise them your soul – it's hard to escape that guilt, isn't it?"

"Shut up!" Sarah shouted, clamping her hands over her ears again. She lashed out and kicked him in the knee. "You're nothing but a bunch of bullies, ganging up on me to make me miserable!"

"The misery's coming from inside, Sar. It's even harder to forgive someone when you feel they owe you restitution first." John raised his voice just a little to make sure she heard. "You're never quite sure they learned their lesson. You don't trust their sincerity. Every stumble proves

275

to you they didn't learn a thing. You know they're going to fail, so why bother accepting an apology? After all, people don't change. They are what they are. When I met Vlad, he clung to everyone, afraid of his own shadow, and now he … stands up and voices his opinion. When I met David, he was about to be expelled from school, and now he's … graduating a university with honors. When I first learned about my father-in-law, I heard long stories about what an uncontrollable drunk he was, but the first time I saw him, he was cold sober. It's almost eight years later, and I have yet to see him touch a drop."

"Stop it! Stop it!" Tears formed in Sarah's eyes. "I *can't* forgive him! He *hates* me! I tried to *kill* him!"

John pulled a hand off an ear. *"He doesn't hate you.* He *forgave* you for that. He loves you, Sarah. He never meant to hurt you. Remember intent versus action? A grudge is a very heavy thing to carry. It takes two hands to lug it around. This is your chance to shed those demons, Sarah; it's now or never. You can take a safe chance or you can run and hide, add another regret to your burden and keep dragging yourself through life under a crushing load. It's up to you."

"Leave me alone!" she cried, pushing backwards into the sofa cushions. The unsympathetic upholstery refused to swallow her. "Leave me alone! I can't! *I hate him!"*

"Don't tell *me.* It's between you and him, and he's right there. Tell *him* why you can't forgive him. Explain it to him." John pushed and pulled until she faced Sasha.

Sarah gasped as she caught sight of her father watching her. She fought John's manipulations, tried to flee, but John was insistent.

"Tell him."

"I will not raise a hand against you," Sasha promised.

Anger overcame the fear. "Because I hate you!"

"You have every right," Sasha agreed. "I understand."

"I said I *hate* you!" Sarah grew bolder as nothing violent occurred. "You hear me? I hate you for what you did to us! I hate you for scaring Vlad! I hate you for making Viktor run away! *He* loved me! He *cared* about me! He died because you scared him away! You killed Mother because you wouldn't stop doing those – *things* – to her," Sarah flapped a hand as if she could wave the sex out of the word, "so she kept having babies! I hate you for making us live on freaking Navara! You never cared! Why would I ever want to see you again? I hate you! I hate you!"

Anger swelled up, and she lunged forward to push him with a powerful two-handed shove. When he didn't retaliate, she punched him with clenched fists, harder and harder as he made no move against her. Sasha leaned back, but didn't defend himself.

Dmitri stepped forward to rescue him, but Sasha waved him away. "No. Leave her," he said with the wisdom of too many years of therapy. "She needs to do it."

"I wanted you to die, and you wouldn't! Everyone else did, but you wouldn't!" Sarah pounded furiously against his chest and shoulders, crying. "A father's not supposed to hurt his children! You're supposed to love us! I *hate* you! I *hate* you! *I loved you!"* she wailed from the midst of her outburst. The raised fist dropped, and she collapsed forward on the broad chest. "I loved you and you hurt me!"

Sasha glanced uncertainly at John, but all John did was nod and smile.

"I was so scared of you!" Sarah blubbered. "You were so big and so loud and you yelled, and I tried so hard to make you happy so you wouldn't do that! I tried so hard! I memorized everything you taught me and I tried to never mess it up, and I loved it when you took me everywhere with the big kids because it meant I was more special and you liked me better, an' I could handle getting spanked now and then if I did something wrong even if it was 'Byeta's fault, but then you whipped me like that and I knew you didn't love me."

"No! No!" Sasha looked as if Sarah was about to bite. He patted her timidly on the back. The tears didn't slow, and he dared put his arms around her. Sarah shifted her weight until she sat half on, half off his lap, allowing him to hold her.

"I never hated you. I never hated *any* of you! It was only the alcohol."

Watching Sarah's oldest nightmare vanquish at last, Dmitri felt his insides crinkle with emotion as well. He knelt by his father's knees, rubbing his sister's back. Sasha reached out to brush a big hand over his head.

John Carver glanced up as he felt a touch on his shoulder.

Tomas motioned toward the door. "We're no longer a part of this." John nodded. Tomas paused just long enough to stuff his handkerchief in Sarah's hand, and they left the room to the healing family.

* * *

Tomas knocked on the door to his mother's suite, entering at her bid. The four rooms had been his mother's private retreat since before his own birth, her actual home within her pretentious estate. Few people ever saw the inside. He doubted her grandsons had, and wouldn't place bets on all of the granddaughters, either.

"Good evening, Mamá."

Andrea sat in an antique upholstered rocking chair in the sitting room, wrapped in a white-and-rose flowered dressing gown of a fabric so light and fine there were more than 250 gossamer threads per centimeter. The room was silent except for the occasional cracking of her joints as she rocked. She didn't look up, just rocked, lost in thought.

"Tea time already, Tomas?"

"It's ten o'clock. You disappeared rather fast this evening. Personally, I thought it went rather well." He took a seat on the sofa.

"It was more pleasant than I anticipated, despite John's rather rude intrusion of work over pleasure."

"It was a very necessary maneuver, and I think it may have done a lot of good. At least, I hope it did. It wasn't planned on John's part; he saw an opportunity to heal and he leapt at it. That's his forte."

A knock sounded at the door and the kitchen helper brought in the tea tray and placed it on the side table between them. *Chamomile.* Leave it to Olga Markovna to know when there was undue tension in the house.

Tomas poured two cups. "I wish we'd done it thirty years ago. He's a very smart man, a very hard-working man. Honorable. He was very dedicated to Maryana. I'm sure things would have turned out differently if we had."

Andrea ignored the tea. "He's a very proud man. He was then, and underneath it he still is. He's been beaten into submission by fate, but the pride is still there. It shows every time he looks at his children. He would never have accepted our help."

"I agree. I think, though, for the children's sake, we should include him more in small gatherings – birthdays and such. At least extend the invitation, whether he accepts or not. I think it would be good for Nik and Marina. Sarah, too."

"Oh, Tomas! I don't know *what* to think." Andrea pressed the knuckles of her small hand to her lips, helpless. "I have hated that man so passionately for almost half my life. I absolutely despised him for stealing my daughter, for ruining her life and ruining mine. I never understood how he could coerce her into such an arrangement, never understood how she could run off with a man who was little more than a homeless vagabond with no past and no future. That man broke my heart and destroyed my marriage. I had no intention of showing him civility today."

Tomas sipped his tea. "But you did. Hate is rather fleeting, isn't it, when you actually have to speak with the person you're supposed to hate. He wasn't what you expected, was he?"

"No."

"Did it ever occur to you Maryana saw that good in him? That maybe

278

he didn't need to coerce her, that it could have been her idea? That she could possibly have truly *loved* him? Enough to leave everything she had for him? I would have done that for Lora. I basically did," Tomas realized as he chose a small fruit tart from the tray. "I took up residence in another country, just like Maryana." Thoughts stirred in his head while he chewed. "Did you ever feel that way about Papa? Did you ever love him that much?"

Andrea glared at him. "Of course I did! We were the perfect match. Both from excellent families, both young and good looking and ambitious, with enough family security to get us through whatever endeavor we chose. We'd known each other for years before our families pointed each other out."

"But did you *love* him?" Tomas pressed. Fyodor Ivanov had been a delightfully pleasant man when Tomas was a boy, but Tomas realized with a start he couldn't think of a single time he'd ever seen his parents romantically inclined; not a kiss, not a held hand. "Did you love him enough to leave your family for him? To lay down and die for him?"

"We had the most spectacular wedding you could imagine," Andrea remembered. "We hired an entire hotel. There were five hundred guests, and the party lasted three days. It made every social column in the solar system, and then some. Not a stitch on my gown had been sewn by machine, even in this day and age. Of course, people still appreciated crafting back then, none of this computer-replicated fakery."

"That doesn't answer my question."

Mamá fell silent. The silence thickened, turned to substance, until it hung about the room like a fog. Tomas waited, intrigued.

Andrea sighed. "I always thought I did. Fyodor was sweet, kind, indulgent, and a peerless wizard when it came to financial intuition. We were a perfect mesh of skills and abilities. We had a profound respect for each other, but after many years I realized that's all there was, all there ever had been. I actually avoided some of our male friends and associates, because I found myself being drawn to them in ways your father never inspired me.

"I was never unfaithful to him, and to the best of my knowledge he remained faithful to me. Physically, at least. I had a secure fortune, an enviable husband, and two beautiful children. I had no right to be unhappy. I didn't realize the extent until we left Maryana in Tbilisi. It killed me inside. It killed him. I knew that, but I couldn't forgive him. It took me twenty-five years of marriage to finally admit that no, I did not love your father. I admired him, I respected him, I cherished him as a friend, as a partner, as a companion, but I never *loved* him. Not as a lover, not as a soulmate, not as a wife. I'm sorry if it upsets you, Tomas, but that's the cold truth." She reached for her tea at last, no longer hot, merely warm, like her marriage.

"I'm so sorry to hear that," Tomas said sadly. "No one would ever have guessed."

Andrea shrugged, fluffing her pride into place. "Showmanship, Tomas. That's what we're really about. Showmanship. Wrap the package, flash the ad, reap the profit, shouting louder than everyone else that we're better, pay attention to us. Every step we take is part of the process. We must watch what we say, what we wear, who we see, where we go, what we do, because we're part of the ad. I'm *old*, Tomas, whether you want to joke about it or not. I can't even pretend it's late middle age any more. I anticipate as many as twenty years left to my life – less, if you bring home any more children." The tone was icy, but he caught the humor in her eye.

"Today I decided I am going to retire, once and for all."

"Mamá!"

"I'm tired of being an advertisement. I want to take my fortune and live it up, as they say." Andrea threw her care to the wind with a wave of her hand. "I'm tired of the scrutiny. I want to do whatever I want, like a spoiled child. I think I've earned it. And if that means entertaining ex-convicts, even murderers, then so be it."

Tomas choked on his tea. He wiped his chin with his fingers and stared at his mother. "Then you forgive him?"

"Let's just say I'm taking it into consideration."

Twenty-six

Time was up. For Galina, it had been both an eyeblink and an eternity. David graduated from university in May with a huge but simple-to-plan party, and the next few weeks passed in a single night. The original date had been February, but Galina postponed it when the race to bring Sarah and Dmitri home began. At first it was out of courtesy; she wanted them to be there. As more information unfolded she picked July, hoping Sarah would be back on her feet and Dmitri released. Time-wise it worked, but it meant starting over, moving from an indoor to an outdoor reception, changing all the dresses and food from winter to summer styles. The invitations had been sent and returned, the catering details confirmed, the translators rented, an entire floor of the *Pyervii Myezhzvyezdnii* Hotel in West Minsk reserved for Milos' Greek family. The languages were different, but some of the ceremony would be the same.

"*Kal'yespera,*" Sarah tried to teach the boys, but she knew only ancient Greek literature, not modern conversational Greek.

"*Cally Spera,*" Nikky repeated, proud to sound important and knowledgeable like Sarah.

"*Oedipus Rex,*" David insisted. "Baklava."

"Don't forget scatology," Sergei reminded him. "Instead of *sköl!*, we should cheer *skata!*"

David raised a thoughtful finger. "Very good point. It's a rare opportunity to broaden our international scatalogical vocabulary."

Sarah rolled her eyes. "*Oedipus Rex* is Latin," she corrected. "Baklava is on the dessert menu, and *don't* use the other word." She tossed him a chip of untranslated Socrates.

The day before passed in a flash of summer lightning. There were last minute confirmations, half-hour weather reports to track a front moving east across Poland and Lithuania, and Milos and his parents arrived at two. Katerina's wedding had been direct from a fairytale, with flowers and ribbons and streamers everywhere, and they'd departed in a reproduction carriage pulled by six white horses. The sweet romantic beauty of it brought a tear to many an eye, but the arrangements had been straightforward, with rows of chairs for the ceremony and rows of tables for dinner. Galina seized the unique chance to pay homage to both her father's love of antiquities and her husband's heritage.

A special director had been hired to supervise the spectacle. There, on the expanse of back lawn, hovering cargo ships lowered decorative columns one by one and added panels across the tops to secure them, creating a life-size outline of an ancient Greek temple. Anyone without an immediate responsibility came out to watch, until a swinging column knocked Nikky over and Tomas banished everyone to the safety of the back porch.

The gowns Galina chose came directly from ancient paintings. Milos loved the idea, and vowed to wear a white tunic and a crown of olive leaves himself, but Galina couldn't see her brothers wearing what amounted to dresses, and chose shorter tunics and loose pants for the boys.

Tomas opened the grand ballroom to accommodate the families for dinner. Soft air wafted fragrantly through the gardens and in the open doors, the white "temple" glowing like a spectre of the past across the lawn. Father attended, escorted by his sister Anastasia. The twins had been preschoolers last time they'd seen her, but shy, quiet Ana – every bit as tall as the leggy twins – was delighted to meet everyone. Sarah could not yet bring herself to shake Father's hand, but she did bid a reserved, "Good evening, Father," when he arrived, and remained in the room.

Katya arrived at seven the following morning, and the rush began.

"You can't be serious!" Sarah wailed, horrified at the news her hair would be curled. Galina's hair now hung in perfect sausages, just like the woman on the amphora in the archaeology text on the computer.

"It's just for a day," Katya consoled her, brushing Sarah's hair before the torture began. "I'm sure the boys will forgive you."

"They might, but I won't," Sarah said, already up in arms over the amount of cosmetics Valeria had painted her with. She adjusted the loose shoulders of her sleeveless peplum. She wore a skin patch at the top of her shoulder where Dmitri had allowed her to have her skin tattooed. David and Sergei began the idea years before in her honor, four small ships in

missing-man formation with a stylized $\mathcal{F}_\mathcal{F}$ underneath, for Fearsome Four.

Vlad had done his the day he turned seventeen, the first day he didn't need Galina's permission to do it. Sarah hadn't had the nerve to ask Uncle Tomas, knowing his stance on body ornamentation, but she knew Dmitri – legally in charge or not – wouldn't let her be left out. Tomas's eyes went cold when he saw it. His battle was not over the mark, but dishonest means of achieving it. He ordered her to keep it covered in public, or he would scrub it off himself. Sarah felt it to be a fair compromise.

"At least my dress is blue. I don't think I could bear to suffer pink on top of all this."

"I'm sure the color would have burned your skin," Katya replied, herself resplendent in pale pink, and raked the hairbrush extra hard.

"Stars and Tsars!" David exclaimed in admiration as the girls paraded down the main staircase. He gave a lewd whistle. "Hell! Either Sarah's cross-dressing, or all this time she's really been a girl." He stretched one of her long, springy curls.

Sarah slapped his hand. "Drop dead! This was not my idea. Between the paint and the lacquer and the clothing, I'm afraid to blink. I might crack something."

Vladimir's mouth hung open. "Gosh, Sar! You look totally stellar! I mean, everybody does," he blushed.

"Not you, too! One more word about my attire and I'll trip you as we proceed to the front and you'll fall on your face in front of everyone. Look at you! You look like you were sleepwalking in your pajamas and got attacked by a bush."

Vlad made sure his crown of olive leaves was still balanced on his head. "Thank you so much. And you look like you forgot to put a dress on over your lingerie."

"Get real. This dress is bad enough. I wouldn't be caught dead in lingerie."

"Behave yourself," Dmitri warned her. He gave her a proud kiss on the forehead, lest he muss her hair. "Don't stand too close to Galina. All the attention is supposed to be on her today, and it's rather rude of her sister to be the most beautiful girl on the planet."

He meant it, too. With her moon-blonde hair smoothed and gathered in a cluster of pale curls, her shapely tall frame draped in the light-blue gown, her large purple-blue eyes made even more striking by Valeria's careful make-up job, Sarah was breathtaking.

She rolled her eyes. "Oh, puh-*lease!* One more word and I'll hide in the bathroom the entire time. If you want to make something out of nothing, look at this." She turned slowly, displaying the low, open back of the dress. It hung below her bare shoulder blades.

"Your back!" Vlad realized with a shock. "Your scars are gone!"

David whistled, running his fingers over the smooth skin. "I'll be damned. When did that happen?"

"This spring. Dmitri's been taking me to have them removed."

"It's beautiful, Sar! I'm so happy for you!" Vlad would have hugged her, but he didn't dare wrinkle either of them.

David shoved in front of Dmitri. He put his arms around Sarah and Vlad. "It's the least he could do. Now remember, when you walk to the front and they ask for the pledges, I don't want to see your lips moving in secret vows, okay? I told you how many times, you can't do those things with each other."

Sarah's elbow caught David in the stomach. "Let's go, Vlad," she said with disgust, and led him away by the hand.

Five thousand stems of flowers. Three hundred and eighty-three guests seated in chairs. Thirty people hired to cater and wait table and keep the grounds clean. Twenty security officers hired to patrol the perimeter against the media and uninvited guests, and the possible obnoxious drinker. Five hired bartenders and five hundred bottles of vintage wine. Ten members of a wedding party. Valeria led the procession, wearing a royal purple gown and accompanied by Milos's best friend, a fellow named Konstantinos Anagnostopoulos.

"And you thought 'Aletneshfaja' was tough," Sarah teased Dmitri.

Dimi laughed. "As long as I don't have to spell it."

Katerina came next, accompanied by Sergei. Height-wise, it would have looked better pairing tall Sergei with Valeria instead of short Katya, but Valeria was the Maid of Honor, and she had to walk with the Best Man.

"Is my hair in place?" Sarah asked Vlad in a last-second attack of nerves.

"Since when do you care about your hair?" Vlad whispered back.

"It's Galina's special day. I don't want to ruin it." Vlad caught his signal and grabbed her elbow, and they started walking.

Nikky followed, and then Marina, in yellow, sprinkling a carpet of petals as she walked. Lastly came Galina, a statue of Athena come to life.

Like her sisters, her hair was smoothed back and arranged in dark gold curls, held in place by a jeweled band around her forehead. Her white Grecian gown, slit up one side and trimmed in gold, looked exquisitely regal on her tall frame. A white and gold cape fell gracefully from her shoulders to form a train. Her arms overflowed with a massive bouquet of red poppies, interspersed with red and white rosebuds. She looked radiantly happy as she slipped her hand around Father's elbow, and they proceeded across the "temple."

Sarah watched their progression from the front, unable to hide well enough behind Katya. Father wore a dark suit, his hair and beard perfectly trimmed. He glanced at Galina, and he *smiled!* Sarah couldn't remember the last time she'd seen Father smile. A shy, lopsided smile Sarah knew by heart, but it didn't belong to Father... That was *Dmitri's* smile! She watched in confusion as Father walked Galina to the front, gave her a kiss, and sat down in the front row next to Uncle Tomas and Aunt Anastasia, and a tall man with a gaily dressed little girl on his lap. A creepy feeling of familiarness itched up her spine, as if she should know the man. Perhaps he was Aunt Ana's son, and it was just a family resemblance.

She caught Dmitri's wink and lopsided smile at her. He sat up front, too, next to Grandmamá. Sarah gave him a brave smile in return, but his smile, echoing Father's, left her unsettled, and she focused herself by thinking about it in terms of genetics and inheritance. When her sisters moved to sit, Sarah remained standing until Val pulled her back to reality.

"All brain, no sense," David said from Grandmother's other side.

The ceremony lasted an hour, the Bishop of Minsk sharing the duties with the Greek Bishop of St. Sophia's. It was a deference to tradition more than anything else; as far as the government cared, Galina and Milos had legally joined the week before, when they'd signed all the paperwork. After the ceremony, Tomas ushered everyone together for group portraits. The man with the little girl had been talking to Father, and he moved in to stand with the Kirushenko clan.

"Why the hell is he in *our* picture?" Sarah whispered to Dmitri, standing behind her.

"Are you that stupid?" Dmitri teased. "You don't recognize your darling brother Alexei and his daughter, Gabriella?"

If Sarah's chin had fallen open any harder it would have bruised her chest. She and Vlad craned their heads around the cluster to get a better look. Alexei had left home half their lifetime ago. A finger or two taller than Sergei, he wasn't quite as broad as David. His dark hair lay short over most of his head save a shoulder-length fringe in the back, and like Father and David, he wore earrings. Father still wore two in each lobe, and David had one on the top and bottom of his left ear, but Alexei topped them both with seven in *each* ear. *Whatever did Grandmamá have to say about that?!* All Sarah and Vlad could remember about Alexei was his violent temper, but the giggling four-year old swinging arms with Marina certainly seemed happy enough. The news gave them someone besides Father to stare at through their meal.

Sarah was happy when the lunch ended and they could wander about. She chatted with John and Dmitri, but David pulled her away with the Fearsome Four.

"We had to talk to him all through dinner," David said. "Here's the meat: he was living with some girl out on some planet, he got caught pumping his hose, they have the kid, and two months later she decides she doesn't want to be tied down and splits, leaving him the kid. Can you dream that shit? And he's raised her himself! Man! Talk about a fucking turnaround! He used to beat the fucking piss out of us!"

Sergei shrugged. "People change."

"I'll believe it when I see it. You ready?" David asked.

Sergei nodded. "We still shouldn't, though. It's not right."

"Do what?" Sarah said cautiously.

"Should nothing! The Fearsome Four are present and accounted for, and we're just going to let everyone know it."

"No way!" Vlad said. "I'm not ruining Galina's wedding."

David glared. "Hold your piss, Chickenshit. We're not knocking down the columns. You feel like sitting here listening to people pretend to like each other for the next eight hours? Just a little harmless fun. In fact, you can pull the first one." He put his arm around Vlad and slipped several large, flat tablets into his hand.

"Go over to the fountain and drop these in," he whispered.

"I'm not poisoning people!"

"They're antacid tablets. They're not going to poison anyone. Every wedding has to have something to make it truly memorable. Remember the pissing horse at Katya's? Loosen up!"

In the midst of the hors d'œuvre table stood a tall fountain, spraying a chilled champagne punch that trickled down four tiers and ended in a serving bowl almost big enough to be called a pond. The churning acidity would spur the bicarb tablets into a mound of bubbles. It would be silent, showy, and harmless.

Sarah broke into a grin. "Oh, David! You are so evil! I'll go with you, Vlad." They walked over arm in arm, halos shining from the purity of their reputations. It took only a minute to pour their own glasses, flip three tablets into a middle tier, and walk the long way around to where David spoke with Uncle Tomas, the perfect alibi. Four minutes later, the yard was abuzz over the foaming fountain.

Tomas investigated, returning to stare hard at David and his underlings. "If I hadn't been speaking to you, David, I would imagine you had a hand in that. It's just your type of sophomoric humor. I hope for your sake you didn't. Don't do that to your sister."

"Mingle, people!" David commanded when Tomas left. "We strike again in one hour."

True to his word, nothing David did ruined the wedding. Sergei took the second prank, slipping the director of music a note accompanied by a hefty tip, and in the midst of a slow dance the music switched to a rather explicit modern song. David struck next, snatching all the corkscrews and creating a frenzy among the bartenders to find new ones. Drinks were switched on unsuspecting guests, or emptied, or diluted with water. Hors d'œvres were rearranged to spell rude words. The flowers in the amphorae on several tables were mysteriously beheaded, bare stems standing proud. It was fun, it was clean, and Uncle Tomas didn't find out about most of it.

Despite Sarah's protests, John dragged her to the dance floor, several fresh flower heads tucked in her curls. Before she could run, Sergei demanded his turn. Sarah escaped after that, and she and Vlad walked around the fringes of the party.

"I will if you will," Vlad dared as they passed a bar set-up.

"Won't we get in trouble?" Sarah glanced at the waiting bartender. Her mind went blank, and she couldn't think of anything Dmitri liked. "I still don't feel great from the last time."

"You're old enough to drink at parties under Uncle Tomas's rules." Vlad thought a second. "Two vodka sunbursts, please."

"What does that taste like?"

"I have no idea," Vladimir admitted, "but I know what vodka tastes like, and I've heard of vodka sunbursts before, so I guess it must be all right." He accepted the two orange-red glasses, and they walked away to pretend to admire a brightly flowering bush.

"Here's piss in your eye," Vlad quoted from the Book of David, and they both took a gulp.

Sarah felt acutely ill. "Vlad? Is it supposed to taste like this? It tastes like the smell of the fuel David uses in his ground bike."

Vlad's eyes were watering. "Like pickled tomatoes. I just killed half my tastebuds. Ugh! "

Together they burst into giggles. The glasses were dumped unceremoniously on the lawn.

No sooner had they headed back to the tables when Tomas intercepted them. "Sarah! The very one I've been looking for. Come, come! You're the only one of the girls I haven't danced with yet."

"I don't dance!"

Tomas took her hand. "Nonsense. A beautiful girl won't do me the honor, here in front of my friends? I promise, I will touch only your hands."

Sarah heaved a sigh. Duty was duty. How could she say no to Uncle Tomas?

"I've hardly had a chance to speak with you," he said while they swayed. "Are you enjoying the party?"

"Yes, sir."

"What have you been up to? I haven't seen you for a while."

Sarah wasn't sure if she smelled a rat or not. It could have been an innocent question, but she didn't think Tomas to be above using her to sniff out information. Over his shoulder, she watched Vlad dancing quite close with a Gypsy-eyed Greek girl.

"Vlad and I have been walking around. Everyone looks so fancy and happy."

"It does seem to be going rather well, doesn't it? You're never quite sure, mixing two cultures like this." Tomas raised his elbow to allow her to turn under his arm, but he bumped the person next to him.

"My apologies, kind sir! Will you swap?" Uncle Tomas twisted his wrist to spin Sarah extra hard into

Father.

Tomas slipped her hand into Father's and stole Katya away.

Sarah froze.

Father froze.

Frightened eyes glanced at each other and turned quickly to the ground.

What to do? If she ran off screaming, Sarah'd embarrass herself, Father, Uncle Tomas, Galina, and just about everyone in the family. If she refused, she'd be insulting Father. She'd made a truce, acknowledged that he had a right to visit with his other children, and he had a right to be a guest in Uncle Tomas's house. She promised never to try to kill him again, but she didn't promise to associate with him. Not in any manner.

Father bowed his big head, every bit as tortured. "My Lady?"

"Sir." Sarah managed to curtsey without falling over. They danced stiffly, as far apart as possible, until the music ended and they could flee.

She pulled Vlad away from the Greek girl and made him walk with her until she found her wits again, along the line of food tables under the canopies. He fed her a chocolate-dipped strawberry, but Sarah'd hardly taken a bite when something grabbed her ankle and she yelped in surprise. The fruit tumbled down the front of her dress into the grass. A hand beckoned her under the table drapes. Sarah glanced at Vlad in amazement, and pulled up the cloths.

"David Fyodor! What are you *doing* under there!" she squealed in a whisper. "No wonder it's been so quiet!"

"Hurry, before someone sees you!"

"In a dress?" A fast glance to see if anyone important was watching, and Sarah hiked her dress and dove under the table, Vlad right behind. David, Sergei, and Nikky were folded up tight; with the new additions, it was quite cramped. An entire tray of dainties sat on the grass with them.

Sarah reached out, retrieved her strawberry, flicked grass off, and took another bite. Berry juice and melting chocolate dotted the folds of her dress. "Why are we under here?"

"Spying!" Nikky burst with joy, allowed in on a Fearsome Four escapade at last. "This is *totally* quantum!"

"You pick up a lot of interesting news this way," Sergei admitted. "Unfortunately, half of it's in Greek, and I didn't grab a translator box."

"I only know Ancient Greek," Sarah said, "but no doubt some of it's similar."

"We're at a party! File the brain power. Check *this*," David gloated, and showed the latecomers a palm-sized monitor screen. "Shh! Shh! Someone's coming!"

Sarah fanned his breath from her face. "What have you been drinking?! Ugh!"

Five heads fought to view the tiny monitor. A microcamera pointed upwards from the ground; as people walked past the table, the spies had a bug's-eye view of the guests. An older Russian woman walked by, stopping at the table right over David's camera. He adjusted a thin wire lying deep in the grass, and the picture zoomed in for a closer view. Enormous thighs jostled for space under the slip-cover dress.

"You pervert!" Sarah whacked David in the ear. "You are absolutely despicable!"

Vlad slid forward for a better view. "Totally electric! Where'd you get it? Can I borrow it sometime?"

"You do and I'll tell Galina!" Sarah threatened.

David hushed them. "Shh! Here comes another one. Bets, gentlemen. Yes or no?"

"No," Sergei whispered.

"No!" Nikky echoed with excitement.

"No what?" Vlad asked.

"Underwear, you ass! Shhh!"

Sandaled feet stepped near the microcamera. A high hemline rested loosely against a shapely young leg. David used the wire to slide the camera farther to the right. The victim leaned across the table to reach something on the far side, and a foot came off the ground. The monitor showed a three-second crotch shot.

Vlad's eyes lit up, while Nikky shook with silent giggles. Sergei clamped a hand over the boy's mouth, grinning.

"The No's have it," David said with a straight face. "Peek-a-boo, *pizdalinka!*"

"That's five!" Nikky squealed under Sergei's hand.

"You are immoral swine, every last one of you! I'm ashamed of you, Vladimir Vasily Kirushenko! Teaching Nikky this is acceptable!" Sarah scolded.

"Who cares," David scowled. "Moral of the story: you flaunt it, we'll haunt it. Shh!"

A long turquoise hem went by, followed by a pair of men's shoes. "...but of course we had to change everything when we found out," the woman said in accented English. "Rudolf was furious with me." The picture jumped as she tripped on the camera wire.

"Whoops. Are you all right?" said a very familiar voice.

"Yes, quite, thank you. My heel caught on something."

"Where?" The man swished a toe through flawless lawn. The image rolled as his foot hit the camera.

"Shit!" David whispered. He yanked on the wire.

The man felt the tug under the soft sole of his custom-made shoe. "There's something down here." He reached down and found the tiny camera, a half centimeter in size. His eyes followed the wire backwards.

"Run!" David jerked the wire free as Uncle Tomas bent over, curious, and lifted the table bunting. The Faithful Five exploded from the back of the table with a yell, taking the tablecloth with them.

Tomas dove to save a huge platter of cheese as it shifted thirty centimeters backwards. He watched his niece and nephews run across the lawn in a comical interpretation of an ancient Greek marathon, Sarah having no trouble keeping up with Sergei and David with her dress hiked almost to her waist.

"Babysitters," he told the Countess Irimescu. "I forgot to order babysitters. When the day is over, I'm going to have to kill them."

Babysitters Tomas found. Nikky found himself dragged by the ear to Valeria. Dmitri was told to corral Sarah or else. John swore to mind Vladimir. Tomas would have preferred to make David suffer at his table, but he knew David was still very much at odds with his father, so Sergei sat next to his grandmother and conversed like an adult for a while. Without his trusty henchmen, David would behave.

After half an hour of polite sitting, the orders began to fade. Nikky went to the lavatory and never quite made it back to Val. Sergei moved tables to talk with Alexei. Vlad conversed with the dark-eyed Greek girl until Sarah's dagger-like stares made him return. He coaxed Sarah onto the dance floor, but before she could sit down she felt a tap on her shoulder.

"I saw you dance with Vlad, and I saw you dance with John, but in five hours you haven't asked me to dance once," Dmitri said with a pout. "Is it something I said?"

"I wasn't ignoring you on purpose," Sarah explained as she took his hand. "I never wanted to dance with *anyone*."

"I'm proud of you, you know? Here you are, all dressed up, with those … lovely stains on your dress, make-up and fancy hair and all, and I haven't had to pull you out from under a bed once. I'm impressed! I mean it. I mean, Father's here, and you actually look happy." His eyes were on the shiny side, and he seemed quite comfortable with himself.

"Dimi, how much have you been drinking? You know Uncle Tomas doesn't like to see anyone drunk. Maybe you should stop for a bit."

"Will you ever stop being a worry-wort? I know my limits and I'm nowhere near them," he assured her. "That's no back-wash brew they're serving; I don't want to insult the host by saying no. I guess I'll take back that statement about happy."

"I *am* happy, I guess. There're enough people around that I know so I don't feel overwhelmed with pressure. I mean, if I feel bad dressed like this, imagine what Sergei and Vlad feel like in those fancy pajamas," she giggled. "Add in all that nightmare therapy I've been suffering, and the medications, and I really feel okay. I guess ultimately I have you to thank for that."

"Only because I told you you'd get there." Dmitri embraced her as they swayed, and she rested her head on his shoulder, content.

A strong finger stabbed him from behind.

"You're dancing with my girl."

"Go find your own," Dmitri told David without missing a step.

"I haven't danced with her. I want my turn!"

"You'll wait til I'm done, you impatient son of a bitch," Dmitri said pleasantly.

"Who the hell are you calling a son of a bitch, you fucking kidnapper!" A big hand slammed Dmitri in the back. "I waited seven years. She's ours now."

Sarah let go of Dmitri. She'd never seen David drunk, but she knew the signs of Too Much, and David had had Too Much. "David, you're too loud. Lower your voice or Uncle Tomas will come over here."

"Let him! Then he can kick this no-good drop-out loser out on his ass."

Dmitri rocked on his toes as if he had nothing better to do. "You got a problem with me?"

"Yeah, I got a problem with you! We kicked you out once; didn't you get the point?"

Sarah saw the hairs rise on Dmitri's neck. "Come on, David. Let's dance." She pulled at his arm. "Even Father danced with me, but you haven't. I've been waiting all day for you to ask."

"Back off, Sarah," Dmitri ordered. "This *boy* has something to tell me. Maybe you'd like to take this discussion to a more private location, so we can be totally honest."

David seethed. "Oh, I very much would. There shouldn't be anybody over by the north wing. I don't think we'd be disturbed."

"Fine!"

"Fine!"

Sarah begged. She pleaded. She hung onto Dmitri's arm and dug her golden sandals into the ground until they pulled up turf, but Dmitri shook her off.

"Leave it alone. It's between me and him. Nobody talks that way to me and gets away with it. You know we don't take shit from asses like him."

"*Please*, Dimi! It's Galina's *wedding*! You can't make a scene! Think about Galina!

"Think about Uncle Tomas!

"Think about your triple-Moon *parole*!"

Dmitri didn't waste words as he came upon David. "Who the hell do you think you're trying to push around?"

"A worthless piece of lying dogshit!" David snapped, glaring down the fourteen centimeter difference in height. Sweat dripped along his forehead into his eyes; he tossed his head to get his hair out of the way. "You think you're going to waltz back here after a few months and stuff her back under your control? I'll break every bone in your scrawny fucking body!"

"Tomas holds her reigns now."

"That's *Uncle* Tomas to you! That never stopped you before, traitor! It's taken me months to undo the damage you did to her."

"*What* fucking damage?" Dmitri spat. "I spent seven *years* undoing the damage Valeria did to her!"

"Right! That's why you locked her away on some shit-ass world where she couldn't even talk to us!" David growled. "That's why she cries in terror the minute she leaves the house, afraid she's never going to return! That's why she dresses like a history text, and has no idea how to relax and have a good time! She can't take a goddamned piss without asking your permission first!"

"What's going on?" Vladimir caught up to them behind the house

292

with that damned Greek girl in tow. He'd seen David and then Sarah crossing the lawn, and where David and Sarah went, there was bound to be something up.

Sarah twitched with dread. "They won't listen to me! Run! Get Sergei! Get John! I think something awful's about to happen."

Vlad yanked his new friend by the hand, and they ran as fast as they could.

"You're out of line, David," Sarah said, offended. "Dmitri never did anything bad to me. Why don't we sit down somewhere and talk this out, okay? You've been drinking and you're upsetting me. Come on." She tried to turn David away, but he shoved her possessively behind him.

Dmitri laughed. "Look who's talking! The little punk who got his ass kicked more than the rest of us combined. You don't know shit about her."

"I know she didn't start stabbing herself until you showed up."

"And just what were you looking for when your head became wedged up your ass? It must be nice to judge people from your throne on the lap of luxury, with servants running to wipe your ass every time you shoot shit. How much did it cost Tomas to buy your diploma?"

Sergei ran up just as David's fist replied, his class ring slicing Dmitri's eyebrow.

Dmitri was smaller and proportionally weaker, but his strength and speed came from years of physical labor and porshie-wrestling on Sigma Tau, not occasional sports and gymnasium weights. He recovered quickly, felt blood, and lit into his brother with everything he had.

Sergei fought to get David from behind; Sarah gave a shriek and grabbed Dmitri, but they were outmatched by alcohol, anger, and determination. David's head split Sergei's lip. Sarah was knocked to the ground and stepped on, adding more grime to the once-pretty blue dress. John came running around the building and dove between the warring parties.

Tomas ran up with a panting Vladimir, assessed the situation for all of five seconds, and tapped the communication function on his *Vsyochas* wristcom. "Tomas Ivanov to security detail: an altercation is in progress on the north side of the house. Please send staff immediately." Nonviolent Uncle Tomas seized both boys by the hair and pulled their heads back. The pain allowed John to push them apart, while Sergei and Sarah pulled them farther away. Security arrived in seconds using Andrea's canopied garden cart.

Everyone stood, breathing hard. Sarah looked like an advertisement for a cleaning service, covered with strawberry and grass marks and footprints, hem torn, hair down and curls unrolling. She pressed against

293

Dmitri, shielding him, one step from tears. Sergei dabbed his lip, checking for blood. David panted, disheveled and sweaty, his lip and cheek swelling, his brother's blood drying on his knuckles. Dmitri's face and chin were spattered with blood; fresh blood still oozed from the bruising wound.

"Security," Tomas said curtly, "you will escort each of these gentlemen to their respective rooms. You will then post yourselves outside their doors, and you will not allow them to exit. If either of them speaks, threatens the other, touches the other, or otherwise creates a disturbance, you are to call for City Security immediately and have them both taken in for disturbing the peace. Is that clear?"

"Yes, sir," the private officers agreed.

"As for the two of you... There are not enough words to convey my disgust. Sergei, please see to it that David arrives at the right room. Sarah, please attend to Dmitri. Thank you." Tomas dabbed the perspiration from his face with his handkerchief, and walked away while his tongue remained civil.

"Better let me take a look at that eye," John said to Dmitri as he yielded to Sarah's pull. "I'll grab my kit out of my flyer and meet you upstairs."

* * *

After breakfasting in their rooms, David and Dmitri sat a cushion apart on the sofa in Tomas's apartment, still warring by seeing who could ignore the other longer.

Tomas stared, playing his waiting game. When truly angry, he would wait five full minutes, sometimes more, unnerving his victim with suspense. Both boys were adults; the most he could do was demand they make peace. He had always had an upper hand with David, more or less. He had become friends with Dmitri, but Tomas just didn't know him well enough yet. Dmitri was intensely sociable and could chatter for hours, but he wasn't prone to gossip, didn't talk much about himself, and kept his thoughts private.

"I am most disappointed in both of you," Tomas began. "Schoolyard brawling is immature enough, but to start a drunken fistfight at your sister's wedding is reprehensible. I thought I taught you to handle your liquor better than that, David?"

"Yes, sir. You did, sir," David said, focused on the corner of a picture frame on the wall behind Tomas' head. "I can only thank you for stopping me before I brought further shame to myself and my family."

"Don't kiss my ass," Tomas said humorlessly. "It only serves to denigrate yourself further. Dmitri, I know for a fact I've told you I don't approve of violence or public drunkenness. You may drink yourself to sleep every night in your room, but the minute you are out of that room, I expect you to be fit for public appearance at all times. Is that clear?"

"Extremely, sir. I apologize," Dmitri said.

Tomas sighed. "I don't know what started this, or what static there is between you, but I want it ended. Here and now. The minute you leave this apartment, all hostilities between you will cease. If they cannot, I will … "

The chime to the door interrupted him.

"Computer: intercom. Who is it?" he asked the air.

"Sarah, sir."

"I'm involved with something at the moment, Sarah. I shall speak to you following lunch."

"It is most urgent I speak with you immediately, sir. *Please!* It cannot wait."

Tomas released the door. "Please make it brief."

She strode over to his chair. "I know what you're trying to do, and I belong here, too. They were fighting over me, and I won't have it! Not at all." She glared at her brothers with a fiery heat.

"Over you?"

"Over *me*," Sarah repeated. "Without using less polite words, I will call them both idiots. Fools. *Porshin!*" she spat for Dmitri's benefit. No animal could possibly be more stubborn and disagreeable than a Sigma Tau Ceti porshie. "They were fighting over who was going to dance with me and it turned into an insult match. For shame! Your anger is making me ill, and if you can't stop, my apologies to Uncle Tomas, but I will need a different living arrangement."

Understanding dawned on Tomas. "So that's what started it."

"Can you believe that? Over *me*. Like I'm worth the bother. You are like my right and left hands; remove either one, and I'm lost."

She attacked with the same steel she used when defending Vladimir, unwavering and strong.

"Shame on you, David! I expected better out of you. Yes, you took care of me while Dimi was delayed, and you did a great job. You dragged me out in public and taught me things I desperately needed to learn. You made me rely more on myself and gave me the confidence I needed to succeed, but so did Sergei and Vlad! You fake it well, but you showed me yesterday you are no gentleman, sir! Inside those respectable clothes you are the same horrid David you always were. The one who annoys me. The one who provokes me. The one who dares me to push myself further than I ever thought I had the nerve to go. The Fearsome Four are still terrorizing the world, and I can't tell you how *good* that feels! I *died* inside when Val flew off and left us! I *needed* to go back to being one of the crowd, exactly as I'd been on that day, so I could pick up where my heart stopped and grow again from there. I can only thank *you* for that. You didn't need to punch Dmitri out to prove you love me. I already knew that. I love you every bit as much, and always will."

Tomas watched her from the side, amused. Sarah seized control like this so rarely, but he recognized the truth in her words.

"And *you*!" Sarah turned on Saint Dmitri. "How could you ever be that jealous of David? *Seven years*! Seven years you had me all to yourself, through good and bad, just the two of us. What you did for me, right or wrong, you did out of *love*! Maybe that's not what you called it back then – putting Val in her place, getting even, rescuing a friend – whatever you called it, you did it from the heart. It is the most noble act I have ever witnessed, and ever expect to. Despite everything, *I love you*, and nothing can ever change that! You don't have to love me back. I wouldn't blame you. I hurt you through my own fear of losing that love, and I will never stop apologizing. You know where my loyalty lies. If you packed your bags and beckoned tonight, I would cry and plead and tantrum, but I *would* leave with you. You know you are the only person in the universe who has my complete and utter trust. We have died many deaths together, and lived to tell about it. The Navarans have a phrase you wouldn't know – *//I'ghanth'ali ot.//** Look it up. It's us." She pressed her lips tightly and blinked hard.

Tomas opened his mouth to fill in the pause, but Sarah cut him off, still rolling

"I think I've had enough damned therapy to know that fight had nothing to do with me. That fight's been brewing for seven years, between two people who used to be friends; it just happened to erupt yesterday. That fight is really about broken trust, isn't it?" Sarah slammed the nail on the head in triumph. "It's about Dmitri breaking a promise to David to follow Val to Earth seven years ago. It's about *David* being abandoned by Dmitri, who was abandoned by Val. Shame on both of you! I got over it. Val got over it. Vlad got over it, but neither one of you can see your way to being friends again? David – Would you be as respectable a person if Dmitri'd been here the past seven years? Would you ever have graduated from a university? Or would you have been content to let Dimi lead the way, getting into trouble together and not caring about anything but having a good time and proving yourselves to each other? And Dimi – would you have gained any of the wisdom and maturity you have today if David had

296

gone off with you instead? Or would your lives have been one long party, your résumé consisting of the number of women you had and the diseases you got from them?"

Tomas and David turned to Dmitri. Dmitri shot Sarah a deadly glare to change the subject.

"I'm going to do something I've never done before," Sarah announced with authority, "and if it doesn't work, you can *both* say goodbye to me, because I won't have two people who still mean so much to each other destroying themselves over *nothing,* and destroying *me* in that process." She squeezed between her brothers on the sofa and picked up a hand from each.

"I'm calling a truce. A Do-over. Neither of you is to blame in the series of events that started this. It's all theoretical *ifs. If* Mother didn't die. *If* I wasn't so stressed. *If* Val wasn't so porshie-headed. *If* Dimi kept his promise. *If* I'd thought of calling for help back when I thought Dimi was dying at the Mirabella. *If* Uncle Tomas didn't come and help us. Any one thing different in the chain would have changed the outcome. I'm calling Truce, and I want it shook on."

There was a pause before David said coolly, "For your sake."

Sarah pushed the hand back. "No! Don't do it because I *ask,* do it because you know I'm *right.*"

"You're right," Dmitri said grudgingly, though he looked the other way. He extended his hand across Sarah. After a moment, David shook it.

Sarah squeezed the hands together. "Now, stand up and face each other and say you're sorry." She pulled them to their feet. "Come on. Say it."

Dmitri raised his eyes to David. "I kept calling to talk to you. You wouldn't answer a single message, and when Sarah tried to tell you, all you did was call me names."

David shifted his gaze to the side. "You pissed me off. Standing up to Val like that, I thought you were some fucking hero, but you let me down. I was fourteen! I wasn't ready to be the oldest yet. You promised you were following us. You left me with *Valeria* in charge, dammit! If she had the nerve to abandon you in the middle of a damned desert, imagine what she could have done to me? When you said you weren't coming back, I cracked so bad, I almost killed her."

"Maybe if you'd answered just *one* of my calls I could have explained it to you," Dmitri argued. "I only meant to stay away a week or two. Maybe if I'd known that then, I would have come back on time. I *needed* to talk to you, man! You were the only person I trusted, the only one who had my back. Maybe I felt like you had abandoned me, too. Maybe if

297

I knew somebody still gave a damn, I would've come home."

"I guess we were both pretty stupid then, huh."

Dmitri held his hand out again. "I'm sorry if I misunderstood."

David shook it on his own. "Me, too."

Sarah beamed proudly. "That's more like it!" She hugged the daylights out of them, then bent down and hugged Tomas in his chair.

"That was beautiful, Sarah," Tomas said with appreciation. "I couldn't have done better myself. I wish John had been here to hear that speech. He'd be as proud of you as I am."

"And I'll bet he didn't think I was listening all that time."

* *I'ghanth'ali ot:* 'My inner link.' Intimacy is a subtle term on Navara. 'Intimate' covers not only mate or lover, but the human concept of closest friend, relative, or blood brother as well. It is used to imply those closest to a Navaran, who share a familial or voluntary telepathic link and are the only ones trusted to be privvy to another's rawest inner feelings. While Dmitri is already genetically Sarah's brother, the deepness of their emotional bond is more along the line of lovers, but without the sexual aspect.

Twenty-seven

Tomas waited for Sarah, killing time leaning against the piano, listening to Dmitri show off. He'd never have his name on a stuffy marquis above the National Symphony, but if you wanted a rip-roaring good time and needed someone to play popular music, Dmitri was very much the man. Although there was nothing so beautiful as a well-played concerto, in many ways Tomas was glad to see him lean away from classical music. It would keep Mamá from exploiting his talents among her friends.

Dmitri stopped to rub his hand.

"I like that," Tomas said. "What was it called?"

"*Into my Out*, by a group called Quantum Slide. They were nano about ten years ago."

Sarah entered, ready for her daily appointment with one doctor or the other. Dmitri slid over and patted the bench. "You still remember that countermelody I taught you for *We the Underground*?"

"Maybe." She'd barely sat when the intercom system gave an unfamiliar, two-toned chime.

"*Incoming message, priority red, destination, Tomas Ivanov,*" said the soothing computer voice. "*Incoming message, priority red, destination, Tomas Ivanov. System override activated, all channels responding.*" Any current use of the communications system disengaged immediately; all channels connected to the incoming call so it could not be lost. Tomas took off at a run for the library, the nearest room with an outside communications station.

Sarah found herself on her feet before she realized it, senses alert and ready to run. The last time some unseen voice announced a red alert, Viktor had died.

Dmitri grabbed Sarah's hand, his own memories just as vivid. "Relax. It's most likely related to his companies. It's probably Val with the results of some legal decision he's been waiting on. We're not about to have an invasion here on Earth."

"No, no one's ever invaded Earth," Sarah repeated faintly. She walked toward the hallway.

"Stay here. It's Tomas's business, not ours. If it's something he wants to share, he'll tell us."

"I'm not eavesdropping," she insisted, leaning against the doorway nearer the library. "I'm waiting for him to finish."

"Right." Dmitri followed her to the door. Only the louder words drifted down the hall.

"No! No! You did the right thing, Sergei. I have the coordinates. I should be there in twenty minutes, maximum. I've got my comm. Stay there. I'm on my way."

There was a tiny pause as Tomas cut the connection on one call and placed another to his answering service in New York. *"This is Tomas. I have an emergency. Hold all incoming calls except priority red and relay them to my personal unit. Call Valeria, tell her to meet me at Town Square Transport Center in ten minutes, without fail. I don't care* **what** *she's involved with! Pull her out of the lavatory if necessary, but she* **must be there** *in ten minutes! I can't wait. Then find John Carver, give him the same coordinates, and have him meet me there as soon as possible. In fact, let his calls through to me as well. Between Valeria and John, call Town Square and reserve me a transport time, make it fifteen minutes from now. Okay? Go!"*

Unflappable Tomas Ivanov tore down the back hall to his office, the absolute farthest corner of the house from the library.

Tomas rushed down the front hall on his way to his flyer, the housemaid Anna almost unable to keep up as she took down his notes. He paused less than a minute when Sarah and Dmitri met him near the side door.

"Dmitri! There's an emergency I have to deal with. Please take Sarah to her appointment for me. Thank you. I don't know how long I'll be gone, but I'll be in touch as soon as I can. Sarah, make sure you keep that appointment." In a whiff of cologne, he disappeared.

"What's …?" Sarah tried to say, but no one was there. *"Shto dyelayet?"* she asked Anna.

"Ni znayu, Miss Sarah," Anna replied, finishing. "Mister Ivanov will call when he knows what time he'll be returning."

"Where'd he go?" Dmitri asked.

"I'm sorry, sir, I have no idea. He's moley-beaming somewhere, and Miss Valeria and Doctor Karverov are meeting him there. Probably New York or Moscow."

Sarah frowned. "John? Why would he need John for a business crisis?"

Dmitri shrugged with mock annoyance. "Who knows? You know how they use John as a private physician. Maybe a business partner jumped out a window. Maybe he was doing private duty with a bureau chief and had chest pains."

"So why would they need Valeria?"

"How the Hell do I know?" Dmitri replied with real annoyance. "To make sure the company's not held liable. You're due at the clinic. If you were as smart as you're supposed to be, I would think that would be the place to ask where John went."

Sarah dragged him down the hall. "We're late."

"I need to speak with Doctor Karverov, please," Sarah told the receptionist at the front desk.

"I'm sorry, Doctor Karverov has been called away on an emergency. You can leave a video message for him, or I can arrange for you to speak with another doctor."

Sarah handed over her clinic ID. "I already know he was called away. I'm his sister-in-law, Sarah Kirushenko. I need to get in touch with him before he returns. Can you tell me where he went, so I can leave a message for him there?"

The receptionist ran the ID. Because of the unstable nature of the patients who came and went, professional privacy was well-guarded, but the ID and palm scan checked out. The girl was the doctor's sister-in-law, and the file included permission for unrestricted access.

"He's at Konstantin Guralny General Hospital in Moscow, consulting on an emergency evaluation. We don't expect him to return for several hours."

Sarah absorbed the news with a straight face, falling back on her training in Navaran indifference to pull her through. "Moscow? Isn't that rather far for a simple eval? Don't they have their own doctors up there? What kind of problem is it?"

"I'm sorry, that's private information."

Only a Navaran could split hairs finer than Sarah. "I didn't ask *who* the problem was, I only asked *what* the problem was. That's not a violation of confidentiality. You send my brother-in-law on a 600-kilometer emergency trip and his wife doesn't even know yet that she has to hold dinner and put the baby to bed before he gets a kiss from daddy, and you can't even tell me *why*?"

"I'm not sure. I think someone said a chemical overdose. That shouldn't take too long."

Sarah felt her blood congeal, but she rolled her eyes and tried to look disappointed. "*That's* all. For all that fuss I figured it would be something interesting, like a severed brain, or a personality that split or something. Okay. I'll try and relay Kat's message to him there. Thank you." She took

Dmitri by the arm and tried to walk to the lift without looking like she was in a hurry.

<*Allash. Taber. kem Oes!*> Sarah cursed in Tau Cetan. "David and Sergei left for Moscow early this morning! Something's happened! Who else would get Uncle Tomas, Val, and John up there together that fast?"

Dmitri's face reflected the same fear. "Shah! You don't know that for a fact. Maybe David lost it and beat someone up."

"You don't understand!" Sarah whispered as she walked backwards out of the lift. "*Sergei does chemicals!* I've seen him, Dim! He says they're legal, but still! He must have done something bad."

Dmitri sucked his lip, thinking. "I know what Sergei does. It's nothing – a mild hypnotic, nothing worse than a drink or two. I swear I heard Sergei's voice talking with Uncle Tomas. It's got to be David. David did chems way back on Navara – Moons know what he plays with now. It's got to be him."

Sarah stared, dumbfounded, as her image of her bold leader burst like a bubble. "*What?!* What you mean he does …?" *Too much!* How the hell could she concentrate on a therapy session with all this going on?

"Wait here," she said as they reached the office. "I'll be out in five minutes."

"Hello, Sarah," Doctor Petrova greeted her. "You look like you're in a hurry today."

"I am." Sarah strung together the few facts she knew and inferred the rest, which was not the same as lying. Scientists did that every day, and she was going to be a scientist. "As you may know, John Carver was called away on an emergency. The emergency has to do with my brother. He's in a hospital in Moscow. We don't know his condition yet. I cannot possibly concentrate on today's session. I came here, I showed up in good faith, so you can write that in your little reports, but I have a real family crisis, and I'm leaving. I need to be home in case John calls with news. I am not going off the deep end; you can call me at home if you'd like, because that's where I'll be. Dmitri's with me, so I'm not alone."

"Why don't you sit and talk about it for a minute … "

"I've got to get home. If everything's okay, I'll be in tomorrow. If it's not, John can fill you in on the details. Bye!" She slipped through the door before it could be locked, grabbed Dmitri, and together they ran for the lift.

"What now?" he asked as they left the building. "We could sit around all day before someone calls."

"Misery loves company," Sarah decided. "Whether it's Sergei or David, they're both part of the Fearsome Four. Vlad doesn't know. We

302

have to get him." She dragged on Dimi's arm.

"I can't sign Vlad out from summer program. For what? So he can twiddle his thumbs with us?"

"He's seventeen; he can sign himself out. Come on. There's a public commlink in the lobby."

"I better not get in trouble for this." Dmitri sighed and followed her back in.

Three hours and a shuttle flight later, Sarah accosted the main receptionist at Guralny General. She held Vladimir's hand breathlessly, having run from the tram stop. Dmitri brought up the rear, trying hard to keep them in sight.

"You had a Kirushenko admitted on an emergency basis a few hours ago. Where I may find him?" Sarah demanded. "He's our brother."

The man checked his display screen. "I have three Kirushenkos listed. First name?"

"David," Dmitri said.

"David F.?"

"That's him!" Vladimir exclaimed, his face paler than the overhead lighting. "Oh my God, it *is* him!"

"He's been taken to the critical-care floor," the receptionist read. "That's on fifteen. Take your right to the directory, a left down that corridor, take the red lifts to the fifteenth floor, and turn left. You'll see the scroll sign."

"Thank you," Dmitri said as he hustled after the pair.

Old fears swelled at the color that always signaled disaster. "Red lifts! That's not good, Dim. That's a really bad sign."

Dmitri spun and held a fist to Sarah's face. "So's this, if you get my meaning. Lock down your bullshit, Sar. I'm sure they've got a Crazy floor here, too."

She held her breath in the blood-red lift, expecting it to open up at a flaming gate of Hell, but it seemed a normal floor like any other. How strange, walking around a hospital as a visitor, not a patient! Sarah couldn't purge the feeling that any minute some official would demand to know where her escort was, and drag her off to an observation room. As they approached the right corridor, Tomas, Sergei, John, and Valeria were clustered in conversation with two law officers and a doctor.

Valeria's gaze drifted down the hall, and her eyes widened. She grabbed Tomas's arm, whispering.

"How in God's name did you get here?" Tomas said angrily as they approached. "Vladimir, why aren't you at school? None of you has any business here. Sarah, you're out of jurisdiction."

"This is all her idea," Dmitri insisted. "I'm just following to keep an eye on her."

"You underestimated my resourcefulness," Sarah told Tomas. "Why didn't you tell me something was wrong with David? He's our brother, too! Serya, *what's wrong?* Why is the law involved?"

"It's kind of serious," Sergei admitted.

Carver turned Sarah and Vlad away from the group. "What happened is David's business. I know you're a strong proponent of patient confidentiality, so I'm sure you'll understand."

"Shove it, John!"

"Sarah, I want you to return home immediately," Tomas insisted. "Dmitri, please take them home."

"No! I won't go. I didn't spend all morning tracking you to be turned away. I'm his sister; I have every right to be here, as much as Valeria or Sergei. My guardians are all here, past and present, so I'm certainly under supervision. Moons above, even one of my *doctors* is here! I'm not leaving until I get some answers!"

Carver beckoned. "Come on, then. You want answers, come on. Over there." He pointed to a sitting area, half a hall away.

Vlad bit; he dragged Sarah.

"I'm not going to play around," John said as they sat. "David's extremely ill. You can't see him now, and I'm not sure when you can. A large portion of muscle in his heart died. Luckily, he was having lunch with Sergei and some friends when it happened. He just returned from surgery. He's got a temp graft but he's off bypass, and in a few days they'll finish growing cardiac muscle of his own. They'll transplant the new piece in there, and if all goes well, he shouldn't have any further problems."

"Shit!" Dmitri breathed, but it seemed to say it all.

Sarah and Vlad's hands fused in mutual support. In Minsk it had been a game, finding and following the clues to where Tomas had gone. Now the game had disappeared.

Sarah tried to stay brave. "John, he's twenty-one years old. How could he have a coronary? That's for old people with neglected health."

"Yes, normally that's true, but not always."

"Is – Is it because of chems?"

Carver's manner sharpened. "Sarah, if you know something, you need to tell me. Any of you. If David's taking some sort of chemical substance, it's crucial they know about it as soon as possible. I don't care if he is

304

or not, but his treatment and his life could depend on it."

"I don't know," Sarah wailed. "Dimi said he does."

"I don't know that for a fact," Dmitri corrected. "I said he did some back on Navara, so it wouldn't surprise me now."

"Vlad?" Carver asked.

Vlad was so upset his bones were nearly audible, shaking in his skin. "I don't know! He drinks, but I've never seen him taking stuff or anything. Just vitamins. He says they help keep him going when he's running everywhere." Sarah agreed.

"What kind? What brand? What did the bottle look like?"

"I don't know! It's white. It didn't have a label."

"Did he ever give you any?"

"No." Vlad shook his head hard. "He told me to get my own; those were his."

"That's fine. There's nothing you can do for David up here. He's not conscious, and he can't have visitors. I'll make sure your names are added to the list so you can access the nursing updates. Go home and do something for me: take Sergei and go through David's room – every drawer, every pocket, under the mattress, under the carpet, find me every bottle of anything that can possibly be injected, inhaled, ingested, or rubbed on. Hand cream, foot powder, aphrodesiacs, vitamins, anything. Put it all in a box, and I will come by late tonight or first thing in the morning to go through it. Dmitri, are you familiar with any types of contraband?"

Dmitri shuddered at bad memories. "I stay clean."

"Well, if it's something you recognize, or Vlad, if you happen to find that bottle of vitamins, page me immediately," John said. "Don't wait a second. Got that? Go back and do that for me. You'll save everyone time, and we'll keep the law out of it as much as possible."

"But what if he ..." Sarah couldn't bear the thought. "Please! I have to see him, John. Just from the doorway, so I know it's really him. I can't take another death. *Please!*"

John rubbed his thumb against his lip, thinking. "I'll see what I can do."

Carver expected to have to restrain Sarah from running into the room, but Vladimir was hit harder by the reality of the life-support bed. John held him up as the boy sobbed shamelessly, Sarah shedding tears as she tried to hug to him at the same time, her concern for Vlad pushing the other crisis just enough to the rear. Dmitri hung an arm from Sergei's sagging shoulder. Sergei towered seventeen centimeters over him; Dmitri couldn't put an arm around his neck even if he stood on his toes.

Grandmother hurried down the hall when they returned well into evening. She wasn't wearing her usual flowing clothing, but a form-fitting pair of pants and a shirt, as if preparing for physical action. For someone in spitting distance of eighty, her body was surprisingly firm and strong-looking.

"Any news?" she asked as Sergei bent to give her a hug.

Dmitri shook his head as Andrea accepted a sad little kiss from Vlad. "Last we heard, there was no change."

Sarah clung to Dmitri, drawn into herself, but Grandmamá reached out and clasped her hands. "Are *you* all right, dear?" she asked with sympathy. "I worried when I heard you'd run up there. I know how hard you take things."

Sarah lifted her head. She tried, then tried again, playing the sentences back in her head, but she couldn't find any disdain, any condescension, any sarcasm. As hard as it was to accept, the sentiment seemed very real.

"I'm okay," she said, giving a light hug lest she manage to break Old Bones. "Thank you, Ma'am."

"Tomas and Valeria left Moscow with David's flyer," Andrea said. "He should be back in another hour. Are you hungry? Shall I have the kitchen fix something?"

Dmitri shrugged numbly. He eyed the gloomy group. "I don't think we're very hungry right now."

"John wants us to look for some things in David's room," Sergei told her. "We're going to head up there for a while."

"I'll have some tea and light fare sent upstairs," Andrea decided for them. "In times of crisis, a little food can sustain you for quite a while."

"Thanks, Grandmamá," Sergei acknowledged, and he headed for the stairs.

Marina and Nikky were in their sleepwear and long overdue for bed, but Tomas wanted everyone present at the meeting in the big lounge, from all household staff who could possibly attend up through Andrea Ivanova herself. Marina dozed against Valeria, while Nikky sat with Vlad and Sarah and tried to look awake.

"I might recognize one or two of them, but I'll have to get the rest analyzed." John Carver rifled through the box of items from David's room. He shook a small white vial of tablets. "I'd say this is, though."

Tomas nodded. He walked to the center of the room. "I called everyone tonight because of the grave incident that occurred today with David. If it wasn't for Sergei and the evac team, he would have been dead

306

before he arrived at the emergency center. He had surgery today, and he will have more next week, but if there are no complications, he will recover in a few weeks.

"He wasn't conscious when I left, but there is a general consensus that his condition was caused by the overuse of certain chemical compounds, most likely obtained without permit." Tomas moved with an aching slowness, his eyes searching the carpet for imperceptible wear. "I've been told some people in this house may have been aware, or partly aware, of what was going on. I don't understand that. I don't know how someone could know something self-destructive was going on, and not try to stop it."

"Because we believed him when he said they weren't," Sarah said. "Why would we think otherwise? I take chemicals and vitamins every day and no one thinks twice about it."

"Yours are prescribed by qualified physicians, and you're monitored to insure no harmful effects," John reminded her.

Tomas paced a slow circle. "I have always had the highest regard for everyone here. I have always believed everyone to be up front and honest with me. I have always given the benefit of the doubt and tried, within reason, to treat the older teens as adults. I have respected everyone's privacy in regard to what went on upstairs. I see now that may have been idealistic. Anything that happens on this property and to this property *is* the business of Mamá and I, no matter who is involved."

Tomas paused behind the grand piano, a hypertrophic podium. "In light of David's near-fatal mistake, I feel forced to take strong if somewhat belated action. At seven tomorrow morning an investigation team will arrive at the estate, complete with sniffer gear. Every room, every piece of furniture, including the private apartments and staff quarters, will be thoroughly examined for legal and contraband substances. No one will be exempt. If it is legal, it will be returned to you. If it is not legal, it will be confiscated and the party involved will be taken into custody by City Security. I suggest if anyone is currently harboring illegal substances, he or she should dispose of them of before tomorrow morning."

"I don't even know what they *look* like!" Nikky said with alarm.

"Me neither," Marina echoed. "Only bad people touch those things. Does that mean David's bad?"

Valeria ruffled Marina's hair. "Of course not. David is a good person. He just made a very bad mistake."

"Don't look at me," Dmitri said. "I don't have a bottle of vodka to my name."

307

"I have enough problems," Sarah said. "My blood's monitored weekly. I'd be caught in an instant."

"I don't even *drink*!" Vladimir pleaded.

Sergei held up his hands. "Everything I have is perfectly legal, and right now anyone who wants it can have it."

"For your sake, let's hope so," Tomas said sternly.

* * *

"I said, get the fuck out of here!" David screamed at John. He sat up and hurled the empty drinking cup at his brother-in-law. The indicators on the patient monitor above his bed danced in response to the strain.

"You hang around here like a fucking vulture! I've got nothing to say to you! You're not the personal savior of this family and you never will be, so leave me the fuck alone! Go cure your own fucking patients and get the fuck away from me! I got enough goddamned people trying to crawl inside my fucking head!" He groaned and dropped back on the pillows, clutching at the knifing pains that stabbed his chest. The tempgraft was meant only to keep a bed-ridden patient alive until further measures could be taken, not power tantrums.

"Okay," John said, though some of the words had hurt. "I came to visit my wife's brother, but if he'd rather not have visitors, that's fine." He went to leave, only to find Tomas and Sarah about to enter. The search three days ago turned up nothing illegal outside of David's room.

"David doesn't want any visitors," John said with a touch of sarcasm. "He finds them upsetting."

"Oh," Tomas replied with disappointment. "No one informed me of that."

"I just found out myself."

"He didn't tell *me*," Sarah insisted, and pushed past John.

David's back was to the door. He flipped over, spitting with rage. "I thought I told you to leave!"

"You didn't tell *me* anything."

David growled and turned away. "I don't want to see anybody."

"Why not? We came a long way. I just wanted to say 'Hi.' We miss you." She took a step closer, bursting with curiosity. She'd never seen David grizzly like this. His hair looked unwashed, was certainly uncombed, and he must not have used beard inhibitor since the incident, for his cheeks and chin were dark with thickening black beard. It made him look like … a young blue-eyed Father.

"Yeah, well, go pour your efforts into some other lost cause." David mashed his hospital pillow around until it was lost somewhere under his neck. "Leave me alone. I don't need all that 'pity poor David' shit. I don't need more whispers."

Sarah walked around the bed, oblivious to the request. "I didn't come to give you any of that. I'm the last person in the galaxy who would do that."

"Go home."

"I don't want to. We just flew two hours to visit you. It's sad when you're all alone in a hospital, far from home."

"Did it ever occur to you maybe I *want* the peace and quiet? That maybe I'm sick to death of your hanging on me and questioning me and acting like a baby? I thought you were supposed to be so fucking brilliant? Why don't you just grow up?"

Sarah's shoulders drooped all the way to her waist. Her face fell only a little shorter. She started toward the door, but the more she thought about it, the more anger overtook dejection.

She stopped at the foot of the bed. "Go to Hell, David Kirushenko! Just go to Hell! I thought we were friends. You visited *me* in the hospital. You were there for *me* when I needed a friend. I only wanted to return the favor. You think you're the only one who's ever been caught doing something stupid? You think you have the bull market on pain and embarrassment? Get in line, Mister!

"You think Valeria wouldn't give her big toe to reverse decisions she's made? You think Dmitri wouldn't? Or Gal? Do you have *any idea* how *hard* it is for me to get out of bed every morning?" Sarah took two steps back up the bedside, not afraid to meet David's sneer with a sharp look of her own. "Knowing that I have to face people who know the very worst facts about me? Wondering if every time I pick up a knife at dinner, people are breaking into a sweat afraid I'm going to use it on myself instead? Look in a mirror, David! No one in our family is perfect, and that means you, too! Nobody gives a … a … a goddamned flying crap on a carpet about what you did! We only care that you'll survive.

"I'm sorry to hear of your accident, Mr. Kirushenko," she said. "May you have a short and successful recovery."

Tomas opened the door in response to the shouting just as Sarah exited. She ducked to the side and walked past.

Ten minutes later she was back.

"I told you to get lost!" David bellowed.

"I just wanted to say I'm sorry for yelling at you," Sarah said, understanding better after speaking to John.

"I'm gonna to give you to a count of three, and then I'm paging the nurse. *Ahdin!...* "

Sarah walked around the bed to face him. David hid under his pillow, but not before she saw the tears.

"I'll go in a second." She sank down until her chin rested on the bed near his face. "I just wanted to let you know that I am an expert on everything you're going through. Think about it. Maybe not the same method, but I guarantee for some of the same reasons. If you want to know how to survive it, I'm willing to talk, or just listen if you want. Ask Dimi; I'm very good at keeping secrets. You know where to find me. We love you anyway." She lifted the pillow and wiped a tear with her thumb, then kissed the bristly cheek. She replaced the pillow and walked around the bed without another word.

"Sar?" he called as she reached the door.

"*Da*?"

"How do you handle – the scared part?"

Sarah stepped over and hugged the broad back carefully, so as not to strain his chest. "You never do." She lay her cheek against his ear. "You just surround yourself with people you love and trust, and draw your strength from them."

Twenty-eight

Tomas entered the hospital room, unsure what to expect. David sat on the bed, staring out the window. A small bag of personal items sat next to him. His hair was combed, and his face smooth again. He didn't turn around.

Tomas knocked on the wall inside the door, with no response. He cleared his throat.

"I came to take you home. They say you're fit medically, but you threatened your counselor. They're meeting to decide what to do."

David's gaze never shifted. "I'm sorry, sir. I was tired of kissing asses to beg for my release and I told them that. I mean, what do they want from me? How can I answer their questions when *I* don't even know who the Hell I am?"

Tomas sat on the bed. "An aftereffect from the chemicals?"

"Sort of, I guess, but more likely the cause. I mean, I know why it happened. I'm not stupid. I guess I'm just sick of these idiots treating me like I am."

"If I may ask, why do you think it happened?" Sociology texts were quick to point out deviancies as being caused by disaffected youth who felt left out by society. David could be a hell-raiser, but Tomas would never have lumped him under the title of disaffected. Not someone who graduated number three in his school class, number 548 out of 6,821 in his college class, and was heading to a prestigious graduate school in America.

"I've been thinking about it a lot, sitting here the last two weeks. I think I kind of understand it, but explaining it to some jackass junior analyst isn't going to change anything. Now I know what Sarah means by what she calls a melt-down. That's what it feels like," David explained. "I feel like I turned into a puddle, and I just can't pull myself back into shape.

"When we arrived in Minsk, everything was so out of control. We'd lost our parents, our home, our friends, Alexei, Viktor, 'Byeta, Dimi and Sarah; we were staying with people we didn't know, in a house that was so far out of our imaginations we were afraid to breathe, 'cause if we got kicked out, we had nowhere. When I lost it with Val, I expected you to beat me like Father – skin me alive, kick us out, throw me in a youth camp. When you didn't – when you treated me like an adult and not some punk who needed his ass kicked – I was scared to death." David swallowed hard, remembering. "I took it as a kind of gift. I knew you were

311

giving me a do-over, and I wanted to prove to you I was worthy of it, no matter how much it killed me. Nobody ever treated me that way before. I never managed to impress my father, but I wanted to impress you so bad I could have cried. I wanted to live in your fancy house and pilot impressive vehicles like you did. Wherever you went, people already knew your name and they respected you. I wanted all that for me."

"And you had it," Tomas said. "It was yours, there for the taking. You only needed to be pointed in the right direction."

David snorted. "I know that now, but I didn't then. I'd never done good in school. My grades were as low as I could get away with. I knew when I hit Northern, I was in big trouble. Sergei was a year behind and I couldn't even figure out stuff *he* was doing. That whole first year I went to every tutoring class they offered, and Sergei explained everything to me night after night until I finally understood. I *couldn't* fail. I didn't want to let you down. I wanted you to be proud of me."

"David, I couldn't have been any prouder of you than I am," Tomas said honestly. "I was proud of you just for accepting my offer. If I'd known your school record beforehand, I would never have said anything. Your efforts showed from the very start."

"I didn't want you to how dumb I really was. I recited spelling and history facts while I swam laps for the swim team. I practiced geometry by dividing up my dinner plate and working out the proportions. I worked out volume by estimating sizes of serving bowls on the table. I worked physics out on the soccer field – angles, distance, force, trajectories, levers." He gave a brief, aching laugh. "I made fun of Sarah when she did that, and there I was doing it myself."

"I had no idea Northern was that difficult for you," Tomas said with a pang of guilt. "If you'd told me, I would have sent you to Leonov. It's not as stringent as Northern. There was never a need to suffer like that."

David gave a distant, sad smile. "But I *did* it! One of the top three students in the best school in the country. I'm still surprised Val didn't drop dead. I know she didn't think I had it in me. Nobody did, me included. You bought me the Aeronavt, and I thought that was the most incredible thing anybody'd ever done for anybody in the history of mankind. It was worth every ounce of sweat to know that bike was mine.

"When I hit University, I lost the structure I had at Northern. Sergei wanted to go to St. Petersburg, but I threatened him to stay in Moscow, because I needed him. My diploma should really go to him. There were always people after me to party, places to go, girls hanging off me. Other people were struggling just as hard as I was, and they took chems to study.

"I knew about chems from Navara," David admitted. "My friends had connections. A couple hits and you didn't give a damn about the freakin' temperature. I knew what to do and how to do it. I didn't dare come home impaired, you know? Same way with liquor. Someone offered me stuff at University and I figured, I already knew how to handle it, right? So I used them to study for exams. Then it was to ease the timeshift when I worked in New York with you. Then it was alerts to study with, and sleepers to catch some rest. Add in alcohol and smokers to calm the jitters from the 'lerts, and either boosters or more 'lerts to counteract the sleepers so I could make it to class on time, and I kind of got lost in the routine. I'm lucky I lasted as long as I did. I made it past graduation. More than a couple of people I know got freaked on the stuff. Someone in my building even died. You shake your head and say, 'Man, it's their fault for not being careful.' After all, *you* know what you're doing, right?"

He gave a laugh halfway between hysteria and depression. "I hadn't been messing with stuff much over the summer; I didn't need it because school was over, you know? I took the 'lerts that morning so I could be on top of things. I didn't want to blow the contract like I did at the Montreal conference last year. Serg and I met some friends for lunch. I had a couple drinks, tossed a couple more pills, and I guess it just reacted bad."

David bit his lip as if trying to keep something inside. "I'm sorry. I didn't do it to make you look bad, sir. I just … I didn't want to fail you again." He looked down at his hands, hands that had beat up undeserving kids for fun, hands that had choked someone nearly to death, hands that reminded him of his father's oversized hands every time he saw them.

"I guess all that fancy education can't erase the bad blood after all, can it?" David did something he hadn't done in front of Tomas in seven years: he started to cry.

Tomas felt as if he'd been blown out an airlock without warning, freezing to death in the dark emptiness of space while his blood boiled and he gasped for air.

"David!" he found the breath to whisper. "Why didn't you tell me? I never meant to put you under such pressure. I would never have knowingly done that. I merely thought you had started to care about things. I was happy that you were able to accept my authority without giving me grief, let alone succeed at Northern. I'm sorry if I pushed you into that."

David sniffed. "You didn't. I just … You had *everything*, and we had *nothing*! You were nice even to undeserving people, and all of a sudden I wanted to be just like you. I wanted you to like *me*. I just don't know who I am anymore. I'm glad I'm not the jackass I was when I got here, but I'm not you, either, and I'll never be as perfect as you, but I don't know anything else. I know I can't rely on the chems anymore, but how the hell am I going to make it through grad school without them? What if I fail?"

Tomas hung a hand from the wide shoulder and patted it. "I'm not nearly as perfect as you think I am, David. I've had fifty-three years to practice getting things right; you haven't. I had my fair share of stupidity at your age, and at least as many failures. You just haven't seen them. I couldn't be prouder of you if you were my own son, and nothing will ever change that, success or failure. If it bothers you that much, ask for a deferment. Take a year off, let the pressure ease. Give yourself time to sort things out."

"But where do I *go*?" David pleaded, his blue eyes even brighter behind the tears. "How do I walk into that house and face everybody, knowing I was lying to them, that I only seemed to be successful, that I just couldn't hack it on my own?"

"I can't answer that for you, David," Tomas said painfully. "That's something that comes from within, something that has to happen on faith. I don't think anyone feels that way about you. You'd be surprised how forgiving the people who love you can be."

"That's what Sarah told me. I don't know where she gets her strength."

Tomas gave a brief chuckle. "Your sister is the craziest person I've ever met, and I say that with deepest affection. She is also one of the most brilliant people I've ever met, and if she says it's so, I'd be willing to stake my money she's right. Come home with me, give it a try. If you find it unbearable, we'll take it from there. You can always stay in my apartment if you want. Shall I go see if you can be released?"

"Yeah." David snuffled, conscience quiet for the first time in years.

* * *

Sarah slipped into David's bedroom. "How's it going?" she asked, more serious and in command than anyone was used to seeing.

David lay on his bed, staring at nothing. His jaw didn't move when he mumbled, "Okay, I guess,"

"Doesn't look that way. Lying around like a paralyzed amœba is supposed to be my routine. You're supposed to be the one standing on your head trying to make me laugh. Should I try that?"

"No. That would probably piss me off."

"Hiding in your room won't help anything. Been there. Doesn't work."

"Haven't decided that yet."

314

Sarah vaulted over him with a leap and sat down on the bed behind him. She flicked her hair around and leaned back against the wall. "Everyone treating you right?"

"Mostly. Scared the hell out of Sergei, though. Guess he'll stop messing with the quasi-legals for a while, huh?"

"We can always hope. Dimi won't give you problems. He knows better."

David twisted around. "Why? He get caught with illegals, too?"

Sarah hesitated. Secrets were secrets. "Not directly. Let's just say we know where that stuff comes from, and who it goes to, and the less you're involved in it the healthier you'll be. If nothing else, you can congratulate yourself on scaring the daylights out of Nikky and Marina. I doubt they'll ever go near something like that. That's good. They needed some sense shaken into them."

"Some consolation prize. Where's your shadow? I haven't seen the Rodent outside of meals since I got back."

Sarah sighed. "That makes two of us. If he won't talk to me, it must really be serious. I promise, when I see him, I'll demand to know. If you'd like, I'll hold him and you can tickle it out of him."

"I don't feel like it."

Sarah pummeled his backside with her feet. "Get up! David Kirushenko isn't an amœba! If you don't stop feeling sorry for yourself, I'm going to get Sergei and order a full-fledged, all-out Fearsome Four war against you!"

David flung an arm at her irritably. "Knock it off! You do, and I'll break your legs."

"Now *that* is more like it."

Vlad sulked at Sarah's gentle inquiries. He stuffed a data card into his computer. "Yeah, so what? I've never kissed David's fat *sraka* yet, and I'm not about to start. I got better things to do than play baby games."

"Since when?" Sarah said indignantly. "More important than your brother's feelings?"

Vlad flipped through the programs on his screen. "*What* feelings? He's jerking you around, just like he does everybody else."

Sarah let him pretend to ignore her for a full minute, then threw those oh-so-familiar therapy words at him. "You're withholding something, Vlad. Out with it."

"Go cry to John."

That did it! David could get rude to her like that, but not Vlad. Vlad was, and would remain, above such things – at least while she still

315

had a say in it. Sarah grabbed the back of his chair and spun it around. "Vladimir Vasily Kirushenko! Don't you throw Attitude at me! I am taller, heavier, and stronger than you. Either you come clean to me or I shall pound you into a ball no one will be able to untangle before the Martian New Year. What happened to no secrets?"

Vlad rose to stand warily by the closet. "Grow *up*, Sarah! You're how old? Get real."

Sarah's face grew harsh. She made a show of rolling her sleeves higher. "So. We do it the hard way."

Vlad took a step back. "What do you care? You weren't here! Who do you think put me straight after you left? If it wasn't for him, I'd still be sitting all pissy in a corner crying. He straightened out! He got his act together! He stopped beating the crap out of me and I looked up to him for a change! I thought he was so astronomical, and all this time he was just some drug-infested nobody who was so hooked on chems he practically killed himself. What do I say to someone like that?"

Sarah rolled her eyes. "Oh. My. Goodness. Somebody help me! I pinned all my hopes on the wrong star! This one's broken! I swear, this whole house is drowning in self-pity! David is, and now you! Nobody's perfect, Vlad! I think I'm the *most* perfect example of that, and you never quit on me, did you? Just because David did something wrong and got caught, you throw him away? Heroes are human, too, Vlad! How could David still be David if he didn't do or say something shocking? Don't you think Dmitri's done things that have knocked my brainwaves flat? It took me a *year* to recover from the fact he was sleeping with girls. I don't think I've ever gotten over the fact that he – and don't you dare tell a soul I told you this he once lost our entire savings gambling I was scared to death when I first found out he smuggled that EPSAR. I guess I knew better then.

"Actions don't define heroes, Vlad. It's what you feel in your *heart* that makes a person a hero, and one bad action shouldn't change that. I shall worship Dmitri to the day I die. I cannot imagine a more valiant, heroic person, despite his flaws. Are you that disappointed with David's mistake that it changes how you feel in your heart, or only in your head?"

"I don't know! I'm just – really mad at him right now. I thought all that stuff was behind him. It's like it was all a big lie or something."

She took his hand. "If you read more literature, you'd know that all heroes have faults, Vlad. That's what makes them heroes; the fact that they can get beyond those faults. Don't give up on him, and in time you'll see I'm right. Nobody expects bad luck to happen." Sarah paused. "Except maybe me."

She gave Vlad's arm a hard yank. "Now, if you don't go in there right now and talk to him, I'll walk in there and toss a glass of water in his face and say it was from you, and then we'll see what he thinks about you!"

* * *

Tomas walked down the aisle in the hangar between the Cruiser and Mamá's long Palatia. The vehicle hangar housed six full-sized flyers – David's flaming red four-person Siberia SkyDevil, Galina's dark blue Solarwind Special, Valeria's white Airwing, Tomas' pearl-gray Copernicus Luxury Cruiser, his racy two-person Baltic Breeze ground speedster, and Mamá's eight-passenger chauffeur-flown Palatia Parliament. In the back was plenty of space for David to park his Aeronavt ground bike, his Overland anti-grav bike, his snow crawler, Nikky and Marina's slow-moving child's groundtracker, and the zippy garden cart that Mamá used to check on the farther reaches of the property. And there was still generous space for the mechanic to move things around as necessary. The hangar, like everything else in the estate, gleamed show-room clean.

"Sergei said I'd probably find you here."

David wiped dust from the electric blue of his Aeronavt. He'd waited two weeks for the repairs after Sarah flipped it, but it looked and rode as good as new. "I went out for a while."

"Feel better?"

"No. When I ride, I think, and I'm tired of thinking. I want to go back to work." David folded the dustcloth and put it back in the proper cabinet so Georgi, the mechanic, wouldn't get upset. He left the hangar, Tomas following.

"Is that wise? Have you come to a decision yet? There's only a week or two before you'd have to leave for school."

David sighed. He scooped a pebble from the edge of the walkway and threw it as far as he could across the back lawn, then walked slowly after it. "I don't know. I just – I have to stop thinking and *do* something! Anything. I can't handle the boredom."

Tomas followed. "That makes sense."

"I've been talking with that guy John recommended."

"Is it helping any?"

"He makes me *think*," David wailed. "I come out of there with headaches from thinking, and all it does is leave me with more questions."

"What do you think about?"

"I don't know. Everything," David said, unable to explain. "Like what

317

I want out of life. How the hell am I supposed to know? I'm twenty-two years old today, and I don't have a clue what I want to do with the rest of my life. I mean, I thought I'd go right into business. That's what I'd killed myself studying for, dammit! But Sarah's right. The people I hung out with were such a bunch of overstuffed – *assholes.*"

"Business and industry are full of those," Tomas chuckled. "I only hope I don't come across that way to others."

" 'Course not. You're not like that at all." They came upon a bench under a flowering tree, and David sat down. The August sun was warm, but already the days were noticeably shorter.

"So, what would you do then?" Tomas asked, sitting. "If you could do anything in the world, no matter how off your head, what would you do?"

David snorted. "Probably … pack up the grounder and ride the entire Trans-Siberian roadway. See the country right at eyelevel. No pressures, no hassles, no ass-kissing, no anything. Just me and the bike and the sky for 13,000 kilometers."

"So why not do it? Take six months or so and go explore."

David shot him a crazy look. "With winter coming on? I'm not that fond of freezing to death."

"In the spring, then."

"I don't know. Maybe. I suppose there aren't as many chems out there in Siberia."

"Maybe not in the rural areas, but you'd be surprised what you'll find, even in remote cities."

David grew quiet again. "I talked with Dr. Lipnitsky this week. He went over a lot of things with me, like susceptibility and genetics. We talked a lot about – you know, Father's problems – and he said any doctor with half a brain should have seen my problems coming from out in space. He said I was high-risk for chemical abuse like that, and I shouldn't even be drinking."

"Prudence is more fortuitous than regret."

"I think back to everything I've done over the years, with and without chems," David said wistfully. "Twelve, eleven, even ten years old, back on Navara, dropping chems in the most putrid stuff you can imagine and daring each other to drink it. Smoking enhancers, getting juiced on caffeine and boosters, or all drifting out on inhalants to escape the heat. My friends and I would pick our targets at lunch, then hang around after school and beat the snot out of some poor kid because we thought he was too smart or too skinny or too emotional, and laugh like hell when he cried – we were three or four to one against kids as young as *eight*! I think Ridahl Shoonoer even pissed on a kid once. Gods, we were awful." David

318

shook his head, remembering. "Dimi covered for me a couple times, but I never got caught. Father would have broken every bone in my body."

"If you were my son, I might have done the same," Tomas said without humor.

"I fell back into some of that at school," David admitted with proper shame. "Not so much at Northern, but at University. You get strung out on alerts, and it's like everything is out of proportion. Noises hit you a hundred decibels louder than they really are. Humorous is hysterical, sarcasm is a vicious put-down, a bump in a crowd is like a blast from a missile. It makes you edgy. I never really beat anybody up, but I threatened a lot. I know I got nasty to a lot of people without reason, and I roughed a couple up."

"It's never too late to apologize."

David stared into the grass. After a moment he nodded. "I know that. There's a few people I want to apologize to, Sergei included. But what it makes me think about most is, how much I hated my father for being exactly *like* that – jumping all over us for the tiniest little infraction, spacing out on vodka or trying to recover his senses from a binge. And I can't stop wondering: Did he feel the same way I did? Is that why he did it, because he felt like he'd physically explode if he didn't? He had a wife and kids depending on him. Did he drink to kill the fear of failure, too?"

Tomas pondered the thought. "Those are interesting questions, David, but I'm not the one to ask." He patted his nephew on the leg and stood up. "As I said, it's never too late to apologize."

* * *

Dear Father,

I have hated you for most of my life. I never understood what you saw in a bottle that made it more important than your own family. I never got the connection between your need to drink and your excessive and unwarranted use of violence against us. I used to believe we were bad, and that you drank so you could find the strength to punish us like we needed. Later on I realized you were just a truly evil bastard who hated every one of us, and it didn't matter what we did, wrong or right, because you were going to beat the piss out of us either way. Every night I prayed you'd die, that you'd crash our flyer and go up in a big fireball. I knew it would upset Mother, but I figured she'd get over it eventually. After she died, I didn't even have to feel guilty anymore. I was absolutely elated when your sentence was announced, and pissed as all hell when you were released.

Today, facing the realities of my recent illness, I was hit by a clarity of

319

insight. Maybe it was insight, maybe the adult genes suddenly kicked on, and in that exact instant I started to think like an adult and not some self-righteous asshole. In that exact second, I understood. It only took a second to realize you were never evil at all. To see that pursuing an education, or pursuing a career, raising thirteen children, or losing a spouse puts a person under a certain amount of stress. Life never goes the way you expect. If one shot of whiskey got you through today, imagine what two will do tomorrow. I know now that being an alcoholic was not your intention, and never was. You never meant for things to get out of control. You never planned on being controlled yourself when you started to seek the bottle's help. It sneaks up so slowly, so silently, that by the time you realize you're trapped, it's too late.

What I'm saying is, I Am Sorry. I am sorry for every bad thought I ever had about you. You are nothing but a man who gave his best and leaned on the wrong friend for support when he feared his best wouldn't be good enough. All fathers are men, and men make mistakes. I am merely a man, and not only didn't I learn from your mistake, I repeated it as well. That makes me twice as stupid. I am sorry for the things I said, the things I did, and the way I behaved.

I guess what I mean to say is, I forgive you for merely being human. I don't remember you a whole lot from the better times, but I am grateful that you were released from prison early, that I survived the incident that pulled my head from my ass, and I can have this chance to reacquaint myself with my truly remarkable father. I love you, I respect you, and I am proud to call you Father.

> *Sincerely,*
> *your son,*

DAVID F. ALEXANDROVITCH KIRUSHENKO

Twenty-nine

S arah hated court visits. Life was good; what right did the court have to remind her it wasn't? This wasn't even her normal progress check; it was worse. After three months, a decision had been reached on Tomas's petition to add Dmitri to the guardianship. All the drugs at the clinic wouldn't have stemmed the nervous acid burning in her chest. Having Dmitri and Tomas there didn't help. Tomas never sweated, but Sarah could read Dmitri easier than a book.

The judge walked in, five minutes late. He looked over the information on his comp screen and cleared his throat. "After careful consideration, this court has ruled to deny the application to add Mr. Kirushenko to Miss Kirushenko's guardianship status."

"What?!" Dmitri exclaimed.

"I don't understand," Tomas said. "Dmitri has cared for her for almost eight years. No one knows Sarah better. He is the person she is most comfortable with. He is her *rightful* guardian, legal or not."

"Numerous issues came up in review, such as the fact that Mr. Kirushenko is a convicted felon and is considered at high-risk for flight with Miss Kirushenko," the judge clarified. "He has minimal education, is not gainfully employed, and at the moment is dependent on relatives. He cannot be responsible for someone else when he hasn't shown an ability to be responsible for himself."

"There were also several reports on file questioning the appropriateness of Mr. Kirushenko's relationship with his sister," the court monitor added quietly. "There were several incidents that pointed to a dangerous level of neglect during his custody."

Dmitri squirmed in his chair as if he meant to polish the seat. "Not that shit again! That's been *proven* false! There were testimonies filed on my behalf … !"

"I have seen no evidence of that whatsoever," Tomas said with more passion than he usually showed in public. His face took on an angry cast, and his hands gestured with defiance. "She's sixteen years old; we're not talking about a small child. What is the procedure for filing an appeal? I will pursue this through a full trial if necessary. What possible difference can his employment or residential status make in a *joint* custody? We all live at the same address!"

"For the time being, the current arrangement stands," the judge said. "Should Mr. Kirushenko be able to prove a change in his educational or employment status, we will gladly review everything again at that time. A change is possible, but we would like to hear Miss Kirushenko's input as to whom she would prefer as her guardian."

All eyes looked toward Sarah, who slumped in her seat, staring somewhere beyond the wall. "Do you have a knife?" she asked.

The judge frowned. "A knife? No. Why?"

"If you did, I would cut my heart out and leave it there on your desk, as that seems to be what you're after. Right hand, left hand – how am I supposed to choose which one to cut off? Just take my heart and spare me the agony.

"Your solution is unacceptable to me," she announced, and walked out of the room.

"Sarah!" Dmitri jumped to his feet, knowing too well her habit of running blind.

"Go," Tomas ordered. "Take care of her. I'll settle this here."

Dmitri spotted her outside the court building. She wasn't running, but she strode determinedly fast, and he ran to catch up. "What are you doing? You can't run away from court! You'll blow any chance you might have of ever being out of the system. You can't run away from Tomas. He's your last hope."

Sarah kept up her pace. "Don't mess with me, Dimi! I'm not running away, I'm running *home*, while I still have one. I have two choices: walk out my overwhelming rage in a socially acceptable manner, or go berserk and choke the life out of the judge and the monitor. I was trying to handle this responsibly."

"It's thirty-seven kilometers back to the house."

"So? We walked that easy on Tau Ceti."

"This isn't Tau Ceti! Will you slow down, at least?" He grabbed her as she waited for a pedestrian cross signal and dragged her toward a sign for a public comm line. "Stop, just one minute! Let me call Tomas and let him know what you're doing, and I'll walk with you, okay?"

Sarah clenched her jaw impatiently. "One minute."

* * *

Dmitri didn't knock. He walked into her room bearing a dish of chocolate pudding and a glass of grape juice. He'd spent the night in Sarah's spare bed, not trusting her or anyone else. He'd seen Tomas nod off in exhaustion. Dmitri slept lightly around Sarah. She lay on her bed in yesterday's clothes, immobilized by anger.

"Lunch time," he announced, and put the dishes on the center table.

"No, thank you."

"It's kind of useless to have a hungerstrike in private. If you want to make a point, you should sit in front of the court with a scrollboard or something."

"I'm not making a point. I just want to think, and I want to be left alone to do it."

"I take it you're not going to group this afternoon. Should I call John for you?"

"I hate group. They're either criminals or really crazy, except for Mia, and that's because she won't speak there, either. We'd have a blast if it was just the two of us. She could sit on one side and ignore John, and I could sit on the other. We'd be a good team."

"One of you is more than anyone should have to handle," Dmitri said dryly. "I'll call and tell him you aren't up to coming in today, but you have to eat the pudding first."

"Maybe," was the empty reply.

David and Vlad tried to cheer her up before dinner. "Look who's the amœba now! If I can't sit like that, neither can you." David shook her arm with affection.

Sarah turned a loathsome eye. "To put it in your own language, David, if you'll pardon my grammar – and I do mean this most lovingly – 'Fuck you.'"

"Whoa! You *are* pissed!"

"What do you want me to say?" Sarah let the Attitude drop. She sat up on the bed; Vlad slid next to her. "If I move, I might lose control, and they'll sigh, take out their checklist, and put a mark next to attachment disorder and noncompliant and can't accept limits, and add a year to my sentence. I'm having such a tantrum inside it's frightening! I'd do myself some serious damage, but the damned drugs dull the impulse so I have time to remember I'm not supposed to do that. I still want to, though."

Vlad rubbed her back in sympathy. "Then just tell them to keep things as they are. It's only a year. 'Mitri's here, Uncle Tomas isn't bad, and you get to stay here just as it's been."

"It's not that simple, Vlad!" Sarah forced the tears back in. She couldn't allow them loose. If she did, her fight to stay calm would be over rather quickly, and her file would take up more space in John's database.

"I love Uncle Tomas, don't misquote me, but I'm in such a bind, no matter how hard I think, I can't come up with a solution that won't hurt *somebody*. I owe Dmitri *everything*! I'm supposed to turn around and say,

'Sorry, Dim, Uncle Tomas can make all my dreams come true. You don't want to hold me back now, do you?' If I accept anything less than Dmitri's guardianship, it's like turning my back on him. I've hurt him too many times, too deeply, to do that.

"On the other hand, Uncle Tomas has been like a Saint to me. His patience has been endless, his kindness extreme, his efforts to help me well beyond anything deemed necessary by laws of kinship or decency. I cannot ignore that. If it wasn't for him, I'd be sitting in an asylum for the criminally insane, permanently beyond repair. Joint custody would solve the problem, but no one outside this house can see that. Whoever said 'Justice is blind' was being sarcastic."

"I'd volunteer, but I think I put myself out of the running last month," David said. "If they think smuggling makes Dimi unfit, I can imagine what they'd say about someone spaced on chems. Sergei's still in school; they probably won't accept that, either."

"I'll be eighteen in five months," Vlad offered with a grin. "Think you could take orders from me?"

Sarah eyed him with a distinct lack of confidence. "Honestly, Vlad? I don't think you could give them. I'll be seventeen in only two, but I'm not allowed to file for Liberated Adult status."

Vlad grasped at straws. "Gal's away for two more weeks, but Valeria would do it. She's a lawyer who already has custody of our brother and sister. I'm sure they wouldn't say no to her."

Sarah's face went cold in less than a second. "I know you meant that with good will, Vlad, but do think before you speak. After seven years of hell, I would beg Valeria to take me back? I might as well kill Dmitri in his sleep. At that rate, I could beg Father to take me in."

"Sorry. I forgot."

"We'll come up with something," David insisted, but he didn't look very positive.

* * *

Valeria knocked bravely on the doorframe. "Dmitri? Can I talk to you for a minute? It's about Sarah."

"Thirty seconds," he allowed.

"I've been … " She stopped inside the doorway. A travel case lay open on his bed, and he was stuffing it with clothes. "What are you doing?"

"What's it look like?"

Valeria shut the door. "Where are you going? Does Tomas know?"

324

"Nope. Don't know myself."

Valeria's insides grew cold. "You're not leaving? Dimi, do you know what happens if you break your parole?"

"Unfortunately." He poked through a case of toiletries, closed it, and stuffed it in the bag. "If I get caught, I'm in really deep shit, but I don't see where I have a choice. This illustrious court system of yours has put Sarah in such a pinch, she's jammed her brain trying to think her way out. Since she can't find a way out, she's made up her mind to run away for a year, until she turns eighteen and they can't force her to choose. We both know that what Sarah's determined to do, she's going to do, law or no law. Being the irresponsible and untrustworthy person that I legally am, I see no other choice than to follow her and make sure she's okay. She'll be living under a rock in Old Gorky Park if I don't."

Val paled. "She ran?"

"Not yet," Dmitri admitted, "but I know where she's hiding. She packed up hours ago."

"You can't do this!"

Dmitri eyed Val with distrust. He snapped his case shut and stood it on the floor. "You pulling a law or something on me?"

"Never. Please hear me out, though. Think of Tomas, Dimi! Before you go off, think of what your actions will do to Tomas! He's still Sarah's guardian – if she takes off, *he* gets in trouble! He swore to oversee your parole as well – you break that, and they come after *him*! How can you do that to him?"

"You think it's something I *want* to do? I can't stop her, but she can't be left alone, either." They wouldn't look for him just on Earth, but throughout the Alliance. Anywhere he needed a bioprint ID, he'd be seized and forced to serve a mandatory five-year sentence. "Tomas will find a way out. He's got more contacts than the UPA has citizens."

Val got in his face, but didn't dare reach out to grab him. "No! You don't understand! As a lawyer I can't tell you this, but as a sister, I will. You can't mess with the Allied Fleet. No one can, not even Tomas. It takes incredible force to get planetary governments to move against the Alliance. Do you have any idea what it cost Tomas to bring you and Sarah home? Between paying off favors, transferring corporate shares, and outright bribery? *Thirty billion credits*, Dimi. He ransomed the two of you for *thirty billion credits*. I know; I've seen the numbers. He sold off twenty-five percent of his holdings in his own companies. He was prepared to go as high as fifty billion, which I would have prevented. Yes, he'll recoup it all eventually, but it still hurt him. If you take off on him or allow Sarah to, you spit in his face. You're telling him his sacrifice was for nothing. He gave everything for you because he knew how much it meant to us to bring you home. That's how much he cares, not just for us, but you and Sarah, too. You can't stab him in the back like that. I'm working every minute I can to find a legal precedent to put you back in charge of Sarah. *I* owe that to everyone. Please! She's got to hang on a little bit longer."

No wonder why Tomas refused to discuss paying him back. Dmitri hung his head. "I didn't know that."

He tossed his case into a corner. "I'll do what I can to slow her. Tell Tomas to alarm everything tonight. If she gets away alone, we're all going to lose."

* * *

John Carver buzzed Sarah into the office. "Group's not til two. Is this a social visit, or something you didn't want to discuss with Dr. Petrova?"

Sarah dropped into a seat. "I hate group," she said sullenly. "It's like being shoved inside a hive of bees. I suppose I should be glad Lara is convinced she's covered with eyes and not mouths, or there'd be another eighty-three voices to add to it. Mia and I are the only sane ones there."

"Because you ignore everyone else?"

"Great minds think alike."

"So what's behind the sudden visit?"

Sarah slouched deeper in the chair. "I'm dying inside, and I can't take it anymore."

"The guardianship?"

Sarah nodded. "I've been thinking about nothing else, twenty-four hours a day, and I think I might have come up with a possible solution. It could work, but it's not my first choice. Not that I have objections to it," she corrected, "it's just not the best choice. Mm – that's not exactly what I mean, either. I trust your opinion, though."

"It's not the best because it exempts Dmitri."

"Ya."

John leaned back in his chair. "Well, run it past me."

Sarah sighed. She stood up and fell into her old anxious pacing. "It's only one possibility. I – I don't know if it would be feasible, or even desirable. It will still break my heart, but not as badly as some other choice might, especially if forced on me by the court. It would free Dmitri up, but I would still be in his life. It would free Tomas up, but without hurting his feelings too much, I hope. It would remove me from Vlad, but just a breath away. And it would only be for a year, anyway.

"I mean – that takes care of everyone's problems, right? Everyone

326

wants me a little more independent from Dmitri and Vlad. I mean – I'll be seventeen soon, I'll be enrolled in school, so I won't be home a lot anyway, right? I'll still be in therapy, so I won't have a lot of free time to get into trouble. I'm supposed to be trying to become independent under the guidance of someone the court feels is responsible enough to show me right from wrong. It could only be someone I'm used to, someone I trust, and someone who is used to my needs and issues."

"Mmhm."

"Now, I haven't proposed this yet to the persons involved. I realize ahead of time the answer may be 'no,' and I'm prepared to accept that answer without a problem," she promised. "I know it's not an easy decision, I know I'm not an easy person, I know there is much to take into consideration, and I wouldn't expect an answer immediately. It would only be for a year," she re-emphasized, as if trying to convince herself. "In theory, I will become my own guardian at eighteen, at which time I will ask Tomas if I may stay at the estate, like everyone else. I have two more weeks to make my choice, so there's still time to discuss details."

"What will you do if the answer's no?"

Sarah blew her breath up through her bangs. "I don't know. Run to the Chinese-Siberian border and hide among the Mongols. Flee back to Tau Ceti and hide in the forest."

"Somehow I can't see a tall, blonde, blue-eyed girl hiding too successfully among the Mongols. Who did you have in mind?"

"It's – it's two people, actually," Sarah stalled. "People who are very important to me. I mean, the court didn't say it was against the *practice* of joint custody, just my first choices. I wouldn't need much space to myself – I'd be willing to live under the stairs. Honestly! I would accept that. I've survived worse. Someone whom I'm very close to, who is like a mother to me and always has been, and someone I've trusted with more secrets than any other person, family included. If I absolutely, positively, have to name someone to be my guardian, I choose you, John." She looked him in the eye, lost, helpless, scared, and out of options. "You and Katya."

John grabbed for his desk as he lost his balance and the chair tried to flip him backwards. "*Me?!* Sar, I know … "

"No! Don't speak! Please, don't speak now. Think on it. Discuss it with Katerina. It was a big risk even to ask, and I'm sorry for surprising you with it. I wouldn't ask if I wasn't desperate. I meant what I said, though. It's *okay* to say no. I have a backup plan in place. I don't want you to do something you feel would be a struggle. You both have your hands full with careers and with Roman, and you owe me absolutely nothing. I am very aware of this, and the complications it could create. Talk it over," she said again. "You know where to find me when you decide either way." She patted his hand and hurried from the office before he could say a word.

She hadn't expected a reply so quickly, but Katya invited Sarah over that night to discuss it. Tomas accompanied her.

Katya brushed Sarah's hair out of her eyes. "I know you're very upset with the court system right now, Sarah," she said gently, "and I wish with all my heart that I could make Dmitri your legal guardian, once and for all. John and I talked about your proposal, and we discussed some details with Tomas. Please understand that such a thing would not be easy on anyone's part. If you lived here, there would be many rules and expectations, and you would be required to follow them. It means John could never again be your doctor, even in a group setting."

"I know," Sarah said glumly. "I knew that when I thought of it. That's one reason why I said 'No' was acceptable. I knew it was a lot to ask, but I was running out of relatives." A hint of amusement crossed her lifeless face. "I never thought I'd live to say *that*."

"Please forgive us, Sarah," Katya said. "I apologize from the bottom of my heart …"

Sarah accepted the answer with a frightening calm. "I know. It's really okay."

" … for not having thought of that on our own. We'd be honored to be your guardians."

It took several seconds for Sarah to connect the words to a meaning. She stared at Katya with disbelief.

John sat down by his wife. "We'd be thrilled to have you stay here. It'll take some adjustments, but, hey – who's more qualified to keep an eye on you than a teacher and a psychiatrist?"

"Actually, we're going to divide you up," Tomas added, in on the deal. "Your room will stay just as it is. If all goes well and you toe the line, you'll spend the weeks here with the Carvers and stay at the estate for the weekends, just like everyone else. You can spend time with Dmitri and the boys, and John and Katerina will have time alone. Just because they're your guardians doesn't mean you can't visit with your family, and they can't visit you. And if you really feel the need, you can always stop by during the week – with the Carver's permission, of course."

Sarah was afraid to breathe, lest it disturb the hallucination she seemed to be having. "For real? You'll really do it?"

Katya laughed. "We'll start the paperwork tomorrow."

Sarah threw her arms around her sister's neck, bruising Kat in the process. "Thank you! Thank you so much!" She hugged John at the same time. She would have hugged Tomas, too, but she was out of arms. "I promise, I'll do anything you say! I'll work so hard you won't recognize me! I won't let you regret it!" She shed the crushing pressure of the last five days in joyous tears.

* * *

Tomas didn't expect to see Katya's face on the viewscreen so early on a weekday afternoon. Two days was a little quick for a ruling on guardianship; courts rarely worked that fast.

"John wanted me to warn you," she told Tomas sadly. "He found out about it too late to tell you when you dropped her off. Sarah's friend Mia committed suicide last night."

Tomas' shoulders sank. "Dear God! She was such a sweet little girl."

"She was only thirteen," Katya said with grief. "John's going over it with everyone today. He says to give Sarah space if she wants, but keep an extra eye on her. Let him know if you think she's getting into trouble herself."

"I will. Her first friend here. I feel terrible."

"No one feels it more than John."

"Of course." Psychiatry was a physically safer practice than something like surgery, but sometimes, if the signs were misinterpreted, the patients still died, and in child psychiatry the pain was no doubt even worse. "He'll be in our thoughts as well."

Tomas sent his expert to evaluate the situation. Dmitri leaned against the doorway to the activity room, dangling a vehicle ignition tag from its holder.

"Look what I got," he said. "It's the tag for Tomas's Baltic Breeze. And with his permission, nonetheless. Where shall we go?"

"I don't want to go anywhere," Sarah mumbled, and followed him to the speeder. She flopped down in the passenger seat and rested her feet on the control panel, head on her knees.

Dmitri started the engines and felt the anti-grav adjusters rise. "I finally have a valid ground pilot's license and a free vehicle. We can't waste it. Let's get something to eat."

"Tough day at the office?" he said after ten full minutes of silence. "Open."

Sarah made a face at the spoon of ice cream he held before her mouth, but she did accept a small taste before Dmitri went back to stuffing himself on the mound of blueberry-vanilla with birch ripple. She sat on the bench in the *botanichesky* gardens like a statue.

"I don't get it. I did everything I was supposed to. I found someone with a somewhat similar background and outlook and attitude whom I could be friends with. And like Mother, and 'Byeta, and Viktor, the minute I got near her, she died. How can I not go back to believing I'm poison?"

"You haven't killed me or Vlad yet. Uncle Tomas looks pretty healthy to me."

"It's not funny, Dim."

Dmitri swallowed a lump of ice cream, then made Sarah take another taste. It was a test. If she would eat something, anything, she was still okay inside.

He waved the spoon as a pointer. "Look at it from a different perspective. Look at the group you had to pick friends from. You yourself said they were all freaks, and if *you* thought they were spacey, they must have really been out there. If you made friends with someone on a terminal illness ward and they died, would you blame yourself?"

"The word 'terminal' would imply they were already dying when I met them. I would still be upset at their passing, though."

"And that's not to say you shouldn't." He took another bite. "But when you make friends with a group of people who are walking on a razor's edge to start with, statistically speaking, one of you is eventually going to fall off. She just happened to be the one that fell. Can I be really nasty?"

"Yeah."

"Now you know how everyone else would have felt if you'd done the same thing. Doesn't feel great, does it." A trickle of ice cream melted over the rim of the container; Dmitri ran his tongue up the side after it. "Every time you pull one of your stupid tricks with glass or EPSARs or other dangerous things, that's how everybody feels about you."

"I never meant to hurt anyone. I was hurting too much inside to worry about that."

"I know. But do you really think your friend was thinking about hurting you when she hung herself?"

For once Sarah saw the greater picture despite her despair. "No. Probably not. Her pain was even deeper than mine. I never set out to kill myself; she'd really tried twice. She only wanted to keep her baby." Sarah dropped her voice to a whisper. The information had been shared in confidence, but what difference could it make now?

"She only held it once. Her mother wanted her to come back and live

330

with her. She didn't want to – you know – with her stepfather still there and all, but the court said she had to. No one would listen to her. No one believed her. I was the only person she actually spoke to, outside of her therapist, and her real father. They were all amazed she came over to visit. Her life was so much worse than mine," Sarah realized. "She didn't have any brothers or sisters to run to."

"That is one of the advantages of a big family," Dmitri had to admit. "Be sad. Regret the loss. But keep in mind she didn't do it to *you*, she did it to *herself*. Maybe that's how she finally found peace."

Sarah reflected on the idea while Dmitri finished his ice cream.

"Thank you," she said after a while, hugging him. "Thank you for always being there."

Thirty

"Ow! Watch my head!" Sarah cried as Dmitri gouged her with the last of the sparkly hairclips. She pulled away and flipped her hair back.

"How do I look?"

"Really good." He stepped back to admire.

She tugged at the hem of her hip-length tunic. The purple, green, blue, and gold pattern was the latest in fashion trends, according to Anatoliy. Her transparent dusty-green tights matched her short shorts, and clung to her legs all the way to her purple sandals. "I'm not too curvy or anything? I don't want to look curvy."

"You're fine."

"My hair's okay?"

"I think I know how to fix your hair by now. You're not too nervous, are you?"

Sarah allowed herself to look as ill as she felt. "I hope I don't throw up in front of anyone. I'd rather stay home with you."

"It's only a party. You're not the host, and you're not the honoree. You park yourself in a seat and speak to anyone who speaks to you. I know you can do that much. Three hours, and you'll come home."

"I wish you were coming with me."

Dmitri flashed a rakish smile. "I'd just get myself in trouble. Stay close to Vlad and you'll do fine. If you can't handle it, give a call. I think someone's going to be manning every commlink receiver in the house."

"Your confidence in me is overwhelming," Sarah said, but she took comfort, knowing it.

David followed Vlad into the room.

"How do I look?" Sarah panicked all over again.

"Beautiful as a sunrise," David said. "Remember, when everyone starts making out, pick someone besides Vlad."

Sarah paled further. "We have to do that?"

"Don't listen to him," Vlad said with annoyance. "It's a party, not an orgy in David's twisted imagination. You look great. Come on." He pulled her by the hand.

"Midnight, Vlad." Dmitri reminded him with a look that said he'd better not be late.

"I know!" Vlad yelled in exasperation. His voice faded down the stairs. "Uncle Tomas told me! You told me! Grandmamá told me! I know how to tell time!"

"You have your 'com?" Tomas double-checked as they got to the side door.

Vlad touched his pocket with waning patience. "Right here."

"No drinking."

"I know that, sir," Sarah promised. "I won't."

"And you know to call me the minute Sarah feels she needs to leave?" Tomas asked Vladimir.

"And if I don't, we'll be back by midnight," Vlad recited to the ceiling. He pulled Sarah out the door.

"Don't do anything I would do!" David bellowed from the balcony.

A summer teen party was the last place Sarah wanted to be on a beautiful August night, but Vlad begged so hard she couldn't refuse him. John thought it a great idea. Dmitri wouldn't take no for an answer. David even lent Vlad his SkyDevil for the evening. Being out at night alone with Vlad was exciting on its own; to Sarah, Vlad was still a child like herself, and she couldn't remember a time when they'd ever been let loose together without supervision. She would have been happy to cruise the city all night, but Vlad wanted to go to the party.

Vlad's friend's house was realistically big, no larger than one hall of The Big House. The homes in this section of the city were closer together, and the entire yard couldn't have been more than half a hectare. Flyers crouched in wait across the front and up and down the streetpath; people flowed in a steady stream between the house and back lawn. Tiny party lights hung from trees and poles and wires, making the yard look illuminated by fireflies.

"You okay?" Vlad checked as they left the flyer.

"So far," she replied without hope.

Sarah hated crowds, hated the crush of people talking about senseless things like brands of toiletries and hair styles, hated the noise and smells and heat from too many bodies in too small a space. Clinging to Vlad as he made his way, Sarah felt no different this time. Vlad knew a good many of the people, introducing her to this group and waving to that one. He had started school late; he was seventeen, but most of his friends were sixteen. This was her alleged peer group John always harped on, but after listening to the chatter, Sarah wasn't exactly sure how these people differed from the troubled ones in her therapy group. They seemed to act, talk, and think pretty much the same

Vlad introduced her to a group of girls, then left for a moment to get them both something to drink.

"So, where are you from?" a Centauri girl asked her.

"I'm living here in Minsk," Sarah replied bravely. "I've just returned from several years on Sigma Tau Ceti."

"What did you do?" a girl with screaming purple hair inquired. "Your parents have interests out there?"

"My brother and I were cultural observers with an Alliance research team."

"What'd you do? Report on clothing trends and the theater scene?" giggled a girl with green curlicues painted on her face.

"Indirectly. Vandijoc was a relatively new farming community. They held dances now and then, but there was no permanent theater," Sarah replied.

"What's the pilot parade like out there?" another girl asked, at least fifty thin bracelets rattling up and down each of her slender bare arms. "Any prime real estate worth shopping for, or are they all a bunch of evolvers?"

Evolvers? Sarah blinked her eyes. No matter what language she tried, the sentence meant nothing in the context of Sigma Tau. She hadn't felt this stupid on her first day of Navaran school.

"There were no pilots," she ventured with a shrug. "There was no airflight at all. We lived in a forested area, so the property was quite beautiful. There was much for the taking."

Laughter broke out among the circle. "She means, what were the pickings like?"

Sarah would have bet money they weren't asking about crops.

"What a spacer!" someone snickered

"She means, were the boys there worth looking at, or were they still evolving?" the purple-haired girl explained. "They did have boys there, didn't they?"

Understanding brought only so much relief. "Yes, there were boys there. They were – fully evolved. Their manners weren't always desirable, but they were not excessively offensive in appearance."

The leader smiled with the warmth of a Plutonian winter. "Small comfort."

Vlad rescued her, not a second too soon. He held out a cup of non-alcoholic brew. "Here, this is tame. Come with me; I want you to meet somebody over here."

Sarah was too glad to leave the girls, but she'd barely taken a step before the comments started. She paused to listen.

"Gods! What a colonist!"

"I hope she's just visiting."

"Poor Vladya! He'd make more friends if he brought a dog."

"That's a good family, too. They must keep her in the attic or something."

"What's wrong?" Vlad asked when she stopped.

Sarah gave him her standard forced smile. "Nothing! Nothing I didn't already know."

Agony. She would bear out the agony, make Vlad happy, but she wouldn't do it again. At least Sergei's friends could hold an interesting conversation. There wasn't a sentient word being spoken anywhere at this party. Sarah leaned against a wide oak in the yard, watching Vlad chatter with a group of friends. He looked so happy, like Dimi did at a party. Vlad's delight gave her some consolation. A girl walked over and kissed him before talking to him. He blushed, but gave her a smile.

"*Pri'vyet*, Blue Eyes."

Sarah startled, and her head snapped around. A boy stood too close to her. Streaks of grease marked his shirt where he'd wiped his fat sausage fingers. Her nose twitched at the scent of beer and salted fish. She pushed tight against the tree.

"Tiger get your tongue?" he grinned through rubbery lips. "Wanna share mine?"

Vlad darted over and pulled her away. "Sorry, she's with me."

"Out of the way, dwarf. Get in line." The boy shoved him aside.

"Come on, Sar…."

"Find your own or take sloppy seconds, but get lost," the boy threatened. "Or I'll do it for you."

"Don't you talk to my brother like that!" Sarah said, forever fearless in defense of Vladimir.

Vlad waved it away. "It's okay, Sar. Come with me for a minute."

"What part of leave the territory don't you get, *zalupa*!" The beefy youth hefted Vlad by the back of his shirt and threw him in the grass.

Sarah helped him up. "Bully! I wouldn't talk to you if you were the last person in the solar system!"

"Drop it, Sar," Vlad warned. He tried to herd her away. "He's a little tanked. It's not worth it."

"That's what you say now, Blue Eyes."

Sarah's dander engaged. Attack her and she'd crumble, but attack her brother and she'd die fighting. "For your information, my eyes are not blue, they are violet, which proves you are either color-blind or never made it past a kindergarten education."

"Listen to the tongue on Sweet Violet, here!" The boy laughed to the comrades who had gathered behind him. "It's a lot more limber than it looks. I could use a good tonguelashing, Professoressa." He grabbed her by the wrist.

"Let go of me!"

"Get away from my sister," Vladimir growled, but an elbow to his chest took the wind out of him.

"TAKE YOUR HANDS OFF ME!" Sarah's voice carried, and a number of people turned to see.

"Lighten up! It's a party! Let's dance." The boy slid an arm around her. "We'll dance a little here, then find a place to dance by ourselves."

Vlad charged, but he was outweighed twice over. Sarah, however, never cared about odds.

The boy's free hand slid low to pull her closer. It was all the additional impetus Sarah needed. The boy stopped breathing as his testicles embedded themselves somewhere behind his sinuses. Two hard fists slammed his soft middle before he had time to bend over; another smashed his shoulder when he collapsed into his own impotent vomit. Four sharp kicks pounded him in the side before Vlad strained himself lifting her physically away.

Sarah stopped, breathing heavy. There wasn't a conversation for fifteen meters, just the strangled gurgling of the boy and his friends talking him through the pain. She straightened her tunic, feeling herself shrinking smaller and smaller under the shocked stares of so many people.

Here I go again.

"I warned him to let go of me," she appealed to the onlookers, then bolted through the crowd, leaving Vlad far behind

Where could she run? Vlad had the handicom; she couldn't call Dimi without going inside to ask to use the family's commlink. He had the security tag for the SkyDevil, too; she couldn't just wait it out in the flyer. Sarah didn't know where she was relative to home or the public tram lines; she couldn't walk away. She wandered back to David's flyer and sat on the nose, but the streetpath had too many shadows, too many people. Couples were kissing and groping against the parked vehicles, and small groups passed things she assumed were less than legal. Sarah didn't want any part of the shadow crowds, either, and worked her way back to the party.

She found a quiet exit on the far side of the house, away from the noise and revelers, and sat on the steps before it. She hugged herself and rocked. It was Vlad she felt awful about. These were Vlad's friends; one or two she'd even met before, and now she'd no doubt ruined his social life, too. He'd probably have to leave the party for creating a disturbance. Or …

Sarah's heart fell over with a thump. She'd hit a guest. A hit constituted an assault, and assault was a bad thing when you were under supervision for attempted murder. Her ears pricked up, listening, but she didn't hear anything resembling a City Security vehicle over the noise of the crowd.

Well, look on the bright side. You didn't freak out completely, you didn't get lost, and you're still holding your own. That's progress.

She turned her head sharply at the rustle of feet. A boy meandered in her direction, cup in hand.

He stopped near her feet and took a drink. Judging by the foam, it was most likely beer. "Anybody else sitting here?" he asked.

Sarah eyed him warily, but shook her head.

He sat on the opposite end of the steps, a meter away. He took a gulp of his drink, hacked, spat, and took another swallow.

He was perhaps a meter eight in height, but his weight lagged far behind, and Sarah doubted he weighed as much as she did. His dark hair hung straight to his shoulders, reminding her of Charlie Aletneshfaja's, but Charlie's had been thicker, and looked cleaner. His face bore the unnecessary scourge of the teen rash. She'd decided to leave when he spoke.

He sprawled back to rest his elbows on the step behind him. "I've been to better parties, but this one isn't too bad. You look kind of pissed, sitting here all by yourself. Someone steal your date or something?"

Dmitri's words to speak if spoken to echoed in her head. "No. I came here with my brother, but you are correct that I am unhappy. Every time I speak to someone, I find myself being insulted and degraded by excessively rude and ill-mannered people."

"Yeah, that would piss me off, too." He started to take another sip but held the cup out instead. "Want some?"

"No, thank you."

"More for me, right?" He took a gulp and sighed. "Which school you go to? Those are pretty fancy threads. You must be part of that posh Leonov crowd, too."

"No. I received my diploma early."

"Prick! That's astro! I wish I could get out early. Where'd you go?"

"I was living on Sigma Tau Ceti IV," Sarah explained for what seemed the millionth time in six months, and she braced for the inevitable accompanying sneer. "I was in Independent Study."

"*Sigma* Tau," the boy mused. "Isn't that way out in the Epsilon Quadrant?"

Sarah nearly fell off the step. "You've *heard* of it?!"

"Not really." He gave a long, noisy sniff, and scratched his nose with the back of his hand. "I read something about it in *Chronicles of the Meritorious*. It's one of those art journals they put out about the exploits of the great ships, you know? That's so rad! You were really there?"

Sarah started to smile, a natural movement that appeared without thought or force. "Four years! Alliance Cultural Observer for the Pelonishalak region, with my older brother. I specialized in language research."

"*Man!*" The boy sat up with a squeal. "What I wouldn't give to do something like that! Sail off between the stars, land on a whole new world that doesn't even know there're other people out here, record everything for the very first time – I'd kill to get off this rock!"

Sarah laughed. "I practically had to kill to get back on it!"

Sarah forgot to fear, entranced that someone actually wanted to hear about the places she'd been. The boy was no scholar, not by any means. He didn't turn up his nose when she mentioned farm work. He never once asked her about fashion or theater engagements, or popular touring musicians she'd never heard of, or told her that she talked funny. He reminded her of David long ago, someone who cared little about anything but hanging out and drinking and maybe raising hell, yet still motivated by dreams. With David it had been his love of high-performance speedbikes, able to memorize pages of statistics and models and manufacturers and engine designs, but he couldn't remember history facts. He could calculate torque ratios in his head, but he couldn't pass maths. For this young man it was a fascination with the adventure of space flight. He wasn't prime officer material, but there were support branches that could benefit from such people. He certainly didn't give off the aura of wealth that often accompanied people in Grandmother's circle; he'd never even heard of the Ivanov Corp.

She had talked with him – actually conversing! – for a whole hour, an hour that felt ten minutes long, when he broke the spell. Out of the blue he asked, "Would you mind if I kissed you?"

"Why?" Sarah demanded. Instantly she realized the situation she'd allowed herself to be led into. There wasn't a terrible amount of light given off by the party lanterns. The people and music made a noise that carried for half a kilometer; there was no guarantee anyone would hear her scream. Or care if she did. She was alone. It was the kind of situation

338

she'd always feared, the kind she'd spent untold hours learning to handle in Petrova's therapy sessions. Sarah edged away.

"Because you've got the bluest eyes I've ever seen, and I just wondered what it would be like to kiss a girl with such blue eyes," he said matter-of-factly. "And – I probably shouldn't tell you, but a bunch of us were checking out the scenery a while ago, and we kind of voted you the prettiest girl here. If I could say I got to kiss you, they'd all be jealous as hell."

Sarah's nose pointed in the air. "And I'm supposed to be pleased by that fact? I did not ask to look this way. I object to having my value measured by physical appearance, when it has nothing to do with who I am."

"I know that. You're the only girl here who was worth talking to. So? Can I kiss you?"

Sarah chewed her lip.

"What's the matter? Do I look diseased or something?"

She gave a confused sigh. "I was trying to think of a reason to say no, but if you are speaking of a one-time occurrence, and you are as honorable as the men you read about, I cannot think of a reason to refuse you one kiss."

"Astro!" He slid closer.

Sarah stopped his advance. *If he can't be bothered to listen to what you want, then he's not worth your bother in the first place,* Katya had counseled her. This would certainly be a test of that theory.

"If and only if you promise not to touch any other part of me, and I warn you, if you're thinking of using your tongue, I will sever any imposing portion with my teeth."

"Keep it in the Arctic, Snowflake! I didn't ask for a ride. I saw you lay out Zhenya over there. He's a fat piece of shit, but I'd rather not have that happen to me, you know? I have a big aversion to pain. I guess you must have had to defend yourself a lot on all those wild planets, huh?"

It wasn't the response she'd expected. "Yes, sometimes," Sarah admitted truthfully. "I just want to be sure our expectations of this event are perfectly clear. One simple kiss, that's all, and nothing more."

"You're really funny. I mean that in a nice way. You're not like the other girls."

"No, I'm not," Sarah agreed, and felt her insides freeze as he planted his lips over hers. They were firm and soft and warm, and he kept them politely close. The unfamiliar scent of his hair and clothes and body filled her nose. Her heart pounded in a mix of fear and response. His knees touched hers, but his hands never did. He *was* an honorable person.

"Sarah Kirushenko!" snarled a furious voice.

Sarah broke away to see Vladimir standing at her feet.

"What the hell are you doing with that greaseball!"

"Vlad! That's very rude." To her new friend she explained, "That's my brother."

Vlad's lips curled tight, his fist shook, his face turned dark with rage.

"*Fuck,* Sarah!" he swore, slamming his fist and his foot down at the same time. "I've spent the last hour tearing my hair out looking for you, and all this time you've been sitting here trading lips with this *monkey*? They nearly drown me in the freakin' punchbowl over your tactics back there! In case you didn't notice, that walrus's friends were just as big as he was!"

Sarah stood up. Vlad's clothes clung wetly. He smelled like sugared fruit. She touched his damp hair and flicked out a piece of lemon pulp. "I'm sorry. I didn't know. I had to get out of there before I did something worse."

"How could it get worse? I'm humiliated quite enough, thank you! Let's go."

Sarah glanced back at her acquaintance. "Do we have to? We were having a rather absorbing conversation about exploration ... "

"I saw what the hell he was exploring!" Vlad grabbed her arm. He pointed his finger at the boy. "Keep your lips off my sister! She's got brothers a lot bigger than you who will hunt you down and hurt you if they find out!"

"That *is* a potentially accurate threat," Sarah admitted. "I'm sorry, but I must go. Thank you for a truly interesting conversation. I enjoyed speaking with you."

"The kiss wasn't so bad, either," he reminded her.

Sarah blushed and turned her head. Vlad pulled at her, but she slipped free. "Here." She removed the fancy clips from her hair and handed them to the young dreamer. "Take these."

"What for?" the boy asked as Vladimir dragged her backward by her hair.

"Proof!" she called out with a wave. "So your friends will know you're telling the truth!"

They fought like an old married couple all the way back to the estate, Sarah protesting Vladimir's attitude and Vlad protesting hers. The argument carried over into the house, where the noise brought the family running.

"You're back early," Dmitri said cautiously.

David moved in for a closer look. "He's wet. Not again?"

"Don't start with me!" Vlad snapped.

Tomas held up a hand. "Start at the beginning."

The arguing flared again.

Tomas hushed Sarah. "Vladimir, speak!"

"She beats the daylights out of some kid who pinched her ass, takes off, and when I finally find her, she's knocking teeth with some lowgrade *guttertrash*!" Vlad ratted with a sneer.

"Dear Lord," Grandmother sighed.

"You poor thing!" Valeria said.

Sergei tried to clap her hand. "Way to go!"

Tomas paled. "You beat someone up?"

David sang out, "*You* got your *ass* pinched! Like this?" He circled around to tweak her backside, but Sarah spun and slapped his hand away.

Dmitri frowned. "Wait a minute. Back up. Did you say she was *kissing* someone?"

"Some freakin' greaseball loser who didn't belong there in the first place!" Vlad continued to rage. "The only way she could have sunk lower was if she'd kissed the creep who pinched her!"

Dmitri was stunned. "You kissed somebody? A boy? You, Sarah Kirushenko? On the mouth?"

Sarah nodded.

"It was disgusting!" Vlad wailed dramatically. "I can't believe she did that!"

"Willingly?"

Sarah nodded again.

"And you didn't scream, or run, or beat him up, or cry yourself silly?"

"No. It's not like we made out or anything. He asked permission for a single kiss, and it didn't last more than three seconds before Vlad came screaming at me."

David crowed with delight. "He's jealous!" He and Sergei bumped fists.

Dmitri broke into a wide grin. "You kissed a *boy*?"

"Yes I did." Sarah tilted her nose in the air. She glared at Grandmamá and added, "And I didn't do a single improper thing."

"She even gave him her *hairclips*!" Vlad moaned.

"You kissed a boy!" Dmitri shouted. He grabbed her up in a bearhug and lifted her off the floor, whirling around the grand foyer. "You kissed a boy!"

"Shah! Dmitri!" Grandmother hushed him. "That is not something to be bragged about."

341

He put Sarah down. "*You* kissed a boy?"

Sarah couldn't stifle her grin. She understood. "Yes I did."

David wiggled his eyebrows lecherously. "What was it like?"

Sarah wrinkled her nose. "He tasted like beer. But other than that ... I guess I don't have any objections."

Her comment brought a round of laughter.

"So, what's this magic Rasputin's name?" Tomas asked.

"I don't know," she realized with disappointment. "We never got that far."

Vlad steamed, the older boys hooted, but it was Dmitri who found the information most amusing. He lifted her off her feet again, laughing until tears came, then grabbed her by the head and kissed her hard just above her nose. "That's my girl!"

Tomas sighed and shook his head.

Thirty-one

S ince his nieces and nephews came to live with him, Tomas threw a lawn party for the household the last weekend before classes, one last time for everyone to be together before the pressures of the school year descended. This year would be no different, save for the number of new people attending.

Adrik had attended for the past two years, and this year Milos was legally family. He and Galina returned from their long honeymoon the week before, full of stories from their ten-country world tour. Father accepted the invitation, still so quiet and reserved it was hard to remember the terror his presence once invoked. Alexei declined, but made a promise to appear at the winter holidays. Tomas once again invited the Countess Ilona Irimescu, a stately, refined woman somewhere in her fifties, as well as several of his closer friends and business partners. And this year, Dmitri and Sarah were there.

A canopy covered a section of back lawn to take the brunt of any weather. It was a holiday Tomas let all the staff have off at once; some attended the picnic, some didn't. The last guest had barely arrived when David appeared with a soccer ball.

He juggled the ball from hand to hand. "I'm not supposed to drink anymore, so I have to do something else. Who's up for a rumble? There's enough for full teams."

Marina and Nikky rushed him. "Me! Pick me!"

Adrik kissed Valeria. "Rest yourself. It's my turn."

Valeria sat down reluctantly, and Milos made Galina sit with her.

Tomas turned to Sasha. "Shall we show the children what the sport is really about?"

Sasha allowed himself to smile. "It's been too many years, but I remember the rules."

"Uncle Tomas, you can be one captain," David suggested. "Maybe Father can be the other."

"I have a better idea," Tomas said. "You and Dmitri be captains. It was your idea."

David won the toss to choose first, and promptly picked Tomas. Dmitri seized Father – who better to block a goal? David snapped up Sergei. Dmitri grabbed John. David chose Adrik, and Dmitri finally called Sarah.

"About time! Since when did loyalty go out of fashion?" she griped.

"Do you want to play, or do you want to win?" he replied.

It still didn't seem fair at the end. Dmitri was stuck with Vlad and Nikky, while David drew the handyman Assam and the groundskeeper Trifolo, and Trifolo's twenty-eight-year-old son Nikita. Five of Tomas's more athletic associates rounded out the teams.

"You've got seven – *seven* – people over a meter eighty," Dmitri argued. "We've got Vlad and Nikky!"

"You chose, fair and square," David insisted. "You've got Father; he counts for two. We'll give you Marina as an extra. That's fourteen to thirteen."

"You're so kind. She'll be killed."

The game *was* vicious. David had led his high-school team to two championships; Dmitri hadn't played in years. Father wasn't used to running, but his long legs could steal a ball before his opponent realized it. The men played politely around Sarah until she plowed through Nikita and one of Tomas's coordinators in her determination to make a score. After that, the game was to the death. Marina took one look at the bloodthirsty crowd coming toward her and ran to the sidelines with a scream. Nikky took a ball on the head so hard it stunned him, but was up and running again before John could check him over.

No one wanted to break for half-time, and Andrea called an end at an hour and ten minutes. Sasha limped on his rebuilt joints; Tomas pulled a shoulder hitting the ground. Milos bruised a rib on Sergei's elbow. Assam had dropped out with a strained back. Nikky was bruised from head to toe but bubbling with excitement. Sarah and Vlad collapsed in a heap, covered with dirt and grass but satisfied. Dmitri and David shook hands. Dimi's team had won, five goals to four.

After lunch, Sarah walked the entire perimeter of the estate with Vlad and Nikky.

"It's not fair," she said wistfully. Her hands plucked leaves from a tree and tore at them. "I feel like I came in at the end of a play. It took me seven years to get out of the lobby, and now it's all over."

"I'm not going anywhere," Nikky promised. He jumped for an overhead branch three times before he caught it and swung. "I thought about going to Northern, but I told Uncle Tomas I'd rather wait for ninth form. There won't be anybody left here by then."

"It's my last year," Vlad said helplessly. "It's not like I can stay in school forever. Galina's married, David'll be gone, Sergei's got one year left in Moscow, and who knows where he'll go after that. When you take out sleep and school hours, it's not like we'll be apart that much more.

344

We'll just make our time count better, that's all. It's only twenty kilometers. If I can get my own flyer next year, it's only a five-minute flight."

"Make it a four-seater!" Nikky begged. "A Wasp 422! A black one, with a white racing stripe. *Fsshew!*" He spun fast, flying his hand in a circle.

"I know," Sarah said with an aching heart. She scattered bits of shredded leaf on the ground. "It's just the principle of it. Why does happiness have to be such a fleeting thing? Why can't we just stay happy, once we find it?"

"Because we'd get bored with it," Vlad reasoned. "Same way you don't want ice cream every night after dinner. Sometimes you'd rather have pie."

"I like pie once in a while, too, but it doesn't mean I can't wish for ice cream while I'm eating it."

The day ended, but not the picnic. So much more was at stake this year, so many permanent changes being made. Everything was as right at that exact moment in time as it ever could be, and any sudden movement threatened the perfection.

"We've given this much thought," Galina said, "but I've decided to accept a promotion to Oslo. We scouted the area while we were on our honeymoon, and we think we've found a town on the outskirts we could live in."

"But what about Vlad?" Sarah grabbed his hand.

"I married Galina, not Vlad," Milos said. "He stays here."

"We'll come back at least every other weekend to visit. That's a promise," Galina added.

Valeria had a guilty look. "I'm afraid Adrik and I have a surprise of our own." She held up her left hand for inspection. There was a gold band on her ring finger.

"I hope no one will be mad. We ran into a … growing complication, and rather than get everyone in a bother so soon after Galina's wedding, we got married yesterday at the Civil Office. We hadn't planned on it, but we figured today would be like our wedding reception, with everyone here."

Galina hugged her. "I told you we should have made it a double-ceremony."

"Complication?" David said without thinking. "You're transferring, too?"

Val blushed. "No. I guess I'm my Mother's daughter, after all.

345

There'll be one more of us in about seven more months."

Cheers rang out across the table.

Marina screamed with delight. "I'm gonna be an aunt again! I'm gonna be an aunt again! And this time I'm big enough to help!"

Tomas pretended to be annoyed. "Well, that overshadows my news. I'm in the process of selling off the industrial and import branches of the Ivanov Corporation. I'll keep control over the other half, but I'm going to allow other people to run them for me. As of the first of September, I am officially semi-retired. I've enjoyed having the freedom these last eight months – that's how I've had time to catch up with Ilona." He pulled the blushing Countess closer. "After eleven years of secret meetings, Ilona and I will make our affair public. We plan to be married in December."

"It's about time," Andrea sniffed. "Really, Tomas. You should have been able to realize your heart faster than that at your age."

"My goodness! So many weddings!" Katya wiped her teary eyes. "Who's next?"

"Don't look at me," Sarah said indignantly.

David snickered. "She's waiting for Vlad to hit puberty." He ducked as Sarah threw a fork at him.

"Perhaps it will be you next time, Sasha, no?" Tomas said.

The big man shook his head. His heart still ached for Maryana, and always would. "I'll never marry again. I have accepted a position as guest lecturer this semester at the Science Institute in Kiev. It will keep me sufficiently occupied, at least for now."

"I'll be keeping a close eye on him," Valeria said. "Nikky and Marina will be spending at least a weekend a month with him."

"What about you, David?" Tomas asked. "Did you make your decision yet?"

"Yeah. The more I think about it, the more I really want to pack up and take off, but I'm heading to New York on Tuesday. I'm doing it for myself, because it's what *I* want to do. Maybe it'll take me longer than two years, maybe it won't, but I'll have proved to myself that I can do it, all on my own. If I can pull it off, I'll use the cross-country trip as my reward. Hell, maybe I'll even take Sarah with me," David said. "If Dimi can take her everywhere, why can't I?"

"Only if you ride slower," Sarah warned him. "If I have to die, I don't want it to be lying in the middle of some wilderness somewhere."

"That sounds like a wonderful plan," Tomas said. "That's the most mature decision I've heard you make."

Dmitri hid behind his waterglass. "And it only took him twenty-two years."

David picked an olive off a tray and threw it at him. "More than you can do, dropout."

"Actually, I'm taking a few classes this fall," Dmitri admitted. "I want to go back to school about as much as I want to cut off my foot, but Uncle Tomas is right. I've never had the freedom like I have now, and I shouldn't waste it. I liked what I did on Sigma Tau. With my experience and a degree behind me, I could get a similar position almost anywhere. I don't know what I'll study – anthropology, maybe, or engineering."

"Don't rule out psychology," John advised. "I'd say you're a natural talent."

"Anthropology?" Sarah said with a straight face. "Based on your experience, I thought you already held a degree – in Woman Studies." She screeched with laughter as he pushed her off her chair.

"Behave!" he ordered. "Or I'll take your same classes, so I can sit behind you and annoy you."

"Did the court ever make a decision for you, Sarah?" Galina asked.

Sarah stood up to tell her news. Katya and John knew already. "The final word came through at nine this morning. After careful investigation, they approved my choice. I move in with Kat and John on the thirty-first." She felt Dimi's hand creep into hers and squeeze; she blinked the tears from her eyes.

"It's not what I ever planned on, but nothing ever seems to be. I'm very, very grateful to them for giving me a way out. I'll stay there during the week, because it's closer to the university and the clinic, but I'll be here every weekend, just like Sergei," she reminded herself. "That way I'll still be close to everyone. I'll be taking classes at the Minsk campus – just four this semester – but I'm starting with mid-Junior status, so that's a help, and if I'm ready, next year, when Vlad applies to different programs, I will apply to the same ones, and I'll go where he goes. That way, someone I know will be close by, just in case. I kind of get the best of all worlds, this way."

John grinned. "Sure, you say that now. You don't know the ogre I am when I get woken up in the middle of night."

"He means that in looks, not temperament," Katya said.

"Did you tell them the other thing?" Dmitri prompted Sarah.

"No! I forgot about that. For those of you who don't follow science journals, you might want to watch for the December issue of *Galaxia Botanica*. It's scheduled to contain a feature article called 'Recessive Inheritance Patterns of Color and Type Among *Pisoligandis typofolia, Sigma Tau Ceti*,' by someone named Sarah I. Kirushenko, of the Chessorak Research Base," she announced proudly.

Valeria jumped up to hug her first. "Congratulations! That's wonderful!"

"Congratulations," Father wished quietly, but his beard curled in a soft smile, and the dark eyes sparkled with pride.

Sarah glowed. "I owe it all to Dmitri. He's the one that challenged me to do it in the first place."

"I didn't do anything but kick you in the ass," Dmitri said, swinging her hand. "You did all the work. You earned it."

Sarah grew somber. "While everybody's here, I just – I want to say how much I – appreciate everything everyone's done for me. Since as far back as I can remember, I've had the most extraordinary family anyone could ever hope for, and I know without a doubt that's true. I hope each one of you realizes just how incredible you are to me. Without any one of you here, I would not have enjoyed the success I've had for the past eight months. For the first time in a long, long time, I'm actually looking forward with anticipation. Thank you, everyone, from the bottom of my heart." She placed a hand over her mouth and closed her eyes. Dmitri rubbed her back in support; she turned and buried her face in his neck.

"It was nothing but our pleasure, Sarah," Tomas said, blinking a little himself.

"Hell, everybody needs a hobby," David said. "If it wasn't for you, we'd still be diapering Vlad. Your coming back simply relieved us of that."

Sarah wiped her eyes. "As long as some good came from it."

Midnight loomed when the last of the party broke up.

"How strange," Sarah mused, looking up at the dark night sky.

"What is?" Vlad asked.

"How many years we used to look for our sun from other worlds, looking for home, and now when I look at the night sky I can't see it, because we're actually back where we started. All I can do is look for the places we've been."

"Mm. When we first arrived, I would look for Navara, imagine I could see your ship on its way here. Later, I looked for the star systems you'd been to. When you hit Sigma Tau, I couldn't even see that with a 'scope. I like this best."

Sarah rested her head on his shoulder. "Me, too."

Katya said goodnight and bundled a sleeping Roman off to the flyer. Sarah followed John.

"Excited?" he asked. "Once we sign the papers, you're stuck. I'm not going to be any easier on you than Tomas was. If you've got any second thoughts, now's the time to bring them up."

Sarah shook her head. "I don't have much of a choice. I'll probably cry the rest of the week, but I'll be ready. Everything's changed so fast; I haven't had time to adjust. I open my eyes, I'm back here. I turn around, Father's back. I blink, Galina's gone. I sneezed, and now David's disappearing. I can't get used to Katya having a baby and now Valeria's having one. I just hope things won't change as rapidly at your house. I'd like some time to catch my breath."

John squeezed her hand. "We're pretty calm and steady. Chaos usually hits in waves, so we should have some smooth sailing for a while. We're happy to have you, either way."

"It really *doesn't* go away, does it," Sarah said. "The happiness? When things are so horrible on the outside that they're tearing you apart on the inside, the happiness is really still there if you know where to look. It's the little glow that feeds your faith, the glue that heals the rips in your soul. It swells and shrinks, but it never goes out entirely. Love is the strength you draw from others, and I'm so much stronger now because I've had the love of so many people, all at once. The more you love others, the more they love you, and the more strength you give them, the stronger you become, even if you can't be with them in person. Fear just makes us forget that. Does that make sense?"

"That sounds like it exactly."

"And that happiness – that feeling of peace and love and the security to believe it will survive – that's the best of everything, isn't it? Knowing the happiness is stronger than any bad thing that can happen?"

John considered it. "Yes, I guess it is. If you know you can fall back on that, you can do anything." He braced himself as Sarah lunged and seized his neck in an overzealous embrace.

"Oh, John! I'm so happy to be alive!"

Epilogue

Eleven months later
July, 2272

It hadn't been something Sarah'd ever thought she'd be doing, but when Uncle Tomas asked Vlad what he wanted to do for his last summer before university, he said he wanted to see where Sarah had been living all those years away.

"No, really!" he insisted. "The farm, the cabin, and everything else that was important to you."

Sarah's stomach fluttered. "I don't know, Vlad. I'm still under court surveillance. I'd hate to travel that far to find out I can't go beyond the Compound gates."

"I'll see what I can do," Tomas promised.

It wasn't what Sarah wanted to hear. Sigma Tau was so full of ghosts. It would be her luck to run into Dmitri's ex, Jaycee. And then there were those … private heartaches. In one way, seeing the Al's would be a relief. Their parting had been so abrupt and heartbreaking, it would be nice to show Mrs. Al things had turned out well. For so many years Sarah wished with all her heart that Vlad could have been there, too, and here was the chance to prove he really existed.

On the other hand, going back to Vandijoc would mean seeing the Aletneshfajas. Charlie had been their best friend through thick and thin, celebrating Sarah's scientific victories or lending a helping hand with their cabin, and waiting out the heartaches of Sarah and Dmitri's darkest weeks after the end of Dimi's marriage. He'd borne the pain of loving her in secret, and the heartbreak of seeing her thirteen-year-old self collapse when he found the nerve to tell her. Charlie had never lost hope that one day, if he were nice enough and kind enough and persistent enough, she just might return his affection.

It paid off. By the time she was fifteen, Sarah no longer saw a sweaty, uneducated, barefoot farm boy who wiped the last ounce of gravy from his plate with his fingers, and never failed to reach inside his pants to scratch in public. She could see the man inside the youth: the shirtless, muscled back gleaming with perspiration in the hot sun, a teenaged boy shouldering a man's job by himself and excelling at it. She could see the intelligence in his mind, his opportunities for learning stunted only by culture and economic need. He never failed to return from Vandijoc without bringing her some small token – a piece of candy, a new pencil for her letters, or maybe just an interesting striped rock. Little by little, Charlie's sweat didn't curl her nose. She noticed the strength in his body, from the bulge of his straining biceps to the tightness of his rump, and wondered what it would feel like to have those strong arms protecting her from harm. She noticed the rusty cinnamon of his mischievous eyes, the curve of his lip, and how his hair really did start out clean-looking every morning. In the early Dark Days, when her fragile mind was so preoccupied with the disaster at hand and her emotional guard down, she realized with a startling shock that she really *did* love him, with her heart, and her mind, and her … *body*.

Emotionally devastated by Dmitri's rage over her cruelty to Jaycee, Sarah simply could not take on any more mental strain. An adult relationship, one with sexual overtones and feelings and responsibilities, was out of the question. The old fears were too strong. She did what she had to do to survive: she buried her feelings, deep, deep down, so far down she could keep them there without conscious thought, a book on a shelf to be taken out and explored when she had nothing else to do. She kept it there for two years before admitting it to John.

Dormant, but not dead. After eighteen months of therapy, of learning how to handle adult situations, of learning not to run in fear of her own inborn human drive for sex, Sarah knew the Book of Charlie still sat on the shelf. She'd open the cover whenever his letters arrived, knew the table of contents and the bibliography by heart, but she could not read the pages, ashamed of how she'd treated him. In her heart she still loved Charlie, and probably always would. He treated her exactly as she would wish to be treated by a boy, and she had never done more than break his heart.

How could she go back and face him now? He wrote her five letters over the past year, each still swearing he loved her. He never mentioned a wife, or even a contracted partner. She never acknowledged his professions, but if she visited, he would take it as a sign of coming back to him. He still loved her. Did she still love him, far back in the book where she didn't dare read? The pressure in pretending otherwise could be deadly. But Vlad wanted to go.

How could she say no to either one?

Seven days.

After four months of planning and petitioning, Tomas received permission for Sarah to visit Sigma Tau Ceti. Sixteen travel days to get there, and they had exactly three days, allowing four for travel, to spend with the Aletneshfajas.

It had been the rainy season when she'd been dragged away in chains some nineteen months ago. Now the Pelonishalak region of Sigma Tau Ceti IV slumbered in the heat of the dry season. Sarah stepped out of the meetinghouse and breathed deeply, soaking in the sunshine. Memories rushed back at the sweet scent of the warm countryside, cocooning her in comfort and security. The bad times had been excruciating, even crippling, but there had been just as many good days as bad.

She closed her eyes to savor every second. "Feel it?" she said to Vladimir and Tomas. "There's no more peaceful place in all the galaxy!" Even the ghastly old dresses were delightful this time. Sarah skipped and spun and laughed. "I didn't realize I missed it this much."

The Chessorak Research Compound felt like home, but there had been changes. Jan Dickerson had moved on. Dale Reston had been promoted to second-in-command in his place. Nora Guillaume was overjoyed to see Sarah, her own days at the Compound now limited by an advancing state of pregnancy. No children over the age of two were allowed at the research facility. She and Marc would have to move on or take up residence in the community.

Marc Guillaume greeted her with a long hug. Sarah returned it with feeling. "I don't know how in Hell you managed to pull this off, but we're sure happy to see you. We had a lot of bad feelings about what happened. It's nice to see it all turned out okay in the end."

"You'd have to ask Uncle Tomas," Sarah beamed. "It was his connections that did it. I honestly didn't think they'd let me back."

"It pays to lay out your plans with infinite detail," Tomas said modestly. "And if that fails, you remind Earth's Ambassador to the Alliance he still owes you a favor."

"Whatever it took, we're mighty glad you're here," Guillaume grinned.

The Compound had a new medical team, a research physician and two techs with a four-year contract.

"We have our health certificates with us," Sarah said without fear. Scars gone, indwelling medications removed, the worst terrors had disappeared, but Sarah didn't want any detailed scrutiny of her records. "I'm sure you'll find our inoculations are up to current standards or more."

"Good," Lark Lanyon said. "It's nice to meet someone who's one step ahead of the game. It's that much less work for me."

"Were they ever able to isolate the reason behind the low fertility rates?" Sarah inquired.

Dr. Lanyon was surprised at the depth of her knowledge. "As a matter of fact, we think we did. At least one possible cause." She took Sarah into the laboratory and called up the information on a screen.

"We've isolated a virus that the natives don't pay particular attention to. It's generally a childhood illness that doesn't cause more than mild fever and aches for a week or two. It's so common that no one ever thinks it worth mentioning. We've isolated six different strains, so it is possible to contract it more than once. However, if a child is approaching puberty or already past it, there's a thirty percent chance the virus will wreak havoc with the reproductive system, rendering the person functionally sterile, or at least making pregnancy much more difficult to achieve naturally. As many as five out of nine couples may not be able to reproduce without medical intervention. There's a natural one in four chance of pregnancy failure anyway, so that lowers it to a three out of nine chance of a given couple actually bearing live offspring."

"Orbital!" Sarah glanced through the statistics. "Is there any hope of developing a vaccine?"

"We have something that looks good on computer models, but large-scale trials are out of the question. The people will have to develop that for themselves. We can't interfere."

"What about just one person?" Sarah proposed. "The immunity wouldn't be passed on, couldn't change society. Every experiment needs a real-life trial."

Lanyon gave sharp laugh. "Too gray an area. It's impossible to get informed consent. It won't correct damage that's already been done, and we'd have to be able to track the person to see if they ever do reproduce. Even then, without deliberately infecting them with the virus, which we couldn't do, there's no proof the vaccine works."

"Of course." Sarah knew, but she couldn't stop thinking how happy Mrs. Al would be if Charlie could someday father a child. "But it wouldn't hurt someone either way, would it?"

Sarah wrote Charlie they were coming, giving him an approximate date the minute Tomas received permission. Two days from the planet, she sent another message, to be forwarded immediately, telling him the probable day. She'd go to the cabin first, show it off, then walk to the Al's along the old paths, but she'd underestimated the Al's anticipation.

Farmers in the Pelonishala region were busy this time of year, with grain coming into harvest and fodder to be cut and dried, but Charlie and his mother wasted the day, sitting on the edge of the wide porch of the main hotel in Vandijoc. It wasn't hard to spot Sarah among the stream of travelers; only one girl in Pelonishala could ever have hair like moonshine.

Charlie waited, afraid to believe, until she smiled at him. He forgot the rule of never touching her, grabbing her off her feet and pressing his tearful face to her neck.

"Sarrah!" he cried, not letting go. <You come back to me! You come back! Praise be to Moons!>

<Charshfe!> Sarah forced her tears away with an oversized smile and hugged him back.

Mrs. Al looked a little less rotund, with more of a discernible indent to her middle. She cried and hugged Sarah repeatedly.

<This brother I write to, Vladimir,> Sarah tried, but Mrs. Al hugged Vlad so hard he couldn't breathe, let alone possibly bow. Sarah leaped to block the onslaught of Uncle Tomas.

<This most respectable *banatishi* Tomas,> Sarah introduced. <He care for me and Dimi-tri, rescue us from jails.> The Al's bowed reverently before Tomas, thanking him.

The Al's farm hadn't changed. The two-room cabin was as bright and clean as ever, almost crowded with the addition of three people. Sarah would sleep on the floor in Mrs. Al's room, and Charlie showed Tomas and Vlad to his space in the loft overhead. Charlie would sleep in the storage loft in their shed.

"I won't hear of it," Tomas had Sarah translate. "We can take the shed. I won't chase my host from his bed."

Vlad frowned. "You mean, sleep in a *barn*? There's beds there?"

Sarah translated, "Charlie insists he will have it no other way. It is the birthing season for the *urpinta*, so he spends most of the nights out there anyway, tending them."

<esa mangato, Ahnax,> Tomas recited with a bow, forever the diplomat.

Charlie walked with them to the old cabin. Sarah could feel his stares behind her, played stupid when he tried to catch her eye, ignored the number of times he managed to brush against her, or take her hand to show her something.

She watched him when he wasn't looking. He had matured in the last year, a little more muscled, a little more confident. The heartache swelled up, churning her insides to butter. Three days weren't enough. Sarah ached to move back to the cabin with Dimi, slide back into a life she'd come to love more than she would admit, but Dmitri was a convicted smuggler and banned from the planet in bold red letters. She pushed the thoughts away, and tried to act like herself.

"What do you think?" she said, whirling around the cabin and checking corners for lost treasures. It had stood empty those nineteen months, as dingy and dirty as when she and Dimi first moved in, but to Sarah it felt as warm and comforting as a favorite shirt. "Isn't it wonderful!"

Vlad curled his lip in disgust. "I can't believe you lived here. It's like a history diorama or something."

Sarah laughed. "You should have seen it when we arrived! That whole half wasn't built yet. We didn't know a fork from a rake, or a needle from a pin. At least we had indoor facilities."

"If you can call it that."

Tomas noted the hole in the ceiling. "A little drafty, isn't it?"

"That's where the EPSAR went off," Sarah said, awed by the sight. "I don't remember most of it. I'm amazed I survived." The official explanation to Charlie had been that Dmitri had discovered the ceiling harbored insects, and removed the wood to eliminate the infestation.

She snapped out of the reverie and raced for the stairs. "Come on! Let me show you my escape route!" Sarah bolted out the window and grabbed for the old handholds, but moss had taken root, and she was out of practice. She slipped on the second foothold and fell the last meter and a half to the ground.

Charlie dove after her, swinging down seconds later to help her to her feet, while Tomas and Vlad raced down the stairs.

Sarah couldn't speak through her laughter. "That never happened before!" she said at last. "See what civilization does to you? Oh, I miss this!"

She made Vlad accompany her to the Al's workshed to help with the evening chores.

Charlie whispered to her while Vlad played with three new baby *urpintan*. <Sometimes, when I sad, I go to your house to think. I miss you and Dimi-tri.> He put his hand on her shoulder, but she twisted away.

<Do not think that, Charlie! I will leave in three days. I cannot stay, no matter what. I here to visit friends, to tell Dimi you are well and not still sad. I told you, Charshfe: I will not marry anyone.>

Charlie looked upset, but went back to work.

Sarah tossed and rolled through the inky-black night. The book had been jarred from the shelf in her heart and it had fallen open far in. Her heart pounded as she thought about him alone in the shed, wondering what he was thinking about.

As if she didn't know.

Psychotherapy and relaxation exercises were not the same as experience. The kind of companionship Charlie wanted was still beyond her ability to give. But if she ever decided to form a more ... *spiritual* union like that with someone (*a normal healthy physiological requirement,* she knew from Petrova's therapy), she hoped it would be with someone like him. Someone who loved her unconditionally. Someone who would be patient and understanding, and listen to her concerns with a desire to please.

Like he would.

Even if I could, I wouldn't do that to him. To taste a dream and then lose it would be cruel. Forbidden things were best left forbidden.

Sarah helped Charlie with the work as if nothing bothered her. Harvest season was underway. Dimi wasn't here to tell her she couldn't use the cutter blade, and she threw herself into the task. Uncle Tomas lent a willing hand, tying and carrying bundles of grain. Vlad worked, too, but not nearly as eagerly. For Sarah, it was like the old days, working and laughing side by side. With four people, the task flew, and they cleared Charlie of three days' work in a single morning.

Sarah offered Charlie a bottled drink at rest time, breaking the green seal. *<Drink! You will like. I bring all the way from Chanchi.>*

Charlie accepted the bottle with a smile. It tasted sharp but pleasant, refreshing on such a warm day. *<I like. Thank you.>*

Sarah broke the color-coded blue seal on her own bottle. She watched him down his with her fingers crossed. The green bottle contained the experimental vaccine, begged off Dr. Lanyon. Charlie knew several people at the Compound; it wouldn't be hard to track him. It might be too late for the vaccine, or it might not work. Or maybe it would. The chance it might was the greatest gift Sarah could think to give him. If only he could find a fertile woman as well.

Sarah dragged Vlad and Uncle Tomas to pasture the porshies, feed the *urpintan* and *joubash,* hoe the gardens, and pick anything that might be ripe. She helped shovel the shed floor, and showed off her skills as a woodcutter while Charlie stood back and laughed. She helped Mrs. Al prepare the evening meal, serving Charlie herself. His eyes caught hers, and she looked away, blushing. She hadn't planned it; it was just the order his plate fell in relation to the seating. Sarah Kirushenko was servant to no man. Except maybe Dmitri, but that was because she owed him so much.

Yet, Charlie was just as loyal, maybe even more. He had to realize she had a dark side – Dimi had told him what she'd done to Jaycee – and still he loved her.

He trapped her after dark as she exited the outdoor sanitary.

<I know you watch me,> he whispered behind her. He nuzzled her ear with his nose. (*specie-specific courtship rituals designed to attract,* she recognized now) <Look at sky. Yellow and silver moons rise together. That means wish will come true. They bring you back to me. That one wish that did come true. I will make new wish. You know what it can be?>

He pressed against her back, his breath a soft flutter on her ear. Her nervous system seemed to short-circuit, and the butterflies in her middle flapped the air from her lungs. She knew now what the feeling was, what it meant, that it was supposed to be there, and that it was okay to feel that way; therefore she didn't panic – yet.

(... touch conveyed by peripheral receptors, synapses connect with second-order neurons in the dorsal column nuclei which connect with third-order neurons in the thalamus which project into the postcentral gyrus of the brain...)

<I come back here because Vladimir wished it,> Sarah said, bordering on Tau Cetan blasphemy. <The Moons did not make me.>

She whirled to face him, hands flat against his chest *(so broad and strong under her fingers a firm curve of pectoral and a small humanoid nipple the power in his ribcage his heart beating right there under her palm his skin so warm right through his shirt)* so he kept a polite distance.

<Charlie, *ganai*! Do not make life harder! I will not stay here. Tomas will return, Vladimir will return, and I will return, too!>

<You feel same way!> Charlie challenged. <I hear those words in voice!> He brushed the loose hair from her face, caressing her ear with his fingers as he tucked the hair behind it. <Tell me truth, Sarrah, after so long. You feel like this for me?>

Sarah wrestled her butterflies for each cubic centimeter of breath. She couldn't look at him. She couldn't lie to him. Here, of all places, she dared not tell even a white lie. *Oh no.* <I feel it.>

(scent-based androgens present in male sweat and urine serve to increase response in females)

Charlie breathed faster. <All this time, I know! You were contracted in your homeland?>

A contract meant more than a betrothal, but less than a formal marriage. It allowed young couples to live together, make sure they were compatible before they were sealed into a permanent bond. A contract allowed for divorce; a marriage generally didn't. Technically, Dmitri had only held a contract that dissolved before his marriage became final. If Sarah said yes, Charlie might be upset, but he would stop the attention. A man did not mess with a contracted woman. It was a safe way out of her predicament, one he would never be wiser to.

<No.>

Light brightened the dark yard as Vladimir opened the cabin door. Sarah jerked her hands down.

Saved!

"Vlad! Come! Come here! Look!" Sarah jumped and dragged him to view the treeless fields. "Oes and Taber are rising together. It's a very lucky sign! You make a wish, and your wish is supposed to come true," she gushed, charged with emotion but trying to change the direction of the flow.

"Quantum stellar!" Vlad stared. Earth had only one moon, and Navara's had been invisible due to orbit. Two rising one before the other was a truly mesmerizing sight. "Does it only work on this planet, or will the wish come true back on Earth?"

"I would think it should. Cosmic forces are cosmic forces. If you win a lottery on one world, you should be able to take the prize with you, no?"

"Makes sense. Make it with me," he said, and took her hands. He closed his eyes. "Okay. I got one. Wish hard."

When he finished, Sarah held one of his hands and reached for one of Charlie's. "We mustn't leave Uncle Tomas too long; Mrs. Al likes him a little too much, and he can't speak enough Pelonishalan to defend himself. Come," she said to Charlie as if he were merely one of her brothers. <We can teach Tomas and Vladimir to play duwhalikae.>

<What you wish for?> Charlie asked.

<That I will arrive home safely.>

The sun rose a third time. Twenty-six hours of visiting remained. At least this time, leaving would be on her own terms, under her own power. Chaos roared inside her. She wanted to stay, stay with Charlie, even though she knew what it would mean. She also knew she couldn't, even if she wanted to. She had a seven-day visa. If she didn't return to the Compound in three days, she would be arrested. She couldn't give up home. If Sigma Tau Ceti lay closer to Earth she might consider it, but even hyperspace calls took ten days each way. She was finally willing to admit – at least to herself – she did love Charlie, and not in a brotherly fashion. If she ever wanted anyone kiss her and mean it, she wanted it to be him. If ever she wanted someone to hold her and tell her they loved her in that nasty biological way, she wanted it to be him.

Twenty-five hours.

She carried on, but the weight between her and Charlie grew heavier. Words stuck in her throat. Even walking seemed difficult.

Tomas and Vlad noticed.

Vlad hopped up next to her on the fence around the porshie field. "You're awful quiet. You talked non-stop in two languages on the way here. You haven't said a hundred words today in any language."

"I know." Sarah sighed, unable to sort out her problems. She gave him a sad smile. "I just miss this place something fierce. It took so long to get here, and already we have to leave again. I wish to the Moons Dimi were here with us. He and Charlie were such good friends. I wish we could all live here; you, too."

"It's beautiful country," Vlad agreed, "but it's not for me. I can't wait to get back somewhere with a real bed and a real bathroom."

Tomas took it in stride. He perched next to Vlad on the sturdy fence, woefully out of fashion in Sigma Tau clothing but commanding nonetheless. "This is fairly civilized. The people are clean despite the level of technology. They're friendly, respectable, and eager to please. I've dealt with cultures that slaughtered your food right at the table so you'd know it was fresh, others where you feared for your life every second you were there. Another one that expected the guest of honor to sleep with the Prefect's wife. If she was happy in the morning, then they felt you were powerful enough to bother doing business with."

Sarah gasped in horror. "That's hideous!"

Vlad's curiosity got the better of him. "Did you?"

Tomas hesitated. "That was a long time ago. Sometimes being a diplomat or ambassador or businessman puts a person in difficult situations that go against his own beliefs, but in the name of peace and good will you must adopt the customs of the culture you're visiting, no matter how strange it may seem."

Vlad grinned. "You did, didn't you?"

"It was a very good deal," Tomas admitted sheepishly.

Sarah stalked off in disgust.

Night brought no relief. Meditation eluded her. She would leave Charlie in the morning. Sarah had never expected to see him again, yet, here she was, and she knew for certain this time would be the last. Katya was her confidant for relationship questions, but Katya wasn't here.

How could she leave him?

She had no choice.

Was Charlie in tears, too?

Natural Human-Tau Cetan fertility impossible due to antigen incompatibility.
Reproductive organ systems physiologically similar.
During initial pair-bonding, activity may be particularly intense.

The right person. The right time. It would feel right. You won't be afraid.

Katya's advice came back to haunt her. Sarah wasn't afraid of Charlie. She hadn't been for years. She trusted him.

No matter how many angles she examined, no matter how many ways she hunted for errors in her logic, Sarah couldn't find a convincing argument to override the outcome. It was a one-time deal that would never come again. Wasn't this what she'd been training herself for these last awful months?

Outside, the night seemed deathly still. Mrs. Al's stentorian snores reverberated through Sarah's head. There were no sounds from the loft overhead. She reached for her clothes.

The heavy door of the workshed opened with a knifing creak. A warm scent of straw and grain and animals wafted out. The flock of *joubash* gave a soft chorus of chugging at the disturbance. A porshie gave a warning grunt at the intrusion, while the other whooshed and stretched its head towards her in the dim light from the moons high in the sky. Sarah hated porshies, but even more she feared darkness.

"Charlie?" she called in a hush. "Charlie?"

"Sarrah?" Charlie's head poked over the edge of the storage loft, directly above her. <What wrong?!>

<Nothing wrong.>. The shed plunged into blackness as she closed the door. Sarah shuffled with her hand out until she found the ladder. She bumped into Charlie at the top, relieved.

<What wrong?> he repeated, pulling her into the sweet mass of *koma* hay. <Why you not asleep?>

<I cannot sleep. Nothing wrong; everything very *right*. I stay awake two nights now, thinking and thinking, but only one thought comes to mind.> He knelt before her in the dark; she reached out and found him, pushed his long hair back from his face, brushed his soft cheek with her fingertips. His chest was bare; he slept only in his pants.

"Charlie?" she began, so nervous she felt sick. *Please, please don't let me be mistaken on this! Let me be ready!*

360

<Remember, long ago, I say I could not be girl for you? I little girl then. Now I much older girl. Much stronger. Even in my land, I will be grown woman in two more moonpasses. I will leave in morning; nothing can change that. Charlie?> Sarah swallowed, heart pounding so hard she couldn't breathe. *(temperature, heartrate, and blood pressure increase)* She walked herself consciously through Petrova's steps, information flashing through her head like so many atomic particles.

<Charshfenaki? For one night, I can be that girl for you. If you want.>

His hands touched her shoulders, so strong yet so gentle at the same time. <You know what you say to me? You know what you mean?>

Sarah trembled, and it took a moment to find her voice. <I know I want to be girl for you, Charshfe. In every way. I want this for longest of time, but I have only tonight. I cannot give you babies, ever, so you can do this without regret. I love you Charshfenaki, but I cannot stay. I want to do this for you. Without contract.>

Tau Cetans had scent glands behind their ears that gave off a subliminal odor their own species found impossibly alluring. Sarah leaned forward, found him, and pushed her nose lightly under his ear, the Tau Cetan equivalent of kissing. A small cry caught in his throat, and he tensed under her hands.

Charlie breathed heavier. He pulled her to him, sniffing her hair. <I never stopped wanting you to be girl of mine. Even for one night, but one night not enough, ever.>

Her lips brushed his ear. <I have only one. I cannot stay, even if Moons themselves came down to say yes.>

<Then we shall ask them to make night sky move slow.> He poked his nose down the side of her neck, growing bolder as she didn't pull away.

(activated by impulses in afferent nerves mediating vasodilation in response to erotic stimuli…)

Sarah could *almost* smell his scent, not quite, like a faint star that appeared only when you didn't look at it. The elusive hint of almost-but-not-quite made her search for it all the harder on him, much to his elation. She knew no matter how hard Charlie tried to elicit the scent of Tau Cetan response from her, she physically couldn't produce it. As a consolation, she'd scrubbed off her anti-perspirants, hoping the stench of her nervousness would mask anything he might miss.

The juxtaposition of emotion was more confusing than she'd imagined. His nose and lips and chin kneaded under an ear, around her throat to her other ear, overloading her with sensations. Half of her froze with fear, but half wanted more. She caressed his neck, consciously forcing the Fear side down, down, flat, until she stuffed it under the carpet of her mind where it wouldn't have to watch.

His hands ransacked her hair, combing the moonshine strands through his fingers with a long-denied hunger. They worked their way downwards as his breath tickled her ear, to her shoulders, to her back, until one strong hand boldly caressed her breast.

Sarah, to her own great surprise, enjoyed the attention, but now she pushed him away, holding his hands in hers to prevent further touching. <You must promise me one thing, Charshfe. If you cannot, we cannot have one moment more.>

<Anything, my Moonshine!> They were practically the same height. He took his hands back and held her close, pulling her hips tight against his.

(*proper functioning is dependent on state of desire and effective vasoconstrictive arousal...*)

He idled by rubbing noses with her.

<Promise you will not... touch me ... in the... girl area there... with your hands. I not like... fingers there,> she stumbled, unable to get past the worst of the old fears. <Promise!>

(*failure of arousal is frequently due to emotional issues, particularly in cases of trauma...*)

Charlie ran the tip of his tongue behind her ear before nuzzling low at the neckline of her dress, unfastening the bodice with a single hand. <Charshfenaki not need hands to make you happy. That I promise. You have initiation yet?>

<No!> Sarah groaned, caught once more between fear and a driving lust she'd never allowed herself to feel. On Earth it would have been an insult for him to inquire about her chastity; she would have slapped him hard, more than once, and left him bleeding. Here on Sigma Tau, it was proper etiquette. A boy expected more out of an active girl, and a naïve girl expected an experienced boy to take the time to teach her what he might want her to do. The conflicting feelings of suffocation and exhilaration surged.

(*reinforced by tactile stimuli from the breasts*)

<I wish on the Moons for it to be you. I want you to do this, but I so afraid, Charshfe!> Sarah breathed sharply in as the bodice to her dress fell open, and he slid the neckline of her blouse downward. Not even a physician had examined the flesh his lips caressed. She felt the slow, deliberate confidence in his moves, smelled the familiar scent of his sweat every time he moved. The resolute darkness of the loft held no directional indicators, no references for time and space, nothing but the warmth of his

body and the pressure of his touch, and the confusing rush of emotion within her. Her mind reeled, dizzy and disoriented.

Was this what Dmitri did to girls? Was this how they felt about what he did? No wonder they never seemed to be upset!

<I tell you, time and time, I could never hurt you, Sarrah,> Charlie murmured as he reached for the fastener to her skirt. <I not school-boy, bragging like porshie in season. We have all of night before us. I promise, you never be afraid again.>

(*estrogen-dependent pheromones secreted by the female sex organs are the most powerful male stimulus*)

(*a thin fold of mucus membrane*)

(*and the resultant accompanying drop in tension*)

He eased her onto his blanket in the hay.

The squall of a hungry porshie woke her. Sunrise filtered through the windows on the far side of the workshed.

<Charshfe! Wake up!> She shook him smartly. <You late!>

Charlie smiled sleepily. <They just jealous, because they did not do what we did.> He rolled over to grab her as she struggled into her blouse. <We should do one time more, to tease them.> He slid an arm around her waist.

<I think four times plenty. You have mind like porshie.> Sarah wrestled away. She straightened the blouse and searched for her bodice. <You forget, Mother will come for joubash eggs very soon, look for you.>

Katya was right. Dmitri was right. Charlie was right. The crushing fear was gone. His activity had been far more pleasure than pain, and the darkness hid any distress. Today, Sarah felt light enough to fly.

< She will be happy to see us.>

<But uncle will not! Do not forget brother! Stop, Charlie! I must dress!> Her skirt had functioned as a blanket for the little sleep they'd had. She gave a tug to reclaim it, leaving him shamelessly naked in the straw. It was the first time she'd actually seen his body, and she blushed despite her knowledge of it.

He reeled in the skirt until she was forced to follow it to him. He tackled her, tracing her cheek with his nose. <Now, you still afraid?>

<Only of what uncle will say if he knows I did this without contract.> Sarah kissed his nose and took her skirt.

Her good humor at breakfast was a far cry from her desolation of the day before. Each glance at Charlie, each wink or wiggle of an eyebrow from him in return, left her awash in a new wave of affection.

363

It had been traumatic to leave him the first time. How could she bear to do it again now?

Tomas caught her alone in Mrs. Al's room as she laced her shoes.

"How's your stomach?" he asked. "Will you make it to Chartaiga?"

"Fine. Why do you ask?"

"You were gone a long time using the facilities last night. I thought perhaps you were ill."

Sarah had to remember to breathe. She smiled innocently. "No! Not at all. Thank you for the concern. I couldn't sleep. I went out and sat on the rockpile by the edge of the yard, to watch the moons for a while."

Tomas picked something out of the back of the armhole of her dress. He handed her a short piece of straw. "I didn't know dried hay grew on rocks here. I never actually slept on a farm before this, but there are many references to it throughout literature. People in those stories were always sleeping in the haylofts, surrounded by fresh air and thousands of stars. When I was young, I always thought that would be the height of adventure." He picked a smaller piece out of the underside of her hair. "Especially if the farmer's daughter were to accompany me."

Humiliation stopped her heart in mid-beat. She blushed as red as the Tau Cetan moon Allash and spun away from Tomas.

"Is it that obvious?" she choked at last.

"If you mean, did Vladimir figure it out, I don't think so. There's a certain look a young man gets when he's done something he's rather proud of," Tomas explained delicately. "You learn to recognize that look with experience."

Sarah's eyes clenched against the embarrassment. The hardest thing she'd ever done in her life, the successful culmination of all those awful hours of therapy and the conquering of all the years of terror, destroyed by mortification just hours after victory. "I'm sorry."

Tomas rested a caring hand on her shoulder; she did her best not to flinch. "There's nothing to apologize for. Was it your decision? Did you enter into it knowingly and willingly?"

Sarah forced herself to whisper, "Yes, sir."

"And are you happy with that decision?"

Yes stuck in her throat, forcing her to nod.

"Then there's nothing to be ashamed of. It happens more than a billion times a day throughout the galaxy, probably a billion times a day on Earth alone. I just wanted to make sure you were okay with your choice."

Sarah pulled away. "Yes, sir. I don't usually... I never... You know that! It's just... You don't know how things were when Dimi and I were here. I can't begin to tell you what… "

Tomas placed a finger across her lips. "You don't have to. If it puts some memory to rest, if you feel better about yourself for it, then, by all means, carry on."

Sarah blushed anew. "Yes, sir."

Goodbye was no easier the second time. Mrs. Al shed a fountain of tears, but she wasn't frightened or violent as the time before. She hugged everyone a dozen times, kissed Sarah, kissed Uncle Tomas, kissed Vlad, kissed Uncle Tomas again, and pressed a basket of food and gifts into his hands for the long trip home.

<esa mangato,> Tomas bowed with a warm smile. <esa mangato, Ahnax.>

Charlie lost his effervescent chatter. He bowed to Vlad and shook his hand, did the same to Tomas. He bowed in half to Sarah, but the smile slid from his face.

Sarah lost herself in his eyes. <I tell you, I not can stay.> She put her arms around his neck in a gesture that could have been interpreted as two old friends parting.

Charlie held her tighter, snuffling longingly behind her ear. "I… love… to you," he whispered in her own language. "I love to you, Sarrah!"

<monad Ahn, risak, Charshfenaki Aletneshfaja! as Ima do sifa lapish, shojen nan i osh eloshin. chenikafche Ima, Ahno, Taberesh i sutho dorenfass. chenikafcheswa, Imara?> *

<Axa,> he whimpered.

Sarah didn't hesitate this time. She was almost eighteen years old, dammit, and she had charge of her own destiny. She placed her lips over his, kissing him an uncomfortably long time.

"Good bye," she said as she backed away. <You will send letters, yes? Tell me of the wife you will have, and the many babies the Moons will bless you with?>

Charlie nodded forlornly, holding tight to her hand. <Maybe – maybe I walk with you, to town? We can make visit last just tiny bit longer.>

Sarah shook her head, feeling *déja-vu* at the pain in her heart. First he would walk her to town, then a little way past, then all the way to

---

* *"I love you, Charshfe. I always will, until the moons fall from the sky. I will think of you every time I see Taber. Will you think of me?" [Note: Taber is the moon that resembles Earth's moon the closest.]*

Chartaiga, then all the way to the gates of the Compound itself. Parting anywhere else would be no less painful, probably worse. He would touch her as she walked, she would blush; he would insist on carrying her things, and she would stupidly let him. They would sit together, and talk together, and she would forget to translate what he said for the others; he'd sneak her kisses and noses when no one was looking, and even Vlad would be able to figure out their secret. And whether they camped that night at the side of the road, or stayed in a hotel in Chartaiga, if Charlie were there, they wouldn't stay apart. Even if she lay directly between Vlad and Tomas, she wouldn't sleep, knowing Charlie was right there, knowing he wasn't sleeping, either. She would pretend to sleep, then slip over to him, and she would not, *would not*, risk doing *That* with other people in the room, especially Uncle Tomas, not even for Charlie.

Even if her heart said yes.

<*Aja!* I know way. It better for both of us if you stay here.> Sarah stepped back, stretching her arm until she gave a tug to free her hand. She raised both her hands to the sides of her neck, dragged them across her cheeks until her fingertips touched her lips. She kissed them, tipped her cupped hands, and pretended to blow the whole mess to him. Charlie "caught" the gesture, touched his fingers to his lips, then repeated the gesture back to her. Sarah crossed her hands and hugged them tightly to her chest with a brave smile. She gave a little wave, then walked backwards until he vanished from sight.

Vlad stabbed her ribs with his elbow. "Hoo-hoo! What did you say to him? He sure looked like he liked it, whatever it was."

"Don't be a vulgar swine, Vlad. You're not David. You're better than that; don't forget it. Look how I hung on you when I first returned. He was our very best friend for many years. I miss him terribly, and I regret I will most likely never see him again in my life. I merely asked him not to forget me." She glanced at Tomas, but he walked on as if he knew nothing.

"Not after that kiss!" Vlad teased. "Where the hell'd you learn to kiss like that? You wouldn't kiss your own hand last year."

"Calm yourself, Vlad," Sarah said dryly, but try as she might, she couldn't suppress the blushing smile that broke out. "Don't be so jealous. We both know just how far I've come."

End

Coming next:

In 2238, opposites still attract. Sixteen-year old Maryana is the darling of the Byelorussian debutante circuit, a knockout blonde with a smile to resurrect the dead and the heiress to her father's galactic business empire. Twenty-two year old Sasha is the son of a chem-whore, a dirt-poor working stiff too withdrawn and demoralized to apply his brilliant mind. When Sasha and his friends crash an upscale party, social-savvy Maryana feels it her duty to make him feel welcome – until she glimpses past his rough-as-pavement exterior, and everything she's been taught to believe doesn't make sense anymore. When her acts of kindness are met with outrage at home, Maryana must make a devastating choice.

Life with Sasha isn't what Maryana envisioned, but step by step she builds up his career and their fortune to award-winning triumph, with an ever-growing family in tow. When their dreams are realized, Sasha accepts what should be a prestigious new job offer, and almost immediately Maryana finds her life once more whirling ever more out of control...

Ancient History

Even the Best stories have to start somewhere

The uncut prequel to *Best Intentions*

Susan Staneslow Olesen is a graduate of The Chase Collegiate School and studied psychology and writing at Wells College. A native of Connecticut, she is a special-needs foster parent with more than 25 years' experience in autism. In addition to working for her public library, she currently juggles a husband, five kids, five cats, three dogs, and an amaryllis plant that just won't die. *Best of Everything* is her fourth novel.

For info and trivia, follow along at
Best Intentions book series on Facebook.com

Priester Wernhers

M A R I A

Bruchstücke und Umarbeitungen

Herausgegeben

von

C a r l   W e s l e

M a x   N i e m e y e r   V e r l a g

Halle (Saale)

1927

Vorwort.

Der Wunsch, die Mariendichtung des Priesters Wernher dem akademischen Unterrichtsbetrieb zugänglich zu machen, hat Herausgeber und Verlag veranlaßt, von meiner im Frühjahr erschienenen Ausgabe einen wohlfeilen Sonderabdruck von Text und Fußnoten mit gleicher Satzeinrichtung, doch ohne Glossar und Reimregister mit knapper Einleitung in der Altdeutschen Textbibliothek erscheinen zu lassen. Mir war dieser Plan in mehrfacher Hinsicht willkommen: ich bin überzeugt, daß die schöne, so eigenartig überlieferte Dichtung für Seminarübungen einen interessanten und lehrreichen Text abgibt, und ich hoffe, daß die Behandlung in akademischen Übungen dem Text selbst, dessen kritische Bearbeitung noch keineswegs abgeschlossen ist, zugute kommen, noch manche Verderbnis erkennen, manche ungelöste oder mehr vorläufig als endgültig gelöste Schwierigkeit beseitigen wird.

Einleitung.[1]

Von der Mariendichtung des Priesters Wernher sind vollständig
nur zwei Bearbeitungen erhalten, die eine (D) in einer ausge-
zeichneten, wohl noch dem 12. Jahrhundert angehörenden Berliner
Handschrift, der nur am Schluß einige 30 Verse fehlen,[2] die
andere (A) in einer Wiener Handschrift des 13. Jahrhunderts.[3]
Beide Bearbeitungen haben gekürzt, A von etwa 5900 auf 4912,
D, das neben Kürzungen auch Zusätze enthält, aber gegen Schluß
ganze Abschnitte weggelassen hat, auf 5137 Verse.[4] Bei voll-
ständiger Erhaltung des Schlusses würde sich sein Versbestand
auf etwa 5166 Verse belaufen. Beide Bearbeiter haben die un-
reinen Reime erheblich vermindert,[5] dafür aber den Versbau oft
merklich vergröbert, beide haben den Satzbau, A auch die Wort-
wahl modernisiert,[6] beide haben die lehrhaften und erbaulichen

[1] Die Einleitung zu meiner größeren Ausgabe, auf die hier ein für
allemal verwiesen sei, enthält eine ausführliche Darstellung der Überlieferung, außerdem einige Beiträge zur Charakteristik des Dichters und
handelt über Reimtechnik, Versbau, Sprache und Heimat Wernhers.

[2] Sehr sorgfältiger Abdruck von Hoffmann, Fundgruben für Geschichte
deutscher Sprache und Literatur 2, 145 ff. Neuhochdeutsche Übersetzung
und Wiedergabe der Miniaturen durch Degering, Des Priesters Wernher
drei Lieder von der Magd in der Auswahlreihe des Volksverbands der
Bücherfreunde.

[3] Ausgabe Feifalik, Des Priesters Wernher Driu liet von der maget,
Wien 1860. Die Ansicht des Herausgebers, daß die Wiener Fassung dem
Original am nächsten stehe, ist unhaltbar und hat auch überall einmütig
Ablehnung erfahren.

[4] Der Umfang des Originals läßt sich aus den Bruchstücken der
Hs. C annähernd errechnen.

[5] Für A vgl. dazu Bruinier, Kritische Studien zu Wernhers Marien-
liedern (1890) S. 63 ff.

[6] Ich benutze die Gelegenheit, um, einer brieflichen Anregung
Friedrich Panzers folgend, auf den Reichtum des Originals an altertüm-

Betrachtungen, mit denen Wernhers Gedicht durchsetzt ist, vielfach
gekürzt, D auch sehr oft nach Form und Inhalt geändert, hie und
da erweitert. Überdies findet sich in beiden Bearbeitungen eine
Unmenge größerer und kleinerer Veränderungen, wobei D sich
mehr stärkere Eingriffe erlaubt, aber wenn es sich schon an
Wernhers Wortlaut hält, im ganzen treuer ist als A, das weit
häufiger willkürlich und planlos in Kleinigkeiten ändert. Keine
der Bearbeitungen ist von der andern abhängig, beide gehen selb-
ständig auf das Original zurück: wo sie übereinstimmen, liegt also
der Wortlaut des Originals vor, abgesehen von etwaigen gering-
fügigen und naheliegenden Änderungen, auf die beide Bearbeiter
zufällig in gleicher Weise verfallen konnten. Übereinstimmende
Verse sind aber in der Minderzahl gegen die abweichenden. Ein-
gehende Untersuchung mag noch in manchen Fällen lehren, bei
wem das Ursprüngliche liegt, an einzelnen Stellen auch aus beider-
seits verändertem Wortlaut das Echte herausfinden, aber auf Grund
der Bearbeitungen den Text des Originals ohne Willkür fortlaufend zu rekonstruieren, scheint mir außerhalb des Bereichs der
Möglichkeit.

Von der Originalfassung sind 2869 Verse, also nicht viel
weniger als die Hälfte in Bruchstücken von fünf Handschriften
(B C E F G) erhalten. Mitgezählt sind dabei auch fragmentarisch,
selbst trümmerhaft überlieferte Verse. Die wichtigste Quelle ist C,
eine Handschrift des 14. Jahrhunderts, die in Nürnberg der Buch-
binderschere zum Opfer gefallen ist, und von der an vier verschiedenen Orten Bruchstücke gefunden worden sind (C[1] in Karls-
ruhe, C[2] wahrscheinlich in Nürnberg, C[3] in München, C[4] in Breslau),[1]
zum Teil vollständige Blätter, zum Teil Blattstücke, zum Teil (C[2])
schmale Streifen, doch vielfach derart, daß sämtliche Streifen, in
die in ein Blatt zerschnitten wurde, erhalten sind. Die Bruchstücke
überliefern gegen 2600 Verse, darunter etwa 600, die auch in
andern Fragmenten (B E F) stehn. Am umfangreichsten ist C[2]

---

lichen Wörtern und Wortbedeutungen hinzuweisen. *gotes âtem = spiritus
sanctus* AD 2405 hätte, wie mich Panzer belehrte, ins Glossar aufgenommen
werden sollen.

[1]) Die Zahlen sind durch die zeitliche Reihenfolge der Auffindung
bedingt; die Stellung der einzelnen Bruchstücke in der Handschrift ist
C[4] V, I, II, C[2] 1—183, C[4] III, IV, C[2] 184—275, C[3] a, C[2] 276—633, C[3] b,
C[2] 634—1840, C[1].

mit 1840 Versen.[1]) Die Handschrift ist wahrscheinlich in Thüringen, möglicherweise auch im nördlichen Ostfranken geschrieben, steht also dem Original zeitlich und örtlich recht fern. Auch sonst ist die Überlieferung schlecht: sie wimmelt von Fehlern, manche Verse sind bis zur völligen Sinnlosigkeit entstellt, zahlreiche Lesarten werden durch andre Fragmente, die dann meist durch die Bearbeiter oder einen von ihnen gestützt werden, oder durch die Übereinstimmung beider Bearbeiter widerlegt.

Von den anderen Fragmenten ist F[2]) mit 581 Versen, von denen 371 auch in C stehn, das umfangreichste. Die Handschrift ist alemannisch-schwäbischer Herkunft, um die Mitte oder in der zweiten Hälfte des 13. Jahrhunderts geschrieben, und stellt eine keineswegs vollkommene, aber doch recht gute Überlieferung dar. Von den drei kleineren Bruchstücken, die nur aus je einem Blatt bestehen, ist der Inhalt von B und E auch in C überliefert, G steht allein.[3]) E, der Schrift nach das älteste aller Bruchstücke (Anfang 13. Jhdt.) hat die weitaus schlechteste Überlieferung, B die beste.

Einen Überblick über die erhaltenen Teile der Originalfassung gebe nachstehende Tabelle.

Verszahl des Originals[4])	Fragmente	Bearbeitung A	Bearbeitung D[5])
1 — 27	G	1 — 27	1 — 27
28 — 41	—	28 — 41	28 — 41
42 — 87	G	42 — 87	42 — 87
88—103	—	88—101	88 —103

[1]) Abgedruckt von Bartsch, Beiträge zur Quellenkunde der altdeutschen Literatur S. 6—57, C[1] von Mone, Anzeiger für Kunde des deutschen Mittelalters 6 (1837), 155 ff., C[3] von Keinz, Münchner Sitzungsberichte 1869, 2, 296 ff., C[4] von Klapper, Zeitschr. f. deutsches Altertum 50, 167 ff.; Bemerkungen zu allen Abdrücken ebda. 62, 154 f.

[2]) Abgedruckt von Greiff, Germania 7, 305 ff., vgl dazu Zeitschr. f. deutsches Altertum 62, 155.

[3]) B abgedruckt durch Docen, Aretins Beiträge 7, 119 und Miscellaneen 2, 103, dann noch mehrfach; am bequemsten zugänglich in Hoffmanns Fundgruben 2, 213; E von Bartsch, Anzeiger für Kunde der deutschen Vorzeit 9 (1862), 112 ff.; G recht unzuverlässig in Bartschs Quellenkunde S. 58; Berichtigungen zu den Abdrücken Zeitschr. f. deutsches Altertum 62, 154 ff.

[4]) Nur annähernd errechnet.

[5]) Ich gebe hier nicht die sonst beim Zitieren verwendete Zählung von Hoffmanns Fundgrubenabdruck, sondern, um ein deutliches Bild von

Verszahl des Originals	Fragmente	Bearbeitung A	Bearbeitung D
104 — 123	G	102 — 121	104 — 123
124 — 131	—	122 — 129	124 — 131
132 — 270	F		
271 — 274	C^4 [1])	130 — 336	132 — 382
275 — 384			
385 — 401	—	337 — 353	383 — 399
402 — 410	C^4		
411 — 428			
429 — 445			
446 — 628	C^2 1—183		
628 — 652	F C^4	354 — 625	400 — 701
653 — 672			
673 — 694	C^4		
695 — 697			
698 — 855	—	626 — 773	702 — 847
856 — 897			
898 — 989	F C^2 184—275		
989—1017			
1018—1082	C^3		
1082—1369	C^2 276—633	774—1408	848—1556
1370—1446	B		
1446—1491			
1492—1538	C^3		
1539—1628	C^2 634—723		
1629—1924	—	1409—1646	1557—1854
1925—1928	C^2 724—727	1647—1650	1855—1858
1929—1970	—	1651—1684	1859—1892
1971—1975	C^2 728—732	1685—1687	1893—1895
1976—2015	—	1688—1721	1896—1939
2016—2020	C^2 733—737	1722—1726	1940—1944
2021—2061	—	1727—1759	1945—1983
2062—2066	C^2 738—742	1760—1764	1984—1988
2067—2364	—	1765—1991	1989—2252
2365—2459	C^2 743—836	1992—2069	2253—2354

dem Umfang der einzelnen Stücke zu übermitteln, eine durchgeführte Verszählung (in meiner Ausgabe rechts vom Text).

[1]) Bis v. 358 sind von C^4 nur geringfügige Trümmer erhalten.

Verszahl des Originals	Fragmente	Bearbeitung A	Bearbeitung D
2460—2469	—	2070—2078	2355—2366
2470—2477	C² 837—844	2079—2089	2367—2373
2478—2500	—	2090—2112	2374—2398
2501—2505	C² 845—849	2113—2117	2399—2403
2506—2515	—	2118—2127	2404—2410
2516—2523	C² 850—857	2128—2135	2411—2419
2524—2546	—	2136—2160	2420—2442
2547—2551	C² 858—862	2161—2165	2443—2446
2552—2646	—	2166—2244	2447—2542
2647—2681	C² 863—896 [1])	2245—2276	2543—2574
2682—2694	—	—	2575— ca. 2607
2695—2726	C² 897—926 [1])	2277—2306	2608—2634
2727—2736	—	2307—2314	2635—2642
2737—2771	C² 927—959 [1])	2315—2347	2643—2677
2772—2783	—	2348—2357	2678—2690
2784—2817	C² 960—991 [1])	2358—2387	2691—2725
2818—2929	—	2388—2469	2726—2826
2930—2934	C² 992—996	2470—2474	2827—2828
2935—2957	—	2475—2493	2829—2843
2958—2962	C² 997—1001	2494—2498	2844—2846
2963—2972	—	2499—2508	2847—2856
2973—2980	C² 1002—1009	2509—2516	2857—2862
2981—3003	—	2517—2538	2863—2866
3004—3364	C² 1010—1370	2539—2782	2867—3168
3365—3405	—	2783—2815	3169—3200
3406—3410	C² 1371—1375	2816—2820	3201—3204
3411—3451	—	2821—2851	3205—3243
3452—3456	C² 1376—1380	2852—2855	3244—3248
3457—3497	—	2857—2888	3249—3289
3498—3502	C² 1381—1385	2889—2892	3290—3294
3503—3544	—	2893—2929	3295—3331
3544—3546			
3547—3646	E } C² 1386—1658	} 2930—3128	3332—3600
3647—3816			
3817—4090	—	3129—3360	3601—3864

[1]) Mit kleinen Lücken.

Verszahl des Originals	Fragmente	Bearbeitung A	Bearbeitung D
4091—4272	C² 1659—1840	3361—3498	3865—4022
4273—5372	—	3499—4454	4023—5050
5373—5378	C¹ 63—68 ¹)	4455—4460	5051—5056
5379—5388	—	4461—4468	5057—5066
5389—5523	C¹ 69—203	4469—4573	—
5524—5608	—	4574—4640	—
5609—5671	C¹ 1—63	4641—4685	—
5671—5726			—
5727—5742			5067—5082
5743—5764	C¹ 203—370	4685—4850	—
5765—5798			5083—5110
5799—5840			—
5841—5873	—	4851—4883	5111—5137
5874— ca. 5902	—	4884—4912	—

Meine Ausgabe gibt den Versuch eines kritischen, mit Hilfe der
Bearbeitungen von Entstellungen möglichst gereinigten Textes von
den in Fragmenten erhaltenen Teilen der Originalfassung. Bei der
Mangelhaftigkeit der Hauptquelle C wird nachprüfende und nach-
bessernde Kritik hier noch manches zu tun finden. In der Ortho-
graphie war Anlehnung an den vom Original vielfach abweichenden
Schreibgebrauch der Handschrift C natürlich ausgeschlossen, eine
gewisse Normalisierung, die über das hinausgeht, was sonst in
frühmittelhochdeutschen Texten üblich ist, daher unumgänglich.
Die strenge Gleichmäßigkeit, die in Ausgaben von Dichtungen der
klassischen Zeit zu herrschen pflegt, wurde absichtlich nicht an-
gestrebt. Ergänzungen sind, gleichviel ob sie vom Herausgeber
stammen oder einer Bearbeitung entnommen sind, in Pfeilklammern
geschlossen, wenn das Ergänzte in der Handschrift fehlt, kursiv
gedruckt, falls etwas dastand, aber weggeschnitten, zerstört oder
unleserlich ist. Die Fußnoten enthalten abweichende Lesarten,
Fehler und Entstellungen, auch unbedeutende Schreibfehler, sprachliche Varianten nur in beschränkter Auswahl,²) ferner Vorschläge

---

¹) Die Verse von C¹ sind fortlaufend geschrieben, aber lückenhaft
und in falscher Reihenfolge.

²) Wer die Fragmente als Sprachdenkmäler studieren will, muß
nach wie vor zu den älteren Abdrücken greifen.

zur Textgestaltung von Bruinier (*B.*),[1] und Sievers (*S.*),[2] mündlich
oder brieflich mitgeteilte von Albert Leitzmann (*L.*), Viktor Michels
(*M.*), und Eduard Schröder (*Sch.*), sowie eigene, die mit *W.* bezeichnet sind, sofern sie schon in meinem Aufsatz, Überlieferung
und Textkritik von Wernhers Maria, Zeitschrift f. deutsches Altertum 62, 151 ff. veröffentlicht sind. Gelegentliche Verweisungen
beziehen sich auf die Paragraphen der Einleitung zu meiner
Ausgabe.[3]

Der Originalfassung gegenüber steht ein paralleler Abdruck
beider Bearbeitungen, buchstabengetreu bis auf folgende Punkte:
stillschweigend sind Korrekturen und nachträgliche Einfügungen,
sowie Überschreibungen in den Text aufgenommen, große Anfangs-
buchstaben bei Eigennamen durchgeführt, sonst getilgt außer am
Versbeginn nach starker Interpunktion, Abkürzungen bis auf v̄, vn̄
aufgelöst, die Vokalstriche (Akute) beseitigt, während die Zirkumflexe
beibehalten sind; ferner ist das in D häufige Zeichen $\overset{v}{\imath}$ aus druck-
technischen Gründen durch *iv* ersetzt, während $\overset{o}{o}$ und $\mathring{u}$ beibehalten
wurden, und die Worttrennung vorsichtig geregelt: eine genaue
Wiedergabe ist hier gar nicht möglich, da beide Handschriften in
allen Nuancen zwischen klarer Trennung und klarem Zusammen-
schreiben schwanken, so daß man, um das wirklich anschaulich
zu machen, im Druck wohl mit einem Dutzend verschiedener Spatien
arbeiten müßte. Sonstige Abweichungen von den Handschriften
(Beseitigung von Schreibfehlern, mechanischen Reimglättungen,
handschriftlich unrein aussehenden, sprachlich aber reinen Reimen
wie etwa *varen* : *bewarn*) sind durch Kursivdruck, der also hier
etwas anderes bedeutet als im Text der Originalfassung, hervor-
gehoben und in den Fußnoten vermerkt. Ebenso notiere ich hier,
in der Regel durch ! gekennzeichnet, die äußerst seltenen Fälle,
wo der Abdruck von D durch Hoffmann (*H.*) sich irrt, und die
etwas zahlreicheren, wo Feifalik (*F.*) eine über seine sprachliche
Normalisierung hinausgehende Abweichung von der Handschrift
bietet, ohne sie in den Lesarten anzugeben.

---

[1] S. o. S. V.

[2] Forschungen zur deutschen Philologie, Festgabe für Hildebrand,
S. 19 ff.

[3] Diese Verweisungen sind ebda. S. 323 ergänzt und teilweise be-
richtigt.

Die ursprüngliche Fassung ist doppelt gezählt: links nach
dem errechneten Versbestand der vollständigen Dichtung, rechts
in Klammern nach den wirklich überlieferten Versen. A hat die
Zählung von Feifaliks Ausgabe in Kursivdruck, D links die Zahlen
von Hoffmanns Abdruck, rechts eine durchgeführte Verszählung,
ebenfalls kursiv gedruckt. Zitiert wird bei Doppelzählung stets
nach den Zahlen, die links stehen. Zahlen in gradem Druck beziehen sich immer auf die ursprüngliche Fassung, Zahlen in
Kursivdruck auf A, durch Komma getrennte Doppelzahlen auf D.

Der Priester Wernher, der sich selbst v. 1296 und 5803
nennt, hat nach eigener Angabe (v. 5799 ff.) im Jahr 1172 ge-
dichtet. Seine Heimat ist unbekannt, und auch sprachliche Kriterien,
die sich aus den Reimen ergeben, liefern kein ganz eindeutiges
Ergebnis. Fest steht, daß er ein Oberdeutscher, und zwar kein
Alemanne im engern Sinne war.[1] Aber auch ostbayrische und
österreichische Heimat ist wenig glaubhaft: der Konjunktiv von
,mögen' lautet *mugen* (*3154* AD), das bayrisch-österreichische *mege*
kennt nur D (171, 26. 180, 20). Aller Wahrscheinlichkeit nach
war der Priester Wernher im mittleren Teil Süddeutschlands, West-
bayern oder Ostschwaben zu Hause. Der Wortschatz spricht eher
für Bayern.

Sein Werk ist eine Bearbeitung des apokryphen, dem Matthäus
zugeschriebenen *liber de ortu beatae Mariae et infantia salvatoris*[2])

---

[1]) Die Annahme mitteldeutscher Herkunft (Bartsch, Germania 6, 121,
Bruinier S. 11) ist ganz unbegründet und haltlos. Gegen alemannische
Heimat spricht besonders, daß Wernher unbedenklich *an, am* auf *ân* reimt
(v. 57. 1575. 3165. 3249. 3747. 4187. 5503. 5743, AD *3201. 3743*), ferner
das Präteritum von *komen*. Die 1. und 3. Pers. Sing. Ind. steht nie im
Reim, lautete also gewiß nicht *kam, quam*, das eins der bequemsten Reim-
wörter wäre (*nam, gezam, man, began, gewan, gân, hân, stân, getân* u. a.),
sondern, wie in den Handschriften auch fast ausschließlich geschrieben
wird, *kom*, auf das es keine reinen und auch nur ein paar unreine Reim-
möglichkeiten (*von, gewon*) gibt. Bestätigt wird *kom* dadurch, daß es auch
im Plural neben *quâmen* (405. AD *2799*) *chômen* (4200, AD *3753*) und im
Konjunktiv neben *quæme* (2471) *chôme, chœme* (982. 3177. 4178) heißt.

[2]) v. Tischendorf, Evangelia apocrypha S. 51 ff.; Hennecke, Neu-
testamentliche Apokryphen S. 103; Steinhäuser, Wernhers Marienleben im
Verhältnis zum ,liber de infantia sanctae Mariae et Christi Salvatoris' (1890).

unter Weglassung der Schlußteile (von cap. XVIII an), die von den Wundertaten des Heilands in Ägypten und nach der Rückkehr handeln, und unter Ergänzung durch Aufnahme mancher Züge aus der Bibel.[1]) Das Verhältnis zur Quelle ist frei: einerseits hat sich der Dichter bemüht, die Erzählung durch viele kleinere und größere Änderungen und Zusätze zu verbessern, lebendiger, anschaulicher, naturwahrer zu machen, andrerseits verbrämt er sie mit einer Fülle von Anrufungen und Lobpreisungen, mit dogmatischen und moralischen Betrachtungen und Belehrungen, meist in schwungvoll-hymnischem Stil, seltener in nüchterner Lehrhaftigkeit. Die schlichte Erzählung des Pseudomatthäus ist zum Muttergottespreis-lied umgeformt.

Drei Teile recht ungleichen Umfangs bezeichnet der Dichter selbst als drei ,Lieder' (1—1284, 1285—3106, 3107— ca. 5900), doch bedeutet *liet* hier nur Teile des Ganzen, nicht etwa ab-geschlossene, selbständige Dichtungen. Wenn man neuhochdeutsch von den drei Liedern Wernhers, den drei Liedern von der Jungfrau spricht, wird daher leicht eine irrige Vorstellung erweckt. Zu-treffender wäre nach heutigem Sprachgebrauch ,drei Bücher'. Das erste *liet* behandelt Vorgeschichte, Geburt und Kindheit der Mutter-gottes bis zum Eintritt in den Tempel, das zweite Jugend, Ver-mählung und Ehe bis zur Verkündigung, das dritte die Geburt des Heilands und was damit zusammenhängt, Flucht nach Ägypten, Bethlehemitischen Kindermord, Ende des Herodes, die beiden letzten Stücke nicht nach Pseudomatthäus, sondern nach der Bibel erzählt, wobei der Untergang des Herodes Agrippa in der Apostelgeschichte als Vorbild für das Ende dieses Herodes gedient hat.

Wernhers Reimtechnik ist noch frühmittelhochdeutsch: ein gutes Drittel der Reime entspricht nicht den Anforderungen der klassischen Zeit, aber die vorkommenden Abweichungen halten sich in ziemlich bescheidenen Grenzen. Im stumpfen Reim werden Wörter mit verschiedenen Quantitäten vor Nasal und vor *r* ge-

---

[1]) Erst nachträglich wurde ich durch die Notiz in der Deutschen Literaturzeitung 1927, 1264 darauf aufmerksam, daß S. Singer schon vor Jahren (Prager Deutsche Studien 8, 304) auf die Möglichkeit einer Be-einflussung durch die *Vita beate virginis Marie et salvatoris rythmica* (Bibl. des lit. Ver. in Stuttgart 180) hingewiesen hatte. Eine Dissertation über das Verhältnis Wernhers zu seiner Quelle, die sich in Vorbereitung befindet, wird auch diese Frage zu erörtern haben.

bunden, nur *o* : *ô* auch vor *t* (367. 495. 887. 3815. AD *3725*),
ferner Wörter mit verschiedener, aber nah verwandter Qualität der
Vokale (*e* : *ë*, *u* : *uo* vor Nasal, *û* : *uo* im Auslaut, vereinzelt *tier* : *mir*
1179, *brût* : *liut* 1313). Im klingenden Reim werden Wörter mit
verschiedenen Tonvokalen gelegentlich noch gereimt (*ergrunden*
: *chinde* 145, *weisen* : *hûsen* 311, *habeten* : *lebeten* 319, *rinder* : *under*
413, *ervollen* : *willen* 417, *venige* : *manigen* 529, *worten* : *furhten* 599,
hôhe : *sâhe* 971, *geburte* : *worhten* 1189, *zebrosten* : *vasten* 1231,
habete : *redete* 1511, *geheizen* : *lâzen* 1603, *unzuhten* : *gerihten* 3615,
kinden : *funden* 3741, etwas öfter *iu* : *û*, anderes nur in den Bearbeitungen überliefert), ungleiche Quantitäten nur vor *r* (*worte*
: *erhôrte* AD *701*, *zierte* : *wirte* 1473, *gerne* : *êren* 3329, *êren* : *herre*
5509, : *herren* 5807, *geinwurte* : *enpfuorte* 5633). Häufiger sind
konsonantische Abweichungen, doch wird auch hier die Bindung
stark verschiedener Lautwerte (Lenis : Fortis, Verschlußfortis : Reibe-
fortis) streng gemieden.

Im Versbau gehört Wernher zu den sorgfältigsten und regel-
mäßigsten unter den vorklassischen Dichtern. Die frühmittelhoch-
deutsche Füllungsfreiheit gilt nur noch am Ende von Abschnitten
verschiedener Größe: hier stehen Verse, die ein recht umfangreiches
Wortmaterial aufnehmen können (Schwellverse). Ihre Messung
(klingende Vierheber oder sehr stark gefüllte Dreiheber) ist nicht
ganz eindeutig. Sonst sind Verse, die über das Normalmaß (zwei
Silben für jeden Takt) hinausgehen, schon ziemlich selten (knapp
10 % aller Verse). Mehr als dreisilbige Takte kommen nicht vor.
Zu dem Erzählvers der klassischen Epik stimmt Wernher im häufigen
Gebrauch einsilbiger Takte (fehlende Senkung), die meist durch
sprachlich starke und stärkste Silben gebildet werden, er unterscheidet sich von ihm durch strengere Übereinstimmung des Metrums
mit dem natürlichen Sprachton ungebundener Rede: seine Senkungen
bilden fast ausschließlich von Natur schwache Silben, metrische
Drückung sprachlicher Starktöne kommt nur in allerbescheidensten
Grenzen vor: *nach dir unweinènde wírt* 909, *unt wie dar nách
unlénge* 3128 sind die stärksten Fälle. Nie stehn Substantiva oder
Adjektiva in Senkung, Verba nur bei ausgesprochen geringer Ton-
schwere (z. B. *zeiner pórte diu hiez áureá* 957, *daz scháf daz é
fuor írre* 1068).

Charakteristisch ist für Wernher eine weitgehende Abstufung
der Hebungen: die große Mehrzahl der Verse hat zwei, seltener

eine ausgeprägte Haupthebung: *eines liedes wil ich beginnen   in
sànt Marien minne,   der ewigen chúniginne :   diu rúoche mine
sinne   unt mine brúst erreinen   von áller slàhte méile,   daz
ich nu mùoze schriben   von ir diu állen wíben   den itewiz hàt
benómen.* Verhältnismäßig selten sind Verse, die bei zwangloser
Rhythmisierung dreigipflig herauskommen (*von dem érsten wibe in
die wérlt* 11, *sit wàrt diu éwige máget erwélt* 12, *swaz Éva súndèn
begie* 20), und niemals enthält ein Vers drei oder mehr syntaktisch
gleichgeordnete Glieder.[1])

Als Wortkünstler steht Wernher auf sehr hoher Stufe: er
beherrscht die metrische Form wie den sprachlichen Ausdruck
gewandt und sicher. Seine Verse sind ungemein flüssig und wohl-
klingend, ohne eintönig zu werden. Sein Sprachvermögen bringt
Schlichtes und Pathetisches gleich treffend zum Ausdruck. Von
der Formelhaftigkeit der frühmittelhochdeutschen Poesie ist er
schon fast völlig frei. Sein Formwille geht dahin, für jeden
Vorgang und jeden Gedanken eigene Prägung zu finden: darin
steht er schon ganz auf dem Wege, den einige Jahrzehnte später
die Klassiker des höfischen Epos gehen.

Von den beiden Bearbeitungen ist D bald nach dem Original
entstanden: die Handschrift ist aller Wahrscheinlichkeit nach noch
im 12. Jahrhundert geschrieben, sicher älter als alle Fragmente,
vielleicht mit Ausnahme von E. Die Sprachform des Bearbeiters
weicht von der des Originals nicht unerheblich ab: *mege* 171, 26.
180, 20, *cham, quam* 151, 40. 165, 4, *gesat* 153, 14. 166, 10. 179, 6.
192, 29. 195, 33. 201, 5. 205, 30, *meit < maget* 176, 16. 182, 11.
188, 19. 205, 38, *chleite < clagete* 152, 17. Bayrisches (*mege, meit,
chleite*) und Nichtbayrisches, Alemannisches (*quam, gesat*) mischt sich
hier in so auffälliger Weise, daß eine sichere Lokalisierung un-
möglich ist. Mehr ein Unterschied im Sprachstil als in der Mundart
sind die vielen harten Apokopen im Reim, z. B. *muot⟨e⟩ : guot* 150, 31.
157, 35, : *tuot* 151, 27, *leit : chleite* 152, 17, *genôte : gebôt* 153, 20,
erschein : eine 160, 29, *werdicheit : leite* 165, 1, auch Epenthesen
wie *zebrast[e] : vaste* 162, 8, *algemeine : erschein[e]* 169, 37, *erschein[e] : gemeine* 176, 21, *harte : vart[e]* 193, 19, *hirte : verbirt[e]*
199, 38. Im Gegensatz zu dieser sorgloseren Sprachbehandlung,

---

[1]) Daher muß es v. 144 heißen *laien únde fróuwen*, 3184 nach A
wèder hie nòch dórt, vgl. meine Einleitung S. LXXIV.

die den Stil des Bearbeiters dem Vulgären, Umgangsprachlichen
näher rückt, steht syntaktische Sorgfalt in der überaus häufigen
Verknüpfung von Sätzen und Satzteilen, die bei Wernher unver-
bunden stehen, und mancherlei stilistische Zierlichkeiten (Antithesen,
Wortwiederholungen und Wortspiele, s. bes. 179, 10 ff., 182, 6 ff.,
209, 38 f.). Unreine Reime werden zum großen Teil beseitigt, der
Versbau ist dagegen unregelmäßiger, archaischer als im Original
(klingende Vierheber, z. B. 172, 40. 177, 29. 182, 8. 9 u. ö., stumpfe
Dreiheber 161, 7. 172, 25. 177, 8. 178, 15).

Die Bearbeitung A ist erheblich jünger: charakteristisch ist
die Beseitigung altertümlicher Wörter, die in D meist erhalten,
aber auch in C oft getilgt sind (so *urschîn* 132. 520. 1213, *chiut*
274. 383, *hiwisch* 420. 3151, *chorter* 457, *jungide* 546, *chreset* 574,
charele 609. 956. 984, *berhtel* 1223 u. a.). Unreine Reime werden
vielfach getilgt, oft begegnen aber auch Vergröberungen des Reims,
nicht nur Apokopen wie in D (*zwar 608, undertân⟨e⟩ 810. 1099,
rât⟨e⟩ 811, pein⟨e⟩ 1086, guote : pluot 1119* u. ö.), sondern auch
Bindungen kurzsilbiger und langsilbiger Wörter (*namen : âmen 189,
geladen : genâden 949. 2461* u. ö.) und auch sonst mancherlei Entstellungen, z. B. *stat : rât 811, : stât 1725; hât : bat 1901, : trat
3331, ewarten : hâten 1479, kêre : werden 1327, weiben : zeiten
1493* u. a. Metrisch unterfüllte Verse (stumpfe Dreiheber) sind
sehr häufig (*65. 67. 134. 153. 175. 231. 314* u. ö.); sprachlich
und stilistisch ist der Bearbeiter von einer ganz ungewöhnlichen
Nachlässigkeit und Ungeschicklichkeit, die sich manchmal zu völliger
Sinnlosigkeit steigert, vgl. z. B. *266 f., 580 ff., 1674 f., 2554 ff.* Der
Bearbeiter ist ein ausgeprägter Typus der Sorte von mittelalter-
lichen Literaten, die gar nichts anderes können als eine schöne
Vorlage in der ärgsten Weise zu verderben und zu entstellen.
Das unterscheidet ihn wesentlich von dem Bearbeiter D: auch
dessen Werk bleibt für unser ästhetisches Urteil weit hinter der
Dichtung Wernhers zurück, erreicht nicht entfernt den Wohlklang
seiner Verse, aber er steht doch als eigenwertige Persönlichkeit
neben ihm, ändert mit Überlegung und Bewußtheit, wo ihm etwas
nicht zusagt und wo er Besseres sagen zu können glaubt, und
was er sagt, ist nie ohne Sinn und Vernunft; seine Arbeit ist eine
wirkliche Umdichtung, A nur eine Verballhornung des Originals.

Berichtigungen.

Zum Text.

17 *l.* den schônen. 53 ff. *l.* an dir noch an dem chinde dîn: êwigez magedîn, nu lâ mich geniezen, 114 *l.* muoze *oder* muge. 117 *l.* schol. 144 *l.* laien unde frouwen. 292 *l.* kûscheit. 321 *l.* alliu. 573 *l.* daz ez sich. 928 *l.* hâte. 1165 *l.* ⟨die⟩. 1235 *l.* karten. 1384 *wohl* churs *statt* salter *zu lesen.* 1488 *wahrscheinlich* blîde *statt* bilde. 1538 siech] *l.* schiech. 1627 iemer *besser zu streichen.* 2065 *die Zahl einen Vers höher.* 175, 11 *l.* 2210 *statt* 2010. 2422 *l.* rehten. 2455 *l.* hâte. 2740 *eher* verwarte *statt* gezwîvelte. 3152 die *besser zu streichen.* 3184 hie, dâ oder] *l.* hie noch.

In der ersten Hälfte von D *sind mir die Zahlen von Hoffmanns Fundgrubenabdruck einigemal an die unrichtige Stelle geraten: es gehört vier Zeilen höher* 147, 5 (*vor* die itewîze), *zwei Zeilen tiefer* 148, 30 (*vor* ersten), 150, 30 (*vor* den offen), 155, 40 (*vor* dune), 171, 35 (*vor* wesen), *eine Zeile höher* 152, 30. 165, 5. 171, 20. 172, 40. 173, 15. 20. 176, 30. 179, 25.

Zu den Fußnoten.

341 *51 b l. 53 b.* 508 *59 b l. 59 c.* 573 *die ganze Note streichen, dafür* ieittenivwet (*so!*) F, ie v̓neuwet C. 1084 *l.* so wirt si?) *zu streichen.* 1188 meinen C *zu streichen.* 1403 egelen C. 1605 *Anm.*] *zu streichen.* 2061—65, 63, 64, 65 *l.* 2062—66, 64, 65, 66. 188, 12 *l.* 180, 12. 2521—23, 2746, 2749 *bis* nü 2751, 2793, 2816 f., 2933 f., 2978—80 *nur die oberen,* 2797 f. *nur die unteren Enden der nicht kursiv gedruckten Buchstaben sind erhalten.* 3004—64 *l.* 3004—3364. 3323 bekumen *l.* bekomen. 3614 mich *fehlt* C.

Maria

vom

Priester Wernher

I.

Eines liedes wil ich beginnen
   in sant Marien minne,
der êwigen chuniginne:
diu ruoche mîne sinne
5 unt mîne brust erreinen   (5)
von aller slahte meile,
daz ich nu muoze schrîben
von ir diu allen wîben
den itewîz hât *benomen,*
10 daz der tôt was bechomen   (10)
von dem êrsten wîbe *in die wer*lt.
sît wart diu êwige maget erwelt,
daz bêdiu *man unde* wîp
lieht unt ⟨den⟩ êwigen lîp
15 mit gezierde muose sch*ouwen*   (15)
dâ zir vil tiurer frouwen:
si gebar den wâren sun*nen,*
*si ist a*ller wîbe wunne.
wie wol siz allez undervie
20 swa*z Eva s*unden begie!   (20)
si hât verbuozet ⟨wol⟩ den val,
ir chûsche *liuhtet ub*eral;
nu schuln wir ir getrûwen,
wan wir in dem tôde *bûwen,*
25 *daz* si uns ellenden   (25)
wider heim gesende
unt uns ru*oche wisen*

1—27 G 2 sancte 5 min zereiñne 6 meile! 8 uon d⁵ 9 et-
wizze   11 uom   12 magde   16 ..... n gedenchet edel frawen
17 die schonne   24 sit wir   25 ellende

A

Einer rede ich hie beginne
in sant Marien minne,
der æwigen chuniginne:
div gerûche mine sinne
5 vn̄ mine brust erreinen
uon aller slahte mainen,
daz ich nu mv̊zze schreiben
von ir div allen weiben
die itewiz hat benomen,
10 daz der tot waz bechomen
uon dem ersten wibe in die welt.
do wart div æwige magt erwelt,
daz beidiv man vnde weip
lieht vn̄ den æwigen leip
15 mit ziêrde mûzze schowen
von der tivren vrouwen:
si gebar die schônen svnne,
si ist aller werlde wunne.
wie wol siz allez vndervienk
20 swaz svnden Eva begienk!
si hat verbûzzet wol den val,
ir chevsche lævhtet vber al;
nv sul wir ir getrowen,
wan wir die svnde bowen,
25 daz si vns ellende
frôlich heim sende
vnde daz si ⟨uns⟩ weise
zv̊ dem frônen paradeise,
da fro Eva ovz geviel.
30 von dem mêre chan si den chiel
harte wol geleiten
ovz disen arebeiten
zv̊ der himelporten.
mit den gotes worten
35 ir wart div warheit gesaget:
si ist mv̊ter vn̄ maget;
si hat der engel niht betrogen:
got hat daz spunne gesogen

9 div   11 no

D

Eines liedes ich beginne
in sente Marien minne,
der ewigen chuniginne:
div gerûche ŏch min sinne
147,5 vnd mine bruste errêinen   5
uor aller slahte mæile,
daz ich nŭ mûze scriben
uon ir div allen wiben
die itewîze hat benomen,
daz der tot was bechomen   10
uon dem ersten wibe in die werlte.
sit wart div here maget erwelte
darzu daz bediu man vnt wîp
daz lieht vnd den ewigen lip
mit der warhêit mûse schŏwen 15
da zir vil tivrer frôen:
10 si gebar den waren sunnen,
si ist aller gnaden ẘnne.
wîe wol si iz allez underuie
swaz Eua sunden ie begie,   20
wan si hat gebŭzet wol den ual,
ir chuske luhtet uber al;
nu schulen ⟨wir⟩ ir getruen,
wande wir in dem tode bûwen,
daz si uns ellenden   25
mege wider hêim gesenden
15 unt uns geruche wisen
zu dem vrônen paradise,
da frŏe Eua uz geuiel.
ab dem mere chan si den chiel 30
wol bringen vnt geleiten
vz den sorgen unt den arbeiten
ze der himelischen borte.
mit dem gotes worte
ir wart div warheit gesaget: 35
sie ist mûter und maget;
20 sine hat der engel niht betrogen:
got hat daz ir spunne gesogen

1*

. . . . *l*
von êwen unze êwen:
*wir schuln si anruofen un*de flêgen.   (30)

45   **H**imelischiu frouwe,
mit geistlîchem touwe
begiuz mînen gedanc,
daz ich ⟨dîn⟩ lop unt dîn sanc
ein te*il gemê*ren muoze,   (35)
50   ⟨unt⟩ hilf mir daz ich gebuoze
daz unreht daz ich ie begie,
wan ich gezwîvelôte nie
an dir *noch an* dînem chindel:
des lâ mich gnâde vinden,   (40)
55   unt lâ mich geniezen
da*z du nie ver*lieze
de*h*einen irdischen man
der dich ze voget wolte *hân!*
dû bist liehter denne der tac: (45)
60   aller tugende wâ*z unt smac*
fliuzet ûz dîner schôze.
nu bedenche froude *grôze*
die dir der engel brâhte,
dô got an dir gedâhte   (50)
65   aller men*nischen nôt*
unt dir die mandunge enbôt
in ditze chl*agelîche tal,*
daz er dich ze einem sal
im selben wolte wîh*en:*   (55)
70   *wie mah*testu mir verzîhen
guoter rede unt guoter *liste?*
du bist diu oberiste
nâch gotes magencrefte:
daz liet ich ⟨ane⟩ hefte   (60)
75   ûf dîne gnâde volle:
du bist daz tou in *Gedeônis* wolle.

Page 5

A

ab ir vil ædelen prust.
40 die nie mannes gelust
gewan noch der svnden val,
si ist mûter ane mal
von ǽwen ze ǽwen:
wir sulen sey an rûfen vū flêgen.

45 **H**imelische vrowe,   147, 25
mit geistlichem tǒwe
begivz minen gedanch,
daz ich din lob vnt dinen sauch
ein teil gemæren mŧzze,
50 vū hilf daz ich gebûzze
daz vnreht daz ich îe begie,
wan ich gezweivelt nie
an dir noch an dem sune dein.
ǽwiges magedin,
55 la daz ich geniezze
. daz dv nie verliezze
denheinen yrdischen man
der dich ze votinne wolde han!
Dv bist liehter dan der tak,
60 vū aller tugende smak
flivzzet ovz diner schôzzen.
bedenche die ǽre grozzen
die dir der engel brahte,
do got an dich gedahte
65 fur aller welde nôt
vū dir den grûz enbot
in ditz iamertal,
daz er dich wolde ze einem sal
sin selbez libe ze weihen.
70 wie mohtest dv mich verzeihen
gûter rede vū liste?
du bist div oberiste
nach gotes manchrefte:
ditz liet ich anehefte
75 ǒf dine genade volle:
dv bist div tovwige wolle.

D

abe ir uil reinen brusten.
die maunes nie geluste   40
noh nehêiner sunden teil,
sie ist iemer muter ane mæil
uon ewen unt ze ewen:
wir schulen sie anrûfen v̄ flegen.

Himelischiv frowe,   45
mit geistlichem tôwe
begiuz den minen gedauch,
daz ich din lob vnd din gesanch
ein teil gemeren mûzze,
unt hilf mir daz ich gebuzze 50
daz uureht daz ich ie begie,
wan ich gezwiuelot nie
an dir noh an dinem chinde:
des la mich gnade vinden
30 vnt la mich ǒch genîezzen   55
daz du nie verlîeze
deheînen irdisken man
der dich ze uoget wolte han!
du bist liehter denne der tach:
aller tûgende wâz unt smach 60
flivzet uz diner schozze.
nu bedenche, frǒe grozze,
waz dir der engel brahte,
do got an dir bedahte
148, 1 aller mennisken not   65
unt dir die mandunge enbot
in ditze chlageliche tal,
daz er dich ze eînem sal
im selben wolte wihen.
wîe mæhtestu mir uerzihen   70
gûter rede vnt guter liste?
dv bist div oberiste
nach gotes magenchrefte:
5 daz liet ich anhefte
vf dine gnade uolle: 75
dv bist daz tov iu Gedeonis wolle.

---

ze sinen   69 wold im selwen   70 mich   71 *das erste* guoter *zu streichen?*
vgl. § 65   72 . . . n (*l.* wan?) du   75 din

147, 30 verlieze *fast unleserlich, aber wahrscheinlicher als* ne irlieze *H.*
148, 2 chlagelliche

Nu wil ich iu den orthaben
bêdiu chunden unde sagen,
daz ich die materie   (65)
80 mit himelischem herie
unt diu starchen mâre
al deste baz bewâre:
Mathêus *ewangeliste*
⟨der⟩ schreib iz von Christe   (70)
85 unt von der muoter di*u in truoc:*
⟨dannen⟩ schreib er zeichen gnuoc,
doch was diu re*de bedwungen*

daz er die schrift diu ê dâ slief
105 mit predige muose *wechen,*   (75)
die suozen lêre entechen,
diu ê was beschatewôt,
diu gotes chint ir brôt
unt ir spîse funden daran.
110 der *îngewundene* van   (80)
der wart ⟨dô⟩ wol begreifet,
fur daz her *geweifet,*
daz diu christenlîche schar
mit chrefte *muose* varn dar
115 ze geistlîchem sturme   (85)
gegen dem lin*twurme,*
dâ der sic scholt ergên.

---

80 himellischen   82 dez   87 idoch   104—123 G   104 schrifpte
6 suze rede   7 e da   8 *für* daz diu *kein Raum, aber so doch metrisch*

A

Nv wil ich ev den orthaben
bede chvnden vn̄ sagen,
daz ich die materye
80 mit himilischem herie
vn̄ die starken mêre
dester baz bewære:
Matheus ewangeliste   148, 10
der schreib ez von Christe
85 vn̄ von der magt div in trŭk;
da von er zeichen schreib genŭch,
doch waz div red bedwungen
in ebreyscher zvngen
vntz an sant Jeronimum.
90 der tet daz durch den gotes svn,
vn̄ durch zweyer pischof rat,
daz er ditz liet getihtet hat
iu die senfte lateine.
daz wazzer wart ze weine,
95 div milich wart ze ôle,

do er vns schreib so wole.

dez heten in geschundet
daz er die red chundet
Cromacius v̄n Eliodorus;
100 die pyscof hiezzen alsus,
die im santen ir brief,
daz er die schrift div vor slief
mit predige solde wechen,
die sv̂zzen lere entechen,
105 die ᴂ waz beschatot,
daz die gotes chint ir brot
vn̄ ir speise funden daran.
der ingewunden van
der wart da wol gelaitet
110 vn̄ fur daz hêr gepreitet,
daz div christenliche schar
mit chreften muge varen dar
ze geistlichem sturme
gen dem lintwurme,
115 da der sich sol ergᴂn.

D

Nv wil ich iv den orthaben
bediv chunden vnde sagen,
daz ich die materige
mit himiliskem herige   80
vnd div starchen mære
al deste baz bewære:
Matheus ewangeliste
der screip iz uon Christe
und uon der mûter div in truch: 85
dannen screib er zeichen gnûch,
doh was div rede betŵngen
in ebreisker zûnge
untze an sant Jeronimum.
der tet daz durh den gotes sun 90
15 vnt durh zweir biscoffe rat,
daz er daz liet gewîtert hat
in die senften latine.
daz wazzer wart da ze wîne,
div milch verwandelt sich in 95
     daz ole,
do er uns screib also wole.
div ŵste wart erbuwen,
do disiv rede nivwe
20 vz wart gechundet.
des het in geschundet   100
Chromatius vnd Eliodorus;
die bisgofe hiezen alsus.
die santen im ir brîef,
daz er die schrift div ê da slief
mit bredige muse erwechen 105
vnt die svzen lere endechen,
div e was beschatewot,
div gotes chint ir brot
25 vnt ir spise funden dar an.
der ingewnden chunclich van 110
der wart do wol begreifet
vnd fŷr daz here gewêifet,
daz div christenlichiv schare
en samet mûse ilen dare
ze geistlichem stûrme   115
gegen dem lintwrme,
30 da der sige scholt ergen.

---

bedenklich, vgl. § 69 d   10 *ingewunde*n, *vgl. § 67*   13 elliv christenlichiv   15 ze dem geistlichen stvrm   17 sol

     90 durt   *102* e   *103* weche

von der vinster *schuln ouch* wir *ersten*
ze dem êwigen liehte.
120   got geschuof uns von niehte,   (90)
der *ist unser* vater guoter.
nu biten wir sîne muoter
daz si . . . .

von dem êwigen urschîne
er chunde wol chôsen,   (95)
von der lilien unt von der rôsen,
135   diu der dorne nienc hât.
nu wolt ouch ich den ir rât
unt ir helfe suochen,
ob si des wolte ruochen,   (100)
daz ich mit diutischer rede
140   daz buoch brâhte her ze wege,
daz si ez alle muosen lesen
die gotes chint wellen wesen,
unt ouch mugen schouwen   (105)
phaffen, laien, frouwen,
145   smechen unt ergrunden
von dem frônen chinde,
   .   daz im die muoter erchôs
diu ir magetuom nie verlôs   (110)
unt niemer mac verliesen.
150   wir mugen ouch wol chiesen,
wie vil gnâdic si sî
der daz chindel sitzet bî
daz lewe unde lamp ist,   (115)
ob allen dingen zoberist:
155   beidiu leben unde tôt,
hirte unt lebendigez brôt,

119*f.* lieht: uz nieht   21 er   22 sin   132—273 F 1—141   135 dorn
43 mv̊zen   44 phaffen vn̄ frowen, *vgl. W. s. 172*   52 kindelin, *vgl. W.
s. 164*   54 zeoberist   55 lip, *ursprünglich?*

A

von der vinster sul wir erstæn
zv̊ dem æwigen liehte.
got geschvf vns von nihte,
der ist vnser vater gûter.
120 nv bite wir sine mûter
daz si vns wol behv̊te
mit ir tȯseutfalten gûte.

Der briester heizzet
      Jeronimus,
der im gezimbert hat daz hovs
125 mit disem bûche hin ze got.
swaz Matheus der frone bot
den ebreyschen vor saget,
dirre herre dez niht verdaget
in der lateine.
130 von dem æwigen scheine
er chunde vil wol chosen,
von der lylien vñ der rosen,
diu den dorn niht enhat.
nv wolde ich ir rat
135 mit ir helfe sûchen,
ob si des wolt gerûchen,
daz ich in tevscher rede
daz pûch prehte her zewêge,
daz ez alle mugen lesen
140 die gotes chint wellen wesen
vñ auch mugen schowen
phaffen, layen, vrowen

wie daz kint die mûter chos
div den magtv̊m nie verlos,
145 noch nimmer mak verliesen.
wir mugen wol kyesen,
wie genedik· si sey
der daz kint sitzet bey
daz lêwe vñ lamp ist,
150 ob allen dingen oberist,
bede læwen vñ tȯt,
herre, fleisch vñ prȯt,

D

uon der vinster schulen ȯch wir
      ersten
ze dem ewigem liehte:
got geschuf uns uon niehte, 120
der ist unser vater guter.
nv bittet sine mûter
daz sie uns hie behv̊te
mit ir tvsentvaltiger gv̊te.

Der leræ̂re heizet   125
      Jeronimus,
der im gezimbert hat ein hus
148, 35 mit disem buche hin ze got.
swaz Matheus der frone bot
ebreisken livten uorsaget,
dirre herre des niht verdaget 130
in der rehten latine.
von dem ewigem urschine
er chunde wole chosen,
uon der lilien vnt uon der rosen,
div der dorne nien hat.   135
nv wolt ovch ich den ir rat
40 vnt ir helfe suchen,
obe si des wolte ruchen,
daz ich mit dvtisker rede
daz buch bræhte her ze wege, 140
daz sie iz alle musen lesen
die gotes kint wellent wesen,
v̄ ovch megen schowen,
die laigen vnt die frowen,
149, 1 smechen vnd eruinden   145
von dem frone kinde,
daz im die muter erchose
div ir magetum nie uerlose
vnt niemer mak verliesen.
an der megen wir wol chiesen, 150
wie rehte gnædich sie si
der daz chint sitzet bi
5 daz bediv lev vnt lamb ist,
ob allen dingen zeoberist,
bediv leben vnt tot,   155
hirt vnt lebentigez brot,

---

122 tȯsētfalte   130 æwige   148, 39 dorne nien] *durch Flecken fast unleserlich, aber sicher nicht* danne eren *H.*

tou unde bluome,
gelt unde ruowe, (120)
wênic unde michel,
160 vor allen sunden sicher,
beidiu vater unde sun,
einvalt unt wîstuom,
grôz unde cleine: (125)
daz ist er alterseine
165 der uns ze nôtdurfte erschein.
er nam hie fleisch unde bein,
sîn snêwîziu sêle
fuor in die phalnzen hêre (130)
⟨· · · · · · · · · · · · · · · ·
170 · · · · · · · · · · · · · · · · · ·⟩
diu chetene ist zebrochen,
gotes ande errochen,
dâ uns der tievil mit bant:
des loben wir den heilant.
175 sîn gezelt stuont in der sunnen, (135)
besigelet ist der brunne,
ungebrâchôt ist ir anger,
ir chorder hât ertôtet den slangen.

Den nît wil ich verdingen
180 unze ich fur bringe (140)
disiu seltsâniu wort:
swaz Mathêus schreip dort
den êbraischen liuten,
daz wil ich iu ze diute
185 sagen unde schrîben, (145)
mannen unde wîben
mit der volleiste
des heiligen geistes.
ich weiz des tieveles strît
190 diche winthalsen gît, (150)
bôsez nîtbechen,
eitergez hechen
der unwirdischen diet,
daz si schelten diu liet,
195 diu in wîslîcher ahte (155)
vergelten niemen mahte,

---

160 von 65 not dufte 69 f. *ich vermute etwa* sante Marîen, dâ
er wolte erschînen, *Michels schlägt vor* sant Marîen wambe: diu frîet uns
von der schande 72 hande 77 vngebrachet 84 iu] hie

A

D

tov vnde blůme,
gelt vnde rûwe,
wenich vnt michel,
uor allen sunden sicher,   *160*

vater vnde svn,
aynvalt vn̄ weistum,
155 groz vnde chleine   *149,10*
ist er alterseine,
der vns ze notdurfte erschein.
er nam hie fleisch vn̄ payn,
sin sneweizze sæle
160 fůr in die phalzen hêre
sande Marien:
die wold vns wol freyen
von den schæmelichen iochen.
div cheten ist zebrochen
165 da vns der tievel mit pant:
des lobe wir den hailant. Amen.

vater unser, gotes sun,
einvalte vnde wîstum,
groz vnt chleine:
daz ist er alterseine
der uns in noten erschêin.   *165*
er nam hie fleish vnde bein,
vnt die reinen menniskeit
hohet er mit der gotheit
von der erde hin ze himele
an sines uaters gesidele.   *170*
do wart div hel*l*e zebrochen
v̄ wrden wir errochen
15 an dem tievil der uns bant:
des loben wir den heilant.
sin gezelt stůnt in der sunne, *175*
besigelt ist der brunne,
ungebrachot ist der anger,
ir chorder hat ertotet den
           slangen.

Den haz ich hie verdinge
vn̄ neit vntz ich furbringe
dise sæligen wort:
170 waz Matheus schreib dort
den ebrayschen levten,
daz wil ich iv bedevten,
sagen vn̄ schreiben
mannen vn̄ weiben
175 mit gotes volleist
vn̄ dem heiligen geist.

Den nit wil ich uerdingen
untze ich fure bringe   *180*
disiv seltsænen wort:
swaz Matheus schreib dort
20 den ebreischen liuten,
daz wil ich iv bediv̂ten

mit der helfe v̄ uolleiste   *185*
des heiligen geistes.
ich weiz wol des tievels strit
diche wanthalsen git,
bosez nitbechen
vnt eitirgez hechen   *190*
der unuerwizze*nen* diet,
daz si schelten div liet,
25 div in wîslîcher ahte
vergelten niemen mæhte,

149, 14 hele   *149, 24* unuerwizzene

     mit grôzem guote widerwegen.

     ich wâne den fluoch fur den segen
     ⟨si⟩ von got enphâhent,
200 die sich daran vergâhent.   (160)
     swer ditze liet bespreche,
     Mathêus muoz ez rechen,
     der ⟨ez⟩ zem êristen schreip
     unt den irretuom vertreip,
205 den Manichêi junger sazte,   (165)
     dô er die zungen wazte
     in uppigem chôse.
     doch ne wolte die rede bôse
     diu christenheit enphâhen,
210 dô si die luge sâhen.   (170)
     der junger hiez Leuciô
     unt wart verworfen alsô
     daz sîn rede wart begraben,
     unt si niemen getar gesagen,
215 wan si mit durren zwîgen stât,   (175)
     unt si der wurze niene hât.
     Mathêus ewangeliste
     der nam im lange friste,
     unz er ez vil rehte gar erfuor,
220 daz weder mos noch muor   (180)
     sîniu wort nemac getruoben.
     des lât ouch iuch genuogen
     unt sant Jeronimi lêre!
     die mugen iu wol gehelfen an der sêle.

225   **B**î den alten zîten   (185)
     got enwas niht chundic wîten:
     notus in Judêâ,
     fremde was er anderswâ.
     dô was der heidenschefte vil,
230 die des tieveles spil   (190)
     an den abgoten begiengen,
     des ouch si schaden geviengen
     an dem lîbe unt an der sêle.

---

198 ih wæne si, *vgl. § 69 c*   201 ditze liet] dich   5 Amachei
9 niht enphahen, *vgl. § 60 c*   11 heiz   12 was   13 betragen   23 sce
26 chudech   27 notus *Sch.*] not⁵, *vgl. Psalm 75, 2 L.*   33 anme

A

D

noh mit grozem gůte wîder *195*
    wegen.
die wane ich den flûch fvr
    den segen
uone got enpfahent,
die sich daran uergahent.

swer ditz liet verspreche,   swer ditze liet bespreche,

Matheus mv̊z ez rechen,   sænt Matheus mv̊z ez rechen, *200*

der ez zem ersten schreip   *149,30* der ez zem ersten schreib

180 vn̄ den irsal vertreip.   unt den irretûm vertreib,

den Manichei ivnger satzte,
do er sine zunge watzte
in upigez chose.   *205*
doh wolt die rede bose
div christenheit niht enpfahen,
do sie die luge sahen.
der ivnger hiez Leucio
vnt wart uerworfen also   *210*
35 daz sin rede ist begraben,
vnt sie nîemen getar sagen,
wan si mit durren zwien stat,
nv si der wrze nien hat.

Matheus ewangeliste   Matheus der ewangeliste   *215*

der nam im lange friste,   nam im so lange friste,

vnz er sich vil rehte erfůr,   untze er ez vil rehte gar erfv̊re,

daz weder mos noch můr   daz weder mos noh mv̊re

185 sine wort mak getrv̊ben: siniv worte en mach getruben:

des vns wol sol genv̊gen   des lat ȯch ivh genůgen   *220*

an sant Jeronimi lære!   *40* vnt sant Jeronimi lere!

der gerůche wenden vnser sære.   die mugen iv gehelfen an der sele.

in dem gotes namen
190 daz geschehe, amen.

Bey den alten zeiten   **B**i den selben citen

was got niht chunt weiten,   got enwas niht chundich witen,

niwer in Jvdea: wan eine erchant in Judea: *225*

fromde was er anderswa.   fremide was er anderswa.

195 do was der heidenschaft so vil,   do was der heidenschefte vil,

die des tievels spil   die des tieueles spil

an den apgoten begiengen,   an den abgoten begiengen,

des si auch schaden enphiengen   des ovh sie scaden geviengen *230*

an dem leibe vn̄ an der sæle.   *150,1* an dem libe vnt an der sele.

---

188 wende   *190* geschehe   *198* schade   *150,1* am

do behielt die gotes lêre
235 diu israhêlische diet,   (195)
als in Moyses geriet
unt ir vater Abraham;
dem wâren si gehôrsam,
Ysaac unt Jacôbe,
240 der in des himeles hôhe   (200)
eine leitern gesach,
dâ in sîn schephâre sprach
facie ad faciem:
wie mahte ez im baz ergên?
245 dô er den engel gevie,   (205)
den er des morgens niht verlie
unz er in gesegenôte,
diu huf im dorrôte
dâ in der engel druhte,
250 hin nâher er sie ruhte.   (210)
zeinem urchunde
hamlîchen dô begunde
der heilige patriarche.
des wunderôte starche
255 allez sîn geslahte,   (215)
als ez vil wol mahte;
si wurden des gefrouwet,
daz er was beschouwet
von gotes anebliche.
260 si suochten venie diche   (220)
gen den himelischen chôren.
hie muget ir ⟨wol diu grôzen⟩ wunder hôren.

Uz dem selben chunne
was ein kint ersprungen,
265 ein man geborn in dise werlt: (225)
got selbe hête im erwelt
sînen gedanc unt sînen sin:
geheizen was er Joachim,
unde was der besten ein
270 den diu sunne ie beschein.   (230)
sîn einvalte was sô grôz
daz ⟨er⟩ sîn sît vil wol genôz
vor got unt vor den liuten.

---

235 israhelitesce 41 lateren gasah 42 gesprah 50 er] ir 52 ham-
lichen *richtig?* 54 do starche 57 wrdes 62 mǔgent *Ergänzung*

A

200 do behielt die gotes lære
div israhelische diet,
als in Moyses geriet
vñ ir vater Abraham;
dem waren si gehorsam,
205 Ysaac vñ Jacobe,
der in des himels hoher æ
ein leitern gesach,
vñ in sin schêpher sach
facie ad faciem:
210 wie moht ez im baz ergen?
do er den engel gevie,
den er des morgens niht verlie
vnz er in gesegenot,
div huf wont im niht bey genot,
215 do in der engel drukte,
hin naher er sich rukte.
ze einem vrchunde
hinchen er begunde
der heilige patriarch.
220 des wundert vil starch
alles sin geslæhte,
als ez von schulden tûn mohte.
si wurden des gefrevt,
daz er wart beschout
225 von gotes anplike:
si sůchten venige dike
gen den himelchôren.
hie mvgt ir wol wunder horen.

Ouz dem chunne ziersam
230 wart ein chint lobesam
in dise werlt geborn:
got selbe het im erchorn
sin gedanch vñ sinen sin:
geheizzen wart er Joachim,
235 der waz der besten ayn
den div svnne ie beschein.
sin gûte waz so groz
daz er sin wol genoz
vor got vñ vor den levten.

D

do behielt die gotes e
div israheliske diet,
als in Moyses geriet
vnde ir vater Habraham;   235
dem waren sie gehorsam,
Ysaac vnd Jacob danah,
der hin ze himele sah
150,5 ein leiter uon der erde gerihte,
da got ze siner gesihte   240
selbe wider in sprah.
wnders im ŏh mere gescah:
do er den engel gevie
unt in des morgens nîen lîe
untze er in gesegenot,   245
div huf im dorrot
da in der engel druhte,
hin naher er sie geruhte.
10 ze einem urchunde
hinchen do begunde   250
der heilige patriarche.
des wnderot starche
allez sin geslæhte,
als ez vil wol mahte.
sie wrden des gefrŏwet,   255
daz er was bescôwet
uon gotes anblike:
si suhten uenie dicke
15 gegen den himelisgen choren.
hie muget ir wnder horen.   260

Vz demselben chunne
was ein kint ersprungen,
ein man in dise werlte geborn:
got selbe het im erchorn
sin gedanche v̄ sinen sin: 265
geheizen was er Joachim,
v̄ was der besten eine
den div sunne ie uberschêin.
20 sin einvalte was so groz
daz er sin uon rehte gnoz   270
uor got und vor den lîuten.

---

nach Sch.   271 … roz bis 357 geistlich die Breslauer Fragmente C ꞏ V.
72 gonoz F   73 der F

200 div   214 hilf   226 venig   233 gedanch!

Joachim chiut *ze diute*
275 . . . .
sô dâ gescr . . . .   (235)
. . . . ge,

liehtvaz . . . .
. . . .
280 . . . ner heilike . . .
. . . .
. . . den engelen . . . . .
. . . .
. . . spile wolde . . . . . .   (240)
285 . . . .
. . . . burde
und . . . .
. . . lriches . . . .
. . . .

290 . . . eruoche uns . . . . . .
. . . .
. . ist aller kûsheit ein gimme.   (245)

. . . .
. . . .
295 . . . .
. . . . . t er arbeite
. . . .
. . . . . . r sank und . . .
. . . .
300 . . . . . niuwen me . . . . .
. . . .
. . . . sten tet er . . . . .
. . . .
. . . . er also scho . . .   (250)
305 . . . .
. . . . uch sine spise.
. . . .
. . . . blikte er under . . .
. . . .
310 . . . . . . er sich erbar . . .
. . . .
. . . der ⟨ze⟩ gotes hûsen

---

274 chût F *bricht ab*   78 licht was   90 . . erucht   96 erweit
302 . . stun   10 d'bar . . .

A

240 Joachim sprichet ze bedeuten
    preparatio domini,
    swa ez geschriben sey:
    daz sprichet vnsers herren beraitunge,

    liehtvaz der sunne,
(245)

    wan er der megede vater wart, 150, 25
    div den engeln waz so zart
    daz si bey den plůmen
250 mit spile wolden růben,
    vnz si můter wurde
    der gotlichen burde,
    vn̄ auch mit æren solde sin
    des himilreiches turlin •
255 vn̄ div wol gereiniget
              chamere:
    div gerůche vns zesamene
    fur ir sun bringen,
    si ist aller æren gimme.

    Joachym der gotes man,
260 der vil æren gewan,
    in siner chintheit
    leit er arebeit.
    do er in der iugent waz,
    wie gerne er sank vn̄ las
265 von sinem schephere;
    die vil starken mære
    v̊bet er in der alten æ,
    mit vasten tet er im wæ.
    menschliche chrankheit
270 er gedultechlichen lait
    in einer senften weise.
    er tailte sine speise
    vn̄ alle sine habe endriv
    (ze himel plikte er vnder dev):
275 ein teil gab er den armen
    (die liez er sich erbarmen),
    witeben vn̄ waisen
    vn̄ ze gotshousern;

D

Joachim chîvt ze dîvte
preparatio domini,
so wâne ich da gescriben si:
daz kivt unsers herren   275
    garewnge.

ein liehtvaz dem sunne
scholt ôh werden bereit
vz siner heilikeit,
wand er der magede vater wart,
div den engelen was so zart   280
daz sie bi den blůmen
wolte beliben vnde růwen,
untze sie muter wrde
der gotlichen bûrde,
vnd ôh mit eren mæhte sin   285
des himelriches tûrlin,
daz den ubeln můz gespart   30
    wesen,
den offen die da sculen genesen
an der sele von rêinem můt:
die vindent si gnadich   290
    vnde gut.

    Joachim der gotes man
eren gnuch er gewan,
in siner chintheit
leid er doh arbeit.
die wile er in ivgent was,   295
gerner sanch vnd las
von sinem schephære   35
div starchen alten mære.
er ûbet sich harte in der e,
mit uasten tet er im wê.   300
sin mennislichen brode
die dewanger also schone
in einer guten wise.
er teilet ôh sin spise
und alle sin richeit endriv   305
(ze himele blikter under div):
ein teil gab er den armen,   40
(die liez er sih erbarmen,
bediv witewen v̄ weisen),
daz ander ze gotes husen,   310

---

245 f. ergänzt F. nach D   248 dem engel   249 l. dem plůmen
255 cham⁵   271 senfte

. . . .
. . . . gen.   (255)
315 ze dem almuosen w . . . .
. . . .
ze sinem selb . . . . . .
. . . .
. . . . se habeten
320 d . . . .
. . . . elliu jâr   (260)
sw . . . .
. . . . niht liegen,
. . . .
325 . . . le lûteret e . . . .
. . . .
gab im got . . . .
. . . . regen,   (265)
daz . . . .
330 . . . . began,
und . . . .
. . . . sich verlie.
v . . . .   (270)
. . . . was sin vil . . .
335 . . . .
. . . .
. . . .
. . . . tic was.
z . . . .
340 . . . . mohte sic . . . .

A ls er wa . . . . . .   (275)
. . . . rank,
er en . . . .
. . . . getelôse.
345 . . . .
. . . . sît noch ê
. . . .
. . . . heln hêt er . . . .   (280)
. . . .
350 . . . er damite . . . . . .
. . . .
. . . . . . ne was daz . . .

---

315 zu den   17 zu sime   19 hetten   21 alle   22 w   27 gab
vn   41 C *reimte* alt : spranc, *was schwerlich echt ist, vgl. § 51 b; vielleicht*
alt : bart, *vgl.* erwelt : vert *1589*   44 gettelosen   46 sint   48 hat

A

zů dem almůsen waz im ger:
280 daz dritail daz behielt er,

daz er die speise hete
die weile er lebte.
Die spende begienk er alle iar.
swaz er sprach daz waz war.

285 Sin sæle levtert er damit.
mit so heiligem sit
gab im got den sinen segen,
himeltov vn̄ regen,
daz er genuhtsam gewan
290 swaz er bowen ie began,
vn̄ vaste fur sich gie.

got verlæh im vil vihe,
daz er chovme vant die waide
ǒf dem velde vn̄ ǒf der heide,
295 bede hev vn̄ gras,
dez ez notdurftik waz.
zů dem het er heil so groz
daz nieman des waz sin genoz.

Do er zweinzik iar alt wart
300 vn̄ im chǒme ensprank sin part,
er wolde sich verbosen
mit denheiner getlosen:
er nam ein chint ze siner æ,
(ich wæn ouch seit noch æ
305 chevscher geburt nie wart geborn)
die er ze mahel het erchorn
ovz Dauides geslæhte,
daz er da mitte mohte
behalten sel vn̄ leip.
310 also schone waz sin weip

D

151,1 den ze râte v̄ ze minne
die got dienten dar inne.
ze dem almusen was ime ger:
daz dritteil behielt er
ze sin selbes tische   315
vnt sinem hiwische,
daz si der uon spise habeten
die wile daz si lebeten.
5 die spende treib er elliu iare.
swaz er geredet daz was ware: 320
erne wolte niht liegen,
neheinen sinen genoz betriegen.
sin sele luterot er damite.
uon so heiliclichem site
gab im got sinen segen,   325
himeltov und regen,
daz ez michel genuht gewan
swaz er buwen began.
10 an swiv sich der herre uerlîe,
mit heil ez fur sih gîe   330
v̄ ergab im sæliclîche.
er was also vihe rîche
daz er chume vant die weide
an dem velde v̄ an der heide

dem chorter also grozen: 335
zu ime en maht sih niemen
          genozen.

15   Als er zweinzic iar alte wart
unt im chume erspranch der bart,
erne wolte sih niht uerbosen
mit deheiner getlose: 340
er nam ein kint ze siner e:
iane wane ich sit noh e
chivsker brût ie wart geborn.
die gemahelen het er im erchorn
20 uz Dauidis geslæhte,   345
daz er damit mæhte
behalten sele vnde lip.
also schône was daz wip

---

293 div   *305* chevser   *151, 11* ergab!

2*

．．．．．．．．．．．．．．
．．．．．．．． gesâhen.

355   ir ．．．．．．．．．．．．．
      ．．．．．．．．．． gir.   (285)
      geistlich ．．．．．．．．
      ．．．．．．．．．． si † gâben
      unt ir opher vil gereite
360   in ir chintheite
      mit frôlîcher gebârde   (290)
      durch ir schephâre.
      sin chunde niht gerasten:
      wachen unde vasten
365   des phlac si âne mâze.
      ir guoten umbesâzen   (295)
      die lobeten den got
      der himel unt erde gebôt
      unt den mergriez zelt,
370   daz er im die hête erwelt
      ze sînem dieniste.   (300)
      si bâten daz er si friste
      ze einer bezzerunge
      den alten unt den jungen,
375   daz si bilde nâmen,
      sô si ane sâhen   (305)
      die manigen guottâte
      die si gefrumet hâte.
      wol frouwete sich Joachim:
380   si truogen niht nîdes under in,
      sie lebeten wunneclîche ensamt.   (310)

      diu frouwe was Anna genant;
      Anna daz chiut graciâ:
      michel ．．．．．．．．

---

358 si *bis* michele 384 C‘I   gaben *sicher nicht richtig: es ist nur*
von Anna die Rede, und C setzt auch 363. 65. 78 *den Plural für den*
Singular. Reimte ursprünglich etwa geistlîchez leben si habete ir almuosen
si gebete? *Schwaches* geben *ist allerdings nicht belegt*   63 si enkonden
65 phlagen   70 die] hie   71 d:nste   72 si!   73 bezerungē   78 hetten
79 vreute   81 wunnenclichen   83 sprichet   84 michele

A

daz ir alle die holt waren
die sey an gesahen.

ir genade cherten si zv̊ ir
ane falsche gir.
315 si het geistlich leben
vn̄ begunde almv̊sen geben
vnde ir opher vil bereit
in ir chintheit
mit frôlicher gebêre
320 durich ir schæpfere.
si chunde niht gerasten:
wachen vn̄ vasten
chunde si sich niht mazzen.
ir gûten vmbesæzzen
325 die lobten alle got
der himel vn̄ ærde gebot
vn̄ der den mergriez zelt,
daz er sey im het erwelt

wol ze pezzeruugen
330 den alten vn̄ den iungen.

Des frevt sich Joachim;
si trûgen niht neides vnder in,
si lepten lieplich bedesamp.

div vrowe waz Anna genant;
335 Anna daz sprichet gracia:
michel genade waz al da,
wan si von ir samen
daz tiwer wûcher namen:
si mûsten die chvniginnen

340 geberen vn̄ gewinnen,
div den himel hat entslozzen,
der alle werlt hat genozzen.

Der die vrowen Annam gebar,
der furste der hiez Ysachar:

D

daz ir alle die si ansahen
der eren vnt der sælden iahen, 350
v̄ sie o̊vh minnende waren
uon ir tugentlichen gebæren.
ir liebe cherten sie zu ir
ane wentliche gire.
151, 25 si hete reinez leben 355
v̄ begunde groz almûsen geben
vnd ir opfer vil gereite
in ir ivgent ioh der chintheite
mit vil frôderichen mût,
als der got meinet gerne tvt. 360
si chunde niht gerasten
von wachen unde uon vasten,
wan des pfleget sie ane maze.
ir guten umbesæzen
30 die lobeten den got 365
der himel vnt erde gebot
vnd die mergriezen zelt,
daz er im die het erwelet
ze sine selbez eren,
vnt baten an ir gemeren 370
sin lop zv̊ bezzerunge
den alten v̄ den iungen,
daz sie bildes da bequæmen
v̄ die suzen lere næmen
35 uon uil maniger gûttæte, 375
die sie gefrumet hæte.
wol frôet sih do Joachim
vnd sin liebiv frô mit im,
wan sie lebeten wnnechliche
ensamte.
Anna was si zerehte genante; 380
Anna daz chivt gracia:
michel gnade div was da,
40 wand uon in der wcher bequam
der frôen Euen schulde benam,
vnd sie die maget scolten 385
gebern,
die got selbe nien mag entwern
deheiner bete die sie an in getvt.
nu dingen ir gnaden, daz ist
uns gv̊t.

Der frôen Annam gebar,
der furste hiez Ysachar: 390

        si wâren verfluochet in der ê
        die an ir geburte   (315)
        gesegenet niene wurten.
405   eines tages dô si quâmen
        unt daz gotes wort vernâmen
        in templo dominî,
        Joachim der stuont dâ bî,   (320)
        dâ sich die êwarten
410   zu dem opher garten
        unt nâch ir gwonheite
        diu schâf dar fur gereiten,
        lamp unt diu rôten rinder.   (325)
        Joachim stuont dar under
415   sam diu einvalte tûbe:
        sîne frasûme
        die wolte er dâ ervollen,
        stiften gotes willen.   (330)
        er hête ophers genuoc,
420   daz im sîn hîwisch dar truoc:
        daz wolte er dâ verbrennen,
        den rouch ze himele senden
        fur diu gotes ougen.   (335)
        grôz was sîn geloube.
425   dô was ie nît als ouch nû:
        ein scriba spranc dar zuo,
        Ruben der êwarte;
        den herren rafster harte   (340)
        unt stoute in alsô sêre;
430   er sprach: ‘du ne scholt nie mêre

---

     402 *bis* den h‘ren 428 C⁴ II   4 nie   wurden   5 komen   10 karten
11 .. wonehaite *bis* dvne 694 F 142—424   12 da C   geriten F   13 vnd
to : e C   14 dˢ stunt C   15 als di wandernde C   16 siner F   vˢsume C
17 da *fehlt* C   20 daz man im dar getruk C   21 do C   25 da F
ie nit] er niht C   ouch] *fehlt* C   26 sprach C, *vgl. W. s. 172*   27 rubyn

A

345 si waz sin liebe ⟨tohter⟩.
loben wol moht er
die gotes ordenunge,
daz er ir ie *gew*unne.
daz waren chlegeliche dink,

350 daz div vrowe vnt der iungelink
zwainzik iar ensamt waren
daz ⟨si⟩ kinde niht gebaren.
daz tet in inrechlichen wǣ:
si waren verfluchet in der ǣ
355 die an ir geburd*e*
gesegenet niht enwurden.
Eines tages do si quamen
vn̄ daz gotes wort vernamen
in templo domini,
360 Joachym stv̊nt da bey,
da sich die ǣwarten
zv̊ dem opfer garten,
vn̄ nach ir gewonheiten
do schv̊f man dar bereiten
365 lamp vn̄ rȯte rinder.
Joachim stv̊nt dar vnder
sam die ainvalde tonbe:
sin versoumunge
wold er erfullen
370 vn̄ stiften gotes willen.
er het da des opfers genv̊k,
daz er dar trv̊k:
daz wold er verbrennen,
den rouch ze himel senden
375 fur die gotes augen.
groz waz sin gelaub*e*.
ǣz waz do neit als auch nv:
ein schreiber sprach da zv̊,
Rvben der ǣwarte;
380 den herren refste er harte
vn̄ strafte in harte ser;
er sprach: ,dv solt niemer

D

sie was sin liebiv tohter.
wol non herzen loben mohter
152, 5 die gotes ordinunge,
daz er ein solih kint gewnne.
iedoh waren ez chlagelichiv 395
dinch,
daz div frôwe vnt der iungelinch
zeweinzich iâr ensamet waren
daz si kindes niht gebaren.
daz tet in inneclichen we,
wan sie hete uerfluchet div e, 400
10 di vngesegent also ersturben
daz si erben niht erwrben.
Eines tages do sie chamen
vnd daz gotes wort uernamen
in dem templo domini, 405
Joachim der stunt dabi,
da sih die ewarten
zu dem opher garten
un̄ nah ir gewonhêite
heten die schaf darfur gereite, 410
15 lember vnd div roten rinder.
Joachim der stv̊nt dar under
sam div einvalte tube,
daz er da sin uersume
eruolte vnd o̊h siniv leit 415
got in dem herzen chleite.
er hete opfers gnuch,
daz im sin hiwish dar truch:
daz wolt er da uerbrennen,
den rȯch ze himele senden 420
20 fur div gotis o̊gen.
grozen habeter glȯben.
do was ie nit als o̊h nv:
ein scriba der trat darzu,
Ruben der ewarte; 425
den herren rafster harte
und bestunt in also sere;
er sprah: ,dv enscolt nien mere

---

der eruarte C 28 h'ren C *bricht ab* harte] starche F, *s. W. s. 167*
30 nie] niht F

348 begunne *152,13* hete gewnne *353* in! *355* geburdē
152,13 ewarten! *376* gelauben

zu unserem opher gân.
wir haben uns alle wol enstân:
got hât dich sô verfluochet   (345)
daz er niht enruochet
435 deheines wuochers von dir.
der dîner fravel ist sô vil:
du muost dich sundern hinnen;
wir ne wellen niht gewinnen   (350)
susgetânen gesellen;
440 wir ne mugen ouch dich zu den besten niht gezellen.'

Von solhem itewîze
mit sînen handen wîzen
swanc er alsô tougen   (355)
die zahere von den ougen.
445 ez dûhte in michel schande,
doch ne was im niht sô ande
daz er daz selbe schelten
mit ubele wolte gelten.   (360)
erne wolte ouch niht mêre
450 wider in sîn hûs. chêren
unt wolte sich vor leide
von sînem wîbe scheiden,
von sîner wunneclicher chonen.   (365)
in einer wuoste wolt er wonen
455 von den liuten verre:
dar hiez ouch im der herre
al sîn chorter trîben,
unt wolte dâ belîben.   (370)
des vihewuochers wolt er leben,
460 zehenten unt almuosen geben
michel baz danne ê,
vil veste wesen an siner ê,
an nihte sich versûmen,   (375)
clagen unde chûmern
465 in der einôde
mennischlicher brôde,
daz diu werlt anders niht enist
wan stuppe unde mist   (380)

---

431 vnserme F   33 hat dih got F, *das ursprüngliche?*   35 en
heines F   39 susgetane F   41 solichem F   46 niht] nie F   ande
bis ein 628 C² 1—183, *bis* ir 652 C⁴ III   49 nit F   53 cronen C
55 in einer wûste (wu : tunge C) verre CF   56 dar] do C   im] in C

A

ze vnserm opfer gan.
wir han vns alle wol verstan:
385 got hat dich so verflûchet   152, 25
daz er niht gerûchet
dencheines wûchers von dir.
diner frevel ist ze vil:
dv mûst dich sundren hinnen,
390 wan wir niht gewinnen
dich ze einem solhen gesellen,
noch wellen da mit die æ niht
vellen.'

Uon solhen iteweizzeu
mit sinen handen weizzen
395 swank er ab so tougen
die trehen von den augen.
ez douht in ein michel schande,
doch waz im niht so ande
daz er daz selbe schelten
400 mit vbele wolde gelten:
da von sin gank, sin chere
wart in daz hous niemere,
vñ wolde sich vor leide
von sinem weibe schaiden,
405 von siner wunnechlichen chonen.
in einer wûste wolde er wonen
von den levten verre:
dar hiez im ouch der herre
al sin vihe treiben,
410 vnde wande da beleiben.
Des vihe wûchers wolde er leben,
zehenden vñ almusen geben
michel paz dan æ,
vil vester an siner æ,
415 an nihte versovmen sich;   153, 1
mit chlage vñ vil chummerlich
wolde er sein in der einode
mit menschlicher blode.

D

zu unserem opfer gan.
wir haben uns alle wol enstan: 430
got hat dih so uerfluchet
daz er nien geruochet
deheines ŵchers uon dir.
din fræuel misseuellet mir:
du must dich svndern hinnen; 435
wir newellen niht gewinnen
susgetanen gesellen;
wir megen ŏh dih ze den besten
niht gecellen.'

Uon solheu itewizen
30 mit siuen handen wizen   440
swanger also tŏgen
die zaher uon den ŏgen.
ez duht in michel schande
vnt iedoh was im niht so ande
daz er dazselbe schelten   445
mit ubele wolte gelten.
erne wolt ŏh niht mere
wider in sin hus cheren
35 vnde wolt sih vor leide
uon sine*m* wibe scheiden,   450
uon siner wnneklichen chonen;
in einer ŵste gedaht er wonen
hin dan uon den livten uerre:
dar hiez ŏh im der herre
allez sin chorter triben,   455
als er da gert beliben.
40 des vihewchers wolt er da leben,
zehenten v̄ almusen geben
michels baz denne e,
uil veste wesen an siner e,   460
got sinen chumber da chunden
v̄ sin angest zallen stŭnden,
chlagen ŏh menniskliche brode
in der wilden einode,
daz diu werlt anders niht enist 465
wan stuppe vñ mist

57 alliz sin vihe dar triben C   59 vihes wchers F   60 unt *fehlt* F
61 michels C, *vgl. 3627*   63 vorsumen F   64 chmeren F, kummeren C
65 *f.* in der mensclichen brod C   66 menneclicher F   67 niht anders
ist F   68 wanne gestuppe C

152,26 din din   *392* div   *152,35* siueu   *410 kein* er!

unt ein schate der gar verswindet,
470 sô sich diu sêle enbindet
von menneschlîcher zarge:
so zergêt ouch alliu froude mit arge.

Als frouwe Anna daz vernam,   (385)
daz Joachim der ir man
475 sô sêre was geleidigôt,
dô wâre ir lieber der tôt.
daz vil wunnecliche wîp
harte cholte si den lîp: (390)
daz er ir hête entwichen,
480 des was ir clage michel,
unt sô verre was gevarn.
si ne trûwete niht bewarn
ir hîwisch dâheime.   (395)
dar umbe was ir leide,

485 daz si ûf der erde
witewe scholte werden
bi lebendigem manne.

si muoste erbleichen danne,   (400)
ir schône wart verderbet,
490 al ir froude wart ersterbet.
die hende huop si hôhe
gen der phalnze frône,
gen dem himelrîche;   (405)
si sprach vil clagelîche:
495 'owî gewaltiger got,
mîne vil inneclîchen nôt
ruoche dû bedenken.

---

469 schade C, scahte F vᵂwindet C   71 menschelicher C, mennes-
chlcher F   72 zergent C ælliu F, alle C   .../wen (so!) C   mit] mir F
74 der *fehlt* C   78 herte hilt C   chelte sie ir F   79 eintwichen F
80 daz C   82 si trŭt C   84 vil leide C   85 uffe C *und öfter* erden C

A

D

unt ein schate der gar uerswindet,
so sih div sele enbindet
153,5 uon mennesklicher **zarge**:
so zergat ŏh elliv frŏde mit *470*
arge,
v̄ elliv werltliebe da gelit,
so daz leben den lip begit.

Als vrowe Anna daz vernam,
420 daz Joachim der ir man
so sere waz geleidegot,
si were gewesen lieber tot.
daz vil minnechliche weip
harte quelte si ir leip:
425 daz er ir wolde gesweichen,
daz chlagte si herzechlichen,

Als frŏe Anna daz ervant,
daz Joachim der ir man genant
so sere was geleidigot, *475*
do ware ir lieber der tot.
daz uil wnnecliche wip
harte cholte sie den lip:
10 daz er ir hete entwichen,
des was ir chlage michel, *480*
vnt so uerre hin was geuarn.
sie entruwot niht bewarn
ir hiwish dahêime.
darumbe saz si mit leide
v̄ weinet herzecliche, *485*
daz sie got so chumberriche
hete geschaffen vnde gesat
an der unsæligen stat,
15 daz sie bi so reinem man
nie herzeliep mit kinde gewan, *490*
vnt dazu bi im lebentigen
daz si witewe solt geligen:
daz waren sorgen ungefüge,
die nehein lip samfte truge.
do muse erbleichen danne *495*
div schone v̄ div gute frŏe Anne.
ir liehtiv varwe uerdarp,
al ir frŏde erstarp.

daz si ouf der ærden
witebe solde werden
bey lebindegem manne.

430 si mŭste erblaichen danne,
ir schŏne wart verterbet,
alle ir frevde ersterbet.
ir hende hŭb si schone
zṽ der pfalzen frone,
435 zv dem himelriche;
si sprach vil chlegelich:
,awe gewalteger got,
min vil inrechliche not
gerŭche dv bedenken.

20 ir hende hub sie hinz im genôte
der uns daz leben gebot; *500*

si sprah vil chlageliche:
,owi got der gnadige v̄ der riche,
du ruche mih arme bedenchen.

---

86 scholde witebe C 87*f.* man : dan C 88 mṽze F 90 alle C, elliv F
ersterbet] d'schreket, *danach noch ein Vers:* ir iam' wart d'wek : t C
92*f.* gegen F, gein C 92 phabize C 94 tugentliche C 95 ouwe du C
97 geruche .. zu bekennen C

jane mac ich niht gewenken,   (410)
    ich ne muoze lîden swaz du wil.
500 ja hân ich angeste vil.
    wâ maht ich reste vinden,
    dô dû mir an den chinden
    neheine froude gâbe,   (415)
    daz dû mir dô benâme
505 mînen karelen alsô guoten
    mit solhem ungemuote!

    swaz du wil daz muoz ergên:
    die tôten heizestu ûf stên,   (420)
    die armen machestu rîche,
510 in selben ungelîche,
    die rîchen lâstu vallen:
    des muozen si dir alle
    grôzer meisterschefte jehen.   (425)

    swar dîn ouge geruochet sehen,
515 dâ ist gnâdicheite mêr
    denne griezes in dem mer,
    dîner guote manicvalde
    mêre denne ze walde   (430)
    iemer zwîger muge sîn.
520 êwigez urschîn,
    gezalt hâstu die sternen.
    si mugen dir dienen gerne
    die du wil beruochen.   (435)
    nu ledige mich von dem fluoche
525 der mich hât erderret,
    mine wambe besperret:
    die scholtu herre entsliezen,
    daz ich dîner heilicheite genieze.’   (440)

    Anna suochte ir venige
530 mit zaheren alsô manigen,

---

498 io CF   99 ich ne muoze] :: h mûz C, *dazu W. s. 166, was ich nicht mehr aufrecht erhalte*   wilt C   500 io hab ich angst C   1 raste C   3 keine vreude nie gegebe C   4 do *fehlt* C   5 minen karelen] hʳre C   gute C   6 sulchem C, solihem F   8f. l. heizest, machest? *vgl.* § 59 b   hiezestu F   14 swaz F   wo dine ougen geruchen C   15 daz ist C   gnedikeit C, genedichaite F   15 f. mere : mere F, *vgl. W. s. 160*   16 griz C   an F   17 manichvalte F   18 ff. me danne zwige in

A

440 ich mak dir niht gewenken:
ich müz leiden swaz du wil.
ia han ich angest al ze vil.
waz frevden mag ich vinden, 153, 25
do dv mir an den kinden
445 denheine frevde gêbe,
daz dv mir do benæme
minen man so gût
mit solhem vnmût!

swaz dv wil daz ist ergan:
450 den toten *heizzest* du ŏf stan,
die armen machest dv reiche
vñ in selben vngelich,
die reichen lastu vallen:
dez mv̊zzen si dir all*e*
455 grozzer maisterschefte iehen.

swar din ougen gerûchent sæhen,
da ist diner genaden mê
danne griezzes in dem sæ.

gezalt hastu die sterne.
460 si mugent dir dienen gerne
die du wil berûchen.
nv ledige mich von den flûchen
da von ich pin verderret,
minem manne sint versperret.
465 die soltu herre entsliezzen,
diner genade la mich geniezzen!'

Anna suocht ir venien
mit ir zeher menien,

D

iane mag ich niht gewenchen,
ihen muze liden swaz du wil. 505
ia han ich angeste vil.
wâ mæht ich reste vinden,
do du mir an den kinden
verzige liebis beschŏde,
daz du mir do die einen frŏde 510
die ih hete benomen hast!
din gnade, herre, suaz du begast!
reht v̄ gnade sint bediv din,
daz laze an mir werden schin!
swaz du wil daz muz ergen: 515
die toten heizest dv ufsten,
di armen machestu riche,
in selben ungeliche,
die richen hohestv ze ualle:
des muzen sie dir alle   520
uon rehte der meisterscefte
                    iehen.

swar diu ŏge rûchet hin gesehen,
da ist sa der sælden me
denne griezes in dem se,
mere der gûte v̄ der bærme 525
                    din
denne zwîer ze walde mege sin.

gezalt hastu al die sterne.
si mugen dir dienen gerne
die du wil beruchen.
nu ledige mih uon dem flûche 530
der mich hat erderret
v̄ mine wambe besperret:
die scholt dv herre entsliezen,
daz ich diner milte genieze.'

40 **Anna** begunde venigen   535
mit zaheren also manigen,

deme : alde   mugen gesin od͛s/e indem mer vische gesin C   518 ze] in
deme F   19 immer F   21 dine F   23 der du wilt :: ruchen C
du] div F   24 dinem F   den flüchen C   25 di mich :: ben gederret C
26 min F   gesperret C, ist besperret F *B. s. 60*   27 du] div F   29 schut
ir venie F   venien C   30 als C

450 hiezzest   454 allen

daz si got erhôrte,
ir angest zestôrte.
dô si nider genicte   (445)
unt wider ûf geblicte
535   in einem boumgarten,
si begunde umbewarten
unt sach an einem aste
die sperchen schrîen vaste: (450)
si gâhten zeinem neste,
540   dâ si ir chindel westen,
unt brâhten in die spîse
ûf einem cleinen rîse,
ûf einem lôrboume.   (455)
diu frouwe nam des goume,
545   wie frôlîchen si flugen
durch daz si jungide zugen.

si sprach: 'owî herre,   ·
nâhen unde verren   (460)
ist dîn trôst geleitet,
550   dîn gnâde ûz gebreitet
fur aller slahte chunder.
du stiftest michel wunder
durch daz du im allem obe lîst.   (465)
dîner gescheffede du gîst
555   mislîche wunne:
von regene joch von sunnen
machestu die erde berhaft;
den vogelîn gîstu die craft   (470)
daz si ir kint meinent,
560   swie si in dem lufte sweiment.
du gebiutest den wilden tieren
daz si kint ziehen:
diu nâter diu dâ slîchet,   (475)
swâ si ir chint begrîfet,
565   si gât im williclîchen bî
unt zeiget daz si sîn muoter sî.

---

532 angst gar C   zustorte C, zerstorte F   35 einen C   bŏngartin F
39 gaheten F, gahte C   zu CF   40 kindelin F, kint C   weste C
41 bracht C   42 vs F   43 birnboume C   45 vrolich C   46 iǔge C,
ir jungide *Sch.*   47 ouwe C, owie F   49 gnade getailet F   50 din
trost F   uz gebreitet] bereitet C   51 vor C   53 ob in allen bist C,
vgl. Glossar   54 dine C   geschefte C, geschefede F   55 mislîche F,

A	D
daz si got erhort	daz si got erhorte
470 vn̄ ir angest zestort.	v̄ ir angest zestorte.
do si ze tal nikte	do sie nider genicte
vn̄ wider ouf plikte	unde wider uf geblicte 540
in einem boumgarten,	iu einem bŏgarten,
do begunde si warten	sie began umbewarten
475 vn̄ sach an einem aste	154,1 unde sah an einem aste
die agilster schreien vaste:	die sperchen schrien uaste:
si gahte zv̊ einem neste,	si gahten ze eimem neste 545
da si die iungen weste,	uf eines bŏmes neste.
vn̄ braht in die speise	
480 ouf einem chleinem reise,	
ovf einem lorboume.	div frŏe nam des gŏme,
die vrowe nam des gaume,	uf einem lorbŏme
wie frolich si flugen	wie vroliche si flugen
da si ir iungen zvgen.	da sie ir ivngide zugen, 550
	5 vnde brahten in ir spise.
	do sprah si also lise:
485 Si sprach: ,owe herre,	,owî, owî got herre,
nahen vn̄ verre	bediv nahen unde uerre
ist din trost gelaitet	ist din trost geleitet, 555
vn̄ din genade gebreitet	din gnade uz gebreitet
fur aller slahte chummer.	fur allerslahte chundir.
490 dv stiftest michel wunder	du stiftest groziu uvndir
dvrch daz dv im allem obe pist.	durh daz du in allen obelist.
diner schepfede dv gibest	diner creature du gist 560
maneger hande wunne:	10 misliche gnade unde wnne:
von regen vn̄ ouch von sunne	uon regen ioh von sunne
495 machest dv die erde berhaft;	machestv die erde berhaft,
den vogelin geist du die chraft	den uogellinen gistu die chraft
daz si ir kint meinen,	daz sie ir kint mêinent, 565
swie si in den luften swaimen.	swie sie in den luften swêiment.
dv gebivtest den wilden tieren	du gebivtest dem wilde
500 daz si ir kint erziehen,	daz ez nah muterlichem bilde
div nater div da sleifet,	15 allez siniv kint ziehen chan
daz si ⟨ir⟩ chint begreiffet.	v̄ hat ŏh sin frŏde daran. 570

---

unmenschliche C   56 joch] und C   57 b'nhaft C   l. machest? s. oben zu 508   58 l. vogelinen gîst die?   60 d' luft C   62 chint fehlt C 63 natir da F   slifet C   64 irgriffit F   65 get in C   66 bezeiget C

477 gahte!   478 weste!   495 behaft   498 swaimen!   502 begreiffent

von dir die vische nâmen
wuocher unde sâmen, (480)
die in dem wazzer fliezent,
570 dîner guote si geniezent.
allez daz der ie wart
daz hât dîn segen wol bewart,
daz sich ie iteniuwet (485)
swaz chreset oder fliuget
575 ûf der erde unt in dem wâge.
nu sage ich dir gnâde
daz du mich alterseine
sô verre hâst gescheiden (490)
von allen ⟨den⟩ sachen
580 die du hâst geschaffen,
von allen den dingen
diu ûz dem urspringe
dînes gwaltes sint bechomen, (495)
dar ûz hâst du mich genomen,
585 gesundert joch gescheiden:
daz muoz ich iemer clagen unde weinen.'

Bedaz si die rede volsprach,
einen engel si gesach (500)
vor ir antlutze stên.
590 diu vorhte begunde si anegên,
si widersaz ez harte;
dô si begunde warten
an sîne schône vederen, (505)
ir sin fuor enwedele
595 sam vor dem winde daz loup.
der engel niht ûf schoup

sîne boteschaft frône:
die frouwen gruozt er schône (510)
mit senftlîchen worten:
600 'dune scholt dir niht fnrhten',
sprach der engel liehte,
'der allin dinc von niehte

---

567 v̌ise F 69 die fische in dem wazzære F 71 daz da C 73 daz
ez C, daz er F ie iteniuwet] ientenivwet F, v˜neuwet C, *vgl. § 62 c*
74 crisct F, kruch^et C 75 und] od�’ C 77 daz du aleine C
80 d˙schaffen C 81 von .ll....... C, *kein Raum für* den 82 uf F
urspringen C 83 mit dinem gewalte F 84 mich *fehlt* F 85 und C
86 daz] des C 87 E C, He F volle sprach F 88 ein F sah F

A

von dir die vische nament,
wûchernt vn̄ sament,
505 die in dem wazzer fliezzent,
diner gûte si geniezzent.
alles daz ie wart
daz hat din segen wol bewart,
daz sich iærlichen niwet
510 swaz chrivchet oder flivget
ovf der erde vn̄ in dem wage.
nu sag ich dir genade
daz dv mich aleinen
so verre hast gescheiden
515 von allen den sachen
die ⟨du⟩ woldest machen,
von allen den dingen
die ouz den vrspringen
dines gewaltes sint bechomen,
520 darvz hast dv mich genomen,
gesundert vn̄ gescheiden:
dez mŭz ich immer wainen.'

Also schir si die red gesprach,
einen engel ⟨si⟩ gesach
525 vor ir antlutze sten.
voriht begunde si ane gen,
si wider saz in harte;
si begunde warten
an die schonen vederen;
530 ir sin fŭr enwedelen
sam vor dem winde daz laup.
der engel niht ouf schoup

sine botschaft frone.
die vrowen grŭzt er schone
535 mit semftelichen worten:
,du solt dir niht furhten,'
sprach der engel lieht,
,der alle dink von niht

D

uon dir die vische namen
bediv wchir vn̄ samen,
die in dem wazzer fliezent,
diner gŭte si genîezent.
allez daz ter îe v̄ ie wart   575
hat dinen segen wol bewart,
daz ez sih ie iteniwet,
swaz chreset oder flivget
154,20 uf der erde vn̄ in dem wage.
nu sage ich dir gnade   580
daz du mich alterseine
so uerre hast gescheiden

uon allem dem dinge
daz uz dem urspringe
dines gewaltes ist bechomen, 585
dar uz hastu mich genomen,
gesundert ioh gescheiden:
des mŭz ih min sûnde weinen.'

25   Bedaz sie die rede uol sprah,
einen engel si gesah   590
uor ir antlutze sten.
div uorhte begunde sie durhgen,
sie wider saz irz harte;
do sie in began anwarten,
ir sin fûr enwedele   595
sam uor dem winde div nedere
v̄ ŏh daz lovb gerne tut.
der engil swang ir den mŭt
30   uz den sorgen also swæren.
mit semftlichen gebæren   600
er gruzte die frŏen schone
mit der botscaft frone,
mit minnelichen worten:
,du solt mich niht erfurhten.
in des gwalte div werlte stat, 605
vnd elliu dinch gescaffen hat

---

89 antlizce C, antlv̂hte F   90. 92 begunge F   93 vedere F   94 als
ein wedele C   95 sam] tut C   von F   97 potesclaft F   98 grvzeter F
99 senftent F   600 du scholt dich C   2 der] dir F   dinhc F   nihte F,
nichte C

154,21 daz daz   520 darzv̊   532 den

chunde wol gemachen,   (515)
der wil selbe wachen
605 uber dîn reinez gebet,
als er kunic ie tet
uber alle die ir gemuote
chêrent an sîne guote.   (520)
dô dîn charele Joachim,
610 als ich dir chundende bin,
von dir ze jungiste schiet,
diu gotes gnâde iuch beriet
daz du swanger wurde   (525)
cheiserlîcher burde.
615 du treist in dînen brusten
des dich wol mac gelusten,
eine tohter hêre.
ja ne wirt ouch niemer mêre   (530)
ir gelîche geborn:
620 si ist ze kuniginne erchorn
uber allez himilischez her.
si schol den gotes sun gebern,
den vil heiligen Christ,   (535)
der aller werlte vater ist.
625 dîn tohter ist hêr unt wîch,
ir ne wart nie niemen glîch

under wîplîchem chunne.
si wirt ein michel wunne   (540)
aller dirre werlte,
630 sô got bûwet in ir gezelte.'

Als diu boteschaft was ergeben,
sine mahte in mêre niht gesehen,
wan er ze churzen stunden   (545)
von ir was verswunden,
635 unt fuor ze sînem meister,
wider ze andern geisten,

---

603 machin F   4 selber C   6 als d⁵ C   9 din alt man C
10 dir] der F   kundigen C   11 vnd dir zu iungest ziet C   12 iuch
beriet] ouch wirret C   13 swangere F   15 unt⁷ C, *s. § 63*   16 lⁱv̊sten F
18 io F   wirt ouch] wart F   19 glich C   20 kunegⁱ C   21 hymelschez F
22 den *fehlt* C   sunt F   23 vil *fehlt* F   24 aller der F   25 din] di C

A

chan wol gemachen,
540 der wil selbe wachen
vber din reines gebet,
als er kvnik îe têt
vber alle die ir gemŷte
cherten an seine gûte.
545 do din man Joachim,
als ich dir saginde pin,
von dir ze iungist schiet,
diu gotes genade evch beriet
daz dv swanger wurde
550 einer keiserlichen burde.
dv treist vnder dinen brusten
dez dich wol mak gelusten,
eine tohter hêre.
ia wirt nimmer mǽre
555 ir geliche geborn:
Si ist ze kvniginne erchorn
vber alles himilischez hêr,
daz si gotes sun geber,
den heiligen Christ,
560 der aller werlde vater ist.
Si wirt weise vū hǽr,
ir wart nîe niht geleiches mêr

vnder weiplichem kvnne.
si wirt ein michel wunne
565 aller der werlde,
so got erbŏwet ir gezelte.'

Als er der botschaft het veriehen
si moht sein niht mǽr gesehen,
· wan er in churzen stunden
570 von ir waz verswunden.

D

im ze dîenest unt ze lobe,
wand er richsent dar obe,
154, 35 der wil in dinen sachen
gnadechliche wachen   610
uber din reinez gebet,
als er kunich îe tet
uber alle die ir gemüte
kerent an sîne gûte.
do diu karle Joachim   615
als ih dir chundent bin,
von dir nv ze iv̂ngeste schîet,
div gotes gnade ivh berîet
40 daz du swanger wrde
einer chunklicher burde.   620
du treist bi dinen brusten
des dih wol mak gelusten,
155, 1 eine tohter here.
ia ne wirt ŏh niemer mere
dehein ir glich geborn,   625
wan sie ist ze frŏen erchorn
uber allez himiliske her.
uon ir sol chomen der
der aller werlte vater ist:
daz ist der heilige Christ.   630
5 din tohter ist der engeln frŏde,
wan sie in gotes beschŏde
gewihet ist v̄ gesegent,
daz uon ir gnade begegent
allem mennisklichem chunne: 635
si wirt der werlte wnne.'

Do diu botschaft was ergangen,
den sie hete beuangen
lipliche mit ir ŏgen,

der hüb sih wider ze den tŏgen, 640

---

ist herlich C   26 ir wart nie kein vrouwe glich C   27 kvnde C   28 michele
bis ir 652 C⁴ III   29 diser werlt C   30 so *fehlt* C   mit ir : in gezelt C
31 Alse F *und öfter*   dise C   wart F   32 sin nīme C   33 wenne C
34 vor F   35 unt] er C   36 wider *fehlt* F   zu CF

154, 38 Initiale   546 saginden   548 do   554 wirt!

die in dem himelrîche sint
geheizen engelischiu kint.   (550)
do begunde fronwe Anne
640 got loben starche danne:
ir schephâre
sagete si gnâde,

daz er sie erlôste   (555)
mit sô getânem trôste
645 von allen itewîzen:
des lobete si in mit flîze.
si wart vil inneclîchen frô,
ir venie suochte si aber dô,   (560)
darnâch gienc si rasten:
650 ja hête sie daz vasten
ein teil geswendet,
doch hête si ir arbeit wol gewendet.

In ir bette si gelac   (565)
eine ganze naht unt einen tac,
655 daz si enâz noch entranc.
si hête reinen gedanc.
ja was ir an der selben zît
als ein man oder ein wîp   (570)
mit swâregem troume
660 sliefe under einem boume,
dem wâre chomen ze schûme
daz er entrunne chûme
vor sînen vîanden,   (575)
unt er darnâch erchande,
665 swenne er erwachôte,
daz alle sîne nôte
wâren verswunden:
als was si an den stunden   (580)
bechomen von ir leide:
670 wunne unde weide
unt vil stâtigen segen
hête ir der engel gegeben.
ir wîbe ruofte si einer,   (585)

---

637 die ime F   38 ge :: hen C   engelsciv F   39 d : vro : w C
anna F   40 got baz lobun dan e C   41 irme C, *l.* dem ir?   44 svs-
getanem F   45 aller itwizce C   ietewizen F   46 lŏpte F   48 venyen C
50 io F   hat C *u. ö.*   51 vaste geswendet C   52 doch hat si alle ir

A

D

155, 10 da div engiliskiv kint
 in gotes ordenunge sint.
Do begunde vrov Anna   do begunde frœe Anne
got loben starke alda,   got starche loben danne.
    si sagete im gnade groz,   *645*
    daz sie alsovil gnoz
    der sinen gute wider in.
    sie erhub ir herze v̄ sin
daz er si erloste   im ze danchen mit flîze,
mit sogetanem trôste   wan er sie uon dem itewîze *650*
575 von ir iteweizze: *15* mit so getanem troste
des lobt si in mit fleizze.   gnadecliche erloste.
Si wart vil inrechlichen frô,   sie wart uil herzeclichen fro,
ir venie sŭcht si do,   ir uenige suhte sie auer do,
darnach gienk si rasten: darnah giench sie rasten: *655*
580 ia het si daz vasten   ia hete sie daz uasten
ze gote verendet   ein teil geswendet,
vn̄ ouch bewendet.   doh hete sie ir arbeit wol
           gewendet.

In ir bette si gelach   In ir bette sie gelach
eine ganze naht vnz an den tak,   ein naht vnd einen tach,   *660*
585 daz si niht az noch trank.   *20* daz sie enaz noh entranch.
si het reinen gedank.   si hete reinen gedanch.
ir waz an der selben zeit   ia was ir an derselben zit
als ob ein man oder ein weip   als einem man der da gelit
mit swerem trovme   begrifen mit swarem trôme *665*
590 slief vnder einem bovme,   slafend under einem bœme,
vn̄ bedouht von sinnen   dem chomen wære ze sune
wie er niht moht entrinnen   daz er entruune chûme
dahin vor seinen veinten,   uor den sinen uianden,
die im sær nach eilten,   vnde darnah erchande,   *670*
595 vn̄ als er dan erwachot,   *25* swenner uon dem slafe erwâchot,
daz alle seine not   daz garliche alle sin not
wæren gar verswunden: uon im wære uerswnden:
also waz ir zestunden   also was sie an den stunden
gar chomen von laide: bechuket uon ir leide: *675*
600 wunne vn̄ liebe paide   bediv ẇnne vnd wêide
het ir der engel geben   unt ẇil statigen segen
vn̄ einen steten segen.   hete ir der engil gegeben.
ire weip rief si ane,

C *bricht ab*   55 en hâz F   57 iô F   61 ze schûme] de schvme F,
vielleicht auch der schûme *oder* ze schûmen   65 irwachete· F
73—97 C⁴ IV   73 rif si eine C, einer rŏfte sie F
    581 kein wol!   *598* zestuden

diu chom ir alze seine.
675 dô ruofte si der magede,
diu was vil ungesagede:
si muose ir harn ofte,
mêre dennez getohte.   (590)
uber lanc gie si dar,
680 dô sprach diu tohter Ysachar,
Anna diu reine:
'nu sage mir waz daz meine:
wannen chumet dir der geist,   (595)
sô dû mîn angest wol weist,
685 daz dû sô harte trâgest
daz dû mich niene frâgest,
weder ich lebe oder tôt sî?
du wârest mir billîchen bî,   (600)
ob ich den lîp wolte laben,
690 daz ich dir daz mahte gesagen.'
diu maget begunde murmeln,
ungezogenlîchen zurnen;

si sprach: 'waz maht ich dir eine getuon?   (605)
dune hâst die tohter noch den sun,
695 dîn man hât dich verlâzen:
ich wil ouch mîne strâze
anderhalben wenden

674 ur alleine C   seime F   75 do rif si aber d⁵ meide C   76 vn-
gesc ... de C   77 harne F   si rif vil ofte C   78 me den ez C
mere danne ir tohte F   82 saga C   waz ez C   83 wanne C   84 min
angest] *kaum leserlich* C   86 niene] nich: en C   88 bellichen F   89 ob]
ab C   90 dir daz] di C   91 f. zurnen : murmeln C   94 dvne] F *bricht
ab*   97 wendē] C *bricht ab*

A

die chomen alze saine.
605 do rief si der magede,
der waz niht leihte ze sagene:

vber lank gie si dar,
do sprach si zwar
Anna div reine:
610 ‚nv sage mir waz daz meine,
oder von wev chumt dir der geist,
seit dv min angest wol weist,
daz dv also trâgest
vñ mich niht enfragest,
615 ob ich leb oder tot sey?
dv wærist mir billeich bey,
ob ich den leib wolde laben,
daz ich dirz mohte gesagen.‘
div magt begunde murmen
620 vñ hezzechlichen zvrnen;
si sprach: ‚waz moht ich dir getün?

dv hast tohter noch svn,
din man hat dich verlazzen.
ich wil ouch mine strazzen
625 al von hinnen wenden
vñ wil daz schier vol enden.‘

Mit solhen iteweizzen
so mv̊st div vrowe enbeizzen:
si labt sich vil chleine,
630 ir frevde mischte si mit weinen.

Der engel für hin vmbe
von gotes ordenunge
da er weste Joachim.
in die wv̊ste gie er zv̊ im
635 ouf dem gevilde
in eines knappen bilde.
er grv̊zt in vil leise,

D

do rufte sie einer magede,
div was uil ungesagede: 680
sie mv̊se ir haren ofte,
mere dennez getohte.
iedoh uber lanch gie si dar,
do sprah div tohter Ysachar,
Anna div uil reine: 685
‚sage mir waz daz meine:
wanne chumet dir der geist,
so du min angeste wol weist,
daz du so stille dagest
v̄ mir antwrte uersagest?   690
du wærest mir billicher bî
v̄ sæhest wie min dinch stende si,
ob ich den lip wolte laben,
daz ich daz uon dir mæhte haben.‘
Div maget begunde murmeln, 695
ungezogenlichen zurnen;
si sprah: ‚waz mag ich dir eine
getun?
dune hast die tohter noh den sun,
din man der hat dich uerlan.
nu wil ȯh ich min straze gan, 700
anderhalben min dinch wenden:
ich kan ez wol uerenden.
waz tustu ze liebe mir?
swaz ih ie gedienot dir,
des en han ich danch noh lône.‘ 705
die frȯe uertrugez schone
v̄ bewêinet doh die itewîze,
uñ swie ez wære an dem imbize,
sie half dem libe also sêine:
ir frȯde wart gemisket mit 710
leide.

Der engel fur hin umbe
uon gotes ordenunge
da er wesse Joachim.
in der ẘste gieng er zu im
uf dem breiten gevilde   715
in eines knappen bilde
v̄ gruzte in also lise,

155, 30

40

156, 1

5

---

604 saine!   155, 35 mih   155, 39 ungezonlichen   630 mischte si!

A	**D**

er sprach: ‚herre weise,   er sprah: ‚herre uil wise,
wes bistu hie aleine?   156, 10 waz listu hie sust eine?
640 wie hastu dich gescheiden   wie hastu dih gescheiden   720
von diner lobelichen chonen?   uon diner loblichen chonen?
wie ist div vnminne chomen?   wie ist div unminne chomen?
var heim schir widere!   wes enuerstv niht widere?
div vrowe ist also biderbe   div frœ ist so biderbe
645 daz dv si trosten mŭst,   daz du sie wol trosten mŭst, 725
wan dv tumplichen tŭst   vn̄ ŏh wendeklichen tust
daz du sey last so lange frist: 15 daz du sie læst so lange frist:
wan si zebarmen ist
allem der sey beschowet,
650 doch hat ir wol gezowet
vm allez daz dir lieb ist.   du uindest da daz dir liep ist.
nv soume dich lenger denheine frist: nv uar heim zu den dinen,
far heim zŭ den dinen   la din gewizzen schinen! 730
(la dine tugende scheinen)   uar uz disem steingeuelle,
655 ovz disem *steingevelle*,   sih waz dine chone welle!
sich waz dein weip welle!   heue dih uz diser chluse,
heb dich ouz der chlouse,   dv mŭst heim zu dinem hûse.‘
var wider heim ze house!‘

                           Do sprah der herre 735
   Do sprach der herre Joachim: Joachim:
660 ‚wan ich ein sunder bin,   ‚wand *ich* ein sundare bin,
da von ich not leide.   20 uon schulden not ih lide.
ich waz bey minem weibe   ich was bi minem wibe
zweinzik iar volle,   zweinzich iar uolle,
daz got des niht enwolde,   daz des got nien wolde, 740
665 daz ⟨wir⟩ ensamt erben   daz ich dehein herzewnne
îe mohten erwerben.   noh liep mit kinde gewnne.
waz solde ich nv da sŭchen?   waz scolt ih denne da suchen?
ia wellent niht gerŭchen   iane wellent des niht geruchen
yrdische levte   25 div irdiskiv livte, 745
670 daz ich mit miner brevte   daz ich mit miner brûte
zŭ ir opfer turre gan: zu ir opfer geturre gan:
darum mŭz ich hie bestan   darumbe muz ich hie bestan
vn̄ ærmechlichen leben,   un̄ sus armeklichen leben,
min almŭsen geben   unde wil doh almusen geben 750
675 minem schæpfere,   iemer minem schepfære,
der mich ze chamer*ere*   der mih im ze kamerare
gesetzet hat dar vbere.   gesetzet hat dar ubere.
were ez mit minem vbele   wærez mit miner ubele

---

649 allem!   655 gestein velle   *156, 19* ihc   676 chamere

A

niht vndervangen,

680 ez wær mir baz ergangen.‘

Des antwurte im der engel do:
,din leben ist an wandel so.
ich bin der engel frone:
got hat gegæben dir ze lone
685 ein tohter bey deinem weibe;
div chom von dinem leib*e*
do dv ze iungist schie*de* von ir.
daz ich sage fur war dir:
din tohter wirt so lobesam

690 daz bede weip vn̄ man
vn̄ auch div himelische schar
mûzzen knievallen dar
da si die chuniginnen
ze troste mvgen gewinnen.

695 var heim in dein gesæzze:
swer mit schatze mæzze
disen yrdischen gibel
hoch vnz an den himel
mit guldeinen spelten,
700 dein tohter moht er niht vergelten.‘

Als Joachim an dem wort
den selben trost erhôrte,
er sovmte sich niht lenger,
er sûcht fur den engel
705 seine venie schone;
er sprach zv̊ dem poten vrone:
,wou ein weile pei mir,
ob ich ze got vn̄ zv̊ dir
genade han erfunden,
710 so vergiz miner svnden.
seit ich ze den æren pin erwelt,
so var mit mier in mein gezelt,
vn̄ enbeizze wir da inne
in der gotes minne,
715 vn̄ gerûche dich erbarmen
vber mich vil armen,

D

156,30 ioh mit sunden niht under- 755
nangen,
ez ware mir lihte baz ergangen.‘

Des antwrte im der engel:
,din leben ist ane wandel.
ich bin des himeles bot frone:
got hat dir geben ze lone 760
ein tohter bi dinem wibe;
div chom non dinem libe·
do dv ivngeste schîede non ir.
uil mandunge sage ich dir:
din tohter div wirt so lobe- 765
sâme
daz aller mennisken name
ioh elliv himiliskiv schare
div muz chnieuallen dare
da div rose ane dorn
ioh div kunigin here wirt 770
geborn.
nu nar in din gesæze,
wan swer dir herre mæze
40 disen irdisken gibel
hohe ûf unz an den himel
mit rotguldinen spelten, 775
der enmæht dir daz kint niht
uergelten.‘

157,1 Als Joachim an dem worte
den richen trost erhorte,
fur den engel viel er bereite,
daz er got unde im gnade 780
sæite.

er sprah: ,herre, nu gewêr mich
einer bete der ih dinge an dih:
5 ob ich daz heil ze dir han funden,
so nergiz der minen sunden.
nu ich ze den eren sie erwelt, 785
nar sam mir in min gezelt,
vnd enbizzen wir darinne
in der gotes minne,

---

686 leiben   687 schiet

A	**D**
daz mich dein segen sterke	daz mih din segen gesterche
in reinichlichem werke.'	ze reiniklichem werche.' *790*
Der engel im antwurtte	der engel im antwrte:
720 mit senftechlichem worte:	,got selbe mit sinem worte
,⟨got⟩ gerŭche dich gesegenen, *157, 10*	der geruche dich gesegenen,
daz dir frevde begegen*e*	daz dir allez daz begegen*e*
vn̄ allez daz dir lieb ist.	daz dir liep muge sin. *795*
min lieber frevnt dv bist	dune bist niht der schalk min,
725 vn̄ miner hŏsgenozzen:	dv bist min husgnozze:
wir han einen herren grozzen,	einen herren haben wir grozzen,
der dich allez dez gewert	der dich alles des gewert
des dein mût gen im gert;	des din diemût an in gert; *800*
er wil dein niht vergezzen.	erne wil din niht vergezzen.
730 mi*n* trinchen noch mi*n* ezzen	min trinchen unt min ezzen
daz maht dv niht beschowen	*15* daz enmahtu niht bescŏen
mit fleischen ougen:	mit fleisklichen ŏgen:
daz ist daz æwige lieht.	daz ist daz ewige lieht. *805*
dv darft mich andigen niht	dune darft mih andingen nieht
735 daz ich dine speise	daz ich die dine spise
ze meinem mvnde weise.	zu minem munde wise.
dv brink der gotes chrefte	nu brinch der gotes chrefte
swaz dv mir wirtschefte	swaz du ze wirtschefte *810*
hivte wellest bieten	mir hivte woldest bieten,
740 mit heiligen mieten,	so maht du dih gnaden nieten
mit deinem opfer drate	
al nach minem rate,	
in deines schepfers gewalt,	*20* uon dines schephæres gewalte,
der al dein gût hat gezalt	der din gûte hat gezalte
745 vn̄ dein almŏsen	und allez din almusen *815*
treit in seinem bŏsem,	treit in sinem busem,
daz dv ie begienge,	daz du ie begienge,
seit dv sein gevienge!'	sit du sin geviênge
	daz du im chundest gedienen.
	25 er wil ŏh dich erchennen v̄ *820*
	lieben.'
Der herre eylinde gienk,	**D**er herre ilent gie,
750 zehant er gevienk	ein læmbel er geuîe,
ein lamp vngemailot,	ein lamb ungemeiligot,
als im der engel gebot.	als im der engil gebot.
er sprach: ,ich torste sein niht getŭn,	er sprah: ,ich engetorstez *825*
	niht getun,
wan daz dv mich, herre, darzŏ	wan daz du mir ratest darzu
755 mit worten hast geschundet.	*30* v̄ mih sin hast geschundet.

---

722 begegenen   *157, 10* begegen   730 mit   *157, 15* min

A

swaz ich han gesvndet,
daz hilf mir ouf halden
gen got dem gewaldigen,
vnz ich das opfer bringe!
760 ia ist daz min gedinge,
daz ich geniezzen muezze
daz ich bey deinem fůzze
hie also nahen stæ,
vnz daz obley ergæ.'
765 Do sprach der engel: ,wesse
ich niht
daz dine gedanke weren lieht,
vn̄ daz ez niht lieb wære
dez himels rihtere,
so hiet ich ez niht gefrumet.
770 Sus waiz ich daz iz dir chumet
. als ez ze rehte sol
dinen sælden wol.'

Do daz lamp wart erslagen,

D

swaz ich nu han gesundet,
da hilf mir uon durh din gute,
daz ich mit reinem gemůte 830
uor dir daz opfer bringe!
ia han ih des gedinge,
daz ich geniezen mǔze
daz ich dinen fůzzen
also nahen bisten, 835
untze die oblei ergen.'
157,35 Do sprah der engel gůt:

,enwesse ih niht in minem mǔt
daz din opfer liep wære
des himeles rihtære, 840
sone hete ihz niht gefrumet.
sust wêiz ich daz ez dir chumet
ze diner sælicheit wol,
wand unser rede damit schol
uf der moltigen erde 845
geûrchundet werden.'

40 do daz lamb was erslagen,

er îlte holz zuo tragen (610)
unt warf ez ûf einen stein;
er brande fleisch unde bein.
dô sich der rouch ûf bouc,
860 der engel al dâ mite flouc
vaste gen den luften. (615)
mit zaheren unt mit zuhten
gestuont der herre eine:
sîn herze was lûter unde reine.

865 **S**în gebet daz was sô nuzze:
ûf sîn antluzze (620)
viel er nider ûf daz gras,
dâ er ophernde was.
er lac bî dem gezîle
870 von der sehsten wîle
unze an die vesperzît, (625)
sô diu sunne schaten gît.
dô chômen sîne hirten:
hin zir herren unt zir wirte
875 îlten si gâhen,
dô si in sâhen (630)
ligen in der molten.
si wânden daz er wolte
sich selben verliesen,
880 vor leide den tôt chiesen.
si îlten in ûf rihten: (635)
er sagete ouch zir gesihte,
wie ez im was ergangen.
dô wurden si bevangen
885 mit ziteren joch mit vorhten:
anders si niene worhten (640)
wan daz si lobeten alle got,
der ûzer angest unt ûzer nôt
diu riuwigen herze enbindet,
890 swâ er den glouben vindet
an den guoten unt an den rehten. (645)
alle sîne knehte
die rieten dem heiligen man
daz er wurde gehôrsam
895 dem engel unt sînen worten.

---

856 tragen *bis* vor 1017 F 425—581   59 do] dz F   60 mtte F
74 zů ir F   77 nider ligen F   82 ze ir F   83 was] ware F   85 iŏch F
89 enbinden F

A	**D**
er eilte holz zv̊ tragen	er ilet sa holz zutragen
775 vn̄ warf ez ŏf einen stain;	158, 1 v̄ leit ez uf einen stêin;
er prante fleisch vn̄ pein.	er brant bediv fleish vnde bein. *850*
do sich der rouch ouf povk,	do sih der rŏch uf bŏvch,
der engel al da mit flouk	der engil aldamit flŏch.
faste gen den luften.	
780 mit semft vn̄ mit zvhten	
gestŭnt der herre aleine	der herre gestunt eîne:
mit louterm herzen reine.	sin herze was luter v̄ reine.

A	**D**
	Sin gebet was im v̄ vns *855*
Sein gebet daz waz so nutze:	nutze:
ŏf sein antlvtze	mit zæhern uf sin antlutze
785 viel er nider ovf daz gras,	5 viel er nider an daz gras,
da er opfernde was.	da er da opferend was.
er lak bey dem zil	er lach bi dem gecile
von der sexten weil	uon der sehsten wile *860*
vnz an die vesper zeit,	uutze an die vespercit,
790 so div sunne schate geit.	so div sunne schatte git.
Do quamen seine hirte:	do chomen sin hirte:
zv̊ ir herren vn̄ zv̊ ir wirtte	hin zir herren v̄ ir wirte
si eilten alle gahen,	si begunden gahen, *865*
da si in da sahen	do si in ersahen
795 ligen in der molte.	10 ligen in der molten.
si wanten daz er wolte	sie wanden daz er wolte
sich selben verliesen,	sih selben uerliesen,
vor laide den tot chiesen.	uor leide den tot chiesen. *870*
si eilten in ŏf rihten.	sie ilten in ûfrihten:
800 er sagte ze ir gesihten,	er saget ŏch zir gesihte,
wie ez im waz ergangen.	wie ez was ergangen.
do wurden si bevangen	do wrden sie beuangen
mit zeheren vn̄ mit vorihten:	mit frŏden ioh mit uorhten: *875*
anders si niht worihten	anders si nîen worhten
805 wan daz si lobten got,	15 wan daz sie lobeten got,
der von sorgen vn̄ ouz nŏt	der uzzer angest v̄ not
die revgen herze enbindet,	div riwigen herze enbindet,
swa er rehten gelawen vindet.	swa er den glŏben vindet. *880*
Do rieten dem man	
810 alle sein vndertan	do was ez ir aller geræte
daz er des engels rat	daz er zehaute sa tæte
volget an der stat.	nah den engelisken worten.

808 *gelawe*   158, 18 *worde̦n*

si sprâchen, si vorhten   (650)
anders . . . .
. . . . niht mêre,
er wurde gerefset sêre
900   an dem lîbe unt an der sêle.
als er des nahtes entslief,   (655)
der engel im aver zuo rief:
'wes sûmest dû dich Joachim?
anderstunt ich bote bin
905   daz du heim muozest varn:
dû ne wellest ez bewarn,   (660)
du muost es engelten
daz Anna sô selten
nâch dir unweinende wirt.

910   du weist wol daz si dir gebirt
eine tohter guote;   (665)
diu ist in gotes huote
von êwen unze êwen.
wie schol ich dich dîner frume flêgen?'

915   **A**n dem andern morgen
do verliez er alle sorgen,   (670)
er huop sich ûf gereite,
erne wolte niht lenger beiten:
er sagete sînen liuten
920   des engels rede ze diute.
die rieten algemeine   (675)
daz si fuoren seine,
als daz vihe mahte gên;
si sprâchen, wolt er dâ bestên,

925   daz muose er âne sie tuon.
ez wâre ein michel wîstuom,   (680)
daz er alsô tâte
als im gechundet hête
der gewaltige bote.

---

897 *ff.* anders harte er wrde gerefset sere F   98 niht mere *bis* aller
989 C² 184—275   99 gerefset] gerauft *in* geraubet (*von anderer Hand?*)
gebessert C   902 zuo *fehlt* C   3 sumestu! F   4 ander] an C
5 heim *fehlt*, mûst C   7 es] des C, ez F, *was aber nur orthographisch*
ist   8 nich . . . . . selden C   9 weinen C   10 siv F   dir *fehlt* C
13 ewe zu C   14 dines wrum̃ C   so flehen F   15 In F   16 alle]

A   **D**

sie sprachen daz sie norhten
158,20 anders den gotes zorn,   *885*
ob er sin gebot hete uerchorn.

Als er des nahtes entslief,   als er des nahtes entsliefe,
der engel im aber zů rief: der engel im aue zurief:
815 ‚wez sovmest dv dich Joachim?   ‚wes sumest du dih Joachim?
anderstunt ich bote pin   anderstunt ih bot ze dir bin   *890*
daz dv heim solt varen   daz du heim mûzest narn.
vñ solt dein weip bewaren,   dune wellest ez bewârn,
                                     du engiltest sin zware
                                     daz Anna lebet so sware
                              25 v̄ so diche nah dir weinende *895*
seit ez also wirt   wirt.
820 daz si dir gebirt   du weist wol daz sie dir gebirt
eine tohter gûte;   eine tohter gute;
div ist in gotes hûte: div ist in gotes hûte
maniger sele sol si wegen   uon ewen v̄ ze êwen.
ze gotes gûte vñ ze sinem segen.‘   wer schol dih diner eren   *900*
                                                      flegen?‘

825 An dem andren morgen   An dem andern morgen
do verliez er sein sorgen,   do uerliez ⟨er⟩ alle sorgen,
er begunde sich beraiten,   30 er hub sih vf gereiten
niht lenger wolt er baiten: v̄ enwolt niht mere bêiten:
er saget sinen levten   er saget sinem lîvte   *905*
830 des engels rede ze devte.   des engels rede ze dute.
si rieten algemeine   die rieten algemêine   ‚
daz si fůren saine,   daz sie furen sêine,
als daz vihe mohte gên;   also daz daz uihe mæhte gen;
si sprachen, wolt er da bestên,   si sprachen, wolt er da   *910*
                                                      besten,
835 daz mv̊st er ane sei tůn.   daz mûse ane sie geschehen.
ez were ein michel weistům,
daz er also tæt
sam im der engel chundet het.

---

die F   17 bereite C   18 erne] er C   lenger *fehlt* F   20 rede]

wort C   21 die] d̦ si C   gemeine   22 daz si vm ẘren engegene C
                          alle geine C

24 sprauchen F   er] ir C   25 mv̊zt ir C   26 missetun C   27*f.* tete
: hette C

830 devten

930 si ruoften vaste hin ze gote
    ûf sîne barmunge   (685)
    mit weinenden zungen.
    si fuoren enalverte
    daz mos joch die herte,
935 beidiu berc unde tal;
    daz vihe chêrten si uberal.   (690)
    si wâren in der ôde
    fumf mânôde
    gewesen joch gebûwen,
940 mit solhen missetriuwen
    daz er boteschaft neheine   (695)
    nie enbôt hin wider heime
    sînem schônen wîbe:
    daz hête si ze nîde.
945 dô si an ir gebete stuont,
    als diche guotiu kint tuont,   (700)
    mit zaheren begozzen,
    der engel unbedrozzen
    der chom ir aber ze siune
950 bî des boumgarten zûne,
    dâ si lac an ir knie.   (705)
    der engel engegen ir gie,
    ir leit er ir gebuozte,
    dô er sie gegruozte;
955 er sprach daz si gienge,
    ir charelen wol enphienge   (710)
    zeiner porte diu hiez Aureâ:
    der wirt begegenôte ir dâ
    âne zwîvel an dem tage.
960 dô was ir trûren unt ir clage
    in den wint verswunden,   (715)
    ir herze was gefrîget unt enbunden.

    Si gâhete engegen dem burgetor,
    des wirtes beitte si davor
965 mit des engels geleite.
    si wolte ir langez beiten   (720)

---

930 riefen C   31 uffe C *und öfter*   32 weinden C   33 enalverte]
alle verte C   34 joch] und C   35 berg! C   36 karten C   38*f.* ge .. sen
funf manden   und ouch gebûwet C   38 fvnf F   40 sulch .. C,
scholi/che: F, *von hier* F *in der Handschrift fast ganz unlesbar, auch in
Palimpsestphotographie nur teilweise und mit Mühe zu entziffern, vgl. W.
s. 156*   41 eine C, *wahrscheinlich* [e]nh[eine] F   42 nie *fehlt* C   46 als]

A

do fŷren si mit aller verte
840 daz mos vñ auch die herte,
peide perge vñ tal;
daz vihe cherten si vber al.
si waren in der ôde
fvmf manôde
845 gewesen vñ mit riwen,
mit solhen missetriwen
daz er botschaft denhein
nie enbot wider heim
sinem schonen weibe:
850 daz het si ze neide.
Do si an ir gebete stŭnt,
sam diche gŭte weip tŭnt,
mit zehern begozzen,
der engel vnverdrozzen
855 chom ir auer ze lovne
bey des bovmgarten zovne,
da si lak an ir chnie.
der engel ir enkegen gie,
ir lait er ir bŷzte,
860 do er sei begrŭzte;
er sprach daz si gienge
vñ wol ir man enpfienge
zŷ einer porten die hiez aurea:
der wirt begegenet ir al da
865 ane zweifel an dem tage.
do waz ir trovren vñ ir chlage
in den wint verswunden,
ir herze wart enbunden.

Si gahte gen dem purgetor,
870 des wirttes baite si da vor.

D

got begunden sie iehen
158,35 siner grozen barmunge
mit lobe sprechender zunge.
sie fûren en al uerte   915
div mos ioh die herte,
bediv berge ¯v tal;
daz vihe cherten sie uberal.
si waren in der einode
ensamet fivmf manode,   920

daz er botschafte neheine
noh boten sante hin hêime
40 sinem tûgendrichem wîbe:
daz hete sie zenide.
do sie an ir gebet stunt,   925
als dicche die gvten tûnt,
mit zæheren wol begozzen,
der engel unbedrozzen
159,1 der chom ir aue ze sûne.
bi des bŏmgarten zûne   930
da lach sie an ir chnîe:
der engel zu ir gie,
ir leit er ir gebuzte,
do er sie mit liebe grŭzte;
er sprah daz sie gienge   935
¯v ir charle wol enpfienge
5 ze êiner borte hiez aurea:
der wirt begegenot ir da
ane zwîuel an dem tage.
do was ir truren ¯v ir chlage 940
in den wint gahes uerswnden,
sie was gefriget ¯v enbunden.

Si gahet engegen dem burgetor,
ir wirtes beitet sie dauor
mit des engeles geleite.   945
si hete wol gewant ir arbêite.

---

so F   gute kind‘e C, *in* F *unleserlich*   48 unu‘drozen C   49 der
fehlt C   gesune F   51 do C, d: F   52 engegen] gegin F, zu C
54 getroste C   56 und irn mā .. phinge C   57 zŷ F, zu C   phorten C
antea C   58 .. geinte ir alda C   60 daz was C   61 deme winde C
62 gefriget unt *fehlt* C   63 gaheten gen F, gahte gein C

158,40 tûgendrichem!   855 ir! lovne *für* sivne *verschrieben?*
858 ekegen   864 begenet   865 tagen

Wernhers Maria.   4

```
           mit gebete undermischen;
           si stalte ir hîwische
           beidenthalp ze sîten.
970        daz mâre vlouc dô wîten.
           si stuont ûf eine hôhe,                        (725)
           daz si verre sâhe
           unt wîten mahte schouwen.
           diu vil edele frouwe
975        diu viel dô nider diche
           mit manigem ûfbliche,                          (730)
           wâ er fuore dâ her:
           darzuo was ir vil ger.
           die liute die dâ wâren
980        die begunden alle frâgen,
           wannen der frouwen schône                       (735)
           der gwisse bote chôme,
           der ir hête daz ûz genomen
           daz ir charele scholte chomen.
985        dô si dô wurden innen
           daz von der gotes stimme                        (740)
           diu rede was erschellet,
           Anna wart gezellet
           ze dem allerbesten wîbe
990        diu in disem lîbe
           was bî den zîten;                               (745)
           ir warten unt ir bîten
           daz wart besûftet tiefe.
           got si ane riefen:
995        alliu sîniu wunder
           lobeten si darunder;                            (750)
           die si dâ vernâmen,
           lop si im gâben;
           mit zaheren si sich beguzzen,
1000       die von den herzen fluzzen.
           schiere si dô sâhen                             (755)
           uber velt gâhen
           Joachim unt sîne schar:
           diu frouwe gâhete dar,
```

---

968 si stalten ir hiuewizcen C   69 baid: nth ... si ... F, beiden-
halben zu den siten C   70 do] vil C   71 stuont] stu ... ch (*wohl*
stunt ouch *oder* stunt hoch?) F   einer C   73 weite C   geschouwen C
75 diu viel do] ... da C (*kein Raum für* diu)   77 w: :r f ... F (*kein
Raum für* waz er fv́rte *G.*)   81 wannen] von C, wenne F   82 queme C
83 daz uz *unleserlich* F   84 daz] wanne C   ir man C   scolte]
unleserlich F, scowen *las G.*   85 si da C   inne C   89 besten

A   **D**

ŏf einen perich stŭnt si hŏ,
daz si verre sehe do.

si viel nider dikke
mit manigem ovfpliche,
875 wa er fûre da her:
da zv̊ was ir vil ger.
die levte mit schalle
begunden fragen alle,
von wannen der bote zæme
880 der selben vrŏ chæme,
der ir hiet ovz genomen
wan ir man solde chomen.
do si des wurden innen,
daz von der gotes minnen
885 div rede waz erschellet,
Anna wart gezellet
zv̊ dem besten weibe
die in diesem leibe
waz do bey den zeiten
890 nahen vñ weiten.

mit maniger rede dar vnder
lobten si gotes wunder

vñ mit zeheren sich beguzzen,
die von ir herzen fluzzen.
895 vil schier si do sahen
her vber velt gahen
Joachim vñ sine schar:
div vrowe gahte dar,

159,10 uf eine hŏhe sie gestŭnt,
als die getrîwen gerne tŭnt,
die liebe frivnte uf dem wege hant
unt dicke an die warte gânt. 950
ir hiwisk stalte sie zen siten.
daz mære flŏch do wîten
daz der herre chomen solte,
v̄ in da enpfahen wolte
15 div frŏe uon *des* engeles lere: 955
des gewndert sere
daz lîvt ioh die lantscaft.
sie lobeten die gotes chraft,
v̄ elliv siniv wnder
div erten sie darunder. 960

frowe Anna div wart ŏch erwelt
unt entikliche gezelt
ze dem allerbesten wibe
div iender wære enlibe.

20 schiere sie do sahen 965
zu in uber velt gahen
Joachim mit siner schâre:
div frŏe hûb sich dare,

---

bis mŭzen 1082 C³ I   90 in dekeime C   91 geziten C
.... den .. ten F, *weder für* do A, *noch für* geziten *reicht der Raum*
92 vnd biten C   93 besufztet C   96 lobte C   99 v'guzen C   1000 von
deme C   1 do .....en, *dem Raum nach* gesahen F   4 gahte C, *unleserlich* F, *vielleicht auch* gegâhte
159,15 des des   887 beste

1005   umb den hals si in gevie,
      an sîner hende si gie,   (760)
      si halste in unde chuste,
      si druchte in an die bruste
      unt enphienc in inneclîchen wol.
1010   si wâren bêdiu sament vol
      des trôstes allermeiste   (765)
      des heiligen geistes.
      alliu diu menige
      diu trat im engegene
1015   unt hiez in willechomen sîn.
      dô tet got vil guot schîn   (770)
      vor mannen unt vor wîben
      daz niemen sîne guote mac volschrîben.

      Ruben den êwarten
1020   den mahte riuwen harte
      swaz er dem herren ie gesprach,   (775)

      dô er diu zeichen ane sach:
      daz er niuwen beleip
      unz er in furder treip
1025   ûz dem gotes hûse,
      dâvor maht im grûsen,   (780)
      dô er diu gotes tougen
      beschouwet an der frouwen.

      nâch den vierzic wochen
1030   diu chamere wart entlochen,
      dâ diu rîcheit inne was   (785)
      der alliu diu werlt genas.

      der wâz vil guoter salben
      begunde dô allenthalben
1035   ûz breiten sîne suoze
      den sundâren ze buoze,   (790)
      zeiner gwissen urstende
      nâch des lîbes ende.

1005 vm C, vmbe F   5*f.* gevinge : ginge C   8 an ir C   11*f.* aller-
meist: von dem heiligen geist C   13*f.* alle di minen   tret im inkeine C
14*f.* giengen, hiezen *B. s. 94*   16 vil guot] wol C   17 *das erste* vor

A

vm den hals si in vienk,
900 an siner hant si gienk,
si halst in vn̄ chuste
vn̄ drukte in zů ir bruste;
si enpfienk in minnechlichen wol,
si waren bede frevden vol.

905 al die menige
giengen *im* enkegene
vn̄ hiezzen in willechomen sein.
do tet got vil wol schein
vor mannen vn̄ vor weiben
910 daz nieman sein wunder chan vol
schreiben.

Rvben den æwarten
begunde riwen harte
swaz er dem herren îe gesprach,

do er die zeichen ane sach,

915 do er die gotes tovgen
an schowet mit den augen
an dem reinen weib*e*
vn̄ an ir werden leibe.
Nach den vierzich wochen
920 die chamer wart entlochen,
da div reicheit inne lak
div al der werlde wak.

der smak der sůzzen salben
begunde allenthalben
925 ovz breiten sin sůzze
den sunderen ze bůzze,
zů einer gewizzen vrstende
nach des leibes ende.

D

umbe den hals sie in gevîe,
an siner hande sie gîe, 970
si chust in div rêine v̄ div gvt
mit vil frolichem můt
v̄ enpfieng in inneklichen wol,
als liep herzelieben schol,
159, 25 ane sunde mæilige minne, 975
wan ze got stûnden ir sinne,
der die gvten beruchet ie.
div menige im engegen gie
v̄ hiez in willechomen sin.
do wart al der werlte schin, 980
daz sin ie vil gut rat wirt
derz ubel durh die warheit
uerbirt.

30 **R**vben den ewarte
den maht do riwen harte
swaz er dem herren ie 985
gesprah,
do er die zeichen gesah
div zemære waren chomen
vnde witen wrden uernomen
in der iudisgen diet,
wie in got mit kinde beriet, 990
wie er in geruchte scheiden
uon kumber v̄ in beiden
35 nah mům̂en frŏde uerlech,
der in div werlte uerzêch.
Nah den uierzich wochen 995
div kamer wart entlochen,
da div richeit inne was
dauon der uerlorn mennisk gnas,
v̄ elliv gotes hantgetat
leben v̄ gnade enpfangen hat. 1000
40 der wâz vil guter salben
begunde do allenthalben
uz breiten sine sůze
den sundæren ze bůzze,
160, 1 ze einer gewissen urstende 1005
nah des libes ende.

Ende von F   19 Rubin C   22 gesach *B. s. 86*   23 nuwent C, *l.* niene?
30 entslozen C   33 der smak C   34 da C   36 svnden C   37 zu
einer gewissen C
906 in   *917* weiben

der vater vil guoter
1040 unt ir vil edeliu muoter
die newolten die himelrôsen   (795)
mit namen niht verbôsen:
si hiezen sie Marîen,
wan als ⟨daz⟩ honic die bîen
1045 ûz dem trôre mugen vinden,
als chan diu chuniginne   (800)

den ⟨heil⟩triefenden fladen
nâch disem lîbe fur tragen
den hungergen sêlen.
1050 an ir ist lobes mêre
danne dehein stimme
⟨iemer⟩ fur muge bringen.   (805)

Dô daz reine chindelîn,
daz êwige magedîn,
1055 in dise werlt wart geborn,
dô wart erleschet der zorn   (810)
der gotes unwirde
unt fleischlîcher girde.
dô wart der mennische
1060 geladet ze gotes tische,
ze der lebendigen spîse;   (815)
die engel in dem paradîse
die enphiengen dô den ir genôz.

honic unde milch flôz,
1065 nôtturftiger segen,
heilfuoriger regen,   (820)
pigmente unde mirre.
daz schâf daz ê fuor irre
daz vant dô crippen unde stal,
1070 dô got lûhte uberal.
uns chom der wîntrûbe,   (825)
diu stimme der turteltûben
wart gehôret vil gereite
uber al die christenheite.

1041 di edelen rosen   44 bynen   46 also   49 der vn-
gewegen sele   50 an] als   52 iemer mêre *L*.   59 mensche
60 geladen   63 enphigen   67 bimente   mirren   68*ff*. daz schaf

A

der vater v̄n div mŭter
930 wolten der tohter gûter
    ir namen niht verbôsen,
    der edelen himelrosen:
    si hiezzen sey Marien,
    wan als daz honik die peien
935 ovz dem trore chan gewinnen,   160, 5
    als chan div chvniginne

    den vil sv̊zzen fladen
    nach disem leibe fur tragen
    den hungergen sælen.
940 an ir ist lobes mere
    danne denhein stimme
    mvge immer fure bringen.

    Do daz reine chindelin,
    daz æwige magedein,
945 in dise werlt wart geboren,
    do wart erleschet der zorn
    gotes vn̄ vnwirde
    nach des todes girde.
    do wart der mensch geladen
950 zv̊ gotes tische vn̄ ze sinen genaden,
    zv̊ der lebendigen speise;
    die engel in dem paradeyse
    die enphiengen do den mensch zv̊
            ir genoz.
    Honik v̄n milich floz,

955 vns chomen die weintrovben,
    div stimme der turtiltovben
    wart gehort berait
    vber alle die christenheit.

D

Der uater uil guter
und ir vil ediliv muter
die newolten die himelrosen
mit namen niht uerbosen: 1010
si hiezen sie Marien,
wand als daz honich die bigen
uzem trore mugen vinden,
also kan sie den kinden,
die ir dienent v̄ getruvent   1015
die wile sie hie enerde buvent,
den heil triefenten fladen
nah disem libe fûrtragen.
sie kan ŏch die bitter der sunden
ioh die totliche wnden   1020
10 mit ir gŭte wol uerdeken.
nu ruche sie uns erweken,
daz wir sie uon herzen mêinen:
so mak sie uns gnade bescheinen.

Do daz reine magdin   1025
            wart geborn,

do wart erlesket der zorn
der gotes unwirde
vn̄ fleisklicher girde.
15 do wart ŏh der menniske
geladet ze gotes tische,   1030
ze dem lebentigen brote
daz die sele nimet uzer note;
der mennish wart engels genoz.

honich v̄ milch vz der erde floz;
got die werlte do segent,   1035
vnt heil von himel regent,
20 pigmente, ole v̄ mirre.
daz schâf daz e fur irre
daz uant do chrippe v̄ stal,
do got luhte uber al.   1040
uns chom der wintrûbe,
div ware turteltube
wart gehoret uil gereite
uber al die christenheite.

kant di krippen   vnd da got luhte uberal   vns kom der wintruben zal
73 f. gereit : kristē̄heit

    160, 6 getruvnt   buvnt   953 do!

1075   **D**er tac daz si geborn wart
        der ist sô liep unt sô zart   (830)
        allen den liuten
        die sich mit der brûte
        hin ze himele wellent swingen,
1080   under ir vanen dingen.
        junge unde alte   (835)
        die muozen die dult behalten
        mit vîre unt mit gesange:
        si wirt vil wol enphangen,
1085   si schol uns willechomen sîn:
        ja liuhtet uns daz magedîn   (840)
        als diu lilie ûz den dórnen.
        si weget ouch uns dâ vórne,
        sô ez uns an die nôt gât.
1090   den sundâren si bî stât
        vil rehte muoterlîche.   (845)
        si wil uns niht entwîchen,
        unz si uns bringet an die stat
        der ie gerte unde bat
1095   allez unser gemuote:
        sô grôz sint ir guote.   (850)
        si hertet wol die lenge.
        unser froude nam anegenge
        dô si in der molde
1100   mit uns bûwen wolde.
        swâ man sant Marîen nennet,   (855)
        sô frouwet sich unt mendet
        beidiu sêle unde lîp:
        ir name uns wîsunge gît
1105   ze unserm heimôde
        ûz irdischer brôde.   (860)
        bezzer name wart nie:
        daz si ze leben ie ⟨gevie⟩,
        des loben wir den heilant,
1110   der dâ herberge vant
        in dem sunnenschîne: (865)
        si enwart ouch nie ze wîbe,
        si ist maget unbewollen,
        si gît uns ⟨froude unt⟩ trôst envollen.

   1080 under] vnd   dringen   82 den tac behalte *bis* dᵉhub si 1446 C²
276—633   84 si wirt] so wirt, *l.* so wirt si?   87 *f.* dorn : vorn   88 *ent-*
stellt? uns vor zorne? *L.*   90 da bistat   93 wanne si uns bren ...
94 der *Sch.*] des AC   ie] ir   98 nam] von   1101 mariam   2 menget

A

Der tak do si geboren wart
960 der ist liep vñ zart
allen den levten
die sich mit der brevte
hinze himel wellent swingen
mit reinechlichen dingen.

965 Si sol vns willechomen seyn:
ia levhtet vns der magede schein
sam div lilye ovz dem dorn.
si wiget vns gen gotes zorn.
als ez vns an die not gat,
970 den svnderen si bey gestat
vil reht mv̊terlichen.
si wil vns niht gesweichen,
vnz si vns bringet an die stat
der ie vnser herze pat.

975 si hertet an der lenge.
vnser frevde nam anigenge
do si der werlde molde
mit vns hie bowen wolde.
swa man Mareien nennet,
980 so frevt sich vñ erchennet
pede sele vñ leip:
ir name vns weisunge geit
zv̊ vnserm heimot
ovz menschlicher not.

985 des lob wir den hailant,
der die herberge vant
in dem sunne scheine:
si wart nie ze weibe,
si ist vnbewollen,
990 die frevde geit den vollen.

D

Der tach daz sie geborn 1045
wart
der ist liep, werde v̄ zart
160, 25 allem dem livte
daz sih mit der brûte
gert uz den sunden swingen,
under ir uanen dingen. 1050
die ivngen v̄ die alten
muzzen die dult behalten
mit vire, gesange v̄ gebet,
wand uns got gnade mit ir tet
v̄ uber uns selbe erschêin: 1055
daz ware lieht brahte sie eîne.

30 sie ist unser frôden angenge,
ir gûte wert wol die lenge.

swa man sænd Marien nennet,
so frôet sih v̄ mendet 1060
beidiv ensamet sel v̄ lip,
wand uns ir name die wisunge git
ze unser heimode
uz irdisker brode.
bezzer name wart nie: 1065
daz sie daz leben ie geuie,
35 des loben wir den heilant,
der da herberge vant
in dem sunne schine:
daz ist div muter sine. 1070

---

4 wîsunge] wege   5 heymote   6 uzir diser   8 der zu leben ie C, daz leben
B. s. 58   14 *ergänzt von Sch.*, trôst unt froude den vollen *L.*
974 des   992 div

1115   Dannen uber driu jâr
         daz si die tohter gebar,   (870)
         ir opher si ûf huoben,
         mit dem kinde si daz truogen
         gen dem tempel frône.
1120   Marîa gie sô schône,
         sô wol ûfgerihte   (875)
         den liuten zuo gesihte,
         daz si nie umbe gesach.
         ze der muoter si niht ensprach,

1125   noch sich darzuo gemuozte
         daz si den vater gruozte,   (880)
         unt sie nie des gezam,
         daz si wîp oder man
         ane wolde schouwen.
1130   si gie vor al den frouwen
         vil gereite zuo der reste.   (885)
         aller kinde beste
         daz suohte manige venigen.
         des wunderôte die menige,
1135   daz si chint was ame lîbe
         unt doch al den wîben   (890)
         ein guot bilde vor truoc
         unt aller zuhte genuoc.
         ' den mageden die dâ wâren
1140   unt in dem tempel lâgen
         alle zît unt alle friste   (895)
         in gotes dieniste,
         den enphulhen si daz chint,
         dem al die dienende ⟨sint⟩
1145   die daz êwige leben
         ⟨unt got⟩ iemer wellent sehen: (900)
         do beleip si gerne under in.
         diu muoter unde Joachim
         die îlten dannen chêren.
1150   diu maget wuohs mit êren
         âne aller slahte laster   (905)
         unt nam sich fur vil vaste,
         ⟨daz ir alle holt wâren
         die si an gesâhen,⟩

1118 si ez   19 frone] schône   20 gin da vore C, vorne *Br. s. 78*
23 umgesach   24 sprach   25 darzu niht   30 allen vrouwen   31 gerechte
32 dirnkinde? *L.*   34 wundert   36 al den *M.*] alten C, allen *Sch.*   37 fur? *L.*

A

Dar nach vber driv iar
do si die tohter gebar,
ir opfer si ỏf hỷben,
mit dem chinde si daz trûgen
995 gen dem tempel frone.
Maria gienk so schone
vñ begunde sich ovf rihten   160, 40
den levten ze gesihten,
daz si vme nie gesach.
1000 zỷ ir mûter si niht sprach,

vñ sei nie gezam   161, 1
daz si weip oder man
ane wolde schowen.
si gie vor al den frowen
1005 vil beraite zỷ der reste.
aller kinde beste
daz sûchte manik venie.
des wunderte al die menige,
daz si mit chintlichem leibe
1010 pede manne vñ weibe
so gût bilde vor trûk
vñ aller zuhte genûk.
den meiden die da waren
vñ in dem tempel lagen
1015 alle zeit vñ alle frist
in gotes lobe vñ sinem dienst,
den enphulhen si daz kint,
dem alle die dieninde sint
die got wellent sehen
1020 vñ himilische frevde spehen.
Si waz gerne vnder in.
div mûter vñ Joachim
die eylten dannen cheren.
div magt waz mit eren
1025 ane aller slahte laster,
vñ nam sich fure so vaste
daz ir alle holt waren
die sey an gesahen.

D

Dannen uber driv iare
daz sie die tohter gebare,
ir opfer sie ufhuben,
mit dem kinde sie daz trugen
gegen dem sale frone.   1075
Maria gie so schoue,
so wol ufgerihte
den livten ze gesihte,
daz sie nie umbe gesah.
zeder muter sie niht   1080
      ensprah,
noh sih darzu gemûzte
daz sie den vater grûzte,
v̄ sie nie des gezam,
daz sie wip oder man
ane wolte scỏwen.   1085
sie gie uor al den frôwen
uil gereite zu der reste.
aller dirnkinde beste
daz suhte manige uenige.
des wnderot die menige,   1090
5 daz sie kint was amme libe,
v̄ doh, als ich fur ware scribe,
der werlte ein bilde uor truch:
daz was zuhteklich gnuch
v̄ gut ze merchen uberal   1095
den mageden in dem sale,
die got zaller zit dienten da.
nu wart ỏh enpfolhen sa
den selben frôen daz kint
dem die sæligen diende sint: 1100
10 alsus beleip sie under in.
div muter v̄ Joachim
begunden danne keren.
div maget ŵhse mit eren
ân aller slahte itewiz,   1105
wan got selbe sinen fliz
v̄ sin hute an sie leite.
des wart im gnade geseite

---

39 meiden   41f. vrist : dinst   43 dem bevalch   44 dē alle di dinent
46 *Ergänzung metrisch gefordert, aber nur ein Notbehelf*   52 sich fur] wr sich
   992 div   994 si daz!

1155   daz si vor liebe weinten
        die got von herzen meinten.   (910)

        Dô sprach frouwe Anne:
        ,got schiubet ûf lange
        sîne gnâde, swenner wil,
1160   unt gît ir ze mâle vil
        daz si niemen ⟨mac⟩ ergrunden   (915)
        noch furbaz gechunden,
        gezellen noch gemezzen:
        wer scholte im des vergezzen?

1165   die mîne vîande
        bestênt an den schanden,   (920)
        die mir ubele sprâchen,
        sine wessen waz si râchen.
        dô ich unberhaft was
1170   unt darnâch schiere genas
        der ⟨vil⟩ lieben tohter mîn,   (925)
        dâ wart wol in allen schîn
        daz daz gotes zeichen
        her ze mir wolte reichen.
1175   nu muoz in allez daz loben
        daz von im ist bechomen: (930)
        leien unde phaffen,
        unt swaz er hât erschaffen,
        daz bechenne in allez an mir:
1180   die wilden vogele unde tier,
        die vische unt al daz wunder   (935)
        daz in des meres grunde
        beidiu fliuzet oder swebet,
        swaz chreset oder lebet
1185   ûf dem ertpodeme
        oder in den luften obene,   (940)
        daz muoz mir bescheinen
        wie ich in ⟨schul⟩ loben unde meinen.'

        Vor ⟨der⟩ gotes geburte
1190   swaz die liute worhten,

1156 von ganzem herzen? *Sch.*   57 di vrouwe   59 wanne er
60 gibt der   62 mac gekunde   63 geceln   65 die *fehlt* viende   68 si
enwosten   71*f.* der liben tochter di ich han   doch mochten si alle wol
enstan   74 her ze] daz er uz C, er uz *B. s. 45*   75 allen   76 kumen,

A **D**

uon allen die in meinten;
uor liebe sie beweinten   *1110*
161, 15 des kindes tugend, zvht v̄ gûte,
suze gebære, reinz gemvte.

Do sprach frowe Anne: **D**o sprah frŏe Anne:
1030 ,got schevbet ŏf vil lange   ,got schîvbet uf lange
sine genade, swen er wil,   sine gnade, swenner wil,   *1115*
vñ geit ir danne so vil   unde git ir ensamet vil
daz si nieman chan vol grunden   daz sie niemen mak ergrunden
noch furbaz kechvnden.   noh furbaz gechunden,
                                 gezellen noh gemezzen:
                                 wer scholt im des uer-   *1120*
                                         gezzen?

1035 Die minen viande   20 die mine viande
gestent in grozzer schande,   die stent nu mit schanden,
die mir vbel sprachen,   die mir ubele sprachen,
vñ ir spot an mir rachen,   sine wessen waz sie rachen.
do ich vnperhaft was,   do ih unberhafte was   *1125*
1040 vñ seit ich nv genas   v̄ darnach schiere genas
der lieben tohter mein,   der herzelieben tohter min,
da worden an ist schein   da wart wol in allen schin
michel gotes zaichen.   daz daz gotes zeichen
nv greifen vñ reichen   herce mir wolt gereichen. *1130*
                                 25 nu mûze in allez daz loben
                                 daz uon im ist bechomen:

1045 layen vñ phaffen,
vñ swaz got hat beschaffen,
daz erchenne in an mir: der mennisk vntez wilt,
wilde vogel vñ tier,   der uogel v̄ swaz in wage spilt,

swaz flivzzet oder swebt,   swaz flivzet oder swebet,   *1135*
1050 swaz chrest oder lebt   swaz chreset oder lebet
ovf dem erpodeme   uf dem erdepodme
oder in den luften obene,   v̄ in den luften obene,
daz sol got den reinen   daz muze mir bescheinen
mit lobe in triwen meinen.'   wie ih in schul loben v̄   *1140*
                                         meinen.'

1055 **V**or gotes geburte noch 30 **E** daz got menniske wrde
swaz die levte taten doch,   ane suntliche burde,

---

vgl. § 31 *b*   79 bekent   81 allez daz   83 oder] und   84 kruchet
87 muoze *Sch.*   88 meinen C   schul loben unde meinen *L. Sch.*] lob und
meinen C, *oder* mit triuwen lobe unt meine *Sch.*   90 swaz *B. s. 50*] wi gut

1033 vol grundē!   *1046* beschaffen!   *161,26* vnt ezwilt

swie guot si dô wâren   (945)
⟨unt⟩ diu chint diu si gebâren,

       doch begên wir niht ir dult.
       wizzet ir wol die schult,
1195   warumbe wir daz mîden,
       daz diu vaste noch diu vîre   (950)
       in gesetzet niht enist,
       unz aller manne bezzist
       si erledigôte
1200   ûz angestlîcher nôte?
       von des êrsten mannes sunden   (955)
       was daz abgrunde
       gerîchet von den sêlen:
       die muosen dar chêren,
1205   solhe unt samelîche,
       arme unde rîche;   (960)
       do enwart nehein gebeine
       sô lûter noch sô reine,
       daz daz mahte bewarn,
1210   sine muosten alle dar varn,
       mit manigem sêre erbîten   (965)
       der ôsterlîchen zîte,
       daz daz êwige urschîn
       erlûhte enmitten under in,
1215   do des crûces insigele,
       daz zeichen ûz dem himele   (970)
       die tiefen helle entrante,
       den tievel geschante
       unt sîne volgâre
1220   die dârinne wâren.

       Dô hiez got uber die sînen   (975)
       ein michel lieht schînen,
       eine grôze berhtel unde glast.
       nu hôret wie des crûces ast
1225   unt der vil heilige stam
       erlôste wîp unde man: (980)
       sît der heilige aller heiligôn
       bêdiu sic unde lôn

1191 gut] heilig   93 f. und doch in den iarn waren   nu ist ir
wol di schult   96 noch] und   98 lezzist   99 f. erledigot : not
1203 geruĉht   4 muzent   6 arm   10 sine] si   13 der ewige schin
14 erblûte mitten   20 *etwa* die dâ in grôzen freisen (pînen? *L.*)

A

swie reht si waren
vñ swaz si kint gebaren,
die ze himel sint geselt
1060 vñ zů den gůten gezelt,
doch begæ wir niht ir tult.
ir sult wol wizzen die schult,
warume wir daz meiden,
daz die vaste noch daz veiren
1065 in gesetzet niht enist,
vnz aller manne bezzerist
si erledegot
ovz engestlicher not:
von des ersten weibes svnde
1070 was daz abgrunde
gereichet mit den selen,
die mûsten dar cheren.

do wart nie denhein gebeine
so louter noch so reine,
1075 daz ez mohte bewarn,
div sele mv̊ste dar varen.
da mv̊sen si erbeiten
der osterlichen zeite,
vnz der liehte schein
1080 erlouht vnder in,
do des chrevzes insigil,
daz zeichen ŏz dem himel
die tiefen helle entrant
vñ den tivel pant
1085 vñ die volger sin
die da waren in dem pein.

Do hiez got vber die seinen
ein groz lieht scheinen:
daz waz dem tievel ain last.
1090 nv horet wie des chrevzes ast
vñ der vil heilege stam
erloste weib vñ man:
seit der heilige Christ
gesiget an des tievels list,

D

swie gůt die livte wæren
v̄ div kint die sie gebaren,

doh begen wir ir dulte niht. 1145
wizzet ir umbe welhe gesciht,
warumbe wir daz miden,
daz wir sie niht viren,
noh in div ere gesatzet ist,
untze unser herre Christ 1150
sie selbe erledigot
uz angestlicher not?
dvrh des ersten mannes sunde
was daz tief abgrunde
gerichet uon den selen: 1155
die musen dar cheren,
solhe v̄ sameliche,
bediv arme vnde riche.

do wart nehein gebein
so luter noh so rêin, 1160
daz daz mæhte bewarn,
sine mûsen alle dar uarn
v̄ mit langem sere erbiten
der osterlichen zite,
daz daz ewige vrschin 1165
erluhte enmitten vnder in,
v̄ des cruces insigele,
daz zæichen uon himele
der helle gewalte entrante,
die sele erloste, den tievil 1170
geschante.

Do hiez got uber die sinen
ein michel lieht erschinen,
ein groze berhtel vñ glast.
nu horet wie des crucis ast
v̄ der uil heilige stam 1175
erlediget wib v̄ man:
sit der heilig aller heiligon
bediv sich vñ lon

161, 35 (line position)

40 (line position)

162, 1 (line position)

5 (line position)

wâren   21 hie   22 licht liz schinen   23 ein groz berk tal   26 der
erlost   27 sit] sin   heiligen

1061 do   161, 34 crhist   1078 zeiten   1088 scheinen!

aller der werlte erzeigete
1230 die sich zuo im neigeten,
unt diu helle was zebrosten: (985)
sît muosten wir vasten
unt mit banvîren
êren die holden sîne,
1235 die ir lîp garten
ze mislîcher marter, (990)
unt solhiu werc worhten
daz si niht envorhten
des lîbes wandelunge.
1240 Moyses ⟨unt sîne⟩ junger
die dâ vor lebeten, (995)
swie vil si tugende phlegeten,

ir dult doch niemen begêt,
diu an ir jârzît gestêt,
1245 wan si den nie gesâhen
des si ze herren jâhen, (1000)
der sît under uns gie
unt sich crûcigen lie,
daz alliu ⟨diu⟩ heilikeit
1250 wurde deste baz bereit,
unt christenlîcher êre (1005)
wurde deste mêre.

David unt Abraham
die wâren fursten lobesam,
1255 Ysaac unt Josuê,
Jacob in der alten ê, (1010)
joch diu tohter Ysachar,
diu unser frouwen gebar,
unt ir vater Joachim:
1260 die hêten allen ir sin
an got ⟨starche⟩ gewendet, (1015)
des enwurden si niht geschendet:
⟨si⟩ sint in himelrîche
den engeln gelîche,
1265 unt dâ sô gefristet
daz in nihtes gebristet, (1020)
wan des alterseine

1229 *l.* al der? 31 zubrochen 33 banvicre 35 karten
36 mislîcher?] gemisscheter 40 Moyses der junge sîne] des? *L.* 43 gedult
44 iargezit 49 ⟨sîne⟩? *M.* 50. 52 dester 51*f. schwerlich in Ordnung:*

A

1095 vn̄ div helle wart zebrosten,
seit mûste wir vasten
vn̄ mit banne veiren
eren die holden seinen.

Moyses vndertan
1100 vn̄ ander gûte weip vn̄ man
die da vor lebten,
swie vil si tugende phlegten,

ir tak doch nieman beget,
der an ir iarzeit gestet,
1105 wan si den nie gesahen
des si ze herren iahen,
der seit vnder vns gie
vn̄ sich chrevzen lie.

Dauid vn̄ Abraham,
1110 die fursten lobesam,
Ysaac vn̄ Josue,
die lebten in der alten æ,
Ysachar vn̄ Joachim:

die heten allen iren sin
1115 an got vaste gewendet,
des wurden si nie geschendet:
si sint in himelreiche
den engeln geleiche.

D

aller der werlte erzeigte
div sih zu im geneigte,   1180
vnt div helle zebraste,
sit wart uns div uaste
geboten v̄ div banvire
durh die holden sine,

162, 10 die solhiv werch worhten   1185
daz sie den tot nien uorhten
durh die gotes minne.
Moyses v̄ sin gesinde
die dauor lebeten,
swie vil tugende sie   1190
pflegeten,
ir dulte doh nieman begat,
div an ir iarzite gestat,
wand sie den nie gesahen
des sie ze herren iahen,
15 der sit under mennisken gîe 1195
v̄ sih crucigen lie
durh liebe der christenheit,
div nu wît ist vn̄ breit.

David v̄ Habraham
daz waren fursten lo⟨besam⟩, 1200
Ysaac v̄ Josue
vnd Jacob in der alten ê
ioh div tohter Ysachar,
div unser frŏen gebar,
20 v̄ ir vater Joachim: 1205
die heten allen ir sin
an got starche gewendet,
des enwrden sie niht geschendet
sie sint inme himelriche
den engeln geliche,   1210
vnd sint da so gefristet
daz in da nihtes gebristet,
wan des alterseine

etwa unt christenlichiu êre   sich begunde breiten unde mêren   57 joch]
und   66 niht   67 wanne des aleine
162, 20 ioachin

Wernhers Maria.   5

daz wir si ûz scheiden
an unsern hôchzîten,
1270　durch daz si muosen bîten
der gotes ledigunge   (1025)
in dem abgrunde,
⟨die helle muosen schouwen⟩
mit allem ir gezouwe
1275　⟨. . . . .⟩
⟨nu⟩ ruofet in die hôhe,

dar si nu sint gefuoret,
von dem tievel ungeruoret,   (1030)
⟨daz⟩ daz heilige ingesîde
1280　vor hazze joch vor nîde
uns armen ruoche enbinden,
daz wir si hernâch vinden
in den himilischen êren,   (1035)
sô wir von disem ellende chêren.
⟨Amen!⟩

1269 hochgeziten   70 da durch daz si muzen bᵉiten   74 gezeume
76 geru : et   79 ingesinde   80 joch] noch   83 unzellichen

A   **D**

daz wir sie uzscheiden

162, 25 an unsern hohziten,   *1215*

durh daz sie musen biten

der gotes ledigunge,

v̄ an des libes wandelunge

die helle musen scŏen

mit allem ir gezôwe.   *1220*

nu rufet sie an alle

uon herzen, niht mit des mundes

schalle,

nv helfe got der gûte   da sie nu sint gefuret

1120 durch sin werdes plût,   uon dem tievil umberuret,

daz wir daz in*g*esinde   30 daz daz heilige ingeside   *1225*

uor hazze ioh uor nide

uns armen ruche enbinden,

alle gemeine vinden   daz wir sie hernah vinden

in den himilischen eren,   in den himilisken eren,

so wir von hinnen mûzzen cheren.   so wir uzem ellende cheren. *1230*

Amen!   Amen!

1121 insinde

II.

1285	Nu vernemet die senften lêre
	von der magede hêre,
	diu uns den heilant gebar:
	guotiu herze, hevet iuch dar (1040)
	dâ ir den trôst vindet
1290	des iu niemer zerinnet!
	bittet sie der underdige,
	daz si flîzeclîchen lige
	ir trûtsun an den fuozen, (1045)
	unz er uns gebuoze
1295	unser leit unt unser sêr!
	der priester heizet Wernher
	der des liedes began.
	von dem er urchunde nam, (1050)
	der ist ouch von Christe
1300	ze einem ewangelisten
	gesegenet unt gewîhet:
	niemen im des verzîhet.
	Mathêus ist der orthabe: (1055)
	der râtet daz wir ûz tragen
1305	die margarîten an daz lieht,
	daz si vertunchelt werde nieht
	in irdischem stoube.
	ja hilfet uns der gloube (1060)
	den wir an die kuniginne haben,
1310	sô wir dem tievil widersagen.
	si ist ein mersterne:
	ja mugen wir si loben gerne
	des himels frouwen unde brût: (1065)
	si beschirmet wol daz liut,
1315	unt alle ir undertâne
	die tuot si sorgen âne.
	si hât gemêret wol daz lôn
	allen gotes heiligôn, (1070)
	wan allez manchunne

1285 dise lere   86 maget   88 herzcē nu hebet   90 uch
zurinnet   91 bit si darunter nige   92 si v :: (vil) ulizclichen   93 an
deme fuz: 99 cristen   1301 geseinet   2 in   3 erthale   4 daz

A   D

A	D
1125 **N**v vernemt di semften lere	**N**v uernemet die senften lere
von der magt here,	uon der magede here,
div vns den hailant gebar:	div uns den heilant gebar:
gûtev herze, hebt evch dar	gutiv herze, heuet ivh dar
da ir den trost vindet 162, 35	da ir daz hæil gwinnet *1235*
1130 des nimmer ev zerinnet!	des iv niemer cerinnet!
pitet sey mit steter dige,	bittet sie der undirdige,
daz ⟨si⟩ fleizzechlich an lige	daz sie flehliken lige
ir trout svne an den fuezzen,	ir trut sun an dem fuze,
vnz er vns gebuezze	untze er uns gebuzze *1240*
1135 vnser lait vñ vnser ser! 163, 1	unser leit unt unser sere!
der priester heizzet Wernher	der pfaffe heizet Wernhere
der des liedes began.	der des lides began.
von dem er vrchunde nam,	uon dem er urchunde nam,
der ist vor Christ	der ist öh uon Christe *1245*
1140 zv einem ewangelist	zeinem ęwangeliste
gesegent vñ geweihet:	gesegent v̄ gewihet:
niht in got verzeihet.	nieman ime des uerzihet.
Matheus ist der orthabe:	5 Matheus ist der orthabe:
der retet daz wir die habe	der ratet daz man uz trage *1250*
1145 vñ die red an daz lieht	die margariten an das lieht,
tragen vū des lazzen nieht,	daz sie werde uertunchelt nieht
	in dem irdiskem stöbe.
	ia hilfet uns der glöbe
	den wir zu der kuniginne han, *1255*
	so wir dem tievil widerstan.
vñ des meres sterne	
Mariam loben gerne,	
	sie ist des himels fröe v̄ brut,
	sie beschirmet wol daz lîvt,
	10 und alle ir undertane
	die getut sie sorgen ane. *1260*
	sie hat den heiligen daz lon
	gemert mit des lebens chrôn,
1150 **wan alles menschchunne**	**wand allez mannes chunne**

---

wir] daz vns C, uns daz *B. s. 51*   5 di di   an] in   11 in ein sterne
13 di himelisschen brut, *vgl. § 67*   18 heiligē   19 wanne allez kunne
     1125 sempften!

1320 ienoch ze helle brunne,
         wâre in diu maget niht chomen

         diu si ûz dem fiure hât genomen.
         si ist ein christalle   (1075)
         ob den engeln allen,
1325 ⟨ein liehtvaz in der vinster;
         si zuchet uns von der winstern,

         daz wir⟩ zeswenthalp gestên,
         sô wir zuo gerihte gên.
         alle ⟨ir⟩ volgâre,
1330 nu bittet den sagerâre   (1080)
         den der heilige geist begôz,
         daz si mîne sunde alsô grôz
         mit gnâden welle bedechen,
         unz ich diu herze erweche
1335 diu noch slâfende sint,   (1085)
         daz si erchennen daz chint
         daz si mit armen umbevie!
         dô si ze cheminâten gie
         bî der smâhen crippen,
1340 dô wart Adâmes rippe   (1090)
         an der frouwen wol geêret:
         si hat ⟨uns⟩ alle froude gemêret.

         Dô sante Marîe,
         diu edele unt diu frîe,
1345 diu maget unberuoret,   (1095)
         ze dem ⟨templo⟩ wart gefuoret,
         daz der kunic Salomôn
         stifte durch daz gotes lôn
         in der stat ze Jerusalêm,
1350 ir êre begunde ûf gên: (1100)
         geprediget wart si wîten,
         wan si in den selben zîten
         erlûhte alsam diu sunne
         ûz allem ir chunne.
1355 ir antlutze unt ir ougen   (1105)

1320 muste zur helle brunne   24 uber di engele alle   26 ziuhet
B. s. 57   27 cesm: einthalp gesten   30 di bitent den sagere   32 daz
si] da her also] so   34 h'zcen   37 f. ummeving : ging   40 rippen   43 sant
maria   44 f. di edele maget und vrie   juncvrouwe unberuret   49 iheru-
salem   50 ir ere] e her   52 geziten   53 er beluhte als   54 kunnde

A

noch ze helle brunne,
wer div magt niht chomen

div vns da von hat genomen.
si ist ein christalle   163, 15
ob den engeln allen.

1155 nv pit die vrowen mære,
den heren sagerere
den der heilige geist besloz,
daz si mine svnde groz
mit vollen genaden deche,
1160 vnz ich div herze erweche
die nu slaffinde sint,
daz si erchennen daz chint
daz si mit armen vmbevienk!
do si ze chemenaten gienk
1165 bey der smehen krippe,
do wart Adâmes rippe
an ⟨der⟩ frou̯wen wol geæret:
si hat vns frevde gemeret.

    Do sant Mareie,
1170 div edele vn̄ div freye,
div magt vnberŭret,
ze dem tempel wart gefueret,
den der kvnik Salomon
stifte durch den gotes lon
1175 in der stat ze Jerusalem,
ir ere begunde ŏf gên:
gepredigot wart si weiten,
wan si in den selben zeiten
louht alsam div sunne
1180 ovz allem irem kvnne.
ir antlutze vn̄ ir ougen

D

ienoh ze helle brunne,
ware in div maget niht   1265
      chomen
div sie uzer not hat genomen.
sie ist ein christalle
uber die engil alle,
ein liehtvaz in der vinster;
sie zuchet uns uon der   1270
      winster,
daz wir zeswenthalben gesten,
so wir an daz gerihte gen.
alle ir uolgære,
nv bittet den sagerare
den der heilig geist begoz,   1275
daz sie mine sunde also groz
20 mit gnaden wol bedeche,
untz ih div herze erweche
div noh slafende sint,
daz sie erchennen daz kint   1280
daz sie mit armen umbevie!
do sie ze keminaten gie
bi der smahen krippe,
do wart Adames rippe
an der frŏen wol geeret: 1285
sie hat uns alle frŏde gemeret.

25   Do sænte Marie,
div edile vnt div frie,
div maget unberuret,
zu dem templo wart gefuret   1290

in der stat ze Jerusalem,
ir ere begunde do uf gen:
erkant wart sie witen,
wande sie in denselben ziten
erluhte sam div sunne   1295
uz allem ir chunne.
30 ir antlutze was so tugentliche,
ir ŏgen also kunchliche,
ir gebærde also reine,
daz sih zv ir glichte dehêine   1300
under allen den frŏen.

1167 frevden   1174 durt

daz muosen an schouwen
die liute mit vorhten.
swâ ander frouwen worhten
lînwât unt sîden,

1360 ir neheiniu mahte erlîden (1110)
der arbeite alsô vil
sô ditze kint in sînem spil
mahte volbringen.
ja worhte si mit sinnen
1365 al des si begunde. (1115)
swaz die alten chunden,
daz enmahte ir niht engân.
des nahtes îlte si ûf stân,
daz si ir venien pflâge,
1370 gote sich ergâbe. (1120)
ir gewonheite
sage ich iu gereite:
alle morgen vil fruo
sô gedâhte si darzuo
1375 daz si ir gebetes huote, (1125)
diu reine unt diu guote,
mit michelem flîze
unz zuo dem inbîze.
sô die frouwen gâzen,
1380 wider an ir werc gesâzen, (1130)
den half si unz an die nône.
sô gie si aver schône
⟨hin⟩fur den altâre,
daz si ir salter lâre:
1385 dâ stuont si unz an die vesper, (1135)
daz alle die swester
daz sanc an viengen,
ir tagezît begiengen:
sô chom geflogen Gabriêl,
1390 der gotes engel vil hêr: (1140)
er brâht ouch ir daz himelbrôt,
daz er der kuniginne bôt

1356 muzen 61 erweit 62 diz 65 allez 70 si sich C
ergebe *bis* gezogenlic 1491 B, *vgl. Sievers, Forsch. z. deutsch. Phil., Festgabe für Hildebrand 19 ff.* 71 *Raum für Initiale* B 71 f. gewonheit
: gereit BC 72 saget B uch C 73 vil *fehlt* C 74 si wol da zu B
76 und di vil C · 78 imbize B 80 an ir werche B, zu wᵉke C 81 an
die] zu C 82 giench B, gink C si *fehlt* B aue B, aber C 83 hin

A

daz mv̊sen an schowen
die levte mit forhten.
swa ander vrowen worhten
1185 leinwat oder seiden,
ir enhein moht erleiden
der arbeit so vil
so daz kint in sinem spil.

Al ir gewonheit
1190 sag ich ev bereit:
alle morgen vil frů
so gedahte si dar zv̊
daʒ si ir gebetes gût
phlak in rehter hût
1195 vñ mit allem fleizze
biz ŏf daz imbeiz.
So die frowen gazen
vñ an ir werch gesazen,
den half si vnz an die nône.
1200 so gie ⟨si⟩ aber schone
hin fur den alter:
da las si ir salter
vil stete vnz an die vesper,
daz alle die swester
1205 daz gesank an viengen,
ir tagzeit begiengen.
Do chom geflogen Gabriel,
der gotes engel vil snel:
der braht ir daz himelprot,
1210 daz er der kvniginne bot.

D

sie mvsen anscŏen
div livte mit uorhten.
swa andere frŏen worhten
linwat unde siden, 1305
ir neheîniv maht erliden
163, 35 also vil der arbeit
so ditze kint frolichen leit.
den tempelherren ze minne
sie worhte mit richem sinne 1310
al des sie begunde.
swaz so wibes hant chunde,
daz enmahte ir niht engân.
des nahtes ilte sie ufstan
daz sie ir venige pflæge 1315
vnde sih got ergæbe.
40 ir site v̄ ir gewonheit
die sage ih iv gereit:
alle morgen vil frů
so gedahte sie darzu 1320
daz sie ir gebetes hûte,
div reine v̄ div gute,
164, 1 mit michelme flize
untze zu dem inbizze.
so die frŏen gazzen 1325
vñ wider an ir werh gesazzen,
den half sie untze an die none.
so gie sie aue schone
hin fur den altære,
daz sie ir salter lære. 1330
5 da stunt sie unze an die vesper,
daz alle die swester
daz gesanch anvîengen
v̄ ir tagezit begiengen.
so chom geflogen Gabriel, 1335
der gotes engel vil her:
er braht ŏh ir daz himelbrot,
daz er der ivnchfrŏen bot:
daz noz sie mit kivshem libe
div nie wart ze wibe. 1340

---

fehlt BCS.   84 daz] da B   salter] gebete C, churs da BS.   spreche C
87 den sanc angevingen C   89 geflogen *fehlt* B   90 vil *fehlt* B   91 ouch BC!
92 enbot B

163, 34 neheniv   *1193* da   *164, 7* here

ûz sîner hant in die ir:
anders âz si niht vil.
1395 swaz man ir gap ze spîse,   (1145)
daz îlte diu maget wîse
armen ellenden
in die stat senden.
al diu samenunge,
1400 alte unde junge,   (1150)
die wurden dô wol innen
der tougenlîchen minne
die si mit den engeln habete.
si selbe ez wol verdagete,
1405 doch was ez unverborgen: (1155)
daz enmahte si niht besorgen.

 Sâlige swester wonten dô
in Salomonis templô:
die wâren dâ gehôhet,
1410 sît sint si gar zestôret.   (1160)
nu habent ez besezzen
rîter vil vermezzen:
die werent ez mit crefte
vor der heidenschefte.
1415 dô diu cheiserinne,   (1165)
diu erwelte gimme,
zuoversiht der werlte,
ir den sal erwelte
dâ si wolte erschînen
1420 bî den heiligen wîben,   (1170)
dô lobte si unsern herren,
daz er sie sô verre
ûz den andern erhuop,
daz si senftlîchen truoc
1425 alle die arbeit   (1175)
die si zuo gewonheit
hêten gesprochen under in.
niemen mahte den ir sin
errechen noch ergrunden.

  1396 daz gehilt C   98 senden S.] ze (zu C) senden BC   99 al]
allen B   1400 alten B, alt C   1 inne BS.   2 tugentlichen minnen C
3 den engeln] den egeln C, dem engel S., vgl. videbant cum ea angelos
loqui *Pseudo-Matthäus cap. VII* hatte C   3f. habet : verdaget B   6 daz
chunde BS.   7 Heilige C   ´9 do CS.   10 sider C   12 ritter BS.,
rittere C   mezzen B   13 crefte BSch.] kreften CS.   14 non B   15 *Raum*

A

D

164,10 anders aze sie niht vil,
als ich ivh bewisen wil:

Swaz man ir gab ze speise, swaz man ir gap ze spise,
daz eilte div magt weise daz ilte div maget wise
armen ellenden den armen ellenden   1345
in die stat ze senden. in die stat senden.
1215 alle div samenunge, al der frŏen samnunge,
alte vñ iunge, bediv alte v̄ iunge,
die wurden wol innen di wrden do wol inne
der tougenlichen minne der tŏgenlichen minne   1350
die si mit dem engel habte. 15 die sie mit dem engel habete.
1220 si selbe ez wol verdagte, sie selbe ez wol uerdagete,
doch waz ez niht verborgen: doh was ez unverborgen:
daz kvnde si niht besorgen. daz enmahte sie niht besorgen.

Sælig swester waren do Sæligen swester wonten do 1355
in Salomonis templo: in Salomonis templo:
1225 die waren gehohet, die waren da gehohet,
seit sint si gar zestoret. nu sint sie gar zestoret.
nu habent ez besezzen sit habent ez besezzen
riter gar vermezzen: riter vil uermezzen,   1360
die wǣrent ez mit chreften 20 die ez werent mit chræfte
1230 vor der heidenschefte. uor der hæidenschefte.
Do div keiserinne, mit den was div maget rêine,
div erwelte gimme, also daz sie stæte schêine

wolde beleiben
bey den reinen weiben,
1235 do lobt si vnseren herren,
daz er sey so verren
ovz den andren erhûb,
daz si ane trûb
mit grozzer arebeit zaller slahte arbeit   1365
1240 gedultechleichen leit die sie ze gwonheit
gepresten vnder in. heten gesprochen under in.
nieman moht ir sin niemen maht den ir sin
errechen noch ergrunden. errechen noh ergrunden.

---

für Initiale B   18 ir] div B, di ir C *S. B. s. 231*   19 daz C   22 also
v῾ren C   23 *f.* erhube: *Reimwort unleserlich, der Raum reicht für* truge B,
vgl. § 3 b   24 daz] da B   senfticlichen C   25 *f.* al die arbeite : gwonheite *S*.
25 erbeit C   26 ze B   27 *ff.* hatten gesprochen   und nimant enmochte
den iren sin erkunden noch ergrunden C   28 den ir] ir B, ir den *S*.

    1230 heidenscheften   *1243* erreihen

1430 si îlte si alle schunden   (1180)
      ze gotes dieniste,
      ze der êwigen gniste.
      si was âne allez wandel
      kûscher denne ein ander;
1435 ir neheiniu was sô wîse.   (1185)
      si âz die gotes spîse,
      die ir der engel brâhte.
      neheines ubeles si gedâhte;
      an der guote was si stâte
1440 in geistlîcher wâte.   (1190)
      vasten unde wachen
      daz enmahte si niht gemachen
      bleich oder truobe:
      des wunderôte gnuoge.
1445 daz beste hête si erchorn;   (1195)
      ouch huop si deheinen zorn,
      die zuht si umbegurte:
      der bôsen antwurte
      newolte si niht geruochen.
1450 schelten unde fluochen   (1200)
      daz was ir seltsâne:
      der sunden was si âne.

      ir hûsgenôzinne
      die starhte si in der minne,
1455 ze bezzerem teile,   (1205)
      ze sâlden unt ze heile,
      daz si die ubermuote
      ersluogen mit der guote
      unt allez unreht vermiten:
1460 alsô lûterlîche site   (1210)
      lêrte si diu suoze.
      nu bittet daz wir sie muozen
      alsô an geruofen
      daz si in der uns geschuofe
1465 in unser teil gewinne,   (1215)
      daz er uns enzunde in sîner minne!

1430 si ilte zu allen stunden C   31 f. dienste : geniste B, dinst : genist C
32 zu BC   34 danne di andern C   35 neheine B, keine C, nehein S,
36 aze B   41 vasten unde wachen S. B. s. 232] wachen und vasten BC
42 daz mohte si B, des moht su C   44 wundert genuge BC   46 ŏch
hube B, ia dʼhub C   in keinen bis nimmʼmere 1538 C³ II   47 zuhte B

A

si eylte si alle schunden
1245 ze gotes dienst vn̄ sinem lobe, 164, 25
dem si lak stetichleichen obe.

ir denhein waz so weise.
si az die gotes speise,
die ir der engel prahte.
1250 denheines vbels si gedahte.

vasten noch wachen
daz chunde sey niht gemachen
bleich noch trûbe:
dez wundrot genv̊ge.

1255 ir housgenozzinne
die sterktes in gotes minne,

daz si ir vbermüte
erslv̊gen mit ir gûte
vn̄ allez vureht vermiten:
1260 mit so reinem siten
lerte sei div sůzze.
nu bit daz wir sey mv̊zzen
alsus an gerůfen
daz si in der vns geschv̊ffe
1265 an vnser tail gewinne
vn̄ vns erzunde mit siner minne!

D

sie mante sie zallen stůnden 1370
werben nah gotis hulde.

sie was ân alle schulde
gut, wolgemůt, milt v̄ wîse.
sie lebet der heren spise
die ir der engel brahte.   1375
neheines arges sie gedahte.
kivsche, diemût vnde stæte
die dri tvgende sie hæte
mit den andern uzerchorn.
nit, hohfart v̄ wiplich zorn 1380
30 vant an ir neheine stat.
wand nie frŏe so hohe getrat
ze sælden v̄ ze eren gliche,
des ist hivte ir lop so riche.
die zuht sie umbegurte: 1385
fluchen v̄ bose antwrte
muste ir sin unerchant;
sie was ân der sunden bant.
uasten oder wachen
daz enmahte sie niht   1390
                  gemachen
35 misseuar noh trube:
des wnderot genuge.
alle ir husgnozinne
die starhte sie in der minne,

daz sie die ubermůte   1395
erslugen mit der gute
v̄ allez unreht uermiten:
ze also luterlichen siten
cherte sie div suzze.
nu bittet sie daz sie uns   1400
                  mûzze
40 wider cheren uon den sůnden
v̄ an ir minne erzunden!

---

49 der wolt C   53 ir ... schen husgenozen C   54 strachte B, sterkten C
in] an B   58 mit ir C   59 vnrechte B, vnrech C   60 als BC   siten C
61 larte C   siv B   di suzen C   62 si sehen muzen C   63 so inneclichen
(inneclich S.) an rufen BS.   66 daz er in ... enzvnde sine mīne C
1256 sterktes!

        Hête ich eine zungen
        diu als ein wâfen clunge,
        gesmidet ûzer stâle,
1470   diu mir die rede gâbe,   (1220)
        ja ne mahte ich christenlîcher schar

        niemer gesagen gar,
        wie sich diu maget zierte
        gen dem himelischen wirte,
1475   der sie gemahelen scholte   (1225)
        unt samt ir bûwen wolte
        durch sîne barmunge.
        eines sites si begunde
        den weder wîp noch man
1480   vor ir geburte nie vernam: (1230)
        swer daz kint gruozte,
        daz si daz gelten muoste,
        sô sagete si gnâde
        ir schephâre
1485   (si blicte hin ze himele),   (1235)
        daz ir diu werlt hie nidene
        senftiu wort zuo sprach
        sô si ir bilde an sach.
        swenne aver si den gruozsal
1490   scholte bieten uberal,   (1240)
        si bat gezogenlîchen,
        daz si got genâdiclîchen
        an der rede vernâme
        unt *guo*ten âbent gâbe
1495   oder sâligen morgen   (1245)
        den liuten *die* mit sorgen
        in der werlte bûwent
        und im iedoch ge*tri*went.
        dannen chom uns diu gwonheit,
1500   daz *wi*r liep unde leit   (1250)
        ûf sîne gnâde schuln ergeben
        der uns verlihen hât daz leben.
        gelernet haben wir *dâbî*,
        swer uns gruozende sî,
1505   daz wir im alsô schô*ne*   (1255)

    1467 ich nv C   ein zunge B*S.*   68 ein wafen] daz eisen (ysen C)
BC*S.* chunge B   69 vz stahele C   70 div rede B   71 do enmocht C
72 nimmer B, keine wis C   73 sich] si C   74 gegen B, gein C
75*f.* sold : wold B   76 samt B*S.*] bi C wonen C   77 duch B sin B*S.*
78 siten C   80 geburt B*S.*   84 irme C, dem ir B*S., doch vgl.* 641

A

Vnde het ich ein zunge
die sam ein wafen chlunge,

ich moht der christenlicher
schar
1270 niht gesagen gar,
wie sich div magt ziert
gen dem himilischen wirt,
der sei mêhilen solde
vñ in ir wonen wolde
1275 von siner barmunge.
eines siten si begunde
den weder weip noh man
vor ir geburt nie gewan:
Swer sei grûzte,
1280 vñ si daz gelten mûste,
so sagt si dank sere
irem schepfere
(si plikte hinze himele),
daz ir div werlt hie nidene
1285 semftev wort zŭ sprach,
swer ir bleide angesach.
swan si den grûzsal
solde bieten vber al,
si bat gezogenlichen,
1290 daz si got der reiche
an ir rede verneme
vñ gûten abent gebe
oder sæligen morgen
den levten die mit sorgen
1295 dise werlt bowent
vñ siner genade getrowent.
dan chom vns div gewonheit,
daz wir lieb vñ leit
ŏf sin genade sulen geben
1300 der vns verlihen hat daz leben.
gelernt hab wir da bey,
swer vns grŷzzinde sey,
daz wir im schone

D

Nie wart so wol sprechender
man
der ie uon buchen sin gewan,
daz ez tohte im einen   1405
ze sprechen uon der reinen
165,1 uollekliche nah ir werdicheit,

an die got sinen fliz leite,
als er sie gemæheln wolte
v̄ bi ir bûen scholte.   1410
eines sites sie do begunde
den weder wip noh man chunde
noh uor ir geburte ie uernam:
swænnez also cham
daz sie ieman grûzte,   1415
5 v̄ sie daz gelten mûste,
so gnadet sie got zehant,
der ir heil so hete gewant

daz ir div werlte zusprah,
senftiv wort da sis ansah. 1420
swa sie aver den gruzsal
sholte bieten uberal,
sie bat herzeklichen,
daz sie got gnadeklichen
10 an der rede meinte   1425
v̄ gûten abent bescheinte
oder sæligen morgen
den livten die mit sorgen
in der werlte bûwent
vñ im iedoh getrûwent.   1430
danne chom uns div gewonheit,
daz wir bediv liep vnd leit
uf sin gnade shuln ergeben
uon dem wir han daz leben.
15 gelernet wir han dabi: 1435
swer so uns gruzende si,
daz wir im also schone

---

87 wort.. | si sprach C   88 *ursprünglich* blîde *nach* A?   89 wem C
aue B   den] daz B*S*., iren C   91 si bot C, do bat si B*S*.   gezogenlic..
Ende von B   94 abvnt C   98 doch C
      1301 gelert

              got biten lônen
              unt irdischem schîne
              der êren verzîhen.
              si was mit guotem willen
1510   senfte unde stille: (1260)
              einen gedanch si habete,
              ob si ze vil geredete,
              †daz si von . . sprich
              verwandelôte sich,
1515   ez enwâre vil nutze.   (1265)
              si *liez* ir antlutze
              vil selten erlachen.
              ir enmahte *an* allen sachen
              niemen gebesten:
1520   ir tugent be*gu*nde ir este   (1270)
              vil wîten gebreiten.
              die mit armike*ite*
              wâren bevangen
              unt siech gewesen lange,
1525   sô si sie geruorten,   (1275)
              die craft si dannen fuorten,
              daz *sie* niht enswar:
              darumbe chêrten sie dar.
              nu biten *wi*r die hêren,
1530   swâ wir an der sêle   (1280)
              ⟨ze tiefe⟩ *sîn* verwundet,
              daz ir daz sî gekundet,
              daz si den *geist* ziere
              unt uns erledige schiere
1535   von aller *uncr*efte,   (1285)
              unt daz si bî dem hefte
              den van selbe *ch*êre,
              daz wir siech werden niemer mêre.

              Dô si begunde wahsen,
1540   dô wart si an dem vahse   (1290)
              schône unt an dem lîbe
              vor irdischen wîben.
              ein herre hiez Abiathar,
              der chêrte sînen muot dar,

1507 irdisschen   9 f. *nach* A?   11 den *oder* ein, *für* einen *kein*
Raum   11 f. het : geret   12 ab   13 ursprich *nach* D *oder* ubersprich
(*für* ub⁵sprich *reicht der Raum*), *aber doch wohl entstellt:* uberspriche,
Reimwort von 1514 *verloren, vielleicht* uberspricke : dicke? *M.*   14 v⁵wan-
delt   15 ez wer den   20 ir iugent   30 *ff.* in so grozen eren   wo

A

got biten ze lone.

1305 si waz sempft vn̄ stille,
selik vn̄ milde,

si waz vil gar nutze.
si liez ir antlutze
vil selten erlachen
1310 wan in rehten sachen.
Div reine vn̄ div bêste
begunde ir tugende êste
weite ze breiten.
die mit arbeiten
1315 waren bevangen
vn̄ siech gewesen lange,
so si sey gerûrt,
div kraft sey vmbegurt.

Nu bite wir die heren,
1320 swa wir an der selen
ze tief sein verwundet,
daz ir sey daz gekvndet,
daz si·den geist zier
vn̄ vns erledige schier
1325 von aller vnchreffte,
vn̄ daz si bei dem hefte
den vanen selbe chere,
daz wir niht schiech werden.

Do si wachsen begunde,
1330 do wart si an der stunde
so schone an dem leibe
verre vor andren weiben.
Ein herre hiez Abiathar,
der cherte sinen mût dar,

D

wnsken daz gotes lone
vnt dem irdiskem schine
der eren nercihen. 1440
si diente got ane wanch
v̄ hete einen gedanch,
ob sie ze vil redet,
daz ez lihte ir scædet,
165, 20 v̄ daz sie uor ursprich 1445
an ir mûte verwandelt sich,
iz en wære uil nutze.
sie liez ir anlutze
vil selten erlachen.
man iah ir an allen sachen 1450
ie der tugende besten;
die begunden ōh esten
v̄ vil witen umbe vahen.

di siechen die sie ersahen
25 v̄ sie angerurten, 1455
die chraft sie danne fvrten,
daz sie niht mere swar:
darumbe cherten si dar,
wand sie da gnade funden.
nu ruche sie unser wnden 1460
bedeken mit ir gûte,

daz wir uzer gotes hûte
iemer komen so uerre
daz uns des tiefils gwalt iht werre.

30 **D**o sie wahsen begunde, 1465
do wart sie in kurcer stunde
an dem hare v̄ an der lich
uber elliv wip so wætlich,
daz ein herre hiez Abiathar
der wante sinen mût dar, 1470

---

wir and⁵ sele ..n v⁵wunt : gekvnt   37 selber   39 *bis* wenken 1628 Cˢ
634—723   42 irdisschem wibe   44 karte

1304 bieten *F.*   165, 20 urspriche : siche   165, 22 wan   1316 langē
165, 27 unser *undeutlich.*

1545   daz er die maget gewunne   (1295)
         sînem lieben sun ze wunne.
         der ⟨vil⟩ kindische man
         der was ouch ir genôzsam;
         der vil rîterlîche degen
1550   wolte si êlîchen nemen   (1300)
         âne valsche minne
         durch erben gedingen.

         diu frouwe daz niht verdolte;
         si sprach, daz si niht enwolte
1555   iemer man geruoren.   (1305)
         werltlîch ungefuore
         dûhte sie sô michel:
         si wolde wesen sicher
         vor mannes gebende
1560   unz an des lîbes ende.   (1310)

         dô bôt er miete grôze
         sînen genôzen
         die des tempels phlâgen,
         daz si die maget gâben
1565   ze chonen sînem chinde: (1315)
         des bat er die gesinden.

         er bôt in golt daz rôte
         unt dingete vil genôte
         daz silber vil wîze,
1570   daz si im hulfen mit flîze.   (1320)
         sîn edele gesteine
         daz was im allez veile;
         er bôt die breiten borten
         unt flêhte mit den worten,

1546 lieben sun] libe   47 *vgl. § 66*   48 gehorsam   49 ritter-
liche   52 gedinge   54 niht *zu streichen?*   55*f.* und nimm⁵ man

A

1335 daz er die magt gewnne
sinem lieben sune.
der was ein kindischer man
vñ der frowen genozsam,
ein vil riterlicher degen;
1340 der wolde sei ælichen nemen
an alle falsche minne
durch erben gedinge.

Div frowe daz niht endolde;
si sprach, daz si niht wolde
1345 immer man gerůren.
werltlich vngefůre
devhte sey so michel:
si wolde wesen sicher
vor mannes gebende
1350 immer vnz an ir ende.

Er bot schatz grozen
sinen genozzen
die des tempels pflagen,
daz si ir ane legen.

1355 er bot in vil genote
silber, golt rote

vñ ædel gesteine:
daz waz im allez vaile,

D

wie er die maget gwnne
sinem lieben svn ze wnne.
der vil kindiske man
der was ŏh ir gnozsam.
165, 35 der herliche degen   1475
gerte sie mit bete erwegen,
daz sie in ruchte minnen
durh erben gedingen.
der e hete er hinz ir gedaht,
doh wart div rede niht uol- 1480
braht,
wand div frŏe des niht uerdolte;
sie sprah, daz sie nien wolte
166, 1 iemer man geruren.
daz werltliche ungefure
duhte sie so chumberriche 1485
daz sie gerne friliche
lebet ane mannes gebende
untze an des libes ende.
got einen hæte sie erwelt,
dem si lip mit sele selt,   1490
5 daz sie wære sin div v̄ sin brŏt,
er bediv ir herre v̄ ir trût.
div antwrte was ungemah
dem bittel vnde gesprah
alle sin genozze.   1495
er bot in mîete groze,
die des tempels pflagen,
daz sie niht scholte betragen,
sie næmen die maget gute
uon dem swærem mûte   1500
10 den sie ir habte furgesat:
darumbe gehîez er v̄ bat.
er bot in golt daz rote
unt dingete vil gnote
mit dem silber wizze,   1505
daz sie im hulfen mit flizze

---

gewinnen   wˢltlichē gefrurē   57 ez duchte   60 biz/unz   lides   65 zu-
koufen   66 daz gesinde   68 gedingte   72 in   74 flehte *B. s. 158*

1339 riterlichˢ!   1344 daz si!   1346 wertlich   1353 pfagen

1575   daz daz kint lustsam   (1325)
        sînem sune wurde undertân.
        diu miete erwegete ⟨si alle,⟩
        ez begunde in wol gevallen:
        si rieten algelîche
1580   unt schunten grôzlîche,   (1330)
        daz si vil gerne tâte
        swes sie der edele herre bâte.

        Dô sprach sant Marîe:
        got hête enzundet sîe
1585   mit bezzerem muote   (1335)
        in engelischer huote;
        si sprach mit zuhte guoter:
        ‚nu weset ungemuote!
        lât varen ditze spil,
1590   wan ich niemer enwil   (1340)

        deheinen man gewinnen
        ze werltlîchen dingen!
        ir enschult mich niht reizen.
        ja hân ich got entheizen
1595   mîne sêle unbewollen: (1345)
        mac ich daz ervollen,
        daz ist der beste rât
        dâ mîn gedinge ane stât.‘
        dô was ein bischof under in,
1600   der was sîn flîzec durch gewin,   (1350)
        durch die gâbe mâre,
        tiure unde swâre,
        diu was im geheizen;
        er sprach: ‚du scholt mich lâzen
1605   dir die wârheite sagen,   (1355)
        der enwil ich niht verdagen:
        got selbe gap Adâme,
        sô wir an der schrift vernâmen,
        Evam ze wîbe:
1610   wâren von ir lîbe   (1360)
        ⟨wir alle niht⟩ ensprungen,
        alte unde junge,

     1577 diu miete erwegete] di mite er wegete C, dâ mit weget er
B. s. 212   78 in allen   79 retten   80 kunten   82 des si   87 mit
guten zuchten, *vgl. W. s. 175*   88 weset nicht   89 lazet var dise
92 w'tlichen   94 hab   96 erwllen   1600 umme gewin   1 gebe *B. s. 137*

A	D

A

daz daz kint lustsam
1360 sinem sun wurde vndertan.
da mit erwægt er si alle,
ez begunde in wol gevallen:
si rieten alle gelich   166, 15
vn̄ schunten grozechlich,
1365 daz si gerne tǣte
swez sey der herre bête.

Do sprach sant Mareie:
got het enzundet sey,
vil reine vn̄ vil stête
1370 in geistlicher wǣte;
si sprach in grozzer gûte:
,weset vngemv̊t!
lat varen ditze spil,
wan ich nimmer wil

1375 denheinen man gewinnen
ze werltlichen minnen!
ir sult mich niht reitzen.
ich han got geheizzen
min sele vnbewollen:
1380 mak ich daz ervollen,
daz ist der aller beste rât
da min gedinge an stât.'
Do waz ein pyschof vnder in,
der was sein fleizzek durch gewîn;

1385 der sprach: ,ich wil dir sagen,
der warhait niht verdagen:
got selber gab Adâmen,
als wir an der schrift vernamen,
Evam ze weibe,
1390 vn̄ weren von ir leibe
die levte niht ensprungen,
die alten vn̄ die iungen,

D

umbe daz kint des er gert,
daz ir sin sun wrde gewert
nah rehte ze elichen dingen.
div miete began in gelingen: 1510
do rieten sie algliche
v̄ schunten grozliche,
daz div frŏe tǣte
swes sie der herre bæte.

Do sprah sænte Marie: 1515
got hete erzundet sie
mit reinegerntem mv̊te
in engelisker hûte:

,wes mv̊et ir ivh, herren min?
lat ditze umbescheiden spil 1520
sin,
20 wand ich niemer man gwinne
ze werltliker minne!
ir ne schult mih niht reizzen.
ia han ich got entheizzen
min sele unbewollen: 1525
mag ich daz eruollen,
daz ist der beste rat
da min gedinge anstat.'
Do was ein bisgof vnder in,
der was sin flizich durh   1530
den gewin;

er sprah: ,frŏe la die rede stan!
ich sage dir wie ez ist getan
umbe die rehten warheit,
als uns div buch hant geseit:
div e ist got liep v̄ genæme, 1535
wan er selbe Adame
frŏwen Euam gap ze wibe:
wæren wir uon ir libe
30 alle niht ersprungen,
bediv alte v̄ iungen,   1540

---

2 tuw⁵   5 warheit, *vgl. § 67 Anm.*   6 der] di   7 selber   adamen
12 alt und iūgen

1364 grozchlich   1376 wertlichen

sô wâre diu werlt ôde,
ringe unde brôde,
1615   sone ruofte niemen an got.   (1365)
frouwe lâ dînen spot:
nim den man ze dîner ê,
daz ez dir ze sâlden ergê!
volge den liuten:
1620   gebir gotes trûte   (1370)
kint alsô reine,
diu gotes êre meinen!
als ⟨uns⟩ ze himele ist gâch,
also schulen ouch hernâch
1625   unser nâchkomen tuon.   (1375)
daz ist der beste wîstuom
des wir iemer mugen erdenchen:
du 'scholt uns an der bete niht enwenchen.'

1614 geringe, *vgl. § 31b Anm.* blode   15 so enrife   16 laz ab ez
ist din   20 gebe der gotis trûten C, gebir die gotes trûten *B. s. 37*
21 di kint   27 den wir   28 scholt — enwenchen *Sch.*] ensalt — wenken

A

so were div werlt ôde,
chlein vn̄ blôde,
1395 so rieffe ⟨nieman⟩ ane got.
vrowe la dinen spot:
nim den man ze diner ê,
daz es dir ze heile ergê!
volge den levten:
1400 gebir gotes trouten
kint also reine,
die gotes dienst mainen!
als vns ze himel ist gach,
also sulen hernach
1405 vnser nachkomen tůn.
daz ist der bêste weistům
des du dir kanst erdênken:
vnserem râte solt dv dich
lênchen.'

Des antwurt in auer ⟨do⟩
1410 rosa iů Jericho,
div magt also liehte:
,ich volg ev mit nihte.
ir sagt mir von Adâme
daz er Evam næme,

1415 doch genoz des Abel
siner keusche hel,
do er daz opfer fure trůk
vn̄ in sin průder erslůk,
danne er bewollen wǣre,
1420 vor sinem schepfere.
got eylte im ze geben schone
zwo guldeine krone:
von der marter eine,
die ander daz er reine
1425 vn̄ vnbewollen was:
da von sin sele genas.
Helyas der weisage,
als ich vernomen habe,
der lebt cheusche hie nidene:
1430 des wart er ze himele

D

so wǣre div werlte ode,
chranch, ringe v̄ brode,
sone rufte nîemen an got.
frǒe la uarn dinen spot:
nim den man ze e,   1545
deiz dir ze sælden erge!
uolge uns ane widerstrit,
wan dir got sinen segen git
166,35 v̄ frǒde mit lieben kinden!
an den soltu heil vinden,   1550
daz du mit den reinen
sin ere můzest mêinen.
daz ist der beste rat
der uon mannes sinne gat,
v des wir megen erdenchen: 1555
nv solt dv uns an der bete niht
wenchen.'

40 **D**es antwrte im ave do
rosa in Jericho,
167,1 diu maget also lieht:
,ichen volge iwes nieht.   1560
ir saget mir uon Adame
daz er Euam næme
uon der gotes hende:
daz tet er ane wende,
doh gnôz mere Abel der gůt 1565
daz er beleip an kivskem můt,
5 do er daz opher furtruch
vn̄ in sin bruder sluch,
denne ob er gemeiliget ware,
uor sinem schepfære.   1570
got ilte im geben ze lone
zwô guldine chrône:
uon der martir êine,
die ander daz er rêine
unt unbewollen was: 1575
daz ist da er mit gnas.
10 Helyas der gotes man,
als ihz vernomen han,

A

von den englen gefueret,
durch daz er vnberůret
was von allen weiben.

got liez an im scheinen
1435 daz er die chevscheit
mit siner gotheit
wil vnderstozzen.
nv hat er frevde grozze
besezzen vn̄ michel ǣre
1440 an leibe vn̄ an sele.

Ich sage ev minen willen:
ir mohtet ǣ gepillen
daz wazzer ovz dem steine,
ǣ ich mich sein vereine.'

1445 Bey handen si sich viengen,
von der rede si giengen.
an dem kindischen weibe
heten si ze neide
daz si was so veste,
1450 die schoniste vn̄ div beste.

Si gebuten ein concilium,
was si darume mohten tůn,
daz Maria div mǣre
als vngevolgik wǣre.
1455 do der gesprochen tak
an ir hochzeit gelak,
ein michel volk chom dar.
ir pyschof hiez Abiathar,
der grůzte sei an der porten
1460 mit den gotes worten.
er stůnt ovf eine grěde,
die hende rekte er běde
gen dem himilischen sal.

D

der wart ze himel gefvret,
durh daz er unberuret   *1580*
was uon allem mæile.
im wart getan ze tæile
div gnade div iemer stat:
damit uns got erzaiget hat
daz er die kivskeit   *1585*
mit der liehten gotheit
167,15 gerne wil under stozen.
nu hat er frǒde grozze
v̄ eren vil erworben,
swîe der lip ist noh un-   *1590*
        erstorben.
des ruchet ivwer bete lan,
wand min mvt ist sogetan
daz ih stæte beliben schol.
got der weiz min herze wol,
min ahte v̄ minen willen,   *1595*
daz ir ê mæhtet billen
20 wazzer uz dem steine,
e daz ih dehein brode meine.'

Zehante sie sih viengen,
uon der rede sie giengen.   *1600*
an dem kindisken wibe
heten sie daz ze nide,
daz sie was also ueste:
darumbe zurnten al die geste.
sie furen als sie tobeten,   *1605*
ein teidinch sie gelobeten;
25 sie gebutten ein gesende,
daz sie chomen an ein ende,
ob Maria die mære
so ungeuolgich wǣre.   *1610*
der gesprochen tach
an einer hohzite gelach:
do chom michel menige dar.
der bisgof hiez Abiathar,
der gruzte sie an der borte   *1615*
mit dem gotes worte.
30 er stunt uf eine grede
v̄ hub uf sin hende bede
gegen dem himelisken sal.

1437 wil!   *1442. 167,19* mohte A, mæhte D, *vielleicht* er *statt* ir
1445 han| *167,27 Initiale*

A

ein stille gebot er vber al;
1465 er sprach: ‚nv horet alle,
wie ev daz gevalle:
Maria div schone
div wil den fursten honen.

swer ir ze weibe gêrt,   167, 35
1470 daz ist ir vnwert.
si chan niht genesen,
si mv̂zze meit wesen.
wir haben hie vrowen vil gezogen,
kvnige tohter vn̄ herzogen,

                                         40
1475 daz nie denheine wart so herte 168, 1
noch sich also gewerte.
ich man evch weise diet,
wie got einen streit schiet,
do die ewarten
1480 vnder in zeworfen haten:
Aaronis gertte gab plv̊men,
lauben vn̄ grv̊nen
begunde si in der arke.
got mak noch starke
1485 sin wunder erzaigen.
wir sein auch sein aygen,

daz bedenchet wol!
ich sag ev waz hie tv̊n sol
alle dise menige:
1490 got mit sinem segene
der sterke evch da zv̂,
daz er daz selbe zeichen tv̊
allen disen weiben
die chomen sein ze ir zeiten.
1495 Arme vn̄ reicher

D

eine stille gebot er uber al;   1620
er sprah: ‚nu horet alle,
wie iv daz geualle,
daz Maria div schone tut:
niemen ist so edel noh so gut,
so riche noh so tîvre,   1625
daz er ir gezem hîvre.

swer ir ze wibe gert,
der scheidet dannen ungewert.
sine trvet niht genesen,
sine mv̊zze maget wesen.   1630
wir haben frv̊en vil gezogen,
kunige tohter v̄ herzogen
der herlichen slahte,
daz uns nie deheiniv in der ahte
also vil ie gemûte,   1635
und iedoh vil grozer gûte
ze rede waren worden
uon allen ir uordern:
deist ein michel herte.
des guten Aaronis gerte   1640
der man ih alle dise diet,
wie er den grozen strit schiet,
do die gotes ewarte
under in zewrfen harte:
div gerte wart wider grv̊en,   1645
begunde lv̊ben v̄ blv̂en
in der heiligen arche.   5
got der mak noh sam starche
siniv tv̊gen erzæigen.
div werlt ist sin æîgen,   1650
der menniske sin hantgetât;
an im reht v̄ gnade stat:
daz bedenchet alle wol!
ih sage iv wie nu tvn schol
disiv menige algemeine,   1655
daz got die warheit bescheine
v̄ sinen willen dabi: 10

die von elichem bande vri
sin komen an den tac hivte,

A

der bringe morgen igelicher
eine gerte.
der got der sey gewertte
bei Aarones zeiten,
1500 ⟨. . . . .⟩
der zaige vns ovf der erden,
wen Maria sule werden.'

vil michel wart ir schal,
der rat geviel in vberal;
1505 ez iahen weip vn̄ man,
div red were lobesam,
si behielten sin gebot.
si dingten an got,
die ane weip waren,
1510 ir venie si do pflagen.
div naht douhte sei vil lank,
si heten manigen gedank.

Als ⟨er⟩ gegert habte,
des morgens do ez tagte,

1515 die alten vn̄ die jungen,
hey wie si zv̊ drungen!
mit pfelleiner wat,
der besten die div werlt hat,
waren si gewirdet
1520 vn̄ reilich gezieret,
igelicher mit sinem geverten.
si brahten alle gerten
lange vn̄ slehte.
do merkte vil rehte
1525 menlich die seinen.
an der selben weilen
ir igelicher het wan,
daz div magt lustsam,
daz kint also schone
1530 in seine gewalt chome.
Die armen vmbesazen

D

der ieglicher uor dem livte 1660
bringe morgen sin gerte.
der got der sie gwerte
bi Aaronis ziten,
nu wir siner gnaden biten,
der lazze uns werden schin, 1665
wes Maria brvt schul sin,
168, 15 v̄ erzæige mit gewalte,
wer ir von siner gebe walte.'

Michel wart do der schal,
der rat gevîel in vber al; 1670
do iahen sie gemæinliche,
div rede wǽre lobliche,
sie behielten gerne sin gebot,
v̄ dingoten hinze got,
die da waren ungehit, 1675
daz er schiede selbe den strit.
20 div naht duhte sie zelanch,
v̄ heten mangen gedanch
vmbe die maget wolgetan,
wer sie ze wibe solte han, 1680
wand sie al der werlte behagete.
do ez des morgens tagete,
der bisgof nam dehein friste,
er chom ze uorderiste.
die richen v̄ die iungen 1685
uaste zu im drungen,
25 wol gebadet, wol gechleit,
als daz ware liet seit:

grozlich was ir geuerte.
sie brahten schone gerte 1690
lange vnde slehte.
do marhte vil rehte
aller mannekliche die sine
v̄ wante der magede gewert sin.
ir ieglicher hetes wan, 1695
doh solt ez anders ergan.

30 die armen umbesæzen

1502 wen] wes *F.*, wem *M.*   1504 in!   1513 habten *A,* al si
gerne habeten *F.*   1514 morges   168,25 lieht   1520 geziert

A	**D**
die torsten niht gelazzen,	die getorsten niht uerlazzen,
die ledige levte waren	die ledigiv livte waren,
si mûsteu dar gahen.	sine mûsen gebaren *1700*
	als man in von hove gebot.
	do kom durh die selben not
1535 Do chom ein greiser man,	uf den tach ein grise man;
harte vorht er den pan;	so harte forhte er den ban.
der was Josep genant,	Joseph was er genant, *1705*
der ist wol bechant;	der ist uns ŏh wol erchant,
168, 35	so wir an den bûchen
	sinen namen wellen suchen.
der was ein witebere,	der was ein witewære,
1540 alt vñ swære,	alter, gut v̄ gewære, *1710*
blŏde sines leibes.	brode sines libes.
der gerte niht weibes:	der engerte niht wibes:
der brahte ein chleines gertlin	er braht ein chleinez gertelin
durich die gehorsam sein.	durh die gehorsam sin.
1545 daz reis also kurze	daz ris also churze *1715*
daz het er ab der wurze	daz het er ab der wrze
gezerret gare vnwæhen,	gecerret harte unwæhe,
daz si da bey sehen	daz div werlt dabi sæhe
daz er niht het willen	sin gemûte niene stan
1550 zv̄ werltlichen dingen.	nah frŏden noh vf liebes wan. *1720*
alle die da waren,	
die daz gebot vernamen,	
die gaben ze hofe	die gerte gaben sie zehofe:
die gerten dem pyschoffe:	die enphiench der bisgof
1555 die enpfienk der æwart.	
der pischof sich do gart	
in die englischen wât.	*169, 1* v garte sih in die heren wât.
ze himel er do sûchte rat.	ze himele suhter den rat.
do gienk er also schone	do giench er also schone *1725*
1560 zv̄ dem tysche frone,	zu dem tische frone,
daz er da erfunde,	daz er da erfunde,
so er verrist kunde,	so er uerriste chunde,
ob dem altare,	ob dem altære,
wie si solten gebaren.	waz gotes wille wære. *1730*
1565 **Nu** vernemt alle besunder	*5* **Nu** uernemet alle besunder
die manikvalten wunder,	div manchvaltigen wnder,
die got dem volke erzeigte	div got der diete zeiget
daz sein gemv̂te neigte	div ir gemvte næiget
ŏf sein maisterheit!	under sine mæisterschaft! *1735*
1570 do der pyschof sin hende preit,	do der bisgof vor der lantschaft
	ze himele hub sine hende,
	do nam ez gut ende.

A

mit zehern wart er begozzen,
sin herze was beslozzen
in der waren minne.
do chom div gotes stimme,
1575 si sprach: ‚in miner ordenunge
wil ich dise samenunge
miner genaden niht verhelen.
ich wil die menie geweren
dez si mich gebeten hat:
1580 mir ist dein geistlicher rat
ane zweivel wol gevallen.
nv legt die gerten alle
zvo dem heiligen tûme
vn̄ lat sei ligen vnze frû!
1585 morgen nemt sei widere,
so zaig ich ŏz dem himile
ev den man so gûten
der Mariam sol behûten:
den ich dar zv̂ han erwelt,
1590 ein toube von sinem stabe vert:
div hebt sich ze fluhte
vn̄ swinget sich in die lufte,
daz sei nieman mak gesehen.
dem sult ir alle iehen
1595 daz er die magt suezze
vor iwer mehelen mv̂zze.
daz sag dem levte,
daz ich daz gebevte!'

Nv rûget evch selbe damit,
1600 daz got aysliche sit
an vns so starke schevhet
daz vns sin stimme flevhet,
div vnsren vordren sâgte
swaz si mit andaht fragten.

1605 Als der ander morgen rot
der vinstren erde lieht gebot,

D

mit zæheren was er begozzen,
sin herze wol beslozzen   1740
in der waren minne.
do chom div gotis stimme,

sie sprah: ‚ih wil dih gewern
v̄ ŏh dise menige niht entwern
des sie mih gebeten hat: 1745
mir ist gelichen din rat.
nu hab daz in diner ahte,
daz dv die gerten hinaht
zu dem heilctum rŷwen legest
unt sie morgen wider gebest: 1750

so zæige ih iv den man so gûten
der Mariam scol behuten:
dem ih die ere han beschert,
ein tube uon sinem stabe vert:
div heuet sih ze der grufte   1755
vnd swinget sih in die lufte,
daz sie niemen mak gesehen.
dem schult ir alle des iehen,
daz er die maget sûzze
uor iv gemaheln mûzze.   1760
daz sage du dem lîvte,
daz ih daz wil v̄ gebivte!'

Nu rŷeget ivh alle damite,
daz got die svntigen site
an uns so harte schivhet   1765
daz uns sin stimme flivhet,
div unser uordern ofte erschein,
wan des ist zwiuel nehein.
do uon dem bisgofe here
eroffent wart div lere   1770
die er got mit diemût angwan,
do frŏet sih wip v̄ man,
vnd als der morgenrot
der vinstirn erde lieht erbot,
daz al div werlte erluhte,   1775
die menige do zit duhte

169, 10

15

20

25

A

sī můsten hin ze hofe gân   169, 30
vn̄ alle ir gerten da enpfan.
do gab man den hersten
1610 ir gerten al zem ersten.

Joseps gerte chleine
div was gevallen eine:
von den andren si entslaif,
daz sey der pischof niht begraif.

1615 Do schamten sich die fursten
der frevel vn̄ der geturste,
daz si mit hohferten
puten dar ir gerten.
swie wol si got erkanden,
1620 vn̄ weren si immer da gestanden,
si heten daz vrkunde
an ir denheiner funden.
Josep der gotes trȯt
der floch die rede vn̄ auch die prȯt;
1625 er douhte sich so nider,
er suchte niht wider
sine gertte zenpfahen.

D

daz sie ze houe giengen,
ir gerte wider enpfiengen.
ze eriste gap man den richen,
den der arme mȗzze ent-   1780
    wichen,
v̄ darnah den smæhen.
sie sprachen, swa sie sæhen
daz zeichen mit den ȯgen,
daz wolten sie glȯben.
35 Josebes gerte div chleine   1785
div was ueruallen eine:
uon den andern sie gesleif,
daz sie der bisgof niht begreif.
do wanten sie algemêine,
nv in daz zeichen niht   1790
    erschêine,
ez chome uon ir sunden
daz got wære erwnden
siner grozen barmunge.
sie wanten herze v̄ zunge
40 dimůtekliche an in,   1795
daz in div tube erschin
div in da was geheizen.
sie rowe daz sie gemeizzen
die schonen gerte hæten.
nu ruche er sie beraten,   1800
170, 1 der al die werlte wiset
vnt sîn warheit briset
mit rehte v̄ mit gûte:
der gefrȯe ir gemute.
ia erschameten sih di fursten 1805
der frauel daz sie getorsten
dar gebieten ir gerte.
si erkanten ir herte
5 v̄ chlagten ir missetat,
daz sie in hohvertiger wat   1810
gotes tȯgen wolten sehen,
daz mit diemut mȗz geschehen.
Josep der gotes trut
der floh die rede vnt die brut;
er duhte sih so nidere   1815
daz er nîen wolte widere
sin klêin gerte enpfahen.

1611 gerten   169, 36 geslief   1614 pischof   169, 39 wænten

1925 . . . . . niht wandeln sîniu wort.

       nu suoche eine cleine gerten dort,   (1380)

1925—28 C ² 724—727   25 *etwa* got wil niht   26 kurcze

A

do si ir niht ensahen,
do sprachen si vil drate:
1630 ‚wir sulen vns baz beraten.'

Abiathar der pyschof
der hiez do ouf den freithof
die chreftigen scharen
alle gemainlich varen:
1635 si baten ir schepfere,
daz er in genedik were.
eine gienk er in daz goteshovs,
die levte treib er dar ŏz.
sich selben gart er sâ
1640 in zwelf tintinabula.
er zoch an sine bruste
daz edel chirchgeruste,
daz got wol gezam;

heizze wainen er began.

1645 Do chom ein engel geflogen,
er sprach ‚ia seit ir niht betrogen,
got wenket niht sinem wort.

nv sûch ein chleine gerten dort,

D

do si do niht ensahen,
170, 10 sie sprachen mit einem mvnde:
‚wir schuln des himels   1820
        urchunde
noh herzeklicher suchen,
ob des got welle ruchen,
daz wir gesehen siniv tŏgen.
er ist gnadich, deist vnlovgen.'

Abiathar der bisgof   1825
der hiez do uf den frithof
15 alle die menige entwichen
v̄ betten inneklichen.

ein gienger in den sal,
daz livt stunt hievor uberal. 1830
selbe gart er sih sa
in zwelf tintinnabula
v̄ in die heiligen wat
die Moyses gebrvefet hat,
niht uon mennisken sinne 1835
wan als im div gotes minne
20 gebot v̄ uorgetihte.
als sih der herre berihte
got ze flegen in dem gwante,
erwelte mirren er brante, 1840
tymiama v̄ wirŏh.
sin sunde wêinter ŏh
so heize uor dem altære,
daz des himels rihtare
geruhte bewisen in,   1845
der bediv gnade unde sin
25 al der werlte teilet
v̄ die sundare heilet,
swa er die rivwe gesiht,
wand im der barmunge giht 1850
ensamet himel v̄ erde
v̄ dienet im so werde.
Do chom ein engel geflogen,
er sprah: ‚ia birt ir niht betrogen,
30 got enwandelt niht siniv 1855
        wort.
nu svche ein chleine gerte dort,

1641 brust   1644 heizzen

din dir ist enphallen:
diu erfrouwet . . . .

† . . . si im von der wîze
die vederen muosten glîzen.
dô wart ein chradem grôzer (1385)

1928 ervreuwet   1971—75 C² 728—32   71 *f. vermutlich entweder*
daz im *oder* daz si im *und* sâhen *statt* muosten   73 thradē

A

div da leit vervallen:
1650 div verriht den zweifel allen,

vn̄ sehet den zwei mit evren ovgen,
dar an die gotes tougen!'
Do si die chleinen rûten
allenthalben gesûchten,
1655 in der arken er sei vant.
er nam sey zehant
vn̄ drank ovz ze der chirchture.
die gerten zaigt er da fure;
er sprach: ‚Josep, gotes kint,
1660 die engel dir holt sint,
die eilent an dich zaigen:
dise gerte ist din eigen.
nv sovme dich niht mere:
wir enpfelhen dir die magt here.'

1665 Joseph erchom vil sere do,
daz mit louten worten so
in der pyschof ane rief.
sine ⟨gedanche⟩ waren tief.
do enpfienk er ziterinde
1670 von des herren hende
daz grûne plûnde reis.
sein part was lank vn̄ greis.
er were gerne entwichen,
sein sorge waren michel,
1675 die bewainot sein not.
Als er die gerten ovf pot
vor weiben vn̄ vor mannen,
ein tovbe swank do dannen,
ein vil wunnechlicher vogel:
1680 der swebte bey dem swipogen,
daz si in alle sahen.
darnach begunde er galen
gen des himels trone.
er waz den vollen schone.

1685 man hort ein schal grozzen
von seinen housgenozzen,

D

div dir ist enpfallen:
div chumet ze frôden in allen,
swie harte sie iv uersmahet.
als sie Josep enpfahet, 1860
ir geseht div gotes tôgen
mit fleisklichen ôgen.'
Do er die chleinen rute
allenthalben suhte,
in der arche er sie uant, 1865
er uam sie froliche in die hant.
do drang er uz der chirhtur
v̄ zeigte die gerte her fur;
er sprah: ‚Josep, gotes kint,
die engel dir gnædik sint, 1870
sie ilent an dih zeigen:
disiv gerte ist din eigen.
nu sûme dih niht mere:
wir bevelhen dir die maget here.'

Josep erchom do harte, 1875
daz mit so lûtem worte
der bisgof in anrief.
sin gedanche waren tîef:
er zwiuelt waz er tæte,
v̄ wes got willen hæte. 1880
doh enpfieng er daz ris.
sin bart was im lanch vnd gris.

weinen begunde er durh not,
v̄ als er die gerte ufbot
uor wiben v̄ uor mannen, 1885
ein tube swanch do dannen,
ein vogel so wolgetan
daz sin got must ere hân:
der swêimet ein wile da
vnd hub sih danah sa 1890
gegen himel hin wider,
danner chomen was her nider.

Do wart ein chradmediker scal
von dem livte uber al:

170, 35

170, 40

171, 1

5

170,36 do | do 1661 eilten 1664 div 170,40 warte 1675 des
beweinot er *F.* 171,8 chradmendiger *Lexer 1, 1701*

von sînen genôzen:
1975 si . . .

A

wan es sey selzêne
dovhte v̄ harte zême.
waz sol ich mere sagen?
1690 Joseph begunde chlagen,
daz er in alten tagen
den chvmer solde tragen.
ein herze er doch gevienk,
fur den pischof er do gienk.
1695 do trǔk der pideminde man
eine chruchen fraissam,
daruber mǔst er sich lênchen.
er bat sein got gedenchen,
daz si in alle liezzen
1700 seines alters geniezzen,
v̄ in des niht endwungen,
daz er die maget iungen
in seine gewalt næme,
wan ez im niht zême.

1705 Do trosten in die herren,
es moht im niht gewerren,
noch er niht trovren solde.
swaz got stiften wolde,
dem mohte nieman widerstan,
1710 wan er wurde vngehorsam.

er bat auer mit minnen,
mit fleize von allen sinnen,
daz si in sein begæben,
seinen siehtom ane sehen.

1715 Der bischof bat in horen,
er sprach: ‚wil dv zestoren

D

si lobten got genot.   1895
wie harte sie wnderot,
171, 10 daz enkan iv niemen gesagen.
er êin muse wol chlagen,
daz er in alten ziten
des kindes scolte biten.   1900
ein herze er gevîe,
fur den bisgof er gie
v̄ leint sih uber sin chruken.

er bat sin got gehuken,
daz sie in alle liezen   1905
sines alters geniezen,
15 vnt in des niht endwngen,
daz er die maget ivnge
in sinen gewalt næme.
er sprah, wie er ir gezæme. 1910

Do trosten in die herren,
im enmæhte niht gewerren,
warumbe er truren scolte?
swaz got stiften wolte,
daz mæhte im niht wider 1915
stan.
wolt ab er des strites nîen lan,
20 des muser wol enkelten:
sie heten freisket selten,
swer wider dem garte
ware strebende harte,   1920
ezen kome im ze ungemah.
Joseph in aber zusprah:
‚swære ist mir ivwer gebot:
des begebet mih durh got,
25 wand ih ir vnwirdik bin. 1925
ichen han die ivgent noh den sin,
daz ih ir wol gedienen mege,
div in so grozzer pflege
komen ist an disen tach.
got weiz wol daz ih enmak. 1930
nu sehet min unchraft an!‘
der bisgof antwrten began,
er bat in ein wile horen,
er sprah: ‚nnde wil dv storen

1695 de   *1698* sei

7*

unt wil du âne sunde
samet ir iemer bûwen
in gotlîchen triuwen,   (1390)
daz mahtu wol geleisten:
2020   du bist des hûses meister

A

daz dir der engel gebot,
daz ist der ewige tot.
ia zaiget daz mægedein
1720 ir herze vn̄ allen iren sin
mit warem vrchvnde,
vn̄ wil dv ane sunde
mit ir immer leben,
in reiner cheusche sweben,
1725 des hast dv gûte stat,
wan ovch ir wille da zv̂ stat.

dich hilfet div chrenche niht.
gotes genade vn̄ sein lieht,
der werlde schepfere,
1730 wesse wol wer dv were,
do er an dich gedahte
v̄n dir die touben brahte.

dv solt gedenchen daran,
wie weilen die zwene man,
1735 Chore vn̄ Abyron,
weilen verworhten ir lon,
daz si an die gotes tougen
niht wolten gelouben.

tû vns daz ze liebe:
1740 mehel die vrowen schiere,
æ wir den hof rŏmen!
dv solt dich niht lenger soumen.'

Do sprach der einvalte:
,got mit sinem gewalte
1745 der weise mich des besten,
wan wie so ich weste
daz ich die sele moht ernêrn,
waz solde ich bezzers gern?
ich wil ev sagen minen sin:
1750 wan ich ein sundere pin,

D

171,30 daz dir der engel gebot,   *1935*
daz ist der ewige tot;
damit mustv uerlorn sin.
ia zeiget dir daz magedin
des himels urkunde,
v wil du ane sunde   *1940*
samet ir iemer bûwen
in gotlichen trivwen,
35 so maht du wol genesen
v̄ maht des huses wirt v̄ meister
wesen.
schaffez drinne swie dv   *1945*
wellest!
daz du vns din alter zellest,
daz gefrumet dir chleine.
niemen weiz wan got eine,
wes er hab an dih gedaht
do er dir die tvben braht. *1950*
er wesse wol wer du wære.
sin lôz daz ist gewære,
40 sin urchunde warhaft.
nu geswîge diner unchraft
v̄ gedenche wol daran,   *1955*
wie zwene herliche man,
Dathan vnde Abyron,
wilen uerworhten ir lon,
172,1 daz sie an die gotes tŏgen
niht wolten gelŏben!   *1960*
nv mache die rede niht ze lanch,
la den strit, volge uns ane wanch:
gemæhel mit frolichem mvt
die maget edel v̄ gut,
5 e wir den hof rûmen!   *1965*
du scholt uns niht lenger sumen.'

Do sprah der einualte:
,got mit sinem gewalte
der bewise mich des besten,
wan swie so ih weste   *1970*
daz ich die sele mæhte ernern,
waz scholt ich tivrers gern?
ich wil iv sagen minen sin:
wand *ich* ein sundære bin,

1720 allē! 1721 waren   1724 cheuse   171,35 husse   171,36 zelest
1746 wie!   1747 ernêren   172,9 ihc

*disem magedi*ne
mit bescheidener rede

minen mahelschaz geben: (1395)
sô si zuo ir jâren chome,
2065 in mînem hûse gewone

A

alt vn̄ vngezeme,   172, 10
waz hulfe daz ich sey næme?
ez ist vmich denhein frume.
ich han hêrliche svne,
1755 vil vermezzen degene,
die mir got gesegene:
die sint hochgeboren,
ze eren wol erchoren.
ich wil an diser weile
1760 disem magedeine
minen mahelschatz gebcn

mit bescheiden reden:
so si zv̊ iren iaren chome
vn̄ in minem house wone,
1765 so schowe si alle div chint
die von mir chomen sint:
an swelhem minem chinde
si die tugent vinde
daz ez ir gevalle,
1770 des sey wir fleizzek alle,
daz si zv̊ dem chere:
des mak si baz ære
dan mein gewinnen.
mit solhen dingen
1775 in min hous v̄ in min hŭt
enphah ich dise magt gŭt.'

Als si die rede vernamen,
die fursten alle chamen
nach sant Mareien,
1780 der edilen vn̄ der freien;
die latten sei ovf den freithof:
si sprachen, daz der pischof
sei wolde besprechen
vn̄ ir ere zechen.
1785 die magt in dem chloster
daz reine kint si trosten;
si zierten wol ir gewant.
die herren nâmens an die hant

D

alt v̄ ŏh ungezæme,   1975
waz hulfe mih daz, ob ih sie næme?
ez ist umbe mih nehein frum.
ich han ave erliche svn,
vil wolgetane degene,
die mir got gesegene: 1980
die sint gŭt v̄ wolgeborn,
zallen sælden erchorn.
an die wil ih ir raten
vnd wil ez uor iv stæten,
15 daz ich ir mit bescheidener 1985
      rede
minen gemahelschatze gebe:
so sie zir iaren bechome
v in minem huse gewône,
so schowe sie elliv div kint
div mir uon got uerlihen sint: 1990
an swelhem minem kinde
sie die tugende vinde
20 daz ez ir wol geualle,
daz dienen wir alle,
daz sie zu dem chere: 1995
des mak sie frum v̄ ere
baz denne an mir gewinnen.
daz ist ŏh al div minne
der ich iemer dar gemûte:
alsus enpfahe ich sie in mine 2000
      hvte.'

25   Als div rede was getan,
die herren hiezzen gan
nah sante Mærien,
der guten v̄ der frien;
die ladeten sie uf den frithof: 2005
sie sprachen, daz der bisgof
sie wolte gesprechen,
ir ere gerne zechen.
die frowen die ir waren bi,
nu ez also komen si,   2010
30 die rieten ir algeliche,
daz sie tæte froliche
swes man an sie mŏte:
daz wrde ir gewant ze gûte.
uf stunt do div rêine,   2015

1755 degen   1762 bescheidener rede *F.*   1776 ephach   1785 div

A

vn̄ fůrten sei an den rink.
1790 ir sele vn̄ alles ir dink
daz enpfalich si got tevre.
si bat daz er si stevren

mit dem heiligen geiste   172, 35
   gerůchte,
swaz rede man an sey sůchte,
1795 daz si an ir antwurtte
besprochen iht wur*te*.
Der pischof stůnt in der mitten,
die levte sweigen hiez er bit*t*en.

do stůnt si sam ein plůme,
1800 div an der wise grůne
scheinet ovz dem dorne:
sam stůnt daz kint da vorne.
si levhtot als div sunne:
ez waz ir aller wunne

1805 daz si di*e* schṑnen vrowen
ane solten schowen.

Do sprach der pischof weise:
‚dv solt ze Paradeise
immer gotes kint sein.
1810 nv sprich, liebes magedein:

daz zaichen daz hie geschen ist
daz wil daz dv denheine frist
dich ŏf habest
vn̄ lenger iht entsagest,
1815 dv mv̊ssest werden hie ze stet
durch gotes gebot vn̄ vnser bet
Josebes gemahele.'
do vielen ir die zehere
von den wangen ovf die wat.
1820 si sprachen: ‚sein ist chain rat,'

D

sie gie zuhtekliche v̄ seine
den herren bisiten
fur die herscaft an den rinch witen
v̄ beualh sich got tiv̂re;
sie sprah: ‚herre, du mih   2020
   stîvre
mit dem heren geiste din,

daz min antwrte muze sin
werde v̄ unbesprochenliche.'
do gebot der bisgof riche
al die menige swigen,   2025
unnvtzen chradem uermiden.
die maget enpfieng er wol:
sie neig im als ein frŏe scol.
da stunt sie sam div blůme,
div an der wise grůne   2030
ir liehten schîn uerre sprenget.
40 die werlt het des wol verhenget,
daz diu rede gelenget wære,
darvmbe wand div werde v̄ div
   mære
173, 1 gab in frŏde v̄ ŏgenweide: 2035
die sælde hete sie beide
an der schone v̄ an der gute.
dar under stunt ab ir gemv̂te
niender me wan eine ze got
v̄ zallem sinem gebot.   2040
5 der herre hub an v̄ sprah:
‚frŏe, din ere v̄ din gemah
wellen wir mit dir ahten.
nv solt dv reine betrahten,
waz gotes wille daran si   2045
v̄ ŏh unser rat dabi.
daz zeichen daz da geschehen ist
daz wil daz du neheine frist
10 noh dehein ufscub habest
v̄ dih niht lenger entsagest, 2050
dune werdest hie ze stete
durh unser aller bete
Josebes gemahele.'
do vielen ir die træhene
ab den hufeln an die wat. 2055
sie sprachen: ‚sin ist dehein rat:

1796 wurde   *1798* biten   *1805* div   *1815* mv̊sset

A

daz si sich wol gehabte
noch niht widersagte.

Do sprach div schône lilye:
,got der het in himile
1825 gesetzet sinen stůl
vñ in daz paradeis fûr,
do er den ersten man
ouz layme bilden began,
der beschûf der werlde vmechreiz,
1830 der allev dink wole waiz,

wan aller herzen tougen
blûent vor sinen augen,
der laitet des meres vnde
vñ daz abgrunde,
1835 erde vñ luft
vñ der helle gruft:
er mit sinen chôren
gerûche mich erhôren,
wan ich daz vrchunde
1840 von sein selbes munde,
von seinen genaden nemen wil.
hie ist herschefte vil,
die wil ich niht verzeihen.
got rûche mir erzaigen
1845 mit sein selbes veste
swaz mir sei daz beste.
Ich han denheinen willen
noch nimmer wil gewinnen,
daz ich mit cheinem maile
1850 miner sele vertaile.
meinen magtom sol ich herten,
doch seit ich ab der gerten
die toube sach fliegen,
so wil ich niht betriegen
1855 daz himelische zaichen.
meinen sin wil ich reichen

D

wer schol daz wenden v̄ chlagen,
daz got selbe ruchet antragen,
173, 15 der an niemen missetvt?
nv sage frôe dinen mut!' 2060

Div maget antwrten began:

,got der den eristen man
uz læime gebildet hat,
v̄ des tronus inme himele stat,
der ŏh geschuf den witen 2065
                    umbechreiz,
elliv dinch er wol weiz;
20 wir mugen in nihtes uerheln,
niht uersagen noh uersteln:
aller herzen tŏgen
div sint uor sinen ŏgen; 2070
des tiefen meres unde
ioh daz uinster abgrvnde,
erde v̄ lufte sint im diensthaft
v̄ erchennent sine chraft:
25 der ruche mih erhoren; 2075
sin gebot shol ich niht storen,
wand ich daz urchunde
uon sin selbes munde
enphangen han v̄ nemen wil.
hie ist ŏh herschefte vil, 2080
der beidiv bet v̄ rat
uon rehte mir ze volgen stat,

swie ich doh niemer gewînne
mŭt ze werltlicher minne,
30 daz ich mit deheinem mæile 2085
min sele uerteile,
noh minen magetûm verwerte.
ich sah abe der gerte
mit samet iv die tuben fliegen:
des wil ich niht triegen 2090
daz himiliske bŏchen.
min herze mŭz ich brŏchen

1824 got der] der got A, der got der *F.* 1843 verzîhen : erzeigen
sicher nicht ursprünglich, ich vermute die wil ich niht verseinen

A	D

A

in ewer aller rat:
swer mich ze hute bestat,
deme wil ich sein gehorsam. 173, 35

1860 mines leibes ich nieman gan,

alten noch iungen
ze chranker wonunge,
ze sundegen sachen:
daz kan nieman gemachen.'

1865 Dise rede douhte sev lobelich:
do sprach mennechlich,
si were eben genůk.
ir leip si also wol trůch
daz sei die levte diche
1870 musten ane blichen.
Do hete der alte
einen mehelschatz behalten,
ein guldein vingerlein: 174, 1
daz enpfienk von im daz magedein

1875 miten in dem ringe.
daz volk begunde singen
des reichen gotes ære.
si wolten dannen cheren,
ze herbergen reiten;
1880 der alte pat sey peiten,
er sprach: ,nv solt ich venien
fur alle dise menige:

die herren die nv hie sint
die sehent wol daz ich daz kint
1885 selbe niht mak bewarn:
ich mŭz reiten vñ varn
dvrich min sache weiten;
wie mohte danne erbeiten
disev magt zeme,
1890 vnze ich wider chæme?

D

in ivwer aller rat:
swêr mih ze hute bestat,
dem bin ich gerne undertan 2095
mit dienste, daz wizzet sunder
wân.
mins libes ich niemen gan,
da belibe ich stætik an.
ob mirz got verlihet,
der nieman nihtes uerzihet 2100
des man mit rehte an in gert,
da wrde ŏch ich niht entwert.'

Div rede duhte lobelich: 40
des iah aller manneklich,
ir antwrte div ware gŭt, 2105
ir sin mit wisheit behut.

do hete in sinem gewalte
einen gemæhelschatze der alte,
ein guldin vingerlin:
daz enpfie sie uon der hant 2110
sin
enmitten inme ringe.
daz uolch an dem tâidinge
uor frôden singen began.
sie wolten cheren dan,
ze herbergen riten; 2115
der alte bat sie biten,
er sprah: ,nu scholt ih min uenige 5
fur alle dise menige
vil billichen suchen,
ob ir es woltet geruchen. 2120
die herren die nu hie sint
die sehent wol daz ich ditze kint
selbe niht mak bewarn:
ia mŭz ich riten v̄ uarn
durh mine sache witen; 2125
wie mæhte danne erbiten
disiv maget schone, 10
untze ih ie wider kome?

1857 *im Original wohl* in den iuwer aller rat 173, 34 hute *durch*
Flecken fast unleserlich, aber sicher nicht hilfe *H.* 173, 38 verzihet: uerzihet 1881 ich! 174, 7 wolte 1886 varen

A

nv gebt vns ze hŭte
funf vrowen gŭte
ovz diser samenunge,
edel vñ iunge,
1895 kevsche vnde piderbe;
die antwurt ich her widere,
swan ir sein niht welt   174, 15
    enberen:
des sol der pyschof mich geweren.'

Do sprachen die gŭten chnehte,
1900 si solden in mit rehte
geweren des er sei bat,
seit er gevolget hat.
si hiezzen die kvniginne
selbe darinne
1905 welen die ir gevielen.
do nam div maget ziere
eine div hiez Rachel,
div waz zv̂ den tugenden snel;

Rebeka hiez div ander,
1910 div was ane wandel;
Sepfora div dritte hiez,
die si niht hinder ire liez;
Abygea hiez div vierde,
die was ane falsche girde.

1915 die fumfte hiez Svsanne,
div mŭste mit ir danne.
michel wart daz wainen,
do si sich mŭsten schaiden.
Mareien schidunge

D

sine wære mit ir gespiln,
anders mŭste sie beviln   2130
v̄ betragen miner uzverte.
nu helfet mir daz ich beherte
mit bete ir ze hŭte
fumve ivnchfrŏen gŭte,

kivsche, gewizzen v̄ biderbe; 2135
die geantwrte ih iv widere,
swenne ir sin niht welt enbern.

des schol mih der bisgof gewern
durh ivwer aller minne:
so bin ih wol gestîvret   2140
    hinnen.'

Do sprachen die guten chnehte,
*m*an scholt in uon rehte
gewern swes er bǽte,
nu er in geuolget hǽte.
20 sie hiezzen die kuniginne 2145
selbe welen darinne.
do nam sie die liebesten vnder in,
hinze den sie truch ir sin:
einiv was Rachel genant,
der alle tugent waren   2150
    erchant;
div ander Rebecca hiez,
die nehein gŭttǽte uerliez;
25 Sephora was div dritte,
div hete reine site;
Abigea hiez div vierde,   2155
div lebet ane alle girde
werltlicher sunden
v̄ giench vngebunden,
wand sie ir hete furgeleit
ze beliben mit der kivscheit. 2160
die fvmften nant man Susanne,
div muste ir volgen danne.
30 michel wart daz weinen,
do ez cham an daz scheiden,
uber al die samnvnge. 2165

174, 18 wan   *1905* geviele   *1912* div   *174, 27* werltlichen

A

1920 tet aller samenunge
gar inrechlichen wê:
si sprachen daz si nimmer mê

in disem yrdischen tal
ir geleiche funden vber al.

1925 fur den pischof si trat,
vrlovbes si bat,
hin fur die phalze frone
mit den vrowen schone.

vber al daz gevilde
1930 in englischem bilde
ze Josebes herberge
si heten ane erge
vil gůt gevertte,
wan sei got gewerte
1935 seines reiches vñ seiner ære,
da si wonent mit frevden immermere.

Div stat heizzet Capharnaum
vñ stozzet an des meres drum:
da sazzen reiche levte.
1940 Capharnaum sprichet ze devte
villa speciosa:
si leuhtet sam dev rosa
vor den andren steten.

D

div Marien schidunge
têt in herzeclichen we:
sie sprachen daz sie niemer me
die reinen uberwnden,
noh ir gliche funden   2170
uber allez irdische tal.
die frowen chuste sie uberal
174, 35 daz insigel rehter gvte:
ir zvhten gehal ir gemvte.
daz ir gesinde ŏh urlŏp nam, 2175
als ez den mageden gezam,
mit zuhteklicher svzze.
zu des bisgofes gruzze
Maria dennoh getrat:
urlŏbes sie in gebat   2180
daz er ir gebieten scholde.
die herren heten sie holde:
40 die wnsketen ir al geliche
sælde vnd frŏde riche,
daz sie die hie geŵnne   2185
⊽ hernah des himels wnne.
175, 1 sie neig in ⊽ cherte dan
mit den frŏen ioh mit dem man
der sie wol bewarn chunde
⊽ *sie* ŏch meinet ane sunde. 2190
sie fure uber daz geuilde
in engeliskem bilde
ze sinen herbergen.
wîe mahte iemer werden
5 loblicher geuerte,   2195
wand sie got bediv gewerte
siner hulde ⊽ al der eren?
nv ruche sie zu uns cheren
sin gnade den sie trvch:
wil sie, so han wir heiles 2200
          gnuch.

Ein stat hêizet Capharnaum,
div stozzet an des meres drum:
da sazzen richiv lîvte.
Cafarnaum chivt ze divte
10 uilla speciosa.   2205
sie lûhte sam div rosa
ob anderen steten.

174, 39 hete   *175, 3* sie] es, *l.* ez?

A

dar was Josepf gebeten:

1945 ez waz in sinem lande.
boten im do sanden
zwene fursten reiche:
si enbuten im minnechlichen,
ob er sey mohte gesprechen,
1950 si wolden mit im zechen
vm ir schef die waren zebrosten:
die chunde er wol chosten,
waz dar ovf gienge,
so man ez an vienge:
1955 er kunde in rehter weile
schef vñ galeien
vil wol bereiten
mit sinen arbeiten.
die mehtigen herren
1960 baten in ferre,

daz er mûste zů in varen,
noch mohte sein niht gesparen.
An dem andern morgen
hûb er sich ovz mit sorgen
1965 der heilige patriarch;
er pat die vrowen stark,
daz si Mariam behûten
durch ir selbes gûte.
er begunde sey bitten,
1970 daz si sey in die mitten
⟨nahtes⟩ legten
vñ ir mit fleizze pflegten.
sein gesinde hiez er fur sich gan:
er gebot daz si vndertan
1975 der edelen vrowen wêren,
vñ allez daz verbæren
daz si niht wolde schowen:
daz lobte ime man vñ vrowen,
daz si ir wolden dienen
1980 durch sein gebot vñ durch ire liebe,
die weil er wære vnder wægen.
er bat daz der gotes segen

D

dar wart Josep gebeten
uon richen fursten zwêin.
des waren sie worden ennêin, 2010
daz ir ieteweder nah im sande:
ia was ez in sinem laude.

ir schef waren in zebrosten:
daz chunder wol chosten,
175, 15 waz sie dar uf tæten.   2215

so uerre sie in baten
daz er in muste nolgen,
doh was sin herze erbolgen,
daz er nah solhen eren
uon sinem huse scholte   2220
        cheren.
iedoh must er hengen,
erne mahtez niht gelengen.
an dem andern morgen
hub er sih uz mit sorgen
20 der heilige patriarche;   2225
die magede fleget er starche,
daz sie an Marien hûte
stæte wæren durh ir gûte,

nahtes bi ir lægen,
mit trivwen ir pflægen.   2230
sin hiwische hiez er fur sih gan,
v̄ gebot daz sie undertan
siner frôen wæren,
unde allez daz uerbæren
25 daz sie leides ermante.   2235
sin svne bat er ôh zehant
in ir dienste gerne stan.
,nu mûz ich ivh', sprah er, ,lan
die wile ich bin underwegen.
der milte gotes segen.   2240

1946 sande   1951 zebrochen   1956 galaien   1960 baten / baten
ferren   175, 20 pfleget   1969 biten   1972 ir!   flezze

2365   an ir chirchgeruste,
       sô si werches geluste,
       daz si durch alte minne   (1400)

       ⟨si⟩triuwen brâhten inne
       an dem ir garwe,
2370   daz si die manigen varwe
       sprankten an diu bilde,
       daz die lewen wilde   (1405)
       unt die trachen swebeten daran,
       beidiu vogele unde man,
2375   diu mislîchen merwunder
       unt allez ⟨daz⟩ chunder
       des diu werlt phlâge,   (1410)
       daz ⟨daz⟩ daran lâge.
       die priester santen ouch dar
2380   wol gezinnelôten har,
       daz si in ze helfe spunnen,
       sô si beste kunden.   (1415)
       dô wart ir strît vil grôz:
       die frouwen wurfen ir lôz,
2385   wâ der purper unt diu sîde
       scholten belîben,
       welche des wert wâre,   (1420)
       daz si daz beste nâme
       unt darane worhte.
2390   den rûhen har si vorhten:

2365 *bis* niht 2458 C² 743—836   65 chirgirdiste   66 so] wanne
69 gegerbe, *vgl. § 31b Anm.*   71 sprengeten   72 leuwen   75 **di**

A

sei alle behůte.
er schiet von dan mit laidem
      můte.

1985 Templi pontifices
die bedahten sich des,
warume sechs magedein
also mv̂zzik solden sein.
Si sanden den edelen weiben
1990 purper vn̄ seiden,
varbe maniger hande

z̊v̊ dem chirchgeruste,
so sey werches geluste,
1995 daz si des begunden,
so si beste chunden.

die priester sanden auch dâr
wol gepursten hâr,
daz si den spvnnen
2000 z̊v̊ der chirchen gezierde vn̄ wunne.
do wart ir streit groz:
die vrowen wurffen ir loz,
welihen purper vn̄ die seiden
vnder in solden beleiben,
2005 ovf swelich daz loz quême,
daz si daz beste nême
vnde dar an worhte.
den rouhen har si vorhten:

D

hab ivch alle in siner hûte.'
do schied er dan mit trurigem
      mute.

175, 30 Templi pontifices
die berieten sih des,
warumbe die sehse magedin 2245
also muzzich scholten sîn.
sie santen den edelen wiben
purpuram unde siden,
coccum v̄ bisse.
sie enbutten in gewisse   2250
bediv sælde v̄ heil,
v̄ daz sie in hulfen einteil
35 an ir chirchgeruste,
so sie werches geluste.
sie baten durh die alten   2255
      minne,
daz sie ir chunstigen sinne
zaigeten an dem garwe
v̄ die manigen uarwe
sprankten an div bilde,
daz die lewen wilde   2260
vnd die draken swebten daran,
bediv uogel v̄ man,
40 div mislichiv merwnder
unde allez daz chunder
176, 1 des div werlte pflæge,   2265
daz daz daran læge.
die pfaffen santen ŏh dar
wol gezinnelohten hâre,
daz sie in ze helfe spunnen,
so sie beste kunden.   2270
do wart ein strit vil groz:
die frŏen wrfen ir loz,
5 wa der purper vnt die siden
uon rehte scholten beliben,
welhe under in gezæme   2275
daz sie daz beste næme.
den ruhen hare sie vorhten:
daz sie daran iht worhten,

---

manige   76 alle   79 santen] sante er   80 gezinnelot   83 stit
85 purpˢ!   90 den] di

175, 34 heile : einteile *175,* 40 mieslichiv *1999* spvnne *2007* worhten

des wolte ieglîch magedîn
gerne uberk worden sîn.   (1425)
do geviel daz lôz an daz kint
dannen alliu wîp sint
2395 gezieret unt gesegenôt,
daz die sîden gruone unt rôt
in ir handen beliben: (1430)
alsô wolte si gesigen,
daz die andern spunnen den har.
2400 diu vil wênige schar
diu enlie daz niht âne nît:
daz verweiz in der engel sît,   (1435)
daz si durch unminne
sie hiezen kuniginne,
2405 wan si von rehten schulden
hête gotes hulde.

der engel der die spîse   (1440)
ûz dem frônen paradîse
sant Marîen brâhte,
2410 do er an den schimph gedâhte

den die magede hêten under in,
er wolte erschrechen ir sin: (1445)
in allen er erschein,
lieht als der goltstein;
2415 er sprach: ‚ez ist ein wîssage
daz ir ze spotte wellet haben:
ir werdet des wol innen,   (1450)
daz si keiserinne
uber al die werlt wesen muoz:
2420 sô wirt ouch iu des tûsches buoz,
so gesehet ir vil gereite
die gerehten wârheite.'   (1455)

dô vorhten si der râche,
mit zuhten si sprâchen,
2425 si wolten ez gerne buozen:
si buten sich ze der kuniginne fuozen.

2394 da von   96 daz si di   99 di har   2401 enliz   2 d⁵
engel in daz seit   3 ir minne   5 schulde   9 sente   10 schinph
13 in allen gâhen? s. § 69 d   14 ein goltzein M.   15 ich wil uch wissage,
vgl. non erit sermo iste in fatigatione missus, sed in prophetiam verissimam

A

do geviel daz loz ovf daz kint
2010 von dem alle vrowen sint
gezieret vñ gesegenot,   176, 10
daz ir seiden grv̊ne vū rot
in ir handen beliben:
also sach man sei gesigen,
2015 daz div ander schar
mŭste spinnen den har.
daz beleip niht ane neit:
daz verwaiz in der engel seit,
daz si denhein vnminne
2020 heten gen der kvniginne,
wan si von rehter schulde
hete gotes hulde.

der engel der die speise
ovz dem fronen paradeyse
2025 sant Mareien brahte,
als er an den schimpf gedahte

den si heten vnder in,
er wolte erschrechen ir sin.
in allen er erschain,
2030 lieht als ein goltzain;
er sprach: ,ich wil ev sagen:
die ir ze neide welt haben,
ir werdet des wol innen,
daz si keiserinne
2035 al der werlde wesen mŭz:
so wirt evres neides pŭz.'

do forhten si die rache;
mit zuhten si sprachen,
si wolten ez gerne pŭzzen,
2040 vñ puten sich zv̊ ir fvezzen.

D

des wolt ieglich magedin
vil gerne uberk worden sin. 2280
Do geviel daz loz an daz kint
dannen div guten wip sint
gesæliget v̄ gesegenot,
daz die siden grune v̄ rot
in ir handen beliben: 2285
also wolte sie gesigen,
daz die andern næmen den hare.
div vil wenigiv schare
div enlie daz niht ane nit.
daz wart ŏh in uerwîzzen sit, 2290
daz sie durh unminne
hiezzen sie ir kuniginne,
15 div uon rehten schulden
was in gotes hulden,
v̄ div der eren chrone treit, 2295
iemer mvter vnde meit.
Der engel der daz himelbrot
tæglichen ir ze tiske bot,
do er an den schimpf gedahte
den die magede heten   2300
under in,
20 den schimpf er ze ernest brahte.
er began schreken ir sin:
en allen gahen er erscheine,
lieht als der tak gemeine;
er sprah: ,ez ist ein wissagen 2305
daz ir ze spotte wellet haben:
ir werdet des inne,
daz Maria keiserinne
25 uber al dise werlt wesen mŭz:
so wirt iv des tuskens pŭz, 2310
so ir gesehet vil gereite
die unverborgen warheite.'
die frŏen harte erschrikten,
do sie den engil an erblikten
v̄ sinen zorn ersahen.   2315
mit uorhten sie iahen,
sie wolten wandeln vnd buzzen,
v̄ butten sih der guten ze fuzzen.

---

prophetatus *Pseudomatthäus VIII*   18 zu keiserinnen *l.* Maria *nach* D?
19 alle di   20 getusches   21 *f.* gereit : warheit   22 *l.* rehten?
   2027 vnder!   *176, 21* gahes, *oder* in *statt* en   *2037* si *aus* di   div

                Nu hôret, lieben, dise sage: (1460)
                an dem anderen tage
                diu kamere des ⟨wâren⟩ sunnen
        2430   diu gie zuo ir brunnen
                an des hoves ende
                unt twuoc ir reine hende.   (1465)
                aller triuwen liehtvaz,
                do si eine wîle dâ gesaz
        2435   unt anders niemen bî ir was,
                ein engel lûter sam ein glas
                der chom ze ir geslichen;   (1470)
                er bat sie wesen sicher
                vor aller slahte leide:
        2440   froude unde weide
                unt daz êwige leben
                daz wolte got von ir geben,   (1475)
                teilen unde spenden
                den armen ellenden,
        2445   die der tievel hâte
                ⟨. . . . .⟩ verrâten.
                er sprach, ez muose chomen ein lieht,   (1480)

                daz enmahte in der vinster nieht
                lenger sîn verborgen:
        2450   si wâre diu alle sorge
                ⌐it dem ole der barmunge
                linden begunde.   (1485)

                do si aller gerniste
                von geistlîchen listen
        2455   mit im geredet hête,
                do verbarc er sîn gewâte,
                bêdiu ougen unde munt,
                daz si in an der selben stunt   1490)
                niht . . . .

    2429 kamerer 32 vil reine   33 ein licht vaz   34 gewas   35 da
enwas   45f. di der tuvel hatte uᵉraten, *etwa* ze sunden verrâten, *vgl.*
3167 *ff.*   47 muz   48 hˢ in   51 oley   52 linderen   53 geruste
56 vˢwarf

A

Nv horet dis*e* sage:
an dem andren tage
div vrowe der sunnen
gienk zů einem brunnen
2045 an des houes ende;
do tuůk si ir hende.
aller æren liehtvaz,
do si eine weile da gesaz
vn̄ ander nieman da waz,
2050 ein engel louter als ein glas
der chom zů ir geslichen;
er bat sey wesen sicher
vor aller slahte laide:
frevde vn̄ weide
2055 vn̄ ewiges leben
daz wolde got von ir geben.

er sprach, ez mûste chomen
ein lieht,
daz moht in der vinster niht
lenger sein verborgen:
2060 si were an alle sorge
mit dem öle der barmunge.
lieben ir sein rede begunde.

do si aller gernist
von geistlichem list
2065 mit ime gereit hête,
do barik er sein gewæte,
pede ougen vn̄ munt,
daz si in zů der selben stunt
mohte sehen weder vinden;
2070 Sus spilt er mit dem kinde:

des nam sey miche*l* wunder.
si het ez gerne erfunden:

D

176, 30 Nu horet, liebe, die sage:
an dem andern tage   2320
div kamer des waren sůnne
div gie zu ir brunne
an des houes ende
vnt dewͨch ir reine hende.
do sie ein wile da gesaz,   2325
aller trivwen liehtuaz,
35 unt anders niemen bi ir was,
ein engel lvter sam daz glas,
mit grozer gute beuangen,
der chom zu ir gegangen   2330
v̄ bat sie wesen ân leide:
gnade, fröde v̄ wêide
wolte got mit ir geben
v̄ daz ewîge leben
40 aller werlte: daz scholte sie 2335
glŏben.
er saget ir uon den gotes
tŏgen,
177, 1 daz ir schiere chome ein lieht,

daz lange in der vinster niht
mæhte sin uerborgen:
sie wære div alle sorgen   2340
mit der barmunge ole
linden begunde v̄ senften wôle;
5 sie wære div die ellenden
wider heim scholte senden
zu ir rehtem uaterlande,   2345
danne sie mit der sunden bande
komen uon des tieuils rate.
do sie aller gerniste hæte
der rede gehoret me,
der engel der mit ir e   2350
sprachte v̄ bi ir stunt,
er uerbarg ŏgen vnde munt,
10 sin antlutze͏ioh den schîn;
also spilt er mit der kvnigin
als man pfleit mit den kinden, 2355
daz sie sin niht chunde vinden:
des began sie wnderen sere
unde iedoh des dinges mere

2041 disev   *2048* da!   *2071* michels

2470 . . . . kort,
daz er dar widere quâme,
daz si sîn ein ende vernâme.   (1495)

    Hie gêt ez an den ernist:
nu muget ir aller gernist
2475 iuwer herze hôhen,
die senften rede hôren,
daz aller bes*te mâre*   (1500)

A

div rede douhte sey ze tief.
ir gedanche schriben eineu brief
2075 in des herzen tolde:
si gedahte daz si wolde
ze einem anderm male
den liehten engel vrageu,
ob er si hete so bechort
2080 daz er verlæzzenliche wort
z vͮ ir gesprochen hete.
si dahte, ob siz gelebte,
daz er dar widere quǽme,
daz si sein antwurtte nǽme.

2085 **H**ie get ez an eineu ernist:
nv mvgt ir aller gernist
ewer herze hôhen,
die semften rede horen,
daz aller beste mǽre
2090 daz dem sundere
wart ie gekvndet,
seit Adâm wart verschundet.
Ein burk heizzet Nazare*t*;
iu einer gegent si stet
2095 div heizzet Galilea:
vnser vrowe div waz da,
div himilischiv kvniginne
div hǽte hous da inne.
do het verznrnet der reiche got
2100 vnde wolte vber der werlte not,
vber vns vil armen
sich genedichlich erbarmen
vn̄ die helle zestoren.
er erwelte oͮz seinen choren
2105 z vͮ siner botschaft
einen engel, *der die* kraft
seiner gotheit
z vͮ der maget preit:
der ist geheizzen Gabriel,
2110 die gotes kraft chvndet er;

D

daz er hete ir furgeleit
uon der chumftigen warheit. 2360
div rede duhte sie ze tief,
ir herze darunder nien slîef:
177,15 sie gedahte waz er meinete,
v̄ daz erz baz bescheinete,
des wolte sie in gerne biten, 2365
so er nah sinen siten

anderstuut zu ir kame,
daz sie sin ein ende uernæme.

Hie gat ez an den ernest:
nu muͤget ir aller gernest 2370
mit liebe v̄ willigen oren
die svzzen rede horen
20 v̄ daz aller beste mære
daz deheinem sundǽre
ie wart gechundet, 2375
sit Adam was uerschundet.
Eiu burch heizet Nazaret;
iu einer gegende sie stet
div genant ist Galilea:
unser froͤe div was da, 2380
aller tuͤgende gimme,
sie hete hûs dar inne.
25 nv was ôh komen div zit,
daz got des viandes nit
niken wolte an uns armeu 2385
vnd sich scholte erbarmen
uber alle sin hantgetat.
do wart erwelt uon sinem rat
z ů der fronen botschaft
ein engel, der die chraft 2390
v̄n die gnade siner gotheite
der reinen bræhte v̄ furpreite:
30 Gabriel ist er genant;
uon dem han wir in erkant,

2075 im Original vielleicht tolbe *,Tiefe, das Innere' zu* telben
,graben' L.   177,16 bitten   *2093* Nazareht   *2106* der die *F.]* d^s
het die

nider zuo der erde;
er vant die gotes werden
in einer keminâten:
dar in sô gienc er drâte.
2505 die chleinen sîden si span, (1505)

daz werc daz si dâ worhte
daz sleif ir ûz den handen:
des boten si niht erkande.
der vorhte er ir gebuozte;
2520 nu hôret wie er sie gruozte: (1510)
‚Ave Marîe,
die dîne bruste frîe,
die . . . .

A

er fûr frôlich
ovz dem himelreich
nider zv̂ der erden;
er vant die gotes werden
2115 in einer keminate:
dar iu gienk er drate.
vil chleine seiden si span,
die si an dem lozze gewan,
do ander daz gesinde
2120 den har mûse spinnen.
Also michel wart der glast
den der englische gast
von gotes augen brahte,
daz div mait sich vberdahte;
2125 ir leip erchom so harte:
si begunde in ane warten
mit vil micheler vorhte;
daz werk daz si worhte
daz slaif ir ovz der hant:
2130 des poten si niht erkant.
der vorhte er ir gepv̂zte;
nv horet wie er sei grv̂zte:
,Aue Maria,
die deine wambe freya
2135 die wil got besitzzen
mit geistlicher hitzzen.

ein vollev genade dv bist:
ia wil der himilische Christ
von dir werden geborn:
2140 dar zv̂ hat er dich erchorn.
er wil bei dir beleiben.
du pist ob allen weiben
gesegenet vñ geweihet,
wan dir alles daz neiget
2145 daz sich kan verstân.
dv solt ze broutbette gan
in dem himele obene:
des wirst dv ze lobene.'
Div maget begunde denken,
2150 die augen nider senken;

D

der Leuiathanes drozzen   2395
mit dem cruce hat beslozzen.
do fur er froliche
uz dem himelriche
nider zu der erde,
da div gotes werde   2400
saz iu einer keminaten,
mit suzzem werche beraten:
177, 35 die chleinen siden sie span,
die sie anme lozze gewan,
do die anderen den hâre   2405
musen spinnen furwâre.
also michel was der glast
den der engelische gast
uon gotes ôgen brahte,
daz div maget sih uberdahte, 2410

v̄ daz werch daz sie da worhte
daz lie sie uon grozer uorhte
40 slifeu uz den handen:
des poten sie niht erchaude.
der sorgen er ir gebuzte; 2415
nu horet wie er sie grûzte:
178, 1 ,Aue, got gruzzet dih Marię,
div uon allem meile bist frie.
aller gnaden bistu uol,
wan Christ uon dir komen   2420
                schol.
unser herre ist mit dir,
er minnet dih, daz glôbe mir,
vñ hat dih darzu erchorn
daz er uon dir werde geborn.
5 bi dir wil er beliben,   2425
gesegentiv ob allen wiben:

dir niget swaz sih chau uerstân.
du scholt ze brutbette gau
iu dem himele obeue:
des wirdes tu ze lobene.'   2430
Div maget begunde denchen,
div ovgen nider senchen;

178, 2 crhist   *2147* ebene

       schiere bringen einen sun,
       der in gnâde wil tuon;   (1515)
       er wirt geheizen Emanuêl:
2550 dehein muoter gebirt niemer mêr
       deheinen *sun sô guoten*:

A

si mohte niht betrahten
noch envollen geahten,
wie dem grůzzen mohte sein.
trŏrik stŭnt daz magedein.
2155 Der engel troste sey aber sa:
‚dine sorge du verla!
gesegent bistu vor allem weibe:
got hat in deinem leibe
im erwelt einen sal;
2160 dv solt der werlde vber al
schiere pringen einen svn,
der in wil genade tŭn;
Er wirt gehaizzen Emanuel:
denhein mŭter gebirt nimmer me
2165 denheinen svn so gŭten:
des entroure niht dein gemvete.‘

Div magt die vorhte verlie,
ein baldes herze si gevie;
ir selbes chevsche si an sach,
2170 zvo dem engel si do sprach:
‚ich kan mich niht versehen,
wie daz mvge geschehen
daz ich kint gebêre
vn̄ doch maget wêre.
2175 ich pin chomen an dise stunt
daz mir ist vil vnchunt
mannes geverte:
mit fleizze ich mich des werte,
als ich wil immer tŭn.
2180 von wev chome mir der svn
den dv mir hast gekundet?
wie sere mich des wundert!‘
Der engel ire antwurte:
‚du solt an der geburte
2185 denheines zweivels pflegen,

wan der himilische segen
vn̄ der heilige geist
wirt des chindes volleist.
die tugende oberiste
2190 zeigent dir die liste,
wie ez mugelich sey

D

178,10 sie nam ez in ir ahte,
wie daz werden mæhte,
v̄ wie dem gruzsal wære. 2435
trurik stunt div gewære.
der engil trost sie aue sa:
‚din sorgen du uerla,
beste aller wibe!
got hat in dinem libe 2440
im erwelt ein sal;
du scholt der werlte uberal
15 bringen einen sun,
der in gnade mak getun;
er wirt genant Emanuel 2445
v̄ der heilant Israhel.‘

Div maget die vorhte uerlie,
einen guten mŭt sie geuie;
ir selber kivsche sie ansach,
ze dem engel si do sprah: 2450
‚ia ne hau ich niht betrahte,
wie daz ergen mæhte
20 daz ich kint gebære
v̄ iedoh maget wære.
ich bin so komen an dise stunt 2455
daz mir ist vil unkunt
mannes liebe v̄ geuerte:
nit flizze ih mih des werte
v̄ ŏh iemer gerne tŭn.
wanne kome mir der sun? 2460

dez muz mih nemen wnder.‘
sa antwrten begunder:
25 ‚du scholt neheines zwivels
pflegen,
wand der himeliske segen
unt der vil heilige geist 2465
der wirt des kindes uolleist.
des oberisten tugent v̄ maht
gezæiget dir wol die ahte,
wie im daz mugliche si

2182 des! *178,24* anwrten 2185 zweives

A

daz er dir wone bey:
mit seines geistes towe
beschat er dich vrowe
2195 vn̄ furdert dich da zů.
ez waz ovch geordent frů
daz ez also werde,
æ himel vn̄ erde
îe geschaffen wurde.
2200 selik ist div purde,
daz wůcher deiner prust
an aller svnde gelust.'

Als er daz wort hete
     gechvndet,
div vrowe wart enzundet
2205 mit rehtem gelouben.
ovf hůb si die augen
gen der himilischen reste.
ir gedinge was so veste;
si sprach in ir gemuete:
2210 ‚got mv̊zze mich behv̊ten.
als ich dich herre hore jehen,
also mvezze mir geschehen:
al nach deinen worten
wil ich genade warten:
2215 dv bist der pote frone.
nv mv̊zze dir der lonen
der dich her hat gesant,
dem allev herze sint erkant.'
Do sprach der engel amen.
2220 von des gelouben samen
wart si zestet swanger.
got soumt ez niht langer
mennisch ze werden
durch vns ovf der erden.

2225 der den himel vil groz
    v̄ al die werlt besloz,

D

daz er dir also wone bi: 2470
178, 30 mit sines geistes tŏwe
bescâtewet er dih frŏwe
v̄ gefurdert dih darzû.
iz wart geordent vil frâ
daz ez also scholte ergan, 2475
e div erde begunde stan
v̄ der himel swebende wrde.
sælich ist div burde
v̄ der wcher diner bruste,
wan dih sunden nie geluste.' 2480

35 Als div rede was ergangen,

div frŏe wart beuangen
v̄ erzunte mit rehtem glŏben.
ufhub sie div ŏgen
gein der himilisken reste. 2485
ir gedinge was so ueste;
sie sprah mit diemûte:
‚got gnade mir, der gûte.
als ich dih herre hore iehen,
also mûze mir geschehen: 2490

40 du bist ez der bote frone.
nu geb er dir daz ewige lone
der dih ze mir sante
v̄ min herze erkante.'
do sprah der engel amen. 2495
uon des glŏben samen
wart sie zehante swanger.
got ensûmet ez niht langer:
179, 1 ia ilter zware
durh die armen sundære 2500
die menniskeit an sih nemen.
do mahte im wol gecemen
div herberge also reine,
sin mûter v̄ mæit al eine.
der wîte er niht uerlie, 2505
do er zu der enge gie:
5 der den himel uil groz
    v̄ die werlt ie besloz,

2203 gechvndet!   2216 lone

A | **D**

der chom mit voller ære
zv̄ der magt here;

der suchte im ein chleine stat:
dar hat er sin gecelt   *2510*
    gesat,
v̄ wart doh geminnert nîe,
da in div gûte enpfie:
sin gewalt stunt ebenriche,
sin mageuchraft ewîcliche,
179,10 ioh wart div menniskeit   *2515*
gehohet uon der gotheit:
div gotheit ungeswachte
die menniskeit anerlachte,
do got menniske werden ruchte
durh mennisken den er   *2520*
    suchte.
er leit an fleiskliche brunne
durh allez mannes chunne,
15 daz er nah champfes site
mit dem viande strite.

da mit er zaiget
2230 daz der himel was geneiget
zv̄ yrdischer molden.
daz lieht waz vnbescholden
in di vinster gevarn,
doch seinen schein chvnde er bewarn.

da wart der himel genæiget, *2525*
als uns div scrift zæiget,
zû der erde; daz ergie
do in unser frŏe umbevie
mit mæitwesentem libe.
div nîe wart ze wibe,   *2530*
sie ist mit der erde gemeinte,
zu der sih alsus uereinte
20 der himel ioh des himels wirt.
sie ist div ân leit gebirt,
der engil frŏde, der werlte *2535*
    heil,
maget ân ende, mûtir ane meil.

2235 Der weisagen meister
bewert mit seinem geiste
daz seine knehte
geprediget heten rehte.
Nv frevt sich Esayas,
2240 daz er weilen chvndinde waz
der maget vnbesprochen;
der himel ist entlochen,
da div kvniginne
nv gebivtet inne.

Der wissagen herre
hat bewâret daz uon verre
alle sine chnehte
heten uorgeseit rehte.   *2540*
nu frŏet sih Esayas,
25 der ez wilen chundent was,

2229 wart erzeiget *F.*   *179,22* meile   *2239* frevte   *2243* kvnigine

sich frouwet der kunic Davît,
sô er an ir fuozen lît,   (1520)
daz von sînem chunne
2650 solh êre ist gerunnen.
Aaron mit sîner gerte
der lobet wol ir geverte,
wan er sie vor diute   (1525)
den ebrêischen liuten.
2655 nu giht der kunic Yessê
der maget wîz alsam der snê,
daz von sînem geslahte
niht bezzers chomen mahte.   (1530)
sîn lampvel zeiget Gedeôn,
2660 daz deste bezzer sî sîn lôn.
. . . vor . en . . g . . . . . .
. . . . magedîn.
wie si alle zuo dringent,
die langen brieve bringent   (1535)
2665 die si von ir tihten:
nu ist chomen zuo gesihte
daz si wîlen frumeclîche schriben,
nu sehent si si ane digen
alle engelische schar;   (1540)
2670 nu vingerzeigent si dar.
die magede habent sich an sie
die si meineten ⟨hie⟩,
sant Margarête
unt alle die ir hêten   (1545)
2675 deheinen dienist erboten:
die sint nu gêret von gote.
wie michel menige mit ir gât,
swâ si sitzet oder stât
in dem himelrîche!   (1550)
2680 si lobent si alle glîche,
die diet ûz allen zungen

2647—81 C² 863—96   48 wanne er an ure suze glit   49 kũde
50 sulche   vᵇnumen   52 lobte   54 erhaften   55 sprichet   56 di
magt als   64 di di   67 biwilen frumelich   71 *Initiale*   meide huben
72 meinete   75 kein dinst   77 michel] himel   81 die] dᵇi, diu *L.*,
B. s. 76.   allen *B. s. 76*] aller

A

2245 Sich frevt der kvnek Daníd,
so er an ir fůzzen leit,
daz von seinem chunne
ist solich ǽr gervnnen.
Aaron mit seiner gertte
2250 lobt wol ir gevertte.

Nv giht der kvnik Jesse
der magt weiz alsam der sne,
daz von seinem geslehte
niht pezzers chomen mohte.
2255 sein lampvel zaig*et* Gedeon,
daz dester pezzer sei sein lon.

wie si alle *zuo* dringent,
die langen briefe si ⟨bringent⟩,
die si selbe tihte*n*;
2260 nv ist chomen zů der slihten
daz si hie bevore schriben;
nv sint si beliben
an englischer schare
vnde vingerzaigent dare.
2265 Die magede habent sich an sey
die sei minten hie,
sant Margrete
vn̄ alle die ir heten
denheinen dienst erboten:
2270 die sint nv geǽret von got*e.*
wie michel menige mit ir gât,
swa si sitzzet oder stât
in dem himelreiche!
si lobent sey alle geleiche.
2275 vor ir ist der engel wunne
mere dan ieman sagen chunne.

D

sih frǒet der kunich Dauit,
der ǒch daz urchunde git,
daz uns uon sinem chunne 2545
bechome solhe ŵnne.
Aaron mit siner gerte
der lobet wol ir geuerte,
wand er sie uor dûtte
dem hebreiskem lîvte. 2550

179, 30 Gedeon den schapǽre furtreit,
den daz nahttǒ uermêit,
wand er ir zaichen furet
div nie wart beruret.
Die herren der alten e 2555
waren ir wnskeute me
denne lebens oder libes,
wand sie des eristen wibes
val sc̨olt undervahen:
die gnade sie uor sahen. 2560
35 des gerten sie ie der suzzen,
daz got ruhte grǔzzen
die werlte mit ir geburte
v̄ mit des kindes geinwrte.
nu sint gewert furware 2565
die guten v̄ die sundære,
die guten ir chrone,
iene der barmunge frone,
wand niemen ist so svnderiche,
wil er buzen herzekliche, 2570
40 im si ǒch gnade beschert,
daz er dem tievil wirt erwert.
des haben wir manek urchunde
uon sin selbes munde
der durh uns ist geborn, 2575
daz im nieman werde uerlorn,
niewan der da missetrŭwet,
v̄ den sin schulde niht gerivwet:
daz ist div frǒde gemeine
die uns brahte div maget 2580
reine.

2255 zaigte   2257 zwene   2259 tihtent   2270 goten

2695   *dâ* habent die hûsgenôze
        mandunge grôze;
        dâ fliuzet cynamôme,   (1555)
        balsamus smecket schône

        under allen den gesellen:
2700   ir sanc ist ebenhelle.
        nu wil ich der geswîgen
        die von disem lîbe   (1560)
        mit êren sint gesundert,
        wan mich des niht enwundert,
2705   daz si die *frouwen gerne sehen*
        unt ir ze keiserinne jehen.

    2695—2726 C² 897—926   95 husgenozen   2700 ur gesallt ist ob
in allen   2 zu disme liben

A

D

180,1   **S**wer uon der gûten sprechen
wolte,

vil sinnes er haben scholte,

dazu tugent v̄ gute,

daz er mit reinem gemute

ir lop mæhte genahen: *2585*

daz ist mir leider unnahen

5 durh min suntliche burde;

doh gedinge ich daz got wrde

menniske dvrh die armen,

v̄ der da wolte erwarmen *2590*

uf mægetlicher bruste,

ein sundarinne div chuste,

div tẘch, div trukent im sin fůzze

v̄ gesteich zu sinem gruzze,

10 ioh daz sie gewan sine hulde: *2595*

sus wart div schuldige âne schulde

v̄ div swarce wol getân:

des dinge ŏch ih sunder wân

so uerre daz ich ernen*d*e

ze sprechen etewenne   *2600*

uber mich uon der heren

div kunigin ist der eren;

doh erfurhte ihz so sere,

daz ich die rede abchere

15 v̄ wende des herzen ŏgen *2605*

ioh mîn ahte uon den tŏgen,

von dem riche, von der herschefte,

uon der sûze, von der trutschefte

der muter mit dem kinde,

welh der hof ist, welh   *2610*
gesinde,

welh ir werdikeit ane ende.

sweu so got dazu sende,

20 der scribe daz ob er mege:

ez ist harte uz mînem wege,

waud ir lob ist so ahtich, *2615*

ir gnade also mahtich

daz sie girdekliche ansehent

die engel v̄ ir iehent

iemer ze keiserinne.

nu helfe sie uns durh di minne *2620*

di got selbe zu ir hat,

und durh den gnadigen rat

Da flivzzet zinamon,

balsamus da smeket schon

vnder den gesellen snelle:

2280 ir sank ist eben vn̄ helle.

Nv wil ich der gesweigen

die von disem leibe

mit eren sint gesundert,

wan mich niht enwundert

2285 daz si die vrowen gerne sêhen

vn̄ ir ze keiserinne iêhen.

188,12 ernenne

wir armen ligen in der nôt
unt enwizzen wanne uns der tôt
begrîfet ungewarnet;   (1565)
2710   diu sêle danne garnet
swaz der lîcham hât gefrumet:
wê wie ubele uns daz chumet!
daz wir ir dienen selten,
des muozen wir enkelten.   (1570)
2715   nu biten wir den gotes sal,
daz si daz tiure gruozsal
des engels an uns bedenke,
unt swâ wir gewenken,
daz si verchiese den zorn.   (1575)
2720   ja wâren si sâlic geborn,
die ûz ir herzen tiefe
ûf ir gnâde riefen.
nu flêgen wir die getriuwen,
daz si uns iteniuwe   (1580)
2725   von allen houbetsunden
unt *ûz dem abgrunde*

. . . . unt gereite:
do si in ir kintheite
neheinen wuocher gebar   (1585)
2740   unz si gezwîvelte gar,
unt ouch vor alter bîbet,
nu ist ir brust gewîhet;

ez ist ir liebe ergangen:
diu frouwe ist kindes swanger   (1590)

2710 ez danne   12 bekumet   13 ir] un   15 nu bitet di gotis
bruth und den sal   16 si daz] si da   20 jo   si!   23 vlehen

A

D

180,25 den er der werlte hab getan,
daz wir die sunde werden âne.

wir arme ligen in der not
ꝟ wizzen niht wan vns der tot
begreifet vngewarnet.
2290 div sele vil lange arnet
swaz der leip hat gefrvmet:
hey wie vbel vns daz chvmet!
daz wir ir dienen so selten,
des mv̊zze wir enkelten.
2295 Nv bite wir den gotes sâl
gemeinlichen vber al,
daz si vns bedenke,
swa wir an ir wenchen,
daz si verchiese den zorn.
2300 ia were er selichlich geborn
der ovz dez herzen tieffe
an ir genade rieffe.
Nv flege wir *die* getriwen,
daz si vns mv̊zze enriwen
2305 von hauphaftiger svnde
vñ o̊z dem abgrunde
erledige alle sele
durch ir svnes ǣre!
‚Ich mv̊z dir sagen mêre,'
2310 sprach der engel here,
‚ein chreftiges zeichen,
daz mv̊z dein herze waichen:

ia ligen wir in der not   2625
ꝟ enwizzen wenne uns der tot
begrifet ungewarnet;
div sele danne garnet
swaz der lip ie gefrumet.
sælich der wol chumet   2630
uf daz tæidinch swâre,
daz er die uogetinne mære
mit dienest erworben hat:
des mak da werden rat.

‚Ich muz dir sagen mere,' 2635
sprah der engil here,
‚ein chreftigez zǣichen,
daz din herze schol weichen,
ze bezzerunge cheren,
div gotes to̊gen leren: 2640

Deiner niftel dink Elizabet,
wie genedichlich daz stêt!
2315 ich sage dir berait:
swie si in ir kintheit·
denhein wůcher nie gebar,
vñ si hat verzweifelt gar,

din niftel Elysabet,
ir dinch frolichen stet
nah wnske ꝟ gereite:
do sie in ir kintheite
nehein wcher gebar,   2645
untze sie uerwarte gar
ꝟ in daz alter getrat,
nu hat sie an der gnaden stat
got selbe gesetzet
ꝟ ir leides ergetzet.   2650

doch ist ir lieb ergangen:
2320 si hat ein kint enpfangen

wol ist ez ir ergangen:
sie ist mit kinde beuangen;

24 iteniuwe] nu v⁵nuwe   2737—71 C² 927—959   40 unz (*so!*) daz
41 bidemt
    180,25 den   *2303* die die   *2318* unze *F*.

2745   unt ist nu worden berhaft:
        ja maht ouch dû die gotes chraft
        an ir schouwen deste baz:
        mugelich ist im allez daz
        daz er gebiutet unde wil:
2750   er ⟨tuot unt⟩ zeiget wunders vil.
        nu ist der sehste mânôt   (1595)
        daz sîn zeswe daz gebôt,
        daz diu alte wambe
        einen vorboten dem lambe
2755   muose gewinnen,
        der sîn kunde bringe.   (1600)
        diu durre ist worden viuhte,
        sîn gnâde wîten liuhte
        nâhen unde verren:
2760   er ist meister aller ⟨knehte unt⟩ herren.'

        Dô diu himilische maget,   (1605)
        als uns Lucas saget,
        gesmachte unt bechorte
        von Gabrielis worte
2765   der oberisten suoze,
        si gedâhte daz si gruozen   (1610)
        Elysabethen scholte
        unt sich des frouwen wolte,
        daz ir sô was gelungen
2770   an der gotes barmunge,
        daz si *muoter scholte wesen*   (1615)

unz an des berges ende

2746 io   49 daz] waz   50 bezeiget   wund⁵   51 der] di   54 sime lamme
55 muze   56 sîn (uns) kunde bringe *M.*] unkundet vinden C, in kunde
vinden *B. s. 52*   59 nahen] witen   60 *Ergänzung nach B. s. 25*   66 f. do
gedachte si an daz gruzen   daz elysabethen scholte   2784—2817 C ² 960—91

A

vñ ist worden perhaft:
ia maht dv auch die gotes kraft
an ir schowen dester baz:
mvgeleich ist im alles daz
2325 daz er gebivtet vñ wil:
er tût vnde schaffet vil.
Nv ist der sehste mano*t*,
daz sein zesewe daz gebot,
daz ir altev wambe
2330 einen vorboten dem lambe
mûste gewinnen,
der im kvnde die minnen.
Div durre ist worde*n* fevhte,
div wûste ist worden levhte
2335 nahen vñ verren,
von chnehte vñ von herren.'

Do div himilische maget,
als vns Lvcas hat gesaget,
gesmakt vñ gechorte
2340 von Gabrieles worte
der oberisten sv̊zze,
si gedahte daz si grv̊zzen
Elyzabeth solde
vñ sich des frewen wolde,
2345 daz ire wole was gelungen
von gotes barmvng*e*,
daz si muoter solde wesen
vñ eines kindes genesen.

si eilte vil gewisse
2350 da si ir niftel wesse.
ôf einem berge si saz:
vnser vrowe wolte vme daz
ire vart niht lazzen.
die vil scharffen strazzen
2355 vñ die vil herten staine
die mohten di*e* vil reine*n*
denheinen weis erwenden,
vnz si an des perges ende

D

div alte get nu perhaft:
so groz ist div gotes chraft,
die mahtv schŏen deste baz: 2655
muglich ist ime allez daz
daz er gebivte*t* v̄ wil:
er tut v̄ zeiget wnders vil.
181,1 nu ist der sehste manot,
daz sine zeswe daz gebot, 2660
daz div trurige wrde getrœste,
div betwngen belœste,

div durre wol gesegente.
so hat er sin gebe geregente,
wand er von gwalte lihet 2665
des ŏh diu nature uerzihet.'

5 Do div himiliske maget,
als uns Lucas saget,
gesmachte v̄ bechorte
uon Gabrielis worte 2670
der oberisten sûzze,
sie gedaht daz sie mit grûzze
ir niftel sehen scholte
v̄ sich des frŏen wolte,
daz ir so wol gelunge 2675
an der gotes barmunge,
10 daz ŏh sie mûter scholte wesen
vnt kindes genesen,
div alte v̄ diu spæte,
div sin uerzwiuelt hæte. 2680
do hub sich uon heime
div edel v̄ div reine
gêin dem berge da si saz
(unarbeitsam duhte sie daz)
uber die steinherten strazze. 2685
ir gûte cham ez cemâzze,
15 daz sie die lieben sæhe
vnde mit ir got ueriæ̂he
siner wndere, diu so riche,
so groz sint unt so trostliche. 2690

180, 43 gebivte 2327 mano*d* 2333 worde 2343 wolde 2346 barmvng͞e
2356 div reine   2357 deheiner wise *F.*   2358 enden

2785 ír niftelen si besprach.

     dô si si êrist an gesach,
     si gruozte sie mit triuwen:
     seltsâne unt iteniuwe   (1620)
     wurden ⟨ir⟩ diu mâre
2790 diu dâ geschehen wâren.
     si kuste die hûsfrouwen
     mit lachenden *ougen,*
     mit herzenlîcher minne.   (1625)
     die mit der kuniginne
2795 *wâren dar gegangen,*
     die wurden ouch wol enphangen.

     Elisabeth diu guote
     erkante in ir gemuote
     von den gotes tougen,
2800 daz al der werlde frouwe   (1630)
     ir ze hove was bechomen:
     si enhête ez ê nie vernomen
     von mennischen zungen;
     der sie dô wolte stungen,
2805 der kunde si wol gelêren   (1635)
     die chumftigen êre:
     daz was der heilige geist,
     rehter dinge volleist,
     der alle froude chundet:
2810 der hête si ouch enzundet.   (1640)
     sâ wart si wîssage vol:
     si rette schône unde wol
     mit sante Marîen,
     diu vor allen wîben
2815 den segen muoz hôren   (1645)
     den niemen mac verstôren;
     si sprach cum magna você:

2786 zu dem ersten an sach   91 *steht vor* 88, *aber mit Um-*
stellungszeichen   93 herzlîcher *B. s.* 94   98 di erkante   99 den] d⁵
2800 aller d⁵   1 kumen   3 menschlich⁵   4 do] da   6 kunftigen
11 sa] zuhant   wissagens

A

ir niftel besprach.

2360 do si ⟨si⟩ erst an gesach,
si grůzte sei mit triwe:
selzene vn̄ niwe
wurden ir div mære
div sprach div seldenbere.
2365 Si kuste die housvrowen
mit lachinden ovgen
vn̄ mit louter minne.
die mit der kvniginne
waren dar gegangen,
2370 die wurden auch wol enpfangen.

Elyzabeth div gůte
erkante in ir můte
von den gotes tougen,
daz al der werlde vrowe
2375 ir zehovs waz bechomen:
si het ez ê niht vernomen
von mennischer zvngen;
der si wolde stungen,
der kvnde sei wol geleren
2380 die kvnftigen ere:
daz was der heilige geist,
rehter dinge volleist.

si wart weissage vol:
si rette schone vn̄ wol
2385 mit sant Mareien,
der edilen vn̄ der freien;
si sprach cum magna uoce:

,mich mv̊z wundren immer me,
wan ich des wirdik wurde,
2390 daz du mit solher purde

D

als sie ir nifteln do gesah,
grozer frȫde nie gescah
frȫen Elisabete
denne sie an der stunde hete.
181,20 sie kusten sih mit triwen 2695
v̄ begunden itenîwen
div seltsænen mære,
waz gnaden an in wǽre

beidenthalp ergangen.
do wrden ȫh enpfangen 2700
mit liebe stæter minne
die geuerten der kuniginne.

Elisabeth diu gute
erkant in ir gemůte,
25 daz da fur ir ȫgen 2705
uon den gotes tȫgen
div Christes muter mære
v̄ des himels brut komen wære:
daz ensæit ir mennisken zunge,
wan div gotes stunge 2710
kunde sie wol geleren
uon den chumftigen eren:
daz was der heilig geist,
rehter dinge uolleist,
30 der alle gnade chundet: 2715
der hete ȫh sie enzundet.
sa wart sie wisheite uol
v̄ began reden so wol
uon der muter ioh dem kinde,
der allez himels gesinde 2720
rihtet v̄ wiset.
sie wart uon ir gepriset
hoher denne ie wibes name
gestige, als iz ir gezâme.
35 sie rief mit lûterre stimme: 2725
,owi aller frȫen gimme,
wa han ich geuordert die ere?
des mûz mih wndern sere,
wie ich des wirdich wrde,
daz du mit solher burde 2730

2365 div

A

mir ze house chomen pist?
dv treist den heiligen Christ,
mûter vnsers herren.
was mak mir nv gewerren,
2395 nv dv mich hast beschowet?
von dir wirt gefrowet
Adâmes geslehte,
vñ ob ich dir nv rehte
mohte gedienen
2400 und dich wol gelieben,
daz têt ich von herzen gier
nieman so willeclich so dier.'

Elizabeth div alte,
nv hôrt waz si zalte,
2405 wie der gotes âtem
hete sey berâten.

si sprach sant Mareien zv̂:
‚min lieber sun spilt harte frů
in des leibes kamere.
2410 seit wir hie ze samene
sein chomen ane neit,
daz kint ist immer seit
mit frevden bevangen.
mohte er her ovz gelangen,

D

mir zehuse komen bist?
du treist den gnædigen Christ,
meîtmûter unsers herren.
waz mak mir nŭ gewerren,
181, 40 sit dv mih hast beschôet,   2735
wan uon dir wirt gefrôet
allez Adames geslæhte?
nu scholt ich dir, ob ich mæhte,
uon rehten schulden dienen:
des gunde ich fur mich   2740
        niemen.'

182, 1 Elisabeth div alte,
nu horet waz sie zalte,
wie der gotes atem
sie hete beraten,
der div broden herze erchert,   2745
div sin gnade durh uert:
er uerdultet vinster nehein,
want swa er ie erschein,
5 da heten vrlovp die sunde
v̄ entwichen an der stunde.   2750
in flivhet elliv achust,
werltliche liebe, svntlichiv glust.
der sælig, den er besitzet,
ist sa gelerte, sa gewitzet
ze guter stæte, ze stæter   2755
        gûte.
er git reinez gemute,
todes vorhte, gotes minne,
rehtes girde, rehte sinne.
10 der geist also here
hiez die frôen mere   2760
sprechen wider die mæit
uon der suzzen warheit;
sie sprah ir lieplichen zû:
‚min sûn spilt al zefru
an minen brusten zware;   2765
er ist fro v̄ frôdenbære.
sit wir zesamen komen sin,
v̄ du mir den gruzsal din
15 ruch*test* erbieten, kuniginne,
sit bin ich worden inne   2770

2396 gefrewet   181,42 fur dich?   182,5 ŏrlovp   182,15 ruchste

A

2415 er enpfienge dich kvniginne.
 grozzer sint seine sinne
 danne sein leip sey:
 der heilige geist wont im bey.

 swie er bei minen rippen
2420 bowe die engen krippen,
 er erchennet wol den heilant, 182, 20
 der dich des wirdek vant,
 daz dv eine soldest sein
 mûter vn̄ magedein.
2425 den leip er allen rûret,
 div frevde in vmbefûret.
 moht er den mvnt erheben
 vn̄ dir rede gegeben,
 dv vernǽmest an seiner stimme,
2430 wie er dich hat in sinne
 vn̄ den hailant mǽre,
 seinen schepfêre.'

 Daz was sant Johannes:
 in dem bovch freut er sich des
2435 bei seiner mûter herzen,
 daz von dem tevren merze
 die waisen ovf der erden
 gefrevt solden werden.

 do der gotes toufer,
2440 der vorlaufer,
 die brust het genomen
 vn̄ ⟨was⟩ ze seinen iaren chomen,
 er weisot ovf den hailant
 mit dem vinger vn̄ mit der haut,
2445 daz er mit seinem troste
 die christenheit erloste,

D

 daz sih daz kint ruret,
 v̄ ez div liebe umbefuret
 gegen diner werdikeit.
 des hat in div gotes wisheit
 bewiste: swie er dih nîen 2775
    sihet,
 der herschefte er doh gihet,
 div dir ze teile ist getan,
 als ŏh ich des mich enstan.
 er erchennet wol den heilant,
 der dih des wirdige vant, 2780
 daz du eine scholtes sin
 muter vnde magedin:
 daz zeiget er mit dem spil,
 des im div nature nien wil
 uerhengen mit der stimme: 2785
 daz tut er dir ze minne.'

25 Daz was sante Johannes:
 ungeborner uerstunt er sih des
 bi siner muter herzen,
 daz non dem tivren mercen 2790
 die sundære v̄ die notigen
 dem tieuel scholten angesigen,
 v̄ daz div maget komen was,
 div des kindes sit gnas
 den nie sunde betwanch, 2795
 v̄ an der der gotes gedanch
30 ioh sin gute ruwen wolte,
 v̄ diu ein blume sin scholte,
 da aller geiste beste
 inne hete reste. 2800
 do der gotes tŏfære
 v̄ sin uorbot mære
 was ce sinen iaren komen,
 als wirz han uernomen,
 er zæigete an den heilant, 2805
 den uns got vater sante,
35 daz er mit sinem troste
 die christenheit erloste,

182, 23 spile   2435 herze   182, 28 mæget   182, 29 dem   182, 30 der
2440 nicht der sîn!   2443 wesot   2446 div

2930　*daz wir dem* tievel an gesigen
　　　 unt von des meres wâge
　　　 ze dem vesten ⟨lande⟩ muozen gâhen.　　　　(1650)

　　　　Daz *ander liet hat ende,*
　　 nu sol âne missewende

A

daz daz lamp an alle maine
sein fleisch vñ sein gepaine
an daz chrevze wolte legen
2450 vñ allen sunderen wegen.
dar nach chom der weissage
zv̊ dem hailigen pade,
da er den herren tovfte
den Jvdas verchoufte.
2455 do wart der himel o̊f getân:
ein toube so lussam
die sach er fliegen vñ sweben
vñ horte sey vrkunde geben
sant Marien kinde,   182, 40
2460 daz wir sulen vinden
in frölichen genaden,
da wir sein zv̊ geladen.
Ich wil an disen stunden
niht vollechlichen kunden
2465 sant Johannes ere:
ich furhte, ich verchere
daz liet von vnser vrowen:
div gerûch ane schowen
vnser pet vñ vnser dige
2470 vñ helf vns, daz wir an gesigen
des argen tiefels vnden
vnde allen vnsren svnden.
              Amen!

Daz *ander* liet hat ende,   45
nv sol an missewende
2475 daz *dritte* werden gesaget
von der div ovf habet
die svnder in ir hûte   183, 1
mit mv̇terlicher gûte.
Nu wil ich ev beschaiden,
2480 waz ir die iuden zelaide
frumten vñ rieten.
von der verworhten diete
so lait si iteweizze vil:
die warhait ich da von wil
2485 kvnden vñ mæren
vñ mit der schrift bewæren.
wir sagen ev von der weile

D

v daz er meil nie gewan.

als er in do to̊fen began,   2810
der himel sih ob im uf tet:
im ze eren da ze stet
ein tube here vf im erschêine,
der nie glich wart dehêine:
die sah er ob im sweben   2815
v̄ horte got urkunde geben
sende Marien kinde,
daz er der si, da man vinde
˙gnade div niemer zegat,
v̄ des riche ane ende stat.   2820
Ich en wil an disen stunden
niht gantzlichen chunden
sænt Johannis ere,
untze ich daz liet furchere
in unser frȫen minne,   2825
ir ze lobe, mir ze gwinne.

Daz ander lieth hat ende,
an daz dritte ich wende
min sinne v̄ min zûnge,
allen den ze bezzerunge   2830
die unser frȫen minnent
v̄ ir gnaden sinnent.
nŭ wizzet daz ich iv bescheide,
waz der kuniginne ze leide
gefrvmte v̄ gerîet   2835
div ubel ivdiskiv diet.
sie leit itwize vil:
die warheit ich dauon wil
5 chunden v̄ mæren
vnde mit den heiligen   2840
              bewæren.

2469 dige *L*.] digen   2473 eine, *vgl. zu* 2578   2475 ander

. . . . zestôren
des swarzen vâlandes nît,
2960   nu si uns die volleiste gît?   (1655)
eine rede wil ich breiten
fur alle die christenheite:

*wîplîch*e sorge:
daz kint, daz ê verborgen
2975   was in ir lîbe,   (1660)
daz kumet ze kurzer wîle
von ir gnâdiclîchen.
diu sorge muoz entwîchen
unt alle unchraft bôse,
2980   *die Even getelôse*   (1665)

A   **D**

daz zvo dem ellenden weibe
der engel wart gesant,
2490 vnz ez wart bewant
daz si den hailant gebar.
die rede sult ir gar · · · · · · · ih sage iv wie sie Christ gebar:
an dem dritten liede hôren. · · · · die suzzen rede svlt ir gar
wie mohte daz zestôren · · · · · · an disem liede horen:
2495 des valantes neit, · · · · · · · die enmak niht zestoren
ob si vns volleist geit? · · · · · · des bittern viandes nit,   2845
eine rede wil ich praiten · · · · · · nu si uns die uolleiste git.
vor aller christenheite:
die hertze einvalten · · · · · · · · div herze der einualten
2500 sulen sey wol behalten, · · · · · div schuln sie wol behalten,
wan ez also war ist   183, 10 wande sie also wâr ist
sam daz der heilige Christ · · · · · so daz unser heilant Christ 2850
von sant Marien wart geborn, · · · uon der magede wart geborn,
vn̄ nie ir chevscheit wart verlorn. · v̄ ir kivscheit nie wart uerlorn.
2505 Swelich weip dise driv liet hat, · Swelh wib div driu liet hat,
so si ze keminaten gat, · · · · · · so sie ze keminaten gat,
in ir zesewen hant bevangen, · · · in ir zeswen beuangen,   2855
si leidet niht lange · · · · · · · · sie lidet unlangen
weipliche sorgen: 15 kumber uon dem sere,
2510 daz kint, daz æ verborgen · · · · wand in unser frôen ere
waz in ir leibe,
daz kvmet in kvrzer weile
von ir genedichlichen. · · · · · · · gnist sie kindes gnædeklichen.
div vnkraft mûz entweichen · · · · die sorgen muzzen entwichen 2860
2515 vn̄ alle sere bose, · · · · · · · v̄ div unchraft also bose,
div Even getelose · · · · · · · · · die Even getlose
in dise werlde gesant, · · · · · · · in die werlte gesante,
do si gotes niht erkant, · · · · · · do si gotes niht erkante
do si vn̄ ir man   20 v̄ mit dem gnadelosen man 2865
2520 wurden vngehorsam. · · · · · · uon gote uallen began.
In ir namen sul wir gesigen,
von der witzzen wirt geschriben,
daz si ane lait
gebar der al die christenheit
2525 von dem tode hat enbunden
mit seinen fumf wunden.
dester wirs wart ir nie,
do si des ersten in enpfie.
si hete semfte genv̂k
2530 al die weile si in trûk.
an allen siehtom si waz,

2494 daz!   2498 christenheit

           niemen kunde getriegen.

3005   die got ûz allen liuten
           erwelte im zeiner brûte,
           unt die sô hât gekindet
           daz si niemer meil gewinnet.   (1670)
           mahte der sunne sprechen,
3010   dehein sîn dinc gezechen,
           der wunschte daz er wâre
           sô schône unt ⟨sô⟩ genâme
           als diu liehte maget ist.   (1675)
           hête diu mâninne list
3015   oder mahte si gekôsen,
           si wolte die himelrôsen
           mit schône ubertreffen.
           si sundert von dem heffen   (1680)
           den vil lûteren wîn
3020   . . . .
           . . . .
           . . . .
           dannen die sêle ersturben,   (1685)
           ob ir vergezzen wurde,
3025   diu uns den arzât gewan
           der uns den siechtuom benam.
           hie schult ir wizzen under diu:
           swâ disiu buochel alliu driu   (1690)
           ⟨werdent behalten⟩,
3030   diu maget wil des walten,
           daz dâ nehein kint
           werde krump noch blint,
           ⟨noch⟩ niemer werde geborn   (1695)
           daz êwiclîche sî verlorn,
3035   sine welle ez selbe fristen

    3004—64 C² 1010—1370   6 zu ein⁵   8 meil *M.*] me, *doch ist tiefergehende Verderbnis wahrscheinlich*   9 sunne *B. s. 156*] sun   gesprechen 11 wnste   14 mâninne *B. s. 156*] manige   16 enmohte *M.*   18 dem] den   20 ff. *völlig entstellt:* und daz gute olei   daz uns heilet unser sere   di uns geslagen hat di schare; *ein Reim* wunden : sunde *oder steckt*

A   **D**

do si des herren genas.
des mv̊zzen si geniezzen
die sich ie verliezzen
2535 an ir helfe here,
vñ auch immer mere
vnz an den iungisten tak,
wan si gewenken niht enmak.

Nv sult ir wizzen vnder dev:
2540 swa dise liet allev drev
werdent behalten,   Swa div buchel driv sint behalten,
div magt wil des walten,   div maget wil des walten,
daz da denhein kint   daz da nehein kint
weder chrump noch blint   werde krumb noh blint,   2870
2545 nimmer wirdet geborn,   v̄ da niemer werde geborn
noch æwichlich werde florn,   daz ewikliche si uerlorn,
si welle ez selbe fristen   sine welle ez selbe fristen

---

schâchære *hinter* schare? *M.*   23 dannen] da von   24 ob] ab   25 arzt
27 *Initiale*   diu] u   32 werde] wedᵇ, *vgl. W. s. 161*   33 ⟨unt daz⟩? *M.*
werde] wirt   35 sine] si   selber

2538 emak   2546 floren

        zuo dem jungisten,
        so der lîp mit manigem sêre
        scheidet von der sêle.   (1700)
        swelich wîp reine
3040   niht hât wan daz eine,
        des ist zwîvel nehein,
        si genïezze ⟨sîn⟩ etlîch teil,
        sô ez ir gât an die nôt: (1705)
        die maget vliuhet der tôt.
3045   in swelhem hûse diu schrift gelît,
        der engel in mandunge gît
        die dâr inne bûwent
        unt ir des getrûwent.   (1710)
        von sant Marîen unt von gote
3050   wart geheizen unt geboten
        allen frumen wîben,
        daz si ez abe schrîben
        unt senden ez ze minne   (1715)
        in dem umberinge
3055   verre unde nâhen,
        dâ man ez gerne enphâhe
        durch der magede liebe,
        daz man ir daran vorhtlîche diene.   (1720)

        Diu maget sant Marîe
3060   geruoche die namen drîe
        †umb uns armen bitten,
        daz uns ir sun gesetze

        zuo der zeswen an den rinc,   (1725)
        sô daz grôze teidinc

3065   ze aller jungiste wirt,
        unt der hêre hûswirt
        mit zorne beginnet scheiden
        die lieben von den leiden,   (1730)

3037 f. ser : sel   41 des] daz   keine   42 si genist etteliche teile
46 manunge   50 si d'wllent (erwelent B. s. 12) daz gebote   54 in dem
v . . . / meringe C, ze dem frône mêringe B. s. 76   56 epfahen   57 meide

A

    ze der zeit iungisten,
    so der leip mit sere
2550 schaidet von der sele.
    Swelich weip reine
    niht hat wan daz eine,
    daz ist zweifel denhein,
    si geniezze sein etlich tail,
2555 vnde gewinne hail
    in ir noten mail.

D

    an dem aller ivngisten,
183,25 da diu sele den lip uerlat 2875
    v̄ ez an den iamer gat.

    von sant Mareien vn̄ von got
    haben die vrowen daz gebot,
    daz si niht beleiben,
2560 si haizzen ez ab schreiben
    die ez mvgen vol enden,
    vn̄ gerůchen ez ze senden
    verre vn̄ nahen,
    da man ez welle enpfahen
2565 durch der magede liebe,
    vn̄ daz man daran ir diene.

    Div magt sant Mareye
    gerůche die namen dreye
    an vns armen letzen,
2570 daz vns ir svn setze

    Div here maget sente Marie
    geruche die namen drie
    umbe uns armen biten,
    daz wir mit reinen siten   2880
    di hulde muzzen erwerben
    v̄ ir helfe so wir ersterben
    v̄ gnade an der urstende,
    so al div werlte hat ende,
    30 da sih hebet daz tæidinch, 2885
    daz groze gerihte v̄ der rinch,
    den nîemen enpfliehen mach,
    wân der eine der den tak
    hie wol vorbesorget hat.
    owi waz trostes im dazu gat, 2890
    als daz urtæile wirt,
    v̄ der uorhtliche huswirt

    zv̊ der zeswen an den rinch
    an dem grozzen taidink,

    swanne got beginnet scheiden
    die lieben von den leiden,

    35 mit zorne beginnet scheiden
    die lieben uon den leiden,

58 man] ma   61 bite   61 f. *sicher entstellt; ein Reim auf* digen *oder*
dicken : gericke? *M.*   63 rehten hant   an] in   65 jungest
    2562 gerůche   *2568* drey   *183,27* bitten   *183,33* eim

        sîniu kint von den chnehten,
3070 die sundâre von den rehten,
        die ubelen von den guoten:
        dâ ruoche Christes muoter
        vaste helfende wesen,   (1735)
        daz ir holden genesen,
3075 unt vil manige diuwe
        die mit grôzer triuwe
        nu ligent an ir fuozen.
        wer mahte uns baz gebuozen   (1740)
        der tôtlîchen vorhte
3080 unt swaz wir ie geworhten
        in getelôsen sinnen?
        ze dem selben teidinge
        gesitzet si bî sîten   (1745)
        dem kunige der sô wîten
3085 rîchsent mit gewalte.
        da enwirt niht ûf gehalten
        al des wir ie gedâhten.
        daz wir hinnen brâhten   (1750)
        âne buozze unt âne bîhte,
3090 daz gestât dâ niht sô lîhte
        sô wir uns gedenken:
        wir ne mugen dâ niht gewenken.
        aller herzen tougen   (1755)
        der enmugen wir niht verlougen.
3095 wir muozen dâ behucken
        swaz wir ie zerucke
        sunden hie gewurfen.
        die der frouwen dâ bedurfen   (1760)
        unt ir helfe gerne sehen,
3100 die schuln ir dienistes phlegen
        in dirre werlt sô schône
        mit geistlîchem dône
        in ir kindes minne: (1765)
        wellen wir die vogetinne
3105 niht hie gestâten,
        sô wirt ez uns dort al ze spâte.

    3070 sundare] sundert er   72 da schol danne   75 dytwe   79 di
totliche   82 zu den selben teydingen   83 bi dᵉ siten   85 rihtet   86 da]
daz   87 allis daz   89 bůz   90 ez dᵉ gat   91 bedēken   95 ie da
buke   97 hie] ie   99 sehent   3100 dinstes gerne pflegen   2 geist-
liem   4 wellen] wol   6 dort ist ez zu spete

A

2575 sein kint von den knêhten,
die svndere von den rehten:
da rûche si vns ze wægen
vn̄ immer æwichlichen pflegen.
Amen!

D

siniv kint uon den chnehten, 2895
die sundære uon den rehten,
die ubeln uon den guten!
da ruche div gute behuten
alle die sih nu dazu mûzzent,
daz si sie mit dienste 2900
grûzzent.

gut ist uns der gedinge
ze dem notlichem tæidinge,
183,40 wan da gesitzet sie bi siten
dem kunige der so witen
richsent v̄ gebivtet 2905
dem himel, der erde, dem livte.
al des wir ie gedahten,
daz wir hinnen brahten
ane bûzze v̄ ane bihte,
daz gestat da niht lihte, 2910
als wir uns gedenken:
wirne mugen da niht gewenken.
45 aller herzen tŏgen
megen wir niht uerlŏgen.
uns kûmet da ze gehucke 2915
swaz wir ie zerucke
184,1 sunden hie gewrfen.
die der frŏen da bedurfen
v̄ ir helfe gerne da sehen,
die schuln ŏh ir nû iehen 2920
ze kuniginne mit dienste.
daz wirt in dort daz liebeste,
ob sie hant ir minne:
wellen ave wir die voitinne
5 niht gewissen hie mit stæte, 2925
so wirt ez uns dort al ze spæte.

2578 dahinter von anderer, aber sehr ähnlicher Hand daz ist daz
and⁵ *183,38* se *183,41* gebivte

III.

Daz drítte liet heve ich hie an: (1770)
    als die ríter zuo dem van
vaste muozen sîgen
3110   in dem volcwîge,
⟨sam schuln⟩ wir zuo dem sternen
fluht haben gerne,
der daz christenlîche her   (1775)
schône leitet uber daz mer
3115   werltlîcher schanden.
si lediget ouch von banden
die riuwigen sêle
durch ir sunes êre.   (1780)

nu gehuget wol, mîn liebiu kint,
3120   diu sant Marîen holt sint
unt sie vaste meinent,
sô si ir sunde weinent:
gedenchet wol wie wir haben gesaget,   (1785)

daz diu êwige maget
3125   Josêbe wart gemahelôt,
unt daz si ⟨muoste⟩ durch nôt
volgen unde hengen,
unt wie darnâch unlenge   (1790)
Joseph was dâheime,
3130   unz er bî des meres reine
ze Capharnaum chêrte,
da er sîne junger lêrte

zimbern grôze chiele,   (1795)
daz si niht zevielen,
3135   als die wintstôze
daran begunden bôzen

3107 heb   7f. ane : vanen   8 rittere   10 volke wigen   11 wir]
wer   st᾽ne   12 habent   13 cristenlichiz   14 leitte   16 ledigete ouch

A

Daz *dritte* liet hebt sich hie an:
2580 als die riter zů dem van
vaste mvzzen seigen
in dem volkweig*e*,
sam sul wir zů dem sterne
fluht haben gerne,
2585 der dem christenlichen her
schone leuhtet vber mer.

Nv gedenket mine kint,
die sant Mareien holt sint,

waz wir han gesaget,

2590 daz div ewige maget
Joseph wart gemehelot,
vn̄ daz si můste vor not
volgen vn̄ hengen,
vn̄ wie darnach vnlenge
2595 Joseph waz da haim,
daz er zů dem mer gemain
bey Capharnavm cherte,
da er seine iunger lerte

zimbern grozze kyel*e*,
2600 daz si niht zevielen.

D

Daz dritte liet heve ih ane:
als die riter zu dem uane
uaste můzzen sigen
in allen uolchwigen,   *2930*
also schulen wir zu dem sterne
fluhte haben gerne,
der daz christenliche here
bringet uber der sorgen mere
uz des tieuels bande   *2935*
zu dem frǒderichem lande,
da got selbe ist der sunne,
ist der tak, ist div wnne,
die nehein trube chrenket
v̄ niemer gewenchet.   *2940*
nu gehuget wol, liebiv kint,
die sente Marien uolgende sint
v̄ sie uon herzen meinent,
so sie ir sunde weinent:
gedenchet wol wie ich han *2945*
                  gesaget,
daz div ewige maget
Josebe wart gemæhelot,
des sie hengen muste durh not,

v̄ wie er mit ir was da heime,

untze er bi des meres reine *2950*
ze Capharnaum cherte,
da er sîn ivngere lerte
uon meisterlichen sachen,
wie sie scholten machen
die notuesten chiele,   *2955*
der chraft nien lihte ceuîele

---

von dē   19 gehuget] gebuwet   mine liben   20 sante   25 Joseph
28 unt wie] daz   30 wanne h' zu der meide reine   32 iung'n
35 winsto^zke

2579 ander   2582 volkweigen   2599 kyelen

10*

ûf des meres unden:
den list er wol kunde.　　　　　　　　(1800)
der vil alte brûtdegen
3140　⟨der⟩ was gewesen under wegen
drî mânôt unt ein halbez jâr,
unz er gefrumete vil gar
des in die fursten bâten　　　　　　　(1805)
die in geladet hâten.
3145　darnâch wart er ⟨des⟩ enein,
daz er fuore wider heim
in die burc ze Nazarêt,
diu mit grôzem lobe stêt　　　　　　　(1810)
in sant Marîen guote:
3150　dar truoc in sîn gemuote.

Sîn hîwisch unt diu magedîn
die hiezen in willechomen sîn:
er wart vil wol enphangen.　　　　　　(1815)
dô stuont ez unlange
3155　unz er des wart inne
an der kuniginne,
daz si lebendigez kint truoc:
do gewan er leides genuoc.　　　　　　(1820)
vil michel wunder in des nam,
3160　wie sie scholte dehein man
iemer haben uberkomen,
diu bî *der* spîse wart gezogen
diu ir von himele wart ge*s*ant　　　　(1825)
in der engelischen hant.
3165　der vil einvalte man
⟨der⟩ hête gedanc unde wân,
daz si mit bôsen sachen
ze solhem ungemache　　　　　　　　(1830)
wâre verrâten.
3170　die frouwen in alle bâten,
daz er sich wol gehabete
unt mâzlîchen chlagete.
si sageten ir unschulde　　　　　　　(1835)
unt swu*or*en bî gotes hulde;
3175　diu vil geistlîchen wîp
diu but*en* s*ê*le unde lîp,

3138 er wolte kunden　　39 alt　　41 mand̄　　42 unz] wanne
45 in ein　　47 nazareth　　49 guote] *l.* huote? *Sch.*　　51 Sin gesinde
52 in] si　　55 unz] wanne　　57 ein lebendingez　　58 er] h⁵　　60 dekein̄

A

Der vil alte proutdegen
der waz gewesen vnder wegen
drey manod vn̄ ein halbes iar, 184, 25
vnz er bereite gar
2605 des in die fursten baten
die in geladet haten.
dar nach wart er des en ein,
daz er fûre wider haim
in die purk ze Nazare*th*,
2610 div mit grozzem lobe stet
in sant Mareien hûte:
dar trük in sein gemv̂te.

Sein gesinde vn̄ daz magedein 30
hiez in willechomen sein:
2615 er wart wol enpfaugen.
do stûnt ez vnlangen
vnz er des wart inne
an der kvniginne,
daz si ein lebendes kint truk:
2620 do gewan er laides genûk.
michel wunder in des nam, 185, 1
wie sei solde denhein man
immer haben vberchomen,
div die speise het genomen
2625 div ire von himel was gesant
in der englischen hant.
der vil ainvalte man
der hiet sorge vn̄ wan,
daz si mit boser sache
2630 ze solhem vngemache
wer⟨e verr⟩aten.
die ⟨vrowen⟩ in alle paten,
daz er sich wol gehabte
vn̄ mezlichen chlagte.
2635 si sagten ir vnschulde
vn̄ swûren bey gotes hulde,

D

uf den hohen unden,
so die winde unsitten begunden.
der alte brûtdegen
der was gewesen underwegen 2960
drie manot vnd ein halbez iâr,
untzer gefrumet vil gar
des in die herren baten
die in geladet haten.
darnah wart er des ennêin, 2965
daz er fure wider heim
in die burch ze Nazaret,
div mit grozzem lobe stet
in sente Marien gute :
dar truch in sin gemûte. 2970

Sin hiwisch v̄ div magedin
hiezzen in willikomen sin
mit frolichem anpfange.
do stunt ez unlange
nutzer des wart inne 2975
an der heren kunginne,
daz sie lebentigez kint truch:
do gewan er leides genuch.
harte wndert in daran,
wie sie iemer dehein man 2980
scholte han uberkomen,
div bi der spise was gezogen
div ir in engelisker hant
uon himel wart gesant.
der uil einualte man 2985
der hete uorhten v̄ wan,
daz sie mit boser sache
ze solhem ungemache
wære uerraten.
die frôen in alle baten, 2990
daz er sih wol gehabete
v̄ mazlichen chlagete.
sie sageten ir unschulde
v̄ swren bi gotes hulde;
div geistlichen wip 2995
butten sele v̄ lip,

---

65 einvaltig   68 zu sulchen ungemachen   71*f.* daz er mezelich clagete
und sich wol gehabete
   2609 Nazareht   *185,3* haute

daz nie man bechôme
zuo der magede schône   (1840)
mit deheinem ungeverte,
3180   noch si des nie gegerte,
daz si uber strâze gienge
unt iemen enphienge,
oder ie gesprâche dehein wort   (1845)
weder hie, dâ oder dort
3185   ze werltlîchem manne,
daz si von dannen
nôt scholte lîden;
sine mahten an ir lîbe   (1850)
dehein wandel wizzen:

3190   si hête sich ⟨wol⟩ geflizzen
sô tugentlîcher guote,
si kunde wol behuoten
ir êren manicvalte   (1855)
⟨unt sich selben⟩ mit gotes gewalte.

3195   **D**er alte mit dem barte
begunde sûften harte
sîn sêr unt sîn ungemach.
zuo den frouwen er dô sprach: (1860)
‚waz trôstes muget ir mir geben?
3200   ja muget ir selbe wol sehen
daz si kindes swanger ist.
warzuo schol der uppige list
daz ir mich wellet triegen?   (1865)
ja betwinget sie diu wiege.
3205   niemen ist sô tumber,
sô alt noch sô junger,

er enmuge die rehten wârheit
unt mîn vil inneclîchez leit   (1870)
wol schouwen unde chiesen.
3210   mahte ich nû verliesen
mit rehten dingen mînen lîp!
von herzen dûhte mich des zît,
daz ich nu tôt wâre.   (1875)
wolte got in sîne gnâde

3177 daz nimant kome   78 maget   80 begᵉte   81 ubˢ di   82 ie
keinē man   84 wedˢ!   85 zu keinē werltlichē manne   88 si mocht
ouch   90 ⟨wol⟩ *Sch.*   91 sô *Sch.*] wol   92*ff.* si konde sich selbˢ wol

A   **D**

daz nie denhein man   185,10 daz nie man bechome
chome zv̊ der maget lustsam   zu der magede schone
mit denheinem vngeverte,   mit neheinem ungeuerte,
2640 noch si des nie gegerte,   noh sie des nie gegerte,   3000
daz si vber die strazze gienge   daz sie uber strazze gienge
vn̄ iemen enpfienge,   unde iemen da enpfienge.
oder ie gespreche denhein wort
weder hie noch dort
2645 ze denheinem werltlichem manne,
von div oder danne
si not solte leiden;
si mohten an ir leibe
denhein wandel wizzen: sîene mohten an ir niht wandels
                            wizzen,
2650 si hiete sich geflizzen   wan sie hæte sih geflizzen
vil tugentlicher gůte,   15 wol so tugentlicher gůte   3005
si kvnde wol selbe behůten   daz sie ir eren gerne hůte
ir ere manekvalde   v̄ sich selbe zaller stunde
mit dem gotes gewalte.   wol bewaren kunde.

2655   **D**er alte mit dem parte   **D**er grise mit dem barte
begunde sevften harte   begunde suften harte   3010
sein sere v̄ sein vngemach.   sin ser v̄ sin ungemah.
zv̊ den frowen er do sprach: ze den frŏen er do sprah:
‚was trostes mvgt ir mir geiêhen?   ‚durh got, wes welt ir iehen?
2660 ia mvgt ir wol selbe sehen   ia meget ir selbe sehen
daz si kindes swanger ist.   20 daz sie kindes swanger ist.   3015
warzv̊ sol der list,   waz schol der uppîge list,
daz ir mich welt betriegen?   daz ir mih so umbefůeret?
ia zaiget ez die wiege.   ich lie sie unberůeret
2665 nieman ist so tumber,   v̄ han sie grozze funden:
so alt noch so iunger,   des bin ich mit leide   3020
                            gebunden.
er mvge die rehten warheit   owe mir dirre warheit!
vn̄ min inrechlichez lait   hie schult ir min herzeleit
wol schowen vn̄ kiesen.   alle scŏen vnde chiesen.
2670 moht ich nv verliesen   mæht ich nv uerliesen
mit rehten dingen minen leip,   25 minen lip mit rehten zugen, 3025
von herzen devhte mich des zeit.   e mich div liv̊te belugen,
                         des duhte mich zit furware.
                         owi wan ich tot wǣre,

---

gehute   ir eren manikvalt   mit des liben gotis gewalt   96 sufczen
97 sêr] leit   3200 selb⁵   4 io
   2664 wiegen

3215   mîne sêle wider nemen!
       waz mac ich ze antwurte geben
       den unsern rihtâren?
       die werdent uns gevâre,   (1880)
       sô daz kint her fur gât
3220   daz sîner ê niht enhât:

       sô muozen wir mit schanden
       disen lîp verwandeln,
       sô si mit den steinen   (1885)
       zepolent unser gebeine:
3225   sô muoz mich riuwen diu vart.
       daz ich ie sô alt wart,
       daz muoze got erbarmen:
       der bezeige sîne milte an mir armen!'   (1890)

       Die frouwen sprâchen im aver zuo:
3230   ,wir sagen dir herre, waz tu tuo:
       habe vil guote reste,
       daz ist dir nû daz beste.
       wirf dîn leit zerucke,   (1895)
       unz got an dir gehucke
3235   sîner barmunge,
       unt er dir ledigunge
       mit sînem trôste welle geben!

       unt nâmest du uns daz leben,   (1900)
       wir mahten dir anders niht gesagen.
3240   daz eine muosen wir vertragen,
       daz sie der engel gesprach,
       den si mit frouden an sach
       diche unde ofte: (1905)
       ob ir daz wol tohte,
3245   des enwizzen wir nieht.
       er was schône unde lieht.

3216 antwort   18 gevâre] gen^{e}e   21 wir doch   30 tu scholt tu
34 wanne got andir gluke   36 unt *M*.] wanne   dir *B. s. 57*] di   37 wolte
38 und nemstu uns allen   39 mugen   40 muzen   41 besprach   44 ob]
ab   46 was] ist

A

wolte got min sele nemen!
waz mag ich ze antwurte geben,

2675 so daz kint her fure gat
daz siner æ niht enhat?

so mv̊zze wir mit schanden
disen leib veranden,
so si nv mit stein*en*
2680 zepolent vnser gebeine.

daz mv̊ze gѳt erbarmen
vñ helfe mir vil armen!'

Die frowen sprachen im auer zv̊:
,wir sagen dir herre, waz dv tû:
2685 habe vil gûte reste,
daz ist dir nv daz beste,

vnz dir got trost welle geben.

vñ benêmest dv vns daz leben,
wir mohten dir anders niht gesagen.
2690 daz eine mûste wir verdagen:
daz sey der engel gesprach,
den si mit frevden ane sach
vil diche vñ ofte,
als ir daz wol tohte,
2695 des enwizze wir nieht.
er waz schone vñ lieht.

D

daz ich daz unsælige leben
mit eren hete begeben,   *3030*
e mich begriffe diser schal,
der nu schiere uert uberal
uon miner ivncfrȯen,
als man beginnet scȯen
185, 30 daz kint ioh die wîegen!   *3035*
mulich ist div werlt zetriegen,
angestliche daz gerihte,
da zaller livte gesihte
daz unreht wirt eruarn.
wîe mak ich daz iemer   *3040*
                bewarn,
wir enmuzzen da mit schanden
ersterben uon ir handen
die uns geværich sint beiden,
ez en ruche got scheiden
35 anders denne ich wæne,   *3045*
der mich ein die sorgen âne
mit gewalte wol getæte,
ob er min gnade hæte?'

Die frȯen sprachen im aue zu:
,wir sagen dir waz tu tv̊: *3050*
habe, herre, uil gute reste,
daz ist dir nu daz beste,
untze daz got din angest wende
v̄ dir sinen trost sende?

186, 1 wand giengez uns an daz *3055*
                leben,
so enmæhten wir dir geben
nehêin ende mere
wan daz der engil here
der frȯen ofte erschein,
v̄ wrden ensamet ennêin *3060*
wir enwizzen welher tȯgen.
der rede ist unlȯgen:
5 âne in so wart nie dehein man
der sie ie bræhte daran,
daz sie iender uon uns quame *3065*
v̄ iemans wort uernæme.
der engil gesprah sie dicche;

185, 27 begegen   *2679* stein   *2695* niht

        der wârheit muozen wir jehen:
        swaz hie wunders ist geschehen   (1910)
        an der brûte lustsam,
3250   daz hât der engel getân.'
        dô zurnte er alsô sêre;
        er sprach: ‚ich wil niht mêre
        vernemen iuwer kôse.   (1915)
        ez was ein man bôse
3255   der iuch alle hât betrogen:
        er was von himele niht geflogen,
        er kom geslichen ûz der stete.
        an sîne tumplîche bete   (1920)
        hât si ir muot gewendet:
3260   des werden wir alle gehônet unt geschendet.'

        Joseph im gedâhte,
        des in got wider brâhte,
        daz er wolte entrinnen,   (1925)
        ê sîn die liute inne
3265   wurden alle glîche.
        er sprach, er muose entwîchen
        durch des lîbes angest,
        unz er mahte langest   (1930)
        die marter ûf schalten,
3270   diu sîniu lit behalten:
        daz wolt er willeclîchen tuon.
        er enkunde sînen wîstuom
        an nihte baz erzeigen: (1935)
        lêhen unde eigen
3275   daz wolte er allez lâzen
        unt kêren sîne strâze
        dâ er sicher mahte sîn.
        er beite unz daz mânschîn   (1940)
        des nahtes ûf errunne,
3280   daz in gewîsen kunde
        sô er sich erhuobe.
        diu ougen wâren im truobe
        von der tage menige: (1945)
        in aller sîner gegene

3253 gekôse   57 stat   59 f. hat si gewendet ir gemute   des
w'den wir geleidet   und alle gescheidet   66 ich mǔz   68 unz] wanne

A

der warheit mv̊zze wir iehen:
swaz halt wunders ist geschehen,
an der prout lussam,   186, 10
2700 daz hat der engel getan.'
Do zurnt er also sere;
er sprach: ,ich wil niht mere
vernemen evr gekôse.
ez waz ein man bôse
2705 der evch alle hat betrogen:
er ist von himel niht geflogen.

ze vbel hat sich ir mût gewent: 15
des ⟨werde⟩ wir alle nv geschent.'

Joseph im gedahte,
2710 des in got widerbrahte,
daz er wolde entrinnen;
æ sein die levte innen
wurden gemainlichen,
so wolte er entweichen

2715 durch den selben ruom.
er wesse niht anders zetûn:

er wolt sein gût lazzen
v̄ varen seine strazzen
da er sicher mohte sein,
2720 als ŏf chome des manen schein.

D

ze sinem liehtem anplicke
frŏte sih ie div gûte
mit reinestætem mûte.   3070
niht anders han wir gesehen:
 swaz wnders hie ist geschehen,
daz chumet uon des engels rat,
der sie ie besorget hat.'
Joseph der zurnete sere;   3075
er sprah: ,ichen wil niht mere
uernemen iuwer kose.
ez was ein man bose,
niht des engels rat,
der ivch betrogen hat.   3080
er kom geslichen uz der stete;
uon siner tumplicher bete
hat sie ir mut uercheret:
des sin wir gehonet v̄ geseret.'

 Joseph im gedahte,   3085
des in got wider brahte,
daz er wolte entrinnen,
e sin div livte inne
wrden allichen.
er sprah, er muse entwichen 3090
durh des libes angest,
untzer mæhte langest
die martir ufschîeben.

die gotwerden v̄ die lieben
mit al siner habe wolter lan. 3095
daz duhte in baz getan
denne ob er des erbitte,
daz er kumber mit ir litte,
wand ez unwendich muste sin.
do beiter untze der mænschin 3100
des nahtes ufgen begunde,
dabi er den wech funde
so er sich erhube.
sin ŏgen waren im trube
uon leides v̄ des alters swære, 3105
wand uber die gegende mære

---

69 schalten] gezalten   77 gesin   78 arweite wanne daz man sin (so!)
81 sô] wanne
    2698 geschen   2716 ez   186, 27 leide? L.

3285 was sîn galter nehein.
       dô er des alles wart enein
       unde vil genôte
       sîne sache gordinôte,   (1950)
       an sînem bette er lac.
3290 der got der alliu herze mac
       von sorgen wol gefrîen,
       derne wolte den kneht sînen
       niht lâzen under wegen;   (1955)
       er hiez im kunden sînen segen
3295 einen engel den er sande:
       der vlouc vil îlande
       in die kemenâten:
       kunden unde râten   (1960)
       wolte er im daz beste,
3300 ê er in wachende weste.
       dô wacte er in alsô schône,
       der gewaltige bote frône:
       der ewangelista saget daz,   (1965)
       daz nie herre wurde baz
3305 von troume enpunden.
       wir mugen daz urkunde
       an der messe wol hôren,
       so die priester singent in den kôren.   (1970)

       Der engel sprach ze dem manne:
3310 ,dîn vorhte ist undervangen,
       Joseph fili Davît:
       dîn schephâre dir den trôst gît.
       war woltest du hine gâhen?   (1975)
       ja scholtu wider enphâhen
3315 dîne gemahelen reine.
       niht langer dû enweine!
       si ist ob allen wîben;
       dir endarf ouch an ir lîbe   (1980)
       niht misselîchen:
3320 du scholt daz volleclîche
       ⟨wizzen unt⟩ gelouben,
       daz alle ir tougen
       von dem heiligen geiste sint chomen.   (1985)

       ir chûsche ist ir niht benomen:

      3285 alter   86 inein   90 hˢczen   92 der wolte   dinˢ   94 kundigē
96 ilende   98 kundigē   3303 sagte   19 nie niht? *Sch.*   19 *ff.* nicht
misseleide   du schalt des volleclich glouben   23 bekumen   24 ist] wirt

A

do er vil genote   186, 30
seine sache ordenote,
an seinem pette er lak.
der got der alle herze mak
2725 von sorgen gefreien,
der wolt den kneht seinen
niht lazzen vnder wegen;
er hiez *im* kvnden seinen segen:
ein engel sant er dar.

2730 da er Joseph wart gewar,
er wakte in also schone,
der gotes pote frone:
Der ewangeliste saget daz,
daz nie herr*e* wurde baz
2735 von trouren enbunden
sam Joseph ze den selben stunden.

Der engel sprach zů dem manne:
,dein sorge ist vndervangen,
Joseph fili Dauid:
2740 din schepfer dir trost geit.
war woldest dv helt gan?
ia solt dv wider enpfan
dine gemahelen raine.
lenger niht en waine!

2745 dv solt endelichen
wizzen sicherlichen,
daz alle ir tougen
  •   sint ane lougen
von dem heiligen geiste chomen.

2750 ir ist niht benomen

D

was sin galter nehêin.
als er des alles wart ennêin
mit im selben v̄ genote
sin sache geordinote,   3110
an sinem bette er gelach.
der elliv herze wol mach
uon sorgen belosen,
derne wolte den frŏdelosen
v̄ den reinen brutdegen   3115
niht lazzen underwegen;
sinen engel er im sande,
der in des gutliche ermande
35 waz er tûen scholde,
v̄ wes got beginnen wolde. 3120

Der engel im do zusprah:
,hingelêit ist din ungemah,
Josep kint Dauit:
din schepfære dir den trost git.
war woltestu gahen?   3125
du sholt wider enpfahen
din gemaheln rêine.
langer du nien wêine:
40 sie ist ob allen wiben
v̄ mŭz iemer beliben   3130
muter unde mæit here:
got lihet ir die ere.
daz scholtu wol gelŏben,
daz allez ir tŏgen
von dem heiligen geiste   3135
                  chumet,
der ie reht v̄ gnade frumet.

2728 in   2734 herren

3325 si muoz iemer maget sîn.
nu lâ des wesen guot schîn,
daz dich got erwelt hât
an den tougenlîchen rât!   (1990)
diene ir iemer gerne
3330 mit flîze unt mit êren,
als du sîst ir eigen:
des enscholtu niht geweigern.
den sun den si gewinnet   (1995)
unt in die werlt bringet,
3335 der wirt geheizen Jesus.
die sunde chan er alsus
leschen unde swenden,
daz die liute enmac geschenden   (2000)
des tievels ruoge unt sîn clage
3340 an dem jungisten tage.
die wârheit ich dir zelle:
er lediget von der helle
die sînen willen haben getân: (2005)
der himel ist in ûf getân,
3345 unt allez daz der ie wart
daz ist gesegenet unt bewart
von sîner magenchrefte,
unt mit der hêrschefte   (2010)
der niemer wirt ein ende:
3350 dar mahtu dînen dienest wol wenden.'

     Joseph der einvalte
niht lenger er entwalte.
sîn froude wart sô michel: (2015)
ja was er worden sicher
3355 vor allem ungemuote
von des engels guote:
diu wunder hiez er schrîben.
unser frouwen sant Marîen   (2020)
bôt er sich ze fuozen;
3360 er sprach: ‚wie wol mich muozen
die sunde iemer riuwen,
daz ich die missetriuwe
ûf dînen lîp ie gewan   (2025)

3326 nu laze daz gut wesen sin   38 mak gescheiden   41 stelle
42 ledigz uns von   45 der] da   gewart   46 geseinet   47 mankreſte
50 dar] da   din dinst   bewēde   52 enwalte   54 io

A   **D**

ir reine chevscheit:
si ist ein raine mait
vn mv̊z immer magt sein.
da von tů din ere schein,
2755 wan sey got erwelt hat   187,1 an den tȯgenlichen rat
zv̊ dem tougenlichen rat.   sin gůte dich erwelt hat.
                                   nu dîen ir mit stætem mute
                                   v̄ habes in lieber hůte,   3140

den sun den si gewinṇet   wan der sun den sie bringet,
vn in die werlt bringet,   den tievil er betwinget:
der wirt geheizzen Jesus.   Jesvs wirt er genant,
2760 die sunde chan er sus   daz kivt ein heilant,
leschen vn swenden   5 wand er die werlt hæilet,   3145
den christen ellenden: div mit sunden ist gemæilet.

                                 uon der helle furet er die
                                 di sinen willen taten hie.
                                 der himel ist im undertan,
                                 ze sinem gebot muz er stan, 3150
alles daz der ie wart   v̄ allez dazter îe wart
daz ist in siner hůt bewart   daz ist gesegent vnt bewart
2765 von siner maisterschefte   uon siner magenchrefte,
vn rehter hêrschefte,   v̄ mit der herschefte
der nimmer wirt ende: 10 die niemen kan uerenden: 3155
da von deinen dienst im wende!'   dar scholtu din dienest wenden.'

Joseph der einvalte   Joseph der vil einualte
2770 niht lenger er entwalte.   niht langer er entwalte.
sein frevde wart vil michel: sin frȯde wart erhaben,
ia waz er worden sicher   sin herze sa entladen   3160
von allem vngemůte   uon sorgen die er hæte.
von des engels gůte:
2775 die wunder hiez er schreiben.
seiner gemahel sant Marien   do bot er sih drate
erbot er sich ze den fuezzen;   unser frȯen ze fuzzen;
er sprach: ,wie mich mvezzen   er sprah: ,wie wol mir můzzen
die sunde immer riwen,   15 min sunde stan ze rivwe, 3165
2780 daz ich missetriwe   daz ich die missetrivwe
ȯf deinen leib ie gewan   uf dinen lip ie gewan

2763 christen] armen *F.*   2773 allem!

umb deheinen *irdischen man*

*fl*ouc ez wîten under in
von gazzen ze gazzen.
die juden viengen ze hazze

A

gen denheinē yrdischen man.
der engel mir gesagt hat
wie ez vrowe vm dich stat.'

2785 der magede herze sich erhůb; 187,20
si wesse wol daz si trůk
den trost aller heiligon:
des seit si got dank vn̄ lon
der potschefte frone;
2790 hinz himel naik si schone
durch vil manik zaichen.
die zeher begunden waichen
ir brust vnbewollen;
si sprach: ,ia mak ervollen
2795 vnser herre vil wol,
des ich immer wesen sol,
swaz er gebevtet vn̄ wil:
er mak mir genade geben vil.'
Die in daz hŏs chamen
2800 vn̄ dise rede vernamen,
alt vn̄ ivnge,
zesamen si sprungen
vn̄ lobten den hailant,
der seine zesewe vn̄ seine hant
2805 het gepraitet vber sie.
merer frevde div wart nie
an den bůchen geschriben.
si begunden ane digen
Christes sagerere.
2810 die starken niwe mere
muosten si bewainen:
Maria vn̄ Joseph die beliben
vngeschaiden.

Daz mere weite do cham
vm die vrowen lustsam:
2815 ez solde niht verholen sein.
ez flouk weiten vnder in
von gazzen ze gazzen.
die ivden begunden hazzen

D

umbe dehein irdisken man.
der engel mich bewiset hat
wie ez umb dih frŏe stat: 3170
du bist ein insigele
des keisers uz dem himele,
der dih hat gemæhelot
durh aller sundære not.'
Div mæit sih frŏen began; 3175
ir sælde die sah sie an,

sie wesse wol die gnade frone:
do neik sie im also schone
der sie geschuof ze den eren:
an sin lop begunde sie cheren 3180
bediv zunge v̄ ir sinne;
sie sprah: ,ia mak div gotes minne
an mir wol uolbringen,
als ich han gedingen,
25 swaz er gebivtet v̄ wil: 3185
er git mir mandunge vil.'
Die zu der rede quamen,
do si daz wnder uernamen,

starke lobten sie den heilant,
der sine zeswen hant 3190
hete gerihte uber sie.
grozer frŏde diu wart nie
under einem gesinde.
uon der muter v̄ dem kinde
30 div richen niwe mære 3195
die musen sie furware
uor grozer liebe bewêinen:
also waren sie ungeschêiden.

Daz mære do uedere gewan
uon der frŏen wolgetan: 3200

witen fur ez ze gazzen.
die iuden viengen ze hazze

2789 potschfte   2813 chom

Wernhers Maria.   11

díu ungewonlíchen wort　　　　　　　　(2030)
3410　umb den *geistlíchen hort,*

. . . . . in dem ríche,
daz man si steinôte.

3452—56 C² 1376—80　　52 rich

A

div vngewonlichev wort
2820 vm den geistlichen hort,
den div maget trvege:
ez douht si vngefuege,
wan si ez nie gesahen.
si hiezzen Mariam vahen,
2825 vñ Joseph den alten
hiezzen si behalten
vnz an den andern morgen.
des si da heten sorgen,
daz hiet in niht geschadet,
2830 vñ heten si sinne gehabet.
die tumben æwarten
erchomen der rede harte;

die pischof vñ ire fursten
gewunnen die geturste,
2835 daz si die maget here
berefsten also sere.
sundern hiezzen si siv do
in ir concilio:
vnser vrowe stûnt ainhalben,
2840 Joseph anderhalben:
also wurden si gestalt.
in wart vor gezalt
manek fraise vñ zorn,
wie si mv̊sen sein verlorn.

2845 si begunden sey an vehten,
daz von ir vnrehte
div æ̂ were zeprochen,
daz belibe niht vngerochen

nach Moyses gebot,
2850 daz in gesetzet were von got:
alle die vnælich
lebten in dem reich,
daz man siv stainot.

D

div ungewoñlichen wort
umbe den himilisken hort,
187, 35 den div rêine maget truch: 3205
iz duhte sie ungefuge genuch,
wand ez e nie wart uernomen.
zesamen waren sie komen:
do hiezzen sie behalten
die frŏen v̄ den alten 3210
untze an den andern morgen.
des sie da heten sorgen,
daz wære in geschadet niht,
ob sie hæten wistûmes iht.
40 die tumben ewarte 3215
die erkomen harte
188, 1 uon der rede, do sie erschal,
v̄ diu ivdenschaft uberal.
die bisgofe vnt die rihtære
uerviengen sie mit swære, 3220
daz sie die maget here
rafsten also sere.
sunderen hiezzen sies do
in ir nitlichem concilio:
5 einhalp stunt des himels brut, 3225
anderhalp der gotes trut.
furgeleit wart in beiden
von dem uolke unbescheiden
manich freise v̄ zorn,
wîe sie musen sin uerlorn, 3230
ob sie deheiner sunden
wrden uberwnden.
sie begunden sie anuehten,
daz uon ir unrehte
10 div e wære zebrochen, 3235
daz wrde wol errochen:
ob sie uor ir geslahte
gerihten nîe*men* mæhte,
sie satz*t*en in varlichen fŷr
die angestlichen selbchŭr. 3240
ez hete in sinem gebote
Moyses geuestent uon gote,
die an der e missetaten,
welh pŭze sie dauon hæten:
15 daz in daz gerihte gemêine 3245

2834 getursten   2846 vnrehten   188, 11 nîen   188, 12 satzen

11*

si strebeten vil genôte
3455   daz si dâ muosten ligen tôt: (2035)
des betwanc si doch nehein *nôt.*

A

si strebten vil genot
2855 daz man siv bede tot.
⟨. . . . .

div magt vorihte niht daz,
wan si îe baz vn̄ baz
trost ir gemv̊te,
2860 swas man sey gemv̊te.
Joseph sein vnschulde pot:
er wart nie plaich noch rot
von denhainer slahte vorhten.
die ivden daz allez marhten,

2865 daz si vnschulden iahen,
vn̄ si die warheit sahen.

Si heten eine gewonheit,
div waz den schuldegen lait,
ein vrtail fraysam:
2870 ir lieber vater Abraham
vn̄ ir vater Moyses
die beweisten si des,
daz si des wazzers vnden
also segen chvnden
2875 vn̄ also tyeffe besweren,
daz sich nieman mohte ernern
die den trank namen
vn̄ ihtes schuldik waren;
des si schuldik beliben,
2880 des si wurden gezigen.

dike chom ez, der ez trank,
daz im div huf ŏz spranch;
ofte sprungen im ŏz die augen,
swer da wolte laugen
2885 seiner missetat
die er begangen hat.
genv̊ge lagen tot

D

ertæilte die stêine
v̄ den swæren tot mit schanden
uon steinwerfenten handen.
daz leiten sie in fûre durh nît,
den der tieuil den sinen git 3250
die im underhorik sint,
v̄ die uor ubele werdent blint
an der gute vn̄ der warheit.
diu tugentrichiv mæit
eruorhte ir zenihte daz. 3255
sie troste ie baz v̄ baz
ir reines herzen stæte,
swie genote ir diu diet tæte.
Joseph sin unschulde bot:
erne wart nîe bleich noh rot 3260
uon neheiner slahte uorhten.
die iuden alle daz marhten,
daz sie bediv stateklichen
uor armen v̄ uor richen
ir unschulde iahen, 3265
swie sie die bernde wambe sahen.

Si heten eine gewonheit,
diu was den schuldigen leit,
ein urteile freissam:
ir alter uater Habraham 3270
vnt ir herzoge Moises
die bewisten sie des,
daz sie des wazzers unde
also gesegen chunden
vnde also tiefe beswêrn, 3275
daz sie niemen mæhte ernern
die schuldige dar chamen
v̄ daz tranch genamen;
mit leide musen die beligen
die uon schulden wrden 3280
bezigen.
ofte gescah, swer iz tranch,
daz im div huf uzspranch;
im sprungen uz ioh div ŏgen,
swer da wolte lŏgen
siner missetæte 3285
die er begangen hæte.
genuge lagen da tot

2864 marekten

ja was diu urteile genamet
aqua zelotipiê,
3500 den schuldigen tet si wê.
si drouten unser frouwen,   (2040)
si wolten *daran schouwen*

3498—3502 C ² 1381—85   98 daz urteil genament   99 celotippie
3500 ez tet dē schuldigē we   tet ez *Sch.*

A

von des wazzers not.

ez hiez aqua *z*elotipie,
2890 den schuldegen tet iz wǣ.
si droten vnser vrowen,
si wolten dar an schowen,
wer der man were
pey dem si daz kint gebære.
2895 Si droten Joseben
auch an sein leben,
ob er niht wolte iehen,
er mv̊se fraise sehen
an sein selbes leibe.
2900 si fragten ob er ze weibe
het gehabt die magt.
der herre waz vnverzagt,
er sprach vil paltliche:
,daz wizze got der reiche,

2905 daz ich sey nie gerv̊rte
seit ich sey haym fv̊rte.
ir wizzet wol waz ich rette,
vn̄ wes ich willen hette.
ze Capfarnaum waz ich gevaren,
2910 ander min dink bewaren;
do ich chom wider haim,
dise sorge mir erschain,
die ir selbe kieset.
ist daz ir mich verlieset,
2915 got mak mit seinem gewalte
mein sele wol behalten.'

Die vil herten Jvden,
die Mariam ane lugen
vn̄ ir ære fv̊rten vaile,
2920 si eylten die vrtayle
segen mit fleizze,
daz si ir iteweizze
mv̊sten bewæren.
vil wulfein gebaren
2925 trv̊gen si gemaine

D

durh des wazzeres not:
sie forhten ez alle ensamet.
ia was ·div urteil genamet 3290
ein wazzer zelotipie,
den schuldigen tet sie wê.
188, 40 Nu drŏten sie unser frŏen,
sie wolten daran scŏen,
wer der man wære 3295
bi dem sie kint gebǣre.
sie drŏten ŏch Josebe
ze uorderist an der grede,
189, 1 wolt er schiere niht iehen,
er muse iamer sehen 3300
ane sin selbes libe.
sie fragten ob er ze wibe
hete gwnnen die maget.
der herre was unuerzaget,
er sprah vil gnendeklihe: 3305
,daz wizze got der riche,
5 daz ich sin niht han getan
noh nie willen gewan:
daz kint ich nie gerv̊rte,
doh ich sie heim furte. 3310
ir wizzet wol wes ich gedahte,
do man mirs zubrâhte.
ze Capfarnaum was ih geuarn,
da muse ich ander dinch bewarn;
10 do ich chom wider hêin, 3315
disiv sorge mir erschêin,
die ir nu selbe chieset,
unt ist daz ir mih nu flieset,
got mak die sele behalten
v̄ ruche des ⟨. . . . . .⟩' 3320

Die ersteinten iuden,
die unser frŏen anlugen
v̄ ir ere furten ueile,
die ilten die urteile
15 segenen mit flizze, 3325
daz sie die itwîzze
musen da bewæren.
mit wlfinen gebaren
raizete sie algemêine

2889 lotipie 2910 bewaru 189, 12 des libes walten *H.*

dô wolten si wesen vil gewis,
3545 daz si mit grozem schalle
ze spotte in wurde allen.
Davides kint Josêp,   (2045)
alse dâ geschriben stêt,
der gerte neheiner friste:
3550 er tranc zem êristen
âne sorge dar fur:
erne vorhte niht daz er verlur   (2050)
lîp oder sêle.
er gedâhte an die lêre,
3555 die im der engel zuo sprach
dô er in jungiste sach:
diu froute sînen gedanc.   (2055)
dô huop er ûf unde tranc
eine schenke grôze
3560 vor sînen hûsgenôzen:

dô stuont er âne wende.
si wîsten in bî der hende   (2060)
umb den altâre siben stunt:
dannen schiet er wol gesunt,
3565 daz nehein urkunde
lugelîcher sunden
an im wart erfunden: (2065)
do begâben in die wuotenden hunde.

Dô gienc ez an unser frouwen:
3570 diu stuont mit spilnden ougen

mitten in dem chreize;

3541—3816 C² 1386—1658   45 valle   46 gespotte   3547—3646 E
47 *Initiale* E   ioseph CE   48 als C   49 begᵉte C   dehainer vrist E
50 *ursprünglich* dranc *nach* D?   zu dem ersten C, zemerist E   51 dar
fur *Sch. B. s. 100*] er dar wᵉr C, dar zv E   52 ern wolte niht also frv̂ E
53 v̂liesen lip odᵉ sele E   54 io gedach .. er C, er dahte E   56 in

A

ovf die vrowen raine;
si sahen sei an mit hazze.
do gesegent wart daz wazzer,
aqua potacionis,
2930 do wolten si sein gewis,
daz si ze schalle
vn̄ ze spote wurde in allen.

Joseph gert denheiner frist,
wan er trank ze fordrist:
2935 ane sorge er dar fûr.
er dahte niht daz er verlur
leib oder sele.
er gedaht an die lere,
die ime der engel zv̂ sprach
2940 do er in ze leste sach:
daz troste seinen gedank.
do hûb er ovf vn̄ trank
eine schenche grozze
vor seinen hŏsgenozzen:

2945 er belaib ane missewende.
si namen in bei der hende
vn̄ fûrten in vm den alter siben stunt:
von danne schiet er wol gesunt.

Do gienk ez an vnser vrowen:
2950 div stûnt mit spilinden ougen

mitten in dem kraizze;

D

der nit uf die vil reine.   3330

do der brunne was gereit,

Josep, als daz buch sæit,
der gerte neheiner friste,
wand in got selbe wiste:
189,20 er dranch ane sorgen darfur, 3335
erne uorhte niht daz er uerlûr
den lip oder sin ere.
er gedaht an die lere,
die im der engel zusprah
do er in ivngiste sach: 3340
diu frŏte sinen gedanch.
do hub er uf unt tranch
25 froliche uor in allen.
sie wanten in nider uallen
v̄ uerderben da ze stete,   3345
iedoh got gnadeklicher tete,
der die sîne niemer uerlat
unt in an den noten bigestat.
Do stunt er ane wende;
sie furten in bi der hende   3350
umbe den altære sibenstunt:
dannen schîed er wolgesunt,
30 daz nehein urkunde
luglicher sunde
an im wart erfunden: 3355
so gnas er uor den hunden.

Nv get ez an unser frŏen:
da maht man wol schŏen
spilntiv ŏgen, frien mût.
uon gote was sie so behut 3360
enmitten inme chreizze:

---

fehlt C   zu i .. geste C, mit vnfrŏden E   57 sine C   59*f.* groz : vor
sime husgnoz E   61 *Initiale* E   62 derwischten C   63 umme C,
umbe E   alter CE   65 kein C, dehein E   66 lugenlicher funde C
67 wrde funden E   68 vergaben C   69 *keine Initiale* E

2936 verlure   189,24 dranch   186,26 tet

diu scheltwort alsô heize   (2070)
diu wâren ir linde als daz tou,
wan sie bôsheit nie gerou
3575 die si mit mannen ie begie:
den willen gewan si nie.
der bischof redete mit ir: (2075)
,daz urkunde kiesen wir
an dîn selbes lîbe:
3580 nu sage wer dich ze wîbe
mit schanden habe gemachet!
des dîn ouge lachet,   (2080)
des mahtestu baz weinen.
du muost den man zeigen,
3585 unt muost die steine lîden
die Moyses solhen wîben
sazte an den buochen.   (2085)
du nemaht uns niht versuochen,
daz dû geturrest lougen:
3590 daz du hâst gefrumet tougen,
daz schînet an dir vorne
von dem gotes zorne.'   (2090)
diu maget im antwurte
mit gezogenlîchen worten
3595 (jâ hête si die zungen
in suoze rede betwungen);
si sprach: ,ich enhân des niht getân   (2095)
daz ich tôdes habe wân.
got weiz wol mîne schulde,
3600 unt hân ich sîne hulde,
sô muoz mîn rât werden:
erne lât mich niht verwerden.   (2100)
hân aber ich gesundet,
daz ich sô bin enzundet
3605 mit werltlîchem viure,
sîn gnâde ist sô tiure:
daz mac er wol erzeigen.   (2105)
swer die sêle wil gemeilen,
der endarf den valschen sin
3610 niht lâzen an in.

3572 als E   73 diu *fehlt* E   d⁵ tou C   74 di bosheit C   75 ie *fehlt* C   77 *Initiale* E   78 sehen wir E   80 nu *fehlt* E   81 habe] hat E   83 dv mahtes E   84 bezeigen C   85 muost *fehlt* E   87 di buch C   88 ne mah E, enda ... C   89 *Initiale* E   turrest C   90 gesundet has E   91 da vor.e C   93 im] in C, *fehlt* E   antworte C

A	**D**

div scheltwort vil haizze
waren ir linde als ein tav, 189, 35
die man ire fure plav.

2955 der pyschof ret mit ir:
,daz vrkunde kiese wir
an din selbes leibe:
nv sage wer dich ze weibe
mit schanden habe gemachet
2960 vn̄ din ere beswachet!

dv mů̊st die pene leiden 190, 1
die Moyses solhen weiben
gesatz*t* hat an den bů̊chen.
dv endarft vns niht versů̊chen,
2965 daz dv geturrest laugen:
daz dv getan hast taugen,
daz scheint an dir vorn
von dem gotes zorn.'
Si begunde im antwurtten
2970 mit gezogen worten,

si sprach: ,ich han des niht getan
darum ir mich sprechet an.
got waiz wol mine schulde,
vn̄ hab ich sine hulde,
2975 so mak mein rat werden:
er lat mich niht verseren.
han aber ich gesvndet,
daz ich pin enzundet
von werltlichem fiwer,
2980 sin genade sey mir tiwer.

---

div scheltwort als heizze
diu waren ir sam daz tȯwe,
wand sie daz unreht nie gerȯwe
daz sie mit iemen îe begîe, 3365
ioh den willen gewan sie nîe.
Der bisgof redet samet ir:
,die schulde kiesen wir
an din selbes libe:
sag an wer dich ze wibe 3370
mit schanden habe gemachet!
des din ȯge lachet,
des mahtestu baz wêinen:
du wirdest ze tæile den stêinen;
die mů̊stu uor uns liden, 3375
wand sie div e solhen wiben
ertæilet an den buchen.
du maht uns niht uersuchen
mit ualslichem lȯgen:
daz tu hast gefrů̊met tovgen, 3380
daz schinet an dir zware:
din reht hilfet dir undare.'
5 Diu maget began antwrten
mit senftlichen worten
(ja hete sie die zunge 3385
in suzze rede betwngen);
sie sprah: ,ich enhan des niht getan
daz ich habe todes wan.
got weiz min unschulde,
unde han ich sine hulde, 3390
so muz min rat werden:
erne lat mih niht erwerden.
10 han aue ich gesundet,
daz ich so bin erzundet
mit werltlikem vîure, 3395
sin gnade ist so tivre
daz erz wol mak erzeigen.
swer sih ze sunden wil neigen,
derne darf den ualsliken sin
niht uerlazzen an in. 3400

---

95 io CE hête si die] hatte sin C 96 suoze] selhe E 97 des] selhes E
98 des todes E 99 weiz min un .. hulde C 3600 gotis hulde C
2 er enlezet C, er lat E d'sterben C, v'derben E 3 *Initiale* E 4 sô
fehlt E 6 tiure] gehiure E 8 vnraïnen E 9 den falk (*so!*) sîn E

2963 gesatz 2972 sprehet

sich selben er betruge,
swer mit im deheine lugen (2110)
wolte beherten.
erne lie mich nie verwerten
3615 von mannes unzuhten:
daz wil ich hie gerihten
aller dirre diete, (2115)
wil ez got gebieten,
die mich hôrent unde sehent,
3620 daz si des hernâch jehent,
daz got der sterkere sî.'
daz wazzer daz ir stuont bî (2120)
daz huop si alsô hôhe
unt tranc ez alsô schône,
3625 sô vil daz si des jâhen
die daz gerihte sâhen,
daz sies genuoc dûhte. (2125)
ir antluzze ir dô lûhte
michel baz danne ê:
3630 ez entet ir niender wê.
si enliezen sie niht stên:
si muoste sibenstunt gên (2130)
umb den altâre;
do erzeigten ir gebâre
3635 daz sie niht enswar.
daz volc daz was ⟨komen⟩ dar,
gesamenet von nîde, (2135)
daz neic dem heiligen magedîne.

Do bedâhten sich die herren,
3640 daz si alze verre

die maget hêten getriben.
dô si an allen ir liden (2140)
ganz was bestanden,
swie si doch erchanden

A

D

sih selben er betrnge,
swer mit im dehein luge
190, 15 gedæhte beherten.
erne lie mich nie uerwerten
uon îemæns unzuhten: 3405
daz wil ich hie gerihten
allem disem gesinde.
div urteil ist mir linde,
wand die mih hiute hie sehent,
hernah sie des iehent, 3410

daz ich der vnschuldek sey.'   daz got der sterker si.'
daz wazzer daz ir stûnt bey   daz wazzer daz stunt ir bi;
2985 daz hûb si ane twanch   20 nu hub sie uf unde tranch
ovf vn̄ tranch   ane stritlichen wanch
so vil daz si des iahen   so uil daz sie des iahen 3415
die daz gerihte sahen,   die daz gerihte sahen,
daz sis genûk douhte.   daz sis alle gnuch duhte.
2990 ir antlutz ir do louhte   ir antlutze ir do luhte
michel paz danne æ: michels baz denne e.
ez entet ir ninder wæ.   ez entet ir niender wê. 3420
si liezzen sey niht sten: sie ne liezzen sie niht gesten,
si mûste sibenstunt gen   sien muse sibenstunt gen
2995 vm den altar;   25 umbe den altære.
do zaigten ire gebar   do erzaigeten ir gebære
daz sey niht enswar.   daz sie niht enswar, 3425
    vnd ir ŏch arges nîen war.
    do begaben sies alle
    mit leide ioh ir sele ualle,
    daz sie die lieben gotes brut
    erbelget hæten uber lvt. 3430

Do bedahten sich die herren,   **L**eide sahen in die herren
3000 daz si al ze verren   v̄ uorhten inz gewerren,
    30 daz sie die maget here
    gemuten ie so sere
die magt heten getriben.   v̄ sie ze ihte heten getriben. 3435
do si an allen iren liden   do sie an allen ir liden
ganz waz bestanden,   gantze was bestanden,
swie si doch erchanden   swie sie doh erchanden

---

30 niender] niht CE   31 liezen E   32 sine *B. s. 43*   mvsten E
33 umme C, vmbe E   altar C   34 ur di gebar C   vn̄ zaigete da
zware E   36 was komen] da was C, *fehlt* E   37 was komen witen E
38 heiligen *fehlt* E   39 erbarmten C, sch̄ameten E, erschameten *B. s. 107*
40 also E   v͛ren C   42 an] in E, *unleserlich* C   44 doch b.... den C

```
3645   daz si truoc daz kindelîn:
       von wannen daz mahte sîn,
       des nam si wunder alle.                    (2145)
       dô si sie ze schalle
       âne schulde brâhten,
3650   vil leide si ir gedâhte,
       des heiligen Christes bluome:
       diu wolte dô mit gefuoge               (2150)
       von dem teidinge
       ir ganzen êre bringen.
3655   si vorhte die vertânen,
       daz si mit bôsem arcwâne
       dannoch fuorten ir haz.                  (2155)
       rihten wolte si baz:
       dô swuor si manige eide,
3660   die enwâren niht meine,
       den grimmigen liuten
       bî allen gotes trûten                     (2160)
       unt bî allen den boten
       die ie kômen von gote,
3665   die in dem himele swebeten
       unt êwiclîchen lebeten
       unt dâ hêten reste                        (2165)
       in der burge veste,
       diu mit sternen alsô rôt
3670   vaste ist genagelôt,
       dâ nie ouge gesach
       siechtuom noch ungemach             (2170)
       von deheiner unchrefte;
       si swuor der hêrschefte


3675   bî der sunnen unt bî dem mânen,
       daz si valsches âne
       âne allen zwîvel wâre                     (2175)
       werche unt gebâre
       unt aller bôsen dinge
3680   ûzen joch innen,
       unt ir lîbes burde
       nie bekuchet wurde                        (2180)
       von deheines mannes gelphe:
```

3645 daz] ir E   46 von welchen dingen C, von wehen (so!) sculden E daz *fehlt* E gesin C sin *Ende von* E 48 schalle] val .. C 49 schult C 50 in gedahten C 51 dannoch gotes bluome *B. s. 52* 55 vorhtē C 58 wolten C

A

3005 daz si trûk ein kindelein:
von wev daz mohte sein,
des nam sev michel wunder
die iuden al besunder.

Dannoch gotes plûme
3010 div wolt iren rûm
mit ganzen æren bringen
von den taydingen.
si vorhte die vertanen,
daz si mit argem wane
3015 dannoch vorhten iren haz.
rihten wolt si aber paz:
do swr̂ si manige ayde,
die waren niht maine,

bey got ir schepfere,
3020 daz si ledek were
aller bosen maile,

D

daz sie trvch daz kindelin:
uon wanne daz mohte sin, 3440
des nam sie groz wnder.
diu reine gedaht darunder,

190,35 wie sie uon dem tæidinge
ir gantze ere scholte bringen.
ia uorhte sie die uertanen, 3445
daz sie mit bosem archwane
dannoh furten ir haz.
rihten wolte sie baz:

do swr̂ sie den grimmigen livten
bi allen gotes truten, 3450

40 die ze himel heten reste
in der gotlichen ueste,

da nîe ðge gesah
sorgen noh ungemach
191,1 uon deheiner unchrefte; 3455
sie swr̂ bi der herschefte
die got vater selbe hat,
ze des gebote stat
der liehte sunne v̄ der mane,
daz sie ualskes ane 3460
an allen zwiuel wâre
der werche v̄ der gebære,

5 unt ir libes burde
nie bekuchet wrde
uon deheines mannes gelpfe. 3465

---

74 bi der *B. s. 47*   76 alliz falsches C   78 geberde C   80 daz uzen . och
(noch *B.*) innen C *B. s. 47*   81 unt] diu *B.*   82 bezuket C
   3010 iren *aus* irem   rûm!   *190,36* uertane   *190,40* hiemel

si bat ir got sô helfen
3685   an *dem* jungisten urteile.
dô sprâchen si algemeine,
si *wo*lten sis verwizzen.   (2185)
mit dienste si sich flizzen,
daz si in der *un*mâze
3690   geruochte antlâzen.

die maget sant Marîen,
si fuorten schône sîe   (2190)

wider in ir herberge.
sus hête diu gotes werde
3695   mit der zeswen ir kindes
des bôsen ingesindes
nît wol uberwunden.   (2195)
die tiefe gedanche chunden,

die sprâchen daz daz selbe dinc
3700   uber allen irdischen rinc
hernâch erschulle
unt allem Israhele gewurre.   (2200)

Bî den zîten was ein keiser,
ein gewaltiger voget der weisen:
3705   der was Augustus genant.
diu rîche hête er alliu samt
in sîne gwalt betwungen: (2205)
diu tâten unde sungen
swaz er eine gebôt.
3710   der vorderôte golt rôt

unt silber wîze gebrande
ûz allen ⟨den⟩ landen: (2210)
cinses wolte er niht enbern;
die liute muosten in gewern
3715   swes sîn wille wart enein:

3684 helfe C*B*.   86 alle gemeine   90 antlazen] genczelich laze
91 marie   92 also schone sie   94 sus] so *oder* si   97 nit] niht   98 tifen

A

bey dem iungisten vrtaile.
Do vil gesworen het div reine,
do sprachen si gemaine,
3025 si wolten seiz verwizzen.
mit dienste si sich flizzen,
daz si in der vnmazzen
gerûchte antlazzen,
die si mit grozzen angen
3030 an ir hieten begangen.
Si fûrten die maget rein
schon hin wider haim;

do het si zestunden
iren neit vberwunden.
3035 Die sich versten kvnden,
die sprachen albesunder,
daz vber aller der werlde rink

daz vngehorte dink
her nach schadet sere
3040 dem volche Ysrahele.

Bey den selben zeiten
was ein kayser weiten
Augustus erkant;
im dienten alle lant.

3045 den levten er gebot,
daz man im gebe golt rot

vñ silber weiz geprant.
prief er ovz sant:
zins wolt er niht enberen;
3050 des mûst man in geweren.

D

,got', sprah sie, ,mir so helfe
anme ivngesten vrtêile.'
do iahen sie mit heile,
sie wolten sis uerwizzen.
mit dienste sie sih flizzen 3470
daz sie zir hulden kamen
v̄ ir die swære benamen,
di sie hæten ir getan 191,10
mit rede v̄ mit bosem wan.
Div gute sant Marie, 3475
diu uon sunden frie
vnt iemer unberuret,
wart wider gefuret
in ir êigen herberge.
sus hete div gotes werde 3480
mit der zeswen ir kindes
des ubeln ingesindes
15 nit wol uberwnden.
die rehte gedenchen chunden,

die sprachen daz dazselbe 3485
      dinch
uber allen irdisken rinch
muse hernah erschellen
v̄ mohte Israhel wol gevellen.

Ein keiser was bi den citen,
ein gwaltiger uoget wîten: 3490
20 Augustus was er genamet.
der hete div riche elliu ensamet
in sinen gewalt betwngen:
div taten v̄ sungen
swaz er eine gebot. 3495
nu fordert er daz golt rot
uon aller werlte gliche,
uon allen steten v̄ allem riche,
uon ieglichem lante
silber wîzze wol gebrante: 3500
25 cinses wolt er niht enbern;
niemen getorst in entwern
swes sin wille wart ennein:

3702 allē isrl', *l.* allen Israhelen?   3 geziten   6 hatte hˢ   10 .ord't
11*f.* und silber wol gebrant   uz allē .. nt   15 inein

michel was daz sîn heil.
do diu niuwe hêrschaft erschal (2215)
uber berge unt uber tal,
swâ die liute wâren,
3720 den cins si im gâben.

under im was ein ander kunic,
vollen hêre unde frumic, (2220)
Cyrinus von Syriâ.
eines buoches begunde er sâ,
3725 dâ man die menige an schribe,
unt die liute darzuo tribe
daz si an die chrônen dâhten (2225)
unt ir *ur*kunde brâhten
an dem gelobeten zîte.
3730 uber alle gegene wîten
niemen was sô biderber,
der getors*te* dâ widere (2230)
gebieten einen vinger;
sô smâher noch *sô* ringer
3735 was ouch niemen in der werlt,
erne muose daz keiserlîch gezelt
mit chamerschatze êren, (2235)
den frô*ne* hort mêren.
die ûz gevarn wâren,
3740 die muosten heim gâhen
zir friunden unt zir kinden,
daz man si gesamenet funde, (2240)
sô man si brieven scholte
als der herre wolte.
3745 swaz drîe pfenninge wac
sô ez ûf der wâge lac,
daz gap ein ieglîch man (2245)
der daz leben *wol*te hân.
der sich ⟨des⟩ wolte werjen,
3750 den ersluogen die scherjen,
die daz gelt enpfiengen

3721 vnd⁵!   22 vollen hêre] ein vollic h⁵re C, envollen *B. s. 187*
24 begundē si da   25 dâ man] daz si   sc⁵ben   26 darzuo] ûz   triben
27 gedechten   28 dar brechten   29 an den gelobtē ziten   32 wider
33 uf gereke sinen vinger   34 geringer   36 erne] er   37 schacze

A

do daz gebot erschal
vber perge vñ vber tal,
swa die levte waren,
den zins si im gaben.

3055 vnder im was ein kvnek,
vollen hær vñ frumek,
Cyrinus von Syria.
eines bûches begunde er sâ,
da man die menige an schribe,
3060 daz ir ovzze ⟨niht⟩ belibe

ze den gesprochen zeiten.
vber alle gegen weiten
nieman was so piderbe,
der getorste da widere
3065 gepieten einen vinger,
so hoher noch so ringer,

er mv̂se dem kaiser ze æren
den frone hort meren.
swa levte ovzzen waren.
3070 die mv̂sen haim gahen,

do man si briefen solde
als der herre wolde.
swaz drey pfenninge wak
so ez ovf der wage lak,
3075 daz gab ein igelich man
der sein leben wolde han.
swer sich des wolte werien,
den erslûgen die scherien,
die daz golt enpfiengen.

D

in so grozzen eren er schêin.
do div niwe herschaft erschal 3505
uber berge vnd uber tal,
daz gebôte muse ergan
an widerstrit v̄ sunder wan.
daz ahten die rihtære
uon Rome, diu so mære 3510
191, 30 dennoch was v̄ so here:
nû ist sie genidert sere.
ein lantgraue hiez Cyrîn
uon Syria dem lande sin.
eines buches der began, 3515
da satzet er die ivden an
v̄ schuf die wirte an scriben
v̄ di livte dazu triben
daz sie an die chrone dæhten
und ir urkunde bræhten 3520
35 an dem gelobeten zite.
uber die lantschaft wite
nieman was so mahtich,

so riche noh so ahtich,
erne muse den zins geben, 3525
den frone hort erheben
v̄ den kamerschatze meren
dem richen keiser ze eren.
die da uz waren gevarn,
die ilten heim daz bewarn, 3530
40 daz sie iht beliben,
sine wrden angescriben
192, 1 zu ir chunne v̄ ir magen,
da si ŏh daz silber gaben,
daz drie pfenninge wach 3535
so ez uf der wage gelach:
daz gap ein ieglich man
der daz leben wolte han.
die sich begunden wergen
die erslugen die schergen, 3540
5 die daz gelt enpfiengen

---

38 gemeren   41 zu irn   43 si brieven] di brife machē   44 als] wi
49 f. weren : scherg . .

191, 30 dennohc   3060 niht *ergänzt F*.   3077 f.; 192, 4 weren AD
: scherien A, sergen D

unt fur die fursten gieng*en*   (2250)
mit cinslîchem horte.
si brâhten in sînem worte
3755 guldîne sûle
unt geladene mûle:
die wagene alsô veste   (2255)
si muosten nider bresten
von des schatzes swâre,
3760 der dem helde mâre
gefuoret wart zesamene
in sî*ne* ⟨vesten⟩ treskame*re*.   (2260)

Dô wart ein chreftiger fride:
diu swert muosten si versmiden,

3765 bêdiu spieze unde sp*er*.
dô newas dehein her,
daz iender des gedâhte   (2265)
daz *ez* sich undervâhte.
do newas niht urliuge
3770 bî d*es* meres piuge,
noch nehein nîtgeschelle.
mit grôz*er* *e*benhelle   (2270)
unt harte fridelîche
stuonden al diu rîche.
3775 *diu* senfte unt diu stille
diu was des kindes wille
daz bî d*er* magede was verholn.   (2275)
der keiserlîche zol

daz sint die namen drîe
3780 die uns hânt gemachet frîe.
· · · · · · · · · · · · · · · ·
der vil stâtige fride   (2280)
uber lîp unt uber *sêle*
daz ist diu geburt vil hêre,
3785 diu von der maget lûhte,
dô got des zît dûhte.

3761 wart] warn   67 iender] imm⁵   69 f. urleuges : puwe   71 nit
geselle   74 alle   77 maget   80 di uns habent gevriet hi   81 wol

A

3080 fur die herren si giengen
mit dem zinsleichem horte.
si prahten nach sinem worte
guldein sevle
vñ geladen mevle:
3085 die wegen vil veste
mûsen nider presten
von des schatzes swere,
der dem helde mere
gefuret wart zesamene
3090 in seine vil veste chamere.

Do wart ein chreftiger fride:
div swert mûsten si versmiden,

peide spiezze vñ sper,
daz man ir ninder funde mer.

3095 do stunden fridelich
alle div reich.
die semfte vñ die stille
was des kindes wille
daz bey der mnide was verholen.
3100 der keiserlich zol

daz sint die namen drey
die ⟨uns⟩ hant gemachet frey.

D

v̄ fur die fursten giengen
mit cinslichem horte.
sie brahten in sinem worte
grozze guldine sule   3545
v̄ geladen mule
v̄ wâgene also ueste,
die daz gesmide beste
⟨. . . . .
. . . .⟩

Do wart ein chreftiger fride:
diu swert uerslugen die   3550
                                        smide,
bediu spiezze vñ sper.
done was dehein her
daz iender des gedæhte
daz ez strite oder uæhte.
done was niht urlivge   3555
bi des meres pîvge
noh *n*ehêin nit geschelle.
mit grozer ebenhelle
vñ harte fridliche
stunden elliu riche.   3560
15 div senfte v̄ diu stille
div was des kindes wille
daz bi der magede was uerholn.
daz man begunde zoln
die breiten werlt alliche,   3565
v̄ sich loste mannekliche
mit gewæge drier pfennînge,
daz sint, als ich gedinge,
die uil heren namen drie,
die uns machent frie   3570
20 uon des uiandes bande,
v̄ selnt uns siner hande
der ein keiser ist der wâre
himels vnd der erde zwâre.

192, 10

---

wir di ... ch und'scheide *vor* ch *noch ein Strich, wahrscheinlich* u, *nicht* i;
sicher ursprünglich digen *oder* dige *im Reim.*

192, 8 danach wohl Verlust von mindestens zwei Versen 3091 friden
3092 si versmiden! *192, 13* en nehein

michel reht was daz,　　　　　　　　　　(2285)
dô Christ nâchwendic was,
daz vester fride wurde,
3790　unt diu schalklîche burde
abe muoste slîfen.
diu rebe was dô rîfe　　　　　　　　　　(2290)
dâ wir den wîntrûben
abe schuln *chl*ûben,
3795　dannen uns flôz daz wizzôt,
daz den êwigen tôt
der christenheit benâme　　　　　　　　　(2295)
mit sînem heilwâ*ge*.
der sun sant Marîen
3800　schol uns an schrîben
an daz lebendige buoch,
wan der des êrsten wîbes fluoch　　　　　(2300)
mit der magede wolte stôren.
die froude schuln wir hôren
3805　diu dâ niemer zegât,
behalten *wir* den ir rât.
die sich des wellent werjen,　　　　　　　(2305)
die tievellîchen scherjen
⟨die⟩ benement in daz leben:
3810　sô mahten wir gerner geben
den cins den drin genen*n*en:
die kunnen daz wol erkennen,　　　　　　(2310)
ob wir si reh*te* meinen,
sô wir des lîbes brôde underneigen.

3815　　**D**ô durch des keisers gebot
der cins was *ge*sa*menôt,*

3788 cristo　90 selicliche　92 dô] da　95 daunen] da von　wisot
96 tot] ..t tot　98 siner　3803 maget　5 zurgat　7 wern　8 di irn
.illiclichen schergen　10 gerner] lib⁵　11 genē/:en　13 ob] ab

A

michel reht daz waz,
do Christ chunftik was,
3105 daz vester fride wurde,
vn̄ alle swere burde
abe mûste sleiffen.
dev rebe waz do reife
da wir die weintrouben 192, 25
3110 abe sulen chlouben.

Der sun sant Marien
sol vns ane schreiben
an daz ewige pûch,
wan er des ersten weibes flûch
3115 mit der magede wolte storen.
die frevde mv̂zze wir horen
die da nimmer zegât,
vn̄ volge wir seinem rât.
die sich des wellent wer*ie*n, 30
3120 die tevfelischen scherien
benement *in* daz leben:
so moht wir gerner geben
den zins den drein genennen;
die chunnen daz wol erchennen,
3125 ob wir sey rehte mainen,
so wir daz leben naigen.

Do durch des cheisers gebot 35
der zins wart gesamenot
in al der werlde chreizze,
3130 do was auch gehaizzen,
die daz gebot niht erfulten,
daz si die frevel gulten
vn̄ daz houbet solten verliesen.
Josepf begunde kiesen,
3135 gedenchen vn̄ trahten,
war er cheren mohte
da er were vnzinshaft.
do weist in d*ie* gotes chraft,
daz er fûre gen Bethlehem:
3140 da mûste daz kint her fure gen,

D

michel reht was daz, 3575
do er nahwendik was,
daz stæter fride wrde,
und die schalklichen burde
abe musen slifen.
diu rebe began do rifen 3580
da wir den wintruben
scholten abe chluben,
danne uns flôz daz wîzzot
daz den ewigen tot
zefuret v̄ gnade tût: 3585
daz ist daz sin here blut.
An dem lebentigen buche
scriben er uns geruche,
an siner holden stat,
da er di rehten hat gesat. 3590

die sih des werent mit sun̄den,
die sint sere gebunden
v̄ uerliesent ŏh daz leben:
so mæhten wir gerner geben
den cins den drin genennen. 3595
got der kan wol erkennen,
ob wir in rehte meinen,
so wir die brode underneigen.

Do der cins was gesamenot
als ez der *k*eiser gebot, 3600
v̄ daz ufgeleit wart,
swer sih daran niht bewârt
daz er daz gelubde erfulte,
der fræuel er engulte
v̄ muse daz hŏbet fliesen, 3605
Josep begunde kiesen
v̄ gedenchen in siner ahte,
war er cheren mæhte
da er wrde zinshaft.
do bewiste in gotes chraft, 3610
daz er ze Bethlehem scholte,
wand Christ da erschinen wolte.

3119 weren   3121 im   3127 cheiser   *192,35* zeiser   3138 de

A   **D**

dannen wir ⟨von⟩ dem weissagen
michel vrchvnde haben.

do enbait er niht mere,   done beiter nîenmere,
er sprach zv der magt here: er sprah ze der magede here:

3145 ,dise rede mak niemen   193, 1 ,dise rede mak niht langer   3615
lenger ovf geschieben: gestan:
daz vnser genoz hant getan,   daz unser gnozze hant getan,
bede weip vñ man,
daz svle wir pilleich tŭn.   daz schuln ŏh wir tun zware,

3150 got hat sinen weistŭm   wand ez uns scaden gebære,
vaste mit dir getailt;   ob wirz ubersæzzen
dein leip ist vngemailt.   v̄ des gebotes uergæzzen.   3620

nv solt dv vrowe wol gehugen,   5 nu scholt du frŏe gehugen,
war wir iærlichen mvgen   war wir iarlichen mugen

3155 vnsern zins bringen,   unsern hŏbetzins bringen,
daz wir iht schaden gewinnen   daz wir ân fræise gedingen
von dem keiser Augusto.'   da ce der rihtære gêinwrte.'   3625
div magt antwurt im do: diu maget im do antwrte:
,des endarft dv niht fragen;   ,des endarft du niht fragen;

3160 vnser kunne vñ vnser magen   unsir friunt unde unser magen
die sint von Bethlehem komeu;   die sint uon Bethlehem chomen;
da sul wir iærlich wonen   10 da schuln wir iarliche   3630
                                                    wonen
mit dem selben vrtaile   mit derselben urteile
daz die purgere alle gemaine   die in die burgære ze heile

3165 in ze rehte wellen sprechen.   vnt ze rehte wellent sprechen.
wie solt wir daz zeprechen?   wie scholten wir die zebrechen?
sinnes sul wir walten;   sinnes schulen wir walten   3635
wir mv̊zzen die æ behalten,   vñ unser e behalten,
æ man vns des leibes beraube.   15 e· man uns des libes rŏbe.

3170 wie wol ich des getrowe,   vil wol ich daz glŏbe,
daz ich bey minem geslehte   daz ich bi minem geslæhte
missetuon iht enmæhte.'   missetun nîen mæhte.'   3640
Joseph geviel div rede wol,   Josebe geuîel div rede wol,
er sprach: ,wie gerne ich sol   er sprah: ,wie gerne ich dir

3175 dines gebotes warten.   uolgeñ schol.
mich dunket daz wir zeharte   mih dunchet daz wir ze harte
gelenget haben dise vart.'   haben gelenget dise uarte;
div vrowe des en ain wart,
sein wer zeit vil gŭte.   20 sin wære uolleklichen zit.'   3645

3180 do kerte div raingemŭte   do cherte diu niftel Dauit
ze Bethlehem die strazzen: gêin Bethlehem die strazze:
si wolt sich briefen lazzen   sie wolte sih brieuen lazzen.
mit andren iren magen.

193, 8 endarf   3174 ger   3176 zeharten

A

ze den selben tagen
3185 erschain ir frev*de vn* wunne,
liehter danne ein sunne.

si fûr frôlich;
ir dienten tougenlich
mit fleizze der engel schar, 193, 25
3190 der vrowen wunnechlich gevar.

Der himilische vater gûter
wolte seine mûter
chumftiger dinge
au ain ende bringen.
3195 aine grozze tovgen
liez er sey an schowen,
die ander niemen sach,
wan si ir scham nie zebrach.
ir wart geoffenot
3200 do ir lieber sun gebot:
bey dem wege sach si stan
paide weip vñ man
bedenthalb ze den seiten
an dem wæge weiten.
3205 ein volk vñ aine schar
chom vil trovrechlichen dar:
die wunden die hende.
in eysnein gebende
waren si beslozzen:
3210 mit zeheren begozzen
si chlagten vnmazzen.
anderhalb bey der strazzen
stûnt ein schar michel,
vor allem leide sicher:
3215 die waren vngebunden,
trouren si niht kvnden.
si heten geistliches spil
vñ ander frevde vil.

Joseph si do sagte
3220 was si gesehen habte.

D

frôde vnde wune
⟨. . . . .⟩   3650
muse ir da begegene*n*
uon des kindes segene.
sie fur dar froliche;
ir dienten willekliche
der engel gesinde gût: 3655
uon den was sie wol behût.

Der himiliske uater guter
der wolte do sine mûter
chumftiger dinge
an ein ende bringen.   3660
ein grozziu tôgen
di*e* sant er ir ze ôgen,
die anders niemen sach,
wand sie di scham nie zebrah
30 magetlicher gute   3665
unt in der kivsche blute.
bi dem wege sah sie stân
bediu wib vnde mau
ietwederhalben zen siten
engegen ir so witen.   3670
ein uolch vnt ein schar
diu chom vil truriklichen dar:
die wnden die hende.
in isinîne gebende
35 waren sie geslozzen: 3675
mit zæheren begozzen
sie chlageten unmazze.
anderhalp der strazze
stûnte ein schar tugentliche,
harte frôderiche,   3680
lieht unt sicher uor leide.
sie heten uolle wêide,
wnneklichiu spil,
alles liebes v̄ eren uil.
40 sie waren schone gechleit 3685
in wizzer wæte gemeit.

Josebe sie do sagete
waz sie gesehen habete
194, 1 uon den zwein scharen,

3185 frevde vñ *F. B. s. 30*] frevnden   *193, 23* begegene   *193, 28* div

A

er gelaubt ez ze trage
vn̄ het denheine frage,
wie dem dinge mohte gesein:
des erschamte sich daz magedein,
3225 daz si daz mere verlie.
vor in an dem wege gie
ein knappe schone ane part;
ir gevert er do wart.
daz was ein wunnechliches kint,
3230 als alle die sint
die ze himel sint erkant
vn̄ gesant von gotes hant.

in dem bilde er in erschain
sam er wer der levt ein
3235 der wolte varen ze Bethlehem.

si sahen in gerne mit in gen.

Do sprach der schone iungelink:
,ich horte wol daz taydink
daz ir het mit einander.

3240 die maht dv ane allez wandel
wol gelauben, Joseph.
daz dein zweivel so stet
gen diser vrowen raine,
mich wundert was daz maine.
3245 Joseph, hore her zvo mir!
die warheit wil ich dir
vil redelichen kunden:
die die hende wunden
vn̄ chlagten so harte,
3250 die habent den weingarte
gotes niht erbowen;

D

der liehten v̄ der misseuaren. 3690
daz gelŏbet er trage
vnde entwalte mit der frage,
wie dem dinge mohte sin:
des erschamte sich diu kunigin.
do sie daz mære uerlie, 3695
uf dem wege sie ergie
ein knappe schone ân bart;
ir geuerte er do wârt.
daz was ein kint lussam,
als ez uon rehte gezam 3700
dem gesinde uor gote,
daz ce sinem gebote
iemer stat v̄ iemer uert,
wan ez fur in niht liebes gert.
in dem bilde erschêiner 3705
sam er der liute wære einer
die ze Bethlehem wolten
v̄ da zinsen scholten.
des selben heten sie wan
v̄ sahen in gerne mit in gan. 3710
do taten sie rede genuge
also sûzze v̄ gefuge
uon der naheten herschaft,
von gotes gute v̄ siner chraft.
ir herze waren reine 3715
in rehter minne gemeine.

Do sprah der iungelinch:
,ich horte wol daz tæidinch
daz e was under iv,
do ich chom gegangen zu iv, 3720
uon den gwaltigen tŏgen:
div mæhte Joseph wol gelŏben.
daz sin sin fremdliche stat
ze den dingen die got hat
ûf dem wege beschêinet, 3725
daz en weiz ich waz meinet.
Joseph, hore herze mir!
die warheit sage ich dir
ze dîvte an disen stunden:
die die hende so wnden 3730
v̄ angestliche gebârten,
die habent die wingarten
gotes niht erbuwen;

A

daz mûz si harte riwen:
daz ist div Jvdische diet,
div die weissagen verriet
3255 die in da waren gesant
von der gotes hant.
⟨. . . . .⟩
daz vil vnschuldige blût
daz ist zv̊ in gerunnen;
3260 dem hirt sint si entrunnen.

ir sunde hant in vertailet:
daz ist daz si bewainent.
mit fevreinen banden
von den valanden
3265 werdent si genichet
vn̄ ewichlich bestrichet.

Die auer die frevde habent
vn̄ sich wunnechleich gehabent,
daz sint die becherten,
3270 die weilen nieman lerte:
die enpfahent den gotes svn
der in genade wil tûn.
die beleibent niht ze der *w*instren;
si gahent von der *v*insteren
3275 in die liehten sunnen,
vn̄ badent ovz dem brunnen
da sich der gaist enpindet,
vn̄ aller pein verswindet
mit gotelichem gepende.
3280 der Juden missewende
wirt der haidensche*f*te trost.
der tiefel gerwet sinen rost
vn̄ e*n*pheht die verworhten,
die di*e* gotes vorhten
3285 niht *w*ellent lernen.'
Joseph horte gerne
daz er imz also beschiet.
di*e* israhelische diet

D

daz mûz sie balde riwen: 3735
daz ist div iudiske diet,
div die wissagen uerrîet
die in da waren gesant
uon des oberisten hant.
die habent vil grimmigez mût;
daz vil unschuldige blut 3740
daz ist hinze in gerunnen;
sie sint dem hirte entrunnen,
194, 30 mit dem si genesen scholten,
ob siz dienen wolten.

ir ubele hat in uerteilet: 3745
des gent sie geseilet
mit vivrinen banden.
in noten v̄ grozzen schanden
sint sie iemer bestricket.
ir ere div ist genicket 3750
v̄ berihtet sih nîenmere:
des chlageten sie also sere.

35 **D**ie anderhalp da frôde hant
v̄ in liehter wate stant,
daz sint die becherten, 3755
die got wilen êrten:
die enpfahent nů gotes svn
der in sin gnade wil tun.
die belibent niht ze der winster;
sie gahent uon der vinster 3760
in die liehten sunne,
v̄ badent sih vz dem brvnne
40 da allez meil uerswindet,
vnde sie der geist enbindet
195, 1 uon totlichem gebende. 3765
der iuden missewende
diu wirt der heidenschefte trost.
der tievil garwet sinen rost,
da er die verworhten
enpfahet, die gotes uorhten 3770
5 nîen wellent lernen.'
Joseph der horte gerne
daz er im die rede so beschîet.
die israhelisken diet

194, 31 mit mit   *3273 f.* winstren : vinsteren *F*.] vinstren : winsteren
3276 kein sich!   *3281* haidenschte   *3283* epheht   *3284* div   *3288* div

A

bewainte er vil haizze,
3290 daz si Abrahames gehaizze
also solten verliesen
vn̄ ewige damnunge erkiesen.

E daz div rede was getan,
der abent begunde ane gan,
3295 div sunne begunde seigen,   195, 10
div naht zv̊ steigen.
als in geswaich daz himellieht,
Joseph der getroute nieht
vollen chomen in die stat:
3300 vnser vrowen er bat,
daz si gerv̊chet vnder wegen
nahtselde pflegen
vnz an den anderen morgen.
do twungen sey die sorgen;

3305 si sprach: ‚swie spat ez werde,
wir sulen die herberge
alswa ninder sv̊chen,
vn̄ wil sein got gerv̊chen,
wan ze Bethlehem in der stat:
3310 vil leiht ich schaden hæt,
solt ich alswa inder sein.
erfult sint die tage mein
daz ich mv̊ter werden sol:

ich bringe kouf vn̄ zol.'

3315 Als ez mitev naht wart,
do gab der magt invart
Bethlehem *ir gruozsal.*
do moht lenger ir zal
haben denhaine frist:
3320 der vorgesprochene Christ
der wolte sich erzaigen
vn̄ sine gv̊te naigen.

D

die began er weinen hêizze, 3775
daz sie Habrahames geheizze
also scholte uerliesen
v̄ den ewigen tot kiesen.

Bedaz div rede was getan,
der abent begunde anegan, 3780
diu sunne nider sigen,
div naht den tach uertriben.
als in do gesweich daz lieht,
Josep der getruote nieht
uolchomen an die stat: 3785
unser frǒen er gebat,
daz sie geruhte under wegen
ane ein bette sih gelegen
untze an den andern morgen.
15 do dwngen sie die sorgen, 3790
daz ir mæitwesender lip
wol erkante sine zit.

sie sprah: ‚swie spætez uns werde,
wirne schulen die herberge
anderswa niender suchen, 3795
wil sin got gervchen,
wan in Dauidis purge:
uil lihte ez uns scade wrde,
20 scholten wir anders iender sin.
erfullet sint die tage min: 3800
daz ich muter werden schol,
daz ist in miner ahte wol.
ich bringe den gewaltigen wirt,
den sin eigen div gebirt,
als er mir herre gebot: 3805
uol varn mv̊z ich durh die not.'
als ez umbe mitte naht wart,
do gab der magede inuart
25 Bethlehême ir gruzsal.
do ne mahte ǒh div ir zal 3810
niht langer haben frist:
der uorgewissagte Christ
wolte selbe do zeigen,
daz sih der himel neigen
scholte zu der *erde*, 3815
do in gebar div werde.

3296 stegen 3303 mororgen 3308 gerv̊hen 3317 ze Bethlehem der
stet sal 3318*f.* do enmohte ouch diu ir zal lenger haben *F.* *195,28* er erde

A

Div vrowe mûst entwalen
bey ainer zellen smâhen.
3325 div himilische porte,   195, 30
div swanger wart von gotes worte
aller werlde zehail,
div sach an einem tail
ein wenigez lǔk:
3330 ir noturft sey darin trǔk,
daz si darin trat
vn̄ ez ze house hat:
daz kom niht von geschihte
daz si algerihte
3335 in dem vinstern hol
solte geberen also wol:
Die Christes predigere
weissagten dise mære

vor, wie si solt gebern
3340 vn̄ ⟨uns⟩ des herren gewern.

do si gie in den stein,
do erlouhte vn̄ erschain
ein michel lieht darinne
gen der kuniginne.
3345 die weile daz si da belaip,
daz lieht die vinster vertraip.

si gebot dem alten manne,
daz er ire ein amme
eilte gewinnen,
3350 die si mit dem kinde
wol bewaren kunde.
die het er schiere funden:
Rachel hiez div aine,
div gahte zǒ dem staine;
3355 Salome damit gie.
der herre si niht verlie:

D

Div frœ entwêlen muse
bi einer smæhen chluse.
diu himiliske porte,
die got mit sinem worte   3820
erwelt uns ze heile,
diu gesah in einem stêine
ein vil wenigez lůch:
ir wille sie dar getruch,
daz sie dar in trat   3825
v̄ sich da hete gesat:
daz enchom niht uon geschihte
daz sie in alrihte
35 in dem vinsteren hol
scholte rûwen so wol: 3830
di Christes predigære
die heten uor manigem iare
uor gescriben v̄ gesaget,
wie div muter vn̄ maget
also scholte gebern   3835
unde uns des herren gewern,
der ze uoget wrde gezalt
fur des tieuels gewalt.
40 do sie gie in den stêin,
do luhte v̄ erschêin   3840
ein michel lieht dar inne
gegen der kuniginne.
die wile daz sie da beleib,
die vinster daz lieht uertreib,
sam da ein fîvr brunne,   3845
oder div perhtel sunne
196, 1 uertribe daz genibele
uz dem ir gesidele.
sie gebot dem man zehante,
daz er sinen flîz wante   3850
heveammen ze bringen,
die sie in ir dingen
wol bewâren chunden.
die hete er schiere funden:
5 Rachel hiez diu eine,   3855
diu gahte zu dem stêine;
Salome damite gîe.
der herre sie niht uerlie,

3329 eine wenige luke   3331f. weder trat : hât noch trat : gesat
kommt dem Original zu, vielleicht trâten : hêten   3340 geweren

      daz er daz allez an truoc,   (2315)
      wan swes diu frouwe gewuoc
      unt swar si in wolte senden,
      daz brâhte er an ein ende.
4095 dô er under wegen was,
      dô chom diu zît daz si genas.   (2320)
      diu geburt tet ir niht wê:

      obstetricum vicê
      stuonden die engel dabî,
4100 do diu maget edele unde frî
      zougte den heilant,   (2325)
      der alliu rîche unt ⟨alliu⟩ lant
      ûf gnâde wolte schouwen.
      ja was ouch bî der frouwen
4105 weder man noch wîp
      noch dehein irdischer lîp: (2330)
      wirdic was des niemen,
      da die engel scholten dienen,
      daz er dâ ⟨mite⟩ wâre,
4110 die hêrschaft ane sâhe,
      daz gotlîch geslahte.   (2335)
      wir hôren ze wîhen nahten
      die geistlîchen hirten
      von des himeles wirte
4115 michel êre chunden,
      doch enmugen sis niht ergrunden: (2340)
      ja ist sîn tûsentstunt mê
      danne dâ geschriben stê.
      daz grôze wuofen unde chlagen,
4120 daz ander frouwen muozen haben,

      sô si gewinnent diu kint   (2345)
      diu von sunden chomen sint,

4091—4272 C² 1659—1840   4101 zougte *Sch.*] zeigte   4 io   9 ⟨bi⟩
B. s. 216   12 wir] wi   17 io   18 dā da   19 *Initiale*   sufczen und
di clag   20 daz] di   hab   22 bekumē

A

er bot in sine miete
der seligen diete.

von siner grozzer gůte
3360 luzel in daz mûte:
swes div vrowe gewůk,
gedultichlich er daz vertrůk.

Die weil er vnder wegen was,
do kom div zeit daz si genas.
3365 div geburt tet ir niht wæ:

obstetricum uice
stůnden die engel dabey,
da div magt sunden frey
zaigte den hailant,
3370 den alle reiche vñ alle lant
ovf genade wellent schowen.
ia was ouch bey der vrowen
weder man noch weip
noch deṅhain yrdischer leip:
3375 wirdik waz des niemen,
da die engel solten diener,
daz er da mit were
vñ die herschaft an sehe,
das goteliche geslehte.
3380 wir horen ze weinahte
die geistlichen hirtte
von des himels wirte
michel ære kunden,
doch mugent siz niht ergrunden:
3385 sein ist tousent stunt me
dan inder geschriben stæ.
Daz grozze wůffen vñ chlagen,
daz andre vrowen muezzen *haben,*

so si gewinnet div kint
3390 div von sunden komen sint,

D

untze er sie brâhte an die stat,
als diu frœ gebat.   *3860*

Joseph der alte,
der uil einvalte,
der senfte vnd der gute,
vil lutzel in daz mute,
196,10 daz er daz allez antruch,   *3865*
wan swes diu frœe ie gewch
v̄ swar sie in wolte senden,
daz chunde er wol uerenden.
Do er underwegen was,
do chom div zit daz sie gnas. *3870*
diu geburt sanfte ergie,
wan sie in âne meil enpfie
v̄ ane sunde gebar:
von rehte ir leides nien wâr.
15 ir waren die engele bi;   *3875*
die taten sie sorgen vrî,
do sie brahte den heilant,
der diu irdisken lant
vns ze hæile wolte scœeṅ.
iane was ŏh bi der frœen   *3880*
nehein werltlicher lip,
enweder man noh wip:
wirdik was des niemen,
da die engele scholten dienen
196,20 dem gotlichem geslæhte.   *3885*
wir horen an der heren nahte

groz ere der werlte chunden,   :
doh mugen wirz niht ergrunden
ia ist sin tusentstunt me
denne da gescriben ste.   *3890*
Daz grozze wfen v̄ chlagen,
daz andere frœen muzzen uer-
                        tragen,
so sie gewinnent div kint
div uon sunden chomen sint,

3359 grozz?! *3361 kein* ie! *3375* nieman *3384* siz *F.*] si *3386* ge-
schreiben   *3388* haben haben

       daz was ir seltsâne;
       si was sîn alles âne.
4125 daz kint daz dâ fur gie,
       dô si daz êrist enphie,   (2350)
       dô was si lûter âne meil:
       dannen gwan si daz heil,
       daz sie niht enswar
4130 dô si Christum gebar.
       daz golt daz diu werlt hât,   (2355)
       diu in dem ellende stât,
       daz enmahte niene widerwegen
       die geburt unt den segen
4135 den uns diu maget brâhte,
       dô sie got sô bedâhte   (2360)
       an allen ir dingen:
       sagen unde singen
       muozen wir iemer dannen.
4140 der val ist zegangen,
       der uns muote sêre.   (2365)
       alle gloubige sêle
       die schuln der hôchzîte
       warten unde bîten
4145 mit geistlîchem trôste,
       dô got sîne christenheit erlôste.   (2370)

       Joseph der heilige man,
       dô er die ammen gewan,
       er gie zuo dem steine:
4150 dâ lac diu maget reine
       in einem grôzen liehte.   (2375)
       ja entrûweten si mit niehte
       an die stat gegâhen
       dâ si den glast sâhen.
4155 dô hête si gewunnen
       den êwigen sunnen,   (2380)
       des schîn niemer zegêt
       die wîle daz der himel stêt.
       daz kint si diche chuste;
4160 ez lac ir an der bruste,
       daz wênic was ze sehenne   (2385)
       unt michel ze jehenne:
       daz den tôt vertrîbet,

    4125 f. gink : enpfink   26 dô] als vō erste   27 di lutt'e   28 dannen] da vō   33 niene Sch.] nimāt C, niemer W. s. 163   34 vō dem segen 42 gleubige   50 do   52 io   56 den] di   57 zurget   62 bekennene

A

daz waz ir seltzene,
vn̄ was sein alles ane.

daz golt daz div werlt hat,
div in dem ellende stat,
3395 daz mohte nieman wider wegen
die geburt vn̄ den segen
den vns div maget brahte,
do ir got gedahte
an allen iren dingen.
3400 sagen vnde singen
muezze wir immer mere.

alle geloubige sele
die sulen der hochzeite
warten vn̄ beiten
3405 mit geistlichem troste,
do got sin volk erloste.

Joseph der heilige man,
do er die ammen gewan,
er gienk zv̄ dem staine:
3410 da lak div maget reine
in einem grozzen liehte.
ia getrouten si ⟨mit⟩ niehte
an die stat gegahen
da si den glast sahen,
3415 do si het gewunnen
den ewigen sunnen,
des schein nimmer zegat
die weile der himel stat.
daz kint si diche kuste;
3420 ez lag ir an ir bruste,
daz wenik was ze sehene
vn̄ michel ze iehene:

D

daz was ir seltsæne: *3895*
sie was sin alles âne,
wan daz kint daz da furgie,
do siz cem ersten enpfie,
daz brûefte der heilige geist
ane suntliche uolleist.   *3900*
196, 30 uon schulden sie niht enswar,
do sie Christum gebar,

der mit siner gêinwrte
v̄ mæitlicher geburte
die sundære getroste   *3905*
v̄ die christenheit erloste.

Joseph der heilige man,
do er die ammen gewan,
er gie zu dem steine:
do lach diu maget reine   *3910*
35 in einem grozzen liehte.
iane getruoten sie mit nîehte
zu ir an die stat gahen,
da sie den glast sahen
von dem ewigen sûnnen   *3915*
den sie hete gewnnen.

daz kint sie dicke chûste;
ez lag ir an der bruste,
daz wenich was zesehen
v̄ uil michel ze iehen: *3920*
40 daz den tot uertribet,

3401 wir den *F.*   3403 hochzeiten   3412 niht

gein dem diu erde bibet,
4165   daz die berge alle
mit michelem schalle   (2390)
weget unt erschuttet,
daz hête dâ gehuttet
in einem engen luoge:
4170   sîn muoter hête froude genuoge.

Do getorsten die frouwen an daz hol,   (2395)
daz des liehtes was vol,
deheine wîs ernenden:

si muosten fur senden
4175   den milten patriarchen.
si wunderôte starche,   (2400)
wannen daz lieht schône
in den stein bechôme
dâ ie vinster inne was:
4180   durch nôt vorhten si daz.
Josêbes kûscheite   (2405)
diu gap im dar geleite,
daz er mahte langen
dâ diu geburt was ergangen.
4185   des kindes was er vil frô,
die gotes gnâde lobete er dô.   (2410)
er sprach: ‚frouwe lustsam,
swaz dû gebute daz ist getân.
wil dû ⟨die⟩ frouwen gruozen,
4190   so gebiut daz si muozen
fur dîn antlutze gên!   (2415)
ich hiez si vor dem hole stên.
erloubestu in die învart,
sô wirt dîn êre wol bewart:
4195   si dunkent mich sô biderbe,
dâ enist niht widere,   (2420)
si kunnen dich wol behuoten.
du scholt ouch in mit guote
danken unde lônen
4200   daz si durch dînen willen her chômen.'

4164 dem] im   bidemet   67 ersuchet   68 gebuwet   69 wenigē
70 vreuden   71 entorsten   72 daz ez   73 ernennen   74 wrsenden!
76 wund°t vil   77 wan   78 dem steine   81 *f.* iosephs kusscheit : geleit,
vgl. W. s. 169   82 im dar] in do   83 dar (*so!*) mochte   87 vil lustsam

A

daz die perg alle
mit michelm schalle
3425 weget vñ schut*t*et,
daz het da gehvttet
in einem engen luge:
sein mûter het doch frevde genvoge.

Do getorsten die vrowen in daz hol,
3430 daz des liehtes waz so vol,
sich denheinen weis niht
gewenden:
si mûsen fur senden
den milten patriark.
si wundrot stark,
3435 von wannen daz lieht schône
in den stein chome.

mit Josebes kevscheit
gewunnen si gelait,
daz si dar mohten gelangen
3440 da div geburt was ergangen.
des kindes was er vil fro,
di*e* gotes genade lobt er do.
er sprach: ,vrowe lustsam,
swaz dv gepivtest daz ist getan.
3445 wil dv die vrowen grvezzen,
so gebivt daz si mv̊zzen
her fur dein antlutze gen!
ich liez sey vor der hole sten.

du solt in des danken ser,
3450 daz si durch dich sint chomen her.'

D

gêin dem div erde bibet,

daz die berge erschuttet,
daz hete da gehuttet
in einem engen lûge: *3925*
sin muter hete frôde genûge

uon den eren, des wæne ich wol.
die frôen an daz liehte hol
197,1 getorsten niht ernenden:
sie musen fur senden   *3930*
den guten patriarche.
sie wnderote starche,
wanne daz lieht bechame,
daz got selben gezæme.

Joseph mit siner kiuskeite *3935*
der gab in darin geleite;

5 er sprah: ,liebiu frôe min,
ich han getan den willen din.
wil du sie nu gruzzen,
so gebîvte daz sie muzzen *3940*
fur din antlutze gen!
ich hiez sie uor dem hole sten.
erlôbestv in die inuart,
so ist din ere wol bewart:
ir sin dunchet mich so gut *3945*
daz du mit in bist wol behut.'

---

88 gebutes   89 vrouwe   93 in eine vart   98 guten   4200 her sint
kumen
   3425 schutet   3430 waz!   3431 den heinen!   3436 dem steine *F.*
3442 div

Si sprach, daz wâre ir vil liep,   (2425)
si enscholten ouch davor niet
langer sich versûmen.
si bat den wec rûmen
4205 sô si în giengen,
daz si wol enphienge   (2430)
des rîchen Christes magedîn.
si hiez si willechomen sîn:
si bat si nider sitzen.
4210 dô chêrten si ir witze,
wie si daz kint bewarten: (2435)
ein bat si im garten
unt wunden ez mit flîze
in diu tuoch sô wîze.
4215 mit lînînen vademen
twungen si zesamene   (2440)
den lîchnamen reine
unt daz heilige gebeine,
daz uns gît ze lône
4220 die untôtlîchen stôle
unt die engelischen wât,   (2445)
unt ouch niemen verlât
der im wil getrûwen.
samet uns wolte er bûwen
4225 unt dolte daz gebende
von wîplîcher hende.   (2450)

Rachel unt Salomê
⟨die⟩ wâren ze chindelbetten ê
gewesen alle zîte
4230 in der gegene wîte.
alle wîplîche site,   (2455)
dâ si gewon wâren mite,
die wâren in chunt von rehte.
do gebôt daz unser trehten,
4235 do si sîne muoter griffen,
daz si nider sliffen   (2460)
zuo der erde fur tôt.
ir varwe lieht unde rôt
diu muoste dô erbleichen.

4202 nicht   5 sô] wanne C, unze *Br. s. 48, vgl. § 31 c*   6 enpfinge̅
10 karten   17 her und reine   22 unt] di   23 der] w⁵   24 daz wolt er
uns buwe   26 wiplichen henden   28 kinde betten   29 mange zite

A   **D**

197, 10 Sie sprah, wie lieb ez ir ware,
sie scholten sich dauor zware
niht langer sumen.
sie bat den wech rûmen.   *3950*

si hiez sey zvo ir gahen
vn̄ begunde sey enpfahen:
si pat sei nider sitzen.
do kerten ⟨si⟩ ir witze,
3455 wie si daz kint bewarten:
ein pat si im garten
vn̄ wunten ez mit fleizze
in die leinwat weizze.
mit leineinem vademe
3460 dwungen si zesamene
den leichnamen reine
vn̄ daz heilige gebeine.

des richen Christes magedin
diu hîez sie wilchomen sin
v̄ bat sie nider sitzen.
do cherten sie ir witze,
wie sie daz kint bewarten: *3955*
ein bat sie ime garten
15 v̄ wnden ez mit flizze
in diu tûch so wizze.
mit lininen vademen
tw̄ngen sie cesamen*e*   *3960*
den lichiname reine
v̄ daz uil heilige gebeine
daz uns git ze lone
die untotliken chrone
vnd die engelisken wat,   *3965*
vnt ŏch niemen verlat
20 der im wil getruwen.
mit samet uns wolte er buwen
v̄ dolte daz gebende
uon wiplicher hende.   *3970*

Rachel vn̄ Salome
die waren ze kindelpette æ
3465 gewesen allezeit
in der gegende weit.
alle weiplich sit,
da si gewandelt heten mit,
die waren in kunt verre.
3470 do gebot vnser herre,
do si sin mûter ane griffen,
daz si nider sliffen
zv̊ der erde fur tot.
ir varbe weiz vn̄ rot
3475 mûste vil gar erb*l*aichen.

Rachel vnt Salome
die waren ze chindelbetten e
gewesen alle zite
uber die gegen wite.
alle wipliche site,   *3975*
da sie gewone waren mite,
25 die waren in chunt durh not.
vnser trehtin in daz gebot,
do sie sin muter griffen,
daz sie nider sliffen   *3980*
zu der erde fur tot.
ir uarwe lieht v̄ rot
diu mûse do erbleichen.

---

30 gegende   32 gewont   35 angriffen, *vielleicht* do si an s. m. g.?,
vgl. § 63   36 si aller   39 v'bleich'
197,26 ce samen   3475 erbaichen

4240 si sprâchen daz si daz zeichen
      ê niemer erfreischten;   (2465)
      ir bischof unt ir meister
      der hête in dicke daz gesaget,
      daz komen scholte ein maget
4245 diu âne man gebâre.
      si jâhen daz si daz wâre   (2470)
      unt errieten ez sô schiere:
      vor vorhten was in leide unde liebe.

       Dô hête daz kint edele
4250 eine ⟨vil⟩ smâhe selede:
      den kunigen was ez sippe,   (2475)
      doch wolte ez in die chrippen
      sich legen lâzen,
      da diu rinder ûz âzen:
4255 dar truogen ez die frouwen.
      si muosten wunder schouwen   (2480)
      an dem sune hêre.
      der wîssagen lêre
      diu wart erfullet daran,
4260 wan er wîset den van
      uber alle hêrschefte   (2485)
      in sîner magenkrefte.
      dâ stuont ein esel unt ein rint;
      daz vil keiserlîche kint
4265 daz erkanten si beide:
      got der gap in eine   (2490)
      ⟨den⟩ verstantlîchen muot
      unt den sin alsô guot.
      si vielen nider an diu knie:
4270 daz geschach ouch vor nie.

4241 nime   43 di hettē   49 Do sprach   50 eine wenige   51 ez
was gesippe   52 krippe   59f. dar ane : wane (so!)   62 mankrefte
65 si do

A

si sprachen daz si daz zaichen
⟨. . . . .⟩ her
nie gefrieschen mer.
in hiet ir pyschof gesagt
3480 dike von einer magt
div ane man gebære:
si iahen daz si daz were.

Do het daz kint edele
ein vil smæhe sedele:
3485 den kvnigen waz ez sippe,

doch wolt ez in die krippe
sich legen lazzen,
da div rinder ovz azzen.

da stûnt ein esel vn̄ ein rint;
3490 daz keiserleiche kint
erkanten si beide:
got gab in ane laide
verstantlichen mvot
mit sinnen also gût.
3495 si vielen nider an die knie:
daz geschach vore nie.

D

sie sprachen daz sie daz zeichen
nîen mere heten gesehen, *3985*
v̄ begunden des iehen,
197, 30 in wære dicke gesaget
daz komen scholte ein maget
diu ane man gebære.
sie iahen, daz sie daz wære *3990*
der elliu werlte ie gerte,
v̄ an der sie got gewerte
gnaden v̄ sælde an ende.
ufhuben sie die hende
v̄ diu herze an der stunde *3995*
mit lobsprechentem munde
35 durh div wnder diu sie sahen;
die chunden sie wol veruahen
mit gutem ioh richem sinne:
daz gab in div gotes minne. *4000*

Do hete der riche arme,
der mit sinem arme
198, 1 al den himel umbesloz,
ein selide smæhe vil ungroz:
doh er wære den kungen *4005*
                    sippe,
er wolt sih in die chrippe
da legen lazzen,
da diu rinder uz azzen:
5 dar trugen in die frǒen.
sie musen wnder scǒen *4010*
an dem kinde here:
der wissagen lere
diu wart erfullet daran,
wand er sih zêigen began.

do stunt ein esel v̄ ein rint; *4015*
daz keiserliche kint
daz erkanten sie bediv:
got der gab in under div
10 einen uerstantlichen mût,
v̄ der sin wart in so gût. *4020*
sie vîelen nider an diu knîe:
daz gescah danor nîe.

3477 wanne an der maget here *F.*   *197, 29* begunde   *3491* erkante

si suohten ir venige   (2495)
mit vor . . . .

4272 *etwa* mit vorhten im engegene *Sch.*

A

si sûchten *ir venige*
uil *vnder der menige*
vor des himeles orthaben.
3500 swaz div zunge niht moht gesagen,
daz zaige*te* ir gebere:
daz da komen were
aller werlte herre.
do wundert auer verre
3505 die ammen die daz sahen:
fur war si des iahen,
daz si ez niemer gehorten.
mit lobelichen worten
lobten si den heilant,
3510 der si dar het gesant.
Joseph der greise man
michel frevde gewan.
do liez div magt mêre
daz kint ruoben ane swere.

3515 Arme levte waren,
die vihes niht enbaren,
die waren an daz velt
vnder ir vihe gezelt.
des nahtes si sich mûten
3520 vñ wolte*n* ez behûten
vor den wolfen rêzzen,
daz si ez niht enfrezzen.
ir wahte si phlegten,
als in geboten heten
3525 ir meister vñ ir wirtte.
ia trugen auch die hirtte
grozze kolben vñ bogen.
do kom ein engel geflogen:
michel was div claritas
3530 vñ der schein der da was,
do der geweltige bote
die mere sagte von gote.

D

sie erten ir schepfære:
daz duten ir gebære,
v̄ daz da komen wære   *4025*
aller werlte herre.
des wnderot verre
198, 15 die ammen v̄ ŏh den grisen.
mit lobe begunden sie brisen,
daz div sinnelosen tiere   *4030*
uersinneten sih so schiere
der milten gotes gute.
der mæit muter gemute
stunt in richer frŏde
durh des kindes beschŏde,   *4035*
daz sie sah v̄ umbevie,
daz sie chust vñ tigen lîe
20 v̄ an ir brust lêite.
der engel schare chomen gereite
v̇ waren ir diensthaft   *4040*
durh die nivwegeborn herschaft.

Armiv liute nahen lagen,
die ir uihes pflagen
an der heren nahte
mit geselleklicher wâhte;   *4045*

sie trugen kolben v̇ bogen.
do chom ein engel geflogen
25 zv in mit grozzem glaste.

3497 *f.* mit d⁵ menige   uil vñ d⁵ venie *A,* vil guoter venige *F. B.
s. 30*   3501 zaige   3517 waren gelegen *F.*   3518 vnder *B. s. 176]* vñ
3520 woltes   3523 *f. echter Reim, aber nicht* phlâgen : hæten *F., sondern*
phlegeten : habeten

A

erchomen waren die knehte:
do troste si mit ⟨rehte⟩
3535 div englische gûte
vñ freute ir gemûte.
Er sprach: ‚ewer sorge verlat!
ich sag iv wie ez ergat:
ein frevde ist errunnen
3540 vber allez mennischen kunne;

der sult ir ouch geniezzen:
des sol evch niht verdriezzen.
Adames schulde ist verlorn;
iv ist ⟨ein hail⟩ geborn
3545 mit fleische vñ mit gebeine:
sin frevde wirt gemaine
aller slahte dieten.
er wil die chlage verbieten
vñ die helle zebrechen,
3550 den grozzen roup rechen,
den der tievel gevie
do er Evam vbergie.
in die kurze Bethlehem
sult ir eilinde gen.
3555 ich sag ev von dem kinde:
seht, daz sult ir vinden
in einer krippe an einem hol:
da sult ir ez mite lob
eren gerûchen
3560 vnde fleizzechlichen sûchen.'
do er des redet genûk,
sin fluk in hinze himel trûk.

do kom im engegene
mit micheler menige
3565 die engel von des himels trone.
si lobten got schone,

D

sie erkomen uon dem gaste:
er troste sie v̄ saget in mære, 4050
wie der heilant geborn wǽre.
er sprah: ‚ivwer sorgen ir lat!
ich chunde iv waz got hat
nu gnaden begangen:
er hat an sih enpfangen 4055
198,30 daz bild siner hantgetat
durh den uaterlichen rat,
daz er die werlt alle
erlose uon dem ualle,
den der eriste menniske tet 4060
uz der wnneklichen stet
in ditze chlagliche tal.
nu ist div schulde v̄ der ual
Adames gar uerchorn;
iv ist der heilant geborn 4065
35 mit fleiske v̄ gebeine.
div frôde ist gemêine,
der schult ôh ir geniezen.
daz die wissagen gehiezzen
ivweren altfordern, 4070
daz ist nu sihtich worden.

ce Bethlehem schult ir gan,
da uindet ir sunder wân
in einer krippe daz kint,
des ensamet elliv riche sint, 4075
40 v̄ die reinen muter dabi.
ein urchunde iv daz si
der trostlichen warheit
die ich iv han furgeleit.'
als er in daz gesagete, 4080
in die lufte er sih gehabete
199,1 gein den himelisken tûren,
daz sie in chume churen.
do komen enkegin im sa
mit michelre menige da 4085
die chore sines gesindes,
der uf der erde in des

3534 ⟨rehte⟩ *F.* 3544 ein heilant *F.* 3545 ein hail mit f. u. m. g.
3547 dietē! 3548 verbiten 3557f. hol : lob *ist kein Reim des Originals,*
sicher hol : wol

A

vil loute svngen si do:
‚Gloria in excelsis deo!'

Die hirtten redeten vnder in:
3570 ‚wir sulen den vnsern sin
cheren hinze Christe,
daz er vns friste,
als der engel hat gesaget
vm daz kint daz div ma*get*
3575 der werlde hat gewunnen
ze frevden vn̄ ze wun*n*en.
verbum in principio
daz ist erschinen also
daz ⟨ez⟩ mens*ch*liche wat
3580 von siner diemvte hat,
pede fleisch vn̄ pain.'
si wurden schier des en ain,
ob in Dauides burge
daz zaichen funden wurde,
3585 daz in ir vngemach
der engel in zv̄ sprach.

si fůren eylande:
Christ si dar sande
da er was bewunden.
3590 do si daz vrkunde funden
vn̄ in der krippe sahen,
si begunden alle gahen,
vor liebe die hende winden
gen dem he*i*ligen kinde.
3595 si bugen sich nider an die knie:
hey wie lieb ez in ergie,
daz si mûsten schowen
die himilischen vrowen!
der nigen si schone.
3600 daz edel kint frone

D

erschinen geruhte
v̄ des mennisken heil suhte.
199, 5 sie huben uf un̄ lobeten got, 4090
siniv wnder v̄ sin gebo*t*,
sin gnade v̄ sine gute.
mit frolichem gemute
v̄ mit liebe sungen sie do:
‚Gloria in excelsis deo!' 4095

Die hirte redeten under in:
‚wir schulen den unsern sin
cheren hince Christe.
wîe zæme uns dehein friste?
10 daz uns der engel hat gesaget 4100
uon dem kinde v̄ der maget,
daz schvlen wir gerne sehen
v̄ gote ŏh beiehen
siner manchualten wnder.'

ennêin wrden sie dar under, 4105
ob in Davidis purge
daz zeichen funden wrde,
so scholte sie wol gelusten,
daz sie daz tûch chusten
15 da der werlt urlosare 4110
mit bedeket wære.
do furen sie ilande:
Christ si dar gesande
da er kint kintlichen lach,
v̄ sin diu reine pflach. 4115
als sie daz ersahen,
sie vielen en allen gahen
der herscefte ze fůzzen
mit zæhern also sûzzen.
20 sie sazten sih an div knie: 4120
owe wie lieb ez in ergie,
da sie in v̄ die frŏen
ensamet musen schŏen!

199, 5 gebote   3574 magt   *3576* wunen   *3579* mensliche
3590f. funden vn̄ *streicht B. s. 90*   *3594* heligen

A

riefen si do an,
daz von rehte lobt weip vnde man.

Die bezaichnunge,
ob die min trêge zvnge
3605 wol gezelen mohte,
wie wol mir daz tohte!
daz got bey der naht
daz reine kint geslaht
der werlde wolte zaigen,
3610 div ŝ was sin aygen
vn̄ auch immer wesen mûz,
da mit tet er vns pûz
der vinster also fraisam,
die bede weip vn̄ man
3615 dolten von der sunde
in dem abgrunde.
div naht vn̄ ir genibele
was so groz hie nidene
daz man si mohte greiffen;
3620 div wolte niht ab sleiffen
vnz daz vns der hailant
bey der magt wart gesant.
Nv sulen wir bey der blûmen
frolichen rûben
3625 vn̄ han gûte reste:
wolte wir wesen veste
vn̄ wolten an der stunde
dem laiden·hellehunde
vnser sele niht geben,
3630 so wir schieden daz leben,
daz wir got gehiezzen
do wir vns tovfen liezzen,
so moht wir bey der blûmen
mit frevden immer rûben.

Amen!

3635 **D**o Christ den hirtten tet bechant
vn̄ in sin botschaft sant,

do lebten manige kunige
edel vn̄ frumige,

D

uon herzeu rieffen sies an
v̄ cherten frolichen dan   4125
wider zû ir hute:
sus troste sie got der gûte.

Do Christ der wære hirte
sine botschaft bescherte
199,25 den hirten also smæhen,   4130
do waren da uerre v̄ nahen
manige riche kunige
v̄ herzogen frumige,
die herliche lebeten

A

 den er niht sant den boten sín.
3640 dar an er machte schin
 daz nieman so arm ist,
 wil der hailige Christ
 sin leben bewarn,
 er mege wol gevarn.

3645 niemen im versmahet,
 swer so zů im gahet.
 ia wolt er ovf der erden
 der schafe hirtte werden,
 die den tievel triegent
3650 vn̄ die sunde fliehent.

 dem wolfe wil er si nemen,
 vn̄ wil in immer geben

 so vollechliche waiden
 daz si vngeschaiden
3655 immer von den englen sint:
 so genedik ist daz kint.

 Daz geborn wart der reine
 Jesus Christus iu einem staine

 vn̄ in einer krippen lak,
3660 div red wol bedevten mak
 sin gůte manikvalten,
 die er vns wolte behalten
 vn̄ vns wolte leren.
 er ist der stain werde,
3665 der ane menschen hant
 von der felsen want
 vil schone waz gesniten;

D

v̄ ⟨in⟩ den eren swebeten: *4135*
den santer niht den engel sin.
daran líez⟨er⟩wesen schîn,
daz nîemen ist so arme,
der sin zuhte wil bewarne,
199, 30 so nider noch so ringe, *4140*
stat der sin gedinge
uaste an unsern trehtin,
er mûze im willekomen sin.
niemen im uersmahet:
der zu ime gahet *4145*
v̄ die sunde durh in lat,
der uindet ŏh hilfe v̄ rat,
daz er dem tieuil enpflivhet.
35 an dem mennisken got nîen
      schivhet
wân ungůte v̄ unreht; *4150*
ieglich guter ist sin chneht:
der diemutez herze treit,
dem ist sin gnade bereit.
er ist ŏh der beste hirte,
des schâf der ræzze wolf *4155*
      uerbirte,
wan er sie beschermen mak
v̄ behûtet sie naht v̄ tach
40 uor aller slahte leide
 v̄ git die ewîgen weide.

Daz Christ uf dem uelde *4160*
die armeklichen selde
in dem steine wolte haben,
v̄ daz geruhte uertragen
daz er in der krippe gelach,
div rede duten wol mach *4165*
200, 1 die sinen diemûte,
 v̄ die manchualten gute
die uns zeiget sine lere.
er ist der steine vil here
der ane mennisken hant *4170*
uon der uelsinen want
gesniten wart ane meile,

3644 gevaren 3645 versmaht *199, 35* den *199, 39* behûte

A

da wart div werlt mi*te*
vil wol behullet,
3670 bedechet vn̄ erfullet
vn̄ der yrdische rink:
dise keiserliche dink
die bezaichent daz lůk,
da in sin můter intrůk.

3675 er wolt mit siner arm*icheit*
geleichen vnser menscheit,
dem doch waz vndertan
der himel vn̄ der werlde plan.

In Christi natiuitate
3680 geschahen vil drate
siben zaichen zestet,
als vns daz bůch zelt.

daz waz daz eine
daz sich hůb saine
3685 ein circulus vm die sunnen,
do si was ensprungen.
der rink was guldein vil rot,
als der hailant gebot,
michel vn̄ weit:
3690 daz wart ᴁ noch seit
an dem himel nie gesehen,
als wir die bůch horen iehen.
den gewaltegen herren bedevtet daz,
der vns ie trostet paz vn̄ paz.

D

v̄ diu werlt uon dem têile
200,5 wart elliv behullet,
bedecket v̄ erfullet: *4175*

daz bezeichent der lůch,
da in sin můter intruch.
frî ist er uon sunden,
sin gewalt so groz zallen stunden
daz in nîemen mak ge-   *4180*
             mezzen:
des schulen wir niht vergezzen.
10 er ist aller steine beste,
erne lat die gruntveste
niht uallen noh wichen.
er wolte sich gelichen   *4185*
unserre armicheit
an der broden menniskeit,
dar umbe daz er uns erhube
uon mennesklicher trûbe
v̄ uns gæbe sin riche   *4190*
mit den engelen gliche.

15 **In** Christes natiuitate
geschahen vil drate
siben grozziv zeichen:
div schulen uns wêichen,   *4195*
daz wir unsir sinne
cheren ce siner minne.
ditze was daz êine
daz sich erhub seine
ein rinch umbe die sunnen,   *4200*
do sie was uf errunnen.
20 der rinch was guldin v̄ rot,
als ez der heilant gebot,
glantze michel v̄ wi*t*:
daz enwart e noh si*t*   *4205*
an dem himel gesehen,
so wir horen iehen.
des himels herren zeigte daz,
daz er ie baz vnde baz
uns armen wolte frŏen;   *4210*
sin wunder liez er schŏen.

3668 mitten   *3675* armůt   *200, 21* wite : site

A   **D**

<table>
<tr><td>

3695 ir sult auch wizzen vm daz
       golt:
der trûbe ez niht endolt,
ez ist schon vñ lieht;
ander gesmeide enmak nieht
sich da zv̂ genozzen:
3700 daz bedevt den kunek grozzen,
der im die krippe het erchorn
vñ ovf der erde wart geborn,
der bey dem gûten herzen
verdolt denheinen smerzen,
3705 der daz vil wol waiz,
wie er der werlde vmechreiz
cheren sol vñ slihten
vñ mit genade verrihten.

Gen deme kinde frone
3710 in der stat ze Rome
daz ander zaichen geschach,
daz ein michel olebach
ovz den kisilingen floz:
daz wunder douhte groz.

3715 bey dem geistlichen ôle
mvge wir kiesen wole
die gotes barmvnge,
die denhein zunge
fur mak bringen.
3720 ia sul wir des gedingen,
daz wir allenthalben
mit der selben salben
die wunden so bestreichen
daz vns div siech ⟨mûz⟩ entweichen.

3725 Ein lugelicher got,
der die sturme gebot,
volkweige vñ die streite,
der stûnt ze der zeite
datze Rome ôf einer sevle:

</td><td>

200, 25 ir wizzet ôh umbe daz golt:
der trube ez niht uerdolt,
ez ist schone v̄ lieht;
ander gesmide enmak nieht   4215
dar zu sih genozzen:
daz bedûtet den kunich grozzen,
der im die chrippe hete erchorn
v̄ hîen erde was geborn,
der bi den guten herzen   4220
verdolt neheinen smerzen,
30 der uon rehte daz wol weiz,
wîe er den witen umbechrêiz
mit gotlicher gute
bediv rihte v̄ behute.   4225

Gêin dem chinde frone
in der stat ce Rome
daz ander wnder gescah,
daz ein michel olebach
uz einem kisilinge floz: 4230
diu geschihte. duhte uil groz.
35 der stein was niht so herte
daz er sih des erwerte,
erne brâht daz ole mære
fure al die burgære.   4235
bi dem geistlichem ole
mugen wir kiesen wole
die gotes barmunge,
die deheine zunge
enmæhte furbringen.   4240
ia schulen wir des gedingen,
201, 1 daz wir allenthalben
mit der sûzzen salben
die wnden so bestrichen
daz div fule mûzze ent-   4245
         wichen.

Ein luglicher got,
der die sturme gebot,
bediv folchwich v̄ strite,
der stûnte an der cite
5 ze Rome hohe gesat;   4250

</td></tr>
</table>

3698 niht   3714 *kein* vil!   3717 div   3724 mûz *ergänzt F.*,
entweiche *M.*   3725 *ursprünglich wohl* ein vil, *vgl.* § 69 a.

A

3730 der tievel vngehevre
den hiezzen si Marte.

er het sey vil harte

betrogen vn̄ vorgesaget,
er solde vallen, so ein maget
3735 ein kindelin gebere   201, 10
daz ane vater were.

si wanden, daz ez nimmer wurde
daz ein magt ane mannes burde
immer kint getruge,
3740 wan ez were vngefûge.

Doch hiezzen si die reste
machen vil veste:
si leiten groz werk daran,
da mit div sevl moht bestan.
3745 als Christ do wart geborn,
do was ir werk verlorn:
div sevl sich do zarte,
so faste vn̄ auch so harte
daz si in allen gahen
3750 ir maister vallen sahen.
vil michel wart daz chrachen:
die levt mûsten erwachen;
von dem gebresten si erkomen;
erschuttet wart do Rome.
3755 von der alten trugenheit
got wolte mit der warheit
selbe rihten den stûl.

der tiefel schreiinde fûr
zv̄ anderen hellehunden,
3760 die da ligent gebunden

D

in erte elliv diu stat:
er was Mars genant
v̄ uil wîten erchant.
er hete die werlte betrogen
v̄ zu im gezogen,   4255
daz sie durh in alle taten
v̄ in ze gote haten.
der hete daz uorgesaget,
swenne so êin maget
ein degenkint gebære   4260
daz ane uater wǣre,
so muse er vallen zwâre.
sie wanten in der burge,
daz daz niemer wrde
daz maget kint truge   4265
ane mannes fuge.
doh hîezzen sie durh gwarheit
di valslichen gotheit
15 mit flizze starche uesten,
vnt allez daz sie westen,   4270
da sie mit scholte gestân,
daz lêiten sie daran.
do Christ wart geborn,
do was ir antwerch uerlorn:
diu sule sich do zarte,   4275
daz nîemen des gewarte,
untze sie en allen gahen
ir meister uallen sahen.
20 michel wart daz chrachen:
diu livte musen wachen;   4280
uon dem slage sie erchomen;
erschuttet wart do Rome.
uon der alten trugheit
got wolte mit der warheit
den stûle selbe reinen,   4285
v̄ zaigete daz man in einen
ze gote erchennen scholte.
als der tieuil do uerdolte
25 den slach uon himel so grozzen,
er fûr ze sinen genozzen   4290
sa uerstozzen in die helle
mit vil wêlichem geschelle.

3730 vngehevwer   *201, 8 l.* allez?   3734 magt   *201, 12* iemer
3754 Romen   *201, 21* erschutte

A

so vaste vn̄ so sere,
so daz er nimmer mere
dar ŏz mak geraichen:
daz waz daz dritte zaichen.

3765 Daz vierde zaichen daz
　　　　auch waz,
daz vnanimitas,
aller fride maiste,
mit des kaisers vollaiste
wart so gesworn
3770 daz der herre ovz erchorn,
der Augustus hiez,
denhainen gewalt niemen liez
an sinem reiche began.
der selbe fridesam man
3775 bezaichent vnsern hailant,
der von sunden vns enpant.

vns kom fride guoter,
do div vil edel mŭter
den sun mit armen vmbe vie,
3780 der den tiefel niht enlie
so vaste reichsen als ǽ,
lumen de patris lumine.

Augustus aber dahte,
daz er wol vol brahte
3785 an der heren Christes naht,
mit welichen dingen er maht
sin herschaft erzaigen

phaffen vn̄ layen.
in sinem gezelte er lak,
3790 sinen gewalt er wak:
div lant vn̄ div reich,
div gar fridelich

D

da ist er gebunden sere,
daz er niemer mere
her uz mak geræichen:　4295
daz ist daz dritte zêichen.

201,30 **D**az fierde wnder daz was
diu michel unanimitas,
aller fride meiste
mit des keisers uolleiste;　4300
der wart erhaben v̄ gesworn,
do Christ was geborn
an dem tage vil heren:
da wolter uns mit leren,
daz er der ware fride si　4305
da wir gnade uinden bi,
35 v̄ der uns sicher mache
von allem ungemache
v̄ uon des tievils gewalte,
des hohfart er ualte　4310
mit siner geinẘrte
v̄ der mêide geburte.
uns kom fride guter,
do diu reine muter
den sun umbevîe,　4315
der den ubeln tot niht enlîe
40 so uaste richsen als e.
dennoh brahter uns sælden me:
daz ist daz ewige leben,
daz er den sinen wil geben. 4320

202,1 Augustus aue gedahte
an der heren Christes nahte,
waz siner chrone tohte,
v̄ mit welhen dingen er mohte
sinen gwalt erzaigen mit　4325
　　　　gute
v̄ sin tugentriche gemute.
in sinem gezelt er lach
keiserliche als er pflach:
5 do frŏt er sich der riche
div im dienten uorhtliche,　4330
v̄ der manigen lande
div da in siner hande

3786 moht
Wernhers Maria.　　　　　　　　　14

A

       im ainen waren vndertan,
       wie die solten gestan,
3795 daz begunde er besorgen.
       an dem selben morgen
       do waz er worden en ain,
       da sin tugent an schain,
       daz alle die da wæren
3800 in den karcheren
       gevangen vn̄ gebunden,
       die niht gedingen kunden
       wider ir veiande,
       daz die eylande
3805 wurden ledek vn̄ frey.
       da wolte got sich selben pey
       lazzen erkennen,
       sin gůte manigen enden:
       der magede svn zier
3810 ze helfe kom er schier
       sinen lieben kinden:
       ab hiez er binden
       die keten also swere
       dar zv̂ der helle charchere,
3815 vn̄ ir tor vil vest*e*
       mŭste gar zepresten
       gen siner zv̂chumft:
       daz zaichen waz daz fumft.

       Welt ir daz sechste vernemen,
3820 so lat ivch sein gezemen:
       Augustus aber gebot
       in ernest . ane spot
       nahen vn̄ verren,
       alle die ir herren
3825 weren entrunnen,
       daz si wider sunnen
       haim vn̄ wurfen vm ir sůne
       gen ir hertůme.
       die daz gebot zebrachen,
3830 die můsen grozze rach*e*

D

       stŭnden ane widerstrit,
       wand nie uordes noh danah sit
       wart dehein keiser so mæ̂re, *4335*
       dem elliv div werlt wâre
       ensamet undertan:
       wie diu scholte gestan,
202,10 daz mŭser besorgen.
       an dem selben morgen   *4340*
       do was er worden ennein,
       da wol sin tugent anschêin,
       daz alle die der wæren
       witen in den charchæren
       geuangen v̄ gebunden,   *4345*
       die gedingen nîen chunden,

       daz man die liezze fri.
       Christ wolte dabi
15 sih selben lan erchennen
       v̄ sin goteheit nennen: *4350*
       der magede sun sŭzze
       mit gnadeklichem gruzze
       chom er sinen kinden:
       er hiez sie abebinden
       die cheten also swâre   *4355*
       da ze dem hellecharchæ̂re.
       die siner hilfe ie baten
       v̄ sin gebiten haten,
20 er loste sie mit siner chumfte:
       daz zeichen was daz funfte. *4360*

       Daz sehste schult ir horen
       mit willigen oren;
       daz zeiget ŏh hince got:
       Augustus aue gebot
       uber elliu siniv riche,   *4365*
       die ir herren frauelliche
       wæ̂ren entrunnen,
       daz die alle wîder sunnen,
25 v̄ daz sie ŵruen sŭne
       ze ir rehtem hertůme.   *4370*
       die daz gebot zebrachen
       v̄ die uolge uersprachen,

    3815 vesten   *3830* rachen

A	**D**
dolen vñ leiden:	die musen liden grozze not:
er wolte in niht en*t*lei*b*en.	in wart ertæilet der tot.
dreyzek tousent vñ mær	drizzich tvsent v̄ mere 4375
hiez der kvnik her	die hiez der furste here
3835 ze weinahten houpten,	durh die fra*u*el hŏpten:
die sein niht geloupten	die daz niht gelŏpten
daz im ernst were. 202, 30	daz ime ernest wære,
die ayslichen swere	die freisten leidiv mære. 4380
bezaichent die verworhten,	daz bezeichent die uerworhten,
3840 die da ane vorhten	die da wellent ane uorhten
dise wer*lt* bowent	dise werlte bûwen:
vñ anders niht getrowent	die schalke ungetrivwen
wan mit vollen leben:	hant sih gerihte*t* ze uehtin 4385
den ist auch ⟨niht⟩ vergeben	wider unseren trehtin,
3845 vñ genzlich vertailet,	der uns hat geheilet;
der helle ouf gesailet	so wirt ŏh in uerteilet
ir sele vñ leip,	sele unde lip ensamet, 35
ez sey man oder weip:	wan swer sih hie schamet 4390
	ze horen daz gotes wort,
	ez gerivwet in dort,
	so er sin buzze muz bestan:
des sol vns got erlazzen.	des geruche er *u*ns erlan
3850 wir mvgen vns gerne mazzen	
sundechlicher dinge	
in des herren minne:	
der die menscheit	der unser brodicheit 4395
mit siner gotheit	mit siner gotheit
3855 bedechet hat so schone,	bedechet hat so schone
der geit sich selben vns ze lone.	v̄ gît sih selben uns ze lone.
Daz sibende was ein sterne: 40	**D**az sibent was ein sterne:
daz bedevtet den mandelcherne	der dute den mandelcherne 4400
von Aaronis gerte,	uon Aaronis gerte,
3860 do die nuzze herte	do die nuzze whsen herte
wuchsen ovf dem dornein 203, 1	uf dem durrem zwîe.
zweie.	
div maget sant Marie	div maget sente Marie
div wart bezaichent da mit,	wart bezæichent damite, 4405
div mit kev⟨schlichem⟩ sit	div mit kivslichem site
3865 vñ ane man*n*es rat	v̄ ŏh ane mannes ra*t*
die mandeln vns geben hat.	die mandeln uns braht ha*t*.
ir nevbornes kint,	ir nivwegebornz kint

3832 enleiden   *3841* wert   *202, 33* gerihte   *3844* auch niht]
auch A, niht *F*.   *3865* manes   *203, 3* rate : hate

A

dem alle createvre vndertan sínt,

203, 5

der hiez daz der sterne louhte:

3870 die iuden daz wunder douhte.
die gelerten vn̄ die alten,
die witze chunden walten,
die sagten bey ir triwen,
ez bedout den kunik nivwen
3875 den div magt solte tragen:
si heten ez von den weissagen
vil dike vernomen,
daz er mit liehte solte chomen.

der sterne der den schein trûk,
3880 an dem abent er sich huob
vn̄ louhte vil schone
ob der krippe frone
vnz an die metein zeit.
ez iach des manik man seit,
3885 do er begunde ovf gen,
er were von Bethlehem
einen fûz niht entwichen:
daz was ein wunder michel.

Do der ahte tak
3890 nach siner geburte lak,
do liez er sich besneiden,
swie an sinem leibe
were denheiner slahte mail:
da mit erfulte er vnser hail.

3895 gehaizzen wart er Jesus:
der engel hær in alsus
der maide vor nante,
do er ire wart bekant.

D

ist so mahtik daz ime sint 4410
elliv riche undertan:
er hiez den sterne wolgetan
uon den wolchen ûfstigen.
do mohten ez niht uerswigen
die gelerten v̄ die alten: 4415
die sinnes chunden walten,
die sprachen zir trivwen,
iz bedûtet den kunich nivwen
den diu maget scolte tragen:
sie heten ez uon den wissagen 4420
uil dicke uernomen,
er muse mit liehte chomen,
wand er ôh uon nîehte
in dem ewîgen lîehte
hete geschafen elliu dinch, 4425
den himel v̄ den umberinch.

der sterne hub sinen schîn
an dem abent do diu kunigin
daz ware lieht gebar.
vil rehte cheret er dar 4430
da er was in dem steine
v̄ sin muter rêine,
unt gab in sîn urkunde
so lange untze an die stunde,
daz er die kunige vz erwêite 4435
vnt sie ze der selde belêite.

Do der ahtode tach
nah siner geburte gelach,
besniden er sich do lie,
swie an im wrde funden nîe 4440
deheiner slahte meil:
daz gescah durh unser heil.
wizzer was er denne der snê,
iedoh enlîez er im die e
uf der erde niht uersmahen, 4445
die wir schulen enpfahen.

geheizzen wart er Jesus:
der engel nant in alsus.

A

nv sul wir twingen vñ zamen
3900 des leibes gelust in sinem namen!

war zv̂ sol vns der leip
der vil armechlich geleit,
so div sele da von scheidet,
ob vns got niht enhailet?

3905 ⟨Ze⟩ Kaldea in der gegende weit
waren bey der selben zeit
benanter kunige drey
edel vñ frey
ovf einem tagedinge:
3910 si waren kûnilinge
alle vnder ainander;
si wolten mit ainander
trahten ir sache
frivntlich mit gemache
3915 vñ vil minnechlich,
vñ wolten an ir reich
beschaiden die terminunge:
die helde also iunge
die zewurfen vngerne.
3920 do kom der gotes sterne
mit micheler chrefte

zv̂ der herschefte.
die kvnige sich bedahten
bey dem schein den er brahte,

3925 daz in der schepfer
da mit gekundet wer.
in gab der ware gotes svn
den sin vñ auch den weistûm,
daz si zesamene swûren,

D

nu dewingen wir v̄ zamen
unser brode in sinem namen 4450
mit vil reinlichen siten!
wirne werden besniten
also uon siner lere,
wir muzzen uns sere
anen gotes hulde   4455
v̄ beliben unser schulde
203, 30 totliche uberladen
der armen sele ze schaden;
wand ez ir allez bechumet
swaz der lip hie gefrumet, 4460
so diu schidunge ergat:
sælich der da iht rehtes hat.

Chaldea ist ein lant
an der schrift also genant:
da stunden nah der sage 4465
drie kunige an Christes tage
35 uf einem tæidinge;
die waren kunlinge:

sie wolten underscheiden
ir riche vū ir eigen,   4470

want sie zeŵrfen ungerne.
do chom der liehte sterne
40 mit grozzem schîm, mit nivwer
chrefte
gahes zu der herschefte.
die herren sih berieten,   4475
waz der sterne scholt gebieten,
v̄ waz er dinges mæinte.
ir wisheit sih uerêinte,
daz in der schepfære
damit gekundet wære.   4480

204, 1 ze samen sie do sŵren,

A

3930 swo der sterne hine fůre,
daz si cherten allez nach:
zů der verte waz in gach.
dromedarios si gewunnen,
die helde sich ovf swngen.

3935 daz zaichen für in allez vor
in den luften enpor;
durch die werlt praite
gab ez in gelaite,
vnz ez si brahte in daz lant
3940 da geborn waz der hailant.

Do die kvnige frey,
die da haizzent magi,
komen ze Jerusalem,
ein schef wolten si da bestên.
3945 ze rate wurden si des,
swen der vbel Herodes
ir verte wurde innen,
er het ez ze vnminnen,
daz si in dem lande weren
3950 vñ in niht ensehen.
·do giengen die herren frumich
vil palde fur den kunik:

der wirt also reich
enpfienk sey frumichlich.
3955 si fragten vm daz kindelein
daz da kaiser solte sein
vber die iuden alle:

do erkomen si mit schalle
die der stete pflagen.
3960 der wirt begunde fragen
die vnchunden geste,

D

zehante daz sie furen
swar sie daz zeichen leite.

ir ravit waren gerêite,
da sẃngen sih ûf die helde   4485
vnt cherten gêin der selde
des kindes v̄ der muter.
got uater guter
204,5 der wîste in daz lieht allez for
in den luften enbor   4490
durh die werlt brêite:
als er in den wech sæite,
untzer sie braht in daz lant
da geborn was der heilant.
div liebe hîez sie gahen,   4495
wan sie sih uersahen
gotes in mennisken ahte,
der in wol genaden mæhte.

10 Do dise kunige drie,
mutes wise, der sunden frîe, 4500
ze Jherusalem kamen,
ein friste sie da namen
mit gemêinlichem rate,
daz ez der kunich iht hate
ze leide oder ze unminne, 4505
als er des wrde inne
daz sie in dem lande wæren
vnde in iedoh uerbæren.
15 do giengen die recken ziere
fur den ubeln wirt schiere: 4510
Herodes was er genant
v̄ rihsent uber daz lant.
er enpfie sie wol furwâre;
do huben sie uf div mære
non dem nivwen kinde   4515
v̄ dem sterne der in luhte.
der kunik enpfieng ez swînde;
20 div rede in fremde duhte:
al der hof erchom ioh div stat.
der herre sie aue bat,   4520
daz sie im furbaz sæiten
v̄ der warheit bereiten

3930 swo!   204,5 enbore   3951 giegen   3961 vnchunde

A

von wannen si daz westen,
daz daz kint mǣre
nv geboren wêre.

3965 Des antwurten im die herren: 204,25
,wir sein gevaren verren
da div werlt hat ende.
in disem ellende
sûche wir daz selbe kint
3970 durch daz vnder ime sint
engel vñ levte.
ia muget ir auch bedevte
sine kumft wizzen gerne:
von himel kom ein sterne
3975 da wir waren alle drey:
michel schone waz im bey.

do wurde wir eu ain
daz wir daz kindel sûchteu haim.

ỏf des weges arbait
3980 gab vns der sterne gelait
her vnz an daz tor;
da entweich vns der sterne vor.
nv want wir hie vinden
daz himilische kindel

D

umbe daz kint so here,
des name, gwalt v̄ ere
so chreftich scholte sin, 4525
wîe in daz wǣre worden schîn.

Die herren *im* antwrten
mit zuhtlichen worten:

,wir suchen daz selbe kint
durh daz untir ime sint 4530
bediv engel v̄ lîute:
daz zǣiget er wol ze dûte.
ir meget ez horen gerne:
uon himel chom ein sterne
da wir waren alle dri. 4535
so michel schonheit was im bi
30 daz sie niemen furbringen mach.
do gv̂nnen wir lieben tach,
wande wir an den stunden
uon gotes gute erfunden 4540
waz daz wnder mêinte.
div schrift uns daz beschêinte,
35 wîe daz zeichen scholt erschinen,
so Christ heilant den sinen
ze helfe wolte chomen: 4545
also heten wirz uernomen.
do wrden wir ze rate,
daz wir strîchen drate
die herschaft ze suchen.
v̄ ob sin got wil geruchen, 4550
so mugen wir niht erwinden
vntze wir die heimut vinden,
40 die daz kint besezzen hat
dem al div werlt ze dienste stat.
205, 1 siu sterne unser wisel wart 4555
v̄ gab uns froliche uart
untze her an daz burgetor;
da entwêich er uns uor.
do gedingeten wir zware
daz unser heil hie wǣre, 4560
v̄ ỏh hie wrden gewert
des unser herze sere gert.

204, 25 in

A

3985 vñ sine mv̊ter sv̊zze,
    div wol mak sorgen pv̊zzen.'

Herodes der verworhte
siner æren er vorhte,
so daz kint begunde
3990 reichsen. zestunde

hiez er die iuden
gedenken vñ gehugen,

ob si westen den list
wa der hailige Christ
3995 solte werden geborn.
michel was sin zorn.

si sprachen: ‚ze Bethlehem
sol div geburt ergên.'

die drey kvnige er bat,
4000 so si komen an die stat
da si daz kint funden,
daz si ze snellen stunden

im ainen boten sanden,

daz er ze den selben landen
4005 chom auch an des kindes fûz,
daz siner sunde im wurde pûz.

D

205, 5 wir wolten daz kint eren
    v̄ sinen gewalt uil heren
ze den sinen fuzzen   4565
diemutekliche gruzzen.'

Herodes der uerworhte
sines riches er do uorhte;
er gewan manigen mut,
waz im ze tûn wære gût: 4570
er gedaht daz er mit swerten
sin riche muse beherten.
10 do besant er di wîsen,
die geerten v̄ die grisen
die der buche pflagen;   4575
er begunde sie fragen,
wes div schrift v̄ die wissagen
              iæhen,
vnt wâ sie sih uersæhen
daz Christes geburt scholte ergan,
dem elliv riche undertan   4580
15 v̄ diensthaft musen sin.
die herren taten im daz schin:
Bethlehem sie benanten,
want sie daz erchanten,
daz in div maget gebære   4585
div uon Dauit komen wære.
die dri kunige er do bat,
so sie komen an die stat
daz sie daz kint fereisten,
daz sie daran leisten   4590
20 des er sie gebate,
daz sie boten drate
nah im hiezzen ilen:
er wolt ȯh ze den wilen
sich bieten an sinen fûz,   4595
daz im der sorgen wrde buz
v̄ al siner missetate
die er gefrumet hate.
die sûzze der worte er bot
v̄ ahtet den bittern tot   4600
25 tȯgenliche in dem mute,
der ubel v̄ der ungute.

3985 sv̊zzen   3995 geboren

A

Die kvnige namen vrloup;
si heten ninder ovfschoup.
do si ŏz der stat
4010 komen ŏf irs weges pfat,
der sterue louht in auer sa,
den kunigen von Kaldea.
do weiste si der sterne,
den si da sahen gerne,

4015 in daz hous rehte,
da si vnsren trehten
solten beschowen
vn̄ die vil edelen vrowen
div in hete getragen:
4020 ia kund iv nieman gesagen
wie liebe si in gedahten.

daz opfer daz si brahten
daz mv̊zze vns wegen
ze dem ewigen leben.
4025 Si sŭchten *venie* lange
mit lob vn̄ mit gesange.

der eine trŭk in der haut
ein golt messe wol gebrant:
da mit bedevt er die kraft
4030 v̄n sin hohe herschaft.

der ander gab den weirŏch,
fur vnsern herren kniet er auch:

D

Die kunige urlŏp namen;
do sie do wider kamen
an ir wech uz der stete, *4605*
nah ir wnske v̄ ir bete

ruchete sie got gewerne
sins geleites an dem sterne.
er kom in aue v̄ fŭre in vor
rehte uon dem purgetor *4610*
205, 30 untze an die sæligen stat
da sih nider hete gesat
mit dem kinde div maget.
div sælde in wol behagete
v̄ erhvb ir herze so, *4615*
daz sie wrden starche fro
v̄ lobeten gotes tŏgen
div sie sahen mit ir ŏgen.
sus brahte sie ir wîsel dar,
der liehte v̄ wolgevar, *4620*
35 v̄ gestunt da ze stet;
damit er in ze wise tet,
daz sie furbaz nîen scholten,
ob sie got eren wolten.
die fursten in daz hus draten *4625*
mit ir opfer, daz sie haten
uon richem willen bereit.
fur daz kint v̄ die meit
vîelen sie herzekliche.
ir mut was uerstantliche, *4630*
40 want den sie mennisken sahen
der gotheit sie im iahen,
v̄ daz sie ane meil wære
diu in mŭter gebære.
206, 1 der eine truch in der hant *4635*
die goltmassen wolgebrant:
damit bedŭter die chraft
v̄ die keiserlichen herschaft
die der kunich aller kunige hat,
dem daz golt wol ze mazze *4640*
5 stat.
der ander brahte wirŏch:
daran erzaiget er ŏch

4025 wenik

A	**D**

da mit vns kvnt wart
daz er were ein æwart.
4035 Der dritte hin fur gahte,
mirren er dem kinde brahte:
da bezaiget er mit
sinen tot, wan æ was sit,
swa man toten begrůb, 206, 10
4040 daz man die mirren dar trůg.

damit si sine gůte,
sinen gewalt, sine diemv̊te
habent wol beslozzen:
des habent si wol genozzen.

4045 **D**o die gotes holden
des nahtes slaffen wolden

vn̄ kurzeweile wolten haben,
ein engel kom in das gadem;
der eilte die rechen
4050 frolichen wechen:
er sagt in das Herodes
gedaht hiete des,
daz er daz kint erslůge.
er gebot daz sey ir wech trůge
4055 anderhalben durch daz lant;
darume were er dar gesant.

Do si den morgen sahen,
vrloup si namen
ze der milten kuniginne:
4060 div grůzte sey mit minne.
do si dannen schieden,
si kusten an die wiegen
da ir herre inne lak:
daz waz in ein lieber tak.

4065 do si hine fůren,

---

daz er got wære v̄ ewart,
der al die werlte bewart.
der dritte mirren darbot: 4645
damit urkundet er den tot
den er sit an dem cruce leit.
ia was do ein gewonheit,
daz man toten mit mirren behielt,
daz ire dehein fůle wielt. 4650
daz opfer was bezæichenlich,
lobesam v̄ wn̂neklich.
ia heten sie fur ware
des kindes herschaft mære,
sin gotliche gůte 4655
v̄ des todes diemute
an der gebe wol beslozzen:
15 des hant sie non rehte genozzen.

Die lieben gotes holden,
do sie des nahtes slafen 4660
scholden,
ein engel liehter in erschein
v̄ gebot daz sie hêim
ein ander strazze musen uârn;
er sprah: ‚ir schult daz bewarn,
20 daz ir den kunich iht me sehet, 4665
v̄ ime des ueriehet
wa daz kint mit der muter si,
want untrivwe wonet im bi.
anders hat er gedaht
denner ivh habe inne braht: 4670
er wil den heilant fliesen;
des schulet ir in uerkiesen.'
do sie den morgen sahen,
sie begunden gahen
25 ze der milten chuniginne: 4675
div gruzte sie mit minne.
mit vrlôbe sie dan schieden
v̄ chusten an di wiegen
da ir herre inne lach:
daz was in der liebeste tach 4680
den sie gelebet haten.
des engels gebot sie taten
vnt namen in eine chrumbe

A

ein anderen wek si erkuren;
si wolten sich behůten,
ob Herodes wolte wůten,
daz er mit siner schande
4070 ir reise niht erwande.
si fůren in ir gegene:
got mit sinem segene
braht sey alle sant
haim wider in ir lant.

4075 Do geschach ze perhtnahten,
als wir ez kunnen ahten,
dannoch zaichen me,
do vns got die nivwen æ
sazte mit der toufe,
4080 da wir vns inne sloufen.
ez kom auch an den selben tak,
des sich div werlt frewen mak
in den namen drein,
danne wir komen sin.
4085 nv dienet im genot,
wan er verwandelot
daz wazzer ze weine!
die zwelf poten seine
wurden da mit veste.
4090 er machet ŏz den gesten
die lieben housgenoz:
do si div zaichen groz
an ir maister sahen,
der gothait si veriahen.
4095 die drey sache alle
sint an den tak gevallen:
an dem selben tage
sul wir gote chlagen
alle vnser missetat,
4100 die wir von des tiefels rat
ovf vns eilen vazzen
mit neide vn̄ mit hazze,
seit vns div můter ie getrůk.
⟨. . . . .
4105 an der trouten vrowen,
der genade m̊z vns beschowen.

D

ioh ein ander uart umbe.
206, 30 sus mit flizze sie behůten,   4685
ob Herodes wolte ẘten,
daz er sie doh niht geschenden
noh der reise mæht erwenden.
sie furen in ir gegene:
got in sinem segene   4690
brahte sie hêin gesunde
ze einer unlangen stunde.

4079 toufen   4094 im veriahen F.

A

Nach den sechs wochen, 206,35
als div zeit waz gesprochen,
do braht div maget here
4110 mit micheler ære
hinze chirchen iren sun;
si douht ir daz wesen frum,
daz si die æ behielte,
swie si der kevsche wielte.

4115 si zunte grozze kerzen;
si was an ir herzen
vil louter vn̄ fro;
si legte turteltouben zwo
auf den altere,
4120 daz ez ir opfer were.

dar chom der alte Symeon;
der enpfienk daz kunichliche lon,
daz zaichen sunderlich,
daz im got der reich
4125 mahte wol gelaisten
⟨. . . . .⟩
der was siech vn̄ blint.
do er daz here kint
an sinen arm genam,
4130 do gesach der hailige man:
ovf taten sich seine augen,
er begunde vmbe schowen
vn̄ lobt den herren den er sach:
sin lob daz er sprach
4135 daz vinde wir an den bůchen,
so wir ez wellen sůchen.

D

Vber die wochen sehse,
do sie des zit wesse,
do braht div maget gute 4695
mit frŏderichem mute
hinze chirchen ir sun,
als div e gebot ze tûn.
daz reht sie wol behielt,
swie sie der kivskeit wielte, 4700
diu in dem himel oben
iemer ist ze loben.

40 sie zunte ir liehte cherzen,
div îe in dem herzen
207, 1 liehter was denne div sunne, 4705
aller engele wnne.
zwô turteltuben sie brahte,
da ir got mit gedahte,
wan under den nogeln allen
niht me lebet ane gallen, 4710
niht so gutes v̄ so reines.
ane die bedorfte deheines
5 andern opferes div reine,
diu mûter ist v̄ maget eine.
dar chom der alte Simeon; 4715
dem hete got ze lon
sines gedinges daz geben,
daz er so lange mvse leben
untzer den waren heilant
enpfienge in sine hant, 4720
v̄ in froliche gesæhe
des der himel ze herren iæhe.
10 do hub er in ûf mit frŏde
des herzelieber beschoude
v̄ des gnaden er gerte. 4725
er sprah: ,nu bin ich gewerte,
herre, des ich îe bat.
du hast mich braht an die stat
daz ih din heil gesehen han.
nu scholt du mich varn lân, 4730
15 herre, in dinem fride
durh des liehtes underdige
daz du der werlte hast gesant:
herre, daz han ich erkant.'

4114 kevse   4122 kunichlche   4126 mit siner volleiste *ergänzt F.*
4134 lobt

A

Ein witebe div hiez Anne;
div was gewesen lange
in dem goteshouse
4140 des nahtes ane grouse,
daz si sich niht envorhte,
noch anders niht enworhte
wan daz si irs gebetes hûte.
div raine vn̄ div gûte
4145 zaigte ovf den hailant
mit dem vingere vn̄ mit der hant,
vn̄ nam daz kindele zehant
daz si in dem tempel vant,
vn̄ iach daz ez wære
4150 der werlde schepfere,

der sele trost vn̄ ir genist.
ez gewan der heilige Christ

ein vrkunde herlich:
er het vm sich
4155 gesament die gûten
die sines gebotes hv̂ten,
sin diern vn̄ sin knehte
die im dienten rehte.
von got sey wir allesamt
4160 an disen dingen gemant,
so wir ze chirchen gen,
daz wir gezogenlichen sten
vn̄ sine herschaft
von aller vnser kraft
4165 minnen vn̄ mainen,
ob aller werlte in einen.

ez sulen vnser sinne
sam die kerzen brinnen

D

Ein witwe diu hiez Anne; *4735*
diu was gewesen lange
in dem gotes hûse
des nahtes ane grûse,
daz sie ⟨ir⟩ nien uorhte.
anders sie niht enworhte *4740*
207,20 wan daz sie ir gebetes hute.
div stæte v̄ diu vil gute
zæigete uf den heilant

vnt umbeviench in zehant;

sie sprah daz er ware *4745*
der werlte schepfære,
der mit mennisklicher wat
sin herschaft bedecket hat.
er wærez der riche Christ,
25 der rehten trost, der armen *4750*
genist:
do heter urkundes genuch.
div muter div in truch
uil werde ir da gesah:
sin lop daz was ir gemach.

von gote birn wir alle samet *4755*
an disen dingen gemanet,
so wir ze chirchen gen,
daz wir da zuhteklichen sten,

30 v̄ daz wir uon herzen meinen
ob al der werlte in einen *4760*
der uns uon nihte geschuf:
unser gebet v̄ unsern rv̂f
schulen wir an in wenden.
ia mag er wol uerenden
swaz uns sorgen obelit. *4765*
er ist der die gnade git
div iemer wert ane wanch,
aller wisheit anvanch.
35 er ist ŏh diu ware minne,
diu da unser sinne *4770*

207,27 gescach *H.*   *207,28* allen   *4160* genant

A

in geistlichem fiwer,
4170 vñ vnser sele ze stiwer
sule wir wesen alle
sam div toube ane galle:
so wirt vns gegeben
daz æwige leben,
4175 daz wir danne beschowen
an ende mit der vrowen.

Do daz mere kom geflogen 207, 40
daz Herodes was betrogen
von den kunigen dreyen,
4180 vor laide begunde er schreien
als er toben wolde.
er sprach, daz er mit golde
si alle widerwege,
ob si gebunden legen.
4185 er hiez in nach reiten,
sůchen also weiten;
er iagt in nach mit fleizze:
er wolt in iteweizzen,
do in Christ kom ze handen,
4190 daz si im niht poten sanden
als si heten gelobt:
des het er sich nach ertobt,
daz si im entwichen waren, 208, 1
vñ ir niht moht gevahen.

4195 do saz er ze rate,
wie er mohte drate
sinen zorn rechen:
des eilte er sich besprechen
mit ⟨sinen⟩ argisten,
4200 die des keine friste
noch pite wolten haben,
si mv̊sten erslahen
die ainvaltigen menige,
div kint in al der gegene.
4205 si rieten allesant,
daz er die kint vber alle sin lant

D

erzunten sol mit sinem vîvre.
dazu hat er uns ze stiure

sine muter geben,
die uns daz ewige leben
uil wol mak erwerben,   4775
die in ir hulden ersterben.

Do daz mære chom geflogen
daz Herodes was betrogen
uon den kunigen drien,
uor leide began er schrîen   4780
als er toben wolde.
er sprah, daz er sie mit golde
wider wæge alle
in ze schanden v̄ ze ualle,

daz sie im niht boten sanden, 4785
do in Christ chom ze handen,
45 als sie heten gelobet.
do was den herren so gezoget
daz sie wol entwichen waren,
daz er nîen mohte ire   4790
geuaren.
doh hiez er in nah riten
v̄ suchen also witen:
do daz niht uervie,
ze rate er mit grimme gie

5 mit sinen mortgelichen;   4795
die rieten ŏh im tobelichen,
daz man div kint elliv ersluge
so gahes mit der fuge
daz Christ under in uerdurbe
e daz er uerborgen wrde.   4800

4177 Do!   4181 wolte   4190 ponten   4199 den ergänzt F.
4200 fristen   4201 han   4205 allesant!

A

vm Bethlehem toten hiezze,
noch deheines genesen liezze;
swas mannes bilde het,
4210 daz man die tote zestet.
do cherte der man grimme
alle sine sinne
wie er daz vol brehte.
er sazte in sein æhte
4215 die kindischen barn,
die vnschuldik waren.
So we dir vntriwe daz du bist!
si wanden daz ir boser list
ze got verholen were.
4220 des tievels trugenere
die waren erblendet,
gehonet vñ geschendet:
Der Magede sun vil wol genas;
daz Herodis wille waz,
4225 daz enmohte niht geschen.
ein engel chom ze Bethlehem;
Joseben er manot harte,
daz er daz kint bewarte;
er hiez in wesen munter
4230 vñ sagt im daz wunter
der kunftigen sorgen,
div dannoch was verborgen.

er ⟨hiez⟩ in fueren Jesum
verre in Egyptum
4235 vnder die haydinische diet.
mit fleizze er im daz riet,
daz er sich da enthabte,
vnz er im auer sagte
wanne er solt wider chêren
4240 mit dem kinde hêren.

Joseph der vil weise,
als er ovz dem paradeise
also gewarnet wart,
er hûb sich schier an die vart

D

So we dir untriwe daz du bist!
sie wanten daz der list
da ze got uerholn wære.
des tieuels uolgære
die waren daran erblendet, 4805
gehonet ṽ geschendet:
der magede sun uil wol genas;
daz Herodis wille was,
daz enmohte niht ergen.
ein engil chom ze Bethlehem; 4810
Joseben er anharte,
daz er daz kint bewarte;
er hiez in wesen muntir
ṽ seit im ŏh dar untir
die kumftigen sorgen, 4815
div dannoch was uerborgen
in des kunges eitirgem rate.
er mant in ilen drate,
daz er furte den heilant
uerre in Egiptelant 4820
under die heideniske diet.
daz gebot er ṽ gerîet,
daz er sih da enthabete,
untzer im aue sagete.
des frôte sih diu maget mit 4825
dem alten,
daz er scholte ⟨behalten⟩
daz unschuldige Christes blut,
daz so gnadik unde gût.

Do Josep gewarnet wart,
er hub sih sa an die uart 4830

208, 10

15

20

4217 wir   4225 gesein A, ergen F.   4230 wunder   4233 ⟨hiez⟩ F.
208, 20 ⟨behalten⟩ H.

A

4245 vñ fuor des nahtes danne
von dem leihten manne
vñ von den gar verwazzen,
die iren sin heten verlazzen
wider daz edele hertům,
4250 daz si an im wolten tůn
frayse vñ vnpilde.

do fůr er vber daz gevilde
vñ begunde von in kêren;

sin lob wolt er mêren
4255 bey der haidenischen diet
da er gegen schiet,
daz sich ir hail mert,
vñ sich ir geloube verkert,
ob si sich liezzen toufen,
4260 in rehtes leben sloufen.

Herodes der tumbe
der hiez do rennen vmbe,
die sinen wůtreiche
hiez er grimmechliche
4265 die degenkint verliesen,
swa si mohten kiesen
die bey zwain iaren
von ir můter komen waren,
a bymatu et infra.
4270 er hiez si allenthalben da
sinen willen laisten

D

uil snelle v̄ unbedrozzen.
der di werlt hat beslozzen   208, 25
vnt elliu dinch in siner hant,
der wolte ditze irdiske lant
mit ungemache buwen: 4835
er floch die ungetrivwen.
die engele waren im bi.
sin můter edile v̄ fri
fure des nahtes dan,
mit ir der uil rêine man   4840
der sie bediu berůchte.
die fremden Christ besuchte.
der mane bot im sinen schîn.   30
der in der pfallenze sin
uerdolt neheine vinster,   4845
die ivden lie er ze der winster;
er wolte mit den heiden sin lop
gemeren
v̄ zu den gnadekliche cheren,

daz sie sich tȯfen liezzen   35
unt im dienest gehîezzen.   4850

Swaz der tieuil angetreit,
ih wêiz er sich niemer geleit
untzer daz uol bringet;
swa er iê nah ringet,
daz chan er wol bestæten   4855
mit bitterlichen ræten.
Herodes der tumbe
der hiez do rennen umbe
al die sinen wtrîche;   209, 1
er hiez sie grimmekliche   4860
die iungen degen uerliesen,
swa sie daz mæhten kiesen
daz sie in den zwêin iaren
uon můter chomen wæren,
a bimatu et infra.   4865
er hiez sie allenthalben da
sinen willen leisten   5

208, 31 vinster : vinster   *4257* hailt

A

æ daz man ez erfraischte.

Die boten sich ovf swungen,
in die purch si drungen
4275 div Bethlehem was genant:
si têten fraise bekant
mit grimmegem hazze.
si liefen in die gazze,
div swert si enbarten,
4280 den herten tot si garten;
si ruktens bey den vahsen,
div kint vngewachsen;
div houp*t* si in abe slûgen,
die si niht begrûben:
4285 si liezzen si alle ligen.
si mohten niht gesigen,
wan si sich niht enwerten:
des leibes si sei beherten.

si lieffen zewette
4290 von bette ze bette,
von fiwer ze fiwer
in der purkmower
in selben ze schanden.
si trûgen an ir handen
4295 die plûtegen waffen:
reht alsam ze den schaffen
die wolfe zǔ springent
vnz si sei nider bringent,
also tobten ⟨die⟩ diebe
4300 ir herren ze liebe.

Do si div kint marbe
inrehalb der purge

D

e iz díu livte uereisten
daz der schade wære ergangen:
der wolf was mit zorne   4870
      benangen.
Die boten sih ufsŵngen,
in die stat sie drungen
div Bethlehem heizzet.
ir herze was gereizzet
209, 10 mit êitirigem hazze.   4875
sie furen uon gazzen ze gazze,
div swert sie erbarten,
den grimmen tot sie garten;
sie zuhten bi den uahsen
diu kint ungewahsen;   4880
div hǒbet sie abeslugen,
bêin v̄ arme genugen,
v̄ rigen siv an div wafen
div bi den ammen slafen
15 scholten an ir brusten.   4885
owî wes mahte sie gelusten
die sogetanen morttaten!
der tieuil hete sie uerraten
v̄ darzu geschundet,
ane des rat niemen sundet.   4890
die gesellen der mêintate
die ilten uil drate
20 rehte alse umbe we*t*te
uon bette ze bette,
uon fîure ze fivre   4895
inrehalp der burchmure,
in selben ze schanden,
vnt trugen in den handen
die blutigen wêre,
sam sie mit einem here   4900
wichlich haten gestriten.
mit wlfinen si*t*en
25 tobeten dise diebe
ir herren ze liebe
durh sin unherez gebo*t*   4905
wider die nature v̄ got.

Do sie diu kint furbrahten,
an div sie uahten

4283 houp   *209, 20* wêite   *209, 24* sitten   4299 ⟨die⟩ *F.*   *209, 26*
gebote : gote

A

gequelten mit arge,
do roumten si die zarge.
4305 si tailten sich in die gegene:
da slûgen si die menige
beide arm vñ reiche   209, 30
alle geliche.
si gedahten an des kuniges wort:
4310 mit fleizze stiften si daz mort;
si zukten sei ze fluste
den mûtren ab der bruste;
si polten an die wente
die fuezze vñ auch die hente:
4315 si enwessen waz si rachen.
als si sey durch stachen,
von in ran milich fur daz plût;
daz gab in grimmigen mût: 35
swie so daz spunne
4320 von den brusten runne,
doch kunden die zagen
ir wûtens niht verhaben,
vnz si gar lagen tot.
do wainten vil genot

4325 die mueter die daz sahen;
si begunden sich roufen vñ slahen. 40
des sint si nv gesellen
des tiefels in der helle.
Do div slaht gefrumet was,
4330 vñ der kinde denhaines genas
in allem dem chraizze,
do begunde wainen haizze
den schaden vil sere
ein vrowe hiez Rachele:
4335 vil harte si daz mûte, 210, 1
daz si in dem plûte
ir lieben frivnt sach sweben.
do wart ir ayniges leben
der vrowen gar vnmere;
4340 si erzaigte ir vngebere
dahaime vñ ovf der strazze:
si wainte ane mazze.
si wolt ovf der erden 5
nimmer mer getrostet werden.

D

unmanliche mit arge,
do rumten sie die zarge 4910
vnt tæilten sich in die gegen,
ôh da nider legen
uil maniger muter frôde
in ir aller beschôde.
witen wart div slahte: 4915
diu zal ist uz der ahte.
owe der stæininen herzen,
div den muterlichen smerzen
ie mahten uertragen!
owi welh ŵfen, welh chlagen, 4920
da div kint waren in der not
halplebentige ⁊ halp tot,
da si lagen allen ende,
hie die fuzze, dort die hende!
owê da man sie hin zuchte 4925
⁊ in daz leben abdrukte,
da der kinde blut nidergoz
den uerkolten in die schôz!
swem ie herzeliep gescah,
der weiz herzeleides un- 4930
      gemach,
waz herzeliep chumbers hat
daz mit herzeleide gestat.

Do der mort gefrumet was,
unt nehein degenkint genas
in allem dem chreizze, 4935
do bewêintez uil heizze
⁊ uil sere div lantschaft.
so swære was des leides chraft:
an den wirten ⁊ den frôen
mûse man iamer schôen; 4940
die stete lagen frôdelose,
die muter sinnelose,
wan sie trostes nîen haten.
iedoh hat sie nu beraten
div grozze gotes gute, 4945
die mit ir selbes blute
⁊ mit der kinde unschulde
erwrben sine hulde

209, 29 si wolten *oder ähnlich zu ergänzen* M. *4328* hellen *4331*
allen *4332* begunden A, begundens *F.* *4334* Rachel *4344* nimmêr *F.*

A

4345 ir mvgt wol wizzen daz,
    daz der mûter manigev waz
    die div kint erzugen:
    der hôret ir niht gehugen
    wan Rachel alaine.
4350 da mit so mvge wir mainen
    die hailigen christenhait,
    div mit grozzer arbait
    vil diche hat gerungen
    vñ schaden auch gewunnen
4355 an ir vil lieben kinden,
    die si niht vberwinden
    mak ouf diser erden,
    der fluste si niht mak getrostet werden.

    Got selbe wolde rechen,
4360 den vbermŷt zebrechen
    den der wuetrich fûrt
    gegen Christes geburt.
    er wold im an gesigen:
    des mŷste er schemelich geligen.

4365 Herodes begunde siechen,
    daz ouf der pette ziechen
    swebte plût vnde wark;
    div suht sich niht verbark
    div im den leip schutte.
4370 got maz im mit dem mutte
    der vnsælden also vil
    daz er mohte denhain spil
    beschowen ovf der erde.
    ez stank der vnwerde
4375 an allen sinen liden.

D

v̄ die ewigen reste:
daz ist aller frôden beste.   4950

    Got selbe wolte rechen,
die ubermut zebrecheu
die Herodes furte
ze Christes gǣinwrte.
gote wolter angesigen: 4955
do mûser schantliche geligen
ze einer churzen friste.
waz hulfen in die liste
der sin herze uol swebete,
do er mit untrivwen lebete? 4960
waz hilfet daz silber oder golt,
da der bose niht uerdolt
rehter tugende invart?
der schatze niemen des bewart,
erne muzze ersterben   4965
v̄ ze valwiske werden.

15 Herodes begunde siechen,
daz uf den betteziechen
swebet blût v̄ warch;
div suht div wart also starch 4970
daz er gar fulen began.
nie mennisk mêre note gewan
v̄ unsælde also uil.
deheine wnne noh dehein spil
maht er geschôen uf der erde 4975
v̄ smachte vil unwerde
20 an allen sinen liden.

210, 10 ze einer churzen friste.

4349 rache   4351 div hailige   4362 gengen   210, 15 betteziehen
4375 *im Original wohl* an allen den s. l.

A	**D**
sin schatz mohte im niht gefriden,	sin gewalt enmohte daz niht
	gefriden,
er můse laidichliche	erne muse leitlichen
von sinem yrdischem reiche	ligen uor armen v̄ richen. *4980*
varen in die hell*e*	
4380 zv̊ sinen wůtgesellen.	
mit den nagelen zart er sine hout,	Mit den nageln zart er die hut,
er hete vil armichliche*n* lout.	er was uil armeklichen lůt.
die weisen arzaten	die wisen arzate
kvnden im niht geraten	chunden im niht geraten
4385 mit wurzen noch mit salben. 210, 25	mit wrzen noh mit salben. *4985*
er prach sich allenthalben	er brah sih allenthalben
ovzen vn̄ inne*n*:	uzzen unt innen:
do entwichen im sine sinne.	do entwichen im die sinne.
von siner grozzen vnfruht	michel wart sin unzuht;
4390 prach in div freche tobesuht,	do dewanch in ŏh div tobesuht *4990*
daz der vil vnraine	daz er armer v̄ unrêine
ab einem wendelstaine	ab einem hohen steine
sich selben ervalte.	sih selben erualte.
dem tiefel wart er gezalt,	da nam in der tieuel ze gwalte.
4395 mit dem er iemerlichen	
mv̊z prinnen æwichlichen.	
Zv̊ Joseph sprach der engel: 30	**C**e Josep der engel do *4995*
	sprah:
,ia solt dv niht lenger	,ende hat din ungemah;
in disem lande beleiben;	
4400 var haim zv̊ den deinen!	wider ze lande scholt du varn;
des kindes veiande	des kindes viande sint neruarn
sint mit grozzer schande	
von der werlde geschaiden.	v̄ uon der werlte gescheiden.
hefe dich von den haiden	nu heue dich hêim uon den *5000*
4405 in terram natiuitatis!	heiden
dv solt wesen gewis,	
daz geschihet an Christ	35 v̄ wîzze daz der heilige Christ,
swaz von im geschriben ist:	swaz uon ime gescriben ist,
in Jvdeam wil er gân;	daz wil er in Judea began!
4410 div menige wirt vil lustsam,	da erhebet sih sunder wân
di er da becheret	daz heil der christenheit, *5005*
vn̄ den gelŏben leret:	als ez uor ist gewîssæit,
Patrum repromissio	v̄ als er hat geheizzen.

4376 im!   4379 hellen   4382 armichlichen *F.*] armichlichev
4387 inne   4389 vnfruht *für* unzuht *verschrieben?*   4394 zuo gezalt *F.*

A

div wirt erfullet also;
4415 des geit den ewigen lon
deus deorum in Syon.'
Joseph cherte do wider haim, 210, 40
als der morgen erschain,
mit sinem graben parte.
4420 er troste sich vil harte
sines iunkherren:

er liez im niht gewerren.

der bey naht æ was entrunnen,
der fůr bey liehter sunnen
4425 wider in sin gesezze.
Herodes der vil rezze
der mûte in niht mere:
er was genikchet sere.

Also mûz ez allen den ergan

4430 die got wellen widerstan
vn̄ siner ordenunge,
ez sin alte oder iunge.
Ditz ist ev vor gezelt,
ob ir genesen welt,
4435 daz ir die werlt schevhet
div hinze helle zevhet,
vn̄ fliehet yrdischen hort
durich daz frone gotes wort,
daz immer ewichlich bestat,
4440 so himel vn̄ erde zegat.
ir sult evch wol behv̄ten
vor der vbermv̂te,
div immer mv̂z vallen.
nv bedenket evch alle,
4445 wie ez dem tivfel ergienk,
do er den vbermût gevienk
vn̄ freuelich fůr:
do er satzte sinen stûl
wider sinen schepfer,
4450 do mûst der lugener

D

der bŏme ist gemeizzen,
da daz heilwæge uon bechumet
daz aller werlte gefrumet.'   5010
Josep cherte do hêin,
als im der morgen erschêin,

mit sinem iuncherren
v̄ der magede uil heren.
gewerren enmohte im niht 5015
uon deheiner ubeln geschiht
noh uon fientlicher lage.   211, 1
der e uon sinen magen
nahtes was entrunnen,
der fure bi liehter sunnen   5020
wider in sin gesæzze.
Herodes der uil ræzze
der enmv̂te in niht mere:
er was geuallen sere.

Also mûz ez allen den   5025
ergen
die got wellent widersten
unt siner ordinunge.
dise warnunge
diu ist iv uor gezellet,
ob ir genesen wellet,   5030
daz ir die werlte schîvhet
diu hinze helle zivhet,
vnt fliehet irdisken hort
durh daz gotes wort,
daz ane zwiuel gestat,   5035
so himel vnt erde zergat.
bewart ivch mit stæter hute
uor der ubermvte,
div iemer uallen mûz
vnt nie gewan statigen fûz!   5040
gedeuchet wie ez ergie
dem tîevil, do er geuîe
hohfart v̄ hohenmut:
do wart er ane wafen v̄ ane blût
uon al den eren gestozzen   5045
mit sinen stritgenozzen

4442 vbermv̂ten   4444 allen

an werltlîchen sachen.
nu ruoche uns got gemachen
5375 im selben genâme,
liep unt gezâme,   (2500)
daz wir geniezen muozen
sant Marîen suoze.

Sît daz der heilant
5390 uns ze helfe wart gesant,
sît begienc er zeichen alsô vil,   (2505)
daz ich enmac noch enwil
mich daran swingen
daz ich si fur bringe:
5395 scholte ich si volleclîchen sagen,
so endorfte ich niemer gedagen.   (2510)
fur wâr sage ich iu,
daz diu buoch alliu
diu wir lesen unde singen
5400 von dem einen urspringe
zesamene sint geflohten.   (2515)
vil wol im daz getohte,
daz er diu wunder begie.
ich weiz wol, sîn gelîch wart nie
5405 unde niemer enwirt.
swer sînen dienist verbirt,   (2520)
der muoz den tôt kiesen
unt die sêle êwiclîche verliesen.

5373—78 C¹ 63—68   75 selbe   77 genese (so!)   78 scē Marie suzen
5389—5523 C¹ 69—203   5401 geulogen   3 begingh

A

vallen vn̄ verderben:
also mv̊zzen alle die ersterben
die zv̊ im gephlihtent
vn̄ sich ze hohe rihtent
4455 an werltlichen sachen.
nv rûche vns got ze machen
ime selben genǣme,
lieb vn̄ gezeme,
daz wir geniezzen mv̊zzen
4460 sande Mareien der sûzzen,

vn̄ der eren manikvalden
die si von sinem gewalte
datze himel hat besezzen:
da sol si niht vergezzen
4465 ir diern vn̄ ir knehte;
da sul wir auch von rehte
immer loben iren svn
per omnia secula seculorum.
Amen!

Seit daz der hailant
4470 vns ze helfe wart gesant,
seit begienk er zaichen also vil,
daz ich enmak noch enwil
mich niht daran erswingen
daz ich sei fure bringe:
4475 solt ich sei vollechlichen sagen,
ich dorfte nimmer gedagen.
fur war sag ich ev
daz div pûch allev
die wir lesen oder singen
4480 von dem ainigen vrspringe
zesamene sint geflohten.
wie wol im daz tohte,
daz er wunders vil begie,
wan sin geliche der wart nie,
4485 noch nimmer mer enwirt!
swer auch sin dienst verbirt,
der mv̊z den tot kiesen
v̄ div sele verliesen.

D

vnt muz ewiklich ersterben:
also muzzen sie uerderben
die sih zu im gepflihtent
unde sih ze hohe rihtent   5050
ane werltlichen sachen.
nv ruche uns got gemachen
im selben genǣme,
werde vnt gezæme,
daz wir hernah geniezzen   5055
sænt Marien der suzzen
v̈ der muter der eren,
so wir hinnen cheren.
ir gnade ist so manekvalte,
diu in sinem gewalte   5060
den himel hat besezzen:
dane schol sie niht uergezzen
ir diwe vnt ir chnehte.
ŏh schulen wir uon rehte
iemer eren den ir sun   5065
der uns gnade mak getun.

211, 20

25

Der heilant hiez die stummen,
5410 die suhtigen zungen,
     sprechen unde singen,   (2525)
     die hufhalzen springen.
     die krumben wurden wol gesunt,
     swâ sîn vil heiliger munt
5415 ein einigez wort sprach.
     sô er die siechen uber sach,   (2530)
     dâ was trôst unde heil
     unt aller mandunge teil.
     er hiez die selpblinden
5420 die vinster uberwinden;
     diu vervallen ôren   (2535)
     diu hiez er wol gehôren.
     swâ er die miselsuht begreif,
     von den liuten si gesleif.
5425 fieber unt diu wernde suht
     diu muosten kêren an die fluht;   (2540)
     diu enmahten im niht vor gehaben.
     er hiez die tôten ûz den graben
     vil gewalteclîche erstên
5430 unt in ir herberge gên.
     die tievelsuhtic wâren,   (2545)
     die muosten im gnâden,
     wan si der bôse geist verlie:
     swaz er wolte daz ergie
5435 allez nâch sîner hulde.
     sunde unde schulde   (2550)
     die vertreip er von den brusten
     die sîner guote luste.
     von fumf girstîn brôten
5440 diu er segenôte,
     darzuo er hiez mischen   (2555)
     zwêne wênige vische,
     fumf tûsent manne
     die satôte er dannen
5445 mit gotlîchen êren,
     daz si erluste mêre   (2560)
     der geistlîchen spîse.
     der wirt was sô wîse:
     zwelf korbe hiez er nemen,
5450 die brosemen dar în legen.

5419 selpblinden *L. Sch.*] selben blinden   25 daz fib⁵   81 *Initiale*
tuuele suchtigh   88 lusten   89 fvnf girstnen   40 gesegenote   41 hiz
er   48 fvnf   44 di gesat er do dannē

A

    Der hailant hiez die stummen
4490 vn̄ die suhtigen zungen
    sprechen vn̄ singen,
    die hufhalzen springen.
    die chrumpen wurden wol gesunt,
    swa sin hailiger munt
4495 wan ain wort gesprach,
    so er sey ane sach.

    er hiez die geborn plinden
    die vinster vberwinden,
    vn̄ die tauben oren
4500 hiez er wol gehoren.
    swa er die miselsuht begraif,
    von den levten si entslaif.
    fieber vn̄ auch div suht
    můsen haben die fluht;
4505 si mohten sich bey niemen enthaben.
    er hiez die toten von den graben
    vil gewaltichlich ersten
    vn̄ in ir herberge gen.
    die tevfelsuhtik waren,
4510 der geist můste von in varen,
    daz er den leip verlie:
    swaz er wolt daz ergie.

    von fumf prôten
    die er segenote,
4515 dar zů er hiez mischen
    zwene chleine vische,
    fumftousent manne
    die satot er alle
    mit gotlicher speise.

4520 der wirt was so weise:
    siben chorbe hiez er nemen,
    die prosem darin legen.

    4493 chrupen   4495 wan!   4497 plinten

si wurden alle ensamet vol: (2565)
daz geviel der werlde wol,
vaste froute sich daz her.
ofte gienc er ûf dem mer
5455 mit truckenen fuozen,
daz wir dar an muozen (2570)
erkennen sînen gewalt,
daz er ze kunige ist gezalt
ob aller hêrschefte.
5460 er schutte mit sîner krefte
die erde zesamene, (2575)
als si wâre an einem vademe.
diz ist michel unde grôz,
wer mahte wesen sîn genôz?
5465 an allen sînen werken
mugen wir gnâde merken: (2580)
die erzeigte er uns besunder.
unt scholte ich diu wunder
alle schrîben unt bediuten
5470 den kunftigen liuten,
der junger wil ich geswîgen, (2585)
daz enmahte mîn zunge niht erlîden.

Die wazzersuht er heilte,
sîne gnâde er ûz teilte
5475 mit michelem vollen.
die liute die bewollen (2590)
mit dem bluote wâren,
er gebôt daz si genâren.
er was an allen dingen,
5480 als wir lesen unde singen,
vil rehte diemuote. (2595)
von den brusten sîner guote
liez er die gnâde sûgen
die armen unt die blûgen.
5485 die griffen an sîne wât,
den wart des siehtuomes rât (2600)
. . . .
sîn volk er wol bewarte,
die mit rehtem glouben
5490 kômen fur sîniu heiligen ougen.

_____

53 *Initiale*   61*f.* zusamene di erde   als si an eime vademe were
63 ditze *B. s. 43*   69 schrîben *B. s. 43*] besc'ben, *vgl. § 31b*   71 d' iũgen
C, der wunder *B. s. 43*   74 uz] vns   78 genasen   81 uil recht' demute
83 gnade] gute   87 des uolgte harte; *völlig entstellt: hinter* harte *könnte*

A

die chorbe wurden alle vol:
daz geviel der werlde wol,
4525 vil vaste frevte sich gotes her.
si giengen ofte ovf dem mer
mit ir truchen fuezzen,
daz wir dar an müzzen
kennen sinen gewalt,
4530 daz er ze kvnige ist gezalt.

siu kraft ist michel vñ groz,
wer mohte wesen sin genoz?

Die wazzersuht er hailte,
sine genade er ovz tailte
4535 mit michelem vollen.
die levte die bewollen
mit dem plûte waren,
er gebot daz si genaren.
er was an allen dingen,
4540 als wir lesen vñ singen,
vil rehte diemûte.

swer getrowet siner guete
vñ an sine wat graif,
aller siehtûm im entslaif.
4545 si wurden wol 'erlost
mit sinem gotelichem trost,
die mit rehtem gelauben
komen fur sin ougen.

---

das verbum harn *stecken, etwa* des si in an harten, *oder auf das Folgende
bezogen* die in an harten; *möglich ist auch Entstellung aus* tarte *zu*
tarn *schaden, schmerzen: etwa* der in sêre tarte   90 vor

        Dô der heilant entslief,　　　　　　　(2605)
        unt in diu menige an rief
        die ûf des meres wâge
        in grôzer freise lâgen,
5495   als er die zeswen ûf bôt,
        sô was gestillet al ⟨ir⟩ nôt.　　　　　(2610)
        er hiez die swâren winde
        von sînen lieben kinden
        entwîchen alsô schiere.
5500   sînen jungern ûf dem kiele
        den was diu liehte sunne　　　　　　(2615)
        vil schiere ûf errunnen;
        des meres unde freissam
        die wâren ir herren undertân;
5505   die scharfen wintstôze
        unt allez ir gedôze　　　　　　　　(2620)
        daz erkante sînen meister
        unt muoste ouch im gehôrsam leisten.

        Nâch allen disen êren
5510   liez sich der milte herre
        die *grimmen* juden vâhen　　　　　(2625)
        unt an daz crûce hâhen,
        dâ mite er *uns* erlôste
        von des tievels rôste,
5515   der von hitze wellet:
        swer dar în gevellet,　　　　　　(2630)
        der ist êwiclîche verlorn,
        der wâre bezzer *unge*born.
        er koufte uns alsô tiure
5520   von dem helle*fiure*,
        von dem alten nîde,　　　　　　　(2635)
        mit sîn selbes lîbe,
        doch er . . . .

    5496 alle　　5502 schiere] snelle　　6 ir] daz　　8 muz　　11 grimmen
B. s. 165

A
Do der hailant entslief,
4550 vñ in div menige ane rief
div ovf des meres wagen
in grozzen fraisen waren,
als er die zesewen ȫf gebot,
so was gestillet ir not.

4555 die grozzen wintstozze
vñ alle ir gedȫzze
daz erkante seinen herren:
des moht in niht gewerren.

Nach aller diser ære
4560 liez der milte herre
sich die Jvden vahen
vñ an ein chrevze hahen,
damit er vns erloste
von des tiefels roste,
4565 der vor hitze wellet:
swer darin gevellet,
der ist immer mer verlorn
vñ were pezzer vngeborn.
er chaufte vns also tevre
4570 von dem hellefevre
vñ von dem alten neide
mit sin selbes leibe.
er liez sich niht betragen:
vnsern tot wolt er veriagen;
4575 von sinen veterlichen triwen
er wolte vns itenewen.
in dem tode er entslief:
sin aygen plȗt schraib den brief,
vnser gruntfeste.
4580 des hailigen chrevzes este
die geit er ze lone
in eterna redempcione.

_____

4553 zesewe

A

Nv hôret waz div schrift sage,
wie an dem merterlichen tage
4585 zaichen geschahen,
daz ez die ivden sahen:
div sunne verbark iren schein
vñ wolte niht lieht sin.
do hûb sich grozzev vinster
4590 ze der zesewen vñ ze der winster
vber aller der werlde podem,
do die iuden begunden toben.
die stern vñ der mane
wurden vinster same.
4595 michel erpidem wart;
do erchom der laide hellewart,
do sich der grunt zarte;
sines schaden er do warte
von vnsers herren lait.
4600 die welde hoch vñ brait
die begunden ir wurzen
vaste vme sturzen.
die plûmen erplichen,
die staine entwichen
4605 vñ prasten von ainander
vñ glosten sam ein zunder.
der kisilink erchlank,
daz daz fewer dar ovz sprank.
Der ivden vmbehank
4610 prait vñ lank
zarte sich entzway.
gefugel vñ tier schray.
daz gepirge wart nie so veste,
ez mûste nider presten;
4615 div grab sich ovf taten,
die toten dar ovz traten:
die voulen vñ erstunchen
die azzen vnde trunchen
mit den purgeren.
4620 die erstanden waren,
si gaben vrchunde
den hailigen fumf wunden,
der gotes vrstende,
der ivden missewende,
4625 die des lebens orthaben

4590 zesewe   4622 de

A

selbe heten erslagen.
waz half die vngeslahten
ir hûte vñ ir wahte,
der schal vñ div vngehabe
4630 die si heten bey dem grabe?
als er die helle zeprach
vñ an dem tivfel sich gerach,
do erstûnt er zeir gesihte,
daz si al gerihte
4635 gar fur tot gelagen.
des wil ich noch fragen:
war taten die getilinge
ir eysneine ringe,
die halsperge also lieht?

---

mit swerten unt mit stangen,
5610   mit spiezen alsô langen,
     dô der heilant erstuont?   (2640)
     ich enweiz warumbe si daz tuont,
     daz si noch wider bellent
     unt ir dankes wellent
5615   die sêle versenchen.
     si scholten sich bedench*en*:   (2645)
     geben si uns den tôten widere,
     sô dunkent si mich biderbe;
     mugen si des niht getuon,
5620   sô glouben an der magede sun,
     den si dâ sâhen erstên,   (2650)
     des si ze jungist muozen gên,
     die ubelen unt die verworhten,
     in des tôdes vorhten.
5625   an sînem gerihte grôzen
     werdent si verstôzen,   (2655)
     si enwellen sich bekêren.
     warumbe werent si sich der grôzen êre?

     Als er erstuont von dem grabe,
5630   dô was ⟨er vollen⟩ vierzic tage
     mit uns in der werlte.   (2660)
     sîne junger er gewerte
     sîner geinwurte;
     den zwîvel er in enpfuorte,
5635   daz si veste wurden,
     ledic von allen burden   (2665)
     angestlîcher dinge.
     ir gemuote was in sô ringe,
     do si ⟨in⟩ muosten schouwen.
5640   unser liebiu frouwe
     diu gesach ir nie sô werde.   (2670)
     der himel wart ûz der erde
     gezimbert an den stunden:
     ir herze was enpunden.

5645   mit in er âz unde tranc;
     er chêrte ouch allen ir gedanc   (2675)

5609 *bis* lobeten 5671 C¹ 1—63   14 ir] eines   17 *Initiale*   20 gleubē
meide   22 gên] ien, *vgl. § 29*   24 in] an   27 si enwollent   32 iunge'n
33 mit siner   36 burden!   aller burden *B. s. 48*   37 wankelich'

A

4640 wes werten si sich nieht
    mit swerten vn̄ mit stangen
    vñ mit spiezzen also langen,
    do der hailant erstunt?
    ich *enwaiz* warume si daz tûnt,
4645 daz si wider pellent
    vñ sich niht enwellent
    der warheit bedenchen,
    sus ire sele versenchen.

    Do got erstûnt von dem grabe,
4650 do waz er vollen vierzik tage
    mit vns ovf der erde.
    sine iunger werde

    frevten sich siner angeschowe
    vñ vnser lieben vrowen,

4655 wan an den selben stunden
    waz ir herze enpunden
    von aller not vñ chlage
    div in vor ane lage.
    er az mit in vñ trank;
4660 er chert allen iren gedank

---

38 geringe   40 unsere libē vrouwē   41 do geschach in *unter Bei-*
behaltung des Wortlauts von 39 f. B. *s. 48*   42 erden
    4644 waz   4654 liebe vrouwe *F*.

vil vaste in sîne minne.
si hulfen im sît gewinnen
vil manic tûsent sêle
5650 mit ⟨râte unt mit⟩ ir suozen lêre.

    Darnâch fuor er ze himele   (2680)
unt trôste ouch si dâ nidene
mit sîn selbes geiste.
der getriuwe herre leiste
5655 daz er den zwelven gehiez
dô er si weinende liez.   (2685)
si wâren in einem gademe
gesezzen zesamene,
do begunde er in erschînen:
5660 mit den zungen fiurînen
si wurden schiere enzundet;   (2690)
ja wart ouch in gekundet
aller lande sprâche.
daz gebot si nie gebrâchen
5665 daz in ir meister sazte.
die zungen wol gewazte   (2695)
die hullen unde clungen;
si sageten unde sungen
von dem heilande
5670 in allen den landen;
si lobeten in grôzlîchen   (2700)
in allen den rîchen.
diu werlt *gruozte* in alsus:
S y o n , r e g n a b i t d e u s t u u s.

5675   **N**u habent die engel uns gesaget,
wie der *kunic* den diu maget   (2705)
gebar der kristenheite
mit sîner *gotheite*
kumftic anderstunt sî,
5680 f o n s e t o r i g o b o n î :
sô h*ât er* sîn gerihte,   (2710)
sô koment im zuo gesihte
o m n e s t r i b u s *t e r r e.*
der gewaltige herre
5685 der teilet sînen knehten
ir lôn *also* rehte   (2715)

5656 weinde 60*f.* di zungē warn fuw‘ine vnd warn schire enzundet
62 io   71 in (*so!*) *bis* 5840 C ¹ 203—370   76 den] vnd   79 kunftig
82 kumt   84 geweltige   85 teilte

     A

vil vaste in sine minne:
des hulfen si im gewinnen
vil manik tousent sele
mit rate vn̄ mit ir suezzer lere.

4665 Dar nach fůr er ze himile
vn̄ troste si hie nidene
mit dem hailigen gaiste.
der getriwe herre laiste
daz er den zwelfpoten gehiez
4670 do er sey waininde liez.
si waren in einem gademe
gesezzen zesamene,
do begunde er in erscheinen:
mit den zungen fivreinen
4675 si wurden schier enzundet;
ia wart in gekundet
aller hande sprache.
daz gebot si nie geprachen
daz in ir maister sazte.
4680 die zungen wol gewazte
die hullen vn̄ chlungen;
si sageten vn̄ sungen
von deme hailande
in allem dem lande;
4685 si lobten in gezogenlichen
allenthalben in den reichen;
den herren grůzten si svs:
regnabit deus tuus.

     Nv habent vns die engel gesaget,
4690 wie der kunik vn̄ div maget
wart der christenhait
mit siner gothait
kumftik vn̄ sponsa domini,
fons et origo boni:
4695 so hat er sin gerihte
vn̄ koment im ze geslihte
omnes tribus terre.
der geweltige herre
der tailet sinen knehten
4700 eben vn̄ rehte

4677 sprachen   4689 gesagt

16*

nâch ieglîches werken:
daz kan er wol *gemerken.*
daz ist der angestlîche tac
5690 dâ niemen nih*t verheln* mac,   (2720)
verstôzen noch verbergen,
noch ung*erochen* werden
vor der kreftigen ma nû.
gedenchet alle d*arzuo:*
5695 sorget ûf daz teidinc,
dâ aller triuwen ursp*rinc*   (2725)
ze sîner zeswen stellet
die schar diu im gevellet!
*diu winst*er zeiget in den tôt
5700 die hie vehtent âne nôt
wider *ir* schephâre.   (2730)
dâ wirt diu rede swâre:
dâ dringet der *arme* fur den kunic,
dâ ist niemen hêr noch frumic,
5705 *wan der hie* gedienet
daz diu sêle dort wirt geliebet.   (2735)

*W*ar denchet ir wuoterîche*?*
ir enmuget daz himelrî*che*
ersturmen mit den schilten!
5710 nu bitet die fro*uw*en milte,
sante Marîen,   (2740)
daz si uns gefrîe
unt . . . nde phlege
dâ sich scheident die wege:
5715 einer gein *dem luf*te,
der ander gein der grufte   (2745)
dâ der vâlant inne lît,
der *swebe*l unde bech gît
sînen undertânen.
5720 wir muozen *uns iemer* ânen
êren unt guoter sinne,   (2750)
wellen wir die *kunig*inne
niht wecken mit den zaheren,
die brût *unt d*ie gemahelen
5725 die got im selben erkôs,
unt diu *ir* magetuom nie verlôs.   (2755)

5689 d⁵ engelische   93 gotes manû?   96 treuwe   97 gestellet
99 den] d⁵   5700 uechten!   4 hêr noch] h⁵nach   6 daz er da wirt
gelibet   7 .ar!   9 . . cht ersturmē   10 milten, *von* m *nur ein Strich*

A
nach igeliches werchen:
die kan er wol gemerken
an dem ængestlichen tage
da nieman niht verpergen mag

4705 vor der kreftigen gotes hant.
nv bedenchet evch liebe allesant
vñ sorget ovf daz taydink,
da aller triwen vrsprink
zv̊ siner zesewen stellet
4710 die schar div im gevellet.
div lenke zaiget in den tot
die hie vehtent ane not
wider ir schepfere:
der tak wirt in swere.
4715 da dringet der arme fur den kvnik,
da ist niemen edel noch frumik,
wan der daz hie verdienet hat
daz dort der sele wirdet rat.

War gedenchet ir wv̊treiche?
4720 ir mvget daz himelreiche
niht ersturmen mit dem schilte!
nv bit die vrowen milte,
sande Mareien,
daz si vns geruche ze freien
4725 vnde vnser sele pflege
da sich schaident die wege:
ainer gen der lufte,
der ander gen der grufte
da der valant inne leit,
4730 der swebel vñ pech geit
den sinen vndertanen.
wir mv̊zzen vns immer anen
eren vñ gůter sinne,
welle wir die kuniginne
4735 niht wechen mit den zehern,
die prout vñ die gemahelen
die got im selben erkôs,
div ir magtv̊m nie verlôs.

---

11 sant   13 *vor* nde *noch ein Strich, wahrscheinlich* i *oder* u: ir kinde
⟨welle⟩ phlegen *M.*   14 dâ] do   25 selb⁵

4709 zesewe   4710 div   4712 vehtent!   4727 luft : grufte
4732 wier   4734. 36. 37 div

bezzer frouwe nie enwart:
mit grôzen triuwen si *bewart*
bêdiu sêle unde lîp:
5730   swer sich inneclîche ergît   (2760)
ûf ir barmunge,
daz enmahte nehein zunge
den vollen *b*ediuten,
wie si weget den liuten
5735   an unsers herren *fuoze*n:
swes wir sie begruozen,   (2765)
daz enlât si niht bes*lîfe*n.
nu chort sie begrîfen
daz si iu niht en*gê*!
5740   *s*ô muget ir darnâch iemer mê
wesen unge*schen*det: (2770)
unser leit si uns wol verendet.

*N*u gedenke wîp unde man,
wie sîn dinc schuln *gest*ân
5745   von êwen unze êwen.   (2775)
swaz wir die maget *f*lêgen,
daz enist niht verlorn.
si ist gesetzet unt erchorn
zeiner gwissen vogetinne
5750   ze an*gest*lîchen dingen.   (2780)
si kan uns armen weisen
wol *helf*en zuo den freisen
werltlîcher sorgen.
ir helfe ist *unver*borgen:
5755   si ist allen den bî   (2785)
die von herzen meinent sî;
die dicke sûftent unde clagent
die sunde die si gefru*met* habent,
den ist si ungeswichen.
5760   ir gnâde ist sô *m*ichel,   (2790)
alsô wît unt alsô breit,
daz alliu diu christenheit
von ir wirt wol gewert,
diu ir zallen zîten gert.
5765   got ist ir herre unt ir sun:
des mac si bêdiu *wol* getuon,   (2795)

5727 *Initiale* 30 innēclichen (*so!*) git 33 vollen] an ... C, anderen
B. s. *221* 34 wiget 37 enlezt 37*f.* be .... ten : begriften 38 chort] kert
39 iu] uch   40 imm'mere   42 uolendet   45 vō ewe wanne zu ewe

A

pezzer ⟨vrouwe⟩ nie enwart:
4740 mit grozzen trivwen si vns bewart
pede sele vñ leip:
swer sich ir inrechlich ergeit
in ir sůzze barmunge,
daz enmoht enhain zunge
4745 envollen bedevten,
wie si weget den levten
an vnsers herren fuezzen:
swes wir sei begruezzen,
daz lat si niht entsleifen.
4750 geruchet sei begreifen,
daz si ev niht enge,
vñ ir genade ev bey geste,
vñ stete frevde ev sende
immer mere ane ende!
Amen!

4755 **N**v gedenke weip vñ man,
wie sin dink sule gestan
von æwen ze æ̂wen.
swaz wir die magt flegen,
daz ist niht verlorn.
4760 si ist gesetzet vñ erchorn
ze ainer voytinne
gen ængestlichem dinge.
si kan vns wol weisen
vñ helfen ovz den fraisen
4765 werltlicher sorgen.
ir helfe ist vnverborgen:
si ist allen den bey
die von herzen mainent sey,
die sevftent dike vñ chlagent
4770 ir sunde die si gefrumt habent.

ir genade ist so brait
daz alle div christenhait
von ir wirt gewert,
d*iu* ir genade gert.
4775 Got ist ir herre vñ ir sun;
des mach si pede wol getů̆n,

D

Bezzer frȯe nie wart:
mit grozzen trivwen sie bewart
den sæligen zaller zit:
swer sih innekliche ergit 5070
uf ir grozze barmunge,
dane mohte dehein zunge
211, 30 ze reht wol beduten,
wie sie weget den livten
an unsers herren fuzzen: 5075
swes wir sie begruzzen,
daz enlat sie ir niht beslifen.
nu bechort sie begrifen,
daz sie iu niht enge!
so muget ir da nah iemer mê 5080
wesen ungeschendet,
35 want sie nnser leit wol uerendet.

Got ist ir herre v̄ ir kint,
des alle creature sint:

---

49 zu ein⁵ gewissen   52 ûz *B. s. 175*   54 hilfe   57 sufczen   64 zu
allen geziten (*so!*)   65 *Initiale*
4774 d⁵   genade!

biten unt gebieten,

    daz wir uns muozen *nieten*
    der êwigen froude
5770 vor Christes beschoude.
    wir *schu*ln ir chlagen unser nôt: (2800)
    si gît daz lebendige brôt
    den sêlen ze spîse
    in dem paradîse.
5775 nu manet die lieb*en* frouwen
    unt lâzet von den ougen (2805)
    die heizen *zahere* fliezen!
    ja mugen wir wol geniezen,
    wil daz hêre *mage*dîn
5780 unser griezwarte sîn.
    nu geruoche si unser bot*schaft* (2810)
    bringen fur die gotes chraft,
    der ir niht verzîhet,
    wan er si hât gewîhet,
5785 gesegent ob allen wîben
    mit s*în* selbes l*îbe*. (2815)
    wir sitzen oder stên,
    in ir hulden schuln wir gên;
    wir trinken oder ezzen,
5790 *wir* schuln ir niht vergezzen;
    wir slâfen oder wachen, (2820)
    wir schuln an allen sachen
    die getriuwen unt die rei*nen*
    *flêg*en unde meinen,
5795 daz si in dem himelrîche
    den en*gel*n uns gelîche, (2825)
    daz wir sie loben muozen dâ
    in eternum et ultrâ.

    *D*ô von gotes geburte
5800 tûsent jâr *wur*ten
    hundert sibenzec unde zwei, (2830)
    dô wart *ein prie*ster des enein,
    Wernher geheizen,
    daz er von *dem* weize
5805 die spriu abe schiede

5769 *f.* vreude : bescheude 72 lebende 78 io 82 brengē 87 *Initiale*
88 hulden] hilfe 89 wir ezen 95 daz] di 97 loben muzen 99 . o!
5801 hundert vnd 2 inein

A

biten vñ gebieten,

daz wir vns mvgen nieten
der ewigen frevde
4780 vor Christes beschevde.
wir sulen ir chlagen vnser not;
si geit daz lebendige brot
den selen ze speise
in dem fronen paradeyse.
4785 nv mant die lieben frowen
vñ lat von den augen
die haizzen zeher fliezzen.
ia mvge wir wol geniezzen,
wil daz hailige magedein
4790 vnser forspreche sein.
nv gerûche si vnser potschaft
bringen fur die gotes chraft,
der sey niht verzeihet,
wan er sei hat geweihet,
4795 gesegent ob allen weiben
mit sin selbes leibe.
wir sitzen oder stên,
in ir helfe sul wir gên;
wir trinchen oder ezzen,
4800 wir sulen ir niht vergezzen;
wir slafen oder wachen,
wir sulen an allen sachen
die hohen vñ die rainen
flegen vñ mainen,
4805 daz si in dem himilreiche
den engeln vns geliche,
daz wir sei loben da
in eternum et vltra.

Do von gotes geburde
4810 tousent iar wurden,
hundert sibenzek vnde zway,
do wart ein priester des en ain,
Wernher gehaizzen,
daz er von dem waizen
4815 die paleas schiede

D

des mak sie bitten vnt 5085
          gebieten,
daz wir uns mǔzzen nieten
der ewigen frǒde
in Christes beschǒde.
wir schulen ir chlagen unser not;
sie git daz lebentige brot 5090
den selen ze spise
v̄ gebîvtet in dem paradise
v̄ den himelen gwaltekliche.

sie ist gnadich vnde riche
ze geben unt ze liheu. 5095
got mag ir niht uerzihen,
der sie im gewihet hat
uber al sine hantgetat.
wir sitzen oder sten,
in ire hulden schuln wir gen; 5100
wir ezzen oder trinchen,
wir schuln ir ie gedenchen;
wir slafen oder wachen,
wir schvln an allen sachen
die guten vnt die reinen 5105
flegen unde meinen,
daz sie in dem himelriche
den engeln uns geliche,
daz wir sie loben da
in ęternum et ultra. 5110
          Amen!

Side numbers: 211,40 (col A, line at speise); 212,1 (col A, line at sitzen oder stên); 5 (col D, at daz si himilreiche)

4781 wier   4783 selben   211,40 gebîvte   4795 *kein* unt!

mit disen drin lie*den*,   (2835)
diu er schreip ze êren
der frouwen diu unsern herren
*truo*c in ir gezelte
5810 aller diser werlte.
im was ein ... priester holt,   (2840)
geheizen was er Manegolt:
der *wîs*te die materje,
als ein guot verje
5815 daz ruoder wîs*et* mit der hant,
unz er chumet an daz lant.   (2845)
er ladete in in daz ⟨sîn⟩ hûs
unt enliez in ouch niht dar *ûz*,
unz er gefrumete unt geriet
5820 daz diu geist*lîch*en liet
wurden gemachet.   (2850)
do enwart niht vil *ge*lachet:
sante Marîe
diu gap in kurzewîle
5825 unt ... gez framspuote,
daz ez si niht enmuote.   (2855)
si habent ze buoze gegeben
allen den die nu leben,
*die di*se rede hôren
5830 mit fleischlîchen ôren,
daz si in *wun*schen beiden,   (2860)
swanne si verscheiden,
daz in diu muoter *fr*ône
der arbeite lône
5835 mit ir anbliche.
wir schul*n* sie manen diche,   (2865)
wan si gnâden ist vol,
sam sie gruo*zte vil* wol
Gabriel archangelus:
5840 benedicta tu in mulieribus.

5806 drien   9 truoc] *nur ein nicht ganz sicherer Rest von* k   10 wˢlde
11 *wahrscheinlich* erzepriester, *oder* kôrpriester, liutpriester?   13 marterie
16 unz] wǟne daz   17 *Initiale weggeschnitten*   lud   18 enliez] liz
19 unz] wanne   23 scē   24 kurzewîle] kunde uile   25 sæligez?
vrouwē spute   27 geben   29 gehoren   30 vlizclichē   38 sam] vnd

A   **D**

mit drin lieden,
die er schreib ze eren
der vrowen div vnsern herren
erzaigte in ir gezelde
4820 aller diser wer*lde*.
im was ain priester holt,
gehaizzen was er Manigolt:
der weiste in der materie
als ain gût verie
4825 der daz schef weiset mit der hant,
vnz ez bechumt an daz lant.
er ladot in in sin hous
vñ enliez ⟨in⟩ niht dar ouz,
vnz er gefrumet vñ geriet
4830 daz div gaistlichen liet
wurden gemachet.
da wart niht vil gelachet:
Maria div got truk
div gab in kurzeweile genůk
4835 vñ so semften mût
daz ez in chom ze gûte.
Si hant ze bŷzze gegeben
allen die nv leben,
die dise rede horen
4840 mit fleischlichen oren,
daz si in wunschen paiden,
swanne si verschaiden,
daz in div maget frone
ir arbaite lone
4845 mit ir selbes anbli*che*.
wir sulen si biten diche,
wan si ist genaden vol,
sam sey grûzte vil wol
Gabriel Archangelus:
4850 benedicta tu in mulieribus.

Do scismatis tempestas   **D**o scismatis tempestas
drevzehen iar gestanden was   drivzehen iâre gestanden was
bey dem babest Alexander,   bi dem pabes Alexander,
do drey herren ander   daz drie herren ander
4855 so vaste wurben vme den stûl   ẁrren ime den stu*l*,   5115
daz er weislos fûr   daz er wiselos fû*r*
ovf dem lande vñ ovf dem mer 212,10 uf dem lande vnt uf dem mere

---

4819 erzougte?   4820 werlte   4845 anblik   212,9 stule : fûre

A

mit vil chlainem her,
do romische reiche
4860 stŭnden gewaltichleiche
an kaiser Frideriches hant,
do er Polan daz lant
dwank mit herverte,
do in got gewerte
4865 siges mit siner schar,
do er zwai vñ zwainzek iar
was gewesen kaiser,
voget der waisen,
ze der zeit vnder dev
4870 wurden div liet alle drev
volbraht von der maget:
daz aine liet saget
von der kumfte Marien,
der edelen vñ der freyen,
4875 wie ir mŭter sei gewan
bey ainem hailigen man
der Joachim genant ist.
daz ander liet zelet die frist,
daz si wart gemehelot
4880 als der hailant gebot,
daz dritte daz si den gebar
der himel vñ erde vil gar
gemachet hat mit sinem list
vñ allez daz darinne ist,
4885 bede groz vñ chlaine:
daz hat er altersaine
allez uber sezzeu,
gezêlt vñ gemezzen.

Swa dise pŭch alle sint,
4890 da wirt geborn denhain kint
dem immer mvge misse gen.
div mŭter mv̊z sich versten
semftichlicher dinge.
ir weget div kuniginne
4895 vor gotes antwurte,
vñ gedenchet ir geburtte
div ir wart ertailet.
von dem wir sin gehailet,

D

mit vil lutzelem here,
do div romiskiu riche
stunten gewalticliche   5120
in des keiser Frideriches hant,
vnt er Polan daz lant
betwanch mit heruerte,
da in got siges gewerte,

do wrden div liet elliv driu   5125
getihte*t* under div:

212, 15 daz erste daz saget
uon der ewigen maget,

wie sie ir mŭter gewân
bi einem vil werden man   5130
der Joachim geheizzen ist.
daz ander zelet die frist,
daz sie wart gemahelot
als der heilant gebot.
daz dritte saget daz sie gebar 5135
der himel vnt erde gar
20 ufhabet . . . .

212, 14 getihte   212, 20 *danach eine zeile ausradiert, in der* groz
noch leserlich ist.

A

daz ist Christ der reiche,

4900 der ladet vns tegiliche.

nv rŭfet in inrechlichen an,

swanne sin mv̊ter in an vns man,

daz er vns ellenden

sine helfe gerŭche zesenden

4905 vn̄ sine englische schar,

div vns laite vnde bewar,

vn̄ vns bringe an die stat

vbi cum patre regnat

et spiritu paraclito,

4910 daz vnser stimme vil fro

mvezze singen immer me:

Gloria tibi domine.

Amen!

Druck von Karras, Kröber & Nietschmann, Halle (Saale)